THE
PROFESSOR
A LESSON IN TERROR

A SHORT STORY BY

R. H. GOSSE

ISBN: 0-75962-349-X

This book is printed on acid free paper.

1stBooks - rev. 4/6/01

To Pam,
whose patience and understanding
allowed me to follow a dream.

1.

To say that Ronnie Fisher was a loser was to give him too much credit. When he was a kid, he grew up with all of the normal aspirations as to what career he would settle on. Unfortunately, he never gave any thought as to what career would settle for him.

He had a loving family that in his second year of college, was completely wiped out in a freak, single car accident. His father had been driving the family home after a night out of dinner and a movie. He had rounded a curve and the car drifted off of the side of the road. There was a slight drop off along the edge of the pavement and when his father steered the car back onto the road, he lost control and ran head-on into a semi coming the other way. To say that the crash was horrific would be a drastic understatement. To put it into perspective, it is noteworthy to report that one of the paramedics that worked the crash scene, a man that had done his job for over fifteen years, tended his resignation the next morning. He did so explaining that he had seen enough.

The loss of his family in this manner was crushing for Ronnie. When he was in his last year of college, he had finally lost the rest of his will to succeed. The nights of reckless partying caught up with him. He mistakenly thought that by pickling his brain in booze, his sense of loss would magically go away. The end result was that he barely got out of school with a degree. If it hadn't been for the fact that he had accidentally gotten some really good dirt on the one professor that was holding his degree in check, he would have never graduated. After all, when you turn in absolutely no work for a semester and only came to class to catch up on your sleep, you can't expect your GPA to be too high.

By blackmailing the professor, Ronnie quickly learned that maybe there was an easier way through life. Hard work was fine, but only if it led to some sort of carnal end, or if not, at least something that would alter the senses. His motivation to this point was that he had watched his parents work hard all of their lives. The question that he kept asking himself was 'What did it get them?' The answer he kept getting was 'Nothing but a bad case of road kill.' That rationalization helped him to decide to use the "easy" way whenever possible.

For awhile, the event with the Professor would bother him. Ronnie wasn't without some amount of conscience. In his dreams he would see the look on the Professor's face at the exact moment that Ronnie relayed his darkest secret to him. In those days, homosexuality was a very taboo subject. One that could easily get you killed or beaten up. In the very least, it would get you fired from your job, especially if you were in the education business.

The fact that the Professor committed suicide a month later ate deeper into Ronnie's soul than he would admit. He always justified the death as 'a fag pining away at the loss of some unknown lover.' After all, how could HIS threatening to reveal the man to his superiors pull the trigger? But in Ronnie's dreams, his subconscious explained it to him. It was like a loop of film that when he would wake in a cold sweat with a gasp, he would have traded his own life to make it stop.

After a couple of years, the dream began to fade until it no longer came. In the mean time, his waking life was truly a bigger nightmare. It was as if as the dream of the dead professor faded away, his waking life slid downward into an abyss. He never kept a job for more than six months. Of course if you listened to Ronnie, the reason for his dismissal was never his fault. He just couldn't understand why the boss was so mad the day Ronnie took a three hour lunch. Or why he was fired when he told the best customer of one business he worked for that 'Vertical stripes made her look fatter than she really was.' Of course there was another time he showed up for work so drunk that he passed out in the break room.

Ronnie's drinking became almost like an Olympic event with him. His small world became even smaller when it began to center around going to whatever job he currently had and the bar that he would spend the remainder of his day until closing time. Then he would stumble across the street to his apartment and sleep until it was time to go back to work and start the process all over again.

Then he caught a break and was offered a job at the Green Oaks Country Club keeping the greens mowed. The money was about a quarter more than minimum wage, all he had to do was show up everyday and ride a lawn mower around until quitting time. It was at the club that he met his wife. She was a waitress in the country club and had the deepest blue eyes, the longest legs, and of course the cutest ass he had ever seen. At first she paid no attention to him, so he began to change his ways. He laid off the sauce and began to buff himself up.

The turning point in the relationship was when she was promoted to dining room supervisor. All of the other waitresses treated her as though she had slept with someone to get the promotion. The truth was that she was a good worker and had seniority over the other waitresses. The dining room had a high turnover rate, but she had stuck there for the last two years.

Ronnie had seen her outside one afternoon after a very rough shift, everyone had given her a really hard time. Her co-workers had been snotty to her and had talked to her in hateful tones. A couple of them had even made crude jokes about her. She was outside crying and Ronnie stopped and consoled her. That won her heart. They talked and found out that they were both orphans, that fact seemed to bond them tighter to each other. The romance was a whirlwind and a year later they were exchanging vows.

Even though this should have been the start of a new and happy life for Ronnie, it was the beginning of his decline once again. In human nature, it seems that scum always seeks its own natural level. Ronnie had a set picture in his mind as to what marriage should be, but his own marriage didn't fit the mold he had made in his mind and it grated on him. Then when Margret was promoted once again, this time to Assistant Manager, his world crumbled. She was making alot more money than he was and it bothered him. The main reason it bothered him was because she liked to throw the fact that she was making more money than he was in his face as often as she could. Ronnie had grown up with the idea that the man of the family should be the primary bread winner. The drinking restarted and one night he decided that he was going to show her who was really the boss of the family.

She was working late that night and Ronnie was free to lubricate himself up with as much liquid courage as he had the money to buy. By the time she got home, he was so drunk he could hardly stand up. As soon as she walked into the house, he started up with what a bitch she was and how he was the man of the house. As he spoke, he became mad. Soon his rage was at the point where it was feeding itself. She was dumb-founded and said that she didn't know what he was talking about. This was like throwing a lit match into a gasoline can, his rage flared.

"Bitch! You can talk when I say you can!" He screamed at her. Ronnie meant to follow it up with a backhand across her face just to punctuate his point. But, being so drunk, he misjudged the distance and hit her on the side of her head, knocking her down. Ronnie stood there for a moment meaning to say that he was sorry, but after thinking for a second he said, "That's what you get for talking back, bitch!"

Ronnie was totally unprepared for what happened next. When his back was turned, Margret got up off of the floor and beat the living hell out of him. By the time she was done, he had two cracked ribs, a broken nose, and it would take almost three days for his right eye to unswell enough for him to see out of again. In his own way, Ronnie had been right, because that was the night he showed Margret who really wore the pants in the family.

As human nature would have it, word of what happened to Ronnie at home spread around work like wildfire. Margret was a hero among her co-workers. Although the guys that Ronnie worked with didn't say anything to him face to face, he knew that they were laughing at him behind his back. Conversations would abruptly stop when he walked into the room. People would look in his direction and laugh or snicker. This, at the very least, didn't do very much to bolster his self-esteem. He crawled even farther into the bottle and that led to more missed days from work. Not alot, not enough to get him into trouble at work, just a few more than normal. Ronnie justified these missed days with the thought of 'How can he work when he was the laughing stock of the country club?'

This was the beginning of the real abuse for Ronnie. If Margret found that he had done something stupid, left the toilet seat up, not recap the toothpaste, not do the dishes right, she would physically take it out on him. One night Margret was cooking dinner and Ronnie walked in and asked her a question, the subject of the question didn't matter, just the fact that she didn't feel like dealing with him. So she picked up the frying pan off of the stove and hit him in the back of the head with it. It took seventeen stitches to close the wound on the back of his head, not to mention the treatment for the burns that he received when the hot grease in the pan had poured down his back.

That was when he decided that he'd had enough and started packing his bags to leave. Margret, who put on a very good tearful show, begged him not to go, saying that she would change and never hit him again. She was true to her word for the next few weeks. At least she had given him enough time to heal. The whole time Ronnie was on the mend, the sex was really good. That was her hold over him, when things got really bad, she would submit to whatever his desires were and be good for a short while.

Looking back at Margret's past, the one thing that Ronnie didn't know about Margret was that she had watched her father slowly beat her mother to death. It wasn't one big beating that she had died from, but the accumulative affects of many years of beatings upon beatings. Too easily she remembered the screaming and hollering, the sounds of things breaking, the quiet meaty thuds of her fathers fists hitting her mother. The one thing that still rung in her ears was the sound of her mother's quiet crying and begging for forgiveness as Margret's father beat her. Subconsciously, this had caused Margret to decide that the first time she was hit, she would return fire. Unlike her mother, SHE was going to keep on giving until there was nothing left to give.

It was right after that incident that Ronnie really began to take his problems with him to work and began drinking on the job. At first he was cautious about it, but when he found out that nobody really gave a damn what condition he was in as long as he got his job done, he started carrying a flask to work. He would drink as he rode around cutting the grass. After a short while, the flask wasn't enough. On the far corner of the course there was a small patch of woods that he would park his mower in, go out through a hole in the fence and walk the two blocks to the liquor store. He started with pint bottles but soon graduated to fifths and spent his days cutting the grass in a self-induced fog.

He was also back to the point of saying the hell with this and just run away. He knew that he could just walk away from the mean bitch he was married to and start his life all over again. He kept thinking that it would be the right thing to do, the smart thing to do. He could always find a new job, after all, he had held onto this one for over two years and that would help him find another job as a greenskeeper easily enough. Ronnie had seen how quick the turnover rate was in the shop and this was one of the better places to work. With his knowledge of cutting grass and experience, he knew that he could easily get a job.

Margret got wind that Ronnie was drinking at work and one night she decided to take matters into her own hands. As she was slapping him around she announced that he had better get his shit together because she was pregnant. She also added that she didn't want her kid to know just how big of a piece of shit loser he really was. Just to punctuate her point, she gave him a knee in the groin that ultimately put him in the hospital the next day.

Of course once again, Margret was really tearful and sorry for what she had done as she was driving him to the emergency room. Margret was being sincere because she was afraid that he would tell someone that she had done this to him. Her fears were unfounded for two very good reasons; First, Ronnie was too stupid to let go of the macho bullshit and let anyone know that SHE had busted his balls. Second, this was the latter half of the eighties and nobody really gave a damn if you were a man getting your ass kicked by your spouse.

Killing your spouse was a different story. If some guy killed his wife, he ended up in prison. But if some woman killed her husband, it was usually thought that it was because he was such a bastard. No one ever thought that maybe it was just because she was mean.

Ronnie spent two days in the hospital with a severely bruised testicle. While he was there, Margret was attentive to his every need. But when she got him home, she gave him a black eye for inconveniencing her. Why, she had missed all of her daytime shows and he should know how infrequently she was able to be home during a week day. Besides that, Margret explained to him, his laying around was going to cost them two days wage, not to mention the doctor bills that he had racked up. Now his paycheck was going to be short and she wanted to buy a new rabbit coat. After all, winter would be here in three months and she just had to have this coat now.

Margret got her new coat and for the next seven months Ronnie endured violent mood swings while watching her balloon up from a size eight to a size twenty-two. It seemed as though her weight was directly related to her ill temper. In short, the bigger she got, the meaner she got.

While this was happening, Ronnie's job performance got better. His fellow workers still talked about him, he didn't hear the things they were saying, he just saw them looking at him and shaking their heads. The consensus at work was that Ronnie was the biggest wimp around. The most common spoken phrase among his co-workers was, "Man, if she did that to me I'd kick her ass from here to tomorrow." Ronnie wasn't stupid and knew that they were talking about him. It began to eat at him and soon he felt as though everyone was talking about him whether they were or not.

Around the time of Margret's fifth month of pregnancy she seemed as though she had gotten an extra dose of meanness. She began taking swipes at him for no reason with what ever she happened to have in her hand at the time. Then one night after nailing him really good in the ear with a metal fly swatter, she announced that he had to sleep on the couch because it was too uncomfortable sleeping with him in the queen sized bed. So as always, he cowed to her wishes as the blood flowed down the side of his neck from his wounded ear.

That was the night that Ronnie's dreams started again. Except that now instead of seeing just the face of his dead Professor, his what would become nightly vision would smile and say, *"Sometimes you get what you deserve."* Then the mouth would open until all he was looking at was a giant mouth with razor sharp teeth coming towards him. Ronnie carried the scream that came from his own lips from the dream world to the waking world. When he opened his eyes he found that he was sitting upright on the couch. The sheets were so wet that for a couple of minutes he was afraid that he had wet the couch. But after smelling the wet sheets for not the second but the third time, he decided that it was just a bad case of the night sweats. So he stripped the sheets and washed them. His sleeping was over for the night.

For the next four months his sleep was cut short dramatically. And although he didn't go back to the bottle, he slipped deeper and deeper into depression. Now, when he was all alone out mowing the grass, tears would be silently cascading down his cheeks. Ronnie viewed his life as a true living hell.

2.

About a month and a half before Margret's blessed event, his 'living hell' suspicions were confirmed. Margret got fired. She didn't even try to find Ronnie before she left and went home. She just got into the car and drove off. Around four o'clock when Ronnie got off from work, Ronnie went out to where the employees parked and found the car missing. On days that they were at work together, Ronnie would get off at four and Margret would get off at four-thirty. Ronnie would spend his time waiting for Margret at the car so that as soon as she got to the car they could leave.

Ronnie had learned the hard way when she had to wait for him once. His elbow still had a dull ache from time to time where she had hit him with a brass candlestick.

Ronnie froze, he couldn't think, didn't want to think, he knew that he would pay hell for this. Why, this was his fault, had to be his fault, he shouldn't have left the keys in the car. Now it was stolen and she would make him pay. Wait, that guilt trip wouldn't work, he was standing there looking at the keys in his hand. Well then, he shouldn't have left the car unlocked. Yes, that was it, he had left the car unlocked and now it was gone. But in his heart he knew that this was also untrue. Checking all of the doors to insure that they were locked was part of his parking ritual. He was border line obsessive about checking the doors. Sometimes he would check the doors, all of the doors, two or three times to ensure that they were secure.

As he stood there, Ronnie realized that if he told Margret now, while she was still with all of her working buddies, her wrath might be forestalled. Surely she wouldn't go off on him in front of her co-workers. So Ronnie mustered up his courage and set sail for the dining room of the country club.

The closer he got to the rear door that led into the kitchen, the heavier his feet seemed to become. As he passed through the door into the vestibule that led into the kitchen, he looked into the full length mirror mounted on the wall for the employees to check their uniforms in. Ronnie saw himself for what seemed to be the first time. He was slouching and actually dragging his feet. This stopped him dead in his tracks and he stood there looking at his reflection with the intensity of someone that had never seen themselves before. God, he looked awful, he thought, so old. How could he look this old? He was only twenty-five, but the person who stood there looking back at him looked like a rough forty. There were lines on his face that helped to give him the older appearance. The lack of sleep also showed under his eyes with two fifty pound bags. Standing up straight and throwing his shoulders back, he found that he felt a little better. Taking a deep breath he noticed that his head cleared. He discovered that his fears had also abated, at least a little.

After all, why was he just about crapping his pants because someone else had taken the car? Things happened. This type of thing happened often. Maybe one of the rich asshole's kids that played golf here had taken it for a joyride to get back at daddy or mommy. If that was the case, Margret and he might get a little money to keep their mouths shut and not press charges against their precious little golden child.

This thought really did bolster his confidence. So he marched through the kitchen and looked through the doors into the dining room to see where his beloved was standing. Only he didn't see her. So Ronnie stepped through the doors and saw one of the waitresses standing at a table filling salt shakers in preparation for the supper crowd.

"Excuse me," Ronnie said gently with a smile on his face, "but could you tell me where Margret is?"

"She's not here." The young girl replied.

A wave of fear washed over him and he was suddenly worried that Margret had gotten sick and had to go home. "Could you tell me where she is? I'm her husband." Ronnie asked.

"You don't know? She got fired today." Was the reply.

He actually felt his lower jaw hit the ground as his mouth fell open in disbelief. "Wha...What?" He managed to stammer.

"You poor guy, you didn't know did you? Maybe I shouldn't tell you this, but I heard that she got caught helping herself to the cash register. They told her to either hit the street or they would call the police." The young waitress told him and then added, "She didn't tell you when she left? Man, that's cold. I feel sorry for you."

"Thank you." Ronnie told her, but he hardly heard himself say it, his mind was buzzing. Margret got fired for stealing? That would go along way to explain how she always seemed to be able to go shopping whenever she wanted to. But Ronnie refused to believe that it could be true. As he turned to leave he noticed that the waitress was speaking again so he said, "Beg your pardon?"

"I was just asking that you not tell anyone that I told you anything." Was her quiet reply.

Ronnie smiled and told her not to worry because he wouldn't say a thing to anyone and then thanked her again.

His mind was a buzz now. He still couldn't believe that she had gotten fired for being a thief. So he headed for the front office to use the phone to call Margret to come and get him. When he got there, the Assistant Administrator saw him and called him into her office. Once he was inside the office, she shut her door and asked him to have a seat.

"Ronald, you have been a very valued employee here. I just wanted to say how sorry I am for what happened today." She told him once they were both settled in their chairs.

"If you don't mind me asking, what exactly did happen? I'm kind of confused."

"That's okay. It all started about three months ago. Every now and then the dining room cash register would either come up short at the end of the night or the food orders wouldn't match the register receipts at closing time. It usually wasn't very much so we just overlooked it. Then last week we really started coming up short. So this week we started watching all of the transactions. Unfortunately, I caught her sticking two twenty dollar bills in her pocket after she under rang a meal."

"Under rang a meal? How do you do that?" Ronnie asked. Up until she had said that, he had been following what she was saying pretty good.

"Actually it's quite simple. You act like you're ringing up a sale, but instead, you only ring up the desert and still charge the customer for the whole meal. Then you pocket the difference after the customer leaves. But getting back, we decided that instead of causing a big fuss and calling the police, we would just cut our losses and ask her to leave. After all, as pregnant as she is, I don't think she needed the extra stress."

"I would like to thank you for that. I just can't believe that she would do something like this. Thank you for telling me, you don't know how much I really appreciate it. I know how busy you are and I thank you for your time."

"That's okay Ronald. I felt that you deserved to hear the truth from someone that was in on it, rather than hear it through the grapevine." The smile on her face was sincere.

"Thank you again." Ronnie said as he stood up, "I really do appreciate it." The smile he gave back to the old woman was as sincere as the one she had given him. Then he asked, "May I use your phone to call for a ride home?"

"Of course you may. Use the one on the secretary's desk if you don't mind."

"Thank you." was his reply as he left the office. His feelings were indescribable at that moment. At first, there had been disbelief, then rage. But now he felt nothing, detached. It was as if he was floating above himself as a casual observer. He saw himself walk out the door and over to the desk where the telephone was and pick it up. He dialed the number and put the receiver to his ear. When he heard the phone ring he was back inside himself again and was

9

startled because he had no conscious recollection of dialing the phone. On the forth ring it was answered.

"Hello?" Margret said. Damn, she sounds normal, Ronnie thought to himself. But then again he really didn't know what to expect her to sound like.

"Margret?"

"Oh, it's you. What do you want?" She said. Ronnie noticed that as soon as she recognized his voice, her whole attitude and tone of voice suddenly changed. He could hear the acid dripping from her fangs. He got a quick visual flash of a set of fangs dripping clear liquid next to a mouth piece of a telephone.

"Everything okay?" Ronnie asked tentatively.

"Of course. Why shouldn't they be? Now what do you want? I'm busy."

"Well...It's quitting time and I need a ride."

"Listen asshole. You got feet, get your own silly ass home. I don't have time for your shit." Margret said and then without waiting for a reply from Ronnie, hung up the phone.

He stood there for a second listening to the silence of an open line and then put the receiver back onto the phone with enough force that it cracked the ear piece when he missed the cradle the first time. Ronnie didn't slam the phone down like you could well imagine someone would in his situation. He just put it down with a lot of force. Halfway through the next day, the secretary would get a small cut on her ear from the cracked plastic.

Ronnie turned around and walked straight out of the door. He turned the corner and went out the main door. Everyone who saw him leave would later remark that they had seen the look of murder in his eyes as he walked across the parking lot heading for the main road out. Ronnie walked on, oblivious to everything and everyone around him.

To say that he was deep in thought was an understatement. The mental conversation he was having with himself was fast and furious. He felt as if his mind had split into two separate halves that were in a conversational battle.

'Oh yeah, my feet will get my silly ass home you bitch. But you definitely are not going to like it when I get there.' A new voice that he didn't really recognize said in his mind.

'Wait, think this out.' The other half of his mind rebutted. This was the voice he was used to hearing. It was his own and the one that he thought in. 'She's had a really bad day and is probably afraid to face you. I mean, to get fired for stealing, you know her day must really suck right now.'

'So what?! If she thinks her day sucks now, just wait until I get home. Her day is really going to suck then. I'm tired of her bullshit. It's almost ten miles home. The least the bitch could do is come and get me.'

'She's upset. I'll just tell her how pissed I am at her when I get home. She won't do this again.'

10

'Right...Remember the last time you decided to make a stand against her? The new dirty little voice asked.'

'Shut up!'

'Got your ass kicked, didn't you?'

'I said shut the fuck up!' He said in such a loud mental voice that it made his head hurt. To his horror, he realized that the other voice belonged to himself. It was the second half of his mind arguing back. But it was older and reminded him of the way he remembered his father's voice had sounded.

'Yeah, you really showed her who was the man of the family that night.' The voice pressed on, 'Be manly enough this time and she'll probably kill you. What a true pussy you are.'

Anyone who happened to see him on his way home that night probably thought that he was one of those guys that every town has. The ones that you sometimes see standing on the street corners either yelling at the cars or talking to themselves. Two of his coworkers saw him on their way home and stopped to see if he needed a ride. He looked straight at them with unseeing eyes. They noticed that Ronnie's eyes had a glazed look about them and his mouth was moving but no sound escaped.

In truth, Ronnie never really saw them, he was on total autopilot for the trip while his mind raged against itself. After asking him a couple of times if he needed a ride and getting no reply as he walked right past them, they said the heck with it and drove away. But the look on his face bothered the two men in the car. There was a feeling that someone was going to die. There was also the feeling that what they had just seen walk by them wasn't human at all. It was death taking a stroll in the late afternoon.

'There will be no more of getting my ass kicked around. I'm not taking anymore of her bullshit. It's time that she paid the price.'

'Pussy!" was all that came as a reply.

'Like hell!'

'Who are you trying to kid? I live with you, remember? You'll get home all puffed up with yourself and she'll smack you in the head. You'll be kissing her ass two minutes after you get there.'

Ronnie. A faint new voice said in his mind.

'Who the hell was that?' Both sides of his mind asked in unison.

Ronnie. It said again.

'Yes?' He thought back.

Ronnie...Come see me. I can help. It replied.

'Who are you?' His undivided mind asked.

Why...I'm your old friend, don't you remember? I'm hurt that you don't recognize my voice. Look ahead of you.

11

For the first time, Ronnie looked up with seeing eyes and saw the liquor store where he had bought so many of his liquid lunches just ahead of him. For a brief second he was tempted to go inside and get something to ease his tensions.

He stopped and stood there looking in through the front door of the small store. As he stood there, the store changed before his eyes. He saw death in the faces of the gathering of men standing around outside. The store itself had changed. It was no longer the spotlessly clean, brightly lit store he had always known. The lights were now dim and the floor was dirty. The whole place had an aura of grungy and he could smell the pungent odor of failure and death. Ronnie thought to himself that it was remarkable that those smells were so close to the smell of feces and urine.

Looking further into the store he saw the counter. Standing behind the counter was his old dead college professor. He was standing there smiling and beckoning Ronnie to come inside with his hand.

Sometimes you need to get what you deserve. The ghastly phantom from Ronnie's past said.

It was then that something snapped inside Ronnie and he ran off down the street screaming.

RONNIE RONNIE RONNIE RONNIE RONNIE RONNIE RONNIE RONNIE RONNIE. Was all that he heard in his mind as he ran. He was grateful when he found that the further away he got from the liquor store the quieter the voice became. Finally, it was no longer there.

When Ronnie finally stopped running he was out of breath and sweat ran down him like a river. He sat down on a bus bench and lit up a cigarette. Looking at his surroundings, he figured that he had run almost two miles. Ronnie glanced at his watch and saw that it was almost six and he knew that he still had a long way to go before he got home. Ronnie couldn't understand what had happened to him at the liquor store, but he felt good that he was able to resist the temptation to go inside and get drunk. The last thing he needed tonight was to show up at home wasted. He wanted to have a clear head when he got home.

Tonight there would be music to face but he was not going to be the one dancing. He would make his stand and to hell with what the consequences would be. It seemed that the run had done him good, he was thinking clearer and felt better than he had in years. Ronnie was convinced that he would no longer be the victim that he had been in the past.

'Bullshit.' The voice inside his mind said, 'Five minutes and you'll be kissing her ass.'

'Like hell,' Ronnie thought back, 'Not this time. She'll be the one puckering up and she had better do a good job.'

'We shall see what we shall see, won't we?'

'What do you mean by that?' Ronnie mentally asked himself.

But the half of his mind that he had been having the conversation with had fallen silent. So Ronnie flipped his cigarette and got up from the bench and started walking again. As with the time that he had been running, he was doing it in mental silence. The only thing that he did decide on was that when he got home he wasn't going to bring up the subject of Margret's dismissal. He wanted to see what kind of story she would give him.

It was almost midnight before he got home. He was sweaty and his feet hurt. Ronnie was glad that he didn't have to go back to work in the morning. After his walk home he doubted that he would be in shape to work, it had been a long time since he had taken a real hike. Ronnie walked into the house and Margret was no where to be seen. With a great deal of caution he walked to the bathroom and took care of business, then he went upstairs and changed into something less sweaty.

Once he was comfortable, he stalked around the house to see where Margret was. With a sigh of relief he discovered that she wasn't in the house. Looking out through the small window in the back door, he saw that she was sitting on the back porch. Ronnie's immediate reaction was to lock the door and let her sit out there all night. But he fought the urge, opened the door and joined her outside.

"There you are," Ronnie said calmly, "I was worried about you. I couldn't find you in the house." He forced himself to remain calm because he didn't want to show his cards.

"Oh Ronnie," Margret said crying, "I'm so sorry. I really should have come and gotten you. It's such a long way home and I was getting scared that you weren't going to come home at all. You really must hate me."

As Margret was talking, Ronnie sat down on the porch beside her. When she was finished speaking, Margret made a move to put her head on his shoulder, Something that she hadn't done in a very long time. Without thinking, Ronnie pulled away from her touch.

"I was right! You do hate me." She said through a renewed veil of tears.

"I wouldn't say that I hate you," He replied and simultaneously thought, 'I loath you bitch. Jesus what an act.' Continuing, he said, "You might say that I'm just not very happy with you right now."

"Ronnie, I have to tell you something, but you gotta promise not to get mad. Please."

'Okay,' He thought, 'Here it comes.' After a second or two of dramatic pause he said, "What could I get mad about? You didn't bounce another check did you?'

"No, I didn't bounce another check!" Margret snapped back, "It's just that when I had my checkup two weeks ago, the doctor suggested that it was time for me to lay off from work and stay in bed. I just didn't tell you because I thought you'd get mad."

'Oh man,' He thought, 'What a lying bitch. With all of this bullshit being spread around there's going to be an award winning crop of roses growing on this concrete slab.' He asked, "So what are you trying to tell me Margret?"

"Today I wasn't feeling very well and the stress got to me. Before I knew it, I had quit my job."

"So that's all you're upset about? You quit your job. Oh well." As Ronnie said it, he was looking in her face and saw her expression instantly change from upset to relieved. Apparently, she thought that he had bought her line of B.S.. Ronnie stood up and turned to go back into the house, when he did he said, "I guess that's that."

"Where are you going?" Margret asked him.

"I have some business to take care of inside."

Margret got up and followed him into the house, up the stairs and into the bedroom. She watched as Ronnie got a stuff-sack out of the closet and began loading it with some of his clothes. She asked him what he was doing, but he didn't answer her. Margret turned the tears back on again and begged him not to leave. When she saw that wasn't working, she reverted back to her normal self and demanded that he put his stuff back and cut out his crap. She tried to lay a guilt trip on him saying that she couldn't believe that he was going to leave because she was too pregnant to work. Pregnant with HIS child.

When Ronnie was finished packing his bag, he turned to leave and only said one thing to her. "Did they let you keep the forty bucks you stole when they fired you?"

This stopped Margret dead in her tracks and her mouth dropped open. It was the classic look called 'Busted'. Ronnie used her state of shock to grab his bag and walk past her out of the bedroom. She followed him down the stairs with a quiet demeanor. She was a few steps behind him coming down the stairs and he reached the front door before she was off of the staircase. Ronnie opened the front door and continued to exit the house leaving the door open behind him. Margret walked to the front door and watched Ronnie as he walked across the porch and down the front steps.

When Ronnie reached the bottom of the steps he took one more step before stopping and turned around to say one more thing to Margret. She had stopped at the front door and was looking out at Ronnie, not saying anything.

"Margret, I'm leaving and I may or may not be back. If I were you, I would take this time to think about your life. Marriage is built on trust, not bullshit." Then Ronnie turned to leave.

As Ronnie was turning, Margret took one step backwards and picked up a small ceramic elephant that was sitting beside the door on a table, then she took one step forward. Her motion was fluid and effortless. Ronnie having his back to Margret, didn't see her step out onto the porch and take aim. As an act of defiance, she threw the elephant at Ronnie as he started to walk away. Her aim was precise and she nailed him in the left shoulder towards the center of his shoulder blades.

At the same instant the elephant hit Ronnie, his sneaker snagged on the unevenness of the concrete pads that made up the front walk that led to the street. It caught him by surprise and he fell flat on his face striking his forehead a pretty good wallop on the concrete.

The elephant, having lost all of its forward momentum after hitting Ronnie, fell straight down and shattered on the walk.

Ronnie was dazed for about twenty seconds.

Kill her. Was the first thing that he heard, Ronnie neither recognized the voice, nor understood what it had said. "What?" Ronnie asked groggily. All he knew was that his forehead, that had been numb, was now beginning to sting.

Kill her kill the bitch kill the bitch kill her kill her now gut her rip her throat out kill the bitch The new voice continued in his mind. It was hypnotic like a chant and getting louder and faster.

On shaky legs, Ronnie managed to stand up. He half turned and looked back at Margret. She was still standing there looking at him and for a half of a second Ronnie considered doing what the voice was telling him to do. He could now feel the blood running down his face from his forehead. As he felt the blood, the voice fell quiet and still looking at Margret, saw that she had began to change before his eyes. She was no longer the woman that he had known, but was evil looking. As he watched, she lost all resemblance to anything human.

What you are looking at is the evil inside of her. The voice said and then quickly added, *She's not even human anymore. No one can fault you for killing something that isn't human. It would be like squashing a bug. Think of it as major pest control.*

The whole time, Margret had been standing there looking at Ronnie to see what he would do. But he was just standing there with a strange look on his face. At first, Margret had been sorry that she had hit him with the elephant. But she consoled herself by telling herself that it was his fault that she had thrown it at him and that it was his attitude that had made her do it.

It was about that same time, Ronnie pressed his fists against the sides of his head and screamed 'No!' It was that instant that Margret recognized the look in his eyes. She had seen those same eyes in a picture of that Manson guy who had killed all of those people in California. A cold shiver ran through her and for the first time noticed the blood running down Ronnie's face.

Ronnie quickly scooped up his stuff sack, both Margret and he ran in different directions at the same time. Margret ran back into the house and Ronnie ran off down the street. Neither saw the other leave.

Margret was scared, she knew that she had pushed Ronnie over the edge. She figured that Ronnie was going to come back into the house and kill her. It didn't take very long before her paranoia was in a self-feeding frenzy. Every little sound (and she noticed them all) was Ronnie coming back into the house. Margret quickly went and locked all of the doors and got a butcher knife out of the kitchen. Ronnie was coming. Ronnie was coming. This thought kept going through her mind over and over again.

Margret knew that she had messed with Ronnie one time too many and now she was going to die because of it. Maybe she shouldn't have hit him all of those times. Now he would be the one to call the bill due and she would pay. She had reached a level of hysteria unparalleled before. Her grip on the handle of the butcher knife was, to say the least, tight. Her knuckles were bone white and would stay that way for a long time. The rivets in the handle made impressions in her palm that would stay there for the rest of the night.

Had the truth been known, she wouldn't have been able to use the knife. All someone would have had to do was to walk up behind her and say 'BOO'. She would have dropped dead of a heart attack. Ronnie had really missed his chance to be rid of her. The coroner would have ruled that her weight, plus the pregnancy had been too much for her heart to handle. It would have been death by natural causes.

Ronnie on the other hand, was still running down the street trying to get the voice inside his head to shut up. He also wanted to get as much distance between Margret and him as possible. He was afraid that he was going to succumb to that voice in his mind and do what it was telling him to do. The blood from his forehead was flowing more now because of his exertion and now, the blood mixed with his sweat was stinging his eyes.

You missed your chance, you know that don't you? His new internal voice asked. It was calm and serene, almost hypnotic. *You should have just reached up and snapped her neck.*

'Shut up!' Ronnie thought back.

That's the problem Ronnie, I've been shut up too damn long. But now you are going to listen, because you can run as far as you want, but how far truly can you run from your own mind?

This stopped Ronnie dead in his tracks, the logic was there. There was nothing he could do. 'What do you want?' He asked.

That you listen for once in your life instead of pretending that you are in control and to listen to another point of view.

'Okay. If I listen, will you please go away?'

Hell no. The voice replied with a slight smirk to it. *You'll listen and I'll damn well do what I want to.*

'Please,' Ronnie thought in a weak voice, 'Please, who are you?'

You know who I am you dickhead. I'm really hurt that you don't recognize me. But that's not important right now. Right now you have to find some shelter and stop your bleeding. Find one of those school bus shelters so you can sit down and tend to yourself.

A chill ran through Ronnie when he realized that the voice in his head was his dead professor.

Get a move on.

Ronnie walked on as he was instructed and a couple of blocks away he found one of those shelters. It was about five feet wide and six feet long with benches running down either side of the interior. Going inside, Ronnie sat down and tried to figure out where he was. For the second time that day, he had run over a mile. Taking off his shirt to swab the blood from his forehead, Ronnie noticed for the first time how chilly the night air was.

Ronnie also noticed that the instant he walked into the bus shelter, the voice inside his mind stopped. As he sat there with his shirt pressed to his forehead he thought about that voice. With a sense of dread it dawned on him that he really did know that voice. It was the one that had been cutting his sleep short for quite some time, it was the voice of the dead professor that had been haunting his dreams for so long.

As Ronnie sat in the bus shelter tending to his injury, little did he know that Margret was calling the police at that very moment.

"City desk. Sergeant Jensen speaking. May I help you?"

"He's trying to kill me!" Margret hysterically sobbed into the phone.

"Who's trying to kill you?"

"Help me, he's coming, he's going to kill me."

"Ma'am please calm down. Is someone in the room with you?"

"No. He's outside and trying to get into the house. He's going to kill me. You gotta help me. I'm going to die."

It was at that point that the phone went dead. Luckily for Jensen, the department had just installed a new phone system that automatically traced the call and gave a printout of the phone number and the address where the call had originated. Within fifteen seconds, Sergeant Jensen was on the phone to dispatch with the complaint and address. Thirty seconds after the phone had gone dead, six police cars were flying to Margret's house. Normally, only one or two cars at the most would have been dispatched, but it had been a very slow night after a very long and slow week. The officers were eager for a little action and when the 'Woman in distress' call went out over the radio net, everyone went to take a look.

About five minutes before Margret made that fateful call, a woman had called Sergeant Jensen and reported that while she had been out walking her cat, she had seen some 'poor man' taking refuge in a school bus shelter. Why the way he had looked he must have been either mugged or in some terrible accident. He had blood all down the front of him.

Jensen called dispatch and the call went out as a 'Check vagrant'. One car was dispatched. Patrolman Lewis and Junior Auxiliary Patrolman Avery were already getting out of their car where Ronnie was, when the call about Margret came across the radio.

"Oh man, we're going to miss all of the fun." Avery said genuinely mad. He only got to ride in the patrol cars twice a month. The rest of the time he spent his volunteer hours being the police departments go-fer. And now he was going to miss the most exciting thing of the month just to help roust some wino.

"Shut up." Lewis muttered under his breath. God he hated the nights he got stuck with the young cop wanna-be's. Nothing but juvenile crap all night about high school and girl friends.

"Hey buddy, you okay?" Lewis said as he shined his flashlight on the young man sitting inside the shelter.

Ronnie looked up, blinded by the bright light and said, "What?"

Both Lewis and Avery said "Oh shit." at the same time and the elder instructed the younger to get the first aid kit. Avery was off like he was shot out of a cannon.

"Hey buddy, you're going to be okay. Just relax and let me help you." Lewis said as he lowered the flashlight and went over to where Ronnie was sitting.

"What's your name?"

"Ronald."

"Did somebody do this to you Ron? You don't mind if I call you Ron do you?"

"No."

"No what, Ron."

"No, I fell down and hit my head and no, you can call me whatever you like sir."

"Drinking tonight Ron?" Lewis asked as he surveyed Ronnie's head. The wound was definitely going to need a bunch of stitches. It was at that moment that Avery showed back up with the first aid kit. Lewis decided to give Avery a thrill and told him to call for an ambulance. Once again Avery was off like a streak. Turning his attention back to Ronnie, Lewis repeated his question. "Been drinking tonight?"

"No sir. I was running and tripped. I hit my head on the concrete."

"Yeah, running in the dark can do that sometimes. How do you feel?" Lewis asked as he put a couple of sterile pads against Ronnie's forehead.

"Sort of confused and my head hurts real bad."

"I bet it does. Here, hold this." He said as he placed Ronnie's hand gently against the pads. Then he continued, "I need to get some information from you if that's okay. What's your full name?"

"Ronald Philbert Fisher."

At the same moment Ronnie was answering Lewis's questions, the police were arriving at his house in full style. The first two officers went to the front

18

door as the rest of the officers surrounded the house and started searching the bushes.

Margret greeted the officers with open arms. She just knew that Ronnie was stalking around in the bushes trying to get back into the house. They explained to her that the bushes were being searched and if he was out there, they would find him. Then they started their end of the information gathering. Within a couple of minutes it was reported back to the officers inside the house with Margret that Ronnie was nowhere to be found. They then put out an All Points Bulletin on Ronald Philbert Fisher.

The APB reached the dispatch just after the ambulance call. When Lewis was satisfied that Ron was going to be okay, he went over to the patrol car to radio in his information. The dispatcher told Lewis about the guy he was tending. Lewis explained what condition Ronnie was in and further explained that there was no way his guy could be doing what was be said that he was doing, they were over a mile away and besides being wounded, his guy was on foot.

The dispatcher told the group over at Ronnie's house where he was. The on scene commander had just arrived, a Sergeant Maxwell, and he realized that Ronnie was over a mile away and there was no way he could be responsible for Margret's hysterics. He had been listening to the radio traffic as he was driving to Ronnie's house. Max went into the house and introduced himself to Margret and then told her the facts as he saw them. This set Margret off and she made a lot of 'friends'. She told Max that he was 'Fucking Crazy' and he was just making up some bullshit so he could get his lazy ass back to the doughnut shop. She just knew that Ronnie was out there somewhere because she had just heard him trying to get back into the house a couple of minutes before they had showed up.

Once again Max tried to explain to her that her husband was over a mile away and not trying to break into her house. He omitted the part that Ronnie didn't seem to be in any physical shape to kill her from the report that he had heard Lewis give over the radio. But Margret just got more irate, louder, and more verbally abusive. It was when she got to the point of theorizing about how Max carried such a big gun to make up for the lack of a dick, that Max told her that if she didn't stop talking he was going to arrest her for a couple of hundred obscenity violations. Max then turned around and walked out of the front door. As he walked outside, he thought to himself that this is one bitch he felt sorry for who ever had married her.

Walking down the porch and up the walk, he saw the smashed porcelain that had been an elephant not too long ago and a small puddle of blood a few feet away and made a mental note of it. When he got to his patrol car he told the other guys that he was going over to where the suspect was, to interview him. Everyone was milling around talking and they just waved him on.

As Max drove to where Ronnie was, he realized for himself that there was no way this guy could have gotten so far away on foot so quickly. He still had a little doubt in his mind until he got to where the ambulance and Ronnie were. When he got there, he went and talked to Lewis first. The paramedics were still working on Ronnie.

"Lew, what's up?"

"Got a messy one here Max. He's banged up pretty bad."

"So how's the kid?" Max asked looking around to see where Avery was.

"Man, be glad you ain't riding with him. First thing he wanted to do was play with my gun."

"So, where is he now?"

"Over there supervising the meat wagon crew."

Max looked over and saw Avery standing next to the bus shelter. "Lucky you." He said to Lewis, remembering how he had to chaperone the kid he got stuck with a while back. A small shiver ran up his spine.

"So, what you got?" Lewis asked.

"One short, very pregnant, raving lunatic bitch saying that your guy is trying to kill her."

"What kind of shape is she in? This guy was a total mess when we found him."

"Not a mark on her. But she's got a mouth on her. She's already pissed me off."

"Well, there's no way this guy could be trying to kill her. Looks like he took a pretty good shot to the head. You can tell he's hurting."

"Mind if I talk to him?"

"Go ahead."

"What's his attitude like?"

"Respectful."

That impressed Max, usually the people they dealt with were belligerent. Didn't matter if they were being helped or not, at some point in the conversation, somebody would point out who was paying whose salary. After what he had dealt with at this guys house, this would be a refreshing change.

"Yew boys 'bout finished with him?" Max asked as he walked over to where the paramedics were working on Ronnie.

"Just about." Was the reply, "All we gotta do is get him ready for transport."

That was when Ronnie spoke up, "Please sir, I can't afford the ambulance ride. I can get to the hospital on my own." Ronnie had no concept of what was going on at his house, Lewis hadn't said a thing to him.

"How do you intend to get there son?" Max asked.

"Walk I guess. I gotta save as much money as possible, I got a kid coming and that's going to be expensive."

"Well, what do you say?" Max asked one of the paramedics.

"We can't force him to go with us. But I do advise that he have a doctor check him out ASAP. He's got a real nasty head wound that we are having a hard

20

time stopping the flow of blood. I also wouldn't be surprised if he had a concussion also."

"It's up to you sport." Max said turning his attention back to Ronnie, "Wanna ride?"

Ronnie thought for a couple of seconds and then shook his head no. The paramedic shrugged his shoulders and started packing his stuff to leave.

When the paramedics were on their way back to the ambulance, Max turned to Avery and said, "Junior, go and help the paramedics put their stuff away. Maybe if you're good, they'll let you blow the siren. I wanna talk to Mr. Fisher...Alone." Avery, looking hurt, took off like he had been shot at. 'Well, at least he's kind of smart.' Max thought to himself, 'He know's how to follow directions.'

"So. What do they call you?" Max asked as he turned his attention back to Ronnie.

"Officer Lewis calls me Ron, but every one else calls me Ronnie."

"Which do you prefer?" Max asked as he sat down on the bench across from Ronnie.

"Which ever you do sir."

Max couldn't help but like this kid for some reason. Maybe it was pity because he had seen what this kid had to put up with at home. But things like Ronnie calling him sir went along way to bolster Max's opinion of him.

"Well Ronnie, I've got a small problem and it's you. You see, your wife called and said that you were trying to kill her. But at the same time, you were found over a mile away really messed up. Wanna tell me what happened?" Max felt that he was an astute observer of human nature, so when he told Ronnie about his wife, Max made a point of watching Ronnie's reaction. The combined look of disbelief and shock told Max that Margret's story was false.

Ronnie's eyes began to tear up, "She told you I was trying to kill her?" He asked.

"Yep."

"I can't believe it. She called the police on me and lied."

"Well, just tell me what happened tonight."

So Ronnie laid out the whole story beginning with the afternoon. How Margret had gotten fired and made him walk home. Her lying to him when he got home and his packing to leave because he wanted some space to think. Of course, Ronnie omitted the part about why Margret had gotten fired and the part about the new found voice in his mind. As he was talking, Lewis walked up quietly and sat down, listening to Ronnie's side of the story.

"So you were leaving?" Max asked.

Ronnie replied that he was and pulled out his stuff-sack from under the bench to support his side of the story. Max took the stuff sack and looked inside, all he saw was what appeared to be a bunch of clothes hastily stuffed inside the bag. He handed the stuff sack back to Ronnie.

"Is that when she attacked you?" Max after a second of thought.

"No sir, she threw something at me, but I tripped over the uneven walk and hit my head on the pavement." The officers looked at each other as Ronnie continued, "I think I blacked out for as couple of seconds. Then I got up and ran. Now here I am with you guys."

"Why did you run?" Lewis asked.

Ronnie opened his mouth to answer but no sound came out. After sitting there a couple of seconds, Max said, "It's okay. Why did you run?"

"I was afraid that she was going to do something to me." Ronnie finally managed to get out.

Max stood up and put his hand on Ronnie's shoulder and said, "It's okay Ronnie. You just sit here and rest. I want to talk to Officer Lewis for a minute." As he said that, he motioned with his head for Lewis to follow him. They walked over to where the patrol car was parked. Following them like a puppy was Avery. The paramedics had chased him off and he had walked up behind Lewis unseen. When they got to the car, it was Avery who spoke first.

"Man...What a puss. Can you believe the story that his wife hurt him?"

Max could believe it, he had seen Ronnie's wife in action first hand. So he told Avery, "Why don't you do something useful? I want you to go to the other side of the road and monitor traffic. That's an order."

Avery had opened his mouth to protest, but when Max had added the part about it being an order, he shut up. It was almost one in the morning and there hadn't been a car drive by since they had gotten there. Rejected, Avery sulked over to the other side of the road and stood there.

"Man, I gotta remember that one." Lewis said as he watched Avery leave, then he turned back to Max and asked, "So what do you think?"

"I believe him. I saw the front walk and there's some kind of broken porcelain on the ground and a small puddle of blood. One thing's for sure, judging from the size of the puddle of blood, he was unconscious longer than a couple of seconds."

"Well, I believe him. What do you want to do?" Lewis asked.

"Let's see if he wants to press charges and you take him to the hospital. Even if he doesn't want to press charges, I'm going to go back and put the fear into little miss bitch."

"Is she really that bad?"

"You wouldn't believe it. Be glad you get hospital duty." Then looking in Ronnie's direction, Max added, "Poor bastard. If it had been me, I probably would have shot her."

When they were finished talking, they walked back to where Ronnie was sitting. Ronnie was trying to get a cigarette out of an impossibly crushed cigarette pack. Lewis reached into his own pocket and pulled out a fresh pack and gave them to Ronnie.

"Thank you." Ronnie said as he took the new pack and then added, "So, what's up guys?"

"That's up to you Ronnie." Max answered him, "If you want, we will run her in for assault."

"But I tripped."

"Yeah, but she threw something at you that could have caused you to trip."

"No. I tripped. Besides, at this stage of her pregnancy and after being fired today, getting arrested may be too much stress for her."

"Okay." Max said, "But Officer Lewis is going to take you to the hospital to get checked out. And just to let you know, I am going to go back and talk to her. Nobody, man or woman, should have to put up with any kind of abuse."

Max and Lewis helped Ronnie up and walked him over to Lewis's patrol car. After they got Ronnie situated in the back of the car and shut the door, Max looked at Lewis and said, "I can't believe it. After what has happened to him, he's still protecting her."

"Yeah, I noticed that. " Lewis replied and then asked, "So, you're going back over to his house?"

"Yep, and I'm going to put the fear of justice in her. Unfortunately, that's about all I can do."

"Okay, I'll catch up with you later for the paperwork."

With that said, Max and Lewis got into their prospective cars and drove off. It wasn't until much later at the hospital that Lewis realized Avery wasn't with him. At four-thirty, Lewis went back to where they had found Ronnie and found Avery still standing beside the road shivering from the early morning cold. He didn't say anything as Avery got into the car and nothing was said all the way back to the station. Lewis did feel a small amount of guilt about forgetting Avery and leaving him standing beside the road. As they pulled into the parking lot he apologized for his error. Avery just shrugged him off saying there was no problem.

As Max drove back over to Ronnie's house, he thought about Ronnie's situation. Over the years as a policeman, Max had seen a lot of different types of abuse and this had all of the tell-tale signs. He wondered how long it had been going on and even why it had started in the first place. Max thought it was sad when two people who were supposed to love, honor, and respect each other decided to start banging on each other. Or more properly, when one decided that it would be fun to start banging on the other one. Since Ronnie wasn't going to press charges against her (Another classic sign, the abused protecting the abuser.), there wasn't much Max could do. So his hands were tied. But he could put the fear of God into her and from his experience in the past, that worked sometimes. And for that poor bastard he had just sent to the hospital, it would be worth a shot.

When Max arrived at Ronnie's house, the Watch Commander, Captain Waters, arrived at the same time. Greeting each other as old friends because they were, they stood and talked for about ten minutes. After hearing what Max had encountered here and Lewis had found at the bus stop, it was agreed that unless charges were pressed, there was nothing to be done. But it was also agreed that the both of them would go inside and give Margret a little pep-talk. Waters then dismissed the officers that were still milling around and Max and him headed for the house. As they walked up the walk, Max pointed out the puddle of blood and the broken porcelain.

Going inside the house, Waters dismissed the officer that had been watching over Margret.

"Mrs. Fisher, I am Captain Waters. I am the Watch Commander and I believe that you have already met Sergeant Maxwell earlier. May we have a word with you?"

"Did you find him?" Margret asked in an afraid sounding voice.

"Yes ma'am, we did." Waters replied.

"So, are you going to put him in jail?" Margret asked in a tone that almost sounded like she was relieved that Ronnie had been caught. Then she threw something in to try and dig the hole Ronnie was supposedly in a little deeper, "You know he tried to kill me earlier."

"That's what we want to talk to you about, ma'am."

"Are you telling me that he's not in jail?" Margret asked starting to sound agitated.

"No ma'am, he's not in jail at this time."

"Well, are you going to put him in jail? You know I heard him trying to get in just before you guys arrived earlier." Margret said, getting a little louder and more agitated.

"Are you saying that you heard your husband just before the police arrived originally?" Waters asked her.

"I've already told everyone that over and over again. Yes, he was trying to break into the house just before you guys arrived. Now, like I asked before, is he going to jail?"

"No ma'am, right now your husband is..."

Before Waters could finish what he was saying, Margret cut him off screaming, "It figures! You men are just covering each other's asses. I guess it would have been better if he would have killed me. I bet he'd be in jail then!"

While Margret was 'Speaking', Waters looked over at Max. Max just smiled back as if to say 'See, I told you so'.

Before Margret could get on a roll, Waters put up his hand in a 'stop' command. When he did this he spoke in a low voice.

"Mrs. Fisher, I'm afraid that if you do not be quiet right now, I WILL arrest you and take you out of here in handcuffs."

Margret's mouth stopped amid stride, she just sat there with it moving up and down with nothing coming out of it. Waters smiled to himself and Max was smiling also, they had shut her up. Waters continued speaking, "Mrs. Fisher, just before you called us and reported the threat to your life, we received another call about your husband."

"What? Who..." Margret interrupted. Again, Waters held up his hand and this time she shut up immediately.

"As I was saying, we received another call about your husband. It seems that he was over a mile away from here with a pretty nasty head wound."

"So what does that have to do with me?" Margret asked flatly. Both Waters and Max were astonished at the lack of concern about her husbands physical condition. They were also astonished at how quickly Margret's attitude had changed.

"Tonight, you and your husband had a fight and he started to leave. Isn't that correct?"

Margret sat silently.

"Mrs. Fisher. Your husband has already told us the events of the evening. So you might as well cooperate with us or this will be a very long night. Do you understand me Mrs. Fisher?"

Margret nodded her head that she did. Suddenly she felt as though her world was crashing down around her, she was scared about how much Ronnie had told them.

"Your husband was leaving tonight, is that correct?" Waters asked Margret again.

"Yes."

"When he was out on the front walk you threw something at him and hit him. Is that also correct?"

"Yes...But I didn't mean to hit him. I was mad and threw a small figurine at him."

"Where did it hit him?" Waters continued the questioning.

"In the back of the shoulder. Why?"

"Then how did he get the gash on his forehead?"

"I don't know, he fell down on the front walk. What did he tell you?"

"The same thing you just did." Max said breaking his silence for the first time.

"So what does this mean?" Margret asked.

"Well Mrs. Fisher," Waters answered her, "It's like this. You assaulted your husband and even thought he said that he tripped, it resulted in a serious injury. Normally I would arrest you right now and take you down to the station to be

25

booked. Then in about three months when your trial comes up, you would get about six months in the county jail."

"Please no." Margret stammered in a small and weak voice almost like a child. Tears began to flow from her eyes again, except this time, they were real.

"I want you to know that the only reason you are not in handcuffs right now is because your husband pleaded, no, begged us not to arrest you. He also said that he wouldn't press charges against you."

Margret's mood change was immediate, "So there's nothing you can do, right?" She asked sounding self righteous. Waters and Max were once again astonished at her reversal in attitude.

"I said that he wouldn't press charges." Waters continued, "But, I can. If I deem that the situation calls for it, I can press charges against you for assualt. Since you admitted that you threw the figurine at him, I can up the ante and make it assualt with a deadly weapon. That will get you about a year in prison."

This deflated Margret's sails immediatly. "So what happens now?" She asked weakly.

"That depends on you Mrs. Fisher. If you agree to stop hitting on your husband, then nothing happens. This time. But if you do something like this again, or the neighbors report any fighting going on here, we are going to come back. Next time, and I really hope that there isn't a next time, we will come and get you and take you downtown. I can also promise you that we will charge you with as many things as I can find to charge you with. Now having said that, do you have any questions?"

Margret said that she didn't and Waters asked her one more time.

"You do understand what I've told you?"

"Yes."

"Then we will be leaving now. Your husband is in Heartcrest Hospital. I believe that you should go there and be with him now, I think that he probably needs you. One more thing Mrs. Fisher. I am deadly serious about you causing any more injuries. I don't know what your past is but that is not the way civilized people treat each other. I will be watching. Your husband awaits."

"Thank you." Margret offered weakly.

"Sergeant Maxwell and I will see ourselves out. Go to your husband, start over again and put your differences behind you."

With that, the two men turned and walked to the front door and let themselves out and walked to the street where their cars were parked. Margret was about to have an anxiety attack. She realized just how close she had come to going to jail. All she could think of was to find her keys and get to Ronnie at the hospital. She realized like she had done earlier that evening that maybe she had gone too far with Ronnie. After all, he was a pretty good guy, he didn't run around and party like the husbands of her friends did. He always did what she wanted with no back talk. If it hadn't been for that one time awhile back when he

26

had hit her. She guessed that she had pretty much been a bitch since that day. But she decided that she would change, she would be better, and she would be nicer and more attentive to him and his needs.

At the same time Margret was inside having her change of attitude, Max and Waters were outside watching the house and talking.

"Do you think she bought it?" Waters asked Max.

"Judging from her reaction when you told her that you could press charges against her, I think she did."

"Yes, I think so also. But the real test will be how fast she leaves here. Don't you think?"

"Yeah. That would be a good indicator. I really think you scared her."

"I can't believe how fast her attitude changed. One second she's poor little helpless me and the next second she's a real iron maiden." Waters remarked.

"I think that a chameleon would have a heart attack trying to change colors as quick as she did. That's for sure." Max replied with a grin. Waters found the comment amusing also and it was indicated through the smile on his face.

They stood there for another minute and then saw some of the lights go off inside the house. A few seconds later they saw Margret come out onto the front porch. They watched as she paused long enough to look out to where they were standing and then quickly walk over to her car and get in. It wasn't until after she had pulled out and drove off before Max spoke.

"Yeah, she bought it."

"Looks like." Waters observed.

They talked for a couple more minutes and then left. Waters went back to the station and Max went back to supervising the patrols.

When Margret got to the hospital, she put on a good show of concern for where and how her husband was. Luckily, she had missed Officer Lewis by a couple of minutes, he was pulling out of the parking lot as she was pulling in. The receptionist at the Emergency Room told Margret that Ronnie had been admitted for a twenty-four hour observation.

Margret was then met by the physician that had attended Ronnie and it was explained to her that Ronnie had required almost thirty stitches to close the wound on his forehead. The doctor further explained that although no one that he knew of had died from the loss of blood from this particular type of head wound, they had a hard time stopping the flow of blood. So not only was the observation period for concussion, it was also to give him enough time to recoup from the blood loss.

When Margret finally got to Ronnie's room, she was not prepared for what she saw. They had wrapped his head in a massive bandage and this made him look a lot worse than he really was. This sight also served to shock her. When she saw the extent of the wrap job they had done on Ronnie, all she could think of was that she must have almost killed him. Standing there in the doorway, she silently swore to herself that she would never do anything like this to him again. Then she swore to her God that if he let everything be alright with Ronnie, she would be a much better person. She stood, unnoticed, by the door for almost five minutes before she walked into the room.

During the quiet time he was getting in his hospital room, Ronnie had been thankful that the voice had stopped in his mind. He couldn't understand why it had stopped at the exact moment he had walked into the bus shelter. It was almost as if it had been turned off amid sentence. After all of the rushing around that had gone on in the emergency room, Ronnie found that he was glad for the peace and quiet. Laying there, he started thinking about all of the things that Margret had done to him. He swore to himself that he would never take that kind of abuse again.

Looking back later, much later, he would reflect that he should have gotten up off of that bed and just disappeared into the night. It would have been much simpler that way.

Margret walked into the room, still unnoticed and walked to the bed. Ronnie was deep in thought while laying in the bed, felt his heart leap in his chest when Margret said his name. He made a visible flinch when she surprised him.

This flinch did more to Margret than all of the threatening the police had done. Margret recognized it the instant she saw it. She had seen her own mother react like that quite a few times to the sound of her own fathers voice. That is, until she died. This made Margret mad, but this time it was at herself.

Ronnie laid there looking at Margret for a few moments. He could see something in her face, it was familiar but he couldn't quite put his finger on it. But there was something definitely good about it, something not directed at him. Then he realized that it was her mad look and it wasn't directed at him.

Finally she spoke. "Ronnie. I am so sorry." Ronnie just laid there looking at her without speaking. "Please forgive me." Margret continued, "Please forgive me for everything that I've done to you."

'Damn, this is a change.' Ronnie thought to himself, 'But I've seen this before. But it is different this time.'

Seeing that Ronnie wasn't going to answer her, she kept on talking. Silent tears ran down her cheeks as she spoke. For the first time, she told Ronnie about her fathers treatment of her mother. About how sometimes she did things out of rage that she regretted later. And that she never meant to hurt him because she really did love him.

When she was finished talking, the all too familiar new voice inside his mind said one thing and only one thing, *BULLLLSHIT!*

Sensing that they were now at what most people would call a pregnant pause, Ronnie spoke for the first time.

"Margret, I'm sorry that you had such a terrible childhood. But, I want you to know one thing. I am not going to put up with anymore of your bullshit."

"I'm sorry. You won't have to, it won't happen again. I'll change."

"What ever," He replied, "I've done everything to kiss your ass just the way you wanted it kissed and you still treat me like shit. I'm tired, tired of it and tired of you." *Way to go! Tell her like it is!* His mental voice said and then fell silent.

"I'll be good." She pleaded, "Just don't leave me. Oh please forgive me. I am so sorry."

"Look Margret, I've had a real shitty day. I just want to rest and get today behind me. You can ask God to forgive you when and if you see him. Because like an elephant, I'll never forget."

"I'll just sit here with you then."

"Do what ever you feel is necessary to make your conscious feel better."

This was a slap in her face, but it was one that she would take without retribution. She went over in the corner and pulled the chair that was sitting there over to the bed. Sitting down, Margret took Ronnie's left hand in her own and pressed her face against it. She just sat there silently. The whole time she was there, until she fell asleep, she never saw the business card in Ronnie's right hand. It had been given to him by Lewis and had Lewis's home phone number along with his work number. It had been given to Ronnie with instruction's that if he ever needed anything, day or night, to call.

Ronnie intended to do just that if he had to. He had meant what he had said to Margret, he wasn't going to take it anymore.

But he would.

3.

After checking on him a couple of times that morning, it was early afternoon before the doctor came in and told Ronnie that he was free to go. The doctor further explained that Ronnie would have to take it easy for the next couple of days. Margret was still there in the room, the chair she had spent the night in was now pulled over to the window and she sat there silently looking outside. She had a faraway look in her eyes that the doctor attributed to either deep reflection, or mind-numbing boredom.

Margret was deep in thought questioning her life. How could she have turned out so much like the man that she hated? She decided that she had better change her life now. With the baby on the way, she didn't want to subject her child to what she had been subjected to as a young girl. Maybe by doing that, she would be able to break this cycle of abuse she had fallen into. Margret was vaguely aware of the doctor when he was in the room.

Ronnie was tired. He had catnapped through most of the morning. It seemed as though every time had started getting some good sleep during the night, the nurse would come in and wake him to check on him. Ronnie was becoming more irritated as the morning wore on. So it was a relief to him when the doctor gave him the green light to go home.

Very little was said on that trip home. Margret was unusually quiet and Ronnie was too tired to comment. When they got home, Margret directed Ronnie to her chair (The most comfortable one) and waited on him hand and foot until he fell asleep.

As Ronnie slept, he dreamed about normal things, safe things. After about seven hours of sleep, Margret noticed him stirring around in the chair. Margret walked over and checked Ronnie to make sure he was alright, she saw that Ronnie was still asleep and was covered with a fine sheen of sweat. Now, his stirring in the chair was becoming more pronounced and violent. She mistakenly thought that he was dreaming about the fight that they had last night. Ronnie was dreaming about her, but not in a way she could have imagined.

In Ronnie's dream he was standing on top of a small plateau. As he turned around he found that he could see the edge all of the way around back to where

30

he was standing. He walked over closer to the edge and saw that he was very high up, the ground looked as if it were thousands of feet below him. The sun was bright but it was not hot. In fact, it was cool, comfortably so. There were no clouds and the visibility was crystal clear. There was a light breeze and Ronnie just stood there enjoying the view. He found that it was peaceful here and he wished that he never had to leave this new place of his dreams.

As he stood there, he heard a faint voice behind him. *Ronnie* it said.

Ronnie turned and saw a man standing by the opposite edge. In a blink of an eye, the man was gone.

Ronnie. The voice repeated, this time right behind him. Ronnie could feel his heart pounding in his chest as he spun around to see what was behind him. But there was nothing there. Ronnie was startled when he felt a hand come to rest on his shoulder and he spun around once again and came face to face with his dead college professor.

'What do you want?' Ronnie asked.

I've got what I want. The apparition replied, *But remember Ronnie, sometimes we get what we deserve.*

It was then with a great deal of dread, Ronnie finally acknowledged and accepted the voice. It was the new voice in his mind that had told him to kill Margret. Ronnie didn't know what to do, so in his dream he started backing up. The Professor just stayed where he was standing. When Ronnie got to the edge, he stopped, standing there precariously balanced on the edge the Professor began to speak to him again.

Ronnie. It really doesn't matter how far you go, I'll always be with you. In fact, I own you.

'Like hell you do!' Ronnie shouted back.

Hell has nothing to do with it because sometimes YOU get what YOU deserve.

With the word 'sometimes', the Professor's mouth quickly grew until with the word 'deserve', it seemed to fill the entire world. Ronnie just stood there looking up, his knees shaking so badly he could barely stand up. Then the mouth opened to reveal razor sharp teeth. They were the size of machete's and had chunks of meat wedged between them. Blood ran down them in rivulets. As Ronnie stood there frozen like a deer in a high power spot light at night, he began to fill with dread that he was going to die.

How 'bout a little blow job Ronnie? The mouth asked laughingly. With that, the mouth started closing and coming down around Ronnie at the same time, threatening to bite him in half.

'Fuck you!' Ronnie screamed as he took one more step backwards and simply dropped off the edge of the plateau. Right over the top of his head, where he had been standing less than a quarter of a second before, he heard the metallic clank and saw the flash of sparks as the teeth narrowly missed him and grated together.

As Ronnie fell, a great sense of peace came over him. He knew that he was going to die, but it wasn't going to be at the hands of that fag professor. He was going to be splattered all over the ground that was rushing up to meet him. For some reason, Ronnie found that comforting, at least it would be quick. A lot quicker than being chewed up. He looked down again and saw that the ground was a lot closer and he knew that it would all be over in less than a second. In his dream, just as he hit the ground he woke up.

Ronnie laid there in the chair disoriented for a few seconds. Then he slowly ran his hand across his face and around his body. He was alive! He was soaking wet, but he was definitely alive. He had heard somewhere that if you dreamed that you were falling and you hit the ground, you died. But he was laying there in the chair alive and it felt really good.

"Ronnie, are you okay?" Margret asked from where she was sitting on the couch.

"Just a bad dream." He replied.

That was the last bad dream Ronnie had for a considerable period of time. Three weeks later Margret had the baby. She was in labor for sixteen hours and Ronnie took secret delight in her pain. When it was all over with, they were the proud owners of a baby girl they named Nancy Anne Fisher.

For the next six months, things were really good and they found that parenthood was a busy time for the both of them. Bottles, diapers, check-ups, and the million other things that go along with owning kids.

It was also a big financial strain on their one income family. Margret had decided (Although she never discussed it with Ronnie) that she wasn't going to go back to work. One time when she was talking on the phone with one of her friends, she remarked that she didn't mind if her husband worked two or three jobs. Margret's spending habits also reflected her attitude. When ever she saw something that she wanted, she got it. The bottom line in the checkbook was no object with her and this caused Ronnie to have to really scramble a few times to cover the checks she had written for the crap she bought.

Ronnie was really beginning to worry that there wasn't enough money to go around. Sometimes it seemed that there was only enough money for the doctors and formula, let alone, Margret's outrageous spending habits. Work was beginning to slow down and there wasn't enough hours to go around. His boss had pity on him and gave him as many hours as possible. Although it wasn't much, this helped a little.

Ronnie's mother had once told him that he had cats feet. No matter what direction he was in when he jumped, he always seemed to land on his feet.

Then one day, Ronnie was taking his lunch at the fourteenth hole. It had a small pond next to a stand of trees that served as a water hazard. There was a bench in the shade with a water cooler next to it. That water cooler had the coldest water on the course. As he sat there enjoying the shade and thinking about as little as possible, there was a sudden, sharp pain in the back of his head. Ronnie actually saw stars floating around him just before he passed out. When he came to, there was a short, fat man standing over him shaking him.

"Are you alright?" The man asked.

"Wha...What?" Ronnie asked weakly.

"I asked if you were okay."

"I think so." Ronnie replied as the fog began to clear from his mind and vision.

"Man, I thought that I had killed you."

"What?"

"I sliced real bad on that last shot and nailed you. As I drove over here and saw you laying on the ground, I thought I had killed you."

"Well, you didn't. I guess that's lucky for me."

With that, the man stood up laughing and offered his hand to help Ronnie up. Ronnie got up but swayed really bad on his feet. The man thought Ronnie was going to fall down, so he helped him sit back down on the bench.

"Whoa there big dog." The man said as Ronnie sat down, "Just take it easy for a couple of minutes."

"Yeah, I guess you're right. I do feel a little dizzy." Ronnie replied.

Surveying the back of Ronnie's head, the stranger said, "Looks like you're going to have a good sized knot on your head."

"What's one more lump on the old noggin. Just another war wound." Ronnie said as he gingerly felt the back of his head.

"I guess the least I could do after half killing you is to introduce myself. I'm Aaron McGuire." The man said holding out his hand.

"Ronald Fisher, you can call me Ronnie." Ronnie replied taking Aaron's hand. After a couple of pumps up and down, they sat there in awkward silence.

"So, do you play here often?" Aaron asked after about half a minute.

"You could say that I play here everyday." Ronnie answered.

"Pro?"

"No. I cut the grass."

This set Aaron off laughing again. This time harder and deeper than the first. "So, are you telling me that I almost killed the help?" Aaron asked after he had gotten himself under control.

"Yep."

"I guess it's a good thing that I didn't, They'd probably raise my membership fees."

"Naw," Ronnie replied straight faced, "Club house rules says that if you kill one of the help, you get six free months." After a couple of seconds they both burst out laughing.

33

With mixed tears, of laughter and relief that he didn't damage Ronnie too bad, streaming down his face, Aaron finally managed to say, "I like you kid, you're alright. So how long have you worked here?"

"Too long, seems like forever. But in reality I guess that it's only been a few years."

"Money good?"

"It's okay. Things are a little tight around the old house right now, got a new kid and the wife can't work. But we make do."

"Ever consider part time work?" Aaron asked seemingly genuinely interested.

"Yeah, but I'm having a hard time finding a second job." Ronnie lied. After working all day and then being up half the night with Nancy, he was too tired to even consider getting a second job.

"Things are tough alright." Aaron said and then sat there for a couple of seconds before continuing questioning Ronnie. "Say, I bet you've seen and heard some really juicy things working here."

"You wouldn't believe some of the things I've seen here. You know that old judge that retired last year?"

"You mean Millvan?"

"Yeah, that's him. One day about a year ago I came around the corner on sixteen and he was standing in the bushes pulling his pud."

"Are you serious?" An amused Aaron asked.

"Yeah. He's deaf as a post and never heard me go roaring by on the lawn mower."

"Oh man, that's good. Anything else?" Aaron asked laughing.

"All kinds of things. You wouldn't believe who's doing who out here in these woods. Why do you ask?"

"I think I have a way to make you some extra money and repay my debt for almost killing you."

"I'm sorry, but I'm not following you. Exactly what are you saying?" Ronnie asked.

"Allow me to introduce myself properly." Aaron said standing up. For a second, Ronnie was scared that he had opened his mouth to the wrong person and he saw his job flying away. Taking off his hat, Aaron said with a flourish, "Aaron McGuire, Editor and Chief of The Daily Constitutional."

Ronnie's mouth dropped open in surprise, Aaron kept talking. "Don't look so surprised kid. They let me out every now and then to pursue relaxation."

"So what do you have in mind Mr. McGuire?" Ronnie asked.

"Oh, now it's Mr. McGuire. A second ago it was the bastard who hit me." Aaron said with amusement in his voice.

"I never..." Ronnie started to say but was cut off.

"Relax kid. I'm just pulling your leg. Anyway, if you could write me a column about once a week, you could make some pretty good money."

"But I really don't know much about writing for a newspaper. What kind of stuff do you want?" Ronnie asked hedging.

"Well, that's a good question. I guess just the juicy stuff you see around here. I'm looking for a gossip column for the Sunday Review."

"If I started writing about what I see around here I might get fired." Ronnie said trying to find objection in what was being offered to him.

"I wouldn't worry about that. All you gotta do is give me the juicy details and we'll clean it up and publish it with a ghost name. We'll even give it a female name to throw any one off of your trail. You know, something like 'Trash Talk' by Betty Leggs."

"I don't know. I haven't written much since college." Ronnie said still hedging. What was said next changed his mind immediately.

"It could be worth $300 a week for one column."

"Shit, sign me up!" Ronnie almost shouted and then added in a lower tone of voice, "Can you do this?"

"Did I tell you that I was part owner and personnel manager?"

"No."

"Well I am. Don't worry, I'll never divulge our secret."

The deal was sealed with a handshake and they sat there talking for almost another thirty minutes.. Aaron explained what type of writing was needed and Ronnie relayed some of the juicier things he had seen.

Aaron was more than happy with himself. He was sure that he had found a way to boost his flagging Sunday paper sales. He had joined the country club a year ago with hopes of getting some scoops himself. So far he had come up with nothing. Every time people saw him coming they would change the topic of discussion or just stand there and smile at him. Now he had his own private spy. One that no one would ever suspect.

When Ronnie got home that evening, he was in a quandary as to whether or not he should tell Margret about his good fortune. He knew that if he kept his arrangements secret, he would have a hard time explaining the extra money. A small amount could easily be explained as overtime. If he did tell her about his new found wind fall, he would run the risk of two things. One, Margret running off at the mouth to someone, or more correctly, the wrong someone. Many years ago, Ronnie's father had told him 'That when it came to a woman, keep your mind to yourself. Just remember that the best rule to live by is telephone, telegraph, tell a woman.' The second thing was that Margret would keep her mouth shut and just increase her ability to spend.

Ronnie believed that it wasn't wise to keep secrets in a marriage. It was okay to keep secrets about a marriage, but to keep something as big as this was going against his grain. Little did he know, Margret still had a lot of secrets that she was keeping herself.

One of Margret's secrets was about a Naval Aviator. He was a Second Lieutenant that she had seen several times. Although there was nothing going on physically between them, she had on a couple of occasions, gotten a babysitter and met him for lunch.

Ronnie decided to tell Margret about his new deal. It was lucky for him that Margret wasn't home when he got there. It gave him time to mull over his problem without her being there. He still hadn't really made up his mind when she showed up almost forty-five minutes later. He helped her into the house with the groceries she was carrying from the car. After listening to her bitch and moan about the soaring cost of food and how she didn't know how they were going to continue to survive on his meager paycheck, he told her his big news.

Margret was elated and kept saying how she couldn't wait to tell her friends. Ronnie then told her that she couldn't tell anyone and that this had to remain a secret. If word of this got around, he could lose his job at the Country Club and that would also put an end to his ability to 'spy'.

Although Margret got really mad about Ronnie silencing her, she didn't do anything about it. She just smiled at him and said that if he didn't want her to talk about something, then maybe he should keep it to himself. For a brief moment, Ronnie saw some of the old Margret in her face and he steeled himself for some type of swift retribution that never came. He relaxed when he saw her relax. But irregardless of what she had told him, Margret did keep his secret.

It was two weeks before the first of his columns came out. He wrote under the pen name of 'Gabrielle "Gabby" Gasbag'. The 'Gabby Gasbag' column was an instant success. His first column was about how he had seen the Sheriff's son selling pot to one of the city councilmen.

4.

Aaron was more than happy with himself because he watched his Sunday circulation go from almost nonexistent to sold-out in one day. Each of the following Sundays, he increased his print by almost two thousand copies and there were no returns. Aaron saw this as the best investment he ever made in his paper. His co-owners were more than happy and wanted to know who Gabby was and where did she get her information from. He explained that to protect her from the public, he wasn't at liberty to reveal any facts about her. They bought his story hook, line, and sinker.

It goes without saying that he got a visit from the Sheriff and the city councilman. Not at the same time, but in the same day within a couple of hours of each other. He explained to the Sheriff that he only printed what was fact and there was nothing he (the sheriff) could do about it.

When the Sheriff got on his soap box about shutting the paper down, Aaron pulled out a faded, worn out copy of a booklet that contained the Constitution in it. Opening the booklet up, Aaron pointed to the first amendment and told the Sheriff to try. Aaron went on to explain that if the Sheriff still had a problem with what had been printed, the paper would be more than happy to print a retraction when Aaron was shown a copy of his son's negative drug test. Not only did the Sheriff leave Aaron's office highly pissed off, but Aaron never heard from him again on this topic. The Sheriff's son also wasn't seen for a very long time. The next time the young man was seen, he was visiting home and wore a military academy uniform and hair cut.

The Councilman was easier to handle than the Sheriff had been. Aaron had been to a couple of the Councilman's private parties and although he hadn't seen the man smoke a joint, Aaron did smell it on him a couple of times. The Councilman invited Aaron to lunch so they could discuss the matter of what had been printed. As Aaron was sitting across the table from the man at lunch, he explained that not only did he have the written word, there were pictures that went along with the story. Aaron went on to explain that he felt that the Councilman was a friend and had decided to just print the words and let people have doubt, instead of printing the story and printing the pictures along with it to seal the Councilman's fate.

The man visibly paled at the news.

The story about the pictures was pure fiction, but Aaron didn't like being pushed around by some elected weasel. He decided that if he laid his cards out on the table early enough, it would save a lot of posturing later. It worked. The rest of the conversation was light and non-political.

The paper did print the Councilman's denial along with the Sheriff's denial of the events. It also made a special point that the paper was neither confirming or denying what had been printed. The paper was completely neutral in this matter.

The next time Aaron talked to Ronnie, which was on Friday when Ronnie dropped off his next article; a scathing report about a preacher and one of the male youth members of the same church out on the bottom nine of the course, the good Reverend was getting his putter 'waxed' as Gabby reported it; Aaron advised Ronnie to invest in a typewriter. That way, if things ever got really nasty, there would be no handwriting samples to find. Just to make sure of Ronnie's anonymity, he would also be paid in cash. He was also instructed that if anyone asked him any questions, he was just a messenger for some old lady. But whatever he did, he was not to elaborate.

When the story about the ill-fated golfing trip came out in the paper, the shit really hit the fan. Of course, Aaron was standing there in his shit proof suit. So the Church's wrath was turned to the country club. After the administrator fielded several dozen calls, there was a meeting called among all of the employees. It was explained that while they didn't think anyone was talking about the things that were seen going on at the country club, the patrons paid a lot of money to play and relax at the club. It was emphasized that what was seen or heard here, was to stay here.

In the mean time, the young man confessed to what had happened and the Church thought it wise to ship the Pastor off on a 'Missionary Mission' to South America. Aaron was more than happy to print a story about the Pastor's new status.

Now, everyone was talking about the column. It was the main topic of discussion on Monday mornings. Everyone but Margret that is. It was eating at her that Ronnie was gaining so much popularity, even though nobody knew that it was him. But, she didn't mind spending the money that Ronnie was bringing home on Friday nights.

The first real fight that Ronnie and Margret had in a long time was about the typewriter Ronnie was instructed to buy. Margret told Ronnie in no uncertain terms that she wasn't going to waste any of 'her' money on something as foolish as that. Ronnie could just learn how to write better. That is when Ronnie got right up in her face and explained to her that it had been suggested he get one, if he wanted to keep bringing home the extra money. That shut her up. When they went to the mall later that night, Margret whined so much about the cost of typewriters that Ronnie said the hell with it and stormed out of the mall.

He was waiting at the car thinking about what he should do and realized that instead of buying something new, he would check out the pawn shops tomorrow to see what kind of bargain he could find. He was standing there deep in thought and never saw Margret approach. The first inkling that he had that she was there was when he saw the fist coming, just before she caught him in the eye.

"God dammit, I've had just about enough of being nice to you, you piece of shit!" Margret screamed at him.

"Wha...What?" Ronnie stammered still slightly dazed from the punch.

"Look," Margret raved on, "I'm not going to waste good money on you when you don't know how long this is going to last."

"But..." He tried to interject, she cut him off.

"As big of a loser as you are, as soon as I waste money on you, you'll get fired and I'll be out what I spent."

Ronnie tried to explain that he was the column and there was no way he could get fired from what he had just about invented. But she wasn't listening to him. He might as well have kept quiet, because the instant her fist had made contact with him, the old mousey Ronnie was back. All of his posturing about how he wasn't going to take anymore of her crap had disappeared with the first punch.

Deep down, it hurt Margret when she had hit him, but she wasn't going to let him know. Truth be known, she found that she liked the feeling she got to see him cowering there. It was turning her on and beginning to make her feel horny. She liked the feeling of dominating him. As they rode home in silence, Margret was reflecting on the way she was feeling. She found that the longer she thought about what she had done, the hornier she became.

When they got home, Margret got out of the car and went straight into the house leaving Ronnie to deal with getting Nancy and all of her baby gear out of the car. Margret went straight into the downstairs bathroom and pulling down her jeans, stood in front of the mirror and masturbated. Her orgasm was so intense that she sat down hard on the toilet and was there for a few minutes, trying to regain her composure. When she was a little calmer, she found that she was still horny, the orgasm she had did very little to take the edge off. Dropping her jeans and panties to the floor, she began masturbating again. This time she imagined that she was hitting and beating Ronnie. Her response was almost immediate, this time her orgasm was even more intense.

Almost forty minutes had passed before she came out of the bathroom. Ronnie was sitting on the couch with a wet wash cloth pressed against the side of his face. Margret said nothing to him as she passed by and went upstairs to change her clothes. At least, that's what Ronnie thought she was going to do.

Ronnie noticed that she looked flushed and started to ask if she was feeling alright, but decided that maybe it would be better if he didn't say anything.

As he sat there, he had been rationalizing why she had hit him. The baby was keeping her up late at night and she wasn't getting much sleep. As he thought about it, he knew that wasn't the reason, Nancy was pretty much sleeping through the nights now, when she did wake up, Ronnie was the one who got up and tended to her. Then his mind returned to something that Margret had said to him in the parking lot. She had told him that she'd had enough of being nice to him. Without realizing it until he rubbed his other cheek, tears had begun streaming from his eyes.

That night, as he slept on the couch, his dream returned. This time he found that he was in the middle of a large void. To him, it was as if he was floating, there was no up or down and he was just suspended there. Unable to move, but completely relaxed.

Ronnie, the all too familiar voice started, *Ronnie.*

'What do you want?' He called back. This time he wasn't scared or even feeling any anxiety. He was calm, too calm.

Ronnie.

'I said 'what' dammit. What do you want with me now?'

My, don't we sound all brave and confident. Too bad you didn't have this attitude earlier, maybe she wouldn't have hit you so hard. In the distance, Ronnie could see a small spot. It was too far away to make out what it was.

'Fuck you.' Ronnie said. When he said that, the spot came rushing towards him and grew larger as it came. It got so big so fast that it gave him the feeling of vertigo. It continued to grow until it became a giant mouth that blocked out everything.

NO, FUCK YOU! The mouth said, Ronnie felt crushed under the weight of the sound itself. Had he been awake in the real world, he felt that his head would have exploded and his body would have been crushed from the pressure of the sound.

'Please no.' Ronnie sobbed.

That's better. The mouth said and then began to shrink until Ronnie was once again looking at his dead Professor standing not more than six feet away from him.

'What do you want of me?'

I brought you here so we could talk Ronnie.

'I don't want to talk to you, I have nothing to say.'

That's okay Ronnie. I have enough to say for the both of us. You, of course, have no choice but to listen.

'Then say what you have to say and then let me the fuck out of here.'

Better watch that attitude Ronnie, because I can do more than bite, this time you are in my world. You won't be able to get away as easy this time. Let's not argue. What do you say we be friends for the moment? Let's shake okay? The Professor said moving closer and putting out his hand.

Ronnie couldn't think of any reason why he shouldn't shake the hand being offered to him, so he tentatively took it in his own. Just as he was beginning to shake it, it latched onto his hand like a vice. Looking down, he saw that it wasn't a normal hand that was gripping his. It was a skeletal hand that was beginning to grip his hand tighter and tighter. Ronnie was beginning to see blood seeping from around those ghastly white fingers. With a rising sense of alarm, he realized the blood was coming from his own hand where it was being cut from those bony fingers.

'LET GO GOD DAMMIT!' Ronnie screamed as he tried to pull his hand away.

HA HA HA HA HA, oh you kill me Ronnie. What's the problem? Can't take a joke? Oh, wait a minute, that's right, you did kill me. Oh well.

With that, the hand was gone. Ronnie looked at his hand and saw that although it was bleeding, it felt a lot worse than it really was. 'Okay, you got my attention you bastard. What do you want?' Ronnie said as he continued to survey his hand.

What do I want? I want to live, but there's nothing we can do about that can we? I came to warn you this time. That bitch you are married to is going back to her old ways. The question is, what do you want?

'I don't follow what you are saying.' Ronnie said confused.

What I'm saying is, are you ever going to stand up for yourself? Or are you going to put up with her shit until she kills you?

'It's not as bad as you make it out to be.' Ronnie said defending Margret.

No it's not, it's worse. You don't know what's in her mind and if you did, you would find that it's scarier than me.

'Bull shit, you're just trying to rattle me.' Ronnie said, his hand was still throbbing and he could feel the blood beginning to drip down his fingers.

Okay, I see that you're a pig headed fool, but I will do you one favor.

'And that is?'

Don't go to the pawn shop tomorrow.

'Why not?'

SHUT UP! The voice roared, once again almost to the point of being deafening. Then the Professor continued much quieter this time, *There is a flea market on the other side of town. Do you know it?*

'Yes.'

Go there and someone very familiar to you will have a much better deal than you can get in any pawn shop.

'I'll see if Margret wants to go.'

Fuck her. You go or else.

'Or else what?' Ronnie asked.

Ronnie, sometimes you get what you deserve. The Professor said as he disappeared in front of Ronnie. He faded away as he said it until there was nothing left but the voice. With the word 'Deserve' Ronnie woke up. Laying there for a few seconds, Ronnie noticed that his hand was still throbbing. He turned on the light and saw that he was bleeding. His hand looked exactly the same as it had in his dreams.

He got up and went into the downstairs bathroom to wash and doctor his hand. After a close inspection, he saw that like in his dream, it was only the skin that was broken and the cuts weren't hardly cuts at all. Looking carefully, Ronnie could almost see the pattern of naked bone wrapped around his hand. He felt the hair on the back of his neck stand up. Wrapping his hand in a towel, he went back into the living room and sat back down on the couch. As he sat there contemplating what he should do, he looked down and saw drops of blood on the floor where they had dripped from his fingers. He quickly cleaned them from the hardwood floor. Glancing at the clock, Ronnie saw that it was four-thirty in the morning, so he laid back down on the couch and tried to go back to sleep.

Sleep was long in coming, partly because what happened rattled him so. Not the dream, but the damage to his hand. It seemed to Ronnie that he had carried his dream world into his waking world. The other part of Ronnie having trouble getting back to sleep was because he always had trouble sleeping with the lights on and he wasn't about to turn them off.

Margret on the other hand, had a very long night of her own. She had been in bed all night pleasuring herself. She would masturbate and then doze off. When she would wake up, she would masturbate again. Just before she came downstairs in the morning, she took care of her needs one last time. When she woke Ronnie from his sleep, Margret was standing in front of him feeling drained, but satisfied.

It was eight in the morning when Margret woke him. Now, instead of being hateful to him like she had been last night, she was almost acquiescent. She asked him why he had slept on the couch and that confused him. Normally, when she had been in one of her moods, he would be banished to the couch. Now she was acting like nothing had happened. When she saw his hand wrapped in a towel, she was almost fawning over him. Ronnie didn't know how to react, so he told her that he had fallen asleep watching television. Margret seemed to buy the story even though the TV wasn't on when she had come down the stairs. With alarm, Ronnie saw that the TV wasn't on but decided that if she didn't question it, he wouldn't press the issue.

Margret was in a good mood, or at least seemed to be. She had decided she would be nice to Ronnie today, even if it killed her. She knew why he had slept on the couch, but wanted to act as if nothing had happened. Hopefully, last night would pass with no repercussions. She still remembered the stiff warning she had received that night a while back from the policeman. The last thing she needed was trouble from the law. So, figuring that if she was nice to him, Ronnie would let the whole matter drop.

Margret cooked Ronnie a big breakfast, something she hadn't done since they had gotten married. As Ronnie was eating, Margret asked him what he wanted to do today. Once again, Ronnie was thrown off guard. She was actually being nice to him. Had he known that Margret was doing this because she was afraid that he would call the law on her, he would have milked it for all it was worth. For a little while, Ronnie became afraid that she was up to something, something bad.

Ronnie had heard a story once about a lady that had been really nice to her husband and then one day, out of the blue, killed him. When the police asked her why she did it, she told them she was tired of looking at him. This memory chilled him. He stopped chewing and sat there looking at her. After a minute, Margret noticed him staring at her. Margret asked him what was wrong and Ronnie quickly said 'Nothing' as he stuffed more breakfast into his mouth. Ronnie decided that if he was going to be killed, it was going to be on a full stomach. It never dawned on him that she could have poisoned his food.

When Ronnie was finished eating, Margret asked him again what he wanted to do today. Ronnie thought for a second and then remarked that he had heard of a flea market on the other side of town and he wanted to go to it. As an aside, he added that maybe he could get a real cheap price on a used typewriter.

When Margret heard the word 'typewriter', she instantly became mad, but she made an academy award performance in concealing her ire. She remarked that it sounded like a really good idea and added that if it was okay with him, she would go up and get Nancy ready so they could get back home early.

Ronnie remarked that it sounded like a good idea as he got up from the table, put his plate into the sink and went upstairs himself to change out of the clothes he had been sleeping in. As he climbed the stairs he found that he was having a hard time remembering the conversation he had with his dream visitor. The one thing that he did remember, other than the fact that he should go to the flea market, was a voice telling him that Margret had gone back to her old ways. He shook that notion off because if she had really gone back to her old ways, he would have been the one cooking breakfast that morning. Of course he would have been prompted to do so by Margret bellowing at him, 'Where the fuck is my breakfast?'.

Ronnie didn't see Margret as she was getting Nancy ready and it was a good thing that he didn't. She was being unnecessarily rough with her. At one point Nancy let out a blood curdling scream just after Margret had thrown her down into the crib. Ronnie stuck his head into the room to see what was going on, he couldn't see Nancy because of the padding around the edge of the crib and all he could see was Margret leaning over the edge of the crib. He asked if there was a problem and Margret quickly answered telling him that she had accidentally stuck Nancy with a diaper pin, but she was alright, just mad.

He took her word for it and never had any idea that Margret was taking her frustration about him out on Nancy. Had he known she was doing that, he probably would have kicked her ass on the spot. Abusing him was one thing but it never occurred to him that she would do it to a child. He asked her if she needed any help and with a slight twinge of acid dripping from her fangs, she told him that she had everything under control. Margret added for him to just go downstairs and wait, they would be down in a minute or two.

Ronnie was outside loading Nancy's stroller into the car when Margret came outside carrying Nancy. He helped her with the diaper bag and put it into the back of the car as Margret strapped Nancy into her car seat. After going back into the house and checking to make sure that everything was secure, he got into the car and they blasted off for the other side of town.

5.

On the trip to the flea market, Margret hardly said a word. Ronnie was happy for the semi-silence and, although she was quiet, she still seemed to be in a good mood. So he just drove on making the minimum of idle conversation. He pointed out new things here and there and commented on how nice the weather was.

Margret answered in all of the appropriate places, but her mind was on other things. She knew that Ronnie was just doing this to get back at her. Why, she thought, he was deliberately trying to piss her off. But she wasn't going to fall for it, no way! She was going to 'kill' him with kindness if she had to. Thinking carefully, she came up with a plan so she wouldn't have to fork out any money on any type of typewriter, no matter how cheap, no matter how old. She would steer him away from whatever he found by telling him that he could probably get a better deal someplace else and not to jump on the first deal he happened upon. Besides, she wasn't going to waste any of her money on him, no sir, she had more important things to spend her money on.

Margret had plans to have lunch with Ted next week and she needed to buy a new dress and she also wanted to pick up the lunch tab. Ted was a much better man than Ronnie and had a promising career in the Navy as a pilot. Ronnie, on the other hand, had a promising career as a grass cutter. That's all he would ever be, this little fluke of writing a column for the paper wouldn't last very long because somehow he would screw it up, he always did. Unlike Ted, who was still learning, Ronnie was already the pilot of a lawn mower and that's the best he would ever do. That thought made Margret let a small laugh slip from her lips. She caught Ronnie looking at her with a puzzled look on his face.

"Just thinking of something funny, honey." She offered in way of an explanation. Ronnie smiled back and then directed his attention back to driving.

'What a loser.' Margret thought to herself and then went back to daydreaming about Ted. Ted with the crisp, clean uniform with the highly polished gold and the seemingly endless supply of money. One day Margret had intended to pick up the lunch check but upon inspection of her purse, she found that she had a lot less money than she thought she did. Embarrassed, she commented that she was a little short on cash right then. Ted, being an Officer and a gentleman, told her not to worry about it and pulled out a money clip that easily held five or six hundred dollars in it. Her attraction to him was immediate. Why, this was a real man, while Ronnie was some kind of sick substitute.

After riding for almost thirty minutes, they finally arrived at the flea market. As Ronnie turned into the entrance, he noticed they were still early and most of the vendors were still carrying things from their cars to the booths. The flea market was still being set up.

Margret took the opportunity to point out that they were so early that they would most likely miss all of the good deals. Ronnie countered with the point that since they were there, they might as well go ahead and look around. This definitely put a knot in Margret's panties, but instead of going off on him, she kept her mouth shut and decided that this might be better. Fewer people set up meant less hassle she would have getting Ronnie to leave. With not much to look at, how could this take very long?

Being so early, they were able to get a parking space right up front where they wouldn't have very far to walk. Getting out, Ronnie set about the task of getting the stroller ready, getting Nancy out of the car and strapped into it.

Margret on the other hand, stood surveying the situation. Although the flea market had looked small from the car, standing, she could see the vendor area stretched out seemingly forever. This disappointed her, now they would be in this God-forsaken place a lot longer than she wanted to be here. So Margret resigned herself to let Ronnie get this out of his system. Maybe when they were done, there would be enough time to go to the mall and do some serious shopping.

Ronnie, once he got Nancy situated, looked up and saw the vastness of the market. He was happy because he knew that he was going to find something here that would suit his needs very easily.

Pushing the stroller up onto the sidewalk, Ronnie and Margret waded into the market and started looking around. The first hour passed very quickly and it seemed as if Margret wanted everything she saw. But Ronnie was intent on finding what he was looking for, or more appropriately, what he had been instructed to look for.

It was almost forty-five minutes into the second hour when Margret found a small dress shop buried deep inside the market. Everywhere she looked inside this small stall, she saw things that she felt that she couldn't live without. There was a dressing screen set up in one corner to try on dresses behind. Ronnie was bored and Margret seemed as if she was going to try on everything that was hanging in there. After ten minutes of watching her try on one dress after another, Ronnie asked her if she minded if he foraged ahead a little ways to see what else was around there. Margret dismissed him with a slight flick of her wrist.

Ronnie was a little disappointed, up until now he had only seen two typewriters and they were so old and in such bad shape that they should have been thrown away instead of trying to be sold. Of course Margret had

46

immediately pointed out the flaws in both of them. Her timing was off though, because she pointed the flaws out after Ronnie had seen them for himself, first. Ronnie did notice that once Margret saw him start to get interested in something, she would zero in and start pointing out problems. She was acting like she was suddenly some type of expert on the matters of writing equipment. Ronnie found that it was starting to become an annoyance.

But now, by himself and untethered other than pushing Nancy, he could look without her critical eye. So Ronnie began his search in earnest. As he neared one corner of the flea market, he saw another, separate part of the flea market across the parking lot. Since it looked a lot smaller and was only a strip, Ronnie decided to go over to it and take a quick look at what was there. So he pushed Nancy in that direction. As he neared it, he saw that there were only a few vendors over there and realized that this detour would only take a couple of minutes at most.

Had anyone been looking at Ronnie as he crossed the parking lot, they would have seen a man pushing a stroller, disappear at the far end of the parking lot with a silver shimmer into nothingness.

At the same instant Ronnie disappeared from everyone else's view, he felt a brief wave of nausea pass over him. Nancy began to cry, not a strong cry like she was hurt, but more of a whimper. To Ronnie, nothing unusual had happened other than the nausea and since he had walked under the awning of this part of the flea market, also at the same time, he didn't notice the sun also looked dimmer.

Looking around for a second, trying to decide which direction to go first, he noticed this portion of the flea market looked much older and dirtier than the section he had just come from. He consoled himself by rationalizing this must have been the original market and the other part had been added on much later.

The first couple of vendors really didn't have anything of interest, but the third one did. As Ronnie walked up to the next set of tables he saw that they were covered with nothing but typewriters. There were all types and models. Some were very old and some were so new looking that Ronnie didn't recognize some of the features on them. Looking up, he saw a sign that said: MAKE OFFER, I LIKE TO DICKER.

For some reason that he couldn't quite put his finger on, he felt ill at ease. Ronnie ignored the feeling and started looking around. He found several units that looked as if they would more than suit his needs. The proprietor of this booth was nowhere to be seen and he kept looking for a few more minutes, tentatively pushing keys on one machine after another. Just as he thought this was going to be a washout because there was no one to dicker with, he heard a jovial voice behind him.

"Sorry to keep you waiting young man."

"That's okay." Ronnie said as he turned around to face the person talking to him.

The voice belonged to his dead professor. Ronnie visibly paled and had to grab onto the corner of the table to keep from falling down. All he could see was the face looking back at him as the world faded away from his eyesight. But just as quick as the faintness had come upon him, it began to fade and Ronnie noticed that it wasn't the professor he was looking at, the man just looked like him, but was much older than the professor of his dreams.

"Hey sonny, you okay?"

"Yeah, I think so." Ronnie said as he instantly began to feel much better. "Do...Do I know you?" He asked.

"Depends, ever been to college?" The older version of his professor asked.

'OhmiGod,' Ronnie thought, 'It is him.' After a second Ronnie replied, "Yes. Why?"

"Well then, you don't know me 'cause I've never been." With that, the man started a deep laugh that lasted for a couple of minutes and ended with a wheezing cough. This made Ronnie feel a little better, but he was still feeling uneasy. "You okay boy? You look like you've seen a ghost."

"You might say that." Ronnie replied and then added, "Are you the owner?"

"Of this magnificent pile of crap? Yes, I confess, I am the owner."

"Well then, how much do you want for this typewriter?" Ronnie asked as he pointed to an old manual unit.

"Well...Let me explain to you how I do things here. You tell me what you're going to use it for and I'll match you up with the unit of your dreams."

"Huh?" Ronnie said, the word dreams sent a chill down his spine.

"A lot of this stuff is junk and I wouldn't want you to waste your money on it. But if you tell me what you are going to use it for, then I can match you up with something that will really do the job for you."

"Are you serious? What if I said that I just needed this old IBM here?"

"You possibly could, if you just wanted to write a letter every now and then, this would be perfect. But if you wanted to do some serious word smithing, you'd be mad more than you'd be writing. Now if you just want a paper weight, this little baby over here would be perfect." He said as he was pointing to a very old manual typewriter. "It really would be better if you told me what you needed it for."

"Well I..." Ronnie started, then after a couple of seconds continued, "I like to write, but I'm not very good. I need something that's easy to work."

"Do you make a lot of mistakes?"

"That's putting it mildly." Ronnie replied.

"Then you need something that will correct spelling, am I not correct?"

"That can be done?" Ronnie asked. Everything about this guy reminded him of the Professor, his mannerisms, his speech, the way he seemed to be able to drill the right question into you. This spooky situation was getting spookier by the second.

"These won't." The stranger replied. He stopped and looked Ronnie up and down, after pausing for a few seconds he replied, "But I got something special under the counter here that will do you right."

"Well I don't know." Ronnie said. He was leery about being offered something that wasn't out on the table to be seen. He didn't have a lot of money to spend and he didn't want to be played for a sucker and get sold some piece of crap that didn't work.

"Don't worry about me ripping you off." The old image of the dead Professor said almost as if he had read Ronnie's mind. The man continued, "Look, this is what I do. I match people up with things that they really need instead of things that they just want. You need something to check your spelling, correct your grammar, and put all of the periods in the right places. I got just the thing."

With that, the gentleman walked around the counter and began to rummage around under it. After a couple of seconds he said, "Here it is." and pulled out a pretty good sized box. "You're going to love this." He remarked as he set the box down on the counter and began opening it up.

"What is it?" Ronnie asked, now more than just mildly curious.

"It's a little something that I dreamed up myself. Unfortunately I never got a chance to use it after I built it. But it does work and very well I might add."

Having said that, he pulled a Frankenstein of a machine out of the box. It was a metal box about two feet square with all kinds of slots and an on and off switch in the back. There were also all kinds of connections that looked like they were meant to plug things into. Sitting on top of the box was a television monitor. Next, the Professor look-alike pulled a keyboard out of the cardboard box and laid it onto the counter. The last thing out of the box was a printer.

Ronnie stood looking at the assortment of gadgets that had been laid out in front of him. Although it wasn't pretty to look at, Ronnie instantly recognized it as some sort of computer. Ronnie had seen computers in the past, but this didn't look like anything he had ever seen. Looking up, he saw that the old man was beaming, like a proud father showing off a new kid.

"Not much to look at, is she?"

"I wouldn't say that." Ronnie replied and then asked, "What is it?"

This set the man off laughing again, "I pull out the latest thing in computers and all he can ask is 'What is it?'."

"I didn't mean any offense, I'm just not that familiar with computers."

"That's okay. No one has ever seen anything like this before. I built it myself and if you don't mind me bragging, not even NASA has something as powerful as this."

"What's it do?"

"What's it do? It computes, it processes, it finishes dreams."

49

R. H. Gosse

Ronnie noticed that for the second time, the word dream had been worked into the conversation. "How's it work?" He asked.

"Well here, let me plug it in and I'll show you." The old man said as he produced a power cord seemingly out of thin air. He then spent the next few minutes plugging things in and turning things on. Finally the big moment came and he flipped on the main power switch. There was a slight hum that grew in intensity and then immediately got quieter when the monitor screen came on. "There you go." The old man said, "Type your name in."

"I don't know, I'm really just looking." Ronnie replied. In some respect he was afraid of the technology he was looking at.

"It won't bite. Go ahead, type your name in."

Ronnie complied and typed his name on the keyboard. The older version of the Professor watched as Ronnie did this and pointed to the ENTER key when Ronnie finished typing. Ronnie pressed it. The screen had displayed his name when he had typed it in and when he pressed the ENTER key, the screen went blank for a second and then printed 'GOOD MORNING RONNIE'. Ronnie just stood there with his mouth open. What a greeting from a machine, and the time was correct also, it was morning.

"How do you like that?"

"All I can say is WOW." Ronnie replied.

"WOW is right. Now try something different. Type in a sentence but make sure you misspell some of the words."

Ronnie typed in 'thias es thee fursmt dya fo mi liff' and was once agin directed to press the ENTER key. Ronnie did so and less than a second later the screen displayed 'This is the first day of my life.'.

"How did it do that?" Ronnie asked with his voice full of excitement. "I mean, how did it know where to capitalize and it even did the punctuation. How?"

"Sure did, didn't it? It has a very powerful word processing program built into it."

"And the program stays in it even when it's not plugged in?"

"Oh yes, and even better than that, if you find a program you like, you can just put the disk in here and load the program into it. Then you'll never have to load that program again. It will always be in there."

"Always?"

"Even when it's not plugged in. The memory is made to stay constant. I'll even throw in a box of programs on disk. Some are back-ups for what's already in there and the rest I haven't had a chance to load yet."

"How did you come up with the idea for this thing?" Ronnie asked.

"I built it for my son in college. You know, to do his reports on. But he died before I could give it to him." The old man's face saddened for a moment and then he continued, "Look, did I show you that you can even plug it into a

50

telephone line? That lets you call up those computer bulletin boards. Even send and receive programs through the telephone line. I hear that's becoming the thing among the computer people nowadays."

"If you built it, then how will I ever be able to use all of the features you built into it?" Ronnie asked.

"Well, you could fumble around for awhile if you want," He said as he reached back into the box, "Or you could simply read the instructions." When he said that, he pulled out a very thick book with a leather cover and handed it to Ronnie.

Taking the book, Ronnie began to leaf through it as he just glanced at the pages. The paper was parchment and were hand lettered with a calligraphy style of text. The book was very easy to read and understand. There were chapters in the table of contents from word processing to computer graphics. Ronnie was instantly in love with it. There was even a chapter about the printer and something called 'Fonts'. He didn't know what Fonts were, but he imagined that if they were as easy as everything else had been on this machine, it would be a snap to learn about them also.

Ronnie was very happy until reality settled in, he realized that he probably couldn't afford something as elaborate as this.

"I see a frown on your face. What's the problem?" The old man quickly asked.

"Well...I really like this computer of yours, but I don't think I can afford it. I have very little money to spend and the most I was hoping to be able to afford was an old typewriter. I'm sorry, I didn't mean to lead you on." Ronnie said in earnest.

"Didn't you read the sign?" The older version of the Professor said as he pointed to the dicker sign.

"Of course I did. But still, you probably want a lot more than I've got to spend."

"But you haven't even asked me how much. You're giving up too easy and taking all of the fun out of it."

"Okay, how much?" Ronnie asked trying to humor the man. He knew there was no way he could afford what he had seen, but since the man had gone to so much trouble, Ronnie didn't want to just walk away.

"Let me see, got a wife who likes to spend money?" The man asked and Ronnie nodded his head yes. "Still have a lot of bills from your lovely daughter Nancy?" The man continued.

Ronnie nodded his head yes again, but totally missed the point that the man had called Nancy by name without Ronnie telling him what her name was.

"Tell you what. Do you have a dollar bill on you?"

"Yes, why?" Ronnie asked.

"Then that's the price. One dollar, American of course."

"That's too low. A dollar for something that does everything this thing does?"

"Well damn. That's the first time I ever had someone tell me that. Tell you what, since that's too low for your conscious, then let's make it twenty pieces of silver. How's that for a price? Twenty dollars."

"That's still too low." Ronnie said, but he was happy that the price quoted was in the realm of possibility of his purchasing power.

"Then let me explain it to you like this," The man said, "I built this for my son and every time I look at it, it reminds me of how he died. It's sad when you have to bury your children, but it's sadder when they take their own lives. Now, if you don't want me paying you to take it away, give me my twenty pieces of silver and get this thing out of my sight."

Ronnie was more than happy with himself as he paid the man and shook his hand to seal the deal. Ronnie got a brief feeling of de'-ja'-vu when he felt the skeleton like fingers grip his hand. It passed quickly and he helped the man pack the computer back into it's box. Once it was packed up, Ronnie stood there trying to figure out how he was going to carry it. Then he decided to take Nancy out of her stroller and loaded the box into it. Lifting the box, Ronnie noticed that it was surprisingly light.

Ronnie thanked the man and started to leave when the man yelled for him to wait.

"Yes?" Ronnie asked as he turned back around.

"You forgot your receipt." The older version of the Professor said as he pulled out a note pad and a red pen and started writing on the note pad. When he was finished he turned it over to Ronnie and said "Sign here." Ronnie shifted Nancy in his arms so he could take the book.

Ronnie noticed that the receipt said that it was for the REVELATION 1. It was written in a red ink that was so dark that it almost looked like blood. Ronnie signed his name and handed the book back to the man, who tore the page out and handed it back to Ronnie.

"As you leave, let me say this. Tell your friends about me. And remember this, I believe that sometimes you should get what you really deserve."

This hit Ronnie like a hammer between the eyes and suddenly, all he wanted to do was leave this place. He wanted to get as far away as he could, as quickly as possible. Pushing the stroller and carrying Nancy, he passed back into the sunlight. As he did, he once again felt a brief wave of nausea pass over him and Nancy shifted so violently in his arms that he almost dropped her. Had anyone been looking in his direction this time, they would have seen a man pushing a stroller with a box perched on top of it and carrying a baby in his arms suddenly materialize with a silver shimmer on the far side of the parking lot.

At the same time Ronnie reappeared to the real world, he got a brief wisp of a smell of sulfur. Looking at his watch, he saw that he had been preoccupied for almost forty minutes. 'Damn.' He thought to himself, 'Margret is going to have a cow with me being gone for so long.'

Ronnie didn't know where to look for Margret so he decided to start where he had left her. Going back to the booth with the dresses he found her. She was still trying on the merchandise.

"I thought you were going to go look around." Margret said when she saw Ronnie.

"I have been. Sorry to be gone for so long, I lost track of time."

"What the hell are you talking about? You've only been gone about five minutes. Why are you carrying Nancy?"

"Because I bought something and I needed the stroller to carry it. What do you mean I've only been gone for five minutes? According to my watch, I've been gone for almost forty-five minutes."

"Then get a better watch asshole. How much did you spend? It better not have been a lot, I found some dresses and you better not have pissed away all of the money."

"Ma'am," Ronnie said as he turned to the sales lady, "Could you please tell me what time it is?"

"Sure," The lady replied as she looked at her watch and then said, "It's almost eleven o'clock."

Ronnie just stood there feeling stupid, he knew his watch was right, he had it for a couple of years and it never gained or lost any time. He knew that when he had left Margret it was ten till eleven, he had looked at his watch when he had walked off. But now looking at his watch, it clearly read eleven-thirty five. But now everyone was telling him that he had only been gone for five minutes. He knew that he had stood there looking at the computer longer than that before he bought it. What the hell was going on? He wondered to himself.

Ronnie was brought back from his deep reflection by Margret's voice.

"....I asked you how much did you spend? What's the matter with you? Have you gone deaf as well as stupid?"

"Uh, sorry." Ronnie sputtered as he cast a glance at the clerk who looked down with an embarrassed look on her face. "I didn't hear you. I only spent twenty dollars." Ronnie told Margret.

"Well it's a good thing because I need some money." Margret said as she piled a bunch of dresses onto the counter. "Pay for these while I look around some more." She told him.

"Sure thing, dearest." Ronnie said as Margret walked away.

The clerk set about the task of ringing up the sale. She and Ronnie stood there in awkward silence. It was announced that the total was one hundred and fifteen dollars. Ronnie pulled out his money one-handed and set it down onto the counter. Counting it out, he found that he only had about a hundred dollars left. He had left the rest of his money at home. Ronnie felt embarrassed and it showed on his face. He didn't know what to do and he sure didn't want to have to tell Margret that she had to put something back. The sales lady, sensing his predicament, told him not to worry about it and she would call it even at seventy-five dollars. She saw the visible look of relief on Ronnie's face.

"Thank you very much." Ronnie said in earnest as he paid her.

"That's okay." The lady told him and then added, "If you don't mind me asking a personal question. Is she always like that?"

'No, this is one of her good days.' Ronnie wanted to say, but instead he said, "You know, it's that time of the year for her." Ronnie winked as he said it.

The sales lady smiled and said, "Yes, those can be trying days sometimes. Thank you for your business."

"No, thank you for your help." Ronnie said as he put his hand on top of the older lady's hand.

She blushed and said, "That's okay. You just hold on and have a good life."

Ronnie picked up the bag of dresses and put them on top of the box in the stroller. Turning around, he walked away.

For a brief moment, Ronnie felt like a whole person. Somehow, when Margret was mean to him when other people were around, it brought out kindness in others towards him. That small amount of balance is what seemed to keep him from either cowering totally or killing her. A thin thread of sanity kept unbroken by the kindness of strangers. He easily remembered the other times when Margret got mad at him in public that lead to kindness from strangers. There was one particularly messy time in a grocery store when he had put some Brussel Sprouts into the shopping cart. Ronnie liked them and apparently she didn't. Margret had picked them up and while discussing his heritage in a very profane way, threw them at him. This had drawn a lot of attention to herself and she was escorted from the store by the manager. The cashier and the manager were super nice to Ronnie as he was checking out. It was at those times, when Margret seemed lower on the food chain in the eyes of other people, that helped to bolster Ronnie's own self image.

Ronnie was beginning to feel as if his sanity was slipping away. A dream that told him to look for someone familiar, an older version of his dead Professor selling him the computer, and he had gained an extra forty-five minutes. Where all of this was leading to he did not know, but he decided that sometimes you just have to hold on and see where the horse takes you.

Ronnie caught up with Margret a couple of booths away. She was looking at some pathetic looking house plants. She and the owner of the plants were talking about fertilizer and sunlight. Ronnie took the opportunity to rearrange the pile of things in the stroller. As usual, Margret was blowing like she was some kind of expert on the subject of plants. Ronnie knew better, Margret couldn't grow a damn thing. He jokingly remarked once that she could kill mold in the toilet. He had gotten a bloody nose later for saying that when they were alone. Looking back now, it had been worth it. But he wasn't going to press his luck a second time. So he just stood there and listened to the conversation.

After a couple of minutes they moved on, Margret having exhausted her limited knowledge of growing plants. Ronnie was now shifting Nancy from arm to arm because his arms were beginning to tire from holding her. He asked Margret if she would hold onto Nancy for a few minutes while he ran out to the car and emptied the stroller. That way, Nancy could be put back into the stroller and they could continue shopping.

Margret blew up. Not in her usual loud and fist swinging way, but in a more of a controlled quiet explosion. All Ronnie could think of was 'Oh shit!' as Margret told him in a quiet but very hatefully firm way "That if he hadn't bought a bunch of trash he wouldn't be having this problem now." After she said that, she pivoted on her heel and started walking to the car. She wouldn't say anything on the way back to the car even though Ronnie tried to get her to talk by pointing different things out. When they got to the car, Margret got out her keys, unlocked the door and got into the car leaving Ronnie to deal with strapping Nancy into her car seat. This was quite some task because her car seat was behind Margret and it required him to crawl across the seat from the drivers side.

When Nancy was strapped in, he went to the trunk and loaded Margret's dresses, the box with the computer, and then the stroller into it. When that was done, he went back and got into the car himself, this was when Margret finally spoke to him.

"It's about Goddamn time. It's hotter than hell in here."

Ronnie had enough of her crap, so he said, "You could have rolled down the fucking window."

Ronnie actually saw stars from the punch he received up side of his head. He sat there thinking about how funny it was, you always heard about seeing stars when you got your bell rung and here he was sitting there seeing them. He was brought back to reality once again by Margret's voice.

"Hurry up and start the car and get the fucking air on. I'm hot."

"I'm sorry if I made you mad." He said as he complied with her wishes, "But Nancy was getting heavy and I just wanted to unload the stroller."

"Well, you wouldn't have needed to unload it if you hadn't pissed away your money on some piece of shit."

He wanted to tell her that he had pissed away a lot less than she had, but thought better of it. After all, she did need some new clothes. She had been losing a lot of weight since Nancy had been born and although she would never get back to where she had been before the pregnancy, her clothes were beginning to look baggy.

Ronnie asked Margret what she wanted to do now and all she said was 'home'. So home is where he drove. The drive was a quiet one and Margret seemed deep in thought, Ronnie was determined not to interrupt her. Had he known what she was thinking about, he probably would have opened the car door and pushed her out.

Margret was seething. She had let him out of her sight for five minutes and he went and bought something. Probably some piece of trash that wasn't worth a damn. Then her thoughts returned to Ted. Ted with the polished gold and big wad of bills. She began to wonder how far she would let the relationship with Ted go. She needed a real man and that's what Ted was. He was a real man. It was on that ride home that Margret decided that she would let Ted get as far as Ted wanted to get.

When they got home, Ronnie unloaded the car as Margret took Nancy and put her down for her nap. Ronnie was just bringing in the box with the computer in it when Margret came back down the stairs. Looking around for a second, she found the bag with her new dresses and picking it up, went back upstairs. In the mean time, Ronnie went into the kitchen and made himself some lunch. He was sitting down to eat his peanut butter and jelly sandwich when Margret came back down the stairs. She was wearing one of her new dresses and Ronnie noticed that she looked really good.

"Wow, that dress really looks good on you. Sexy, if you know what I mean." Ronnie remarked wiggling his eyebrows as he said it.

"Yeah? Well, keep your dick in your pants. I'm going to the mall and I won't be back for quite a while. I'm going to meet some of the girls there and we're going to be shopping for the rest of the afternoon."

"But I was hoping that we could spend the afternoon together."

"Get real," She replied, "Why would I want to spend the afternoon cooped up here with you? Besides, when I get back, you can take me out to dinner."

"But Margret, I..."

Before he could finish, she had already walked out of the front door. He just sat there looking at the front door as if he was expecting her to come back, by him mentally willing it. When he heard the car start up and then drive off he knew that she wasn't going to come back. When he heard the car drive off, he also heard that all too familiar voice inside his head.

What a Bitch!

'Shut up, I don't need your shit right now." Ronnie thought back.

You know she is going off to see her lover.

'What the hell are you talking about?' Ronnie mentally questioned.

But it was at that point that the voice decided to remain silent. 'Great.' Ronnie thought, 'You throw something out on the table and then shut up.'

Sitting there thinking, Ronnie decided there was an upside to this. The upside was that he now had the afternoon to himself. Nancy would be asleep for a couple of hours and when she woke up, she wouldn't be any problem at all. He was used to keeping her entertained on the many times he was home alone with her. After he was finished with his lunch, he began to go through the box with the computer in it. After twenty minutes he had most of the contents spread out on the dining room table. After he had everything out of the box, Ronnie picked up the leather bound book and turned to the chapter marked 'Getting Started' and began reading.

6.

At the same time Ronnie was finishing his lunch, Margret had pulled into a convenience store and went over to the telephone. After finding some change in her purse she called Ted. He was at the dorm and had the afternoon off. Ted told Margret that she was lucky to get ahold of him because he had just walked in and was wondering what to do with the rest of his day, he told her that if she had called five minutes later, chances are that she would have missed him. After a few minutes of talking it was agreed that they would meet at a little English style Pub downtown by the name of 'Le Bistro'.

After Margret got off of the phone, she went and sat in the car for a couple of minutes trying to decide what to do. She didn't want to show up without any money and she had forgotten to pick Ronnie clean before she had left the house. She started the car and began driving to her rendezvous she saw a grocery store where she knew she could cash a check. Without a second thought, she pulled into the parking lot and went inside where she cashed a check for a hundred dollars. The clerk remarked that it was a lot of party money and Margret replied saying that she needed some cash to go yard saleing. No other questions were asked as the clerk counted out the money.

Margret was more than pleased with herself as she got back into the car. When she had been standing in front of the clerk she had a brief surge of anxiety but Margret quickly found that this had been a lot easier than she thought it would be. The only fly in the ointment was that there was only about ten dollars in the checking account. Margret was aware of that fact also. She had been toying with the idea of doing this for a long time, but had always been too nervous to actually go through with it. Now she found out that there was nothing to be nervous about. It had gone very easily with no questions asked. This, in Margret's mind, was like getting free money.

On her way to the Bistro she passed another supermarket of the same chain. Since her check cashing card was good at all of the chain's locations, she decided to try her luck again. Parking and going inside, she went through the same routine and once again her efforts were rewarded with another hundred dollars. Margret never stopped to consider the consequences of what she was doing. To her, she had just gotten two hundred dollars of free money. Money that she could do with as she pleased.

She was ten minutes late getting to Le Bistro, Ted was already there and had gotten a table in a dimly lit corner away from the mainstream of foot traffic. When she got there she had to look around for a minute before she found him at the table. She gave him a kiss on the cheek before taking her seat next to him. Anyone observing them would have thought that this was two lovers engaged in courtship.

They spent several hours there eating, drinking, and talking before they left and went to the Officer's Club at the base. Later, Margret told Ted about what an asshole Ronnie was. If she hadn't been drinking she probably would not have mentioned him, but the alcohol lubricated her tongue in the way that oil lubricates a sticky gate hinge. At first, Ted pulled away from her when he found out she was married, but she quickly explained that their marriage had been over for quite a while. Margret was very persistent and very persuasive. She wove an intricate web of fiction. She told Ted about how Ronnie would come home from work drunk and abuse her. Putting on an academy award performance, Margret got all misty eyed and told Ted about how when she saw Ronnie come home from work like that, she would fear for her life.

After another hour there, they retired to Ted's room in the dorm. After explaining that his roommate was on a cross country training flight and wouldn't be back for three days, the green light was on. After an hour of foreplay, the heat and urgency of need took over and Margret surrendered herself to him, mind and body.

7.

Long before Margret was getting her 'ticket' punched, Ronnie had decided that the dining room table wasn't the place to set up the computer on. He cleared off the desk in the living room. When he was finished clearing the desk, he saw that it was time to get Nancy so he went and got her up from her nap. Then he took her downstairs and made her lunch. When she was finished eating he cleared out the corner next to the desk and moved her playpen there she he could keep an eye on her while he worked with the computer. He put Nancy into the playpen and got the book back out and turned back to the chapter titled 'Getting Started'. Laying the book on the desk, he began hooking things up using the hand drawn pictures in that chapter as a guide. It took him thirty minutes to get everything connected properly.

When Ronnie was satisfied that everything was ready to go, he plugged the computer into the outlet. As he pushed the plug into the outlet, there was a flash and Ronnie received a mild electrical shock. Inspecting his hand he saw there was no damage done. What he had no way of knowing was that the instant the metal prongs on the plug touched the metal parts of the receptacle, the spark welded the two metal parts together. In a quite literal sense, the computer hooked itself to a permanent source of energy.

Ronnie tried to unplug the cord from the outlet and found that he could not. So he felt the outlet to see if it was hot and found that it wasn't. Sitting there, he wondered what he should do. Should he try to force the plug out or should he just say screw it and continue on. Ronnie decided on the latter. Now it was time to turn it on and breathe electrical life into this new machine of his. He saw himself as some sort of mad scientist as he reached behind the computer and flipped the main power switch on. There was a final pop and a small puff of smoke as the electrical connection was made even more complete and permanent. Ronnie quickly turned the switch back off fearing that he would break his new toy. Cautiously, he flipped the power switch back on again. This time nothing happened other than the unit began to come on. Instead of hearing the soft hum that would grow in intensity until the monitor came on, he thought that he heard breathing.

Ronnie listened carefully and realized that it did sound like breathing. There was no mistake about it. In-out. In-out. It grew louder and louder and just as he was beginning to become alarmed, the breathing stopped and the monitor came on.

GOOD AFTERNOON RONNIE was printed across the screen on the first line. WHAT WOULD YOU LIKE TO DO? Was asked of him by the second line.

For the next hour using the book, Ronnie learned how to find the menu, enter and exit programs, and how to make the processing program work. "This is so cool." Ronnie said to nobody in particular after he was able to enter something into the processing program and then get it to print off on a sheet of paper in the printer.

Ronnie took a brief break to change Nancy and then he sat back down at the computer. For the next four hours he sat and learned. When the time had elapsed, he sat back and felt that he was now proficient and confident enough to use the computer. He knew that he still had a lot to learn, but he also knew that as time passed he would get better at it. The most important thing was he had learned how to use the word processing program, the spell checking and correction program, and the grammar correction program. Ronnie was extremely delighted with himself.

As Ronnie was learning the computer, the computer was learning Ronnie. The way he thought, the way he spelled, and most important, the way he formulated his thoughts. It wasn't a fully independent functioning unit yet, but that would come with time.

Ronnie looked at his watch and saw that it was almost six o'clock. Deciding that Margret would be home at anytime, he turned the computer off. He noticed that as the power left it and the screen blinked off, there was a sound that almost sounded like a groan. He got up, picked Nancy up and took her upstairs to get her ready to go out. Ten minutes later they were both back downstairs ready to go out and get dinner as soon as Margret got home.

After another half hour had passed, Ronnie decided that he might as well feed Nancy. So he fixed her some dinner and fed it to her. After that task was done, he sat back down and waited. After sitting there for a while, he saw the computer book laying on the desk. Going over to the desk he picked it up, as he did, he thought that he heard 'Turn me on' as soft as a sigh in his mind. Shaking his head, he went back over and sat back down and started reading. Time passed very quickly as he sat there and looking at his watch again, he saw that it was nine-thirty. Thirty minutes after Nancy's normal bedtime. He took her upstairs and got her ready for bed. After reading her a bed time story, he kissed her goodnight, turned off the light and turned on the night-light.

Ronnie went back downstairs and after sitting there for a few minutes, picked the book back up and resumed reading. One thing in Ronnie's favor was his ability to read something once or twice and be able to remember it in total. Even though he was getting madder by the minute about Margret not being home yet, his reading time was not being wasted. He was learning a tremendous amount of information. Ronnie attributed this to the fact that the book was easy to read and understand.

At ten-fifteen, Ronnie went over and sat back down in front of the computer, then he arranged the book next to him on the desk. Turning the computer on, he started going through the routine to bring up the main menu. He hardly noticed when, at the beginning, the computer greeted him with 'GOOD EVENING RONNIE'. Once the main menu was displayed, he began scrolling down through all of the entries until he found a file named 'HELP'. This file was not listed in the book so he typed in 'LOAD'. Within a few seconds the screen began filling with information that was presented in letter form.

HELLO RONNIE,
APPARENTLY IT DID NOT TAKE YOU VERY LONG TO FIGURE OUT HOW TO WORK THIS COMPUTER. CONGRATULATIONS! THIS SYSTEM IS SO MUCH MORE THAN ANY OTHER COMPUTER SYSTEM YOU CAN BUY THROUGH A STORE. THIS SYSTEM WILL TAILOR ITSELF TO YOU. THERE IS NOTHING TO BE ALARMED ABOUT. SOMETIMES, SOME OF THE RESPONSES YOU WILL RECEIVE MAY BE STRANGE. BUT IT MAY BE DUE TO THE FACT THAT THE SYSTEM IS WORKING. THINK OF IT AS WHEN YOU ARE DOING SOMETHING AND SOMEONE ASKS YOU A QUESTION THAT YOU ONLY HALF WAY HEAR AND GIVE AN ANSWER THAT, TO OTHER PEOPLE, DOES NOT MAKE SENSE. THIS PROBLEM WILL GO AWAY AS YOU USE THE SYSTEM MORE AND MORE. IT WILL BE A LEARNING PROCESS FOR BOTH YOU AND THE COMPUTER.

THERE IS ONE THING THAT I DID NOT TELL YOU WHEN I SOLD THE SYSTEM TO YOU. THERE IS A SPECIAL FEATURE THAT YOU HAVE TO ACTIVATE THAT I THINK YOU WILL FIND VERY USEFUL AND MAKE THIS SYSTEM EVEN MORE INTERACTIVE. ONCE YOU HAVE READ THIS LETTER, PRESS THE DELETE KEY AND FIND A FILE BY THE NAME OF 'VOICE'. LOAD THIS FILE AND FOLLOW THE PROMPTS. ONCE THIS FILE HAS BEEN LOADED AND ACTIVATED, THE COMPUTER WILL FOLLOW VOICE PROMPTS INSTEAD OF YOU HAVING TO TYPE COMMANDS IN. IT WILL ALSO LEARN YOUR VOICE AND ACT AS AN ADDED SECURITY MEASURE TO KEEP UNAUTHORIZED PEOPLE FROM USING YOUR SYSTEM.

ALSO, WHEN YOU ARE USING THE WORD PROCESSING PROGRAM, YOU CAN JUST SPEAK TO THE COMPUTER AND IT WILL TRANSFER YOUR VOICE INTO TEXT THAT WILL BE DISPLAYED ON

THE MONITOR. OF COURSE, AT ANYTIME YOU CAN STILL USE THE KEYBOARD AND TYPE. BUT YOU HAVE TO TELL THE COMPUTER WHICH SYSTEM YOU WANT TO USE. IF YOU WANT TO USE THE KEYBOARD, SIMPLY SAY 'OVERRIDE VOICE' AND IF YOU WANT TO GO BACK TO THE VOICE SYSTEM, SIMPLY SAY 'OVERRIDE KEYBOARD'.
I HOPE THIS COMPUTER HELPS YOU WITH YOUR WRITING AND GOOD LUCK WITH 'GABBY'.
PRESS DELETE NOW

Ronnie felt the hair on the back of his neck raise as he read the letter, but it stood at full attention when he read that last line about Gabby. 'How the hell could anyone know about that?' He wondered. No one outside of McGuire, Margret, and him knew who Gabby was.
Looking back at the monitor screen, he saw that the press delete message was now blinking. So he pressed the delete key and another message was instantly displayed.

PRESSING DELETE WILL PERMANENTLY ERASE THIS FILE AND REMOVE IT FROM THE MEMORY. IF YOU WANT TO CONTINUE AND DELETE THIS FILE, PRESS Y FOR YES OR IF YOU WANT TO KEEP THIS FILE PRESS N FOR NO.

Ronnie sat there for a moment trying to decide what to do. Did he want to keep this file or not? Making his decision, he pressed the 'Y' key. Instantly, the screen went blank and the message 'RETURN TO MAIN MENU Y/N' came on. He once again pressed Y and almost immediately the main menu was displayed. Scrolling up and back down the list of files, Ronnie saw that the HELP file was no longer listed there.
He began looking for the VOICE file and after a few minutes found it. He put the curser on the file and typed in load. As he sat there waiting for the program to finish loading, he flipped through the book really quick. Just as he thought, just like the HELP file, there was nothing about this voice system listed in the book. Maybe this was something put into the computer after it had been built, he wondered. Then he came to the conclusion that this computer was getting to be a better and better deal the more he learned about it and used it. Suddenly there was a burst of sound and the computer spoke for the first time.
'HELLO RONNIE,' the voice was cold and mechanical sounding. As it spoke, the words printed onto the screen at the same time.
'THIS IS THE VOICE ACTIVATION SYSTEM. FIRST I WILL NEED TO LEARN YOUR VOICE. THERE IS A LIST OF TWENTY WORDS THAT I WILL ASK YOU TO SAY. I WILL PRINT EACH WORD ONTO THE

SCREEN, WHEN YOU SEE THE WORD PLEASE SAY IT. IF I AM ABLE TO LOG YOUR VOICE PATTERNS INTO MY MEMORY I WILL RESPOND WITH THE WORD 'GOOD' AND THEN WE WILL CONTINUE TO THE NEXT WORD. IF I AM UNABLE TO LOG YOUR VOICE PATTERNS IN, THE WORD WILL BEGIN TO BLINK. PLEASE REPEAT THE WORD. PLEASE SPEAK SLOWLY AND CLEARLY. IF YOU ARE READY TO BEGIN, PLEASE RESPOND BY SAYING 'YES'.'

Ronnie said yes and the screen went blank, just as he began to fear that something was wrong, the first word printed onto the screen. APPENDIX was the first word. Ronnie said the word and was rewarded with 'GOOD'. Then the next word was printed onto the screen and the process was repeated. Ronnie got so caught up in the procedure that he hardly noticed that it took almost an hour and a half to complete the program. Now the computer spoke again.

'THANK YOU RONNIE, THIS NOW COMPLETES THE PROGRAMMING PORTION OF THIS PROGRAM. I HAVE COMPUTED THE WAVEFORMS OF YOUR VOICE AND YOU NOW HAVE COMPLETE VOICE CONTROL. DO YOU WISH TO ACTIVATE VOICE SECURITY?'

"What's voice security?" Ronnie wondered aloud to himself.

'VOICE SECURITY,' The computer answered almost immediately, 'IS A FEATURE WHERE NO ONE BUT YOU WILL BE ABLE TO ACCESS EITHER CERTAIN FILES OR THE WHOLE SYSTEM IF YOU WISH. THINK OF IT AS A PADLOCK ON YOUR SYSTEM THAT YOUR VOICE IS THE ONLY KEY. IF YOU WISH TO USE THIS FEATURE, PLEASE SAY YES AND STATE EITHER FILE OR SYSTEM.'

'Oh, this is so cool,' Ronnie thought. "Yes." He said and after a second he said the word "System."

'THIS NOW COMPLETES THE PROGRAMMING AND SECURITY PORTION OF THE SYSTEM. IS THERE ANYTHING ELSE THAT YOU WOULD LIKE TO DO RONNIE?' The mechanical voice asked.

'Man, that voice is going to get on my nerves.' Ronnie thought to himself and then he had an idea. "Yes. How can I change your voice?"

'I DO NOT UNDERSTAND YOUR REQUEST.' The computer answered him, both on screen and to his ears. 'PLEASE RESTATE YOUR REQUEST.'

Ronnie thought for a moment and then remembered something that he had seen on an old science fiction movie about space a long time ago. "How can I change the parameters of your voice?" He asked.

'WAVE FORM AND DURATION PARAMETERS MAY BE RESET THROUGH SET-UP FILE. DO YOU WISH ME TO ACCESS THIS FILE?'

"Yes."

The screen went blank for a second and Ronnie could hear something start up inside the computer that sounded like the disk drive running. Looking at the disk drive where the computer disks went into, he saw that the red light that usually came on when the drive was on was off and remained off. Suddenly the screen flashed dark red and a flashing logo came spinning slowly from an infinite spot in the center of the screen. When the sound stopped inside the machine, the computer spoke.

'WARNING-THIS IS THE SYSTEM SET-UP FILE. DELETING OR CHANGING INFORMATION CONTAINED IN THIS FILE COULD CAUSE SERIOUS HARM TO THE WORKING PERFORMANCE OF THIS SYSTEM. WHICH PARAMETER DO YOU WISH TO CHANGE?'

"Voice parameters." Ronnie answered.

'ACCESSING VOICE PARAMETERS.' The computer replied and once again the screen went blank. A couple of seconds passed and then the screen came up green with the words 'VOICE PARAMETERS' printed in the center. Without being prompted, the computer went into a sub-routine.

'THIS IS THE VOICE PARAMETER CONTROL SET-UP FILE. HOW DO YOU WISH TO CHANGE MY VOICE?'

"Can you change it to sound less mechanical?" Ronnie asked.

'I DO NOT UNDERSTAND THE PHRASE -LESS MECHANICAL- DO YOU WISH ME TO PROVIDE YOU WITH SAMPLES OF WAVEFORM AND DURATION SO YOU CAN CHOOSE THE PARAMETERS THAT YOU PREFER?'

"Yes," Ronnie replied, "Do that."

'I WILL BEGIN GIVING YOU SAMPLES OF WAVEFORM AND DURATION. SAY THE WORD STOP WHEN YOU FIND THE WAVEFORM AND DURATION THAT IS MORE APPEALING TO YOU.'

After saying that, the computer began speaking. It started by reciting the Constitution of the United States. At the beginning, Ronnie couldn't distinguish the words from just plain noise and then the noise faded away and Ronnie couldn't hear anything at all. After five minutes the computer was into the human range of speaking and after another minute Ronnie said stop.

He had stopped the computer at a vocal range that somehow reminded him of something that he couldn't quite put his finger on. It was familiar but still sounded machine made. Sitting there thinking about it he noticed that unlike spoken language, the words were crisp and sharp. Subconsciously, the new computer voice he had chosen was an octave lower than the voice from his dreams, the one that he now heard in his mind from time to time. Ronnie decided that this was better than what he had started with.

'DO YOU WISH THIS TO BE THE NEW PARAMETER FOR THE VOICE OR DO YOU WISH ME TO CONTINUE?'

"Yes, this will be the new parameter. Do not continue."

'THIS IS NOW THE NEW VOICE PARAMETER SETTING. DO YOU WISH TO CHANGE ANY OTHER PARAMETER OR DO YOU WISH TO RETURN TO THE MAIN MENU?' The new voice asked him.

"Main menu." Ronnie replied.

Once again the screen went blank and the sound deep inside the computer started up again. After a few seconds the main menu was displayed on the screen. Looking at his watch, Ronnie saw that it was now well after midnight. So he put the voice security on for the system and turned the computer off. Just before the screen went blank the message 'GOOD NIGHT RONNIE' was both flashed onto the screen and spoken aloud.

Ronnie just sat there for a couple of minutes looking at the blank screen. This was the best investment he had ever made, he thought to himself. Just as he started to get up, the old familiar voice spoke up inside his mind.

So, where's the whore?

"Shut up." Ronnie answered aloud.

Well...Where is she? It's almost one o'clock, do you know where your whore is? The voice asked making fun of an old public service announcement that had been on television.

"She and her friends probably stopped at a night club and are having a few drinks. So do me a favor and just shut the fuck up."

I'll shut up when I want to. But, if you want, I'll tell you where she is.

"Okay smart ass, where is she?" Ronnie asked.

You gotta say please.

"Fuck you!"

You'll never know what I know. The voice inside Ronnie's mind taunted in a very sarcastic tone. *Or are you afraid to know what I know?*

"I'm not afraid of anything when it comes to you. After all, all you are is a figment of my imagination." Ronnie said, both trying to bolster his confidence and defend himself at the same time.

Oh, I get it. You like pussy after someone else is through with it. Is that it Ronnie? Does the thought of sloppy seconds give you a boner?

"Shut up!" Ronnie said loudly, almost yelling.

So that's it, Ronnie likes it already lubed up huh?

"I said shut up!" This time Ronnie did yell.

Tell you what old boy, I'll give you this one for free. Right now she's asleep in the arms of another man.

"You are a liar!" Ronnie said loudly, the anger plainly evident in his voice.

Okay, get an attitude if you want. But I'll tell you what, just to prove to you that I am not a liar, I'll give you two things for free. Then you'll see that I'm being honest with you. She will be home at two-fifteen A.M..

"Okay, two-fifteen. What's the other thing." Ronnie asked somewhat calmer.

Mention the name Ted to her and watch her reaction. I'm sure that you will find that I have a lot of insight on this matter. Just remember that I'm the only friend you have. I'll always give it to you straight and not like he's been giving it to her straight this evening.

"You are a lying asshole and I can't wait to prove you wrong."
Unfortunately Ronnie, sometimes you get what you don't deserve.

After saying that, the voice was silent and Ronnie was glad for the silence. But he couldn't get what had been said to him to go away. He tried not to think about it, but it just became a nagging thought. Kind of like a piece of music that you hear just a fraction of and then are stuck with it for the rest of day going over and over in your mind. Ronnie got up from the chair at the desk and walked over to his chair in front of the TV. Within a couple of minutes of turning the TV on, he was fast asleep.

8.

At the same time Ronnie was feeding Nancy her dinner, Aaron McGuire was meeting three of the major stockholders of the newspaper for dinner. Aaron had been expecting this dinner meeting ever since Ronnie's column about the preacher. This was going to be the meeting where they would try to stop the Gabby column and probably try to fire him. At least they would try to do that. Aaron was more than ready for them and he intended to use every resource at his disposal to ensure that the Gabby column wasn't going to be shut down. No matter what these gutless wonders had to say about it.

Aaron had seen an increase of sales that was phenomenal. One of the reasons he was here to see this happen was because of a deal he had made about five years ago. He had been an editor of a newspaper in New York when one night as he was leaving his office, he and three of his coworkers were held up in the elevator. After they finished handing over their wallets and watches, the lone masked robber decided to shoot all of his victims.

Aaron had been standing at one end of the group when the robber opened fire on the other end of the line of people. He shot each person and Aaron stood there in disbelief as he watched his friends go down. Then it was his turn and he stood there facing the gun pointed at him. He closed his eyes as he saw the trigger being pulled. There was a click and nothing happened. The round in the chamber had misfired. Aaron opened his eyes when he heard the second click and the next round misfired as well. He started to reach for the gun when the gunman swung the gun upward catching Aaron under the chin. Aaron fell to his knees as the elevator stopped and the doors opened. His next clear recollection was of some woman screaming as he looked around at his dead and dying friends. The gunman had run off as soon as the doors had opened and was never caught.

During an extended vacation to recover from the trauma of his ordeal, Aaron had heard of a small newspaper that was looking for an investor. So he traveled south-west and bought fifty-one percent of The Daily Constitutional. The other forty-nine percent was owned by the previous owner and a couple of prominent business owners around town.

The previous owner was a much older gentleman by the name of John Whitfield. He had retained twenty-five percent of the stock and had sold the remaining stock in ten percent increments. The last four percent was spread around to his grandchildren.

The deal had been that Aaron would run the daily operations of the newspaper and they would be silent partners. And silent they were too, until they either started bitching about the lack of sales or the cost of the overhead. Whitfield wasn't so bad. He had run the paper for many years and knew the upside and downside of the newspaper business. The other two, on the other hand, tended to be very vocal. Now that the paper was making a few waves in the community, Aaron had been expecting the dinner lecture.

As he walked into the restaurant, he saw the three stockholders sitting at a table in a dark corner. He walked over and without ceremony, sat down as he greeted them.

"Howdy boys. Anything new?" He said as he sat down, picked up a menu and was not looking at anyone in particular.

"Aaron, so nice of you to join us this evening." Whitfield said to him.

Aaron looked over the top of his menu at the three gentlemen seated in front of him. Just as he was deciding whether or not he wanted to cut the BS short and tell them to kiss his ass or listen to them first, the waiter showed up and started taking their orders. Once the waiter was dispensed of, Aaron decided to let his partners speak so he could see just how little was on their minds.

"Okay gentlemen. I know that this is a business dinner, so what's on your minds?" Aaron told them.

"Aaron," Bernie Fryer, the head of a good-sized law firm, spoke up, "There seems to be a small problem at the newspaper."

"Oh?" Aaron replied, "And what kind of problem are we talking about?"

"You know very well what problem we are speaking of." Jacob Renfroe said. He was the owner of a small chain of sporting goods stores that had spread out in a few small towns around the area.

Aaron started to speak, but was cut off by John, "Look Aaron, let's not beat around the bush. This Gabby Gasbag column is stirring people up around town. After the column about the good Reverend..."

"People are threatening to sue us." Bernie interjected cutting John off.

"What people? Who?" Aaron asked calmly but with enough sarcasm in his voice to start pushing everyone's hot buttons.

"Gentlemen," John said as he raised his hand, "We are here to discuss matters at the paper. If we get to loggerheads now, nothing productive will come of this meeting. Now let's all get a drink, relax and calmly discuss the situation."

The waiter, summoned by John, came back over to the table and took their drink orders. During the few minutes it took to get their drinks no one spoke.

When the first round was finished and the second round was well on it way, they began to talk again.

"Look Aaron," Bernie said, "We're not looking to shut down the column, all we are asking is that you tone it down a little. I want you to know that I couldn't be happier of the results from the column. For the first time in a long time the newspaper is operating in the black. I'm also told that the circulation demands are still rising."

"Yes," Jacob interjected, "I'm also really happy with the results. But the column about that Preacher, that was overstepping the boundaries of good taste."

"I didn't know that journalism had to stay within good taste." Aaron snapped back, his voice rising a little. The triple bourbon he had just downed was beginning to lubricate his Irish blood.

"Gentlemen..." John said as he raised his hand again. This time he was interrupted by the waiter, the food had arrived at the table. The conversation stopped as the meals were handed out and after ordering the third round of drinks, John resumed control of the conversation. "Gentlemen, there is no reason to get testy. We're just here to protect ourselves if litigation becomes a result of this Gabby person."

"Look," Aaron said to the three of them, "I can understand your concern. Let me assure you there is nothing to worry about. We can prove everything that has or will be written in this column. I've been in the paper business long enough to know you can't print unsubstantiated material. Besides, I haven't seen anything that doesn't support what has already been printed."

"So far." Jacob interrupted, "But how far will you let this go before you say enough?"

"Jacob," John interrupted him, "How can he answer that?" How far would you let it go if you were in his shoes? After all, he's done something that I couldn't do, He's almost tripled the circulation."

"For now." Bernie threw in, "But what if the paper starts losing readers because of something that was printed?"

"How could it be any worse than when I came here? I've been struggling to keep this paper floating. Now, when I'm starting to see some return for my hard work, you guys are crying like a bunch of babies."

John could see the feathers starting to ruffle, so once again he jumped in and took the conversation over. "Yes," He said, "It has been an uphill struggle. But let me remind all of you that we are here for other matters than just the Gabby column. Aaron, just think over the position the Gabby column could place us in. That's all we are asking. Now, let's get to some of the other business. Since the circulation is up, how is the press handling the extra load?"

"Well, I'm running the press at a slightly higher speed." Aaron answered him, "So now instead of being finished at four in the morning, we're getting finished at three-thirty. Also, running at the higher speed has resulted in a slight drop in ink consumption."

For the next two hours they ate, drank, and discussed the small details of the newspaper business. Jacob and Bernie could hardly keep up with the conversation between Aaron and John. Not that it really mattered, they were now somewhere in the fifth or sixth round of drinks. All they knew was John seemed to be satisfied with the answers he was getting and as long as John was satisfied with what he was hearing, then they were also.

It was on the seventh round of drinks that Bernie started up again about the Gabby column. "So Aaron," Bernie said as he leaned across the table to get closer to Aaron, "Who is she?"

"Pardon?" Aaron replied, not understanding what Bernie was asking about.

"Who is she? I know Gabby isn't her real name. Who is she?"

"Look Bernie, I can't tell you. I'm the only person who knows who she is and I promised her that I would not divulge her identity as long as her facts were correct."

"Like hell!" Bernie said, raising his voice almost to the point of shouting, "We foot the bills too! We have a right to know."

Looking at his watch, Aaron saw he had been there a lot longer than he had intended to. Now that the conversation was turning loud and ugly, he decided now was the best time to make his exit. Standing up he said, "Look, it's my job to see that the paper comes out at the right time with the right facts. You know the paper would have folded and you guys would not be here with some extra change in your pockets if I hadn't come along. More important, if Gabby hadn't come along. There isn't enough news around here to fill up the paper. Now I, for one, am not going to look a gift horse in the mouth and as long as Gabby is coming across with some good paper-selling dirt, I'm going to print it. If you don't like what I'm doing, then come up with the dough and buy out my share. Then you can run the paper full time like I do."

Aaron turned to start for the door, stopped and said one more thing. "If anyone has a problem, or tells you they have a problem with the paper or the Gabby column, tell them that I said to kiss my ass and come and talk to me."

Aaron looked around the table to see what the reaction was. Bernie and Jacob were doing that drunk head bobbing thing with the look of shock on their faces. John was smiling a big smile and giving him a thumbs-up sign under the edge of the table. Apparently Aaron had said something that John agreed with. After giving John a smile and a wink he left.

As he was walking out he thought about the thumbs-up sign John had given him. John served as a kind of a buffer between Aaron and the whiners. When John had sold him the paper he had known exactly what he was doing. By selling him fifty-one percent of the stock, Aaron could always use the old 'Buy me out" argument. "The chief cook and bottle washer of a company should have free reign to run the company without fear of anybody. This is especially true when it comes to the press. Just protect my retirement." John told Aaron as the final papers were being signed.

Walking out into the night air, Aaron breathed deeply. The fresh air seemed to clear his head a little. He was late and he had to get back and check the proof plates so the Sunday edition could be run. He also had to proof the Gabby column since he hadn't even looked at it since Ronnie had dropped it off on Friday. Somewhere deep inside him, he hoped that it was a real ass burner. The office was only four blocks away, so he decided instead of driving over, he would walk. It would also help to sober him up, although by looking at him, you couldn't tell that he felt half plowed.

When he got back to the office, the first person he ran into was the new go-fer he had hired. A kid by the name of Avery.

"Hey kid!" Aaron yelled at him as he walked up to the loading dock.

"Yes Sir!" Was the response he got as Avery ran over to where Aaron was now standing.

"Do you know how to drive and do you have a license to prove it?"

"Yes Sir I do."

"Then here," Aaron said as he handed his car keys to the kid, "Do you know where the Cattleman's Club is?"

"Yes Sir."

"Good. Walk over there, get my car and drive it back over here and put it in my parking place. Can you do that?"

"Yes Sir!" An enthusiastic Avery replied.

"Good. Oh, one more thing."

"Sir?"

"Mess up my car in any way, shape, or form and I'll use your ass to clean the press with. Understand?"

"Yes Sir."

"Oh, Avery, one last thing."

"Sir?"

"Why the hell are you still standing here? Why aren't you back already?" Aaron yelled at him.

Avery turned and took off out the door and down the street. Walking over to the door and looking out of the window, Aaron saw Avery running down the street in the wrong direction.

"That kid is dumber than dogshit." Aaron laughed to himself. Then he turned around and going into the press room, he started barking orders.

"What? Do I have to be here for you guys to do anything? Sweet Jesus, we got a paper to put out!" He said for the first time what was to become the most common phrase heard for the rest of the night.

After checking with the typesetter, he saw everything was being laid out. Looking at his watch, Aaron saw that they were actually forty-five minutes ahead of schedule. He told the proof-reader to hold the Society page because he was still waiting for the Gabby column to be completed. When the Proofer started to balk, Aaron held up his hand and told him not to worry, he would have it for typesetting within the half hour. That seemed to appease the man.

Aaron went into his office, shut the door, and sat down behind his desk. Taking the Gabby column that was in an envelope out of his desk drawer, he opened it. 'Well, what's it going to be this week?' He thought to himself. After the conversation he had earlier, he felt even if the column said nothing but that the town was full of assholes, he would print it. Taking the paper out of the envelope, he began to read it. As he did so, his eyebrows lifted.

"Holy shit!" He said as he read the column a second time. Seems like Ronnie had overheard a conversation between a couple of lawyers who just happened to work for Bernie Fryer's law firm.

It seems that while the two lawyers were hiding from work at the club, they had been laughing about how they padded their expense accounts. About doing a fifty dollar job and getting paid a couple of hundred for it in cash by the client, turning in the fifty and pocketing the rest. Getting some little paralegal or secretary to draw up a will or a simple power of attorney and charging a wad of cash for it. Wills could squeeze out an extra hundred while POA's could net fifty to seventy bucks.

The capper that made Aaron laugh so hard he actually had tears streaming down his cheeks, was how the older lawyer was explaining to his junior partner how to skim assets off of probates and trusts. Ronnie had named names, but the biggest kick was that Ronnie had gotten the name of the law firm correct.

"Bernie is going to shit his pants tomorrow." Aaron laughed to himself. Then he quickly corrected the spelling and almost sent the column to the typesetter like it was. But after pondering how much Maalox Bernie would go through tomorrow, he decided to make a few changes. Instead of using the lawyers names, he just used their initials. For the name of Bernie's law firm, he changed it to read 'A prominent local law firm'. For the ending, Aaron remarked it was no wonder that legal fees were too expensive for the common man to afford and there should be some sort of judicial reform. For an extra kick he added that Gabby hoped that nobody would take the law firm to court for malpractice.

Rereading the column he decided that he liked the flow and this is what they would print no matter what the outcome. He took the story out and laid it onto the typesetters table so it could be laid out. Then he went and started checking the couple of million things that he would have to check tonight.

9.

In Ronnie's dream, he saw he was once again standing in the high place. Looking down over the edge, he could see a city spread out below him in twinkling lights. It was peaceful here, looking up he could see the stars spread out across the sky above him. They were so bright and he hadn't seen the stars like that since he was a kid. He felt as though he could stay here forever. Suddenly there was a breeze that began softly and gained in strength until he felt as though he was going to be blown over the edge. It was then that he heard a single word that started softly and gained in strength like the wind. *TTTTTEEEEEEEDDDDDDDD* the familiar voice said in the wind. When the last syllable was out the wind abruptly stopped. There was no other sound.

A few seconds later he was woken by the sound of the front door closing. Ronnie sat up quickly and was blinking his eyes to clear away the sleep from them. Then he looked at his watch. Two-fifteen on the nose. He felt a hot flash come over him and a sudden need to urinate.

Margret walked past the living room and stopped when she saw Ronnie sitting there. After looking at him for a few seconds, she finally remarked, "Isn't it past your bed time?"

"Where the hell have you been?" Ronnie asked her, the irritation plainly evident in his voice.

"If I wanted you to know, I would have invited you along. Besides, what's your problem? I told you when I left that I was going out with the girls."

"Bullshit! Tell me where you really were."

"Look you piece of shit, don't cop an attitude with me! I was out partying with my friends." After saying that, she started to turn and walk away.

"Margret." Ronnie said, he had decided that now was the time to drop his bombshell.

Stopping and turning back around to face him, she said, "What now? I'm too tired for your bullshit."

"Going to Ted?" He asked as he watched her face.

Margret's mouth dropped open and she just stood there for a couple of moments while her thoughts were in a blur. How could he know about Ted? She thought to herself. How much does he know? What did he know? All she could think of was that she was busted. Finally, she stammered a reply, "Who?"

"What?" He coyly asked her. Her reaction was more than telling, and now he knew that the information he had been given, was correct.

Margret was confused. 'Maybe he didn't say what I thought he said.' She thought to herself. 'He's so calm. He should be shitting a brick, pissed off mad right now.' She observed. "What did you say?" She asked him. Her attitude was a lot softer, almost subservient.

"I asked if you were going to bed."

'PHEW!' A big mental sigh of relief. "Yes, I just didn't hear what you said. Sorry." She replied. Her demeanor noticeably changed.

"That's okay. I think I'll go up with you." He told her. 'Oh you bitch,' He thought to himself, 'You are going to pay for this.' He got up, turned off the lights and followed her up the stairs.

Once they were in bed, Margret tried to be submissive to him but he blew her off saying that he was too tired. Then he acted like he had fallen asleep and waited until he heard her soft snore before he rolled onto his back. It was almost dawn before he fell back asleep and he used his time awake to plan ten different ways to get even with her.

First there was the 'Follow her, catch them both in the act and kill them' thought. As he laid there thinking about it, he could see himself doing it. It was so easy, he could feel his hands slip around her throat and he would rejoice at the solid feel of her neck vertebrae crunch beneath his fingers as he squeezed until his fingers almost met each other through her throat. That soon dissolved to kicking both of their asses and then finally to confusion about what he should do.

When sleep finally found him, he first dreamed about normal things. But after awhile he found himself standing in a liquor store. At first he didn't recognize it, but slowly came to recognize it as the liquor store that he had bought so many of his liquid lunches in the old days.

He was the only person in the store and as he stood there looking around, the store slowly mutated around him. It was no longer brightly lit and spotlessly clean. It was now dim and grungy. The floors were so dirty that they looked as if they were made of dirt. Looking at the shelves that supported the liquor bottles, he saw there was a thin layer of green slime on them. The pungent odor of failure and death, vaguely reminiscent of urine, was so strong that it almost made him sick to his stomach.

May I help you? Ronnie heard that all too familiar voice behind him. He spun around and was surprised to see he had been standing with his back to the checkout counter. He found himself looking into the face of his dead professor. There was a sick grin on his face and Ronnie could smell a breath so foul that there were no words to describe it other than the rot of death. And that really didn't do it justice other than to give it a label.

Well Ronnie, what's your pleasure? The foul smelling spectrum asked as Ronnie set a bottle of Scotch onto the counter. Ronnie didn't realize that he had been holding the bottle of Scotch until he saw his own arm and hand set the bottle down onto the counter.

'Why are you asking me that?' Ronnie asked.

It's your dream, you must have called me. The professor replied as he took the bottle from the counter and unscrewed the cap. Flashing a big grin that sent shivers down Ronnie's spine, the professor raised the bottle to his lips and took three very long pulls on the bottle. Setting the three-quarters full bottle back onto the counter he remarked, *Some things you never get used to being without. Want some?* Again, flashing that foul grin. This time Ronnie noticed with some shock, the glint of steel in this apparitions mouth. It looked like, instead of teeth, he had miniature machetes in there.

'What do you want?' Ronnie asked him. 'I didn't invite you here.'

Well Ronnie old boy, you're right. This time I came to visit you. Have a drink.

'No.'

You know you need it. Your wife is a whore and you are a waste of life. Drown your sorrow, be a man and have a drink.

'I'm not going to drink with you, so quit asking. I do not drink anymore.'

Suit yourself. The Professor said as he picked the bottle back up and hit it again. This time Ronnie could swear that he heard the clink of metal scraping glass. When the bottle was set back onto the counter this time, it was three quarters empty.

Oh man that's smooth. The Professor remarked as he stepped from behind the counter.

'So what the hell do you want?' Ronnie asked again.

To tell you that I told you so.

'Kiss my ass!' Ronnie shot back.

Now is that anyway to act after I helped you? You could be a little more grateful. I told you where she was and when she would be home. I even told you who she was with. That ought to be at least worth a thank you.

'How about a hearty Fuck You instead?' Ronnie asked mockingly.

The Professor's hand was so fast, Ronnie never saw it coming. All he knew was the feel of bony fingers grasping his throat and slowly closing. Nothing was said for a moment as Ronnie began to see spots before his eyes. His breath was cut off between his lungs and mouth.

Although the Professor was standing in front of him, as the Professor spoke it seemed as if the sound was coming from far away. *No, I don't think so.* The Professor said as he slowly tightened his grip on Ronnie's neck. *In fact, I think you need to learn how to be a little more respectful. I think that I need a thank you and I need it now.* To punctuate his point he squeezed Ronnie's neck a little tighter.

Ronnie began to fear that his thorax was going to be crushed and as everything began to go black from the lack of oxygen, he managed to squeak out a very weak "Thank You". Actually, Ronnie said nothing because there was no wind passing through his throat to form the words. His mouth just moved in a soundless thank you.

Instantly the hand and the pressure were gone. But Ronnie had already started a downward slide and ended up on the floor. This is a strange sensation, Ronnie thought to himself. Here I am unconscious in my own dream. Suddenly he felt something warm flowing over him. It was a warm liquid feeling that was relaxing, but slowly, the feeling began to burn. Soon, Ronnie felt as if he was on fire.

Ronnie opened his eyes to see the Professor standing over him, sucking on a bottle of liquor and pissing on him at the same time.

Ronnie screamed and rolled away from the unearthly golden shower he was getting. At the same time, the Professor lowered the bottle and zipped his pants up.

Man, you scared me this time.

'You pissed on me you bastard!' Ronnie shouted at the Professor.

Hey, I was just trying to revive you. I was going to pour it on you, but I decided that it would be too much of a waste.

'You fuck! You pissed on me!' Ronnie shouted, still full of rage.

Well, you scared me. I thought I had killed you and I'm long from being finished with you. Remember Ronnie, respect. Next time I might not be in such a good mood and let go.

'Fuck you!'

What's the matter Ronnie? You look a little pissed. The Professor laughed at him.

'What do you want? Why are you tormenting me?' Ronnie said as he broke down and began to sob.

Let me think a minute. Hmm, let's see. I'm dead and bored. So tag, you're it.

'Please leave me alone.' Ronnie said in a weak voice. He sounded drained and spoke with the enthusiasm of a man with no hopes or dreams.

Can't do it, sorry.

'Why?'

The professor's mouth began to swell until it was the only thing that could be seen. Now those miniature machetes were full sized and quickly growing larger. Just when it seemed impossible to get any larger, the mouth spoke. *BECAUSE YOU KILLED ME!!!*

With that, the mouth snapped closed and Ronnie managed to roll away just in time. Scrambling to his feet, he saw the mouth was opening behind him for another try. He didn't notice that the machetes in the upper and lower sets and very back, had letters on them. The upper left machete had a 'Q' while the lower left had a 'Z' on it. The upper right had a 'P' and the lower right had a 'M' on it.

As Ronnie scrambled out the front door of the liquor store he heard the mouth clang shut behind him. This time everything was lit up from behind Ronnie by the flash of sparks created by the blades clashing together.

At the same time the flash was seen by Ronnie, he woke up. He found himself laying there bathed in sweat. He looked around and saw the room was bright, so he looked at the clock and saw that it was almost eleven. He laid there for a few more moments wondering what would have happened had the mouth closed on him. As he was pondering that thought, he began to notice the aroma of bacon coming from downstairs.

10.

Ronnie crawled out of bed and went into the bathroom. After taking care of his immediate needs he went to wash his hands and face in the sink. As he stood there looking into the mirror he noticed that he had one bruise on one side of his neck and four smaller bruises in a vertical row on the other side. His throat felt sore and he filled a glass with water and drank it, the cool liquid felt good in his bruised throat.

After a couple of minutes of silent reflection and disbelief of what had happened to him, he went downstairs. As he neared the bottom of the staircase he heard Margret call out to him.

"I thought I heard you up stairs. Hurry up, your breakfast is getting cold."

"Where's Nancy?" He asked as he walked into the living room. His throat was really beginning to bother him. Breathing wasn't making it hurt as he had walked own the stairs, but he now found that talking was really irritating.

"She's next door with Heather." Margret replied.

Heather was the daughter of the next door neighbors and at sixteen years old, she was one of the best babysitters on the planet as far as Ronnie was concerned. Sometimes Heather would just come over and take Nancy for a walk. The few times when Ronnie had used her services, she would always refuse payment. At first, he had insisted that she take the money but she would always refuse. Once he managed to slip a ten dollar bill into her purse while she was playing with Nancy. The next morning he had found the bill stuck under the windshield wiper of the car in an envelope. Ronnie never gave up trying to give her money, but there was no way he could get her to take it.

"Honey, what happened to your neck?" Margret asked him sounding all concerned.

"What?" Ronnie asked. He was taken aback when she had called him honey and he had not heard the rest of her question, he was deep in his own thoughts. He could not remember her ever calling him Honey. *Yeah, she's playing it cool.* The voice whispered in his mind.

"What happened to you Dearest? There are bruises on your neck." Margret continued as she walked over to where Ronnie had stopped walking. As she got there, she reached up and gently touched his neck. Ronnie winched as she did so and surprised himself as he did so. Margret thought it was from his neck being sore, but Ronnie realized that he had involuntarily did so from her touch.

"I don't know." He replied. *Respect.* The voice whispered.

"Does it hurt?" She asked gingerly with concern in her voice as she tried to examine his neck. Margret inwardly began to worry, she hadn't seen those bruises last night when they had gone to bed. But here they were this morning. She began to question herself as to whether or not she had done something to him in her sleep. She didn't think that she had, but it was hard to tell. Thinking back to her dreams last night there were no strange ones that she could remember, nothing that would lead to something like this. There were only two dreams that she could remember. One was of having a verbal argument with somebody she never saw, and the other was about Ted. In that dream, it seemed like her and Ted were looking for someplace to have sex, but that was all she could remember of it.

"No, it's okay. Just sore." Ronnie replied as he was pulling away from her. 'Just sore' was an understatement. His throat felt like it was on fire.

"Drink your orange juice. It's cold and should sooth your throat." Margret offered.

"So, what's up this morning?" Ronnie asked her.

"Well. We're here by ourselves for a couple of hours and I made you some breakfast. Let's go from there."

"Feeling guilty about something?" Ronnie asked her and instantly Margret felt a pang of guilt. Looking at Ronnie as he had said that, Margret realized that he had been smiling as he asked the question and that maybe she had taken what he had said the wrong way.

"No," She quickly replied, "I just thought that it might be fun to have some time alone."

"It smells good, let's eat." He told her as he walked to the table. *Man, look how cool she's acting.* The Professor piped up again, *What are you going to do about it?* "I'm going to eat." Ronnie said aloud.

"What did you say?" Margret asked puzzled.

"I said let's eat." Ronnie quickly covered as he realized that he had spoken aloud instead of just thinking his reply.

"Okay then, sit down. Eat."

Walking over to the table, Ronnie saw scrambled eggs and bacon. There was also toast and grape jelly on the table. The smell and sight of the food made him instantly ravenous. As he began to eat, the Professor spoke up, *How do you know it isn't poisoned?* Thinking about it, he saw that was a good observation and suddenly lost his appetite. He set his fork down and sat back in his chair as he looked at Margret. She was shoveling food into her mouth. As he watched her chew, he imagined that mouth of her's full of machetes. He could almost hear the metallic clinking as she chewed.

Sensing she was being watched, Margret looked up from her plate at Ronnie and swallowed. She noticed that he had a strange look on his face. "What's wrong?" She asked him.

"Sorry, but I guess my throat is a little sorer than I thought it was."

Margret felt an instant flash of rage. 'How dare the little bastard not eat after I spent time cooking this shit.' She thought to herself. "That's okay. Just drink your orange juice to help your throat feel better." She said as she forced a smile.

"So. Did you have a good time last night?" Ronnie asked her between sips of juice.

"Yes." She replied with a sly smile on her face. "We went to the mall and when that closed, we went bar hopping." She had to resist the urge to tell him that she had more orgasms in one night with Ted than the whole time they had been married.

"Well that's good. I'm glad you had a good time." He replied nonchalantly.

"Yes. It definitely was a good time." She replied dreamily.

11.

At the same time that Ronnie was pondering as to whether his eggs were poisoned, Bernie Fryer was just opening his eyes. After Aaron had left the restaurant last night, it seemed like Jacob, John, and he had about another twenty rounds of drinks. He barely remembered getting home. He didn't care what time it was, all he knew was that it was really bright outside and he just wanted to get to the bathroom without throwing up.

Almost crawling into the bathroom, he pulled himself upright at the sink. He didn't dare turn the light on, even though it was dark in there, there was enough light to do what he had to do. Opening the medicine cabinet, he pulled out the aspirin bottle. Filling a glass full of cold water, he open the bottle and put it to his lips. When about half of the bottle was in his mouth, he picked up the glass of water and began drinking. He didn't stop drinking until the glass was empty.

Bernie felt an instant, massive wave of nausea sweep over him and he had to sit down on the toilet. Not that he could have helped it, his legs sort of buckled and he had to sit down somewhere and the toilet was the closest thing. He didn't feel like standing back up to urinate, so he tucked his penis between his legs and relieved himself. When he was done he continued to sit there and after a few minutes, he began to feel better. Not great, but better.

After sitting there for another ten minutes, Bernie decided that he felt good enough to face people. So he got dressed and went down the back stairs that led straight into the kitchen. When he got there he found his wife humming as she chopped celery to put into the tuna fish salad she was making for lunch. The smell of tuna was about to make him sick again. She always did that to him. Whenever he was out late and came home drunk, she would make a big bowl of tuna for lunch. That was her way of getting back at him. She knew that when he was hungover, tuna was the one thing that would bring him to a really pretty shade of green. He didn't even have to eat it (Which he usually didn't.), the smell alone was her revenge.

Bernie never complained though, he knew how much of an asshole he was and also just how lucky he was that she had stayed with him all of these years. He knew it hadn't been easy and was grateful that she was here now making lunch. Even if it was repulsive to him. Personally, he liked tuna, but not after he had been drinking. He went over and poured himself a cup of coffee after kissing her good morning. Bernie then sat down at the table and picked up the newspaper.

"So how was your meeting last night?" She asked him, "You got home pretty late."

"Long and hard to follow." Bernie answered her. He sat the paper back down and sipped his coffee.

"I bet it was hard to follow," She replied with amusement in her voice, 'When you got home last night you were singing some nasty song about some one called Barnacle Bill the Sailor."

"Well, those newspaper guys are pretty heavy drinkers. It's a wonder we even get a newspaper at all, the way they go at it." Bernie told her that, trying to justify the condition he was in when he had arrived at home.

"And of course you had to keep up with them right?" She remarked.

"Of course." He said as he opened the newspaper.

After looking over the front page, he went straight to the Society Section and found the Gabby column. The first time he read it the facts in the column really didn't really sink in. It was near the end of the story the second time he read it when it dawned on him that the initials in the story were mighty familiar.

"That Goddamn Irish son of a bitch!" He said loudly, "That rat bastard McGuire!" He felt that the part about legal reform was a direct slap in his face. The fact that his employees were ripping him off was a secondary point to his rage.

"Bernie! Such language. What's your problem?" His wife asked him. She was unaccustomed to hearing that sort of language, that loud in her kitchen. Especially on a Sunday morning.

But Bernie was far from hearing her, he was in the middle of rereading the story for a third time. 'If this is true,' He thought to himself, 'Those two little rat bastards are unemployed. But if this is bullshit, Aaron McGuire's ass is mine.' He vaguely became aware of his wife talking to him.

"Is there something wrong dear?" She asked concerned about what had brought on such an outburst from him.

"Fucking-A right there's something wrong!" He snapped back at her. This time she only frowned at the use of his language.

"Anything I can do?" She asked.

"I'll be in my office." He said as he got up from the table, "No interruptions. Understand?"

His wife merely shook her head that she did. She knew him well enough after seventeen years of marriage to know that when he got into this type of mood (Which wasn't very often.), it was best he was left alone.

Slamming the door of the den that had been made into an office, he immediately went for the phone. Checking his Rolodex, he dialed Aaron's home phone number. It was answered by an answering machine. After debating as to whether he should leave a message or not, he hung the phone up and immediately called John Whitfield. It was answered on the third ring.

"Hello?"

"John? John, is that you? This is Bernie." He said.

"Bernie? Good morning. How are you feeling today?" John said when he realized who it was that was calling him.

"Don't give me that shit. Where's Aaron McGuire at?"

"Bernie, how should I know? You sound troubled. Is there something wrong?"

"Goddamn right there's something wrong. Haven't you read the paper yet?"

"Actually Bernie, I just got up and was in the bathroom when you called. So the answer to your question is no, I haven't read the paper yet. Why, what's wrong?"

"That Goddamn Aaron used the Gabby column to write a slam piece on me and my law firm."

"What?" John asked shocked and then added, "Aaron wouldn't have done that. Are you sure?"

"Hell yes. He gave some initials of a couple of my guys and told how accounts were being skimmed. Not to mention pocketing money after jacking the prices up." An irate Bernie told John.

"You say that he used initials? Did he mention the name of your law firm?" John asked.

"No. He's too damn smart for that. But I am going to have his ass for this."

"Bernie. You know that unless he mentioned you, your employees, or law firm by name, there's nothing you can do." A calm sounding John told Bernie in an attempt to poke holes in Bernie's rage.

"His ass, John, I want his ass for this. He can't slam me like this and get away with it." Bernie raved on.

"Look Bernie, if you have a problem with the newspaper, you're going to have to talk to Aaron. As you know, I'm not involved with the daily operations any more. Now if there's nothing else I can do for you, try to have a better day."

Bernie started to say something in protest, but realized that John had hung up on him. This served to fuel his fire even more and he tried Aaron's home number again with no success. Then he called the paper and getting the newsroom, he asked if Aaron was in. He was told yes, Aaron was there, but he was in his office in a meeting and couldn't be disturbed. Without leaving a message, Bernie hung up the phone.

Without changing out of his grubby clothes, Bernie went out, got in his car and drove straight to the newspaper office. He parked in the loading dock and went in through the rear entrance. Walking through the press room, he asked a kid who was standing there where Aaron's office was.

Avery, who was very tired from working his first all nighter, just pointed in the direction of the newsroom.

Bernie marched into the newsroom and looked around. He saw a dark office with 'EDITOR' painted on the glass door. Without stopping to knock, Bernie went straight into the office and slammed the door shut. Finding the light switch, he flipped it on.

Aaron was stretched out on an old sofa along one wall. The door slam had woke him up, but when the lights flipped on, he sat up covering his eyes bellowing.

"What's the problem? Can't you see that I'm trying to sleep? Or are you stupid as well as blind?" He said not knowing who he was talking to, he was still half asleep.

"Wake up you lazy, two timing, slandering son of a bitch!"

Hearing Bernie's irate, loud voice standing right here in his office, Aaron became instantly awake.

"Bernie, so nice of you to drop by! If you would have called ahead, we could have had brunch." He said, trying to set a calm tone to this confrontation.

"Cut the bullshit you dogshit Mick!" Bernie shouted enraged, "Who do you think you're fucking with? Huh? Nobody, and I mean NOBODY fucks with Bernie Fryer!"

As Bernie was venting, Aaron stood up. If this escalated to more than a one-sided shouting match, he didn't want to be caught sitting down. There was no doubt in his mind that he could easily kick Bernie's butt a couple of times in a row and if Bernie wasn't so full of steam, he would heave realized it also. Aaron stood there, a good foot and a half taller and seventy-five pounds heavier than Bernie. Aaron wasn't afraid of having to put a stompin on Bernie if he had to, and should Bernie have produced a weapon, Aaron would have probably have killed him with it. But Aaron just wanted to diffuse the situation.

"Look Bernie, I can understand why you're pissed off. Hey, I was trying to protect you..." Aaron started to say.

"PROTECT ME?" Bernie shouted cutting him off, "How were you trying to protect me by writing those bullshit lies in this rag you call a paper?"

"Now Bernie, calm down a Goddamn second," Aaron said sternly, starting to loose his happy thoughts, "I didn't write the Gabby column."

"You are a fucking liar!" Bernie said in a quieter voice, "After that crap last night, you came back here and wrote that trash about my law firm. You did it just to get back at me."

"Hey, I wouldn't do that. The only thing I did was to edit the column. I'm the one who substituted initials for the names and took the name of your firm out of the column."

"Bullshit!"

"Bernie, if you don't calm down, I'm gonna have to call security and have your ass thrown out of here. Now...Like I was saying, I took your name out of the column. So you should be thanking me."

"Like Hell! You wrote that crap and I'm going to expose you. You're Gabby aren't you?"

"I wish. Look Bernie, I can prove what I'm saying. And if it isn't true, I'll print a full front page of me kissing your ass with an apology."

"Then prove it asshole." was Bernie's reply.

Aaron picked up the telephone and pushed a button, a couple of seconds later he spoke, "Jack, bring me the file with today's Society section's hard copies." This was a file that was made when the stories were typeset. About a minute passed before Jack arrived at Aaron's door. Taking the file from him, Aaron shut the door and walked over to his desk. Pulling up his chair, he sat down and started going through the file. Finally, he found the piece of paper that the column was originally written on that contained the Gabby column. He handed it over to Bernie.

"Here, read this." He said.

Bernie started reading the poorly written, badly spelled column. He could see where someone had crossed out the names of his soon to be fired lawyers and he saw where Aaron had crossed out the name of his law firm. Aaron's changes were in the margin and Bernie sure didn't miss where Aaron had written in the additional comments about legal reform at the bottom of the page.

"This doesn't prove anything." Bernie said, "You could have written this yourself."

"Look around stupid." Aaron said, "There's about ten thousand examples of my handwriting in this room alone. None of them matches that piece of paper in your hand bonehead. You would also find that my handwriting is the changes that were written in. If I have to, I can also provide handwriting examples from everyone who works here. This is a legitimate, submitted column."

"Then tell me who Gabby is and I can prove for myself this is bullshit." Bernie said. He now felt that he was losing control of this confrontation. Truth was, the second he walked into Aaron's office, he never had control. But he still wanted to get his hands on whoever Gabby was.

"Bernie, nice try. But I told you last night I couldn't and wouldn't tell you who Gabby is. But I do have a better idea, why don't you call your working buddies and see if it's true. If this turns out not to be true, then I'll pull the column forever and still print the front page apology."

"You bet I'll check my people out asshole, then we'll sue your ass out of existence. Got that?"

"Yes Bernie, I hear what you're saying." Aaron said, trying to suppress a smile. He wished he had a dollar for every time he had heard that threat. Then he added, "Bernie, one more thing."

"What's that?"

"Shut the door on your way out!" Aaron bellowed at him as he stood up.

"Fuck you!" Was the reply. Bernie turned and walked out of the office, leaving the door wide open.

"Damn, what a stupid little fuck." Aaron remarked to himself as he sat back down. He put his feet up on his desk and reclined in his chair, a grin slowly spread across his face until he couldn't contain himself any longer and started laughing.

His laughter was cut short by the phone ringing. Looking over at the phone, Aaron saw it was his private line. There were only about six people that knew the number and they had all been sworn to the pledge of death to never give the number out.

"Hello?" Aaron asked as he picked up the receiver.

"Aaron, it's me John."

"Good morning John. How are you this fine morning?" Aaron asked. He surmised that John was calling about the Gabby column. But he was also genuinely interested in how John was doing. Aaron was accustomed to hearing from John after the dinner meetings. John would call him and report what had happened after Arron left the meetings.

"You really sound like you're in a good mood for this early after a Sunday edition. I didn't want to call you so early, but I'm afraid I might have some bad news that's going to get rid of your good mood."

"Are you okay John?" Aaron asked concerned.

"Oh. It's not me. Fryer called me up, raising hell about the Gabby column."

"Yeah, I know."

"What? Did he call you? I didn't think that he would be able to figure out about sleeping you on that old ratty couch in my office. Sorry, I mean in your office."

"That's okay." Aaron said chuckling, "Old habits die hard. But to answer your question, No, he didn't call me. I just threw him out of my office about two minutes before you called."

Now it was John's turn to chuckle. "Good. So tell me, is the column true?"

"According to Gabby it's gospel."

"So we're covered?" John asked.

"She's got names, dates, and times. She has all of the facts."

"Good. I hope this ruins that little prick Fryer. I wish I hadn't sold him that ten percent now."

"Yeah, he's a whiner alright. But don't sweat it, you did what you had to do and I've handled people a lot worse than him."

87

"Well, I just wanted to forewarn you that he's out for a piece of your ass. But I guess you already know that."

"That's alright John. I can handle him and the paper is safe on this one." Aaron said. Deep in his heart he was hoping Ronnie hadn't dropped a turd in his lap.

"Well, I guess I'll talk to you later then. Have a great day Aaron. Good bye."

"You too, good bye John." He said as he hung the receiver up.

After a few minutes of contemplation, he got his Rolodex out and found Ronnie's home number. He sat there for another ten minutes before he finally decided to call Ronnie. Picking up the phone once more, Aaron dialed Ronnie's phone number.

12.

Breakfast had been over for awhile and Ronnie was sitting in the living room reading the paper when the phone rang. Margret was in the kitchen doing the dishes so he answered the phone. When the phone rang Margret froze, she just knew that it was Ted calling her. She was near panic when she heard Ronnie say hello.

"Ronnie, this is Aaron McGuire. How are you doing this fine morning?"

"Fine Mr. McGuire. How are you doing?" Ronnie said, surprised that Aaron was calling him. Had Ronnie listened carefully to the background noise in his own house, he could have heard Margret exhale when she heard the name McGuire.

"Just fine Ronnie. It's Aaron, remember?"

"Sorry." Ronnie said, he found it hard to call people higher in authority than himself by their first names.

"That's okay. I called to see if you've read the paper yet."

"I was just starting to go through it when you called. Why?"

"Just curious. Listen, I changed your column a little. Nothing major, we can talk about it on Friday."

"I hope I didn't do anything wrong." Ronnie said.

"No, of course not. Like I said, it's nothing major. But just to let you know, it seems like your column has raised a bit of a fuss already this morning."

"Mr. McGuire...Aaron," Ronnie corrected himself, "I'm really sorry. If there's anything I can do..."

"Ronnie," Aaron said cutting him off, "Don't worry about it. But there is one thing that I need to know. Are the facts you stated true?" Aaron asked not pulling any punches and then held his breath for Ronnie's answer.

"Of course. I only write what I see and hear, just like you told me."

"Good boy!" Aaron exclaimed and greatly relieved, "I want you to keep doing that and don't change a thing. I hope you understand that I had to check and make sure. I have to watch out for the newspaper's interests."

"I understand." Ronnie replied, for a moment he had been afraid that this column was his last. "Do you want me to take it easy in the next couple of columns?" He asked.

"Hell no! You just keep writing what you find out. Okay?"

"You're the boss."

"Great. Well, I'll talk to you later then. Have a good day."

"Good bye." Ronnie said and then hung up the phone. He immediately turned to the Society page and began reading.

13.

After leaving Aaron's office, Bernie went out to where he was parked and stood on the loading dock for a few minutes to get his rage under control. Just as he started to go down the steps, he looked around and saw Avery leaning against the wall on the other side of the dock. Bernie had an idea and decided to do some fishing, so he turned around and walked over to where Avery was standing.

Avery had been standing there trying to get up enough energy to walk home. It had been a very long night and he was bone tired. Just entering the working world and not knowing what to expect, this all-nighter was nothing like he had ever experienced before. While being out all night doing something fun, was fun, being out all night because of work, just sucked. Now add on the fact that he had to walk home and it's easily seen how hopeless he felt his life was at that moment. He was not even aware that someone was walking up to him until Bernie spoke.

"Hello!" Bernie said in a pleasant tone.

Avery nearly jumped out of his skin.

"Hey, I didn't scare you did I? Sorry."

"That's okay. It's been a long night and I'm getting ready to walk home."

"Which way are you going?" Bernie asked.

"Over to Mulat Cove."

"Hey! I'm going the same way, want a ride?"

"Well, I don't know..." Avery said, unsure of this stranger who had approached him.

"It's okay son," Bernie said as he stuck out his hand to introduce himself. He was used to disarming hostile witnesses and befriending them to get what he wanted. "My name is Bernie Fryer."

Avery instantly recognized the name as some kind of big wheel around town. Taking the offered hand and shaking it he said, "Steve Avery. Glad to meet you Mr. Fryer."

"So Steve, you sure I couldn't give you a ride?" Bernie said as he pointed over towards his car, an almost brand new, jet black Corvette.

"That would be great." Avery quickly answered. He liked this guy, he had a really hot looking car and had called him by his first name, Steve. Nobody called him by his first name, usually it was Avery, Dillweed, or Dickhead. Although the list seemed endless, those were the top three favorites. He couldn't help but like this guy.

"Then let's go!" Bernie said cheerfully.

They walked over and got into the car. 'This is great,' Bernie thought, 'This kid is playing right into the palm of my hand.'

After a minute of driving, Bernie asked Avery if he was hungry and Avery admitted that he was. He wouldn't tell Bernie, but Avery had forgotten his lunch last night and was about to starve now. Bernie pulled into a small diner and after reassuring Avery that breakfast was on him, they went inside.

Bernie selected a booth over in the corner where he would pump Avery for all the information he could. The waitress, a young lady by the name of Lisa, dropped off their menus. Bernie sat looking at her ass as she walked away.

"Know what I'd like to eat." Bernie remarked and then looked at Avery, who was nothing but all smiles.

"I don't know what to get, it all looks so good." Avery remarked as he looked over the menu.

"You like eggs?" Bernie asked.

"Of course."

"You like steak?" Bernie inquired again.

"Yes."

"Then it's settled." Bernie said as he flagged Lisa down.

"You guy's ready to order?" Lisa asked as she walked up to the table.

"Yes. We'll both have steak and eggs. Well done and over easy. Throw in two sides of pancakes while you're at it. We'll also need a pot of coffee." Bernie answered her.

"Hungry this morning?" Lisa remarked as she wrote down the order. Then she left and returned a minute later with a carafe of coffee. Once again, Bernie watched her as she walked away. When she disappeared around the corner, Bernie decided that it was time to start making the kill with Avery. He was going to find out who Gabby was, one way or the other. If he could use this kid to do it, so much the better. So waiting a few minutes, he started making small talk about how he wished he had taken up journalism in college. Then he added he felt that being a lawyer was almost the same, "You find the guilt and punish it." He told Avery.

Avery remarked that he knew just what Bernie was talking about. He went on to explain how he used to 'work' for the police department until he had gotten a better job offer at the paper. Bernie knew pure fantasy when he heard it, but he just kept nodding his head and acting like he was really interested in everything the kid had to say. All Bernie was interested in was the subject of Gabby.

They had just finished off the coffee when the food arrived at the table. Lisa set the plates down and took the empty pot to be refilled. When it was back, Bernie began to work on Avery. Between bites and mouthfuls, Bernie began to spin a web of total fabrication.

"You know Steve," Bernie said in a low voice like he was telling a great secret that couldn't be overheard, "I shouldn't tell you this, but there's a small problem at the paper."

"What's that?" Avery asked, his ears perked up from hearing that there was a difficulty that he normally wouldn't be privy to.

Looking around as if he was checking to see if anyone was in earshot, Bernie continued in the low voice, "You have to promise not to tell anyone that I told you."

"Done." Avery quickly answered, "What's the problem?"

"You see, I was at the paper this morning because of a small legal problem. Have you heard of the Gabby Gasbag column?"

"Kind of. Why?" Avery lied, he hadn't heard anything at the paper other than 'do this' or 'do that.'

"Well," Bernie started, he could see that he had this kid hook, line, and sinker. All he had to do now was to reel him in. "It seems like she writes a lot of lies about people around town. Now it's getting the paper into trouble."

"How so?" Avery asked as he chewed on another piece of steak.

"It's kind of complicated, but the end result is going to be that the paper is gonna get sued out of existence for slander."

"Why is the paper going to be sued? Why don't they sue this Gabby person?" Avery asked.

"Because nobody knows who Gabby is. If we knew, then the lawsuit could be directed at her instead of the paper."

"If it's lies, then why print it at all?"

"Well...This is really top secret." Bernie said in a hush as he leaned closer to Avery across the table. This time he was acting like he was going to reveal a secret so dark and deep, the planet would stop spinning as he spoke, "The real owners of the paper are friends of hers and have her on the payroll. All she has to do is write something for the paper. Doesn't matter if it's true or not."

"Don't the owners know what's going on? Seems like they should be worried they are going to lose their business if she keeps on doing what she's doing."

"They have so much money they don't care. If they lose the paper, they'll just take it off their taxes. They don't give a damn about us working stiffs. Believe me, I don't want to lose my paycheck because of some arrogant snobs that have nothing better to do than play tennis and swim in heated pools all day."

Avery was stunned, "You work for the paper too?" He asked.

"Of course. I do all of the legal work. You know, contracts and the occasional asshole who tries to sue us because he got caught doing something wrong and we exposed him. But this Gabby thing goes way beyond that. I can defend the paper against problems when the truth is printed, but I can't defend against lies."

"Doesn't Mr. McGuire know who Gabby is?"

"Apparently not. I believe Aaron said that the column is delivered. So he's never seen her."

"What can be done?" Avery asked concerned.

"Well...If someone was to follow the messenger around, they might be able to get a line on who Gabby is. Hell, might even be worth some type of reward."

"What type of reward?" Avery asked eagerly.

"I know that I'd put up a thousand dollars to find out who she is." Bernie replied, he had considered just offering Avery a couple of hundred. But he wanted to make sure the hook was firmly planted, so a thousand seemed like a good amount of blood money.

When Avery heard the amount, his mouth dropped open. "I'll do it." He said without a second thought. Bernie just smiled at him and Avery continued speaking, "So, do I tell Mr. McGuire when I find out?"

"You can't tell anyone." Bernie quickly said. "I'm putting the money up, so you tell me. That way, if there's any sort of trouble, it will be directed at me."

"Remember Steve, you can't tell anyone about this. If you do, you will implicate yourself."

Avery didn't understand what that meant, but he did know there was no way he was going to miss out on this chance for an easy grand. So he agreed, although he did think it was strange that Bernie made him swear it was just between the two of them and that McGuire couldn't know they even had this conversation. After a minute of silence, Avery spoke up again, "Mr. Fryer, can I ask you a question?"

"Of course Steve. What's on your mind?" Bernie said as smooth as silk. Now that he had Avery in his pocket to do his work, he figured the kid was stupid enough to ask him for instructions.

"If you were going to do this, how would you go about it?" Avery asked, not disappointing Bernie.

Bernie thought for a couple of seconds and then replied, "Well...You know everyone at the paper don't you?"

"Of course." Avery answered immediately, he suddenly feared that the offer was going to be withdrawn because he had asked for advice.

"Then watch who comes and goes. If you see a strange messenger come in, find some way to find out who he is. If you see a woman you think is Gabby, get her license plate number or ask someone who she is." Bernie paused for a second and then asked, "You can do this can't you?"

"Of course I can. I know all about undercover operations. Remember, I used to work for the police department." Avery lied.

94

"Yes." Bernie said, hoping to jump on the covert bandwagon, "That's exactly what this is Steve, an undercover operation. A VERY secret undercover operation. Remember, only you and I know. It could be very dangerous for the both of us if anyone found out."

"You're right," Avery repeated, "No one must know, it could be very dangerous for the both of us."

Bernie just smiled to himself, he had this kid eating out of the palm of his hand and now this kid thinks he's part of the CIA. This was better than he could have hoped for and for only a grand. Whenever Bernie had used 'extra' help in the past, it had cost him almost ten grand up front.

After breakfast was over, Bernie dropped Avery off at his house. Bernie gave him a business card with his private number on it. He also made the point that sooner was better, for all of them, than later.

Avery hardly heard what Bernie said. In his mind he was now the next 007, a spy, going off to fight the ultimate evil.

"Bernie, you are sooo bad." Bernie laughed to himself after he drove off. Now he would have this Gabby's ass in the sling that it deserved to be in. When he got home he went straight into his office and made two phone calls. They were brief and almost exactly the same. Basically it was 'Get your shit out of my office before I get there tomorrow.' There was little protest from either party that he talked to.

When he finally came out of his office he found his wife in the family room reading a book. She looked up at him and saw he looked like he was in a better mood.

"Where did you go?" She asked him.

"I had to run to the office for a little while."

"Important business?"

"Yes, very important. There was a problem with one of the accounts." He replied.

"So...Is the world saved for now?"

"Yes and it's going to be a very good day followed by a bunch of better days."

"That's good." She replied as he settled down in his easy chair.

14.

Ronnie sat and read his column. He saw that the changes were minor and he liked the legal reform add-on Aaron had put at the end. Other than that, the column was mostly as he had written it. He was just setting the paper down when Margret walked back into the room.

"Who was that on the phone honey?" She asked.

Ronnie almost said it was Ted, but decided to tell the truth. "It was Aaron McGuire."

"What did he want?"

"He just called to let me know about some changes he made on my column."

"He changed your column?" Margret asked trying to sound indignant.

"Nothing major. It actually made the column a little better. I'm still learning and getting used to writing."

"Well as long as you're okay with the changes. Then I guess there's nothing to worry about. So...What do you want to do today?"

"I dunno, lay around and take it easy."

"Sounds good to me." she answered him. After a couple of minutes of awkward silence she added, " I see you got your computer set up. Does it work?"

"Yeah, I got it together last night. It's really neat and seems to work great." he told her. For some reason, talking about the computer seemed to excite him.

"Are you going to use it for your column?"

"Yeah. It has spell checking and error correction. It's going to be a big help with my writing."

"That's nice dear." Margret remarked and then turned her attention to the remote control for the television.

Ronnie watched her as she flipped the channels. 'Look how cool and calm she is....BITCH!' He heard himself think. Then he realized by her own actions, she was admitting she was guilty, or at least felt guilty about something. She never called him the things that she was calling him today. Only when she was scared about getting into trouble about something, did she act nice to him. Thinking back, he remembered how she had acted after that night the police had rattled her cage about abuse. She had acted just like this. He raised his hand to his throat and rubbed it. Maybe she had done this to him while he was sleeping and was now afraid that he would report her. He tried to rationalize to himself that was what had happened. She had grabbed his throat while he was sleeping and he had dreamed the Professor was the one who did it. He felt a chill as he remembered the Professor's bony handshake and the way his hand had looked the next morning.

It's too bad that Ronnie couldn't read Margret's thoughts. As he was sitting there thinking she had done this to him, she sat there also thinking she had done this to him. Actually, she was sitting there afraid that she had done it to him. She sat there flipping the channels without really seeing them because she was deep in thought. She couldn't remember trying to strangle Ronnie, she was trying to remember how he had looked this morning when she had gotten up. She couldn't remember if the bruises were on his neck or not. If those bruises had been inflicted by her on him, then it must have happened while she was asleep. As far as she could remember, she had only dreamed about Ted last night. There had been nothing about Ronnie that she could remember invading her sleep. Of course she had already forgotten the dream about her arguing with some one that she couldn't see.

'RONNIE'

Ronnie blinked and looked over at Margret, but judging from her actions, she hadn't called his name. He looked around and as his gaze fell on the computer he heard the computers mechanical voice,

'RONNIE COME OVER HERE AND TURN ME ON'

Ronnie jerked his eyes away from the computer and looked at Margret and saw that apparently, she wasn't hearing anything. He also noticed that as long as he wasn't looking in the direction of the computer he wasn't hearing anything. After about half a minute he looked back at the desk.

'RONNIE RONNIE RONNIE COOOME ON TURN ME ON LETS PLAY A GAME'

He averted his gaze from the computer and forced himself to look at the television. He found that he was actually having to force himself not to look at the computer. Even though it was a struggle not to look, like before, he noticed that he wasn't hearing anything. A couple of minutes passed before he looked again.

'RONNIE COME ON LETS PLAY A GAME YOU LIKE GAMES DON'T YOU LETS PLAY TURN ME ON'

Without realizing what he was doing, Ronnie got up and walked over to the desk.

'THERE YOU GO COME ON TURN ME ON TURN ME ON TURN ME ON'

Ronnie watched with disconnected concern as his hand went up and reached behind the computer, felt the power switch and turned it on. He sat there trying to remember why he was here as the machine warmed up. As the monitor flickered to life he heard himself say "System voice and security off.". Margret looked at him right after he said that, thinking he had spoken to her. But when he failed to respond when she asked him 'What?' she chalked it up to hearing things.

GOOD DAY RONNIE the screen had printed across it, WHAT WOULD YOU LIKE TO DO? It asked him. He placed his hands on the keyboard and typed in GAMES. The screen went blank and a second later a menu came up on the screen. He saw all of the usual games listed. Tic-Tac-Toe, Hang man, Chess, Checkers, the list went on and on.

Reading down the menu he saw a game that he wasn't familiar with, it was called Oracle. He decided to see what it was, so he typed the letter next to the game and once again the screen went blank. Thirty seconds later the screen printed, THE ALL KNOWING ORACLE. DO YOU WISH TO ASK A QUESTION?

Ronnie typed in yes and the screen prompted him to type in his question. Being the smart ass that he was, Ronnie decided to see just how all knowing this Oracle really was, so he typed in "Who is Margret fucking?" and pushed enter. The response was immediate, the screen printed NOT YOU, THAT'S FOR SURE.

Ronnie sat there dumbfounded and almost immediately the screen printed a second line, I TOLD YOU LAST NIGHT THAT THE NAME IS TED.

Ronnie pushed his chair back and started to reach for the power switch to turn the computer off, before he could, the screen printed, I WOULDN'T DO THAT IF I WERE YOU. YOU MIGHT MISS AN IMPORTANT MESSAGE. Ronnie's hand stopped halfway up.

"Like what?" He said aloud.

AARON MCGUIRE IS GOING TO CALL YOU THIS AFTERNOON

This time his response was immediate, he finished reaching up and turned the power switch to the off position. But the computer didn't turn off, it just printed another line, I WAS RIGHT ABOUT THE TIME LAST NIGHT AND THIS TIME ABOUT THE CALL. REMEMBER RONNIE, RESPECT. As he saw the word respect, he heard that mechanical voice in his head. Looking at the screen he saw that it was blank and the computer was off. Ronnie felt as if he had come out of some sort of trance.

He looked over and saw that Margret seemed to be engrossed in a cooking show. She looked over at him and smiled, that smile sent a shiver down his spine. Looking back at the computer, he decided to turn it back on and play some games. He found that he liked the chess game the best. After a couple of hours had passed, Margret suggested they get Nancy and go to the mall and then out to dinner. This sounded good to him so he shut the computer off and went to get ready to go.

When he came down the stairs, he found Margret was gone so he assumed that she had gone next door to get Nancy. He went to the front door and looked out and found he had been right, Margret was coming back from next door carrying Nancy. It was then that the phone rang.

"Hello?" Ronnie said as he answered it.

"Ronnie?" A voice inquired.

"Yes."

"Ronnie, this is Aaron, I hope that I'm not bothering you."

"No, not at all." Ronnie managed to croak out, when he had recognized Aaron's voice he felt his knees go rubbery.

"Listen, I hate to bother you again, but I was wondering if you could stop by my office after work tomorrow. I would like to go over some things with you that might help you with your writing."

"You mean that I'm not in trouble?" Ronnie asked, suddenly fearing Aaron had reconsidered what he had said this morning and Ronnie was going to lose his writing job.

"Of course not." Aaron said laughing, "Ronnie believe me, you don't have to worry about that. This is just to help your writing."

"I can't get there before five-fifteen."

"That's okay."

"Good, I'll see you then."

"I'll be here." Aaron said and then hung up.

Margret walked in just as Ronnie was hanging up the phone and she asked him who it was.

"Wrong number." He replied and then thinking quickly he added, "Some guy asking if some chick was here."

Margret's blood froze in her veins, she just knew that Ted had tried to call her. So trying to act all cool and calm, she asked Ronnie if he was ready to go. He replied that he was, they left and spent the rest of the day shopping. Rather, Ronnie spent the rest of the day watching Margret shop.

15.

The next morning came all too early and Ronnie went to work. Three hours after he left, Margret woke up. Within fifteen minutes of waking up, she was on the phone to Ted. Luckily, he answered the phone on the first ring. They spent the next two hours exchanging sex talk and decided that they could meet again tomorrow night.

After being at work for a couple of hours, the Superintendent came by and told Ronnie that there was a meeting at ten o'clock at the shack. When ten came around, Ronnie pointed his mower towards the Greens Shack and drove to it. When he got there he saw all of the other maintenance people there. Standing around with everyone else, he found that nobody knew what the meeting was about. Not even the Superintendent.

After waiting fifteen minutes, a golf cart came down from the Club House with two men in it. As it got closer, Ronnie could see that Mr. Bernstein, the owner of the club, was driving. Seated beside him was a man that Ronnie had never seen before. They parked the cart and walked over to where the crowd of employees were gathered and stood silent as the group spread out in front of them. After the group had settled down, Mr. Bernstein began to speak.

"Gentlemen. There is a serious problem here at the club. Somebody has been talking to someone about the things that go on here and these things are ending up in the newspaper. This cannot continue. People pay a lot of good money to come here and relax. If our patrons start getting worried about having their actions reported, they are going to stop coming here. If they stop coming, we stop making money. We stop making money and we can't afford to continue paying you. That's when we all lose our jobs."

He paused for a moment to let that sink in and then continued, "The gentleman next to me is Mr. Benson. He is the attorney for the club. He has a few words for you. Mr. Benson."

Mr. Benson began speaking. He explained this was a problem that had the potential to lose a lot of money for the club. If it didn't cease now and they found out who was doing it, that person would not only be fired, but also be open to all kinds of legal repercussions. He made it sound like that by the time they were finished with you, not only would you be penniless, they would have taken away your birthday also. He was very convincing.

When he was finished speaking, both men returned to their golf cart and drove away. Everyone was milling around and discussing what they had just been told. Floyd Fritz, the Superintendent, broke up the assembly by telling them, "God was finished speaking and now it was time to get back to busting their asses."

Ronnie was walking back over to his mower when Fritz yelled at him.

"Ronnie! I need to see your sorry ass in my office now."

Ronnie just about laid a load in his pants, he just knew that he was busted and was fixing to lose his job. He turned and walked straight into the shack and went into the office to wait for Fritz. Five minutes later, Fritz joined him.

"Don't look so scared son." Fritz said as he walked into the office.

"Mr. Fritz, I don't know anything about what they were talking about. I just do my job and mind my own business." Ronnie told him. He figured that at this point, it would be better to deny everything than to confess.

"Is that what you think Ronnie? That I brought you in here to grill you about some pain in the ass the boss has? Fuck them. I think it's funny that somebody is ratting on some of the things going on around here." Fritz said with a big grin on his face, but then he added, "Of course publicly, I have to support the position of management. But just between you and me, piss on them."

"Well, I just thought that after the lecture we just had that..." Ronnie didn't finish the statement.

"I understand. The reason I brought you in here is that I was going over the personnel records. I see you haven't had a raise or a promotion in over three years."

Ronnie just sat there in shock, he couldn't believe he had been working there that long. He did manage to say "Yes Sir."

"Well Ronnie, it's time for your raise. Just how much of a raise, depends on you. To get a promotion, you have to pass an aptitude test that has only one question. Do you want to try?"

"Sure." Ronnie said, he figured that he had nothing to lose.

"Okay, here's the question. Take all of the time you need to answer it. Are you ready?'

"Yes Sir."

"Good. Here it is. On a lawn mower's throttle there is a turtle and a rabbit printed on it. What do those symbols stand for?"

Ronnie couldn't believe it, this was so simple, he answered almost immediately, "The rabbit means fast and the turtle means slow."

"Congratulations Ronnie. You are now the new Assistant Superintendent. Your pay has just increased by about three-fifty an hour." Fritz said excitedly as he stood up and poked his hand out to be shaken.

"I can't believe it!" Ronnie stammered and then took and shook the offered hand. "What do I do now?" He asked.

"Mainly, you ride around all day doing what I tell you to do, solving problems, and keeping the rest of the guys looking busy. These guys will screw around at the drop of a hat. You start your new duties tomorrow. Why don't you take the rest of the day off and go celebrate with your wife?"

"But I still have to finish the back nine."

"Ronnie, you are a boss now. Don't worry about it. Besides, I said that one of the things you have to do is what I tell you to. Remember? So get out of here and go home. Go screw your wife or something. Okay?"

"Yes Sir." Ronnie replied.

"Oh Ronnie, one more thing. Now that you're my new assistant, you have to call me Floyd. Not sir, not Mr. Fritz, not even asshole, it's Floyd. Understand?"

"Yessi...Okay Floyd."

"Good. Now get out of here."

Ronnie couldn't believe his luck. Not only had he gotten a raise, but he had been promoted also. He couldn't wait to get home and tell Margret about his good fortune. He headed out to the parking lot and found the car. As he was driving home, he remembered Aaron's phone call and decided even though it was almost lunch time, he would go ahead and stop by Aaron's office. As he drove over to the paper, he was wrestling with whether or not he wanted to continue the Gabby Column. With his new position and the raise, along with the pep talk from the owner of the Club, he didn't want to jeopardize his good fortune. He ultimately decided to talk to Aaron about it and get a second point of view.

When he arrived at the paper, he parked by the loading dock and went inside. Going to Aaron's office, he saw that he wasn't in. Standing there for a minute looking around, he saw a young man standing over in the next room. Ronnie decided to go through the doors and ask where Aaron was.

16.

Avery had gotten to work early that morning with two things on his mind. First was the secret mission he was on and second, the thousand dollars. In his mind he had spent that grand about ten times and in ten different ways. He planned on being Bernie Fryers eyes and ears until he could come up with the needed information. He only hoped that it wouldn't take too long.

Avery was on his eleventh plan to spend the money, when he saw a strange man approaching him. Thinking back, he felt that for some reason, this guy looked familiar. But he could swear he had never seen him before in his life.

"Excuse me," Ronnie asked, "Do you work here?"

"Yes. May I help you?" Avery replied.

"Could you tell me where Mr. McGuire is?"

"Who are you and why do you want to know?" Avery asked.

'Uh-ho.' Ronnie thought to himself, but remembered what Aaron had told him to say. "I'm a messenger and I have a delivery for McGuire." Ronnie answered with a little authority to his voice.

"Well, I can take it for him." Avery said. He couldn't believe this chain of events. The very first day of looking for a strange messenger and here he was in front of him. If he could get the Gabby column from him and give it to McGuire, then he could be assured that he had the correct person. This person would lead him right back to the Gabby bitch and his thousand dollars.

"I'm sorry, but I was given instructions to hand deliver this directly to Mr. McGuire. So...Is he here or not?" Ronnie said as he started to become irritated at the way this kid was treating him. But Ronnie decided to refrain from getting rude with him unless he needed to.

"If you would please wait by his office I'll go get him." Avery replied with a big smile, he was now sure that the right person had just been dropped in his lap.

"Thank you." Ronnie said as he turned back towards the office as Avery headed in the general direction of the store room.

Aaron was in the store room doing an inventory of supplies and ink. When he saw Avery come into the room he was instantly annoyed because the kid couldn't find enough things to keep himself busy and was always bothering Aaron for things to do. It would be okay if Avery did a good job, but he always did a half ass job of whatever task he was given.

"Mr. McGuire, are you in here?" Avery called out.

"Over here behind the shelves. What the hell do you want?"

"There's a messenger here for you." Avery explained.

"What does he want?"

"He say's that he has a delivery for you."

"Then sign for it and put it in my office. I'm busy right now."

"Can't. He say's that he can only deliver it to you in person."

"Dammit, I'm never going to get this inventory completed." Aaron said angrily as he put his clipboard down. "Where is he?" He growled at Avery.

"I told him to wait by your office. I hope I did the right thing."

Aaron didn't answer him and left the store room muttering under his breath. Avery followed him out. When Aaron got to where he could see that the messenger was Ronnie, his mood softened considerably. Avery did not miss the change in mood and tried to stay close enough behind Aaron so he could observe what was going to happen without being obvious.

"Ronnie," Aaron called out, "You're early. I wasn't expecting you until late this afternoon."

Ronnie saw Avery behind Aaron looking in his direction, so he replied, "I have the information that you requested."

Aaron half turned and saw Avery behind him. When Avery saw Aaron look in his direction, he tried to look busy, but it was too late. He had been caught watching.

"Step into my office and let's see what you got." Aaron said as he pointed to his door. Going inside, he shut the door and sat down behind his desk, motioning to Ronnie to take a seat as he did so.

"Glad to see you. How come you're early?" Aaron asked once they were settled.

"I got promoted today and the boss gave me the rest of the day off. So I thought that I'd swing by here and talk to you. I hope I haven't come at a bad time."

"It's never a bad time for me to talk to you." Aaron replied with a smile that was genuine. "I'm glad you came by, I wanted to tell you that I really like what you've been doing with your column. It's coming along a lot better than I hoped it would."

"Great!" Ronnie replied and then added, "The column is something that I want to talk to you about also. You see, with this big promotion it might be harder for me to get material. I don't know if I can keep writing."

Aaron's defenses instantly went up, there was no way he was going to lose his cash cow, but he could sense there was something that Ronnie wasn't telling him. "Ronnie. I get the feeling that this isn't the whole story. Is something wrong?" He asked.

After a minute of silence, Ronnie spoke. "Yes. Today at work, they had a lawyer come and talk to us. He said if they found the person who was supplying the information, they would fire him and sue that person off the face of the planet."

"Ronnie." Aaron said laughing, "I can't tell you how many times I've heard that. Let me assure you that you have nothing to fear. As long as you write the truth, no one can touch you. And as long as you're writing for me, you have the legal resources of the paper behind you. Don't worry."

"Are you sure? I don't want to lose my job, either of them." Ronnie asked.

"Hey, I wouldn't just leave you hanging. You have a responsibility now. Did you know that you have a small fan club started?"

Really?"

"Yes, and I can't keep the Sunday edition on the racks, there's such a demand for it. It's all you Ronnie. Before the Gabby column started, we had about a quarter of the papers that we printed come back from the racks as returns. Now, I can't keep them stocked. We are increasing our run every week and still selling out."

"Damn. I had no idea my column was that popular." Ronnie said in disbelief.

"That's right, you are popular and you are the reason the paper is selling out. Look, let me lay all my cards out onto the table. If it wasn't for the Gabby column, this paper would have shut down a couple of weeks ago. But now that everyone is buying to see what you are going to write next, the paper is running in the black for the first time in a long time."

"Okay," Ronnie said, "If it really means that much, I guess I could keep writing."

"That's my boy." Aaron said relieved, "You just keep turning out the columns and don't worry about anybody suing you or getting fired. The paper will protect you. After all, how can you fight the truth?"

"You can't." Ronnie replied.

"That's right. Like this last column you wrote. Look how people were getting ripped off and not even knowing it. Now it's going to be harder for another lawyer to pull the same scam those guys were."

"I never thought of it like that."

"Look Ronnie, I have an idea. Why don't you write a couple of fluff pieces. We'll run those and maybe that will take some of the heat off of you at work."

"I don't quite follow what you're saying."

"Write a column about high gas prices, or one bitching about the potholes in the roads around town. Anything to show that all of the information for the columns is not being gathered at the club. Believe me, the fervor at your work will die down quick enough." Aaron explained.

"I get it. That will throw them off track and show the gossip is not just coming from one place."

"Precisely."

Now that Aaron was sure he wasn't going to lose Ronnie as a valuable source of information and revenue, he started talking about how the column should be formed, and a bunch of other small details. When he was finished, he got up and walked over to a bookshelf and selected two books from it, They were old, well worn text books on journalism. Giving them to Ronnie, Aaron explained that Ronnie should read these books when he got a chance and they would help him in his writing.

When the meeting was over, Ronnie looked at his watch and saw almost an hour had passed. He told Aaron that he had to get home and tell his wife the good news about his job. Aaron smiled and told him how happy he was for him.

Avery was gathering up the trash that seemed to always accumulate in massive proportions, when Ronnie and Aaron emerged from the office. He watched them as they talked for another minute and then shake hands. Avery followed Ronnie out of the building and watched Ronnie get into his car as he was putting the garbage into the dumpster.

Had Ronnie looked into his rear view mirror as he pulled out of the parking lot, he would have seen Avery writing down his license plate number.

17.

Avery was pleased with himself as he walked back into the building, he couldn't believe it had been this easy to find the delivery guy. Now he was one step closer to Gabby, but all he had right now was a license plate number. He knew he was going to need a lot more than that to collect his thousand dollars. But he didn't know how he was going to go about turning the plate number into a name and an address. After his stint as a Junior Auxiliary Patrolman, he knew how easily the information could be obtained. Unfortunately for him, he had burned his bridges behind him and had left the impression of just another loud-mouthed teenager, when he proclaimed his freedom (in front of almost the whole patrol shift) from the mundane rigors of law enforcement. Avery knew once he had that information, all he would have to do was to follow the person around until he met up with someone that might fit the mental image that Avery had of Gabby. That problem perplexed him for a good portion of the afternoon.

After Avery had finished cleaning the bathrooms, he was dumping the trash for the thirtieth time that day when he found himself almost alone in the news room. Looking around he saw that most of the reporters were gone, but there was one old man sitting over in the corner slowly typing away on a piece of paper. The contents of that paper keenly held the interest of the old man, but was unknown to Avery. The only other person in the room was a young lady who also looked as if she was very hard at work.

Avery decided to go over and talk to the man and see if he had any ideas on how to go about finding out what he needed to know. So he continued dumping the trash cans until he got to the man's desk. Once there, Avery interrupted him.

"Excuse me," Avery said politely, "Are you a reporter?"

The old man looked up at him and replied, "Well I sure as hell ain't the cook."

"Good one." Avery replied, acting as if that was the funniest thing he had ever heard. "Mind if I ask you a couple of questions?" He continued.

"Not really," The reporter said as he leaned back in his chair. "I'm not getting anywhere with this." He said as he indicated the paper he had been typing on. Then he continued, "So, what's on your mind Mr. Reporter Wanna be?"

"Have you been a reporter long?"

"Only all of this lifetime. Why?"

"Oh...I was just wondering."

"Look kid. I've been in this business long enough to know when someone is trying to butter me up. So why don't you just tell me what you want, so we can both put an end to this pain and suffering quicker."

"Okay. I was wondering how you would go about finding out who somebody was if all you had was the license plate number of their car."

"That's easy." The reporter replied and after looking at Avery for a moment, he asked, "Who is it and why do you want to know?"

"Well. I don't know who it is. But the reason I want to know is..." Avery's mind was a blur trying to come up with a story that the reporter would believe. As usual, Avery hadn't thought his plan through before putting it into motion. But quickly enough, he came up with a story. "I was supposed to go out with my girlfriend last night. As I was walking over to her house, she lives a block away, I saw her get into a car with some guy I've never seen before. They drove off and all I got was his tag number. I just want to know who he is. That's all."

"Did you ask her?"

"Yeah. But she told me that she had forgotten about our date and was over at a girlfriend's house."

"So she lied to you. Hell of a way to run a relationship, not to mention a railroad. Look kid, take my advice, dump her and move on. There are other fish in the ocean as they say."

"I would, but I really love her. I just want to find out who this guy is so I can get a look at him in the yearbook to see if I really have a chance."

The reporter sat there looking at Avery for what seemed to be forever before he asked, "Do you have the tag number on you?"

"Right here." Avery said as he pulled the scrap of paper he had written Ronnie's tag number on, out of his pocket.

"I don't know why I'm doing this. I guess I feel sorry for you or something. I have a friend over at the DMV who can get me the information you want. But this is going to cost you."

"What ever the cost, it'll be worth it." Avery replied with a huge grin on his face.

"Let's just say that you owe me a favor. Okay?" the reporter said as he picked up the phone.

"If a favor is all you ask, then this is a bargain." Avery remarked as he watched the reporter dial the phone.

Avery fell silent as the reporter spoke into the receiver. It was apparent the reporter had some sort of intimate relationship with a woman who worked at the DMV. After a couple of minutes of small talk and laughing, the reporter asked about Avery's information. A few seconds later he picked up a pencil and began writing Ronnie's name and address on a memo pad. When he was finished he talked for another minute before hanging up the phone.

The reporter sat for a few seconds before he spoke, "Seems like your girlfriend has a taste for older men." He said as he gave Avery the piece of paper he had been writing on.

"What do you mean?" Avery asked.

"According to this guy's date of birth, he's about twenty-five years old."

"Oh." Avery muttered as he looked at the piece of paper containing the information about Ronnie. "Thanks a lot, I owe you." One very happy Avery told the reporter.

"You bet you do kid. I'll be sure to let you know when you can repay your debt." The reporter called out as Avery walked away.

Avery wandered off as he put the slip of paper in his wallet. Now that he was sure the information was safe, he went about finishing the job of dumping the trash. He had the information he needed, but now he needed a plan of attack more than ever. The incident with not having a cover story before talking to the reporter had taught him that he needed to be careful. Spies don't usually live long if they don't take the time to cover their tracks. Avery thought to himself.

As he stood, hiding from work, behind the dumpster and sitting on the garbage can he had just dumped, Avery decided that after work he would track down the address and then stake the place out. If he was lucky, he would be able to get a lead on Gabby before the week was over. After he finished his chores for the day, He found Aaron and asked him if it was okay if he left a few minutes early. Aaron just glared at him and told Avery okay. Avery was out the door almost before Aaron's lips quit moving.

It took Avery twenty minutes to find Ronnie's street and another ten minutes to find his address. As he drove by, he saw the car that he had seen Ronnie driving was not there. He drove to the next block and turned around, coming back, he stopped the car across the street one house up. He sat there for a minute debating whether or not he should check out Ronnie's house by daylight or ride his bike back over here tonight.

Looking at his watch, he saw that it was almost time for his mother to go to work and that meant that he had to get the car home. She only let him borrow the car if he followed her rules, the main one being that he had her car back in time for her to go to work and that he fill the gas tank twice a week. Tonight and the bike would have to do. He didn't know what he would find under the cover of darkness that he couldn't see now, but he did know that secret agents were more productive in the dark.

Avery put the car into drive and went home.

18.

After leaving the newspaper, Ronnie drove straight home. When he got there, he found Margret just hanging up the phone.

"What the hell are you doing here?" She asked surprised.

"I got the day off..." Ronnie started to say but was instantly cut off by Margret.

"You did what?! You stupid asshole, we can barely afford to eat when you do work and here you are taking the day off!" Margret yelled at Ronnie.

"But Margret, I have some really good news..." Ronnie started to say but saw her swing at him. He side stepped it and she missed. Ronnie's quickness seemed to make her madder.

"I can't believe you," Margret yelled as she swung at him. "You just had two days off and here you are taking another day off! We need the money you stupid prick!"

"Margret, shut up!" Ronnie yelled back at her.

Margret was in full battle rage now. "I don't know who you think you're talking to, but you sure as hell don't talk to me like that!" To punctuate her point, she picked the broom up from the corner and swung at him. This time he wasn't so lucky and she caught him across the wrist.

"Owww Goddamn it! What the fuck is your problem?"

"You're the problem you piece of shit. Always pissing away money on junk!" She yelled as she pointed to the computer. "You don't give a fuck about my needs!"

"What?" Ronnie asked totally flabbergasted. He couldn't believe what he was hearing. This was the old Margret that he had lived with, she had only lasted a day being nice. For some sick reason, he found this more comforting than the way she had been acting yesterday.

"You heard me! What are you, deaf as well as stupid?"

"Margret, you don't understand. The reason I'm home early is because..."

But she didn't let him finish. "Don't give me some kind of bullshit about wanting to spend time with me. You just got the day off because you're lazy!"

Ronnie couldn't take anymore from her and blew up. "You should talk about lazy," He yelled at her, "I'm the one with the job bringing home the money!"

But that was as far as he got. When he mentioned money, Margret launched. She was kicking and swinging when she collided with him, she even tried to bite him as he fended her off. He didn't hit or swing back, but just covered himself to keep from really getting hurt and pushed her away. Ronnie was just about to make a break for the door when she stopped her attack and withdrew.

"What the hell is your problem?" Ronnie shouted at her.

"Fuck you, you worthless turd bag."

"Goddamn, I sure am glad I got a chance to come home early." He said. Margret made a move towards him and he backed up, maintaining a safe distance from her. If there was such a thing.

"Why don't you get your worthless ass back to work?" She said snidely.

"Because as I said before, they gave me the day off. I came straight home to give you some cheery news."

"What cheery news? Why are you here?"

"They gave me the day off to come home and celebrate my raise and promotion with you." He told her.

"They promoted you? They must really be getting desperate. How big of a raise did they give you? Knowing you, you'd get all excited if they gave you another nickel an hour."

"Over three dollars an hour." Ronnie told her.

This shut Margret up, after a few seconds passed she asked, "How much?"

"Over three bucks an hour and a promotion too!"

"To what? Head manure spreader?"

"You're looking at the new Assistant Superintendent." Ronnie said with some pride.

"Bullshit."

"Really. I had to pass an aptitude test and everything. I start my new job tomorrow."

"Do they know that they promoted a moron?" She asked sarcastically. "They'll fire you when they figure it out."

"Very funny."

"I wonder how long you'd keep your promotion if they knew who Gabby really was." She taunted.

This time he made a move towards her. It was swift. So swift that it surprised her, she hadn't expected him to move so close so quickly. As much as she noticed his speed of movement, it was the look in his eyes that caught her attention. They were narrow and full of a rage so huge that she became concerned Ronnie was going to do more than just come closer to her. When he got next to her, he would reach out and somehow crush her. But Ronnie stopped just out of reach.

Still, the look in his eyes bothered her. Margret had seen just how easily Ronnie could kill her and realized just how vulnerable she really was.

"I hope you know," Ronnie said in a too quiet of a voice. Margret could hear how he strained to control the rage in his voice. "That if you tell anyone about Gabby, there will be no money coming in. I will be fired and without a job. Not only from the Golf course, but from the paper as well."

Margret remained silent although the look on her face was deadly serious. Ronnie felt he had won this round of the battle. But he also knew that perceived wins were deadlier than actual wins. They had a way of lulling the winner into a false sense of security. That was when the defeated usually came up from behind and kicked your ass.

"Margret, I don't know what your problem is," Ronnie continued, the emotion in his voice had softened a little, "But I am damn sure getting tired of it. The boss made me take the afternoon off and you attack me for it."

As he spoke, she looked down at the floor and when he finished, she looked up at him. Her eyes were now filled with tears. Although she wasn't making any type of crying noise, tears were streaming down her cheeks. Ronnie felt his heart melt at the sight of her tears and felt mad at himself that he had made her cry.

You better watch it. Ronnie heard the Professor's voice say, *Rattle snakes usually look pretty harmless just before they bite.*

Margret noticed Ronnie looked as if he was in a trance for just a second. She didn't know it, but it coincided with the Professor's advice. Then as quick as he had zoned out, she saw his eye's focus back on her again. She was not aware she was crying, to her, Ronnie was the embodiment of all of the things that was wrong with her life. Ted on the other hand, represented all of the things that could be right. Ted was a real man, while Ronnie was a sham.

"Well Margret. What is your problem?" She heard Ronnie ask when she became aware that he was talking to her again.

"I don't know. Sometimes I get really mad and I can't control myself." She said trying to sound demure.

"No shit...You need help." Ronnie told her, "If I get you an appointment with the doctor this afternoon, will you let me take you?"

"I don't need a doctor!" She snapped back at him.

"Maybe he could give you something that will help calm you down." He offered.

"I DO NOT need a doctor!" She raised her voice to a yell as she said this.

"Well you need something. I don't know how much more of your garbage I can take."

"Isn't that a mighty nice sentiment. I have some kind of problem and you want to toss me out the door!"

"Margret, that's not what I said. It's just that you hitting and yelling all of the time is getting mighty old."

"You don't love me you bastard." She screamed at him. As she did so, she was coming towards him and he cowered. But she passed right by him, pausing at the door only to pick up her purse. Then she was gone and Ronnie went over to the door and watched as she got into the car. He stepped out through the door and onto the front porch as she started the car.

"No. Stop. Don't go." Ronnie said quietly in a droll tone.

Margret saw Ronnie standing on the front porch saying something. So, giving him the finger, she put the car into reverse and flew out of the driveway.

"Yes, I love you too dear." Ronnie said to himself as he watched her drive away. He stood there for a minute to see if she was coming back. When it became apparent that she wasn't, he went back inside.

As he walked through the door, he realized that he hadn't seen Nancy the whole time he had been home. He went straight upstairs to her room. When he got there he found that the door had been tied shut, a piece of rope was tied to the doorknob on Nancy's door to the door knob of the closet door. This made it impossible to open the door more than a quarter of an inch.

"What the hell?" He remarked to himself as he tried to loosen the knot. The door had been pulled on so many times from the inside that the knot had tightened to the point of being impossible to loosen. He ended up having to cut the rope to open the door. Once inside the room, he was greeted by a horrific sight. Nancy was sleeping on the floor a couple of feet from the door and at some point during the morning she had taken her diaper off. There was urine and crap all over the room and all over Nancy. It was apparent that she had walked in it and had used it for finger paint to decorate her walls.

It was at this point that if Margret had been around, Ronnie would have killed her. But since she wasn't there, it was of no use to dwell on that happy thought. So he gently picked Nancy up and took her into the bathroom to give her a bath. Once she was clean, he got her dressed, took her downstairs and fed her.

When she was finished eating, he put her in the playpen with a bottle and turned on the television. He found Sesame Street and pulled the playpen in front of the TV. He then got a bucket, sponge, and various other cleaning supplies. Going back up the stairs he cleaned the room up. It took him almost an hour to get the shit off of the walls and out of the cracks in the hardwood floor.

When he got back downstairs he found Nancy laughing and yelling at Bert and Ernie. He then spent the next forty-five minutes playing with her until she began to get sleepy. He put her back into the playpen and turned down the TV. Soon, Nancy was asleep. Looking around, his gaze settled on the computer.

'RONNIE TURN ME ON LET'S GO COME ON TURN ME ON TURN ME ON' Ronnie heard in his mind. So he walked over and turned the computer on to warm up while he went and got a soda. When he came back the computer was on and waiting for him. He sat down and after playing a couple of games of Solitaire and a game of Chess, decided to make a Gabby file.

Ronnie thought about what Aaron had said about just writing a couple of fluff pieces and decided this would be an excellent time to write one. After putting his byline onto the screen he just sat there. Not one idea came into his head, he was totally blank. So he played with the voice mode until he hit upon an idea. He would make a file with the Gabby columns that he had already written.

He got the file folder he kept in the desk drawer that had the previous columns he had written after they had been clipped out of the newspaper. Once he got everything arranged, he took each of the columns, said the date and then read the column out loud. It took a few tries before he got the hang of it, but was soon on a roll. The voice program worked perfectly. Soon he was creating files in the word processing program like he was an old pro at it. He found not having to type and just speak out loud made everything much easier and go much faster. After he finished each column, he saved them to disk and then printed a copy of each one. He then stapled the newsprint copy to the printed copy and put them back into the folder.

As he read the last column into the computer, he unwittingly read a mistake into the column that he didn't catch until after he had printed it out. He took the paper, wadded it up and threw it into the trash. Going back, he pulled the file back up, corrected the mistake and then reprinted it. Satisfied, he took that copy and stapled it to the newsprint like he had done with the rest.

Now that he was satisfied the back columns were complete, he sat there for a few moments contemplating his next column. He had some thoughts about a pothole column so he went ahead and wrote it. He pointed out the three worst streets that he knew of in town and speculated about where the road tax money was going. When he was finished he printed the column out and read it. It was pretty good, although it wasn't a hard-hitting Gabby column like he had written in the past. He added this column to the folder. Sitting back he had an idea and wrote about how you always saw a bunch of road department people standing around while only one or two, at most, worked.

As he read over what he had written, Ronnie realized this column was too close in subject matter to the first one. So he rewrote the first column combining the second column with it. Now he had a column that was harder hitting than either of the columns by themselves. In the column, Gabby suggested there were too many people who were getting paid big money to do nothing and that's where the tax money was disappearing to. He also pondered the question of where a person had to go to get one of these high pay, no work jobs.

When Ronnie was finished, he printed out the results and read it. This time he liked what he had better than the two separate columns. So he dated it for this Sunday and saved it to disk, he then took the other two columns and wadding them up, tossed them into the trash. He then printed out a second sheet of the combined columns and placed it in the folder also. This would be the work he would turn in on Friday.

Having completed his newspaper work almost a week early, he went around the house and gathered all of the garbage up and took it out to the can for pick up. Had Ronnie delayed for a couple of seconds before going back into the house, he would have seen Avery in his mom's car cruising into his neighborhood.

19.

After Margret left the house, she drove around for a half hour trying to think of something to do. She didn't want to be at home with the loser she was married to and she couldn't think of anywhere to go. Part of the reason she had acted towards Ronnie like she had was because he had walked in right after she had been telling Ted how much she had enjoyed the things that he had done to her and was elaborating on what was going to happen tomorrow night. Ronnie had caught her off guard and surprised her.

As she was riding around, she did decided to try and call Ted to see what he was up to, but there was no answer at his dorm room. That's when she decided that she needed some money. So she repeated her journey of the other day, cashing checks at different grocery stores she had check cashing cards for.

When she was finished doing that, she had netted about six hundred dollars. Margret wasn't happy she had only gotten that amount, thinking that she needed as much money as she could get. Then she had an idea and went to a local big chain discount store. It only took her twenty minutes once she was inside the store to do her shopping and write a check for ninety dollars for the merchandise. She then took her newly purchased stuff to the same chain store at a different location and returned it. Although they gave her the minimum of hassle, they did refund her money in cash. Before she left that store, she repeated the process and set sail for the next store of the same chain.

By the time she had finished late that evening, she returned home with almost fifteen hundred dollars. This is much easier than working, she thought to herself as she parked the car. When she went inside, she found that Ronnie had fallen asleep in the chair in front of the television. She stood looking at him, asleep and fidgeting in the chair and couldn't remember what she had seen in him in the first place. She decided that it must have been a case of lust at first sight.

Margret went straight upstairs and didn't even bother checking on Nancy before locking herself into the bedroom. As she sat in bed counting her money, she began to think about Ronnie. She couldn't remember where the marriage had begun to fail. In her mind, it had always been Ronnie's fault for everything that had gone wrong. If he hadn't hit her that first time, then she probably wouldn't have had to take matters into her own hands. Besides, he wasn't very much of a man. She thought to herself, not like Ted. As her thought's rambled on, she began to think about the way she treated Ronnie and felt a brief pang of sadness. But she justified her actions to herself by remembering the way her father had treated her mother. She also found that thinking about hitting Ronnie was turning her on, so she took matters into her own hands and began to masturbate. But this time she wasn't getting any satisfaction, so she began to think about Ted and her orgasm was almost immediate.

20.

When Avery got home, he was almost two minutes late and his mother was waiting for him at the door. She was in a high state of aggravation. He would have been home on time, in fact, with time to spare, had he not stopped and filled the gas tank. The cashier had taken a long time to check him out. Now that he was inside his house, his mother chewed him out unmercifully. Avery just stood there and took it because he knew better than to interrupt her when she was on a roll. He just waited until she ran out of steam like he knew she would. She always did. Then he explained to her about the gas station and the check out girl.

This seemed to satisfy her and she gave him a long list of things to do before she got home, then reminded him this was her night to work a double shift. That meant she wouldn't be home until dawn and Avery smiled to himself. It will be good not to have her around tonight, he thought to himself. This way he could go off and check out Ronnie's house after dark. Everyone knew secret agents were more productive after dark.

He just smiled as he waved goodbye to her as she left. Once he was satisfied that she wasn't coming back for some unknown reason, he set about completing the chores she had left for him to do. Clean the kitchen, bathroom, living room, and the laundry. He was used to doing all of the housework. While he was folding one of his mother's titanic bras he wondered if James Bond ever had to fold one of his mother's bras. Avery knew that as soon as he got his thousand dollars, along with his new job at the paper, he would move out. Out of this hell he was forced to live in rent free.

After almost three hours of hard work and pipe dreaming, he was finished. He made himself a quick dinner and then went to set out the things he would need for tonight. He waited a short time before going out to the garage and getting his bicycle. He had to ride almost five miles to get to Ronnie's house. He had selected a dark blue windbreaker to wear. That was the darkest thing that he owned. He slipped a flashlight down his sleeve, the elastic cuff kept the flashlight from falling out.

It took him quite awhile to ride over to Ronnie's house and it seemed as if the whole ride was uphill. It was well after ten when he finally arrived. He saw the car he had seen Ronnie drive off in was now parked in the driveway. He saw that the downstairs lights were on, along with one of the upstairs rooms. He parked his bike on the other side of the hedge and cautiously approached the house.

He crept up to the windows and looked in, even though the shades were drawn, he could see Ronnie sitting in front of the television. From this angle he couldn't see that Ronnie was asleep, but he could see that Ronnie was moving around. Looking around from his limited point of view, he saw the computer sitting on the desk.

Avery then moved to the next window but couldn't see anything, so he moved on. He went from window to window catching small glimpses of the interior of the house. Finally, he found himself behind the house where the kitchen was. Looking through these windows, he found there was nothing to be learned. Then he saw the garbage cans.

"Ah-ha." He said quietly to himself and then went over and opened the first one. This can seemed to be full of diapers and shit covered paper towels, he quickly closed the lid. The smell was awful. The next can was not even half full, but it contained what could be called 'waste basket' trash. He started going through it and found one of the Gabby columns. It wasn't dated and didn't have a byline, so it just looked like a short story. Reading it, he saw it was some kind of story about potholes.

He began digging through the trash again and found the story about the road department. He noticed this story was about the same length as the first one he found. So he renewed his search in earnest because he had a gut feeling that he was on the right track. Then he found the column about the lawyers.

"All Right!" He exclaimed loudly. He realized that, not only had he found the messenger, but there was a very good chance that he had just found Gabby.

A dog in the yard of the house behind him began to bark. So he quickly replaced the lid on the garbage can and headed for his bike. He got on his bike and peddled away as fast as he could. It was midnight when he got home.

After putting his bike away, he went inside just in time for the phone to start ringing. He answered it and found it was his mom checking up on him. Had he been a few more seconds getting there, he would have missed her call and that would have been very bad. Luck had been truly on his side that night. He assured her he was alright and was getting ready for bed. She told him that she loved him and would see him in the morning.

The whole time Avery had been talking to his mother, he was digging through his wallet looking for the business card that Bernie had given him just the day before. After he hung up from his mother he found the card behind his drivers license. Looking at the clock, he saw it was ten after midnight and he debated for a couple of minutes before picking the receiver back up. After all, Bernie had told him to call as soon as he knew something. So he dialed the number and listened to it ring. Just when he feared that nobody was at home (About the sixth ring.) The phone was answered.

"Hello?" A feminine, sleep laden voice asked.

"Hello, is this Mrs. Fryer?" Avery asked as pleasant as possible.

"Yes." Was the reply.

"Is Mr. Fryer there?" Avery asked, still being pleasant.

"Hold on, I'll get him."

Avery heard her talking to someone and assumed that she was waking Bernie up.

"This better be good." Bernie said as he got to the phone, sounding half asleep.

"Mr. Fryer, this is Steve."

"Who?" Bernie asked abruptly.

"Steve...Steve Avery. I have some really good news for you."

"Talk to me Steve." Bernie said, his tone had changed abruptly. Now he sounded fully awake and happy to hear from him.

"I have the information you wanted."

"Way to go Steve!" Bernie almost yelled. "What did you find out?" He asked.

"I found out who Gabby is and I have a name and address."

"Are you sure?" Bernie asked.

"Of course. I even have proof."

"Well then, tell me what you have my boy."

"I think it would be better if we met somewhere tomorrow. Then we could exchange information." Avery said cautiously. Even though he liked Bernie, he wanted to make sure he wasn't going to be cheated out of his money.

"What?" Bernie asked.

For an embarrassed moment Avery thought that Bernie had forgotten about the thousand dollars. "You know," Avery said, "I give you what you wanted for what you said you'd give me."

"Right-Right. We could do that. When and where?"

"I dunno. What do you suggest?"

"How 'bout I pick you up at noon and we go to lunch?"

"That would be nice Mr. Fryer. But I get my lunch hour at eleven-thirty tomorrow."

"You'll be at the paper?" Bernie asked.

"Yes. Is there a problem with that?" Avery asked.

"No, not at all. But I think it would be better if I didn't pick you up at the paper." Bernie said, he didn't want to take the chance of Aaron seeing him picking up one of his employees.

"What if I waited for you across the street from the First Rock Bank?" Avery asked.

Bernie thought for a second, yes that would be better. That was two blocks away from the paper. "Sounds good to me." He told Avery, "I'll see you there at a little after eleven-thirty tomorrow."

"Great! I'll see you then. I promise you won't be disappointed." Avery reassured Bernie just before he hung up the phone.

Avery was in a good mood now, by this time tomorrow night he would be rich.

At the same time, Bernie was ecstatic. This was the fastest that he had ever gotten results for such a small amount of money. "I ought to hire the terminally stupid more often." He laughed to himself as he hung the phone up.

"Who was that dear?" His wife asked him, she was still half asleep.

"A guy I have doing some research for me." He replied.

"Why did he call so late?" She asked him, still half asleep.

"It's my fault. I told him to call me as soon as he found out what I needed to know. You know, work stuff."

"That's nice." She replied as she started to drift back off to sleep.

"You bet it is." Bernie commented.

Bernie was too keyed up to sleep, so he rolled over and began to nuzzle and fondle his wife. She didn't protest and after a few minutes of coaxing from Bernie, they made love for the first time in a long time. Even after they were finished, he found it hard to fall back asleep.

Now he had Gabby's ass right where he wanted it. And like a fly on the window, he was going to squash it.

21.

When sleep finally did find Bernie, instead of dreaming of his secretary like he usually did, he dreamt that he was sitting in front of a keyboard of one of the computers at work. He was typing at a furious pace. Looking around he saw that he wasn't at his office, but somewhere that he didn't recognize. He saw that he was in an empty room. Still, he continued to type.

He looked at his hands and saw he was typing so fast that his fingers were a blur. When he slowed down, he heard a deep booming voice that seemed to overwhelm and vibrate every fiber of his being.

'KEEP TYPING, I DIDN'T TELL YOU TO SLOW DOWN YET.' The voice said.

Fear overtook him and he started typing faster. He didn't know why he was afraid or even who he was afraid of. For the first time he looked at the computer screen and saw that he was typing "GABBY'S GOOD, GABBY'S GREAT, I LOVE GABBY." This was repeated over and over again until almost the entire screen was filled and he was adding to it. As fast as he typed a line at the bottom of the screen, a line disappeared from the top. No matter how fast he typed, he could never fill the screen entirely. He had a sense of panic and he just knew that there would be hell to pay if he didn't get the entire screen filled.

Without slowing down, he looked down at the keyboard again. To his horror, he watched the keys turn from regular keys on a keyboard to miniature machetes pointing straight up with the keyboard letters printed on them. He tried to be careful, but found that he couldn't slow down. He watched as his finger tips shredded to the consistency of hamburger. The meat dripped through the keyboard as his fingers shredded back towards the palm of his hands. All too quickly and to his horror, he found that he was just typing with the bones of his fingers. He saw one of his fingernails stuck on the letter T machete key and watched as the fingernail slowly split under it's own weight. The sharpness of the machete blades was akin to that of a laser. He saw the two halves of that single nail fall, disappearing into the keyboard.

As he typed, splinters of bone began to flake off. He watched as his hands were slowly consumed until he was using the bloody stumps at the ends of his forearms to continue typing. He was trying to keep up, but when he looked at the computer screen he saw that he was falling painfully behind. He now only had a quarter of a page filled. The Gabby comments were disappearing at the top of the screen. With a sinking feeling, he realized that he had been wrong. He wasn't trying to fill the screen with writing, he had to keep the screen filled with writing. The keyboard began to grow larger and the voice started again.

'FASTER FASTER FASTER KEEP TYPING FASTER FASTER FASTER.'

Then the laughter started.

It seemed to go on and grow until he felt the bones in his body vibrate with the sound. He saw that now his forearms were half consumed by the machete keys, which had grown in size tremendously. He now had to use the stumps of his arms, which ended just below his elbows, to push a key. He found that he could barely push each key because they had grown so large. There was blood everywhere, on the keyboard, on the screen, the walls, and all over him.

The keyboard began to take on a fluid motion and the back keys were well over his head as the keyboard curled around him. He found that he was no longer able to reach the top two rows of the keyboard. There was nothing left of his arms just above where his elbows should have been. Now the keyboard was completely over the top of him, but he still tried to type because he knew that he had to keep the screen filled with the Gabby message. Although he couldn't see the computer screen anymore because the immense keyboard was blocking his view, he knew if he didn't start hurrying, his time was just about up. It's a shame that he couldn't see the monitor, because if he had, then he would have known just how futile that thought was. At that moment, the last line of print blinked off of the screen. Bernie's only indication of what had happened was when the machete keys suddenly pointed towards him. His only thought was that this was what it must be like to be in a shark's mouth. The keyboard began to close and he felt the machete keys press against his back at the same time they pressed against his stomach.

With sickening horror he realized that he was going to be bitten in half and consumed. Just as he felt the sharp pain of the blades cutting into him, he woke with a scream. Bernie sat there for a couple of minutes, disoriented, before he realized he was at home, safe in his bed. Still, he felt there was something wrong. He looked at the clock and realized that it was after nine in the morning. He jumped out of bed and rushed into the bathroom. Standing in front of the sink, he noticed that his fingers were beginning to sting and looking at his hands for the first time, saw the tips of his fingers were covered with cuts. Each were about a quarter of an inch in length and there were at least ten cuts on each finger. Bernie felt the floor sway beneath his feet.

"What the..." He cried out and had to grip the sink top to steady himself on his wobbly legs. He eased himself onto the toilet seat. As he sat there looking at his fingers, they began to bleed in the same manner that paper cuts do. You get to see the cut for a little while before the blood actually comes. Bernie pulled a bath towel off of the rack beside him and buried his hands in it. The stinging pain from the cuts was almost more than he could endure.

After sitting there for a few minutes he got up and threw the bloody towel into the bathtub, then he began to search the medicine cabinet for Band-Aids. He almost called out for his wife to come and help him, but he remembered that this was Tuesday, her day to go out in the morning for shopping and lunch with her girlfriends. He finally found a box on the top shelf, but looking inside he found that there were only four band-aids. Pulling one out, he began to unwrap it to put it on. When he raised his finger to apply the band aid, he saw that there were no cuts on it. He stood there in disbelief as he looked at his finger, then he examined the rest of his fingers and found no cuts on any of his fingers.

This perplexed Bernie for a moment because he knew that he had seen the cuts. But now, there was nothing to prove it. Then he remembered his proof. He spun around and pulled the towel out of the bath tub and upon examination, found no blood on the towel. Once again he felt the ground sway beneath his feet, so again, he had to sit down on the toilet. This time he had to put his head between his knees to keep from passing out. Although the cuts were gone, the nerves in his finger tips wouldn't let him forget the stinging pain of the cuts for almost an hour. And that was long before his finger tips were no longer tender to the touch.

When Bernie finally felt like he wasn't going to pass out, he decided to call his office. His fingers were so sore that he had to use a pencil to dial the phone. When he had pressed the first number with his finger, the pain was so intense he thought he felt all the hair on his body stand up. Looking around he saw the pencil lying there, so he picked it up and with the pencil sticking out of his closed fist, continued to dial the phone. When his secretary answered the phone at his office he explained that he was finishing some business at the house and wouldn't be in until sometime in the afternoon.

Not that it really mattered whether or not he showed up first thing in the morning since he owned the business, he just didn't want any prospective clients sitting there waiting for him to show up. After he was finished on the phone, he went to his downstairs office. After sitting in there for a little while, he opened the safe he had installed in the floor under his desk. He poked around in the safe for a minute before he extracted the thousand dollars for his meeting with Avery. After counting the money to make sure the amount was correct, he sat back in his chair with his hands cradled in his lap waiting for the pain to subside. He found that handling the money was worse than trying to dial the phone.

22.

After putting the garbage in the cans and going back into the house, Ronnie got Nancy up from her nap and spent the rest of the afternoon playing with her. Dinner time came and passed and he fed Nancy her dinner. When she was finished, he cleaned her up and went back into the kitchen to make himself some dinner. Another peanut butter and jelly sandwich. When he was finished eating he spent the next few hours playing with Nancy before getting her ready for bed at eight o'clock.

When she was sound asleep (It took three stories to get her there.) He went back downstairs and began to watch TV. It wasn't very long before he was asleep himself. Working at the Country Club required very early hours so it wasn't hard for him to fall asleep early.

Ronnie entered the dream state shortly after falling asleep and found himself standing in the high place once again. He turned around and found that he was alone. It was dark and looking down over the edge, he saw the twinkling lights of the town far below him. Ronnie judged that it was early morning because of the lack of activity on the streets far below. He stepped back and looked up at the stars. He saw the milky way in a way that he had never seen it before. Here, way up over the ground below, the sky was clear and free of the pollutants that hung in the air over the valley below like a ground fog. There were so many stars visible it was hard to distinguish between the constellations. The view amazed him, never had he seen the sky like this before. Not even from his childhood, when there wasn't as much air and light pollution.

He laid down on his back and just laid there looking up at the stars. After a few minutes a shooting star blazed overhead and although he couldn't hear any sound from it, it was low enough that he could see the flame wavering behind it as it burned up from the friction of the atmosphere.

Ronnie remembered that he had heard at one time that when you looked at the Milky Way, you weren't seeing the Galaxy. You were actually seeing the light from the stars and nebulae in part of the Sagittarius Arm of the galaxy that lies between our sun and the galactic center. As he laid there, he wondered if there was another person out there looking back at him.

That's a pretty lame question Ronnie. A voice said, jolting Ronnie back to reality. He sat up looking around and saw the Professor.

'I was wondering when you'd show up.' Ronnie said with a disgusted tone to his voice.

You don't sound glad to see me.

'I was at peace, you know, resting. You disturbed me.'

No Ronnie, I don't know about rest. It's not easy being dead you know. There are all kinds of things to do...

'Like what?' Ronnie asked interrupting him.

Little things, details. You know, like rotting, fucking with you, jamming with Elvis, looking for Little Richard, and of course, fucking with you. It's always the little things that keep you the busiest.

'Don't let me keep you. Besides, Little Richard isn't dead yet." Ronnie replied as he began looking at the stars again.

Shit, no wonder I can't find him. Seems like you are a little preoccupied here. The Professor remarked, *Maybe we should go to someplace where there are less distractions and we can talk.*

Ronnie started to tell the Professor not to bother because he wasn't going to listen to what he had to say. As he opened his mouth he saw the Professor raise his hand and snap his fingers. As the Professor did that, Ronnie's entire field of vision seemed to be filled by those fingers. He even thought that he could see minute pieces of flesh fly off of them when they were snapped. Instantly, he was no longer sitting where they had been, but was now standing in the grungy liquor store. The Professor was standing on the other side of the counter looking at his finger tips.

I hate it when they do that. The Professor remarked.

'Too bad. Did it hurt? I sure hope it did.' Ronnie replied.

Watch your mouth boy. Remember, I can really fuck you up if I want to.

Ronnie did remember, but somehow didn't think that it was going to happen. Not tonight at least. So he asked, 'Why did you bring me here?'

I just wanted to talk to you. I really enjoy these little face-to-face meetings we have.

'That really makes my day. But all bullshit aside, what do you want?'

How about a little drink Ronnie? The Professor asked as he turned around and pulled a bottle off of the shelf behind him.

'You know that I gave that stuff up. Why are you here? Why won't you give me a straight answer?'

Because I don't have to. The Professor replied as he opened the bottle and then began to drink it.

'Don't tell me this is a social call.' Ronnie replied.

The Professor continued to drink until the bottle was empty. When he was finished he set the empty bottle on the counter and pulled another bottle off of the shelf. As he was spinning the cap off from this bottle he emitted a huge belch that actually shook the building. Bottles rattled on the shelves and several fell off, shattering on the floor. Ronnie's eyes watered from the smell of the belch when the noxious gas reached him.

Damn, I miss this stuff. Is this a social call? I don't know... No it's not, I came by to let you know something. The Professor said and then began to drink the second bottle down.

Ronnie stood there patiently. When the bottle was drained he asked, 'Well, what's the big news?'

When I get around to it, I'll tell you. Besides, we have all night. Let me ask you a question Ronnie. Does your life still suck?

'As a matter of fact, no. I would say that things are really going rather well asshole.' Ronnie said smugly. Quicker than he could see, the Professor's hand shot up and gripped his throat. There was a slight pressure, but he could feel the power behind the grip. A grip that could easily crush Ronnie's throat.

Lip off one more time, little dick, and you're going to see whether or not it's possible to breath out of your asshole. Remember Ronnie, respect.

'Sorry.' Ronnie said and the hand released it's grip.

Apology not accepted, but I'll let you slide this time. Aw, look at that. He said as he pointed to the broken bottles on the floor. *That is the true meaning of alcohol abuse. Normally, I would use you to clean that up with, but I'm in a really good mood. You know why Ronnie?*

'You know I don't, but I imagine you're fixing to tell me.'

You're right. I'm happy because tonight, I get to fuck with somebody else. That's right Ronnie. There's going to be another player I get to add to my little circle of friends.

'Does that mean I'll be seeing less of you in the future?' Ronnie asked happily.

Fortunately for you, no. This friend is only going to be with us for a short period of time. Let me rephrase that. He's going to be here for a long time, but only with you for a short time.

'Is that what you wanted to tell me?'

No.

'Then when are you going to tell me?'

Okay, since you asked so nicely, I guess I could tell you. He stopped and looked at his watch. *Goodness, how time flies when you're having fun. I'll tell you two things for being so patient. First, there is a guy who is on to the fact that you're Gabby.*

'Shit!' Ronnie exclaimed.

Don't worry Ronnie, my boy. It's not as bad as you think. There's nothing that a little damage control can't handle.

'Oh man, I'm fucked.'

Like I said, don't worry about it. By this time tomorrow night, the problem will be fixed. Hey, I gotta go, I'll be seeing you.

'Wait!' Ronnie said.

What now?

'You said you were going to tell me two things. What's the other thing?'

Oh yeah, I did didn't I? Well, hold onto your seat, Margret is still fucking Ted. In fact, that's where she'll be tonight. Oh, one more thing, you'll have to work late tonight. Looking at his watch again, he said, *Gotta go, see you later.* With that, he disappeared.

When the Professor disappeared, the liquor store surroundings disappeared also, and Ronnie woke up. He laid there, kicked back in his chair for a few moments before looking at his watch. He saw that it was five in the morning and he knew he had forty-five minutes before he had to leave for work. He picked up the television remote, turned off the tv and stood up. His muscles were stiff and sore from sleeping in the chair and they screamed when he stretched, protesting their call to action after lying immobile for an extended period of time, in a less than natural position.

Ronnie's first thought was that the bitch never even bothered to wake him to come to bed when she came home. Then he heard a quiet whisper in his mind that gave him his next thought, *Maybe she didn't come home last night.* So he shuffled over to the front window and looking out, he saw the car parked in the driveway. That sight threw another log onto the fire of irritation that was beginning to burn within him.

'Oh yeah Bitch, you're going to get yours.' He thought to himself as he began walking to the kitchen. He found that even though he was sore from sleeping in the chair, he felt very refreshed. Like he had slept a long time and was thoroughly rested. He also found that he was very hungry, so digging through the refrigerator, he found eggs, bacon, and a can of biscuits. Breakfast was on. Ronnie fried three eggs and the entire package of bacon. The whole time he was cooking, the biscuits were in the oven.

As he sat at the table eating, he found that his appetite seemed to surpass his normal state of morning hungry. He was famished. He ate the entire pound of bacon after he inhaled the eggs. The biscuits went down so easy with butter and strawberry jam lathered on them that he almost didn't realize that he had plowed through them until he came to the last biscuit. This one he left due to a sudden pang of guilt from having eaten all of the breakfast food. He sat there watching the sky become lighter and thinking about Margret. The thing that was bothering him the most, was that she had just left him down there asleep in the chair after she had been out doing God knows what.

Ronnie tossed the frying pan into the sink along with his plate. The cooling grease dripped from the pan and into the sink, where it slowly gathered in a rivulet and headed for the drain. Fuck her, Ronnie thought, let her clean something for once. He turned to go take a shower and saw that last biscuit sitting there. Snickering to himself, he picked the biscuit up and took a bite out of it. To call what he did a bite, is like calling a volcano a flame. When he set the uneaten portion of the biscuit down, all that was left was the outside edge of the crust and over half of that was gone.

"Hell, there ain't even enough to slap butter on." Ronnie said to himself. Imagining Margret's reaction to the mostly eaten biscuit amused him greatly. He hoped it would get the same reaction from her that you get by flipping the bird to a policeman just as he is about to hand you a speeding ticket. Inflammatory, to say the least.

He went upstairs to use the shower and get dressed. He found the bedroom door shut and locked. Behind the door he could hear Margret snoring loudly. For a brief moment he imagined himself kicking the door open and flipping on the lights. But he decided that all the damage he wanted to do was sitting on the breakfast table downstairs. He reached into the hall closet and pulled out a small screwdriver he kept in there for opening the locks on the doors from this side. He then quietly picked the lock on the bedroom door and slipped inside.

Margret was sprawled out on the bed nude and snoring heavily indicating that she was in a deep sleep. Ronnie had a brief thought of removing his clothes, crawling into bed and taking Margret. Forcibly if he had to. But he resisted the whispers in his mind and turned to his dresser. He opened the top drawer and pulled out his work shirt. Opening a lower drawer, he got a pair of pants out. Then he went to the bathroom and took a shower.

When he was finished, he quietly went downstairs and out the front door. Getting into the car, he drove off to his job and his new responsibilities. This was a new day and he felt like a new man. All it had taken was a good nights sleep and a breakfast fit for a king. With so many things seeming to go his way today, he decided even his relationship with Margret was going to change. When he got home tonight, he was going to issue her an ultimatum. It was going to be either his way or the highway...He was through taking her bullshit.

23.

Avery had been watching the clock all morning, there was no way he was going to be late for his lunch date. There was too much on the line and he had big plans for the money. To him, a thousand dollars was a huge sum of money, almost enough to retire on and live like a king. However, the part of him grounded in reality, knew just how little a thousand dollars really was.

When eleven-thirty came, he was out the door like he had been shot out of a cannon. His only delay was when he punched his time card and that was almost on a dead run. He sprinted down the block and crossed the street without looking, taking the second block faster than he had taken the first. Ahead, he saw the back of the bank. He passed the bank and crossed the second street again without looking. He passed scant millimeters in front of a delivery truck. The driver never saw him, only noticing some movement in front of the truck on the passenger side. Avery felt the truck slap the shirt that he was wearing loose over his pocketed Tee-Shirt.

"Better look next time." Avery said to himself, "It wouldn't do to get killed just before payday."

He looked up the street just in time to see Bernie's Corvette turn the corner and come towards him. It stopped at the curb where he was standing and he got in. He did so unknowing he was being observed by Aaron McGuire who was sitting in the Fondue Restaurant where Avery was standing.

Aaron liked Fondue and often went there on Tuesdays, to sit and review the want ads before sending them to be typeset. Normally, he wouldn't have seen Avery, but Bill the waiter was standing at the table and exclaimed "Damn fool kid!". Aaron looked out the window to where Bill was looking just in time to see Avery have his narrow miss with fate. At first Aaron was afraid Avery was looking for him and just sat there looking at Avery standing on the curb. Then Aaron recognized Bernie's Corvette when it pulled up to the curb and watched as Avery got in. Then the Vet took off with it's new passenger. Aaron began to wonder what this was all about, having forgotten the want ads for the moment. What ever it was, Aaron smelled a rat.

"Mr. Fryer, how are you today?" Avery asked as he got into the car. When Bernie took off he had to hang onto the door handle to keep from being thrown around in the seat.

"Great. How about you Steve?"

Avery looked at Bernie and saw he didn't look so good. "I'm doing just fine. Are you okay? You don't look so good." He asked.

"Didn't get much sleep last night. So, do you have the information I was asking about?"

"Of course. It's right here in my pocket. May I ask where we're going for lunch? I'm starving."

"I know a little pub where you can get the best steak in town."

"Great." Avery answered enthusiastically.

In a couple of minutes, Bernie was parking in front of some place called Le Bistro that Avery wasn't familiar with. Going inside, the waitress and some guy behind the bar seemed to know Bernie. The guy asked if Bernie was here for 'The usual' and Bernie answered by saying "Of course. Set us both up."

They settled in a booth in the corner and the waitress, who had followed them to the table remarked, "I know what you want to drink Bernie, but your friend here looks a little young for Scotch. What would you like to drink Hon?"

Avery, who found it difficult to bring his eyes up higher than her ample bosom, mumbled that Iced Tea would be fine. When she was gone, Bernie leaned toward him and said in a low voice, "Nice set of hooters wouldn't you say, Stevie my boy?"

Avery, feeling like he was going to burst with a terminal hardon replied, "That is the biggest understatement I have ever heard."

"Okay Steve, here we are and lunch is on it's way. Now show me what you got." Bernie said impatient to get the proof in his hands.

Pulling a couple of sheets of folded paper out of his pocket, he began to explain to Bernie the events since the last meal they had shared. He showed Bernie the columns about the road department and the potholes and explained how and where, he had found them. Bernie was just about to tell him these didn't prove anything when Avery produced the next sheet of paper and handed it over. This was the misprinted column about the law firm. Reading it over, Bernie realized the kid was on the right track. Avery continued his commentary about his surveillance of Ronnie's house. He told about seeing the computer where he had found the columns. When Bernie heard the word computer, his ears perked up. He knew that where there was a computer, there were computer disks. He also knew anyone who wrote, usually kept their stories on those disks.

"Okay Steve, looks like you're on the right track. Do you have a name and address?"

"Yes I do."

"Well, what is it?" Bernie asked gently.

"Mr. Fryer, I'm kind of embarrassed to have to bring this up, but I've shown you proof. It's your turn to show me the pay off. Give it to me and I'll write the name and address on the back of this piece of paper." Avery said, as he gently pulled the paper that contained the column about the law firm back to him.

"Looks like you're an old hand at this." Bernie said as he produced an envelope that contained ten, one hundred dollar bills. He handed the envelope over and Avery began to write. When he was finished, he handed the paper back to Bernie.

"Yep. I'm a real product of the American educational system." Avery remarked as Bernie took the paper from him.

Lunch arrived at that point and they both began to eat. Avery thought this was the biggest steak that he had ever seen, it hung off either side of the plate. Covering the plate like it was, the baked potato that came with it had to be brought on another smaller plate.

Now they were both in exceptionally good moods, but for different reasons. Bernie was happy because he now had both Gabby and Aaron in his hands, and he was going to squeeze. Avery was happy because he was now rich.

When they were finished eating, Avery insisted he pick up the tab for the meal and left a handsome tip. He wanted the waitress to remember him and she would, because it wasn't very often that somebody left a tip that was bigger than the check had been.

Bernie took Avery back to the newspaper and let him out a block away. When Avery got out of the car, he thanked Bernie for the business and remarked if he needed anything else to call him. Bernie told him not to worry, that since Avery had done such a good job, he might have something for him to do every now and then.

Bernie believed in not burning any bridges until he was absolutely sure he was finished with them. And who knows, he just might have some extra credit work for Avery sometime in the future. The kid had been very efficient in this matter. It was good to have a disposable asset and the kid was very disposable.

After dropping Avery off, Bernie pulled the pieces of paper with the columns on them out of his pocket and unfolded them as he drove. Finding the correct one, he looked at the address and then set off to find it. Twenty minutes later, he was driving by Ronnie's house. To Bernie, the house looked as if there was nobody home. There wasn't a car out front and the shades were drawn. He had an immediate impulse to stop and go inside, but he resisted it and decided to come back tonight when the owners of the house were home. That way, he could bully this Ronald person into confessing whatever information he knew on the subject of Gabby.

Ronald will talk. Bernie thought to himself. He had all kinds of ways of making people talk and this guy was no exception. With that thought, he rounded the corner and drove off, heading to his office for the first time that day.

24.

It was both a good thing and a bad thing Bernie didn't stop. Margret was rolling around inside the house in a total state of fury. She had gotten up that morning to find the car she needed today, was gone. (Never mind she didn't tell Ronnie she needed it.) And a mess in the sink. The sink drain was clogged with the congealed bacon grease and there was no breakfast food left in the fridge. Then Margret saw the mostly eaten biscuit laying on the plate in the center of the table. The biscuit was the lighted match dropped into the gasoline can and she blew up. She screamed every obscenity and swore every curse that she could think of, down on Ronnie's head.

So the good thing for Bernie, with Margret's track record, she would have probably attacked him at the door because he was a man. Unfortunately, the bad thing Bernie didn't stop was that Margret was so mad she would have told him anything and everything he wanted to know about Ronnie's involvement with the Gabby column. So unfortunate indeed, that he didn't stop. Bernie could have had all the information he needed, from where Ronnie worked, to when and where he dropped the finished column off.

After she calmed down a bit, Margret decided she would get even with the rat bastard (Ronnie) if it meant she had to draw her last breath to do it. At first, she didn't know how to go about it, so she set about the afternoon pondering how she would exact her revenge. Then it occurred to her she would be meeting her answer tonight. She would set her plan into motion by filling Ted with so many lies about Ronnie that Ted would have no recourse but to put a major load of whoop-ass on Ronnie. Yes, Margret thought to herself, that is exactly what she would do. This thought put the first smile on her face for the day. She went over and picking up the phone, called Ted to confirm their meeting tonight.

As she talked to Ted on the phone, she made sure she sounded very upset. She also avoided the question every time she was asked, if there was anything wrong. As cold and calculating as a general going off to battle, she began to set her trap. She didn't know for sure if she would be able to get Ted to play along and do what she wanted, but she felt confident she could. After all, pussy is a mighty powerful bargaining tool. After she hung up the phone, Margret made herself lunch before going to get Nancy up from her nap. Going back downstairs Margret fed her a very late lunch. A glance at the clock told her that it was only a few more hours before Ronnie was due to get off from work. She put Nancy into her playpen before settling down to watch her afternoon stories.

Margret sat there watching a world of beautiful people in intriguing circumstances. In a weird way, Margret felt the soap operas she was watching was more realistic than the life she was living. She looked over at Nancy, who was playing with a set of stackable rings and felt a sudden rush of resentment. It was Ronnie's fault that she had gotten pregnant and was now trapped here, in this life. Margret also felt if she had somewhere to go, she would just leave. Walk away and never look back. But now that could wait, she wouldn't do anything until after Ted smoked Ronnie's ass. Then she would just walk away without any regret or remorse. It was a fantasy that she would lose herself in, along with the fantasy of the soaps, for the next couple of hours.

25.

Ronnie's day had been great. He was still learning the ropes of being a supervisor to a bunch of people. The task that troubled him the most was remembering to call Mr. Fritz by his first name Floyd. He figured it was due to the fact he had been raised to show respect for the people that he was subordinate to. Ronnie kept catching himself and apologizing as he corrected himself. Floyd just laughed and told him he would get the hang of it.

Ronnie's hardest minute had come first thing in the morning. When every one had arrived, Floyd announced there was going to be a meeting and for everyone to hang around before going off to their prospective tasks. Floyd motioned to Ronnie to follow him. When they were alone in the office, Floyd told Ronnie the subject of the meeting was to announce Ronnie's promotion. Ronnie instantly began to worry how his colleagues would take the news. He knew that sometimes when people got promoted, friends would turn against each other. Ronnie didn't want that to happen because he felt everyone who worked there acted like pals. They didn't hang around each other, but they had always been a tight working crew.

Ronnie also knew the majority of the guys who used to talk about him, about how Margret was kicking his ass at home and that he wasn't man enough to stand up to her, were gone. So the legend about how he was such a wimp at home had died a natural death with their leaving. That was one dragon Ronnie was glad he didn't have to fight.

After their brief discussion, Floyd and Ronnie rejoined the group of men that had assembled in the break room. If you could call it a break room, it was just one end of the shack that served as a storage area. There were a couple of worn out couches that had come from the main building of the club. They had been thrown away and some of the guys had brought them here. There was also a small table directly under the air conditioner where many lunches had been eaten and shared. The men crowded into this small area and Floyd's speech was short and sweet.

"Gentlemen," Floyd said and the room quickly quieted, "Yesterday morning, I promoted Ronnie Fisher to Assistant Superintendent. That means that he's now all of you gentlemen's immediate supervisor. He is my direct assistant and if he tells you to do something, it is the same as if I told you to do something. If there is a problem with something, tell him. If you need something, tell him. But give him a few days to get used to his new position. Also, if any of you have a problem with this promotion, I will be more than happy to write you a nice letter of recommendation for your next job. Do I make myself clear?"

When Floyd asked that, he looked around at everyone's faces. There were only smiles and nods of approval returned to him. Floyd knew if anyone from outside the shop had heard the speech, he would have sounded like a real hard-ass. But his men knew two things, first, he was one of the best bosses to work for, and second, he meant the last part about finding a new job.

He stood there for a couple of moments looking at everyone, before adding one last comment, "Now that we're done Bullshitting, get your asses back to work."

A snicker ran through the group and everyone began filing out. The majority of them didn't leave before they had a chance to congratulate Ronnie on his new position. There was a lot of back slapping and "Way to go" along with "Couldn't be happier that it's you" as they left. Ronnie felt a great sense of relief nobody seemed to be against his promotion and everyone seemed happy that he had gotten it. That set the mood for the day.

About mid afternoon, Floyd sent Ronnie out to check the cut job being done on the greens. Ronnie spent the next hour riding around looking at the grass before Floyd called him back on the radio Ronnie now had to carry. Ronnie returned to the shack to meet with Floyd.

"Ronnie," Floyd said as Ronnie walked in, "How's things looking out there?"

"Everything is looking great. What's up?"

"Seems like we're having a problem with the irrigation pump at the pond on the back side of fifteen."

"Sounds like a problem, isn't tonight the night the sprinklers are supposed to run?" Ronnie asked.

"Yeah, but I called the irrigation company and they are sending a guy to work on it. The good news is they seem to think that it's a relatively small problem. Bad news is, he's about a hundred miles away from here on another job. So it's gonna take him awhile to get here."

Ronnie just stood there looking at Floyd for a second before asking, "So what's the bottom line Floyd?"

"You're going to be late for dinner."

Ronnie felt a shiver run up his spine. At the exact moment Floyd told him he was going to be late, he remembered the Professor telling him that he was going to have to work late. It seemed as if he could feel the hair on the back of his neck standing up.

"Ronnie, are you okay?" He heard Floyd ask. The question seemed to zap him back to reality.

"What?" Ronnie asked.

"I asked if you are feeling alright. You looked kinda funny for a moment." Floyd said concerned.

"I'm perfectly fine." Ronnie replied, then thought he should add some sort of explanation. "I just felt a little dizzy for a second. It's nothing, I just skipped lunch today and I guess it's starting to wear on me. How late do you think it'll be before the guy gets here?"

"At least a couple of hours. Why don't you go up to the kitchen and tell Francie to feed you because you have to work late tonight. If she gives you any crap, tell her to call me. Okay?"

"Sounds good, but I'm gonna call home first and let the wife know that I'm going to be late."

"Sure, take however long you want, it's going to be a couple of hours before he gets here. Go eat and relax, call your wife. This is just part of the job. A crappy part, I know, but a part all the same."

"No problem Floyd, I'm not complaining. This is just part of making the big bucks, right?"

"Unfortunately yes. It is part of being the boss. Now get out of here." Floyd told him.

Floyd watched as Ronnie walked out the door and he was now convinced that he had made the right choice when he had promoted Ronnie. He had worked with a lot of different people in his time and had found that when you laid last minute overtime on people, it usually divided them into three groups. The first group will bitch and moan loudly about either plans or inconvenience. The second group will do the job, but cop an attitude about it. The third group will smile at you and go do their job. No bitchen, no attitudes, no B.S.. Just do the job and be happy about it because they realize it's just part of working. Floyd knew it was from this third group that you got your best workers and even better 'Management' type individuals. Besides, he was really starting to like Ronnie.

On his way out of the shack, heading for the kitchen, Ronnie stopped and used the phone. As he stood there with the receiver in his hand, he was torn between calling Margret to let her know he would be late or not calling her at all, just letting her guess when he would be there. But he decided to take the upper hand and show some responsibility, so he dialed his number and the phone was answered on the fourth ring.

"Hello?" Margret's voice asked on the other end.

"Margret, this is Ron...." He started to say but was cut short.

"I know who it is. What the fuck do you want?" She replied hatefully.

"I'm just calling to let you know I have to work late tonight."

"You what?" She yelled at him.

"I have to work late."

"Bullshit! You get your ass home when you're supposed to or else!"

"I have no choice, this is part of my job. One of the pumps is broken and I have to wait for the repairman to arrive." Ronnie explained.

"What part of, I don't care what your problems are, get your ass home on time or else, don't you understand?"

"Look Margret, this isn't up for discussion. I'm going to be late tonight because I have to work late. If there's a problem with that, then we'll discuss it when I get home." Ronnie said flat out.

"You don't talk to me like that you little piece of shit! Get your ass home on time or else!" Margret screamed at him.

There was so much hate in her voice Ronnie could swear he could feel it radiating from her. "Look Margret, I'm not happy I have to work late, but..." It was at that point that she slammed the phone down, hanging up on him.

Ronnie just stood there looking at the dead receiver in his hand for a moment before hanging up. He could feel the outrage rising within him. He had the only job in the family and after her fit yesterday about him coming home early, he couldn't understand why she was getting so mad about him getting the extra overtime. Suddenly, Ronnie felt a great sense of calm come over him and he knew what he had to do. He would confront her tonight when he got home. He felt by tomorrow morning, there would be a solution to his troubles. He didn't know what that solution would be, but there would be one.

After the phone call, he turned and walked out of the shack towards the kitchen of the club to get some food. His mind was a whirlwind with the argument he was going to have with Margret when he got home. The quarter of a mile he walked to the kitchen seemed like the longest quarter of a mile that he had ever walked.

26.

When Margret slammed the phone down, she stood there for a couple of minutes in a fit of rage. How could that little bastard do this to her? She was supposed to meet Ted tonight and she wasn't about to let that little prick Ronnie stop her. He would pay for this. Why, by the time she got through priming Ted with bogus information, Ronnie would be lucky if Ted didn't kill him. Deep in her heart, she hoped that Ted did kill him. Then she could make a fresh start. Just to be able to walk out of this life and into a brand new one would be perfect. A new life, with a real man who has a good career and lots of money she could throw around on anything she wanted. At no point during her fantasy did she think of Nancy. In fact, Margret's new start didn't include Nancy.

Margret looked over at the playpen and saw Nancy, "Shit" escaped her lips. Somehow she was going to have to get rid of the kid tonight. Pondering this new problem for a moment, she picked up the phone and dialed Heather's house. Heather's mother answered the phone and Margret tried to make small talk for a couple of minutes. But when Margret saw she wasn't getting anywhere with the older woman, she got around to the reason of the call. She inquired about Heather being busy tonight, explaining she had to go out and help a friend of hers, but Ronnie had just called and told her that he had to work late. Heather's mom told Margret she would have to ask Heather herself and went to go get her daughter.

'Yeah, go get your daughter you old bitch.' Margret thought to herself as she heard the receiver on the other end being laid down. The 'sweet as honey' routine for the neighbor was getting on her nerves. She rationalized if this is what it took to get what she wanted, then she would play the game and be so nice and sweet, the recipients of her attention would go into sugar shock.

When Heather got on the phone, Margret told her story again about helping a friend and Ronnie working late. She continued to explain to Heather she knew this was short notice, but she would really appreciate the help. Heather explained to Margret there wouldn't be a problem and she would be glad to do it, but she was in the middle of writing a report for school. Margret had a burst of anxiety thinking that Heather couldn't babysit. She was greatly relieved when Heather asked if it was possible for Margret to drop Nancy off at her house. Then she could watch her there and get her school work done at the same time. Margret told Heather that would be perfect. So the deal was done and Margret hung up the phone.

A couple of minutes later she called Ted and told him her plans were changed a little. Sounding all breathless and upset, she told him she would have to meet him somewhere. Ronnie had just left in a drunken rage with the car and she didn't want to be here when he got back, lest she suffer the consequences of his condition.

Ted was all concerned and told her he would meet her wherever she wanted. Hell, he would even come and pick her up at home if she needed it. Margret quickly told him no, explaining she was afraid that Ronnie might come home and catch them leaving. "That would be dangerous for the both of us." She told him.

They agreed to meet in forty-five minutes at a convenience store about three blocks from Margret's house. She told Ted it would be much safer that way. Ted assured her that she had nothing to worry about as long as he was there. She told him that was fine, she did feel safe when he was around, but there was no telling what kind of evil Ronnie was capable of when he was drunk.

After Margret got off of the phone, she got Nancy ready to go to Heather's house. Looking at the clock she saw she was already beginning to run behind, so she stuffed some diapers, a few toys, jarred food, and a can of formula with a couple of bottles into a diaper bag and took Nancy next door. Margret went back to her house and quickly got ready, then she took off down the street and headed for the convenience store.

27.

Bernie had a very good afternoon. After planning his little line of bull he was going to tell Ronnie, he took care of some of his case work. He was in such a cheerful mood, even the secretaries remarked (Not to him of course) that he should come in late more often. They rarely got to see this side of him. Only when he had won a big settlement for one of his clients or had won a seemingly unwinnable case, was he this cheerful at the office.

Bernie planned on casing Ronnie's house until someone arrived, so he called his wife around two-thirty and told her he had to work late and not to wait dinner on him. He was just so backlogged with work that he had to catch up on. He went on to explain to her the main fly in the ointment was one of his trust accounts was having problems and was going to require an after hours meeting with the clients.

Bernie's wife never asked any questions about the office unless he was in one of those rare moods when he volunteered information. Mainly, she was out of the loop and only saw his employees at the meager Christmas party he threw once a year. At those parties, she only stood in the corner or beside him and listened to 'shop talk' that was well above her head. To her, even these few occasions were as boring as the law books Bernie brought home sometimes, for some after work reading and trial preparation.

With all of his bases covered, Bernie waited until after six in the evening to leave the office. He drove straight to Ronnie's house and saw the house was dark except for one light downstairs. It was dim and looked like it was deep inside the house. There still wasn't a car parked out front. Bernie went to the end of the block and turned around, parking down the street where he had a good view of the house. That way, he could get a good look at whoever came home. Sitting there with the night getting increasingly darker, he began to wonder if anyone was ever going to come home. Another half hour passed and his thoughts began to turn to Avery ripping him off.

He decided that if this did turn out to be a dead end, he would get his thousand back out of Avery even if it meant killing him and selling his organs. Bernie could stand losing the grand, but he couldn't stand being taken for a ride.

Bernie sat and amused himself for awhile deciding what he was going to do to Avery until he saw it was eight o'clock. Sitting there debating what to do, he decided to get out of the car and do a little recon of his own on Ronnie's house.

He walked up the street and entered the yard at the corner. Staying by the fence, he walked around the house, behind it, and came out on the other side. He found there were no windows on the far side of the house, so he made his way around behind the house back to the other side he had just passed. He saw the windows on this side had nice, high bushes next to them. He worked his way between the bushes and the house. At the first window towards the rear, he raised up and tried to look through it. The shade was drawn and he could only see through a quarter of an inch gap between the shade and the edge of the window. He couldn't see much, so he worked his way to the next window. This one was a little better, there was a half inch gap to peer through. Looking inside he confirmed his suspicion there was nobody home and as he craned his neck to get a better view, he saw the computer sitting across from him on a desk.

He made his way to the next window but found that he couldn't see anything at all through it. So he squatted down and ran through his options. Looking at his watch he saw that fifteen minutes had passed since he had left his car. This is taking too long, he thought to himself and decided that he would try to gain entry to the house. That way, he could get a look at what was on the computer. If he was lucky it would be something that was compatible with the computers at work. Then all he would have to do then is rip off the computer disks, go back to work and see what was on them. Bernie knew that he wasn't a wizard when it came to computers, but he wasn't a novice either. He could work just about any system on the market.

He went around to the back of the house and forced the back door. It wasn't very hard, only the bottom knob lock was on and no deadbolt. He leaned against the door, putting his weight against it and he could feel the door shift against the bolt. The door felt flimsy, so he stepped back, raised his foot, and kicked straight out. He caught the door right next to the knob and he heard the wood splinter as the door swung open.

"Should have been a locksmith." Bernie chuckled to himself, as he walked through the open door and closed it behind him. He took care to use the back of his hand as not to leave fingerprints. Now he was inside and stood there listening for signs of life inside the house. He was standing inside the kitchen and nearly jumped out of his shoes when the refrigerator kicked on right next to him. It was one of those older models that made a lot of noise when the compressor kicked on. Slowly, he walked through the kitchen and paused at the door going into the dining area that opened into the living room. Again he paused to listen for sounds of occupancy. He heard nothing.

Cautiously, he walked through the living room to the front door and peeked out through one of the little panes of glass in the door. Seeing nothing, he put the deadbolt on. Bernie figured that it would give him a couple of extra seconds to get out through the backdoor if someone came home while he was inside. He walked back to where the computer was sitting, pulled out the chair and sat down.

Looking at the computer Bernie realized that he had never seen one like this before. It looked like someone had assembled it out of spare parts. The Frankenstein of computers, he thought to himself with a smile. As he scanned the contents of the desk, he only found one disk that had no markings on it to indicate what was on it. He decided to turn the computer on and see if there were any internal files. He fumbled around behind the computer until he found what he thought was a power switch. Flipping it, he listened as the machine slowly came to life. Just when he thought the computer wasn't going to come on at all, the screen lit up.

"About fucking time." He said to himself. Then the computer spoke.

'GOOD EVENING BERNIE.' The computer both spoke and printed on the screen.

"What the hell?" Bernie remarked. He had an immediate sense of alarm that the computer spoke to him and knew his name. His immediate thought was he was being set up. So he quickly glanced around to ensure that he was still alone.

'I AM SO GLAD YOU COULD JOIN ME THIS EVENING.' The computer continued.

Bernie felt the chill of a cold sweat as it broke out on his body. A cold sweat caused by the fear he had been caught somehow. He closed his eyes as he muttered, "This can't be happening."

'BERNIE, THIS IS HAPPENING.'

"How...How can this be real? How can you understand me?" His throat was dry and he had a feeling of impending doom.

'I UNDERSTAND A LOT OF THINGS. WHAT WOULD YOU LIKE TO KNOW?'

Goddamn talking computer, Bernie thought to himself, his fear somewhat abated. After a moment of sitting there feeling paranoid and a quick glance around the room to ensure he was alone, he asked, "I can ask anything?"

'AS LONG AS I KNOW THE ANSWER, YES, YOU MAY ASK ANYTHING.'

"Shit. This is too easy. Okay computer, who is Gabby Gasbag?"

'IS THAT WHAT YOU REALLY WANT TO KNOW?'

"Yes. That is what I really want to know."

'ARE YOU SURE?'

He couldn't believe it, the damn computer was trying to mess with him. "I said yes you mechanical piece of shit."

'SAY PLEASE.'

"Okay," he replied beginning to get mad, "Please tell me who Gabby Gasbag is." Bernie wanted to add more about how the computer was a reject from the junkyard, but he resisted the temptation.

'THAT'S BETTER. RONALD FISHER IS THE COLUMNIST KNOWN AS GABBY GASBAG.'

Bernie couldn't believe it. This mechanical piece of shit had just told him what he needed to know. "Really?" He exclaimed.

'YES. IS THERE ANYTHING ELSE THAT YOU WOULD LIKE TO KNOW?'

"Like what?" He couldn't think of anything else to ask, he had just gotten what he wanted.

'ALL OF HIS INFORMATION COMES FROM THE COUNTRY CLUB HE WORKS AT.'

This was too good to be true, the machine was spilling it's guts to him. "Is there anything else you want to tell me?" He asked.

'YES, ONE MORE THING.'

"What's that?"

'IT IS A GOOD THING THAT YOUR NAME IS FRYER.'

"Why is that?" Bernie asked, intrigued. This computer was truly a marvel. He had never seen a machine like this before, it was almost as if it had its own personality.

'BECAUSE YOU DON'T LOOK LIKE A ROASTER.' The computer answered.

Before Bernie could reply, he watched in horror as a blue spark leapt from the keyboard to his hands that were laying on the desk. For Bernie, it seemed like time slowed down to a crawl, everything was happening in extremely slow motion.

When the electricity hit him, all of his muscles went into a spasm and he instantly became rigid. The force of his legs straightening out, propelled him backwards in the chair. The casters on the chair rolling easily on the hardwood floor. The last two things he saw were the keys on the keyboard looked like miniature machetes with letters on them. The second thing was the lightening bolt of electricity as it came from the monitor screen and hit him dead center of his forehead.

That was when everything went white and Bernie Fryer existed no more. As he left this reality, he felt as though he was being pulled out of his body through the spot the electrical finger touched on his forehead and he could swear he could hear laughter in the electrical crackle.

The electricity continued to flow through him as he continued to slowly roll backwards in the chair. Still, the arc was continuous and the smell of ozone filled the air along with the smell of burning flesh. Smoke began to fill the room from the cooking action caused by the high current flow heating up Bernie's head.

Thick smoke. When Bernie was in the center of the room, the arc of electricity coming from the computer jumped from him to the wall outlet behind him. His body continued to roll backwards toward the outlet as if the force of the magnetic field the spark was creating was drawing him toward it.

When the chair got to the wall on the opposite side of the room, the tendrils of electricity seemed to take more control as they swivelled the chair around. The main arc was now coming from the top of Bernie's head to the outlet. With a crackle, two offshoots of that main arc ran down opposite sides of Bernie's face and then jumped to his hands. His arms slowly raised as if obeying the electric command. His head began to lower as the main arc pulled it down. A clear liquid similar to raw egg whites dripped from his face as the fluid in his eyes, now split open from the heat, ran from between his clenched eyelids.

His body fell out of the chair propelling it back towards the desk. Bernie's lifeless body came to rest against the outlet on the wall. That was when the arc stopped. The outlet glowed for a couple of seconds and the melted plastic of the cover began to cool. Some of what was left of Bernie's hair imbedded in the butter soft plastic of the outlet cover. Much later, after the plastic had cooled, it would require a pair of scissors to separate Bernie from the outlet.

The air was thick with smoke and the putrid smell of fried Bernie.

The computer printed 'HAVE A REAL HAPPY DAY ASSHOLE.' on the screen before turning itself off.

28.

If there was anything to be said about Ted, it was that he was punctual. He was at the convenience store exactly forty-five minutes to the second after he got off the phone to Margret. He saw her walking up the street and when she saw him, he saw her face light up. She ran the rest of the way to the store and when she got there, they embraced. Acting like young lovers who haven't seen each other in a long time. Getting into his car, they left the parking lot and Margret suggested they go get some dinner. Being early, they would miss the dinner crowd by a long time and have the rest of the afternoon to themselves.

Now that they were together, Margret put her plans to use Ted against Ronnie on the back burner. There would be enough time later to ease into the topic of Ronnie. This is like fishing. To get the big fish you can't just yank on the pole and start reeling the line in when you feel the nibble, you have to do it slowly, without the fish realizing it's being caught. Margret thought this to herself as they drove away from the convenience store.

Ted asked her if she like Italian food and she told him she didn't care what they ate, as long as they were together. That decided, he took her to a little hole in the wall, just outside the base called 'Ace Hole's'. Although the place was nothing to look at from the outside, it had the best Italian food in town. It was one of those best kept secrets that somebody tells you about, but you never see advertised.

Ted had an Aloha Pizza (Made of pineapple and ham), while Margret dined on Veal Parmesan with Fettuccine Alfredo. She made a couple of comments about his pizza, she had never heard of what he was eating, so he gave her a sample and she found it delightful. The Veal was like none she had ever tasted before. When the bill came, she insisted on paying it. Ted, being a modern man, let her. He was very surprised when she pulled out the wad of bills she was carrying.

Seeing Ted look at her money, Margret quickly explained she was saving up for a divorce and the deposits for an apartment. Ted told her to put her money away because he would pick up the check. Margret made a big fuss about it, saying leaving that bastard Ronnie was probably a pipe dream and her money might as well go to good use.

"Is he really that bad to you?" Ted asked.

"Sometimes. Mainly, when he's drunk is when he tries to hurt me." Margret replied blinking back the fake tears.

"Why do you stay with him? Just walk away."

"Because..." She started to say, but then started crying harder. After a couple of moments, she regained her composure and continued, "Because I'm afraid of what he'd do to me. He told me that if I ever left him, he would kill me."

"If he ever lays a hand on you I'll..." Ted started to say, bristling with all of those macho hormones running through his veins. But Margret cut him short.

"Please Ted, let's not talk about unpleasant things. When I'm with you I feel like I have a future. When you're not around, it's like I'm in darkness. Especially when Ronnie comes home drunk and starts hitting me because I haven't ironed one of his shirts or gotten dinner on the table fast enough." She told him, pausing every now and then to sniffle for effect.

"Whatever you want." Ted replied as he put his hand on top of hers and then continued. "Well, what would you like to do now?"

"Why don't we go back to your room and see what kind of trouble we can get into." Margret said with a sly smile.

"I know what kind of trouble I'd like to get into, if you know what I mean?" Ted said as he raised his eyebrows and wiggled them.

"Just call me trouble." Margret said with a dead serious look on her face. Without intent, she never spoke a truer sentence.

They both sat looking at each other before Margret broke into a wide grin. They got up and left, heading for his dorm room, where they would stay until the very early hours of the morning. Ted enjoyed her passion, Margret enjoyed his stamina.

Although Margret didn't say anything to Ted, she found out something about herself that night that deeply troubled her. The other night when she had masturbated at home, it had taken the thought of Ted to bring her to orgasm. But tonight with Ted, the only way she could find release was to think about hitting Ronnie. So when Ted thought he was doing his finest work, little did he know it wasn't him that was tripping Margret's trigger, but her fantasizing about hitting and punching Ronnie.

It was two-thirty in the morning when she asked Ted to take her home. He argued she needed to stay with him and not go back to that hell she was living in. For a moment, it seemed she was considering his request, but she told him no and explained she needed to get home while Ronnie was passed out. That way, she could be there in the morning when he woke up and he would never know how late she had been out.

"I say the hell with him." Ted said as he watched Margret get up and begin dressing.

"No. I have to be there. It will be just awhile longer and then I'll have the money I need to get away." She told him as she unsuccessfully tried to put her pantyhose back on. She finally gave up and balling them up, stuffed them into her purse.

"Margret," Ted said as he got up and took her into his arms, "Margret, don't be silly. I have all of the money we'll ever need. Don't worry about it, we can get an apartment and you'll never have to worry about another thing."

"Ted...You don't know how tempting that is. But I'm afraid Ronnie will always be a problem. There has to be a way to get rid of him. That way, we can be together forever with no loose ends dragging behind."

"What do you mean?" Ted asked as he pulled away a little.

Shit, I've scared him off. Margret thought to herself. Covering herself because she didn't want Ted to pull so far away she couldn't reel him back in, she said, "I don't know. I'm just afraid that if I run away, he will hunt me down and kill me."

"Why would you think that?"

"Because he's told me a couple of hundred times when he's hitting me that if I ever left, he'd hunt me down and kill me."

"But Margret, you have nothing to worry about. You'll be safe with me and I'll make damn sure that bastard never lays another hand on you."

"I'll tell you what. Let me think about it. But I must go home now so he won't think something is up. I need time to get some of my things out of the house, which is going to take a few days. Please Ted, take me home."

"If you must go, then I'll take you. But I look forward to the day when we can be home together." He tightened his embrace and one of his hands found its way down to her butt.

"Lover, there will be enough time for that later when this whole Ronnie business is behind us. But I really need to go home now." Margret pulled away from him and finished dressing.

Ted, seeing she was serious about going home, grabbed a pair of shorts and put them on. Then he selected a shirt and put it on. They went to his car and left, heading to where she lived. As they neared Margret's neighborhood, she suggested to Ted he drop her off at the end of the ally that ran behind her house. That way, she explained, she could sneak into the house through the kitchen and better her chances of not being caught.

Ted did as she asked and sat at the end of the ally as he watched her walk down it and then turn. She stopped briefly and waved goodbye to him. He could just barely see her but he did see the wave. Not knowing whether she could see him or not, he waved back. He drove off right after Margret disappeared from view. Margret, thinking she had gotten away with another night of good loving, walked through the back yard and around the side of the house heading for the front.

29.

Ronnie got home about nine-thirty. It had been a very long day. He would have been home earlier, but had stayed to make sure the pond they had begun pumping water out of to run the sprinklers, was refilling after the main pump came back on line. After he was assured that everything was going well, he went and called Floyd at home to let him know they were back up and pumping water again.

Floyd was happy that Ronnie had called with the information and told him to come in around noon tomorrow to make up for having to work so late. This made Ronnie happy because now he could sleep in late. After getting off the phone, he locked the shack up and headed for his car. Which, by now, was the only one left in the parking lot.

After he got into the car and started it, Ronnie realized just how tired he was. But this was a happy kind of tired. He knew he had accomplished something, something important. Something that just a short while back, he would have had no concept he would be in charge of. Something of great importance. So he pointed the car for home and blasted off.

When Ronnie got home, he had a feeling Margret wasn't there even before he got out of the car. He could see by the dimness of the house Margret had left the shell lamp on. It was a lamp made out of sea shells, painted a horrible flourescent green and white and served as a night light downstairs. It sat on top of the television and Ronnie hated it. To him, it was the most gaudy thing that he had ever laid eyes on. But when Margret had seen it, she fell in love with it immediately and couldn't live without it. So, not wanting to make her mad, he put up with it and no longer gave it any thought.

As he walked to the front door, he wondered if Margret had taken Nancy with her, but he really didn't think so. More likely, Nancy was next door with Heather. Ronnie really had to go to the bathroom so he decided to go inside before going next door. When he opened the door, he immediately saw how smoky the house was. The smell was the next thing to assault his senses and he immediately thought Margret had left something in the oven and it was burning.

Taking a deep breath, Ronnie ran through the house in the direction of the kitchen. The smoke grew thicker as he got deeper into the house. Intent on getting to the kitchen, he didn't see Bernie laying on the floor in the shadows. Even when he tripped over one of Bernie's legs, he still didn't notice Bernie there. As he got up, he just assumed it was some crap that Margret had left laying on the floor. Besides, his focus was on getting to the kitchen to see what was on fire.

As he entered the kitchen, Ronnie flipped on the light switch expecting to find the room full of smoke. What he saw stopped him dead in his tracks. The kitchen was mostly clear of smoke. He went to the stove and found that it wasn't on. Ronnie didn't notice the backdoor frame was split. He then turned around and went back into the dining room, turning on lights as he went along to get a better look and see what was smoking. As he passed the table and it no longer blocked his field of view, he saw Bernie laying on the floor for the first time.

Ronnie froze with fright, not knowing what to do. He didn't know Bernie, so he didn't recognize him. But he did realize what it had been he tripped over. Ronnie noticed the man on the floor wasn't moving and thought that maybe when he had tripped over him, he had somehow knocked the man unconscious. Backing up slowly, he reached around the corner without looking and got the broom from where it was kept just inside the kitchen door.

Once Ronnie had the broom in his hand he felt braver. He walked up to the stranger laying on the floor. "You better not move. I have a weapon." He said confidently. The sound of his voice surprised even him. But there was no indication that he had been heard.

"Hey you, asshole. I don't know what you think you're doing in my house, but if you move you're going to wish you were dead by the time I'm through with you." Ronnie said not knowing how ironic the statement was. Ronnie stood there for a moment before noticing just how still the man was. He tentatively poked him with the broom handle trying to get a response out of him. Nothing. Cautiously, Ronnie got closer and poked him harder. Still nothing and now that Ronnie was closer he noticed it looked like the man wasn't breathing.

Suddenly, Ronnie got scared again. What if this guy had done something to Nancy and Margret? He skirted around the guy and ran upstairs. Checking the bedrooms and the bathroom, Ronnie found that he was alone. So he went back downstairs. When he got to the bottom step, he cautiously peeked around the corner, expecting to see that the stranger had been playing possum and would be gone.

Bernie was still laying there in the process of assuming room temperature. Ronnie walked over to Bernie's body and shook Bernie's shoulder, trying to roust him. When Ronnie shook Bernie, Bernie's head rolled to one side, his hair stuck in the plastic outlet cover served as a pivot point. For the first time, Ronnie saw just how black Bernie's face was. The outer layer of the skin had first blistered and then burned black from the electricity. Ronnie reached for Bernie's wrist to feel for a pulse. The first thing he noticed was what appeared to be steam rising up from Bernie's head, but Ronnie found that Bernie's arm was very cool to the touch.

Ronnie stood back up and quickly walked over to the telephone and called the police. He explained to the Desk Sergeant on the other end that he had just come home and found a dead guy in his house. Ronnie gave the address and after answering a bunch of questions, hung up the phone and started waiting for the police to arrive.

As he was waiting, Ronnie went next door to inquire about Nancy and found she was there asleep. Heather's mom told him Margret had left her there late in the afternoon. He explained to her he had come home and found some guy dead in his house. Heather's mom was horrified and told Ronnie to call the police, to which Ronnie replied that he had and was now waiting for them to show up. He asked if it was okay if Nancy spent the night because he didn't want to wake her up and take her back over to his house where the dead guy was. Heather's mom told him not to worry about it and wouldn't hear of Ronnie taking her back home with him.

By now, David, Heather's dad, had joined his wife at the front door to see what the commotion was all about. Once he heard what had happened, he went and put his shoes on to go back over with Ronnie and help him. Ronnie was glad for the company because he didn't want to be in the house alone with the corpse.

Less than six minutes had passed when the first squad car of the night showed up. It contained Sergeant Maxwell. Max had been the closest one to Ronnie's address when the call came over the radio. Max had been running an errand and was in the neighborhood. Although the address was familiar, he didn't recognize it until he saw the house. Immediately Max became afraid the dead body he was here to verify was going to be Ronnie's.

Max felt a great sense of relief when Ronnie came walking out of the house heading for the cruiser. The sense of relief instantly turned to dread. He thought the body was that little loud-mouthed bitch the kid was married to. Max had seen it a couple of times before, the person being abused would put up with it until one day they just snapped. It didn't happen very often, but it did happen. In the rage, they would payback all of the abuse they had endured.

Max remembered back to a case he had seen once when he was a very young Officer. This lady had been married to a guy for eighteen years and every Friday night he would go and get drunk on his way home from work. He would come home very late and pop her a couple of good ones before passing out for the night. The next day they would go on like nothing had happened the night before. One night she had enough, there was no warning, no outward sign that she had enough and was fed up. She just waited until he passed out and stabbed him three hundred and sixteen times. When she was finished she called the police herself.

When Max saw the guy, it was like looking at hamburger with eyes. Max always remembered the number of times she had stabbed her husband, he was standing outside puking and over heard one of the Senior Officers remark the guy had been stabbed once for each month they had been married.

This was the main reason Max hated spousal abuse cases. Max realized that he had been daydreaming alittle and saw Ronnie was now standing at the curb, patiently waiting for him to get out of the car. Max got out and walked around to where Ronnie was standing.

"Hello Ronnie," He said as he put out his hand to be shaken, "It is Ronnie, isn't it?"

"Yessir." Ronnie replied as he took the hand and shook it. He didn't recognize Max and was confused why this policeman would know his name.

Max could tell by the look on Ronnie's face that he didn't recognize him, so he said, "I guess you don't remember me. I was here the night you tripped and banged your head."

Then it clicked for Ronnie and he remembered Max. "Hey, I didn't recognize you. That was a crazy night for me and some of it is still jumbled up. How are you doing?"

"Real good. Now if you don't mind me asking, what you got going on here tonight?"

"Well, I came home from work, I had to work late tonight, and I found this dead guy between my living room and the dining room."

"Do you know him?" Max asked.

"Nope, never seen him before." Ronnie said and then after a quick moment added, "To tell you the truth, I haven't really gotten a good look at him yet. Once I saw he was dead, I left him alone and called you guys."

"That's good. What about your wife, does she know him?"

"I don't know. She's been gone since late this afternoon and still isn't back yet."

"Where did she go?"

"Beats me. She left our daughter with the neighbor and went out."

"You got a daughter?" Max said surprised, he didn't know how he had forgotten that Margret had been pregnant when he met her. "Last time I saw you she was still pregnant."

"Yep." Ronnie replied proudly, "And we named her Nancy. She's asleep next door."

"Is she a daddy's girl?" Max asked with a smile.

"Of course."

"Okay Ronnie, let's go in and see what you got."

Ronnie agreed and they went into the house. Ronnie turned on the living room light as Max went and inspected Bernie's body. The first thing Max noticed was how Bernie's face looked burned, almost cooked. Reaching down to check for a pulse, Max also noticed that Bernie's fingernails were black and there were burn marks on his hands. Max warned Ronnie not to touch anything and then started looking around the house. In the kitchen, he saw the splintered door frame that Ronnie had overlooked and speculated this must have been the point of entry.

At Max's suggestion, he and Ronnie went back outside while Max called for back-up. Once the call was made, Max pointed to David and asked Ronnie who he was. Ronnie explained he was the next door neighbor, David, and the father of his babysitter, Heather. Max told Ronnie to wait there and went over to talk to David. Ronnie watched as the two men talked for a couple of minutes. When Max came back to where Ronnie was standing, he made a point of telling Ronnie he had been checking his story with David. Ronnie asked him what David had said and Max just replied he had confirmed Ronnie's story. Not that he had been worried about it, but it was just his job to gather as much information as possible.

A few minutes passed before the crime lab showed up along with three cars of policemen who apparently had nothing better to do. The crime lab people went inside and checked Bernie's body out while Ronnie was asked to tell his side of the story at least two dozen more times. It seemed to Ronnie that just when he finished telling his side of the evenings events, someone new would show up and ask the same questions all over again.

Around midnight, Ronnie began to feel the strain of the evening's events and it was beginning to manifest itself in irritation. It was chafing him that he was still being interrogated while he still didn't know who the asshole was who had broken into his house. When he was asked to tell his story again, he exploded, telling the policeman that he wasn't going to answer any more questions until somebody started answering HIS questions. Namely, who was this guy laying on HIS floor, in HIS house dead? The policeman developed a real attitude at that point and told Ronnie he was going to answer the questions or go downtown to be held as a suspect in the murder of one of the towns most prominent citizens. Ronnie asked the cop why, if this guy was so prominent, did he break into his house? The policeman walked off in a huff, a couple minutes later Max showed up.

"What seems to be the trouble Ronnie?" Max asked.

"There's no trouble here, but the policeman who was just here asking me questions told me if I didn't cooperate with him he was going to take me downtown as a murder suspect. That the guy in there is some kind of prominent citizen and basically that because I'm not, I must have killed him."

"He did what?" Max asked, irate.

"That's what he said. What the hell is going on here?"

Max looked around to see if they could be overheard and motioned for Ronnie to follow him outside. Once they were outside and Max was sure no one was eavesdropping, he turned to Ronnie and said, "Ronnie, you aren't going to believe who that guy is."

"Try me."

"The dead guy in your living room is a man by the name of Bernie Fryer. Are you familiar with that name?" Max asked.

Ronnie noticed that as Max spoke to him, he had been watching Ronnie's face intently. As if he was looking for some sort of reaction that never came. "No. Should I be?" He replied to Max. There had been so much going on this evening you could have asked Ronnie who Jesus was and he wouldn't have been able to give an accurate reply, so anything having to do with the Gabby column was nowhere near his thoughts.

"Probably not." Max replied and then continued, "But here's what I can't tell you. Bernie was a big time lawyer downtown. Had his own law firm and everything. He also came from an old time family from around here with a lot of money."

"So if he's such a model citizen, what the hell is he doing in my house?"

"That Ronnie, is the six million dollar question."

"I'm sorry Sergeant Maxwell, but that is one question I can't answer for you or anyone else, no matter how many times I get asked. I just came home and found him there, that's all I know."

"I know Ronnie. No one is saying this is your fault and I want you to point out the asshole who told you that. It's been awhile since I got to chew some ass. Oh, one other thing. Call me Max, all my friends do."

"Thanks...Max. But don't worry about the cop, I mean, he was probably just excited and I'm tired of telling my side of the story. I guess maybe what he said just hit me the wrong way."

Max smiled at Ronnie and said, "If that's the way you want it. But if you have any trouble with anyone, tell them to come and see me. Okay?"

"You bet Max." Ronnie replied as he smiled back.

Max started to turn to walk away and stopped, acting as if he wanted to say something else. So Ronnie spoke up, "How come I get the feeling that there's more to this story than you're telling me?"

Max's face really looked as if he was struggling with some great decision and after a moment he spoke, "You're right Ronnie, there is one more thing. However, I don't know if I can tell you."

"Well, if you're worried about me telling anyone, my lips are sealed. If you decide not to tell me, that's fine too." Ronnie replied nonchalantly.

Max stepped closer and lowered his voice, "You gotta promise not to tell anyone because this is not fact, but pure speculation."

"Scout's honor." Ronnie replied as he put up the Scout Sign with his right hand.

"Do you get the newspaper?" Max asked.

"Yes."

"Have you seen this new gossip column that's been in the paper lately? It's by someone named Gasbag, I think."

Ronnie felt as if he was in a state of shock. "Yes." He mumbled. He was just beginning to put law firm and lawyer together.

"Well, this last Sunday there was a column about a couple of lawyers ripping off some of the good townsfolk. I didn't think about it or make the connection until one of the lab guys said something. Some of the guy's think it's Fryer's firm that the column was written about..." Max meant to continue, but as he spoke he watched all of the color drain from Ronnie's face. Max caught Ronnie's arm just in time to keep him from falling backwards.

Ronnie was in a state of semi-consciousness when he realized he was sitting down and Max was shaking him saying "...you okay?"

Ronnie weakly mumbled yes and put his head between his knees.

"Are you sure? Man, you scared the hell out of me. Do you need anything? Is there something I can do for you?"

"No, I'm okay. Max...We have to talk. I think I might know why he's in my house."

"What are you telling me Ronnie?"

"Max," Ronnie said, looking serious, and straight into Max's eyes, "I have to tell you something, but it has to be a secret. You gotta promise me that you won't tell anyone."

"What is it Ronnie?" Max asked, suddenly afraid this nice kid was going to confess to killing old Bernie in there.

"You aren't going to believe me, but you know that column you were talking about? The Gabby Gasbag column?"

"What about it?" Max asked, feeling strange because this murder confession was not going like it should be.

"I'm Gabby Gasbag."

Max's mouth dropped open, "What?" he asked.

"That's right. I'm Gabby Gasbag. Nobody knows it and it has to stay a secret or I'll lose my job. Both at the Country Club and at the newspaper. I needed the extra money when Nancy was born and I got offered the job of writing the column." Ronnie suddenly felt better, as if a large weight had been lifted off his shoulders.

"You're Gabby Gasbag?" Max asked in surprised disbelief.

"Yes."

"No shit. I'll be damned. So why do you think Fryer was in your house?"

"Maybe he was here to confront me...I don't know. I came home and found him there, I really can't say what his motivation was. I don't know how he could have found out who I was, that's supposed to be a secret. If he found out who I was, I imagine it would be pretty easy to find out where I live. Oh man, this can't get out, I'll be ruined."

Max just squatted in front of Ronnie for a couple of seconds and then said, "Your secret is safe with me Ronnie. I won't tell anyone and I don't see any reason why we have to include this little fact in the investigation." He patted Ronnie on the shoulder. Max was relieved this hadn't turned out to be a murder confession after all. As Max stood up he added, "Listen Ronnie, I've got to get back. If you have any problems with anyone, tell them to come and see me. If you need anything, let me know. Okay?"

"Yes. And Max...Thanks."

Max gave Ronnie the thumbs up sign, turned and walked away towards the house. He was barking orders as he walked and inquiring of everyone he saw as to whether or not they had something to do.

Around midnight the coroner showed up and went inside the house. It was almost one-thirty before they took Bernie away in the back of the coroner's station wagon. After the body was gone, Ronnie went back into the house. There was a lot of activity still going on inside and he found Max sitting on the couch writing on a clipboard. Ronnie walked over to where Max was sitting and sat down.

"So, what's the verdict Max?" Ronnie asked as he sat down.

"Oh...Hey Ronnie. Finishing up the paperwork so we can get out of your hair."

"Not bothering me at all. In fact, I imagine the neighborhood is getting plenty to talk about for the next month or so from this."

"I can imagine. Say, has your wife showed up yet? I need to talk to her and get her version of tonights events."

"No, she's not home yet. She should be coming home anytime now." Ronnie sounded troubled and frustrated. He didn't mean to sound that way, it just came through in his voice.

Max sat there looking at Ronnie for a couple of seconds and then asked, "If you don't mind me getting personal, does she do this often?"

"Do what?"

"Take off and stay out half the night?"

"No...Not really. Every now and then, but nothing that I would call often. She likes to go out with her girlfriends every now and then."

"Do you know where she went?"

"No." Ronnie replied with a sigh. "She never lets me know where she's been, or even when and where she's going."

"Do you think she's cheating on you?"

"What?" Ronnie asked shocked, his mind instantly turning to Ted and the Professor.

"Do you think she's cheating on you? I hate to be negative, but I've seen it before. Maybe she has a boyfriend." Max said as he put his clipboard down..

"I...I don't think so. No, she couldn't possibly..." Ronnie started to say, but he just couldn't find the words to finish out his thoughts. How could he tell his new found friend he knew that she was cheating because the dead Professor who kept plaguing him in his dreams had told him so.

"Well, probably not. In my line of work you get to see a lot of the scum of the earth. After awhile you start seeing scum even where none exists. Sorry, I didn't mean to imply anything."

Looking at Max, Ronnie could see that he was genuinely sorry for suggesting that Margret was getting her ticket punched by someone other than Ronnie. "Don't worry about it Max. I can fully understand your position." Then Ronnie changed the subject, "It sure did take the coroner a long time to get Mr. Fryer out of here. Was there a problem?"

"No," Max said with a smile, "That old SOB likes to take his time. I keep accusing him of doing his autopsies in the field instead of his office."

"Did he have any ideas on how Fryer died?"

"Yeah...I was meaning to tell you when I saw you. It seems like he got electrocuted on the outlet over there." He pointed to the outlet next to the taped outline of Bernie's body.

Ronnie looked and saw the cover plate of the outlet was missing. He had no way of knowing, but since the cover had been melted and contained a good amount of Bernie's hair in the melted plastic, the coroner had taken it along with him as a weird keepsake. "How could that have happened?" Ronnie asked as he was making his observation of the outlet.

"Doc thinks that maybe Bernie was messing with the outlet for some reason when it backfired on him. I think it might have been arson. I saw a trick once where you short the outlet and let it overheat. Then two-three hours later bingo, you got a good house fire going. Of course, that's just my opinion and nothing official." Max told Ronnie, and then after a moment of thought, added, "Doc said that it was the damnest thing he had ever seen."

"What was?" Ronnie asked.

"Doc said that Fryer's head was cooked. When you get electrocuted, you get burned from the heat of the electricity. Doc said it looked like Fryer's head was completely done. Said he'd know better by tomorrow, but that was his preliminary observations."

"Damn. I've never heard of that before. Completely cooked you say?" Ronnie said as he felt his stomach turn over at the thought. But he didn't want to seem squeamish in front of Max.

"Yeah, Damn is right. If I were you, I would get an electrician here first thing in the morning and check out your wiring. I hate to think that a fire could start because of it. Besides, we'll need a copy of the report from an electrician to go into the file of this investigation."

"No problem. I wouldn't feel safe until the wiring checks out."

"In fact, have the electrician bill us for the check out and send us the original copy of his report. That way, we can include it in the cost of the investigation." Max offered.

"I'll do that. If you don't mind me asking, how long does that have to be there?" Ronnie asked as he pointed to the tape outline on the floor and going partially up the wall.

"We're through with it, so I guess you can remove it as soon as we leave."

"Good. It gives me the creeps looking at it."

"Know what you mean Ronnie." Max picked his clipboard up and started writing again. Then he stopped and said in a hushed voice, "I would be grateful if our discussion here tonight didn't show up in a newspaper column anytime in the near future."

"Don't worry, it won't. I just appreciate you not telling anyone about our discussion earlier."

"What's a small secret among friends?" Max said with a smile.

"You bet." was Ronnie's reply as he turned his attention back to the tape outline. He sat there thinking about what Max had said about Fryer's head being cooked. The thought sent a shiver up his spine and a knot to the pit of his stomach. It was hard for Ronnie to imagine the amount of power it would take to come out of the outlet and do a thing like that. But what bothered Ronnie the most, was the speculation about it being Bernie's law firm and the Gabby column. For Ronnie, there was no speculation, he had written the column himself and knew. The million dollar question was how did Bernie find out who Ronnie was and find him so quickly?

Even though it was very late, Ronnie decided to give Aaron McGuire a call and let him know what had happened. So he went upstairs and found Aaron's phone number in the phone book. Ronnie sat on the edge of the bed, debating whether he should call or not and finally decided to go ahead. The phone was answered by a very sleepy sounding Aaron on the fifth ring.

"There better be somebody really important dead to wake me at this hour of the morning." Aaron growled.

"Aaron, this is Ronnie Fisher. I hate to wake you, but there is something really important I need to tell you."

"Ronnie? Ronnie, what the hell are you calling me for?" Aaron grumped back at him.

"Tonight Bernie Fryer broke into my house..." Ronnie started to tell him but was cut off.

"He did what?" Aaron raved at him, now sounding fully awake. "That stupid bastard. How do you know it was him? Did the police get him?"

"Yes and no. It was the coroner that ended up getting Fryer about twenty minutes ago."

"What?" Aaron demanded.

"I had to work late tonight and when I got home I found Fryer dead in my living room."

"Son of a Bitch!! Was anyone else hurt?"

"No. My wife and daughter weren't at home when he broke in. But that's not the reason I called. I'm wondering how he found out who I was and where I lived."

"Don't worry about it Ronnie." Aaron said as he remembered watching Avery get into Fryer's car. "I think I know exactly how he found out and I will take care of it tomorrow. How did he die?"

"You can't use this until the official report comes out from the police, but he was electrocuted."

"He was what?" Aaron asked in disbelief.

"Seems like he was messing around with one of the outlets and got zapped." Ronnie omitted the part about Fryer"s head being cooked.

"Hells bells. I can't believe he's dead. I also can't think of anyone that deserves it more either. Don't worry about it. I'll take care of things on my end. You just lay low and I'll plug the leak. Like I said, don't worry about it." Aaron said trying to reassure Ronnie.

"I won't if you say so." Ronnie replied unassured. "What should I do about this weeks column?"

"Just turn it in as usual. But if I were you, I wouldn't write about this. Find something else."

"I've already got it written. This one is about the Road Department."

"That's good. I'm glad to see you took my advice. Just turn it in and we'll go on from here."

"Okay...Great. I'll see you later. I just wanted you to know."

"Good. I'm glad you did. Good night Ronnie."

"Good night." Ronnie hung the phone up and he sat there looking at it for a couple of minutes. He knew Aaron had told him not to worry about being found out, but it did trouble him. If it was this easy, what if somebody else decided that they needed to discuss what had been written about them? Ronnie decided that from now on he was going to have to be a lot more careful. If it wasn't such easy money, he would give up the column in a second. But three hundred a week was just too sweet of a deal to give up.

Ronnie felt tired and laid back on the bed. Closing his eyes, he fell asleep almost instantly and started to dream almost as quick. Once again he was at his high place. Looking around, Ronnie saw that it was early morning just right after dawn. Standing there he watched the colors of the sunrise slowly fade away. It was peaceful here, a dimension away from the madness that was happening below him inside his house. He tried to walk over to the edge of the precipice but found he couldn't quite get to the edge itself. No matter how far or fast he walked, it always seemed to stay the same distance away from him.

Ronnie could still see over the edge to the town in the valley below. Although the sun had now risen through a quarter of its arch, there didn't seem to be any change in the activity far below him. Suddenly, there was a booming voice that seemed to rattle the world itself.

I HAVE NO TIME FOR YOUR BULLSHIT RIGHT NOW, The voice said, *GO BACK FROM WHICH YOU CAME.*

Ronnie opened his eyes and looked at the clock on the bedside table. He saw that it was almost two-thirty and realized he had been asleep for less than half an hour. He wondered if Margret was home yet, but somehow knew that she wasn't. Where was Margret? Ronnie wondered. He hoped the police weren't still there when she did show up, tonight there was going to be a showdown. Her not being there was just laying fuel on the fire. He decided to go back downstairs and see if the police activity was showing any signs of coming to a close.

When Ronnie went back downstairs he found no change in activity. Policemen were still bustling in and out of the house. Looking around, he saw Max standing off to one side in what seemed to be a heated discussion with two guys dressed in suits. When it was finished the two guys walked off and Max saw Ronnie standing there. Max smiled and walked over to where Ronnie was standing.

"Hey Max. How's it going?" Ronnie noticed how tired Max looked.

"I've had much better days, that's for damn sure." Max replied, sounding as tired as he looked.

"What's wrong?"

"The crime lab finger printed in here right after they got here. Now it seems that they can't find the prints they lifted and the detectives want another set done." Max explained.

"Just do another set. That seems simple enough." Ronnie offered.

"Yeah. We could have done that, but we can't do it now. The crime scene has been contaminated by every swinging dick that didn't have anything better to do tonight than stopping by to see what's going on."

"So another set is pretty much an impossible dream right now. Right?"

"Something like that."

"Well, I don't want to add to your troubles, but I was just wondering when you guys were going to pack up and be finished."

"Oh, so that's how it is. Come get the body and get the hell out." Max said taunting Ronnie, then Max smiled.

Ronnie felt relief at the sight of that smile, for a brief moment he was afraid he had made Max mad. "No, not at all. I was just wondering how long things like this normally took.

"Relax Ronnie. I was just kidding with you. Right now it looks like we'll be done within the hour."

"Great, thanks. I just wanted to know. I've never seen anything like this before."

"Luckily, most people haven't. Unfortunately, you are getting firsthand experience. I promise we'll get finished as quick as possible."

"Thanks man." Ronnie said and then headed for the kitchen.

When Ronnie got to the kitchen, he noticed the broken door for the first time. Damn, he thought to himself, this is going to take a few bucks to fix. After inspecting the door frame, he turned around and got himself a coke out of the refrigerator and made himself a peanut butter sandwich.

As he ate, he enjoyed the flavor of the peanut butter and the sugary sweetness of the coke. Peanut butter was one of his favorite foods and he remembered his mother one time, when he was little, telling one of her friends he could eat peanut butter until it dripped out of his ears. Ronnie found later that he had the same fondness for ham. Standing there, eating as he looked out the window into the backyard, he saw a shadow cross the backyard and head around the side towards the front of the house.

Ah-ha, the prodigal bitch returns. The up until now, silent voice spoke in his mind.

Ronnie set the coke down and walked into the dining room just in time to see Margret come bursting in through the front door. He had heard her, even before she got into the house, she was screaming and hollering.

"What the hell is going on? Why the hell are you pigs here? What has that asshole done now?" She asked in an excited, over amplified voice.

For a brief moment, EVERYTHING stopped inside the house as all eyes turned to her. Max, who just happened to be standing near Ronnie, turned and looked at Ronnie. Ronnie smiled and said, "There she is."

Max went over and began talking to her.

30.

Margret had expected to sneak into the house and quietly go to bed. She turned around from waving goodbye to Ted and headed for the kitchen side of the house. As she rounded the corner she could see there were a lot of people inside the house. It seemed like all of the lights were on downstairs and she began to get mad, thinking Ronnie was having a party without asking her permission first. As she got closer to the front of the house, she saw the cars parked out front were police cars.

That was when she started screeching because she was scared, she thought they were here to get her for all of the bad checks that she had written. Then, in the millisecond it took for that fear to pass, a new fear took it's place. The new fear was something had happened to Nancy. It was all Ronnie's fault and he would pay for whatever had happened. She would see to that. Everything that happened was his fault and now her plans of getting quietly to bed were ruined also.

She was still yelling when she walked into the house. Margret stopped yelling when she saw everyone stop what they were doing to look at her. She stood there in awkward silence for a moment, thinking there seemed to be a lot of police in her house when she noticed one walking in her direction. She noticed that he looked vaguely familiar.

"Are you Mrs. Fisher?" Max asked, not bothering to reintroduce himself from the first time he had talked to her.

"Yes." Margret replied.

"I'm Sergeant Maxwell. May I have a few moments with you?" He asked politely.

"About what?" Margret demanded. As she asked this, she looked around Max to where Ronnie was standing. She saw that he was just standing there looking mad.

"We have a little problem here and I need to talk to you about it."

"Is my daughter alright?" Margret asked, making a good show of concern.

"Yes, everyone is fine." Max replied. He noticed that Margret seemed to be forcing her concern.

"Then what makes you think that I know anything about whatever has been going on here? I've been out of the house since late this afternoon."

"That's what your husband told us. I just want to know if you might have noticed anything unusual happening around here before you left." Max asked trying to be polite as possible.

"Not really. What is this all about? What's happening here?"

"Let me ask you this, do you know a man by the name of Bernard Fryer?" Max asked, watching her face for a reaction the same way he had watched Ronnie's. There was none.

"No, I can't say that the name is familiar. What is going on?" She asked, starting to sound more testy than she had been.

"Well Mrs. Fisher, it seems like Mr. Fryer broke into your house this evening and in the act of...Well frankly, we don't know what he was doing inside your house because nothing seems to be missing. Anyway, while he was touring your house, he got himself electrocuted."

"He what? You mean he died in here?" Margret asked stunned.

"It would appear so."

"Where?" She asked not really wanting to know, but it was all that she could think of to say.

"Right over there." Max said as he pointed to the taped outline on the carpet and wall.

"So what happens now?"

"Paper work. Right now, I really need to know where you were tonight for my report."

Max noticed once she had asked about the health of her family, she never asked where the baby was. He knew that this was unusual and felt Margret was up to something. He was too trained as an observer not to notice her behavior. What was she up to? He wondered and then decided that one way or another he was going to find out for himself.

"I was out."

"I know that ma'am. You already stated that and I personally noticed it. I need to know where you were and if there is anyone who can verify that you were there."

"Are you talking about an alibi? Excuse me, are you accusing me of killing this guy?" Margret snapped at Max.

"No ma'am. I'm not accusing you of anything." Max told her. Now he knew she had been up to something. Her body language was screaming it to him. "It's just that I have to establish your whereabouts around the time of Mr. Fryers death for my report."

"Well, I'll make it easy for you." Margret told Max as she pointed her finger at him. "I don't know shit about any Mr. Fryer. I was alone tonight and there isn't anyone that can back my story up."

"Okay. Then tell me where you were alone *at*." Max said to her. He didn't like her pointing her finger at him and he would like what she did next even less.

"That is none of your fucking business." She said as she poked him in the chest with her finger.

"Look lady," Max said as he lowered his clipboard, his voice was quiet and full of authority, "It's late and I'm tired. But I have to warn you that if you poke me one more time, I'm going to arrest you for assault on a police officer. Do you understand me?"

Margret only nodded her head yes.

"Now," Max continued in his lowered voice, "I really don't give a good Goddamn where you were or what you were doing. I don't even care who you were doing. I need these questions answered and we can either do it here and I can close out this investigation, leave and never have to deal with you again. Or, I can take you down to the station, put you in a small room where you will sit until you decide to cut the crap and give me the answers to these questions. It's your choice, how would you like to do this?"

"I'm sorry," Margret said turning on the charm, "But this whole situation is a little disarming."

"I can understand your point of view. But please understand mine. I just have a job to do." He had seen snow jobs before, but nothing like this blizzard on feet standing in front of him.

"I went off for some quiet time. I went over to the park off Concourse Avenue. I was there until after midnight, then I just walked around before coming on home."

"I'm not familiar with the park you're talking about. Where did you say it was?" Max asked. He knew she was lying because of the reaction he had seen on her face when he had told her that he didn't care who she was doing.

"Over off of Concourse. It's right next to that square drainage pond with the wooden privacy fence around it."

"Is that the one right on the airport's flight path?"

"There are a lot of planes going over all of the time. So I guess the answer to that is yes."

"I know the one you're talking about. You were there the whole time?" He asked trying to trip her up on her story. He wanted to see if she kept with the left at midnight part of the story.

"I was there until midnight, then I started walking home. But not straight here. I'm afraid that I went farther than I had intended and it took me longer to get back."

"Did anyone see you at the park? Maybe someone walking a dog or just walking around that would remember you?" He thought Margret was either telling the truth or one of the best liars that he had come across in a long time. He quickly discarded his thoughts of Margret's wholesomeness and settled on his latter observation.

"No, I'm afraid not. I didn't see anyone the whole time I was gone. I can't really say if anyone saw me."

"I see. Well, thank you. I guess that's about it for now. I can always get with you at a later date if it turns out I need anything else." Max told her as he started writing on his clipboard again.

Max just happened to look over the top of his clipboard at Margret's feet and saw she was wearing a pair of white leather sandals with very thin straps. One across the toes and one across the ankle. He saw the straps were pulled tight on her feet. He couldn't place what it was that seemed strange to him about her shoes, so he just filed it away in the part of his mind he stored unusual facts and oddities.

It was almost five in the morning before the police were finished and finally out of the house. As Ronnie walked back into the house after seeing Max out to his patrol car, he decided to call Floyd in another thirty minutes and let him know he was going to be late coming in. Once inside, he saw Margret looking at Bernie's taped outline on the floor and wall. He quietly walked up behind her before saying anything.

"What a night." He remarked.

"How long does this shit have to stay here?" She asked him with a smudge of irritation in her voice.

"The police said we could remove it as soon as they left."

"Then what's taking you so long to get it off the floor?"

"I'll get to it in a minute. First, I want you to answer a question for me." He told her, trying to think of a way to remain calm and still ask the question burning inside him.

"Well, make it snappy. I want to get to bed." She snapped back at him.

"Okay, I will. Where the hell were you tonight?" He asked. The question just seemed to hang in the air and the silence was thick.

"I was out. Okay?" She said and then turned to go upstairs.

"That's not good enough." Ronnie said as he caught her arm and stopped her.

"Let go of me asshole!"

"Margret. I asked you a question. Where the hell were you tonight?" Ronnie asked, struggling to remain calm and not let his anger flare up.

"If you don't let go of me right this second, the police will be back here and there will be two taped outlines on the floor." He could hear that she was close to losing control in her voice.

"Shut up!" He shouted at her. "I'm so tired of your bullshit. Now you are going to answer this question and you had better tell the truth because I might already know the answer."

"You don't know shit! I was out and that's that. Now get out of my face before I hurt you."

"Fuck you! Do you talk to your boyfriend like that or do you just save it all up for me?" He snapped back at her, coming dangerously close to losing the control he was desperately hoping to keep.

As usual, Ronnie never saw it coming. All he knew was the sudden reality of her fist being driven into his solar plexus, hard and deep. The blow caught him unexpectedly and knocked all of the wind out of him. He stood there gasping for breath. Everything was beginning to get foggy around him and his head was beginning to feel lighter and lighter. Without knowing, Ronnie sank to his knees.

Margret's eyes narrowed to slits and she smiled. The next thing she did was drive her knee up into the bottom of Ronnie's chin. The only thing that kept Ronnie's teeth from breaking when they were driven together was his tongue. As he had been on his knees gasping for breath, it had been sticking out just enough and his teeth came together on the end. His tongue was cut deeply on both bottom and top. When that happened, the fog that Ronnie was in turned to blinding white pain. He still couldn't breath and now his mouth was rapidly filling with blood.

Margret saw that Ronnie was now totally immobilized with pain, so she turned and ran to the staircase. Looking back one more time to make sure that he wasn't following her, she saw that he was still on his knees in the middle of the room. Margret stopped and added her last two cents worth.

"I don't know what your problem is," She yelled at him, "You left a huge mess in the kitchen this morning and you didn't come home when you were supposed to. But I do know this, if you fuck with me anymore, you'll be in a world of hurt asshole. You can take that to the bank because I mean it. I'm through with your bullshit!"

She bolted up the stairs and locked herself in the bedroom. Although Ted had just about wore her out, she found herself filled with desire at the thought of what she had just done to Ronnie. She quickly stripped and began to masturbate, bringing herself to three quick and tremendous orgasms.

While Margret was upstairs indulging herself, Ronnie was still on his knees in the living room. The only thing that had changed was he had stuffed the bottom of his shirt into his mouth to stem the flow of blood and he was beginning to get his breath back. He slowly got up and walked to the downstairs bathroom. He was still light headed and felt as if he was going to fall down at any second. Inside the bathroom he pulled the blood soaked shirt from his mouth and began to spit the blood from his mouth into the sink..

Ronnie fumbled around blindly on the counter top and found the cup that was kept there. He filled it with water and rinsed his mouth out. When the cold water hit the cuts on his tongue, which was throbbing with each heartbeat now, his mouth awoke with fresh blinding pain. The light over the sink seemed too bright and his teeth felt painfully sore. He spat bright red blood into the basin. Ronnie kept repeating the process until the water he was spitting back into the basin was clearer. The throb was still there, but as he rinsed his mouth the bite of pain from the cold water hitting his tongue became less and less.

Standing there inspecting his mouth in the mirror, he saw that it looked like the wounds on his tongue were clotting. His tongue felt like a lump in his mouth and saw how the cuts on the top and bottom of his tongue matched the pattern of his upper and lower front teeth.

Goddamn bitch! Ronnie thought to himself and the tears began to flow. He stood there silently crying. When he pulled himself together, he looked at his watch and saw it was after five-thirty. He knew Floyd was at work and went back into the living room for the phone. Sitting down on the couch with a towel, Ronnie dialed the number to the shack. The phone was answered almost immediately by Floyd.

Ronnie explained to Floyd all of the events that had transpired since he had left work the previous evening. Of course, he omitted the part about Margret decorating his mouth in bright red. But he did have to explain why he was mumbling when Floyd asked him what was wrong with his speech. He told Floyd he had tripped over Bernie's body and had bitten his tongue when his chin hit the floor. Floyd was shocked and told Ronnie not to even worry about coming in that day. He was to just stay home, get some rest and take care of business. Ronnie thanked him and hung up.

Ronnie stood up, and after standing there for a minute, he turned and started for the stairs.

31.

When Max left Ronnie's house that morning, he kept thinking about Margret's shoes. There was something about them that bothered him. It had been on his mind ever since he saw them and although he couldn't put his finger on it, he knew he would figure it out sooner or later. Margret's shoes weren't really important, this was a simple and clear cut case of accidental death during the commission of a crime. There was no doubt in his mind that Fryer had broken into Ronnie's house to either intimidate Ronnie or start a fire. There was also the possibility Fryer was going to steal something that would prove Ronnie was Gabby and then expose him to the public. That brought about the possibility of blackmail. With the types of columns being written, there might be a small group of people who would pay to find out who had exposed their deepest secrets to the reading public.

But his thoughts kept coming back to those shoes. What had been so unusual about them? What was the thing that he was missing? For some reason that he couldn't explain, this was one of those things he couldn't shake off. It was becoming like one of those tunes you hear on the radio and then can't get off of your mind for the rest of the day. Before going back to the station to do more paperwork, Max decided to check out Margret's story by getting a mileage check of how far away the park was she had supposedly walked to. He stopped the cruiser and got a city map out of the glove box. He then turned the car around and went back to Ronnie's neighborhood. He stopped the car just short of Ronnie's house and opened the map. He quickly located where Ronnie's house was and marked it with his ink pen. Then he located the park and marked it also. Max saw that it was a good distance away from where he was now. So he picked the most direct route and shifted the car into drive. After noting the mileage on the odometer, he headed for the park.

Max drove slowly and looked for any gap between houses or cut-throughs someone could use to shorten the trip. He found none and a little while later, he found himself at the park in question. Max looked at the odometer again and found that he had driven almost five miles. Four point eight to be exact. He noted the mileage and route on the map and then pointed the cruiser in the direction of the station, heading there to finish the paperwork from last night's fun.

The sky was beginning to lighten with the impending sunrise when he finally pulled into the police station parking lot. Max parked in the maintenance area so his car could be checked out, refueled and then sent back out for the next patrol to use on this new day. This was a practice forced on them when the city had cut the budget of the police force. Every car, unless it was broken down, would be out on patrol until it was absolutely worn out.

Although the department had seen an increase of mechanical failures, they had also seen a dramatic decrease in people calling to complain about seeing a squad car parked in front of someone's house during off duty hours. The next time the budget came around, there were less people complaining about the misuse of property. The police force got the increase they had been asking for, plus a small percentage over what they had asked for. The public seemed happier because they weren't seeing unused police cars sitting around. The chief decided this was a good public relations gimmick and decreed this would be the policy forevermore.

It seemed to be a good system. Good that is, unless the guy who had the car before you had one of those two or three chili cheese dog lunches. Then the car would have the tendency to be a little ripe when you got into it. Max walked over to the metal desk where he had checked out the car to begin with and began shuffling through the papers stacked there. Finally, he found the piece of paper that went to his car and filled it out. He wrote his name, beginning and ending odometers, and stated there were no problems with the car.

When Max was done with the maintenance sheet, he went on into the station and found the desk he shared with two other policemen that were on other shifts. Unlocking his drawer, he pulled out the necessary forms and began filling them out. Two hours later he was finished and took the forms to the Captain for review. Another thirty minutes passed while he and the Captain discussed what had happened. It was mutually agreed upon that Fryer had "gotten his" while fucking around where he shouldn't have been. Since the man was dead, it seemed pointless to charge him with a crime, so Captain Waters agreed to go with the conclusion of accidental death during the commission of a crime.

"Okay Max. What's troubling you about this case?" Waters asked as he leaned back in his chair.

"Nothing, why?" Max answered.

"Bullshit. I've known you long enough to know when you are putting on your poker face. So what's up?"

"Is this part of the official discussion, or is this just two old fishing buddies talking to each other?"

"I knew there was more to the story. How do you want it?"

"Anyway but on the record." Max replied as he looked Waters straight in the eye.

"Of course. Lay your cards out on the table and confess your sins." Waters replied with a smile on his face. Max and he had been friends for a long time and he knew when his buddy had something on his mind.

"Well, it might not be anything. But I think Mrs. Fisher is lying about her where abouts last night. She said she had walked to the park, but I measured it, it was almost ten miles round trip."

"So where do you think she was?"

"I dunno."

"Do you think that she had anything to do with Fryer's death?" Waters quickly asked.

"No. Her reaction was too genuine to the fact that someone had died in her house. Plus there was no reaction to Fryer's name. I believe her when she says she didn't know him. So no, I don't think she was involved." Max said the last part with a tone of reflection in his voice.

"Then if she's not involved, what's bothering you about her?" Waters asked puzzled.

"It's just that Mr. Fisher seems like a pretty straight Joe. I hate to think that she's up to something behind his back."

"Boyfriend maybe?"

"Possible. I just don't know."

"Max old buddy, you know this wouldn't be the first case of the hen getting out of the henhouse. Happens all the time. Besides, you're not a marriage counselor. People have to work out their own problems. All you do is keep the peace."

"Yeah, I know. I just hate to think she's doing that to him."

"Just let it go Max. We'll rubber stamp Fryer's death after we get the report back from the coroner. Now go home and get some rest, you got mids again tonight."

With that said, Waters went back to shuffling papers on his desk and Max got up and left the office. As he headed for the locker room to change and go home, Max ran into one of the new female recruits. She was a lot of fun to be around because she had a very warped sense of humor and could tell some of the funniest (and dirtiest) jokes Max had ever heard. She had ridden with him a few times when she was just a cadet and he felt that they had a rapport going. He stopped her and asked if he could have a couple of minutes of her time. She agreed and they went to the back of the office where they could talk in private.

"So what's on your mind Mad Max?" She asked him after they were settled.

"I want to ask you about shoes." Max replied with a smile.

"They go on your feet. Anything else you want to know?"

171

"Seriously," He replied as his smile widened, "I need to know some things about women's shoes." Max then explained the events of his shift and the type of shoes Margret had been wearing.

"So what do you want to know about her sandals?" She asked Max sounding confused.

"She said that she walked to the park and then back. I measured it and it was almost ten miles round trip."

"Then she's lying."

"Why? How do you know?"

"Because those types of sandals you described are more for show than a hike."

"What do you mean?" He asked. He really didn't need the information because his suspicions had been confirmed.

"With those thin straps, her feet would have been rubbed raw. Not to mention the openness of the sandals would let in all kinds of road trash. I had a pair like those and walked around downtown one time in them. They hurt my feet so bad that I had to call in sick for a day. I was working at a pizza place at the time, to pay for tuition and almost got fired for calling in. But what could I do? I couldn't wear shoes because my feet were raw from so many blisters. I was hurtin' for certain."

Max just sat there thinking about what he had just been told.

"If there's nothing else, I have to go. We were here for some paperwork and my ride is about to leave."

"No, there's nothing else. Thanks...thanks a lot."

"Anytime Max." She said as she got up and left.

Max sat there for a couple of moments thinking before heading to the locker room. The situation with Margret lying to him troubled him. He knew she was up to something, most likely a boyfriend. But he couldn't arrest her for simply lying to him (he could, but he didn't want to force the issue) and he hated to think about what would happen when and if Ronnie ever found out she was cheating on him. Ronnie's reaction might be detrimental to Margret's health.

Max decided to stamp the whole affair with 'Forget it'. He was tired and just wanted to get home so he could get to bed. If the coroner's report came back with even a small hint of foul play he would be on her like white on rice. Until then, there was nothing he could really do.

32.

Aaron looked at his watch as he walked from his parking place to the building. It was almost eight-thirty, unusually late for him to be arriving at the paper. But he wanted to see who he could catch goofing off on the loading dock. Not that he really cared, his guys worked long and hard hours for him, so he never got mad at their little indulgences of time. He knew that when the steel was in the forge, they would go full force until the die was cast without complaint. Hell, sometimes even he would be out there helping the B.S. story hour take flight with one colorful story after another. Today he just wanted to catch Avery standing there with his dick in his hand as usual.

As he rounded the corner, Aaron caught a flurry of movement on the back of the dock. He smiled inwardly to himself that he had succeeded in his plan. Climbing the stairs that took him from ground level to the floor level he saw Avery sweeping the vestibule in front of the double doors.

Avery was all smiles and said good morning to him. His reply was a simple, "My office, ten minutes." Aaron didn't even slow down as he walked on past Avery into the press room on the way to his office. He saw everyone was busily at work and everything looked normal. Let the kid sweat, he thought. He had intended to chew Avery's ass and if he was lucky, reduce him to a pile of crying and quivering employee. But seeing Avery already screwing around this early in the morning, Aaron decided to have some fun with him. The ten minutes served two purposes, to make Avery sweat, and to give Aaron enough time to come up with a scary bedtime story to turn up the heat. He wanted to teach the kid a lesson, that in this business you never sold out your sources. That could get you a permanent case of dead, for either you or your source.

Ten minutes came and went quickly and Aaron made him wait another five minutes outside his office while he sat at his desk shuffling papers. Aaron finally motioned him inside and told him to take a seat, they sat and looked at each other over the desk in silence. The silence was almost more than Avery could bear.

Avery was in a mild state of panic. He knew he had been seen sitting down on the loading dock and figured that he was about to be fired. Rationalizing in his mind, he decided he had been fired from better jobs than this one. He remembered the money he had and decided that if he was going to be fired, then the hell with it. He was a rich man now and could get by for a while. At least, that's what Avery thought while he had been outside. But now sitting here in front of Aaron, it was all he could do to keep from wetting his pants. Aaron was that good of an intimidator. He had been able to knock all of Avery's cockiness out of him, leaving him hoping that he would survive this talk with the boss, without saying a word.

Finally, Aaron figured he had sweated the kid long enough and spoke.

"You really fucked up this time kid."

Avery started to say he had been working when he was seen, but Aaron stopped him. "There's not much you can say in your defense. Because of you, a man is dead." Aaron said in as stern of a tone as he could muster.

The statement seemed to put Avery into some kind of mental vapor lock. How could somebody be dead because he was out sitting on the loading dock? His mind raced and all he could manage was a semi-intelligent "Huh?".

"How much did Bernie pay you to sell out Gabby Gasbag?"

That turned Avery's brain back on. Oh shit, he thought, Mr. Fryer killed the man he had spied on. "I don't understand what you're talking about. Who's dead?" He quickly replied.

Aaron came up out of his seat and smashed his meaty fists down on top of his desk. "Don't give me that bullshit kid!" He shouted at Avery. "I know damn well what you did. Bernie Fryer picked you up and took you to lunch yesterday. Is that what he paid you? A lousy piece of meat? And you, a little piece of dick snot, told him some information he didn't need to know. He died for your sins boy. The responsibility for Bernie Fryer's death rests solely on your shoulders."

"But...How?" Avery stammered. He couldn't believe that Fryer was dead. How could this be his fault? All he did was provide some information. The guilt Aaron had just laid on him was running rampant through his mind, and teenagers by their very nature, always try to find a way to deny fault in their character.

"I'm going to tell you a story." Aaron said in a calm voice as he sat down, "And you're going to listen. You see, you don't know who you are dealing with. In this business you meet a lot of scummy people. Some of them wear fifthly clothes, but a lot of them wear suits. The suits are the ones that you have to lookout for. The filthy clothes will just take your possessions if you let them. The suits will take your life. In this business you never tell anyone anything you know. And that's because you never really know who you're dealing with or what they are capable of. The junkie down the street may take your money if he finds you half dead beside the road, but he might be the one who calls an ambulance. While your best friend, the president of a bank will just pass you by and let you lay there. Do you understand me?"

Avery was noticeably quiet and only nodded his head yes. Aaron saw that Avery's eyes were getting a little misty looking and was happy with the performance and the reaction he was giving and receiving, so he continued.

"Now, I really hate to be the one to tell you how big the pile of shit it is that you've stepped in, but I'm gonna do it anyway because I like you. I find it hard to believe that a man of your age hasn't heard of the mafia. Well, one of the elderly mothers of the oldest organized crime families lives here in town. She approached me awhile back about doing a column of some of the gossip that she was hearing. I told her to send me some of her work and I would see what I could do. I was instructed later, that no matter what her work looked like, it was to go to print. I'll never forget what he told me, 'If Grandma wants to write for the local paper, then she's gonna write for the local paper or else.'." Aaron said the last in a mock Italian accent, dropping the accent he added. "I never got around to asking what 'or else' meant and I really don't want to find out. It turned out that her stuff, while being real rough, was pretty hot. But it was really the work of a rank amateur. So I hired Ronnie Fisher to pick up her columns, clean them up and type them. Since he has been doing this, I have found out the old lady has taken a real liking for Ronnie. So it's natural to assume the little circle of protection that has been surrounding her has been extended to him also. I have a feeling when Fryer was seen breaking into Ronnie's house, that little circle of protection went into action and offed him."

"You think this was a mafia hit?" Avery spoke up for the first time. "If the mafia killed him, why didn't they take the body with them?"

"Boy," Aaron said as his eyes narrowed at Avery, "You really don't know very much about how the world works, do you? They left the body there as a warning to anyone else who might have thoughts about continuing Fryer's work. It's the same line of thought as natives on those islands in the Pacific Ocean who put the head of their enemies on poles and decorate their island with them. I mean, just because they kill you doesn't mean they go through the hassle of getting rid of you. It's smarter and easier to leave you behind to serve as a warning."

Avery put his hand to his throat and held it there as if he was trying to keep his head from flying off his shoulders. He was as pale as a white sheet.

Aaron was pleased with himself, he could see Avery was buying the story, hook, line, and sinker. After a moment of what looked like self reflection, he added some more good news for Avery's benefit, "The only thing I can think of, is for you to lay low. Hide out and forget that you ever heard the name Fryer. If I were you, I would also hope that old Bernie didn't talk before they killed him.

"What would he tell them?" Avery shot back, not understanding the direction Aaron was taking his fairy tale.

"Knowing that weasel, he probably told them he was working for you. Or at the very least, given them your name and address in hopes they would leave him alone and go after you. Bernie was a slimy one all right. He would have said or done anything to save his own miserable hide." Aaron didn't think it was possible, but he saw Avery pale even farther.

"What...What should I do? What can I do? What will happen to me? I really didn't mean any harm to anybody, Mr. Fryer told me that it was real important to the paper to find out who Gabby was. I don't want to die." He pleaded with Aaron.

"Well, forget that you ever heard of Bernie like I said. I would also forget about Fisher also. And I would most definitely stay as far away from his house as possible. Yeah, laying low seems like your only recourse."

"They are going to kill me aren't they? No matter what I do, they're going to get me and kill me." Avery said with a trembling lower lip from being on the verge of tears.

Aaron was more than happy with the reaction that he was getting and would have continued terrorizing the kid, but he had work to do and decided to cut the kid some slack. "Look kid, the simple fact that you are still alive and we are having this conversation is a good thing. I mean, if they were looking for you, you'd probably be dead right now. So at least there's a little hope for you. Not much mind you, but some hope none the least." Aaron sat back in his chair and looked at Avery. The kid was looking better, still pale and Aaron noticed that his hands were shaking a little.

"Maybe if I went to the police and explained my side of the story..." Avery started but Aaron cut him off.

"That would be the ideal thing wouldn't it? But you don't seem to realize how deep the mob's hands are in this community. If you went to the police and 'explained your side of the story' as you put it, it would be the same as you running up a flag and saying 'Here I am, come get me'. I can guarantee that you will be in the hands of the bad guys before the sun goes down." He told Avery. The last thing he wanted, was for Avery to go running off to the police and spill his guts. Especially after the load of horse manure he had just shoveled out.

"Mr. McGuire, I don't feel so well." Avery said. Ever since he had heard the word 'Mafia", he felt as if he would die on the spot, or at the very least, wet his pants. His stomach was one big knot that threatened to force his breakfast up. He couldn't believe he was in so much trouble for just telling someone a small piece of information. How could he have been so stupid? Inwardly he knew it was the smell of money that had made him stupid and now he was going to pay the ultimate price for it. There was a chance that they were not looking for him. After all, McGuire had said if they had wanted him, he would be dead right now. It was a slim chance, but he was willing to grasp for any chance that came along.

"I know how you feel kid. Tell you what, take the rest of the day off and go chill out somewhere. Go see a movie, go home and watch TV. Just get yourself together and come back tomorrow ready to work. Remember what I said, forget you ever heard of Bernie Fryer or Ronnie Fisher. If you don't, and go shooting your mouth off, you might draw the wrong type of attention to yourself. YOU know what I mean."

"Yessir."

"Good, now get lost."

Avery thanked him and left his office quickly. Aaron sat there and watched Avery leave, waiting until he was sure the kid was gone before bursting into laughter. He guffawed until his chest hurt and tears were streaming down his face. Aaron couldn't believe the kid had bought such an outlandish story. Aaron was in a very good mood for the rest of the day.

33.

Avery, on the other hand, only kept his composure long enough to get to where his mom's car was parked. As he opened the car door, he felt the vomit rise. There was nothing that he could do to stop it and he lost his entire breakfast before settling into the dry heaves for a couple of minutes. His chest hurt and he was crying like a baby as he got into the car and drove home, the tears blurring his vision. At every corner and stop light he imagined that assassins were waiting for him.

When Avery finally reached his house, he had to sit in the driveway for a couple of minutes to regain his composure before going inside to face his mother. He knew she would want to know why he was home from work so early and decided that instead of telling her he had been sent home, he would tell her that he had come home because of lack of work. That would save him from having to explain to his mother he was now on the endangered list and couldn't tell anyone, especially the police. If he did that, it would also mean he would have to tell her about the thousand dollars he had stashed in his room. He knew she would demand that he turn it over for 'safe keeping'.

Avery knew 'safe keeping' meant that he would never see the grand again. She had a way of making money disappear. Every time he had given her money in the past to hold for him, it would be gone when he asked for it later. If he persisted in pressing the point, she would jump down his throat about not pulling his fair share around the house. No matter how much arguing would pursue, it always ended with him sulking away without his money.

When he felt that he was calmer, he left the relative safety of the car and went into the house. Once inside, he greeted his mother and told his story about coming home early. The story was the one about the lack of work and not the real story as he understood it. She just smiled and waved him on, she was engrossed in a game show on the tv and wasn't in the mood to stop and discuss his reason for being home. Avery slinked away to his room to spend the rest of the day hiding. Once inside, he felt better, safe and secure. He sat on the edge of the bed lamenting over the situation he now found himself in and decided that no amount of money was worth the gut wrenching terror he was feeling now. He was so scared that had somebody chose to knock on his door at that moment, he would have probably dropped dead on the spot from fright. Once again, he broke down into tears.

34.

Ronnie stood at the foot of the staircase, he was aware that the Professor wasn't whispering things in his mind. Usually by now the Professor would have been making all kinds of suggestions about what to do with Margret. Ronnie was partially grateful of this, but he was also partially sorry the instructions weren't coming. Other than the constant throb of his tongue, his mind was blank and he didn't know what he wanted to do. Part of him wanted to go upstairs and knock the crap out of Margret for doing that to him, while the sane part of him just wanted to let it go. To let this abuse from her go unchecked and to eventually fade from his memory.

But something inside him was beginning to emerge, telling him that this had to stop. That he must take no more. Ronnie didn't recognize who it was telling him that, it had just been too long since he had listened to his own consciense.

Ronnie made his decision and started to climb the stairs slowly. Each footfall brought fresh pain in his mouth. He was beginning to feel light-headed again and his stomach was upset from swallowing so much blood. When he got to the top of the stairs he had to sit down for a few moments until he felt better. Once the initial wave of nausea passed over him, he felt as if he could go on. Ronnie stood up and started for the bedroom. When he got there, the door was locked.

That was the last straw. To be locked out of his own bedroom was more than he could take at the moment. He didn't give a damn if Margret was inside or not. Ronnie took one step backwards, turned around and brought his foot up next to the door knob behind him. Bringing his knee forward, he put all of his weight into the backwards thrust of his foot. It worked! The lock on the door not only split the door jam, but the hinges gave way and pulled loose as the door exploded inward.

Margret was laying on the bed with a look of shock on her face. Not only had he caught her in the middle of giving herself pleasure, but she had never considered that he would have the balls to come through a locked door. She quickly pulled the bed sheet up, trying to hide what she had been doing before he broke her concentration.

Ronnie stood there for a couple of seconds looking at her and then shouted, "You WILL NOT lock me out of my own bedroom! Get your lazy ass up and go get your daughter, Right...Fucking...NOW!!"

Before she had a chance to reply, Ronnie turned and went into the bathroom. Margret had never seen this type of reaction out of him before and it scared her. The image of his scrawny butt standing there in the doorway after the door had literally exploded inward was a vision that she would not quickly forget. There was something different about him and it wasn't even on the same lines as the time he had hit her. When she had looked into his eyes this time, she swore that she saw murder in there. His eyes were so dark and cold. That is what scared her the most, because she knew it was her that had pushed him over the line. The fact the front of his shirt was covered with blood just made his actions more animal-like to her.

Once she was sure that he was in the bathroom, she jumped out of bed and put on a pair of jeans and a T-shirt. She then quickly and quietly went downstairs and next door to get Nancy.

While she was leaving, Ronnie ran more cold water in the sink and rinsed his mouth out. This time the blood he was spitting out was minimal. Inspecting his tongue in the mirror, he saw the wound was mostly clotted except for a couple of bite marks on the edges. He decided that he was going to live after all.

Thinking back to the way he had kicked the door open and the look of surprise on Margret's face made him feel good that he had not taken his anger out on her, but the door instead. It also made him mad to see that she had been up there taking care of her own needs. Whenever he had approached the subject of sex with her, she was either too tired or too busy. Now he suspected maybe it was that she was too much of a bitch. The look of embarrassed shock on her face had been worth whatever it would cost to repair the door.

The thought about having to repair the door reminded him that he had to call the electrician to check the wiring out. So he stripped off his shirt, wadded it up and threw it into the garbage can. He went back downstairs and found a telephone book. Looking through it he found the one that Max had recommended and dialed the number. After explaining who he was and what had happened, it was agreed that someone would come by this morning to take a look at the wiring.

While Ronnie was on the phone, Margret returned with Nancy. Although she didn't say anything, she kept a wary eye on Ronnie. When he got off the phone he looked at her and told her that the man would be by this morning to check the house out. Then he explained further that he was going to lay down and while she was waiting for the man to show up, to get the tape up off of the floor.

Margret started to bristle at the fact that he was commanding her, but before she could say anything, he was already gone, heading up the stairs. She walked to the bottom of the staircase just in time to see him disappear around the corner.

181

She was bone tired and wanted desperately to go to sleep. But after his little display of temper this morning, she was afraid to close her eyes. There was no telling what that little piss-ant would do to her if he caught her sleeping. For the first time in many years, Margret was truly afraid.

Ronnie stepped over the broken door and laid down on the bed. Even though it had been a very long day, he found sleep to be elusive. He tossed and turned and couldn't find a comfortable position to lay in. It seemed that right as sleep did find him, Margret was there shaking him awake. She informed him the man was there to check the wiring. Ronnie got up and went downstairs.

He followed the electrician around for thirty minutes as the man checked one thing after another. Finally it was announced that the fault had been found. The electrician diagnosed the problem as a faulty outlet in combination with a fused circuit breaker. The man proclaimed that it was a fatal accident waiting to happen. The breaker and outlet were replaced and Ronnie agreed to pay for the parts. It was a good thing the electrician wasn't very thorough or he would have discovered two breakers fused. The one that he found and the one that the computer was plugged into.

Once Ronnie's part of the bill was settled and the repairman left, Ronnie walked back into the living room and sat down. Margret was in the dining room slowly pulling the tape off of the floor. Ronnie noticed that she was unusually quiet and he decided to leave her alone. After a few moments of tense silence, just the sound of the tape peeling off the floor, Margret spoke first.

"Ronnie, I'm sorry if I hurt you this morning." She looked at him with puppy dog eyes.

I bet. Ronnie thought to himself, but kept his mouth shut.

"Aren't you going to say anything?" She asked him. She was starting to get that sniffy quality to her voice, the one that would lead to her easy on, easy off tears.

"Why should I? What is there to say?" He replied tersely.

"You could say that you accept my apology."

"Is that what you want Margret? For me to accept your apology so everything will be alright?"

"But I mean it. I really am sorry for what I did to you." Her eyes beginning to leak.

"That's the problem Margret. You always mean it. But it doesn't stop you from inflicting pain the next time. But hey, just to make you happy, I accept your apology. Happy now?"

"I'm serious Ronnie. You think that I'm kidding but I'm not. I am sorry for what I did to you." The tears were coming faster now.

"Well, we'll see just how serious you really are." Ronnie replied, paying no attention to her display of grief.

"Wha...What do you mean by that?" She asked amid sniffle.

"If you are sincere about being sorry, then you will take measures to make sure it doesn't happen again."

"Like what?"

"How the hell should I know? Get some professional help. See a preacher, call one of those hate management hot lines. But do something." He told her. Ronnie was amazed. Normally, she would have been attacking him by now for talking back to her the way he was. Maybe she was being sincere.

"I will Ronnie, I promise." as Margret said that, she walked up to him and put her arms around his neck. She felt him instantly stiffen.

Ronnie decided to press his luck and added, "One more thing Margret. I know what you've been up to and who you've been up to with. It had better stop now or else."

Margret's reaction was one of stunned amazement and all she said as she lowered her eyes was, "I will, I swear."

Ronnie felt he was in the pilot's seat now. Margret was being submissive to him and he liked it. He showed her what she had done to his tongue and she freaked out, insisting that he go and see a doctor. Ronnie told her they didn't have the money and he felt like he was going to live. She started crying again and this time, Ronnie thought that the tears were sincere.

After Margret went to feed Nancy her lunch, Ronnie decided to play with the computer. He went over and sat down at the desk and turned it on. When the screen came on, the only message that was displayed was 'DATA SORTING' and the computer would not do anything else. He sat there for five minutes before deciding nothing was going to happen and turned the computer back off. Ronnie felt disappointed that he was unable to use the thing and it never occurred to him that Fryer might have broken it last night.

He went into the kitchen and made himself a sandwich, but found that the act of chewing used more muscles in his tongue than he knew was possible for one organ to possess. So for the time being, eating was off of his list of things to do. He felt a small flash of anger towards Margret for forcing him on this new miracle diet. When he had walked in here, he was just a little hungry. But looking at the sandwich laying on the counter, his stomach was roaring like an angry lion. The hunger was becoming a knot in his stomach and all he could do was obsess about how hungry he was.

Then Ronnie remembered something about some doctor named Stillman and something about a water diet. If he remembered correctly, the diet was based on the premise that if you drank enough water, you would cease to be hungry because your stomach was full. Ronnie decided that whatever the idea was behind it, it was worth a shot. He got a glass out of the cupboard and after filling it under the tap, began to drink. After the third glass, he found that his hunger was beginning to abate. So he continued to drink. He found that four and a half water glasses was his limit and it was true, he was no longer hungry.

Thirty minutes later his hunger was back with a vengeance and he had to pee so bad that he almost didn't make it to the bathroom in time. As he stood there urinating, he decided that Stillman was full of crap and must have owned stock in a water company. So after he was finished he went back into the kitchen and made himself a cup of soup. He crushed a bunch of crackers into the bowl to soak up the broth. The first spoon full made his tongue hurt like it had just been injured all over again. The hot liquid seemed to find every nook and cranny of the puncture wounds on his tongue. So he sat the bowl in the refrigerator to cool for a couple of minutes.

The taste of food made his stomach start up in all of its full glory again. As he stood there waiting for his lunch to cool down enough to eat, the need to urinate struck once again. This time when he went, he marveled at the pleasure he was deriving from taking a simple leak. Ronnie began to think about the simple joys of taking a leak. This was one of those that make your fingertips tingle. Yes sir, this wasn't one of those simple leaks, no sir. This was one of those that all of mankind would look back on throughout history as the major leak.

35.

While Ronnie was in the bathroom marveling at the concept of urinating, Margret saw the mailman come. She started to say something to him about getting the mail. After hearing him laughing in the bathroom, she decided to let him keep his good mood and get the mail herself. It was a good thing she did, because there were seven notices from the bank and the grocery store about bounced checks.

Margret felt as if her skin was on fire from the fear, she realized that if Ronnie had seen these notices first, his reaction would have been totally unpredictable. Especially this new and improved Ronnie, the one that wasn't putting up with her crap anymore. She honestly felt bad about what she had done to him earlier. Not at first of course, but when she saw those teeth marks on his tongue, that's when the feeling began to creep in. Looking back, Margret realized the moment she had stepped over the line. She resented herself for kneeing him in the jaw when he was down. And now, like a serpent, her little quest for money with the checkbook was beginning to rear its ugly head.

When she heard the bathroom door open, she quickly folded the notices up and put them in a side pocket of her purse. She didn't know how she was going to do it, but she knew that she had to resolve this problem before Ronnie found out. She decided even though she had spent part of the cash, she would go and start paying back the stores that she had written the bad checks to.

A short amount of time had passed since she had heard the bathroom door and Ronnie still hadn't rejoined her in the living room, so she went to see what he was up to. She walked into the kitchen and she saw him leaning over the sink with a bowl of soup. He had just taken a sip from the bowl and now had a grimace of pain on his face that would come back to haunt her that night in her dreams. The look of agony on his face as he ate while looking absently out of the kitchen window made her sick to her stomach. It was at that instant that she realized she was no better than the man she had so despised when she was growing up.

She stood there looking at him and Ronnie turned his head and looked at her. At that instant, Margret no longer saw Ronnie standing there, but her own dead mother looking back at her. Blood was running from her mouth and down the front of the simple blue shift dress she was wearing. Margret's mother opened her bloody mouth and asked "Why?" When she said that, Margret saw something fly out of her mouth and land on the counter top. Margret looked down and saw in disgust what appeared to be the tip of her mothers tongue lying there in a small dollop of spit and blood. Margret just stood there with her eyes wide open in terror, she found that she didn't have anything to say in response. When she blinked her eyes, her mother was gone and Ronnie stood there as he had been the whole time. Slowly chewing and looking at her. Margret quickly looked down again and saw there was nothing on the counter top.

Ronnie had been standing there eating his lunch the best he could when he looked over and saw Margret standing there looking at him. To Ronnie, she had a strange wild look about her. He asked her what the problem was and started to get alarmed when she didn't answer him. He wasn't alarmed something had happened, but that she had finally slipped a gear and was about to commence attacking him. As he looked at her, he noticed it seemed she wasn't really looking at him because her eyes weren't focused on him. The second time he asked her what the problem was she seemed to come back to reality, but still didn't say anything.

Margret was horrified that she saw herself in her father's role and Ronnie was in her mother's role. She remembered growing up, alone and scared in her bed at night, as the fights raged on in the kitchen. The sound of things breaking, her father shouting and her mother sobbing. Every now and then she would hear the meaty slap of her father hitting her mother. She had vowed that this would not be the way for her when she got married. But now here she was and the vicious cycle was repeating itself. Except she wasn't the victim, but the tormentor. She quickly slapped a smile on her face when she noticed Ronnie looking at her strangely.

"I'm sorry, I was daydreaming. Did you say something dear?" She asked to cover herself.

"Not really, I just saw that you looked strange and was wondering if there was a problem."

"No. I was standing here watching you eat and I guess my mind wandered. Sorry."

"Nothing to be sorry about."

"Is there something that I can do for you?" She asked him and he shook his head no as he sipped from his bowl.

Saying nothing, Margret turned and walked out of the kitchen and went to check on Nancy. A few minutes later, Ronnie reappeared and asked her if she had paid Heather's parents for the overnight babysit. Without missing a beat while she was flipping the channels on the TV, Margret replied she didn't have any money when she went over there. Besides, she added, they had insisted that she owed them nothing.

As he walked to the door, Ronnie replied that the way to keep a good babysitter was to pay them whether they wanted the money or not and walked out the door. Looking through the window, Margret saw he was going next door.

Ronnie had been out of the house for less than a minute when the phone rang. The first call was from the grocery store's accounting office informing her, three of her checks had just been returned from the bank. And if she didn't mind, could she come by there sometime really soon and pay them the money she owed?

Margret was apologetic and courteous all over the phone to the lady who was calling her. She told her that her car was broken down right now, but as soon as it was fixed, tomorrow morning, she would be there to straighten things out. Margret then told the lady she just didn't understand how this could have happened, but that she would resolve this little faux pax just as soon as she could.

Almost as soon as she hung the phone up, it rang again. This time it was the bank calling to ask her if she had gotten her purse stolen or something because there seemed to be a lot of bad checks coming back with her signature on them. The young lady went on to explain in a very nice way that unfortunately, 'Free Checking' at her lending institution wasn't really free. Almost as an after thought, the young lady added that they really needed her to come down to the bank as quickly as possible to clear up this minor oversight. And as long as we're on the subject, the young lady told her with no emotion what so ever in her voice, that your account with us is frozen until we see you in person with some green in your hand. So please refrain from signing your name to any more paper with our name attached to it. Have a nice day!

Margret was about to have a panic attack Ronnie was going to come home and ask her who was on the phone. So she 'yes ma'amed' and 'you betted' to get the woman off of the phone as quickly as she could. Margret told her she was sooo sorry that this had happened and that it wouldn't happen again, but it would be tomorrow before she could get there because her car was broken. But not to worry, she would be there tomorrow afternoon for sure.

Margret got off the phone and just stood there with a 'phew' feeling when the phone rang for the third time. She nearly jumped out of her skin when the striker hit the bell inside the phone. Her first reaction was to turn the phone off but decided on the second ring to see who it was. This time it was Ted. Margret sounded breathless and scared as she started crying and was telling him she couldn't talk right now and she had to get off of the phone before Ronnie came home.

Ted told her not to worry about that asshole she was married to, and if he asked, just to tell him she was talking to one of her girlfriends. He went on to tell her after last night, he just had to call her and see what she was up to.

Margret was standing where she could see next door and saw the front door as it swung open. She quickly told Ted that Ronnie was on a rampage and he was coming back. She quickly added it wasn't safe and she would call him when it was. "Please don't call until you hear from me." she added with a begging quality to her voice and then hung up the phone.

She looked out through the window and saw Ronnie was crossing between the yards and then she looked back at the phone. She saw the ringer on-off switch and switched it to off. She didn't want to chance a fourth phone call when Ronnie was back in the house, her nerves couldn't take the strain. Once she was sure the phone was off, she quickly walked to the couch and sat down. She turned off the TV and picked up a magazine and started looking at the pictures, acting as if there was nothing going on.

When Ronnie walked back into the house, she asked him how it had gone and he told her even though they had insisted that they weren't owed anything, he had insisted that they take twenty-five dollars. Normally, Margret would have jumped on Ronnie about pissing away money when they had been told they owed nothing. But she knew it was better not to argue about this today. It was just Ronnie's nature to make sure that debts were paid. That way he felt that no one would be able to come back at a later time and pull some number about being owed for some favor done at an earlier date. She knew that was the way he was and usually got into an argument about it with him just for the sake of arguing.

Besides, her most pressing problem was to keep Ronnie from finding out about the creative financing she had been up to. At the very least, she hoped he wouldn't notice that the phone was turned off. As she was thinking about the phone, she remembered the phone up stairs. Without drawing attention to herself, she quietly and calmly went upstairs and turned that one off also. The rest of the afternoon went by pretty uneventful. Margret had one tense moment when she saw Ronnie heading for the kitchen and he stopped by the phone and was looking at something.

Her first reaction was he was looking at the phone itself and she felt the fear rise within her. But it turned out that he was just looking at a magazine laying beside it.

For Margret, time marched by too slowly and the day finally turned into night. For Ronnie, the afternoon wore slowly on also. He found that for some reason, he couldn't sleep during the day. There was nothing to do except veg with Margret watching TV. He tried to sleep, but it just wasn't going to happen. He even tried to play with the computer a couple of more times. But both times he turned it on, it still had the same 'DATA SORTING' message displayed on the screen and it wouldn't respond to anything he typed into the keyboard.

After the second time, Ronnie was afraid Fryer had broken more than himself during his nocturnal visit. That Fryer had done something to his computer before having his shockingly fatal accident. Ronnie was tired and decided it wasn't worth the brain power to deal with it. Around seven-thirty that evening he went upstairs to bed and finally dozed off.

36.

When Ted hung up the phone, he was torn between going over to Margret's neighborhood, finding her, and taking her away from her terrible life. Or doing the smart thing, facing up to the fact that she was just a convenient piece of tail he had grown to like. Down deep he knew there was really little he could do about her situation. He would be finishing flight school in a couple of months and the next two years of his life would not be conducive to dragging around a wife or girlfriend. Ted already knew most of the next two years would be spent aboard ship.

By instinct, Ted knew Margret would call him when she was able to. He reasoned that all he would accomplish by going to her neighborhood would be to draw attention to himself and possibly put Margret further into danger. Not to mention jeopardize his career in the military. Ted decided that for now, he would stay put and not do anything. But if the chance ever arose...He would put the scum she was married to in his place.

If Ted had known all of the facts and been able to view the entire situation from a distance when he hung the phone up that day, he would have never answered it again.

37.

When Max got to the station for duty that night, the first thing he did was check on the pathologist's report to see if it was back yet. It was. Max read that the coroner had found that Bernie had died from heat trauma to the head and heart as a result of electrocution. There was a brief description about how in addition to Bernie's head being fully cooked, there had been an electrical burn hole in the center of his chest going through to his spine. Bernie's heart, which had been in a direct line between the entrance hole and the contact point in the spine, had also been cooked solid. The coroner went on to speculate that there had been no foul play in this horrible accident. Max looked through his mail box and also found the report from his electrician friend was there. This report stated that there had been a severe malfunction of the circuit breaker that supplied the outlet that fried Bernie. The report went further to say that this was just an unfortunate accident waiting to happen due to the defective circuit breaker. Had Max's electrician friend been able to see Fryer's body, he would have quickly changed his conclusion.

Even though everything was one-plus-one-equals-two in front of Max, he had a gut feeling the correct answer was closer to three. On his way into the squad room for roll call, Captain Waters saw him and called him over.

"Afternoon Cap. How's it going?" Max said as he got into speaking range.

"Pretty good Max. The reason I called you over was to tell you the paperwork is back on Fryer."

"I know, I saw it already."

"Good. I guess you can close this one out. It looks like a simple case of Fryer breaking into this Fisher guy's house for some unknown reason and getting his balls toasted in the process. Wouldn't you say so?"

"You call the ball boss. That's just what I was thinking."

"Good. Finish out the paperwork and have it on my desk before you roll out tonight. Okay?"

"No problem, it's just about finished anyway. I was just waiting for those last two reports to come in before I signed my name on the dotted line."

After Max said that, Waters turned to the guy that was standing next to him concluding his conversation with Max. Max went on into the squad room and got ready for the briefing. He couldn't help but think there should be some way of letting Ronnie know that his wife was up to something other than her current height and weight.

When roll call got underway, Max forgot all about Ronnie and concentrated his efforts on tonights hot spots. He was supervising several cars tonight and needed to know where the areas were that he most likely would be in tonight. Which in this small town was no where, unless you counted keeping the teenagers from their usual parkin' and sparkin' spots and wearing out the parking lots of the eight fast food places during their endless cruising.

Max looked back at his own youth and remembered he was also one of those youths. Except in his day, it was Duce Coups and Roadsters. Big muscle street rods. Now days, it was just a bunch of pimply teenagers out in their momma's cars. Too inexperienced to really know how to drive. Max dreaded the nights when one of the local youth would decide they were one of the Andretti boys and end up stuck to a tree or telephone pole. Brick mailboxes did the trick too. It didn't happen very often, just once or twice a year. But it always seemed they would pick Max's shift to do it, leaving him the unpleasant task of finding the parents and explaining just how big of a splat their precious little Johnny made when he hit that tree at a hundred plus. The worst for Max was when there were passengers in the cars and he would have to find their parents also. Telling someone their child is dead because of something stupid they did was one thing, but having to face down a parent because they just happened to be along for the ride was another. Those were the worst and usually it was a date situation when little Johnny decided to show his ass trying to be bad, lose control of the car, find the immoveable object and not only waste his life but the life of the girl he was trying to impress.

38.

Ronnie slept for a long time before actually dreaming. There were smaller dreams, like the ones that everybody has throughout the night but can't remember the next morning. The only dreams worth counting are the ones that you remember the next day. It was almost two-fifteen in the morning when Ronnie accidentally woke Margret up as he got out of bed. She came half-awake and didn't remember it the next morning.

When Ronnie started dreaming, really dreaming, it was about one-thirty. When he became aware of his dream, he found himself standing in the wheel house of a small boat. He looked out through the front window and saw he was in what appeared to be quiet water. He looked down and saw he was actually piloting the boat himself. Looking back through the windows, he noticed for the first time that he was heading for a rock jetty. So he turned the boat and felt the rock and sway of the boat as it settled into its new course. Ronnie steered along the side of the jetty for awhile. He was really enjoying this, he never had much experience with boats but he always enjoyed what little exposure he had.

Looking around the cabin, Ronnie saw there was a door leading out onto the deck and it was open. He could see the bay he was sailing around the edge of and saw that it was immense. Looking the other way, he saw there was a door on either side of the cabin and they were both open. Outside one door he saw the rock jetty silently slipping by. Looking up at the top of the jetty, he could see sea foam shooting straight up as if huge waves were breaking on the other side of the rock wall. Ronnie looked down at the water on the opposite side of the boat and saw it was a light gray that matched the sky. Looking ahead at the jetty he saw the clouds were much darker on the other side of the wall. Almost black.

Since the boat was riding steady, Ronnie decided he wanted to go outside and see the rest of the boat. Looking down under the window, he saw a rope hanging down with a loop in the end. Acting like he had done it before, he put a bit of port lean to the wheel and hung the loop over one of the pegs. Standing there for a second to make sure the boat would keep true to it's course, he then stepped out through the door on the jetty side. The wind felt cold, raw, and moist on his face. He could hear the thundering roar of the surf's constant pounding on the other side of the sea wall. Breathing deeply, Ronnie could smell the briny fish smell that went with what he remembered as the sea.

Surveying his situation, Ronnie saw the catwalk he was standing on led around the wheel house to the other side. He followed it and as he was looking towards the stern, saw he was traveling on a small shrimp boat. The booms were down and he was dragging nets. Ronnie paid no real attention to this and just stood there looking at the bay he was traveling down the side of. As far as he could see straight out, there was nothing but calm water. Looking behind him, he could see what appeared to be the coastline, but it was too distant to recognize what coast it was. Ronnie quickly realized this wasn't just a jetty he was sailing down, but a huge sea wall to keep the ocean out and the immense bay calm.

He stood there on the deck mesmerized at the water he was passing and feeling the slight roll of the deck beneath his feet. Ronnie felt at peace, there was so much calm there and he wished that he could stay there forever. This was so much better than the high place he visited.

Ronnie came out of his trance and checked the progress of the boat to make sure he wasn't getting too close to the sea wall. Much to his displeasure, he saw he was headed straight for the sea wall. The boat hadn't turned, the sea wall had. He was sailing straight for the corner of the sea wall where it turned and paralleled the coast. He knew his speed and for some reason, he also knew the capabilities of this boat. Ronnie knew he was in trouble, especially dragging nets.

Ronnie jumped back into the wheel house and jerked the rope off the wheel. Grabbing one of the pegs on the lower right hand side of the wheel, he gave the wheel a healthy spin. The boat slowly started to turn and Ronnie kept the wheel spinning until the rudder hit the blocks, jerking the wheel to a stop. In a fluid movement he cut the throttle back and the boat slowed, but continued to turn. Ronnie didn't want to let the nets settle on the bottom, so after a second, he jammed the throttles forward to the stops. With relief he saw that although it would be close, he was going to miss the sea wall.

Ronnie quickly straightened the wheel out to resume his straight course and held his breath waiting for the boat to jerk to a stop from the nets fouling on the bottom.

The jerk never came.

He stood there wondering how he had known how to do all of this. The most experience he had at being on the water was the one summer he had spent as a kid with his grandfather on the coast. Ronnie had a warm happy feeling that went along with the memories of his grandfather. Grandpop had a small ten foot row boat they would go fishing in almost every weekend he was there. Ronnie was even allowed to drive the boat every now and then. The little fifteen horse power engine looked like something left over from World War 2. Grandpop always said, "She ain't fast, but she'll always get you there."

Ronnie thought, with some amusement, the weekend fishing trips were probably more for Grandpop's beer drinking entertainment than to foster Ronnie's nautical abilities. Ronnie felt some confusion about where he had acquired the knowledge he was using to run this vessel. He pondered that question as he forgot he was in a dream.

Now safe and secure in the knowledge that everything was safe and he had avoided disaster, he roped the wheel off and went back out onto the catwalk. He looked back over the stern and saw the corner he had just barely avoided decorating with the boat quickly retreating behind him. For the first time, he saw a second boat turn the corner and follow in his direction. Looking carefully, Ronnie saw that the other boat was almost identical to the one that he was on. The paint was different, but it was also dragging nets. In his mind, the other boat was of no concern, so he went back to admiring the calm water surrounding him.

Suddenly, the deck pitched as the hull of the boat glanced off of a post in the water and Ronnie lost his footing. Before he could react, he was over the railing and plummeting towards the water. He hit it and plunged below its surface. He felt the water and even tasted the salt it contained. He could feel the coldness of the water as it filled his clothes and ran next to his skin. Ronnie was frantically trying to get back to the surface and after a great deal of struggling, his head broke the surface. He was aware of two things as he sucked in a huge lung full of air. The first was just how heavy his clothes felt now that they were soaked with water. The boots on his feet felt like concrete blocks and he was becoming tangled in the yellow slicker he noticed for the first time that he was wearing. As he started swimming to the boat that was merrily cruising along on its own, Ronnie saw he wasn't going to make it back to the boat. He realized that second thing as the net boom passed over his head.

Ronnie calmed himself when he saw that by treading water, he could slowly make his way to the sea wall and climb up on it. It was only a couple of hundred feet away. So he waited for the boat to completely pass him by before starting the slow swim to safety.

Once the boat passed, Ronnie started swimming in earnest for the sea wall. Just when he felt he was starting to make some headway, he felt a steel cable hit him in the side, pulling him under. Horrified, Ronnie realized he was on the inside of the net. He tried to grab the cable as it spun him around, but he missed and the cable that held the nets to the boat started spinning him around and around. He became aware that now, not only was he spinning around, but he was also going deeper and deeper underwater. Ironically, he was more aware of the nausea that was being caused from the spinning motion than the salt water pouring down his throat and filling his lungs, drowning him.

Just as he started to lose consciousness, Ronnie found himself laying on his back on a very hard surface. Looking around, he saw that he was in some sort of abandoned warehouse, or so it appeared. The ceiling was very high and he could see huge, thick, wooden rafters supporting the second floor. He saw the walls around him were either brick or some type of ceramic block. As he looked at his surroundings, Ronnie now saw that the room he was in was in towards the center of the building and it was round. Although the lights he could see hanging down were off, the room was brightly lit. The ceiling above him was mainly made up of massive sky lights and they showed the day outside was bright and sunny, the sky was bright blue and cloudless. As he sat up he saw a stainless steel table was the hard surface he had been laying on. From his new position of half sitting with his elbows on the table behind him, he saw that the room he was in was at least seventy feet in diameter and was sectioned off by packing boxes stacked in make shift short walls.

Well, I'm glad to see that my patient is finally awake. A familiar voice from somewhere on the other side of the room said, startling Ronnie.

'Wha...Where am I?' Ronnie asked as he sat fully upright.

Whoa, don't go too fast. Let me help you.

Ronnie looked around and saw the Professor standing next to him dressed in a long, white lab coat. Ronnie suddenly realized that he was still dreaming and swung his legs over the edge of the table. When his feet touched the floor he nearly fell down, there was hardly any strength in his legs to hold himself up. It was the steady hand of the Professor holding Ronnie's arm that helped him get his footing.

'Thanks.' Ronnie mumbled, feeling very unsteady on his feet. He looked down towards his feet and saw the leg of the table he had just gotten off of. The stainless steel contrasted with the dark red tile on the floor. But Ronnie didn't notice that as much as he noticed how dirty the floor was. Piled next to the table leg were scraps of meat that had been lying on the floor so long they were beginning to look like jerky. Ronnie noticed a piece of what looked like rib bone with meat still attached. The bone had been neatly sawed on both ends as if it had been removed from something or someone. The meat on the rib bone also had the jerky look to it. Ronnie saw the ends of the bone were black and the overall bone had a varnished look. It seemed as if this particular specimen had been on the floor for time immortal.

Looking around, Ronnie saw there were specimens of this nature all over the place. As he surveyed the floor, he saw there was a trail, a clean place to walk, swept through the area he could see. It was as if this place was cared for by the laziest person around. Looking to where two of the box walls came together creating a corner, Ronnie saw there were fresh specimens of meat and dirt swept into that corner. Maggots also crawled around in the corner. Not a lot, just enough to repulse Ronnie with the fact they were there.

Ronnie brought his gaze back to the table that he had just gotten off. He saw that it was an autopsy table complete with a head block on one end and a drain in the other. Looking at the table he saw that it was the cleanest thing in the room.

He noticed that the drain wasn't hooked up to anything and there was a bucket hanging from a hook under the open hole in the table. Ronnie forced himself to look into the bucket and saw chunks of meat and congealed blood.

Ronnie felt an overwhelming sense of confusion sweep over him as his mind tried to adjust to his new surroundings. The last thing he remembered was being on the boat, or more correctly, being tossed overboard and drowning. The sudden change in realities was almost more than his mental state could take, a sort of reality shifting jet lag. He just couldn't comprehend how he had gotten from where he had been to where he was now.

You're in my world, remember? You're dreaming. The Professor said as if he were reading Ronnie's thought's.

'Where am I?' Ronnie stammered.

Damn, you're either just confused or stupid. Personally, I think you're stupid. As to how you got here, I brought you here. Your little nautical adventure was becoming very unproductive. Besides, there was something that I needed to remove from you.

'What are you talking about? You had to remove something? What was it?' Ronnie asked confused.

Simply this. The Professor said as he wheeled a surgical tray from behind where he was standing. He pulled the towel that was covering it off and held up a pair of hemostats. Clamped in it's jaws was a black piece of growth. It looked almost fetal in nature, but more evil, malevolent. It also looked vaguely familiar. Almost like someone Ronnie knew in a blackened misshapen growth.

'What is it?' Ronnie asked.

Just a small problem you had, but I removed it for you. Nothing to be concerned about really. The Professor said as he tossed the growth, hemostats and all, into the bucket. *You have a couple more of them, but they're nothing to be concerned about right now. Besides, I did this one for free. Do you know what a good doctor would cost?*

Ronnie looked back into the bucket one more time and knew the thing he had been looking at was somehow Bernie Fryer. He started to say something, but the Professor cut him off.

Like I said, there's nothing for you to be concerned about. There is a more important reason why I brought you here. There's something that I want to show you.

'And what is that?' Ronnie asked, he was beginning to feel better.

Awww...Always in a hurry to get to the point aren't you? You never want to slow down and have some fun.

'I can't imagine anything you would want to do as being fun. Besides, I'm really sick of your crap. You just pop in and out of my mind and my dreams as you damn well please.' Ronnie said without realizing he was raising his voice. He did know he was beginning to get angry. He realized that this was just a

197

dream, but now that he was here, he remembered all of the things the Professor had done to him in his dreams. He continued, 'You know, you have no right to interfere in my life. After all, you're dead. Aren't you supposed to be heading for the light or something like that?'

Look boy, The Professor yelled at him, clearly mad, *You are the last person to lecture on the sins of interference. Seem's like I was doing alright for myself when I was alive. But some little piece of cock dripping like you had to interfere with me. To butt in. Let me clue you into a small fact of life. I know you never exposed me to my faculty friends. But it was the argument we had in my office that was overheard.* The Professor had been pointing at Ronnie the whole time he had been talking and Ronnie realized that he was now floating a couple of inches off of the floor. Ronnie was mildly startled when he saw he was no longer earth bound. Still, the Professor continued to talk. *I had a life, until you came along. I never hurt anyone or even did anything with anyone that wasn't in a receptive frame of mind. But because of you, I was exposed and the threats made my life a living hell.*

Ronnie was about seven feet off of the floor now and was afraid that if the Professor let him fall, he would get hurt. So he quickly said, 'Look man, be cool. I didn't mean what I said. You said you wanted to show me something. What is it?'

Oh yeah, I forgot. The Professor said nonchalantly and snapped his fingers.

With that snap, they were no longer in the warehouse/morgue. They were now standing side by side on top of a concrete column. It was night and the area was lighted by street lights, the type you see on an interstate that light the big clover leaf exchanges. Ronnie was startled by their height and became momentarily disoriented. He became dizzy and almost fell from the beam they were standing on. Once again, the Professor came to the rescue and steadied him.

Ronnie was looking around and saw they were standing under an interstate overpass. Right under it, not more than what Ronnie guessed to be a foot over his head he could hear the cars going over him. He looked and saw the Professor had sat down and quickly followed suit to sit beside him. Ronnie saw they were sitting on top of a beam that was supported by a huge concrete column. On top of this beam was the concrete cross beams that actually supported the roadway. Even though it was night, Ronnie had to admit to himself that this was a moderately busy interstate. Cars were constantly going by on all sides of him. Over, behind, in front, and even under him. He sat there watching and listening to the melodic rhythms of the tires as they rode over the rough concrete.

After a few minutes the traffic started to wane along with Ronnie's interest. He found he was quickly becoming bored but decided not to say anything. Whatever it was that they were there to look at was keeping the Professor's attention. Which in Ronnie's view meant the Professor wasn't messing with him. That fact kept Ronnie's mouth shut quicker than his screaming boredom. The traffic was quickly thinning out and now there was just the occasional car passing by.

Another block of time passed and Ronnie's boredom won out and he asked, 'Why are we here? What are we going to do, play in the traffic? Spit on cars as they go by?'

Shhh. The Professor said as he put a finger to his lips. *You'll see. Any second now.* looking off into the darkness, he added, *There. Here it comes now. Watch.*

Ronnie looked off in the darkness in the direction the Professor was but didn't see anything. 'What are you looking at?' He asked.

That. The Professor said as he pointed to a pair of headlights as they topped the plateau the over pass was on.

Ronnie watched the headlights as they steadily grew closer. They had topped the hill a long way off and even at interstate speeds it took a long time for the car to reach the nocturnal illumination of the interchange lamps. A turn signal came on and the car headed for the off ramp that would take it under the overpass and then turn right.

Ronnie quickly realized that the speed of the car was too great for ramp. He watched in horror as the car seemed to speed up as it approached the curve and continued straight. The outside of the curve had a good sized amount of upward tilt to it and the car ramped up as it headed straight into the guard rail and through it. The car's brake lights were on the whole time but never slowing down. In fact, to Ronnie, it seemed like at the very last instant before the car hit the railing it was as if whoever was driving this car had floored the accelerator.

The car sailed through the air in a straight line. That last little burst of speed really helped to get some air and distance. Ronnie could see liquid spilling from the rear of the car from where one of the cement guard rail supports had punched a hole through the steel gas tank. He could see the car was beginning to lose altitude in its nose-heavy trajectory and was heading for the ground, nose first.

The car hit the ground with a tremendous thud, smashing the hood and the front wheels almost back to the windshield. Now a slave to it's momentum, the car continued forward, flipping onto its roof. As the roll continued and the weight of the vehicle crushed the trunk area, Ronnie thought it was going to be able to make one more loop as he watched the car stand straight up on it's rear bumper. But the car had lost a lot of its momentum when it had crashed into the swampy soft island of ground trapped in the interstate interchange. Ronnie saw the car actually stand on it's rear bumper for two long seconds before settling back onto its roof.

The gasoline that had been flying through the air with the car had fallen all over the ground before the car had settled back onto it, wheels up.

Ronnie couldn't believe what he had just seen and commented about it to the Professor.

Wait. The best is yet to come. The Professor replied as he sat watching the spectacle.

Ronnie returned his attention to the wrecked car and sat there looking at it. He felt powerless to do anything about what he had just seen because of his high perch under the overpass. Then he saw movement and realized that something was slowly falling out of the area where the engine had been. Straining to see in the illuminated darkness, he saw a spark from the thing that was falling. Ronnie instantly realized that it was the battery falling.

Instantly, Ronnie could see up close and he now found himself watching the chain of events unfolding from only a few feet away, directly in front of the upside down car. He watched the battery slowly fall out of the crushed engine compartment.

The battery itself was crushed. Its manufactures never intended it to support the full weight of the car multiplied by G force and not have the casing split. But there was still some juice in it. That baby was designed to get one last start out after you left your car parked on the dark side of the moon for a month with the lights and radio on. It was guaranteed to start your car on the first time. Every time. Ronnie watched as the battery, void of any water and much lighter now, slowly dropped as the heavy cables unfolded and let the battery head for the ground. The battery landed on the ground partially on top of what was left of the hood. Another spark formed as the positive battery cable, broken by the crash and then the batteries fall from it's resting position inside the engine compartment, pulled loose. It dropped and made contact on the metal hood.

The minute spark created by the contact with the metal hood, ignited the gas fumes on the ground and the fire spread quickly.

Ronnie found himself back at the high vantage point under the overpass. He watched as the flames crawled up the engine compartment and began running up the undercarriage until it hit the gas tank itself. The fireball was tremendous. Even as far away as he was, Ronnie still felt the soft hot push from the blast and then he noticed the wind shift as the air rushed back towards the center of the blast area. The fire as well as the heat was tremendous. Ronnie could hear glass breaking and after a minute, there was a muffled explosion inside of the car.

A can of Root Beer had been floating around in the back seat of the car for a couple of months, after flying around the interior of the car and bouncing off things, was full of pressure and couldn't take the intense heat anymore. It became a pressure bomb. The explosion shredded what was left of the front seat that it had ended up under, after making its rounds of flying around the interior. The soda inside the can that hadn't turned to foam the instant it was released from its confines, partially put out the fire in the interior of the car. As the fire began to reclaim the area the Root Beer had put out, the sugar in the soda caramelized and caused the fire to burn hotter.

'Why did you show me this?' Ronnie asked as he looked over at the Professor.

Didn't you find it amusing? I thought it was splendid!

'You would, you bastard.' Ronnie replied sharply.

Watch your mouth boy. Remember, if you dream you are falling and don't wake up before you hit the ground, you die. I could easily push you off.

'You could, but I don't think you will. You need me. So...Is this why you brought me here? To watch a car wreck?' Ronnie replied, his tone much tamer.

Damn. You're no fun. I guess that this little display was wasted on you. We have one more stop to make before we get down to work. The Professor said as he snapped his fingers and once again their location changed.

Ronnie found himself sitting on the floor of the liquor store. He stood up but didn't see the Professor anywhere. Then he heard a bottle break. He followed the sound around the corner and found the Professor chugging a bottle of Bourbon. When the bottle was empty the Professor dropped it to the floor where it broke when it landed on the previous bottle.

Have some. The Professor invited Ronnie.

'No thanks. You know damn well I don't drink anymore, why do you insist on continuing to bring me here?'

Because, The Professor said as he leaned real close to Ronnie's face, *This is one of the few places I enjoy out of your pathetic little life.* The smell of liquor on the Professor's breath was beginning to make Ronnie's eyes tear.

'This isn't my place. I never went to a place that was this filthy.'

Yes you did. You just never really saw it in its true light. Sometimes a drink will cloud your eyes. But I don't have to tell you that, now do I? Look around boy. Do you think that you're just looking at dirt on the floor? Grime on the windows? Crawly things all around? No...That's not what you're seeing. The grime on the windows is the clouded dreams of a drunkard. The dirt on the floor is ambition when it is abandoned. And of course, that makes the crawly things all around Hope...Hope that has been lost. So you see, every liquor store really looks like this. You just gotta open your eyes. You have to learn how to look and really see things for what they really are.

'I really hate to say this, but I understand what you're saying. It makes sense to me.' Ronnie replied thoughtfully.

Yeah? Well, it's too bad you don't have any more refined memories. But I guess this will have to do. Damn, I sure do miss this stuff. The Professor remarked as he picked up another bottle.

Ronnie looked down and saw it was a bottle of Martell Cardon Bleu Cognac. So, his specter liked the finer, higher dollar spirits. Ronnie thought to himself.

Unlike the rest of the bottles the Professor had picked up, he didn't immediately open the bottle and start drinking. Instead, he carried the bottle with him as he walked back towards the front of the store.

'So...What now boss?' Ronnie asked as he followed the Professor.

Well, The Professor answered as he stopped walking, *We have a lot of work to do at your house. I have a surprise for you. We need to get there soon.*

'What kind of surprise?'

You'll see. Now go back and meet me downstairs.

'Go back where?'

Listen stupid...Let me think, I guess I should have said wake up and meet me downstairs at the computer.

'Okay, but tell me why, first.'

I bet you're a lot of fun on your birthdays and Christmas. Tell me what you got me. Tell me. Tell me. Tell me. The professor cried, mocking Ronnie. Then he added, *Just get your sorry ass downstairs.*

The Professor snapped his fingers again and Ronnie's eyes opened. He was still lying in bed. Margret was lying next to him, snoring loudly. At first Ronnie was just going to lie there and go back to sleep. But he heard a voice drift up from downstairs.

Ronnie, get down here. There's work to be done.

Ronnie sat up in the bed and rubbed his eyes. Debating for a moment, he carefully crawled out of bed trying not to wake Margret up. When he was just about out of bed, he accidentally bumped her foot and she stirred, partially waking up.

"Wha...What's going on?" Her sleepy voice asked.

"Bathroom." Was all he said and she rolled over. A few seconds later she resumed snoring, this time louder.

When Ronnie was satisfied she was still asleep, he resumed his path to downstairs, heading for the computer and the Professor. As quietly as possible, Ronnie went down the staircase and found the Professor sitting on a table chair he had placed next to the computer. Ronnie walked over and sat down at the desk.

About time. The Professor remarked.

"Hey, I'm here. What now?"

Turn the computer on and I'll show you.

"The computer has been locked up all day, it won't work. It wouldn't work for me earlier."

That's because I was busy and didn't have time to play with you. Now turn the damn thing on so we can get busy.

Ronnie reached behind the computer and flipped the power switch on. After a half a minute the screen came on and the message 'MEMORY FULL' appeared.

"What now?" Ronnie asked.

You got paper for the printer?

"Yes."

Then load it in. We have a lot of things to print tonight.
"If you say so. Why is the memory full?"
You'll see once we start printing.

Ronnie loaded the printer with as much paper as it would hold. The Professor then directed Ronnie through different files and showed him which ones to dump to the printer. Ronnie noticed that instead of file names, the majority of the memory was filled with dates. The Professor showed Ronnie how to group the files and the printing job started.

Looking over, Ronnie saw the Professor had opened the bottle of Cognac and was sipping it. He offered the bottle to Ronnie, but Ronnie just frowned and shook his head no. The Professor shrugged and went back to sipping from the bottle and looking at the computer screen. Ronnie looked at the screen and saw pages of text quickly flashing across the screen. He looked at the paper hopper and saw the blank pieces of paper disappearing one after another. The printed pages were piling up in the printer exit tray.

"What is all this stuff?" Ronnie asked.

This my boy, is Bernie Fryer's life. Or at least, the good parts. I kind of borrowed his memories last night and I arranged them so they could be printed off.

"You borrowed his memories?" Ronnie asked in a tone of voice that was a cross between sarcasm and disbelief.

Okay, if you want to be like that, I took them. Is that better? Besides, he wasn't going to use them anymore.

"You took his memories? I can't believe it. How did you do it?"

You don't want to know. Besides, there's so much stuff here. Juicy stuff. Old Gabby Gasbag has got a load of ripe stuff here.

"I don't believe you. I'm not going to write a bunch of columns from the memories of a dead guy."

Get over it. You will write what I allow you to write. Besides, like I said, there's some real juicy stuff here. And as an added bonus, the columns are already written. Wait until you read them. Then you can tell me you won't use them. Not that it will really do any good to tell me what you think.

"How did you get his memories?" Ronnie asked persistently.

Let's just say I traded for them.

"Traded what?"

He gave me his knowledge and I gave him some power. About ten kilowatts worth of power I think. Sorry...But I think your electric bill is going to be a tad higher this month. But hey, we all gotta give something in the pursuit of dirty laundry. And believe me, this laundry is the dirtiest I've ever seen.

Ronnie saw the printer had stopped and he loaded more paper into it. Pressing the enter key, the printer resumed it's task. Ronnie just sat there for awhile reloading the printer and watching the Professor type on the keyboard.

Ronnie also made sure the pages didn't accumulate under the paper exit as they were coming out. Every now and then the Professor stopped typing and took a sip from the bottle of Cognac.

Finally, the Professor stopped typing and sat back. He took the bottle off of the desk and took the cap off. Ronnie noticed the swallows were deep and long as the Professor drank. When he was finished, the Professor let out a foul smelling burp and looked at Ronnie.

I guess we're about finished for tonight. Why don't you go back to bed? You still have to get up in the morning for work.

"Do you want me to turn the computer off?"

No. You can leave it on. I can turn it off, I just can't turn it on yet. Now go to bed.

Ronnie opened his eyes, waking up, and found himself sitting alone at the computer in the dark. He felt half asleep as he looked down and saw his hands on the keyboard, his fingers were sore and there was a pile of paper next to the printer. The printer was still spitting paper out. Ronnie got up from the chair and went back upstairs. This time crawling over Margret without bother or concern as to whether he was going to wake her or not. Once he was back in bed, he went instantly back asleep.

In the morning, the alarm clock went off heinously early. Ronnie woke just before the alarm went off feeling fresh and revived. It seemed that it had been a long time since he had slept so soundly. As he stumbled to the bathroom in the dark, he thought about the dreams he had last night, they had been so vivid and real. Thinking about them, he decided that they had just been dreams. If he had been up most of the night like he had dreamed that he had been, then he would be bone tired right now.

After Ronnie finished showering and getting dressed, he went downstairs and found the computer off. Or at least it sounded off, Ronnie didn't hear the printer running as he walked down the stairs. He had half expected to find it on and when he saw that the monitor was off he felt a wave of relief sweep over him. So it had been just a dream after all, Ronnie thought to himself. But he froze in his tracks when he saw the pile of paper stacked neatly on the other side of the computer next to the paper output slot of the printer.

Turning a light on because it was still dark in the living room, Ronnie picked up a couple of pages and looked at them. At the top of each page was a date and the sheet was filled with what appeared to be a blow by blow description of everything that someone had done during a one day time period.

Looking at the pile of paper, Ronnie saw there was easily seven or eight hundred sheets of paper there. He stood there in disbelief of what he saw. He felt so good, so rested. How could he have stayed up all night? He laid his hand on top of the computer and found it was still warm. Ronnie looked at the top of the desk to see if the Professor's bottle of Cognac was sitting beside the computer, but he found nothing.

Well, at least I dreamed something. Ronnie thought to himself. Then he decided the Professor had probably taken the bottle with him. He smiled to himself and shook the thought off. Ronnie quickly gathered the sheets of paper, looking for a place to stash them, he opened the bottom desk drawer and found the bottle of Cognac there. Ronnie froze in his tracks, temporarily blinded by indecision. He couldn't believe he was actually looking at the bottle the Professor had snagged out of his dream. Ronnie's first impulse was to take the bottle and pour it down the kitchen sink.

Ronnie decided better of it. He didn't want to go back to the liquor store again with the Professor. And that was exactly what would happen if the Professor found his booze missing.

So he just sat the stack of paper in the drawer next to the bottle and shut the drawer. Looking at his watch, Ronnie saw that it was getting close to the time to leave for work. He went into the kitchen and made himself a quick breakfast before he left. Even though the day had a few rocky moments right off in the beginning, the rest of the day was much better.

39.

A couple of hours after Ronnie left for work, Avery left for the paper. It had been a long and sleepless night. His paranoia had run rampart all of yesterday and ALL of last night. Every time the phone rang, he thought it was hit men calling to check and see if he was home. When the pizza man came after his mother had called and ordered dinner, he just about had a heart attack when he heard the knock on the front door. Looking out his window, he saw a strange car parked outside.

When Avery finally arrived at the paper, he set about his morning tasks without his usual enthusiasm and juvenile mouth running he normally attacked his tasks with. Sure, he liked to screw around whenever possible, but he also knew the boss couldn't yell at you when you looked like you were doing your job. Besides, today he didn't feel like screwing around. He was dead tired and afraid to go to sleep. He just wanted to lay low and not let anyone even notice he was there. A couple of hours passed and even the typesetter commented to the printer on how quiet Avery was this morning. The printer just smiled and commented it was good to have the little kiss-ass out of his hair for once. The typesetter laughed and nodded his head in agreement before returning to his task of laying out the type on tomorrow's stories.

Forty minutes later over coffee, the printer commented to Aaron that there was something wrong with Avery. Aaron told the man thanks and said he would check into it. Aaron knew that the press was no place to be if you couldn't keep your mind directly on your task. A running press was a place that you could easily loose a finger, an arm, a life, if you didn't pay attention. The last thing Aaron wanted to do was use a piece of Avery as ink for a couple of thousand copies of whatever they happened to be running at the time.

After the printer left, Aaron snickered to himself that he guessed the kid had gotten his message after all. He wondered silently just how far he should let this form of torture go. Aaron decided that it could go on for a bit. The presses wouldn't be running until later this afternoon and he would let Avery stew in his own juices for awhile longer. Then, just before they started the presses, he would cut the kid some slack and let him go home early.

Aaron took a stroll around the office and found Avery dumping trash into the dumpster outside. Standing where he couldn't be seen on the loading dock, he watched Avery as he set about his task. Aaron noted to himself that the kid looked jumpy as hell. About then a motorcycle with an impossibly loud muffler cranked up across the street with an explosive roar.

Aaron could swear he saw Avery turn blue from the lack of oxygen from not breathing. Just as it looked like the kid was beginning to swoon, he explosively inhaled and gripped the edge of the metal container to steady himself. When Avery turned around, Aaron saw that the kid was crying.

Aaron quickly retreated so he wouldn't be seen and went straight back to his office. He knew letting Avery stew in his own juices was one thing, but humiliating the kid by being seen watching as the emotional break down was going on was beyond how far Aaron would let this go.

Another hour passed and Aaron summoned Avery into his office. Once the kid was seated across from him, Aaron saw just how bad Avery looked. There were deep, dark circles under his eyes from the lack of sleep and his hands were shaking slightly. Trying to decide which approach to take with Avery, Aaron decided to be direct and let the kid off as easy as possible.

"How you feeling today Sport?"

"Fine sir. Why do you ask?" Avery replied respectfully.

"You seem to be under the weather or something today. You having troubles at home?" Aaron asked in a consoling tone.

"Not that I can think of."

"Have trouble sleeping last night?" Aaron asked flat out.

Avery just sat there as if he wanted to say something but his mouth just moved with nothing coming out.

"Look kid, I've been in this business a long time. You're not the first person I've seen that was scared turdless because they were afraid some mafia asshole was going to show up and ventilate them." when he said that, Aaron could tell he had hit the nail right on the head. The expression on Avery's face told the whole story and Aaron read it word for word.

"But..." Avery started to say, but Aaron held up his hand and cut him short.

"Let me finish. Like I said, you're not the first. There is a bright side and let me assure you, there is one here. You're just too young and inexperienced to know what it is. Anyway, the bright side is, if these guys, professionals and don't make the mistake to kid yourself they weren't, were after you, you wouldn't have survived last night."

"Are you sure about that?" Avery asked relieved but wanting Aaron's reassurance.

"Hell yes. These types of guys are very professional. They have to be, their very life depends on it. You either take care of business when you have to or you will get taken care of. Believe me, if old Bernie so much as even thought your name while they were playing with him, their next stop would have been your house until you got home. Or as early enough in the evening as it was, they most likely would have done you and your family while you were sleeping."

"So you're telling me the danger has passed?" Avery inquired looking very much relieved.

"Probably..." Aaron said and then paused, acting like he was deep in thought. He continued speaking when he saw the dramatic pause had dampened Avery's spirit a bit. "Yeah, you're going to be alright. They wouldn't have waited this long. Two people in one day would be too much for this little town not to notice. A body a day would be more like their pace. So I guess since you survived last night, you should be safe today."

Avery sat there for a moment thinking about this and realized that if McGuire knew all of this information, he must have sent him home on purpose yesterday. So he said, "May I ask you a question?"

"Sure kid, anything."

"If you knew all of this, why did you send me home yesterday without warning me?"

"I don't quite follow you."

"You sent me home knowing I might get killed and didn't tell me?" Avery asked, starting to sound upset.

"Simple. Every man must face his own destiny alone. If you had hid out last night, you wouldn't now know for sure they're not looking for you. Besides, if you had bought it here at the paper, somebody else might have gotten hurt also. Not to mention all of the paperwork I'd have to fill out because of your death." When Aaron finished speaking, he leaned back in his worn leather chair and folded his hands together over his belly.

Avery sat there digesting this new information for a couple of moments before he spoke, "I guess I can understand what you're telling me. Basically, a person can't run away from their problems and you were protecting the other people that work for you."

"Welcome to manhood boy. Look, let me do something for you. Go home, eat something and go to bed. Come back tomorrow ready to work and we'll all take life one day at a time. Okay?"

"Thanks, I will." Avery said as he was getting up from the chair.

Aaron didn't say anything as Avery left his office. What could he say? He had just finished laying out a huge pile of manure and Avery had wallowed in it. The seeds Aaron had planted would follow Avery all through his life and eventually mold him into the person he would become. After thinking about it, Aaron decided that theory was probably crap also. Avery would just end up being some middle class ass-kisser with a load of bills and a belly full of ulcers. Aaron did realize whatever happened to Avery, this little experience would be a major factor in shaping his life.

Aaron also knew he deserved an academy award for the performance he had given in front of the kid. It had been hard enough to keep a straight face when he had confronted Avery the first time about Gabby's mafia connection, but when Aaron had him in his office this last time, he found it damn near impossible to keep from laughing and telling Avery the main fear he had been running from all night was himself. As Roosevelt had said in 1933, 'The only thing we have to fear, is fear itself.' Aaron knew that sometimes, fear is a very powerful motivating factor.

40.

It was around ten in the morning when Ronnie decided he needed to call home. He didn't know why, but he just had one of those gut feelings he should. The first time he called the line was busy. So he thought nothing of it and called back about fifteen minutes later. This time the phone rang and Margret sounded upset when she answered it. She wasn't crying or anything like that, but Ronnie could hear it in her voice.

"Margret, is everything okay?" He asked her.

"Of course." She replied flatly.

What Ronnie didn't know and Margret wouldn't tell him, was she had been fielding telephone calls all morning from stores wanting to know when she was going to come in and take care of all of her bad checks. She was trying to figure out how she was going to get to the places to pay them back when the phone rang one more time. Margret debated whether or not she should answer it, but curiosity got the better of her and she picked up the phone.

This call seemed to be like all the rest she had been getting all morning, asking when she could come and clear up the small money matter that had occurred. But this call, unlike all of the rest, added an element Margret had not even considered nor heard of. The lady Margret was speaking to mentioned that in addition to the face amount of the checks themselves, there was an additional charge of fifteen dollars per check. Margret's blood froze in her veins as she asked what the woman was talking about. The woman explained that not unlike other stores, they also had a bad check charge that was assessed to each check. When Margret inquired about the other stores having this charge she was told that 'Oh yes, everybody has these charges now-a-days.'.

When she got off of the phone, Margret was overwhelmed at the fact that now, not only did she owe for the checks, but all of the stores were tacking on extra to what she owed. She had spent some of the money and didn't have enough to pay back just the face amounts of the checks, let alone the extra fees. Margret stood there next to the telephone not really knowing what to do when Ronnie called. She did know she had to start paying back what she owed as soon as possible to keep Ronnie from finding out what she had done.

After Margret assured Ronnie there was nothing wrong, she mentioned that she needed to go grocery shopping so they would have food for supper. Ronnie told her he would be happy to bring her the car at lunch time, but she would have to bring him back to work and then pick him up at the end of the day. She told him there was no problem with that arrangement and would be ready to go as soon as he got there.

Margret was ready to go when Ronnie arrived, she had even made him a lunch to take back with him. Nancy played in the carseat as Ronnie drove back to the Country Club. Everyone seemed to be in good spirits. Ronnie could tell something was wrong though, Margret seemed to be real jumpy. Maybe she had been on the phone telling her boyfriend Ted to take a walk and it hadn't gone well, Ronnie thought to himself. He almost mentioned it but decided that it might be better to let sleeping dogs lie and passed over the subject. When they arrived at the club, Ronnie kissed Nancy good bye and told Margret not to be late. She assured him she would be on time and drove off. Ronnie then turned and went into the break room of the shack and ate his lunch, something he hadn't done in a long time.

Margret went to the first couple of stores she had visited and paid the bad checks she had there. She found out there was indeed a bad check charge and paid it also. Margret realized there was no way she could come up with the money to pay for all of her checks and the check charges also. Margret knew she had to think of a way to come up with the extra money or Ronnie was going to find out about this whole check incident. It was at the third store that Margret thought she had found her salvation.

41.

The state was trying to legalize gambling and the grocery store Margret was in had just installed video poker machines. It was a quarter a play and you could up the ante by pumping more quarters into the machine for a maximum bet of five dollars. In the first three hands, Margret had taken five dollars and tripled it. At last, Margret thought, she had found her savior. Then she hit a long losing streak and before she knew it, she was down almost two hundred dollars. But she kept playing, going over to the change cage time after time to buy another roll of quarters. She just knew the losing streak she was on would end soon and she would be riding high again.

The change of luck never came and by the time Margret was done, she had lost over half of the money she had been holding. Feeling depressed, Margret went and quickly bought a few groceries to make dinner with. On her way out of the store she stopped at the service desk and paid the checks she had floated at that store. As she paid for the checks, her depression seemed to deepen. When the clerk tallied the check charges, Margret realized just how little money she had left. She felt helpless and frightened.

As Margret was driving home to put away the groceries she had bought, she decided her luck had just been bad today. Today's performance didn't mean her luck would be bad all of the time. Hell, she could even go back later tonight and have better luck. Or better yet, she could have just moved to another machine when she felt like her luck had run out on the particular machine she was playing. The rest of the trip home, Margret was in much better spirits and there was a strategy session going on inside her head that would have made any General of any Army envious. This quickly overcame the depression she had felt inside the store, it also helped her to rationalize away the fact she had just pissed away a lot of money that wasn't really hers on chance and a video game.

Instead of concentrating her efforts on trying to plan her playing strategy, she should have placed more emphasis on actually learning the game of poker. The mistakes she made at the video game were grievous. She would get a pair of three's and up the ante to five dollars. Then she would throw away three cards and play a blind double. A blind double is where she pumped in another five

212

dollars for a maximum bet of ten dollars before she could look at the new cards she had been dealt. If she had won one of these rounds, the payoff would have been twenty dollars. But not knowing when to hold or fold, Margret had spent her afternoon donating money to the machine.

Time got away from Margret at the house and by the time she realized what time it was, she was already thirty minutes late to pick up Ronnie. Rushing around, she grabbed Nancy and headed straight out the front door. Fifteen minutes later she was at the Country Club and found Ronnie waiting for her at the entrance.

Ronnie was furious, but he didn't say anything. Margret offered a weak excuse for being late, but Ronnie paid no attention and just glossed over her apology. He told her not to worry about it. What he didn't tell her was he had never expected her to show up at all. Let alone late.

But he had waited, at first just to see how late she would be. Then he decided that if an hour passed, he would walk home and righteously kick her ass. While Ronnie was sitting there he imagined she wasn't even at home at all, but off with Ted getting one more in for old times. Ronnie began to fantasize about Ted and Margret's last conversation. 'So sorry I have to go and I can't see you anymore, so here's something to remember me by.' he wondered just how far they got before the clothes hit the floor.

Ronnie was deeply engrossed in his thoughts when Margret finally pulled up. He was going to confront her with her indiscretion, but when he saw Nancy sitting safely buckled into her carseat in the rear, he knew Margret hadn't been with Ted. Ronnie knew Margret wouldn't have taken Nancy with her. That would take away from her illusion that she was free to do what ever she felt like. When it comes to love, children are the big inhibitor.

Or, at least, is what Ronnie had learned from her. On the few times he had approached Margret on the subject of sex (which was when he saw that she was in a good mood), she would stave him off by telling him she was too tired from chasing Nancy all day. Or dealing with Nancy had given her a headache. So the probability she had taken Nancy with her on an erotic rendezvous was nil.

Margret told Ronnie she had gone home after she had dropped him off at work and went shopping later. Margret then bemoaned the fact the checkout girl was the slowest thing she had ever seen on the planet. Why, she had just gotten home when she realized what time it was and came straight to get him.

To Ronnie, the story was plausible enough. He did know how Margret sometimes lost track of time. As he sat there mulling over that last thought, Margret continued to drone on about things that had kept her from being on time. Ronnie was thinking Margret did lose track of time when she was doing something she wanted to do. But if he was into something, Margret watched the seconds pass by like she was the grand time-keeper of the world.

Ronnie remembered one time when they had gone to the mall shopping. Margret spent almost three hours trying on dresses and clothes. As they were leaving the mall, Ronnie remembered that he needed a wood file and went to the tool department with Margret in tow. Two minutes had passed before she started up about him taking too long. Then she almost had a hemorrhage because it took them a full five minutes to find the tool and get checked out.

On that particular ride home, Margret had dogged him unmercifully about the four dollars he had spent on the file. Ronnie thought back with clarity how he had fought back the urge to mention something about the hundred and fifty dollars she had spent on her clothes. Looking back now, he knew he had done the right thing by not mentioning it, but he also realized if he had stood up to her back then, maybe she wouldn't be the raving bitch she was, sometimes, most times, now.

After they got home, Margret put Nancy into her playpen, then went and quickly cooked dinner while Ronnie took a shower and changed clothes. When he came back downstairs, she was still cooking so he went over to the computer and turned it on. After waiting for it to warm up, it came on with the message 'COMPILING DATA'. After punching a few keys, Ronnie quickly saw nothing seemed to work and he turned it back off.

He sat there for a couple of moments and then opened the bottom desk drawer. Ronnie saw the stack of paper still lying there in the drawer undisturbed. Looking further back in the drawer, he saw the half empty bottle of Cognac still there. Reaching inside the drawer, he peeled about two inches of paper from the top of the stack. Looking around like a school kid sneaking a look at his father's collection of Playboys, he began reading the pages of paper in front of him.

Ronnie was amazed at the amount of detail contained on those pages. He read through them quickly and saw they were the last few days of Fryer's life. As he neared the last few pages, he saw the blow by blow chain of events that led up to Fryer's death. Ronnie read about the meetings with Avery and how this Avery guy had sold Ronnie out for a thousand dollars. He continued to read about how Fryer had waited for him and then frustrated, broke into the house. To Ronnie's amazement, he read how the electrical shock had not come from the wall outlet as he believed it had, but had originated from the computer itself.

At least Ronnie now knew how he was found out and by whom. He was contemplating whether he should call Aaron and inform him of this new found information when Margret announced dinner was ready. Ronnie quickly restacked the paper and returned it to the drawer. He then went over to the table to see what culinary delights Margret had whipped up in the kitchen. To his disappointment, he saw it was another macaroni-n-cheese and hotdog kind of a night. Ronnie knew that he could always count on her to put the same thing out, time and time again.

During dinner Margret announced she had been thinking about going back to work. Ronnie was stunned and couldn't think of a reply when she hit him with the second part of her plan. Margret informed him she needed the car to go job hunting tomorrow if he didn't mind. Of course she would take him to work and pick him up, on time, she promised, if she could use the car. Ronnie, still in a state of shock because he had figured she would never go back to work again, stammered that it was okay with him. He then asked her what had led her to this decision and she told him she just wanted to help out with the bills. She also added it wasn't fair that he should have to shoulder the entire burden himself. Besides, she had heard about a good paying job as a waitress on the other side of town and she wanted to check it out.

Ronnie agreed that if that was what she wanted to do, he would support her decision all the way. He also added that now with the writing job and his promotion at the Country Club, they weren't going to be financially hard off for very much longer. But if that was what she really wanted to do, then she should go for it.

The rest of the night was uneventful and Ronnie tried one more time to use the computer, once again he got the 'COMPILING DATA' message. Frustrated, he turned the computer off and watched tv until it was time to go to bed.

As Ronnie slept, he was dreamless until around two in the morning. This time when the dream started, Ronnie found himself sitting down in front of the computer and the Professor was sitting next to him. As Ronnie looked around the living room, he noticed everything had the surreal clarity only found in the dream state. The Professor said nothing and only pointed to the computer itself. Reluctantly, Ronnie reached behind the computer and turned it on. It wasn't until the screen came on that the Professor spoke for the first time. Ronnie noticed that before the computer came on, the Professor seemed to be looking for something.

Okay, The Professor said as the screen lit up, *What did you do with it?*

'What are you talking about?' Ronnie asked, not knowing what was being looked for.

My bottle of Cognac. Where did you hide it?

'You're supposed to be all knowing. Find it yourself.' Ronnie told him. Since Ronnie wasn't the one who put the bottle into the desk drawer, he felt no obligation to let the Professor know where it was.

We don't have time for hide and seek tonight. We have a lot of work to do. Just tell me where it is.

'No.'

Okay smartass, tell you what, I'll just find it myself.

'Give it your best shot.' Ronnie replied glibly. He figured if the Professor had to ask and couldn't remember where he had put his own bottle, then he wasn't as powerful as he thought he was.

215

Without bothering to reply, the Professor reached down and opened the bottom desk drawer. He flashed Ronnie a big toothy grin that had the hint of steel as he reached in and pulled the bottle out.

'If you knew it was there all along why did you ask where it was?' Ronnie asked as he watched the Professor unscrew the top from the bottle.

To see just how big of an asshole you are.

'Like I really need this shit from you...'

Actually, The Professor said, cutting Ronnie off, *You really do need this shit. You won't believe what I've been up to.*

'What have you been up to?'

You know all of the stuff I got from your friend? Well, I've been going through it and you won't believe the things I've found. It looks like we have a best selling book on our hands here. Not to mention almost six months worth of columns for your newspaper buddy. The Professor stopped talking and took a long pull from the bottle he was holding. Before he spoke again he belched.

Ronnie could almost see the green cloud of fumes heading his way before it actually got to him. The smell was putrid and made his nose run and his eyes sting. 'God damn!!' Ronnie cried as he leaned back trying to find some clean air to breath.

Sorry about that. The Professor offered and then started speaking. *It seems like your friend wasn't as clean as the driven snow. In fact, he was dirtier than a honey wagon driver who has fallen into his work.*

'How about cutting through the crap and just giving me the readers digest version.' Ronnie replied as he sought fresh air. The green cloud of fumes was taking its time to dissipate.

You really must learn some patience. But if you insist, I will give you a synopsis of what I found. It seems like Mr. Fryer had a small coke business on the side. Not only did he have some of the more prominent town citizens as customers, but also a Congressman and some folks in state government. Coke wasn't the only thing he was into either. Seems like he was a major player in a fraud scandal at one of the local banks. He also royally screwed some folks out of their inheritance and was so creative with his taxes that the IRS actually gave up trying to collect what he owed them. Of course his friend in Congress had something to do with that. I guess having a friend in government can be helpful at times. Especially if you're trying to get government off of your back.

'Is there anything else?' Ronnie asked when the Professor stopped speaking.

All kinds of things. The list literally goes on and on. Once we start printing you'll get to read them for yourself.

'What about this book you were talking about?'

Well, I was thinking. There's enough stuff here, I can pull some of it together and you can send it to a publisher. I knew a couple of people that would eat this type of stuff up and print it. Believe me, this stuff is really good. The implications alone should propel it onto the book racks with a force that will carry it up the book charts. The Professor said with real enthusiasm.

'Okay. Let's say we print this book, have you got a name for it yet or is it to be an untitled work?'

The name was the easiest part of it all. I was thinking it should be called "Confessions of a Dead Man". Ironic, don't you think?

'To say the least. When do we start?'

Right now. Load the printer with paper and let's go.

Ronnie got another ream of paper out of the cabinet and loaded the printer as he was instructed to do. The whole time he was doing this, the Professor was typing away at the keyboard. After a few minutes of this, the Professor sat back with a satisfied look on his face and explained to Ronnie that they would print the Gabby columns first. Then when that task was done they would move on to the book itself and start printing it. There was very little for Ronnie to do except sit back and watch the printer spit out one printed page after another. Ronnie sat in silence as the machine set about its task. Other than the noise the computer was making, the only other sound was the Professor drinking noisily from his bottle and typing on the keyboard.

It seemed like a great deal of time had passed before the computer stopped its printing task and Ronnie gathered up the printed paper before him. He sat there reading the different columns containing information about how Fryer had set about most days trying to figure out a bigger and better way to make money and succeeding at his goal. Ronnie learned how, while Fryer was doing volunteer work with civic organizations, he would be dealing coke to his high society friends at almost double its street value. Ronnie also learned Fryer had gotten into this lucrative business when a now circuit court judge had asked him how to get rid of a large amount of coke the judge had 'accidently' taken home with him from the police evidence room. Fryer never asked how the judge had obtained the powder, but there was a sort of explanation offered to him.

The explanation came in the form of a comment from the judge that it would be impossible to convict someone when there was no evidence left. As predicted, the original owner of the coke (who just happened to be Fryer's client) did go free and was never convicted of his crime. Fryer's client never asked what happened to almost two pounds of pure coke and Fryer, who had it safely locked up in his safe at home, never offered to give back his clients merchandise. The judge never brought the subject back up because he was satisfied with the envelopes of money he was getting from Fryer as the coke was sold and Fryer gave him his cut of the profits. In cash and always alone. Just Fryer and the judge.

In those days, the drug trade was slow and it took Fryer almost four months to get rid of what he had. But that four months was enough time for Fryer to get used to having extra cash around. He never filtered any of the drug money through his business or bank accounts. So to him, it was just free lunch money. He did use some of the money in his business, but never on the surface. He used it to hire outside help like Avery to take care of special problems that arose from time to time. A wealthy client would come in with a son or daughter (or even themselves) and would offer to pay handsomely to get what ever legal mess they had gotten themselves into taken care of. Most times it was a simple DUI. Fryer would go and see a police friend of his and for a couple of hundred dollars, the results of the breathalyser test would either disappear or get changed to just below the legal limit.

On more complex matters, the price would be a lot higher depending on the degree of difficulty or how much stuff had to be covered up. Bernie's crowning achievement was when he got an ex-mayor's kid off from a manslaughter charge. It seemed the young man was bored and rebelling from his father's authority. He had gone out and robbed a small gas station in the middle of the night. Although he never intended to kill the clerk, the kid pushed the clerk and the clerk had stumbled over a gas hose and struck his head on the concrete pump island. The clerk lingered in a coma for almost a week before he died, although it was rumored he had been brain dead from the time he had arrived at the hospital. There were no surveillance cameras, so there was no positive ID on the mayor's kid. The fly in the ointment was a pizza delivery guy who just happened to be pulling into the station to get gas in time to see the kid shove the clerk.

The public outcry was just short of a lynch mob and EVERYONE wanted to see the kid ride 'Old Sparky' into oblivion. After a visit down to skid row and five grand lighter, Fryer had arranged for the pizza guy to leave this reality forever. Now, with no eye witnesses and purely circumstantial evidence, the case was thrown out of court. After all, the ex-mayor and his son maintained the story that the boy had been home all night studying for an English exam.

And of course, out of the goodness of his heart, Fryer then offered to represent the distraught family of the victim in a wrongful death lawsuit against the company that had employed the unfortunate clerk. After a month of battling the corporate lawyers, Fryer won an unprecedented four million dollar settlement for not taking better precautions against things of this nature. That was when Fryer really won the reputation of a man who could take matters into his own hands and get things done.

Ronnie couldn't believe what he had been reading. As he shuffled through the columns, he saw there was indeed some very good stuff here. He also saw there was enough columns here and he wouldn't have to write anything for a very long time. Then the thought occurred to Ronnie that maybe this was just one of the Professors cruel jokes. So he asked the Professor about the columns.

'Are you sure this stuff is on the level?'

Somehow I knew that you'd ask me that. You are a very mistrusting person by nature. Do you know that?

'Whatever...Answer me. Is this stuff for real or are you just yanking my crank?'

If I was yanking your crank, big boy, you'd be enjoying it a lot more than you think.

'I doubt that. I'm not into your particular type of game. Now tell me, is this for real?'

Oh...You never know until you get a chance to walk on the wild side of life. I think you'd enjoy it more than you think. The Professor replied as he laid his hand on Ronnie's shoulder, *as for what you're reading, yes. Every word is true according to Fryer himself.*

'How do you know he was telling the truth?'

Because when I got this information, he never had a chance to speak. It's hard for a man to lie about what he's been up to when you get the facts straight from his memory.

That seemed to satisfy Ronnie and he asked, 'What about the book you were talking about?'

Reload the paper tray and we'll get started on that as soon as you're ready. That is, if you still want to pursue this.

'Of course.' Ronnie replied quickly.

Then let's get started.

Ronnie reloaded the tray and after the Professor typed for a few seconds and the computer started printing again. Once this printing job started, Ronnie took the pages that contained the Gabby columns and straightened them up. He sat there for a long time as the printer spit out one page after another reading the columns that had been printed. He found the Professor had been right, Fryer had been one of the most corrupt individuals he had ever run across.

After a half hour of constant printing, the Professor told Ronnie that he estimated it was going to take at least two days of printing before the job would be complete. Ronnie told the Professor he didn't mind and as long as the book was as good as the columns he had read, he didn't mind putting in the extra time. It was then that Ronnie looked at the clock and saw that it was almost four in the morning. The Professor commented on the time and told Ronnie to go to bed, they would continue tomorrow night.

It was at that point that Ronnie woke up and found himself in his bed upstairs. Margret was snoring loudly next to him. He craned his neck to see the alarm clock and saw that it was just a few minutes before four. Thinking to himself that he had just had a mighty strange dream. He rolled over and resumed sleeping. When his alarm went off, Ronnie awoke once again feeling fresh and throughly rested. His mind wandered back to the dream he had last night and thought to himself that it had been a really strange one.

As Ronnie was brushing his teeth, he began thinking about the Professor himself. Ronnie realized that ever since the computer had been brought home, the

Professor had been invading his dreams less. He also realized that now, everytime he saw the Professor in his dreams, the Professor seemed to be taking on a softer, less menacing image. Ronnie thought to himself the Professor also seemed to be more human-like, less ghoulish.

Ronnie started for the stairs after getting dressed and remembered Margret had asked him for the use of the car. So he turned around and went into the bedroom and woke Margret up. As usual, Margret woke with her less than usual good spirits until he reminded her she was the one who wanted the car. Once he said that, Margret smiled and told him she would be ready to go in ten minutes.

Ronnie went on downstairs and froze when he saw the stack of paper next to the computer. He walked over and turning on a light, began to look at the printed pages. Before he got a chance to start reading, he heard Margret walking around upstairs. So he quickly stuffed the printed paper into the bottom desk drawer. He then went into the kitchen and made himself a quick breakfast. Ronnie ate quickly and as he was coming out of the kitchen, Margret was just coming down the stairs with Nancy slung over her shoulder. It had been ten minutes like she had told him and they went outside. Margret drove him to work and dropped him off.

42.

When Margret got back to the house, she was walking into the house with Nancy when she realized she had left her purse in the car. She quickly went inside and put Nancy down in the middle of the floor before going back out to the car to get her purse.

Their driveway had a slight slant going down to the street. Margret opened the door and sat down inside the car. The door, reaching the end of its opening arch, swung back and caught her in the leg. The pain was tremendous, and in rage, Margret shoved the door back open again. Almost at the same time but slightly after, she grabbed the strap of her purse and started to stand up. Once again, the door reached the end of its opening arch and not having spent the energy that was used to open it, it began to swing back again. This time, the top corner of the door caught her in the side of the face.

Since the door had a lot more force in it than she had been prepared to deal with and being caught by surprise, the door forced the side of Margret's head against the top of the door frame. Margret saw stars and blacked out for a couple of seconds. When she regained consciousness she was sitting back in the car seat again with the car door pressed against her legs. The side of her face the door had caught was numb and the other side of her head was sore, tender to the air and touch. Fearing her cheek bone was broken, she gingerly touched her cheek with her finger tips. There was no feeling and she saw, there was no blood on her finger tips when she brought her hand away from her cheek. As she sat there trying to regain enough strength to walk back into the house, she could feel as well as see her eye beginning to swell shut. At the same time, the sleeping nerve endings in her cheek and eye socket were beginning to wake up. The pain was immense.

When Margret had calmed down enough to regain her footing she stood up. The simple act of standing brought about a fresh wave of pain and her world fogged over for a couple of very long seconds. She had to grip the roof of the car to keep from falling down. When her vision came back to its painful clarity, she eased the car door shut and slowly walked back to the front door of the house. Each foot fall bringing a fresh coat of pain to the misery she was in.

Once inside the house, Margret looked and saw that Nancy was still in the same spot she had laid her and had fallen back asleep on her blanket. Margret continued on through the living room on her way to the downstairs bathroom. Stopping only long enough to grab a washcloth from the small linen closet next to the bathroom door. She went inside and turned on the light and the brightness of the light created a starry effect in the eye that was swelling shut. The light also caused a fresh wave of pain from the intensity of the light.

Margret stood inspecting her face in the mirror and saw that the car door had caught her in the lower corner of the eye socket. The swelling she was experiencing was a tad-amount to a good old fashion shiner. Margret turned on the cold water tap and let the water run for almost a minute as she continued to inspect her face. She put the wash cloth under the stream of cold water to let it start soaking in the coolness. As Margret waited for the water to turn the right degree of cold, she felt her cheek bone very carefully with her finger tips. She was relieved to feel that it didn't feel like it was broken, but realized how lucky she had been. Another quarter of an inch towards her nose and she might have received some irreversible damage to the eye itself. She tested the water and found it to her suiting and turned it off. She wrung the excess water out of the wash cloth and carefully folded it, then placed it over her wounded eye. The coolness was soothing but it seemed to wake up even more nerve endings.

Margret stepped back and with her free hand, put the lid down on the toilet and sat down. She sat there trying to relax and hoping the pain would go away soon. After fifteen minutes, it seemed her prayers were being answered, the pain was starting to diminish. The whole time she was sitting there she could feel her anger rising within her and although her rational mind knew this wasn't his fault, her ire was being directed at the thought of Ronnie. Why, if that inconsiderate bastard hadn't woke her this morning she wouldn't be in this situation right now. The rational part of her mind told her he was only doing what she had requested. The irrational part told her he would have either walked or taken the bus. At worst, he could have returned the car at lunch time like he had done yesterday. She had a right to use the car and her name was also on the title. It didn't matter to her that she had not paid a cent to help buy the car, it only mattered to her that Ronnie didn't have exclusive rights to use it. Once agin the rational side of her brain reminded her that Ronnie had only done as she had requested. At the end of her mental argument she was having she came to the conclusion that Ronnie would pay for his transgression.

When Margret was feeling better, she reinspected her face and saw the swelling had stopped, but it was going to be one heck of a black eye when it the internal bleeding stopped. The pain she was in was still great and she could feel a king sized headache coming on. The king sized headache matched the king sized lump on the other side of her head where it had hit the top of the door frame.

Margret opened the medicine cabinet, took out a bottle of aspirin, opened the top and put six tablets in her mouth, swallowing them the best she could.

Margret went back into the living room and sat down looking at Nancy sleeping peacefully on her blanket in the middle of the floor. She just happened to look down at her legs and saw that there was the start of a good sized bruise from where the car door hit her. Now she really felt like damaged goods and she absolutely knew Ronnie was going to pay for this.

Nancy woke up and Margret fed her breakfast. Once that chore was done, Margret went back to fantasizing about how she would make Ronnie hurt for this. After awhile she realized time was passing her by and quickly went upstairs and changed clothes. When she came back down she had an outfit for Nancy and got her ready to go also. Then they were off to the supermarket.

On the way to the supermarket where the poker machines were, she stopped by the bank and bought a hundred dollars worth of quarters. Then Margret continued her pilgrimage to the market where she not only lost the hundred she had brought with her, but another two hundred and fifty more.

When she came out of the supermarket, she was almost busted and totally disgusted. Wondering what she should do, Margret decided since it was so easy to get the money in the first place, she would just do it again. Then she would be able to come back to the poker machines and change her luck. So she set sail. Nancy was beginning to get cranky from the lack of lunch, so before Margret went to the first store, she stopped and bought lunch at a fast food restaurant. After lunch was finished and Nancy was changed, she once again set out to get as much money as she could.

By the time she was done she had put almost two hundred miles on the car and twenty five hundred dollars in her purse. She also saw it was almost time to get Ronnie, so she pointed the car in the direction of the Country Club and sailed on. She wanted to be there on time today, yes she did, because Ronnie had a bill to pay and she was going to collect.

43.

Almost two days had passed since Ted had spoken to Margret last. He sat on his bunk thinking about how scared she had sounded the last time he had talked to her. He was wondering what horrors the bastard she was married to was subjecting her to. He felt it was very unlike her not to have called him by now. That reinforced the feelings Ted was having that something had to be done about Ronnie.

Ted had a three day break in duty and unlike all of his comrades (Who were out partying constantly. Only stopping by the dorm long enough to change clothes or get more money.) Ted sat patiently waiting for the phone to ring. He just knew as soon as he left his room, she would call and he would miss it. Now, after a day and a half of waiting he was beginning to obsess about Margret. He knew the neighborhood she lived in although he didn't know the exact house. He was tempted to go cruise her neighborhood until he saw her. Then he could squelch his fears that something horrible had happened to her. But since she had told him that it was dangerous for her and she would call him as soon as it was safe, he decided against it. He didn't want to place his beloved Margret in any more jeopardy than she was already in.

Absence was doing its job of making his heart grow fonder. In his mind, Margret had gone from just a convenient piece of tail to Ted needing her like oxygen.

Ted knew once he got Margret away from her abusive husband, there would be nothing the slimy bastard could do. As Ted sat there thinking about it, he decided that if they made their move when it was time for him to ship out, there would be almost no way they could be traced in their escape. Her husband didn't know he was in the military and it would just look like she had just up and disappeared. Then Margret and he could live the rest of their lives together.

As Ted sat and pondered his situation hour after hour, he took the idea of getting the divorce on the run and expanded it. He decided they could get Margret her divorce at his next duty station and then with his flight schedule, he could mail the divorce papers to her soon to be ex-husband from the other side of the United States. Maybe even from the other side of the world depending on where he would be doing his flying at the time.

It never occurred to Ted that the divorce papers would have the name of the state they were drawn up in printed all over them.

There were several times he almost called her, just to hear her voice, her laugh. He could close his eyes and see her in his memories. He remembered everything about her, the way she smelled, how her hand fit in his, and the way she would suck her breath in and hold it when he made her come. He needed her badly. But being the good little military man that he was, he would wait like he had been ordered to.

44.

Avery made it through a day of work without getting killed and it was truly a miracle. Although he had gone home early yesterday to sleep, he still couldn't get the idea he was the next item on someones hit list out of his mind. Just as he had gotten to sleep after laying awake in his bed for a painfully long time, a car came around the corner and when the driver down-shifted to stop at the stop sign at the next corner, the car emitted a series of back fires. Avery found himself on the floor wide awake. He also found as he laid there waiting for the bullets to start shattering his room, that he had wet himself. That was pretty much the end of his sleeping career for that night. He did, however, drift off to sleep around four in the morning only to be awakened a couple of hours later feeling more exhausted than when he had gone to bed to begin with.

Aaron had noticed that Avery was dragging, but after watching him for a half hour, determined he wasn't a safety risk and didn't send him home. When it was finally time to go home, Avery went straight there and went straight to bed. He didn't even stop to eat dinner.

When his mother went to wake him later, he was in such a deep sleep that she couldn't rouse him. She had watched a daytime program on that particular day about drug addiction and feared her son was in the clutches of some dreadful addiction. The signs were all there as they had been explained on the Donahue show. Loss of appetite, strange behavior, paranoia. As she stood there in his room debating to herself what her actions should be, she looked over at his dresser and saw his underwear hanging out of the drawer. She frowned at the sight of his clothes hanging out of his dresser because she had gotten onto him so many times about his sloppy house-keeping.

Opening the offending drawer, she began to straighten it up and found his hidden wad of cash in the back corner. At first she thought it was just some one dollar bills rolled up. He had done that in the past to make it look like he had alot more money than what he really had. She pulled the roll out and began to count it. To her slack jawed amazement, there was over nine hundred dollars there. As she stood there looking at the money, she began to put two and two together and came up with her uninformed version of four. He had been coming home early from his job and now he had much more cash than he should have. She now had the evidence that he wasn't working at the job he had been given, but dealing drugs instead.

She quietly shut the drawer and went downstairs with the money. She sat in front of the television crying because she didn't know what she was going to do with her now errant son. She didn't know where she had gone wrong. She had tried to raise him the best she could after her husband had run off with the floozy from the bar he frequented on the way home from work everyday. She had vowed her little boy would grow up to be as straight as an arrow. Now, here he was a drug dealer. Oh, whatever would she do? She didn't know for sure, but she did know she would put her faith in the Lord and he would show her the answer to her problems.

On the second time she asked the Lord out loud whatever should she do, a commercial came on advertising a twenty-four hour help line. This was almost as if it was an answer to her question and she was sure the Lord had seen it in His infinite wisdom to give her the answer in this form. She hardly debated for a second before picking up the phone and dialing the number.

In a town as slow as this one is, she had the complete and immediate resources of the help line at her disposal. She explained her only son was a big drug addict, taking only God knows what and was now passed out upstairs in a drug induced stupor. Why, she even feared for her life because when he came home hopped up on who knows what, there was no telling what he could do to her. The volunteer at the help line gave her the phone number to a rehab center and told her to call them immediately. Avery's mom thanked the nice volunteer and hung up after promising she would let them know how everything turned out.

Without hesitation she called the rehab center. What she didn't know was this particular center wasn't very reputable. After explaining her plight to a couple of different people, they took her name and address and told her someone would be there in fifteen minutes to pick her son up. With tears in her eyes, she thanked them for helping her and her unfortunate son.

Fifteen minutes later to the second, an ambulance silently pulled up out front and two of the biggest men she had ever seen got out. They came to the front door carrying a straight jacket and a black plastic coated stick that was about three feet long with a rounded metal tip. They explained to her that they were going upstairs and put the jacket on her son and take him to the center where they could start his treatment that would put him on the path to Wellville. She told them what room he was in and they asked her to stay downstairs no matter what kind of noises she heard. They also told her that this might get rough, as it almost always did and they didn't want her to get hurt. But not to worry because they were professionals and did this all of the time.

She smiled at the two attendants, Mike and Larry, as they mounted the stairs and headed for Avery's room. Once inside, they shut the door and turned on the lights. Avery was still sound asleep as they decided the best way to put the straight jacket on him so they could transport him back to the rehab center.

"He seems to be sound asleep. Why don't we just try to put the jacket on him?" Mike suggested.

"Because that's no fun. I won't get to use my equalizer on him." Larry said as he held up the black metal tipped stick.

"You and your damn toys. Lets just see how far we can get with the jacket and if he wakes up and gets out of hand, you can zap him."

"Promise?"

"Have I ever lied to you before?"

"Well, there was that time when you told me that you could hold your breath for an hour."

"Shut up and lets get this done. I want to hurry up and get back to the center. It's almost time for the meds to be passed out and I wanna get back so I can do a little shoppin' out of the drug cart. If you know what I mean."

"Yeah, I know exactly what you mean. What are you shopping for tonight?"

"There's this kid in my neighborhood who said he would pay two dollars for every hit of Valium I can get him. He also said he would go as high as three-fifty per hit of any hallucinogens I can find."

"Not bad, not bad at all. Looks like you'll be able to afford that new car after all."

"You bet buddy. Let's get this over with. You pull him up and I'll slip the jacket on him."

"Okay, but at the first sign of trouble, step back and I'll zap him."

"Great. But this time make sure I'm not touching him first."

"Hey, I said I was sorry didn't I?"

There is an amazingly strange part of the human psyche that will allow a person to incorporate the things that are going on around them into the dream they are having. This is exactly what happened to Avery. He was lying there having a dream about his current object of desire, Maryann from Gilligan's Island, when it was interrupted by a dream about two mafia hit men standing in his bedroom discussing the best way to kill him. The dream was so alarming to him, even in his sleep, he began to wake up and found there WERE two men in his room coming closer to him.

Avery was lying there partially asleep and partially paralyzed with fear. He watched through barely closed eyes as Larry walked around to the head of his bed, then he felt Larry's hands slip beneath his neck and pull. Avery came up to a sitting position and Mike grabbed his arm to start slipping the straight jacket on.

Avery came instantly awake and swung as hard as he could with his free hand. Mike and Larry were caught by surprise and Avery got a lucky shot square on Mike's jaw. Mike saw stars as his legs refused to support his weight any longer and folded beneath him. Avery continued the motion until he was standing on his feet. He stood looking directly into the startled face of Larry.

"You little son of a bitch!" Larry cried as he stepped back and raised his souped up version of a home made cattle prod. All Avery saw was what he thought was the barrel of a gun being raised in his direction.

From somewhere deep inside him, Avery mustered up the courage to face this oncoming threat. In one fluid movement he reached out and grabbed the cattle prod by the shaft. As Avery stepped forward, he forced the prod upward under Larry's chin. At that same instant, a very surprised and very unfortunate Larry pushed the trigger he had spent so much time recessing into the shaft. At the very moment, the metal tip touched his chin and the movement of Larry's finger was complete on the trigger, the circuitry in the prod came to electrical life. With a static like crackle, twenty-five thousand volts of electricity flowed through the tip and into Larry's chin.

Larry stiffened and wet his pants before falling to the floor unconscious. Avery was left standing there with the prod in his hand looking at what he had just done and secretly not believing he had just immobilized the two guys by himself. He looked over at Mike and saw the man was beginning to stir. Avery looked down at the prod he was holding and turned it around to hold it by the hand grip made out of a bicycle hand grip.

Mike was beginning to come out of the daze the sucker punch had given him. As his eyes focused, the first thing he saw was Larry laying face down in what appeared to be a puddle of water. He looked up and saw the grinning face of Avery as Avery touched the tip of the prod to the side of Mike's head.

Mike had really meant to say 'No' but never really got a chance to say it. He thought he did, but the word never escaped his lips before Avery depressed the trigger. With a crackle, the cattle prod did its job and Mike was now rendered as unconscious as his friend who was sleeping peacefully in a pool of his own urine.

Avery stood there for a second time in amazement and then grabbed his clothes that had been lying on his dresser. As he ran from his room, he swooped down and grabbed his shoes as he bolted through the door. He ran down the stairs taking them three at a time half expecting to find his mother downstairs dead. There was a noticeable look of shock on both his and his mother's face when he found her standing in the middle of the living room.

He screamed at her to run because there were two murderers upstairs as he bolted past her still in his underwear. As Avery ran out on the front porch, he looked behind him and saw that she was following him. He mistakenly thought she was running also when in reality, she was just going to the door to see where he was going.

She stood at the front door and watched her son as he ran down the street in his underwear screaming there were killers in his house. When he was out of sight, she turned and realized the two highly trained professionals were not following her son. After a couple of seconds of debate, she decided to go upstairs and see for herself what had happened to those nice young men.

She slowly climbed the stairs and timidly looked into her son's bedroom. She was greeted with the sight of what she thought was two dead men lying on the floor. Her eyes widened in shock before she turned and ran back downstairs. All she could think of was her drug crazed son had killed those two guys. Had she stood there for a couple of seconds longer, she would have heard Mike start to softly snore.

Avery was two blocks away before he stopped running and slipped behind some bushes in the front yard of a house. While he was standing there, he quickly began to put on his clothes as he gasped for air. Two blocks was a long way for him to run at a full out pace and the fact he had barely taken a breath the whole trip accounted for his lack of oxygen now.

When he was finished dressing, Avery went to the front porch of the house he had dressed in front of and rang the door bell. The door was answered by an elderly gentleman who was listened to Avery stammer something about wanting to use the phone to call the police because there were hired murders in his house trying to kill him.

The gentleman stood there for a couple of moments slightly confused at the story that had come out in spurts from the now babbling Avery. Then as if the light of perception went on over his head, the gentleman told Avery to hold on for a moment and disappeared into the house. Less than a minute later the man returned with a portable phone and handed it out the door to Avery. Avery put it to his ear after the man told him the police had already been dialed.

Avery listened as the phone rang and then was answered by the police department. Avery (Now breathing much better than the first time he told his story) explained as calmly as possible that a couple of hired killers had broken into his house and had tried to kill him. He went on to explain that if it hadn't been for the grace of God he would be dead right now. But he had somehow been able to subdue his attackers and had left them unconscious in his bedroom.

The policeman Avery was talking to asked him where he was and told him to stay put, there would be a cruiser there in less than a minute because there was one in a nearby neighborhood. Avery thanked the officer and hung up before handing the phone back through the front door to its owner. He then thanked the gentleman for the use of the phone and then went to the curb to wait for the police to arrive. As he sat at the curb, Avery anxiously looked up and down the street watching for either the police to arrive or signs that there was activity in the street in front of his house. From his vantage point, all Avery could see was what looked like a big station wagon parked in front of his house.

The ambulance that Mike and Larry had arrived in was a much older style ambulance from another decade and looked nothing like the modern day ambulances Avery was used to seeing. Not having stopped and read what had been painted on the side of the vehicle when he had run past it during his hasty retreat, Avery had no idea what he was looking at a couple of blocks away from him.

True to the policeman's word, the cruiser pulled onto the street where Avery was sitting in less than a minute from when he had hung up the phone. Avery saw the cruiser and flagged it down. As the cruiser pulled up to Avery, Avery's mother finally decided that she had to do something and called the police. The call was answered by a policewoman and Avery's mother informed her she had called to report her drug crazed son had killed two men in his bedroom and had run off in the night dressed only in his underwear. She then gave her address and asked if they would please hurry.

The policewoman that had answered the phone insured Avery's mother they would get someone over to her house as soon as they could. She also added if the son should come back, it might not be a wise thing to let him back into the house. Avery's mother had never considered he might be dangerous to her, so, now armed deeply in her paranoia, she went and made sure that all of the doors and windows were locked.

At the same time his mother was securing the fort, the officers that had responded to Avery's call was getting a blow by blow description of how he had single handedly taken on the two thugs and overwhelmed them with their own weapon. Avery had already surrendered the prod to the two officers and they had been amazed to see how the home made weapon worked.

They loaded Avery into the back of the cruiser for his own safety and took him back to his house. On the way over, the call about the drug-crazed teenager dressed only in his underwear came over the radio. Since Avery was dressed and very coherent, they immediately saw the stories didn't match. When they arrived at Avery's house, the two officers saw the ambulance from the rehab center sitting in front of the house. They didn't say anything in the car in front of Avery about the ambulance. Avery was now telling them his mother had been there also, but he had warned her when he ran by her and hopefully she had gotten away also.

One of the officers told Avery not to worry and wait in the cruiser while they went and saw what was going on. Since there were no door handles in the back of the cruiser, Avery had no choice but to comply as the two officers got out of the cruiser and went to the front door of the house. On the way up the walk to the front door, one of the officers shined his flashlight on the vintage ambulance and saw the cheap magnetic sign for the rehab center stuck on the front doors.

Mike and Larry were still upstairs passed out. The prod to the head went a long way to disabling them for an extended period of time. After this experience they would have a working knowledge of why the people they had zapped in similar fashion in the past were always subdued well after they had gotten to the rehab center.

The officers went to the front door and knocked. Within a minute, Avery's mother answered the door with a huge sigh of relief. She started crying as she told the two officers her drug-crazed son had killed the two poor men upstairs. Both of the officers went upstairs and found to their great relief the men weren't dead, just unconscious.

They rousted Mike and Larry and after ten very confusing minutes, started getting their side of the story. One of the officers questioned Larry about the prod and was told that it was standard procedure if one of their pick-ups got unruly, they would zap the person and there would be no more problems. Larry added all he knew was the old woman had called in for a pick up and somehow the little bastard had gotten the drop on them.

The other officer, after listening to Mike and Larry's side of the story, went downstairs to talk to Avery's mother. She was greatly relieved when she was informed the men weren't dead, they had just been zapped with their own toy and had only been asleep. She then explained she had called the rehab center because she couldn't wake her son and she just knew it was because he was on some kind of dope. She added she had just wanted to do the right thing for him.

The officer then asked her if she had proof her son was into drugs. She replied that the only proof she had was her son's behavior and roll of cash, which she produced and showed to the officer. He then asked her if she had any other proof and was told no.

It was just about that time that his partner started down the stairs with Mike and Larry in tow. Once every one was down in the living room, the officers asked everyone to wait there while they stepped into the dining room to compare notes. After a brief conference, they decided to go and talk to Avery himself. As they started for the front door, Larry asked if would be okay if he went out to the ambulance to get some dry clothes to change into and was told it was alright with them but not to leave until this whole matter was sorted out. No questions were asked and no inquiries were made as to how Larry had gotten so wet and truth be known, if it wasn't for the fact that his underwear was soaking wet, Larry himself really didn't know what had happened either. Oh sure, he had seen a lot of his pick ups piss their pants when they were hit with the electricity and Mike and he would take great amusement in it happening, pride prevented him from admitting that was what had happened to him.

To draw the attention away from his moist state, Larry remarked that some days, every day was a Monday as the two officers and him walked out through the front door together. Everybody laughed at Larry's remark as they walked across the porch towards their separate destinations.

Avery had been sitting in the cramped backseat of the cruiser now for almost fifteen minutes while his mind was running rampart through different scenarios as to what was going on inside his house right now. With the windows rolled up, he was unable to hear if there was fighting or even gunshots going on inside his house. This added fuel to his over active imagination. Just as he was beginning to think something had gone terribly wrong inside his house and he was going to be trapped inside the back of the cruiser until his killers came out to get him, the front door opened and the two officers walked out followed by Larry. Everyone was smiling and Avery had one more thought that froze the blood in his veins. He remember what Aaron had told him about the police being in bed with the mafia in this town and he realized he had made the worst mistake of his life. He had safely gotten away from the killers only to call the people who would gladly deliver him back into their hands. He now knew his life was fixing to be over and felt the hopelessness as it settled upon him like a leaden shroud.

As the two officers got closer to the cruiser, Avery felt his heartbeat speed up with desperation. He knew he had to do something if he was to live to see the sunrise but he really didn't know what he was going to do, so he began to survey his situation. He was locked in the rear of the cruiser that served as a rolling prison. It was designed to withstand bigger, badder, and meaner people than he could ever hope to be. It was just a fluke he had been able to get the drop on the first two assassins of the evening, now he was going to need a miracle to get away again. Avery quickly decided whatever he did, it was going to have to be outside of the cruiser.

The two officers reached the cruiser and without debate, the first one opened the rear door and stepped back. Avery started to get out of the car and the other officer put his hand against Avery's chest and told him to hold on and sit there because they needed to talk for a second. Avery quickly complied by sitting back in the seat and not continuing his rush to get out of the car. He didn't want to tip his hand that he was onto what he thought was going on. He just knew as soon as he was outside the cruiser, he was going to set the new land speed record for a pair of tennis shoes.

The officer that had told Avery to wait started explaining that his mother had called the men and they were from a local rehab center. The two men Avery had subdued in his bedroom were not assassins but just a couple of orderlies that had come here to take the now bewildered Avery to the rehab center for treatment of his drug addiction.

This new information was just about too much than he could handle, it was so left field that he never could have seen it coming. Avery weakly explained he wasn't into the drug scene and would happily submit to whatever drug test they wanted him to take. In fact, Avery added, they could even search the house and his room. But it would be a waste of their time because they wouldn't find anything.

The officer that Avery's mother had shown the wad of cash asked Avery about the cash. At first, Avery wanted to tell the officers he had gotten the money from Bernie Fryer for some work he had done, but decided against it and told them that he had gotten it from saving up. He added that the only reason his mother didn't know he had it was because if she did, she would have taken it from him by now and he would never see it again.

The officers believed Avery and finally let him out of the back of the cruiser. They took him inside his house and everyone sat down for a conference. Thirty minutes later, Mike and Larry left empty handed (although the officers kept Larry's toy for further investigation.). Avery's mother was apologizing to everyone for having caused so much trouble. She had been so sure she was right from what she had seen on the daytime television talk show. Avery explained he had been really tired and had gone to sleep because he had worked late and then missed a couple of night's sleep because of insomnia.

45.

The second thing Ronnie noticed when he got into the car, the first being that Margret was on time this time, was Margret was being very cold and distant. Then Ronnie noticed her face seemed different. It wasn't that he was being inattentive to her, but from his angle of view of her driving, he couldn't see her black eye and how the other side of her face was swollen. Ronnie asked her if there was a problem and Margret took off her sunglasses and turned to look at him for the first time.

Ronnie was shocked to see the way her face looked and asked her what had happened. In a very cold tone, she told him she had been hit by the car door earlier that morning. When he asked her if she was okay, Margret's reply was; "A-lot you fucking care." Margret replaced her sunglasses before putting the car into drive and speeding off.

Ronnie kept pressing the point to find out if she was okay and Margret finally told him to "Shut the fuck up," and then added, "I don't need your bullshit right now."

They rode in silence for a few minutes before he asked her how the job hunting had gone that day. It must have been the right thing to ask because her tone softened a little almost immediately and she told him that it had been good. She didn't get the job today because the owner of the restaurant hadn't been there, but she was supposed to come back tomorrow for an interview.

Margret on the other hand, was just biding her time. She wanted Ronnie calm and relaxed when she swooped down on him with her own case of whoop-ass. She still didn't know what she was going to do to him, but she knew she would think of something when the time was right.

When they arrived home, Margret went inside and sat down, leaving Ronnie to take care of Nancy. When Ronnie got into the house he saw that Margret was now stationary so he put Nancy in her playpen and went into the kitchen to see about dinner. It made him mad that he had to see about cooking dinner after she had been off all day. But he decided with her injuries, it was the least he could do to help. He found some hamburger in the freezer and a box of hamburger helper in the cupboard. So dinner was on.

235

After dinner was cooked and eaten, Ronnie also took care of the dishes. When that task was done he went back into the living room and sat down with Margret in front of the television. A couple of mindless hours passed and then he decided to play with the computer.

This time when he turned it on, it came up and didn't give him the 'SORTING DATA' message it had been giving him. After looking through the menu he found a poker game. He downloaded the game and spent an hour playing it. The whole time he was playing, Margret was bitching at him about one petty thing after another and he was having a hard time concentrating on what he was doing. Her constant interference was making the game he was playing very unenjoyable. After an hour of listening to her bitching and moaning he turned the computer off.

Margret had been sitting there trying to decide what she was going to do to Ronnie, but was dismayed that she couldn't think of anything that was good enough. Of course she had thought about hitting him, but that would be too simple and wouldn't give her the pleasure she was looking for. She wanted to do something to him that would make him suffer for an extended period of time. As she sat there watching him watch television, she felt a slight revulsion at the sight of him. But when he had gotten up and started playing with his damn computer, the ire rose within her like yeast making bread rise. So, whenever it seemed like he was starting to get into his game and having fun, she would start talking to him and distracting him. She saw the disturbances were starting to get on his nerves and that was what she wanted. She kept it up until he finally turned the computer off. When Ronnie did that, Margret felt like she had won. This round at least.

Of course, the instant the computer was turned off, Margret couldn't think of another single thing that she wanted to say to Ronnie.

They sat in silence for awhile and Ronnie finally announced he was going to bed and got up and went upstairs. Margret sat there for a little while racking her brain as to what her next move would be but found that she still couldn't think of a single thing. Disgusted, she went upstairs and went to bed also.

Both Ronnie and Margret laid in bed for a while before going to sleep, both deep in thought. Ronnie was thinking he had to get the next Gabby column to Aaron and somehow think of a way to approach the subject of the new Gabby columns about Fryer's past that were already complete. Margret on the other hand was trying to think of a way to fuck Ronnie over.

Right as she was falling asleep it hit her, the perfect plan. She would use Ted to exact her revenge. She would get in touch with Ted and tell him that she hadn't been able to talk to him because of Ronnie. Then, when he saw the way her face looked, she would tell him that Ronnie had done it to her. If she was lucky, Ted would either kill or at the very least, severely hurt Ronnie. Yes, that would be what she would do and she would do it first thing in the morning. Now

236

contented, Margret fell asleep with the knowledge she had hit upon the perfect plan.

When a person goes to sleep, it seems as if they shut their eyes and then reopen them in their dreams. In reality, there is quite a time span between the time they go to sleep and actually start dreaming. Some ancient cultures used to think the reason for this was the act of dreaming itself was because you were close to death. They believed sleep was actually a very close dance with death itself and this closeness is what allowed you to dream. It was at those times that you were getting a chance to see what is on the other side of life. It was also common knowledge this dream place was a place that one misstep, one mistake, and you never woke up and would stay in the dream world forever. In Ronnie's case, this belief was almost a true statement.

To Ronnie, he felt sleep sweep over him and his eyes closed, then it seemed he reopened his eyes just a couple of seconds later. When he opened his eyes he found himself sitting in front of his computer again. Except this time, he wasn't right in front of the computer but sitting slightly to one side. The Professor was sitting directly in front of the screen and Ronnie saw the computer was already on.

Howdy partner. 'Bout time you got here. The Professor said to him. He sounded happy, almost glad to see Ronnie.

'Well here we are. Another night of fun with an asshole like you.'

Awww, what's the matter? Don't want to be rich and famous?

'Of course I do. But I thought you couldn't turn the computer on by yourself.'

Oh that...Well that used to be true. I'm getting stronger now and I find that I'm needing you less and less for the menial tasks. The Professor replied nonchalantly as he typed on the keyboard.

'So you need me for the ball breaking stuff right?'

My, don't we have an attitude? What's the matter Ronnie? Fall asleep on the wrong side of the bed?

'It seems like no matter what side of the bed I fall asleep on, I always end up with you.' Ronnie replied sharply.

Isn't that sweet. The Professor replied as he stopped typing and laid his head on Ronnie's shoulder. Ronnie could smell the Professors putrid breath hot on the side of his face. The smell was powerful and seemed to assault Ronnie's nose. Ronnie tried just breathing through his mouth, but the smell was so strong that it continued to assault his senses.

To his horror, Ronnie saw the Professor raise his hands and place them on either side of Ronnie's face. When the hands were in position, the Professor caressed him. Had anyone been looking at this it would have seemed like a lovers caress. To Ronnie, it seemed like he was being rubbed raw with a skeletal hand. Even though the Professors hand was fleshed out, there was a distinct feel of bone on Ronnie's face. Ronnie was instantly repulsed by the feel and he drew away from it.

'Cut that shit out,' Ronnie said as he pulled away. 'Since you don't need me to turn the computer on and you only want me for the ball breaking stuff, then why am I here now?'

In case something goes wrong. I'll need you to fix it.

'So you do need me huh? What if I say no? What if I decide not to cooperate and tell you to go get fucked instead?'

Oh...You will cooperate. The Professor said with a chuckle.

'I wonder. What if I did refuse to do your bidding? What would you do then?' Ronnie asked full of himself and self confident.

Like I said, you Will cooperate. There are ways of making you see things my way. Remember when I used to hurt you?

'Yes.' Ronnie replied somberly.

Now that I'm getting stronger I can hurt you a lot worse. The Professor said as he leaned close to Ronnie's ear and whispered.

'Okay, I believe you.' Ronnie said as he pulled away from the Professor's face. 'So...I'm just supposed to sit here and if something goes wrong, then I'm supposed to be Mr. Fix-it.'

You got it Buck-a-Roo. Just sit there and be good, or else.

'Great. I get the big 'Or Else'. Somehow I think I'm going to get the big 'Or Else' no matter what I do.'

Believe what you want, but do it on your own time. Now is my time and I say that it's time to print.

When the Professor said that, the printer came to life and started spitting pages out. When the printer had come on, Ronnie almost jumped out of his skin. He hadn't noticed it was even on let alone loaded with paper. The Professor sat back with a satisfied look on his face and watched the paper as it came out of the printer. Ronnie watched as the Professor opened the bottom desk drawer and pulled out a bottle of Cognac. Ronnie saw this was a new bottle, full and the seal still intact.

Ronnie almost asked where the bottle had come from, but decided against it, his thought was it was better to let sleeping dogs lie. Besides, Ronnie really didn't care where the bottle had come from. What was bothering him was the Professor was now using the bottom drawer as his own. But thinking about that point, Ronnie decided maybe it wasn't so bad. After all, all of the printed paper in that drawer was work the Professor had done. All Ronnie had done was load the printer and shuffle the paper as it came out.

Ronnie had been too engrossed in the conversation with the Professor to notice what was going on around him. Had he been more aware of his surroundings, he would have noticed Margret's head sticking around the corner listening to his one-sided limited, verbal exchange.

46.

When Ronnie had gotten up in the middle of the night (As he was in the habit of doing lately) he had woken Margret up. Normally she would have rolled over and gone back to sleep as she always had done in the past. But this time when Ronnie had crawled over the top of her he had woken her up more to the surface of waking than he had done in the past. Margret half rolled over, opened her eyes and saw Ronnie standing there naked in the doorway of the bedroom. Sleepily, she asked him if there was anything wrong. When she didn't receive a reply she came fully awake fearing something was wrong.

She laid there in bed listening to see if she could discern what the problem was without having to actually get out of bed. She couldn't hear anything and after a few minutes decided to get up and see where Ronnie was. After a quick tour of the bathroom and Nancy's room, she found he wasn't upstairs at all. She walked over to the staircase and looked down it expecting to see darkness. Instead, she saw a glow coming up from downstairs. At first she thought it was the glow of the television set and almost went back to bed. But she noticed the glow was constant, unlike a television which will cast a glow that varies with the brightness of what is being shown. So she decided to go downstairs to see what was going on.

Margret crept down the stairs as quietly as she could, avoiding the couple of creaky steps near the bottom. As she neared the bottom of the staircase she could hear Ronnie talking to someone. She froze.

Who the hell could he be talking to? Margret wondered. Taking one more step down, she peeked around the corner and saw Ronnie sitting at the computer. Puzzled, she watched for a minute and then saw and heard Ronnie start talking to the computer. She stood there trying to hear the conversation but Ronnie was speaking too low for her to make out what he was saying. What she could hear didn't make any sense to her but she did notice that he was carrying on a one sided conversation, pausing each time as if he was listening to a response to what he had just said. As she watched the events unfold in front of her, Margret noticed Ronnie was even turning his head as if he was talking and listening to

239

someone sitting next to him. Then he said something about 'getting the big or else', whatever that meant, and then folded his arms and sat back.

She was just about to say something to him when the printer started up. For some reason, the printer starting up caused her to lose her nerve and as quietly as she had come down the stairs, she quickly retreated back to the bedroom. It was a shame she had left when she did. If she had waited for another moment, she would have heard the desk drawer open and seen a bottle of liquor levitate over the top of the desk.

Margret sat alone in her bed for a long time trying to decide what it was she had seen that had spooked her. She realized she had never seen Ronnie sit and talk to an inanimate object before. As far as she knew, to make a computer work, you had to push the keys on the keyboard and not just sit and talk gibberish to it.

Yet, there had been something spooky about what she had seen and she couldn't put her finger on what it had been. To her, it had been more of a feeling than the rational input of what she had seen. But still, she had seen him and was wondering what he was printing down there in the middle of the night. Then his reason for being down there hit her, he must be down there working on his Gabby column. After all, he had to turn it in tomorrow so it could be printed in the paper. Yes, that's it. That's what he was doing. She had seen him sitting there plenty of times writing the column out long handed and he would sometimes speak outloud the words he was trying to put down on paper. Ronnie had told her he would do it that way because it made the words flow easier. She thought about it as she drifted off to sleep.

Later in her dreams, Margret found herself running and she was afraid. There was something or someone pursuing her. She didn't know who or what it was, but she did know it would be really bad if she stopped and the unknown pursuer caught her. She ran and ran and ran. Still the thing behind her was getting closer. She didn't dare look behind her, she knew the sight of it would petrify her in her tracks. She did look down, however, and saw the ground looked as if it was made out of paper. Under her feet, she could see numbers passing by and realized the numbers were to the checking account she was writing bad checks on. Looking up in front of her and to either side, saw she was running across a giant checkbook. It was then she knew the thing after her was the authorities.

Her immediate reaction was to stop running and turn around to face what was behind her. But she found she couldn't force herself to do it. Somehow she knew if she did stop, the circumstances of what was after her would crush her. So she took the easy way out and continued to run.

Morning came too early with Ronnie waking her to see if she needed the car for her job interview today. She told him she would be ready in a few minutes and Ronnie disappeared through the bedroom door. Margret lay there for another minute bone-tired from her dream-filled night. She felt as though she had actually been running all night long.

The minute passed and Margret gathered enough strength to get up and get herself and Nancy ready for the pre-dawn ride to the Country Club.

47.

That morning, Ronnie woke up feeling refreshed as he always did after this new round of what he now thought of as his computer dreams. After he woke Margret up he went downstairs and as he expected, found a pile of paper next to the computer. He also found a stack of Gabby columns waiting there for him so he didn't have to go searching through the drawer for something to turn in to Aaron today. He opened a different drawer and pulled out a large envelope and put the columns inside it. Then he sealed the envelope and went on into the kitchen to make himself some breakfast.

When he was finished eating, Ronnie went back into the living room just in time to meet Margret coming down the stairs with Nancy slung over her shoulder. To his shock, he saw that Margret's black eye looked a lot worse this morning than it had looked last night. When he commented about it to her, she just shrugged her shoulders and said, that even though it looked worse, it felt a lot better. After that exchange, they left.

48.

Around nine in the morning Margret decided to give Ted a call to see if he was around and he answered on the second ring. After exchanging love talk for a few minutes, Ted asked Margret if she could meet him somewhere or if that wasn't possible, if he could come over and see her. She told him it wasn't such a good idea and Ted explained to her this was his last day off he would have for at least two weeks. He explained further this was because he had a training flight and survival school he had to go to.

The thought of being with Ted for the day wasn't unappealing to her. In fact, she was beginning to feel that slippery warmth begin in her loins as she was talking to him. That was what helped her to decide. Yes, she told him, she would meet him at ten-thirty at Aceholes.

After Margret hung up the phone she went next door to see if she could get a babysitter for the day. Although Heather's mother wasn't very happy about the last minute asking, she agreed to babysit Nancy for the day after Margret explained she had to go look for a job.

To Margret's amazement, the older woman never asked her about the black eye and she figured the old bag must have seen what had happened to her yesterday morning with the car door. After making a big deal out of thanking Heather's mother for taking Nancy on such short notice, Margret went back over to her house to collect Nancy and the things she would need for the day.

When Margret left their front porch on her way back home, Heather's mother turned to her husband (who was home because he only had to work a half-day today) and told him when Ronnie had given Margret the black eye, she hoped it had hurt like a son of a bitch. To that proclamation, her husband only smiled. Although he would never admit to it, he was hoping Ronnie hadn't hurt his hand when he hit her.

They would never say anything to anyone about their feelings, but they had no use for Margret with all of her screaming, cussing, and bullying. They did have pity for her poor husband, Ronnie, and would have given him the moon if he would have asked them for it. But Margret was another matter, they had seen through all of her pretense when they had first met her. They had seen how one second she was practically foaming at the mouth telling Ronnie what a stupid prick he was and when she had seen them watching her, the next second she was acting so sweet, sugar wouldn't have melted in her mouth. They were old, almost too old to have a daughter as young as Heather, but they weren't fools and they knew an act when they saw one.

Ronnie and his beautiful daughter were another subject. Ronnie had never been anything but respectful towards them, and little Nancy was as cute as a bug. One thing that had impressed them about Ronnie over Margret was how she would avail herself to them for babysitting at the drop of a hat and never mention anything about compensation. Whereas Ronnie would always insist on paying. That made them feel as if Ronnie respected them and the fact that a job done was worth paying for. Even when they had insisted he not pay, he would get out of the house and they would find the money he had offered them laying on a table or on top of the television. From their old school of thought, it was refreshing to meet someone who respected the thought of fair compensation.

Five minutes after she had left their house, Margret was back with Nancy and made another big show out of thanking them for what they were doing. Heather's mother was a little abrupt with Margret and almost shut the door in her face after Nancy had been handed over. Margret hardly noticed and went back over to the house to get ready to meet her lover.

Now that Nancy had been taken care of, Margret dressed quickly so she could get on her way. She was thinking if she was quick enough, she could hit a couple of stores on the way to Aceholes and cash a couple of checks. She just hated the thought of not getting some money before starting her day of whatever Ted wanted to do.

After checking the checkbook to insure she had enough checks for the day, she left the house and stopped at the first department store she passed. She went inside and bought some jewelry. As she looked down at the security blue of the check, she saw the account number and instantly flashed back to her dream from last night. She must have drifted off in her own world for a moment because the next thing she knew, the clerk was asking her for a second time of there was anything wrong. Margret quickly said no and began to write the check. Some little piece of her rational mind asked her if she really meant to do this. Are you really going to write this check when you know there's no money in the account to support it?

As Margret was so good at it, she ignored her inner voice and handed the check over when she finished writing it. The clerk asked for Margret's I.D. and for an instant, all Margret could think of was that now she had been caught and would pay the consequences for her actions. With a shaking hand, she handed over her drivers license and stood there prepared to run if it looked like she was going to be arrested.

Margret watched as the clerk copied the information off of the license and Margret sighed an inward sigh of relief as the clerk smiled and handed the license back. She was too afraid to say anything and quickly left. Margret sat out in the car shaking for almost five minutes before she got her courage up to leave.

She knew that whatever happened, she couldn't go back into that store to do a return like she had been doing all over town. She was trying to decide what she was going to do when she saw the next department store ahead. Without hesitation, she pulled into the parking lot and went inside.

This time her anxiety attack didn't hit until she was putting her checkbook away. Margret almost snatched the bag out of the clerks hand as she turned to rush towards the exit. This time it only took a couple of minutes for the shakes to stop. As she pulled out of the parking lot she knew this was another store she would be unable to return to.

She now had almost fifteen hundred dollars worth of jewelry in the two bags beside her and she had to think of some way to exchange it for cash. She drove along trying to decide what she was going to do when she turned onto the street that led to Aceholes and ultimately, the military base. As she looked out the windshield, she saw the solution to her problem. As with most roads leading to a military base, both sides of the road were littered with pawn shops.

Margret saw a sign that said this particular shop paid top dollar for gold and she pulled into the parking lot.

As she parked the car, she looked at her watch and saw she had plenty of time before she had to meet Ted. She didn't really know what to do or expect in the pawn shop because she had never been inside one, but she did figure it wouldn't be a good idea to have the price tags still on the stuff she was trying to sell. So she quickly stripped the jewelry of its prices and put all of the jewelry into one bag. Margret took a couple of deep breaths, got out of the car and went inside the pawn shop.

Inside, Margret found the pawn shop was nice and clean, not at all what she had expected. Even though she had never been inside one, she had a predisposed idea of what it should be like. This was supposed to be the place where drug addicts came to sell the stuff they had stolen to buy more drugs. It was also supposed to be the place where people sold their most cherished, personal stuff in despair to get money to be able to afford the meager things in life.

Margret walked up to the counter and set the bag of jewelry down on the glass. After a couple of seconds of waiting, an old gentleman came shuffling out from behind a curtain that separated the main sells floor from the back room. The man had snow white hair and a very healthy tan. Although it was hard for Margret to take her eyes off of the pistol strapped to his hip, she saw that the man in front of her looked well weather-worn.

"May I help yew?" the man asked with a smile. Margret noticed that he didn't have any front teeth. Top or bottom.

R. H. Gosse

"Your sign out front says that you buy gold jewelry."

"Yep. It sure do."

"I have some jewelry here I would like to pawn."

"Let's see wha'cha got." The man said as he laid out a black velvet cloth onto the counter.

"How much can I get?" Margret asked prematurely.

"Well ma'am, usually I get to look at the stuff yew wanna sell before we start dickerin about the price." He replied, his smile never faltering.

"Sorry." Margret said as she felt her cheeks flush with embarrassment. She dumped the contents of the bag onto the piece of velvet. Then as if in defense she offered, "I've never done this before. I'm not really sure what to do."

"That's okay, everybody has a first time no matter what they is doin'." He replied as he slipped a jewelers loup into his eye and started examining the pieces of jewelry in front of him.

"So what do you think?" Margret asked after giving the man a couple of minutes to examine her loot.

"Rat pretty pieces. Why is yew sellin 'em?" He inquired as he examined a diamond bracelet for a second time.

"Excuse me?" Margret asked, not really understanding why the man had asked for a reason she was trying to unload the jewelry.

"Why is yew sellin 'em? I always like to hear why people want to unload the memories to a stranger like me."

"My husband is sick." Margret told him figuring that some medical sob story would fetch a higher price. "And we need the money for hospital bills. They just keep coming in and he hasn't been able to work for almost six months. Our savings are gone and we are just about broke." Margret was comfortable with the lie she was telling and it seemed the man was buying it, so she continued. "My husband didn't want me to sell my stuff, but I can see no way to pay the bills, buy his medicine, and put food on the table without doing this. In fact, he would probably have a fit if he knew where I was right now."

The gentleman had heard all kinds of stories in his life, he had been in the pawn business for more than thirty years. Even though Margret thought he was buying her story hook, line, and sinker, he knew pure bullshit when he heard and smelled it. He had seen the junkies keep trying to come in day after day with tv's and stereo's and he had seen the truly needy come in with their most valued life long possessions. To him, Margret fit neither of these descriptions. She was clean looking and the finger print check would tell him if she was in trouble with the law.

He also noticed that all of the jewelry that Margret was trying to sell him looked brand new. There was no wear in the gold and there also was no sweat dirt that accumulates on the cracks and crevices of rings, bracelets, and the back of watches. The stuff looked brand new.

246

After debating for a moment he said, "Looks like yew gotta 'bout two grand worth o'stuff here. Best I can dew is eleven hundred." He looked Margret straight in the eye when he said that, knowing anyone who walked in with that much jewelry would know about how much it was worth. He was looking for a disappointed look in her eyes. It wasn't there.

When Margret heard eleven hundred she was ecstatic, she had figured she was going to be offered five hundred. But she didn't want to seem over anxious at the first offer. "Is that the best you can do?" She asked.

"Yep, this is jest a small shop. Eleven hundred is a lot more then I can afford. So...That's my offer, take it er leave it."

Acting disappointed, Margret replied, "Well, if that's the best you can do, then I'll just have to accept your offer."

The man just smiled back at Margret and pulled out some forms from under the counter. Fifteen minutes later, after filling out three forms and having both of her thumb prints taken, Margret was walking out of the front door with the cash safely stashed in her purse.

Looking at her watch she saw she had just enough time to go meet Ted. As she drove towards Aceholes, she reflected on her new found experience and decided that it hadn't been so bad after all. This also seemed like an easier way to get the money back than it had been going and doing the return thing at the stores. Margret decided that from now on, she would stick to buying jewelry and then taking it to pawn shops for cash.

Margret left the pawn shop and drove down the street to Aceholes. Turning into the parking lot she saw Ted's car already parked there so she parked beside it. Going inside, she found Ted sitting in a booth and she walked over and sat down next to him. Ted stood briefly as she neared the table. When he saw her face his mouth dropped open in surprise and shock.

"Margret my love, what happened to you? Are you okay?" Ted asked her concerned.

At first it didn't register with Margret what Ted was talking about. Her new found joy with pawn shops had over shadowed her original intent here (other than getting laid.) then she remembered her shiner. "Please Ted, I really don't want to talk about it right now."

"If you insist. But really, are you okay?" Ted asked as he took her hand in his.

"I am now that I'm here with you." She replied as she tightened her grip on his hand.

They ate a quick lunch and she followed Ted to his dorm. Once inside his room they got down to business. After a couple of hours of loving, Margret decided to try and launch her plan on Ronnie's destruction. As they laid there in the after-glow of good sex, Margret started crying. Ted tried to comfort her but was only successful in making her cry even harder. Or so he thought.

When it seemed she was calming down, Margret told Ted it was only when she was with him she was truly happy. Ted lay there in silence and listened to her. She told him, much to his shock and dismay, how Ronnie had come home drunk the other night and beat her because she hadn't kept dinner waiting for the four hours he was late coming home.

When Margret saw that Ted was playing right into her hands she elaborated on her story. She told him how the beatings were becoming more and more frequent for lesser and lesser things. Now she saw Ted beginning to take interest in her story she decided to throw one more bone on the pile for him to chew on. In a meekish tone of voice like she was ashamed to bring up the next fact, she told Ted that Ronnie was starting to suggest she take on some of his friends from the bar he hung out at.

Ted asked her what she meant by 'take on' and from a veil of fresh tears she told him that it meant he wanted her to have sex with Ronnie's friends while he watched. Ted became visibly mad at this new found fact saying somebody needed to put Ronnie in his place. Then after a couple of long minutes (for Margret) of thought, Ted asked her if she would go away with him. Almost at once Margret told him she would, but someone would have to take care of Ronnie before they could really and truly be together.

The silence was thick and Margret added she figured if someone showed strength to Ronnie, he was just barbaric enough to appreciate it. The silence continued and just when she thought maybe Ted wasn't taking the bait after all, Ted asked her if that was the only way she knew of they could make a fresh start.

With an inward smile and an innocent tone to her voice, Margret told him she could think of no other way.

Ted told her he would think about it while he was away and would have a solution to her problem by the time he got back. Margret started crying again and when he asked her why she was crying, she told him it was because for the first time in her life she wasn't afraid and he made her feel safe.

Looking at her watch, Margret saw that it was getting close to the time she had to pick Ronnie up. So she got up and got dressed. Once she was ready to go, she kissed Ted good bye and they made love talk for a couple of minutes before she left.

Margret got to the Country Club early and Ronnie noticed she seemed to be really happy when he got into the car. He also noticed she was in a better mood than he had seen her in a very long time. She didn't even complain when Ronnie told her he needed to stop by the newspaper. Then he asked her how the job hunting had gone and by the way, where was Nancy?

Margret explained that Heather's parents were watching Nancy and the job interview had gone very well. In fact, she added, she thought she had gotten the job but wouldn't know for sure until the following Monday. That seemed to appease Ronnie and they rode in silence to the newspaper.

49.

When Ronnie walked into the press room from the loading dock, the first person he saw was Avery. Although Ronnie didn't really recognize Avery or know who he was (or really cared), Avery recognized Ronnie instantly and took off in the other direction like he was strapped to a rocket. Ronnie wound his way through the building and found himself standing in front of Aaron's office door.

Looking inside, he saw Aaron talking on the phone. When Aaron saw Ronnie standing outside, he motioned for Ronnie to come in and quickly got off of the phone.

"How's it going kid?" Aaron asked as he stuck out his hand.

"Real good." Ronnie replied as he took the offered hand and shook it. Aaron motioned to a chair and Ronnie sat down. When he was settled he continued speaking, "I have the next column for you." Ronnie opened the envelope he was carrying and pulled out the original column he had written for this weeks edition and handed it over to Aaron.

Aaron read through it quickly and pulled an envelope of money out of his desk drawer and handed it to Ronnie. "This looks really good kid, keep up the good work. So I have to ask you, how's it going after your little adventure the other night?"

"Things have settled down around the house. But..." Ronnie's voice trailed off.

"What's the problem Ronnie?"

"Well...It is a problem. And one of a strange magnitude."

"A strange magnitude huh? This sounds intriguing. Just lay it out and we'll see what you got."

"It seems like I found out a lot of information about Mr. Fryer. I can't reveal my sources, but I have been told this information is very factual." As Ronnie told Aaron that, he pulled the other columns out of the envelope and handed them over also.

Aaron sat there for almost ten minutes reading the twenty stories that were written in column form. When he got done he sat back and pulled a cigar from somewhere out of a desk drawer. He didn't say anything as he prepared the cigar and lit it. When he exhaled a large cloud of smoke he looked at Ronnie and asked, "Are you sure that all of this is true?"

"That's what I was told."

"Are your resources reliable?"

"Very."

"Well I'll be Goddamn. Looks like old Bernie was up to a lot more than his usual brand of bullshit. Who told you this stuff about him?"

"I'm sorry Aaron, but I promised that I would tell no one who it was that gave me this information. And I have to respect that agreement."

Aaron held up his hand in a 'stop' fashion and said, "That's okay. You have to respect your sources and I can respect that. Forget I ever asked the question."

"So...Do you think you can use this stuff? Or should I just throw it away?"

"Hell yes, I mean, no. We aren't going to throw anything away and yes we are going to use it. Looks like you've written yourself a little vacation here. Tell you what we'll do. I can't pay you for all of these columns right now and I don't know how many of them we'll use. Just keep coming here each week to pick up your money. If it looks like we have to back off of the subject for some reason I'll let you know a week in advance so you'll have enough time to bang out something else for me. How's that sound to you?"

"Like a winner. In the meantime, I'll keep my ear to the ground in case something juicy comes along."

"You do that kid and we'll both end up retiring as rich men. Now get out of here and let me think about how I'm going to start this shit storm."

"Thanks." Ronnie said as he stood up. This time it was his turn to offer his hand.

Aaron took the offered hand and pumped it a couple of times with a very big smile on his face. He watched Ronnie leave and then reread the columns. He couldn't believe what he was reading, but even if only half of what he saw was true Bernie had been one dirty bastard. Part of him told him to shelve the columns and forget about them. But the newspaper man in him told him to forge ahead. What had been that old saying? Damn the torpedos, full speed ahead. He knew the papers he was holding was full of torpedos.

Aaron knew this was probably going to rip this town apart, setting neighbor against neighbor and probably piss off folks from the state capitol all the way to the nation's capitol. But Aaron also knew that one way or another, he was going to sell one hell of a lot of newspapers.

50.

It was a pretty good evening for Ronnie, and Margret was nice to him in ways that she hadn't been in a long time. Ronnie began to get suspicious as he sat there thinking about how she was acting. Margret was upstairs putting Nancy to bed and changing into 'something more comfortable' (her idea) and Ronnie had a few minutes to ponder why she was being so nice to him.

Usually, she only acted this way after she had done something to him. But since he wasn't dead right now, poisoning his dinner didn't seem like a possibility and since he had suffered no physical abuse from her, he was flummoxed. A few minutes later Margret came downstairs wearing a black teddy she had gotten on one of her 'shopping' sprees. She sat down on Ronnie's lap and started nuzzling his ear. They were intimate for the first time in a long time.

After the act of loving was complete, Ronnie lay there still trying to decide why Margret was acting the way she was. He almost commented that she was really being nice to him, but decided that it probably wasn't a good idea to whack the hornet's nest when the hornets were being nice.

That night Ronnie had no dreams, none that counted, and he awoke the next morning feeling fresh and alive.

Margret was still asleep and Ronnie went downstairs to make breakfast. As he passed the computer, he saw there was a new stack of paper laying beside the printer. He stopped and looked at this new addition and saw the first page, which was the last page printed, had a name and address on it. He picked up the next page and saw it was a cover letter to the person the first page named.

Ronnie read the letter and saw it told this person they had shared the same Professor in college and the Professor had recommended him so many years ago, that if Ronnie was to ever start writing to find him and send him a manuscript. Which he was now doing. Ronnie read on and saw his own name was the one in the signature block along with his return address below it.

Ronnie stood there looking at all of the paper below those two sheets he had in his hand and saw there had to be at least two hundred more pages of the book that had been printed. He stood there for another couple of seconds before he heard footsteps above his head and realized that Margret was up also. Ronnie quickly shoved the new pages into the bottom desk drawer with the rest and continued his journey into the kitchen.

He cooked a big batch of scrambled eggs, bacon, and toast. He was setting everything out on the table just as Margret was coming down the stairs with Nancy. When breakfast was over and after Margret finished the dishes, she came into the living room and asked him what he wanted to do today. He replied that he really didn't care and whatever she wanted to do would be fine with him.

Margret told him she had heard that a new mall had just been opened in the next town over and wanted to know if he felt like taking her there. Ronnie replied that it seemed like a good idea to him. So after getting ready, they left and spent the rest of the day at the new mall.

It was almost an hour away from their house and the mall was spectacular. Ronnie had never seen anything like it before. It was three stories tall and had every kind of shop you could imagine. Margret really didn't buy anything and spent the day mostly window shopping. Ronnie found a video arcade and spent almost ten dollars playing games he had only seen in the magazines.

As they were leaving the mall with the few things they had purchased, Margret brought up the subject of dinner. Ronnie said he wanted to go out, but Margret offered to cook something if he would stop at a grocery store on the way back home.

Just before they got onto the interstate highway, Margret saw a grocery store that belonged to the same chain as the one she had bounced so many checks at back home. She persuaded Ronnie to stop so she could go ahead and do some shopping. Grocery shopping was one thing, but she also intended to cash the check she would write for a good amount over her purchase. She had a check cashing card from the chain and knew that even though they were in a different city, they would take her check. She was also counting on the fact that since they were in a different city, this store wouldn't know about her checkered past. Pun intended.

Ronnie stopped and parked, but declined to go inside saying he would just sit in the car with Nancy so they wouldn't have to go through all of the motions of getting Nancy out of her seat. Margret pretended to be disappointed, but looking in the backseat, saw that Nancy was fast asleep. Margret was happy, although she didn't act like it, that Ronnie was staying in the car. This way she wouldn't have to come up with a reason why she was cashing the check for over. She asked him what he wanted for dinner and he told her anything that she wanted to get. He did, however, mention that a nice taco salad sounded good to him.

Taco salad, Margret thought to herself. It figures Ronnie would be satisfied with the mundanely simple things in life.

Once inside the store, Margret quickly picked up the things she needed to make the salad. She picked up a few more items before heading for the checkouts. She was checking out and the total came to twenty dollars and some cents. Margret asked the young woman who had checked her out if she could write the check for over. The young woman smiled and asked Margret if she had a check cashing card. Margret replied she did and the woman told her it could only be for twenty over the amount. Margret quickly wrote the check and handed it over with her card.

The fly in the ointment came when the woman punched the check cashing card numbers into the cash register. After taking just long enough for the computer the register was hooked to took to think, the display on the register flashed 'Supervisor Override Required' and a three digit code. The clerk was puzzled and Margret asked what the problem was. The clerk told Margret she had to get the manager, but not to worry, it was probably because her card was from another city. Margret started to raise a fuss about being short on time, but the clerk reassured her not to worry, this would only take a second.

Margret wasn't worried about the checks she had written back in her home town because she was, after all, in another city. The clerk went to get the manager, who was standing two registers over from where Margret was. He came over with a big smile on his face. As he came over he was reaching for the keys he needed to put in the register to override the code. But when he saw the three digit code being displayed his hand stopped rummaging around in his pocket. The code told him he was standing in front of a major bad check writer.

The store chain had just installed this system that linked all of its stores back to one central office via computer. In this computer there were two different codes for bad check writers. One code meant a simple 'NO' that was reserved for a person who had a bad check but hadn't gotten it taken care of yet. The other code meant 'HELL NO' and was reserved solely for the people who had written so many bad checks at their stores the chain was starting to consider legal action.

It was this latter category that Margret fell into.

The manager explained as nice as he could that there was no way he could take a check from her and in fact, she would have to wait while he called in to his main office to see what he was supposed to do. Margret was in a state of shock and offered no resistance as she followed him towards his office in the front of the store. While they walked the manager was explaining to her the problem would probably be quickly resolved and she would be able to get on her way with her groceries. As he stopped to unlock the door to his office, Margret felt the anxiety attack coming on and bolted for the front doors.

The manager, unsure about what to do, didn't pursue Margret once she was outside of the store. He went quickly into his office to call in for instructions. Once Margret was outside and saw the manager wasn't following her, slowed to a quick walk towards where the car was parked.

Ronnie saw Margret as she was walking across the parking lot and wondered why she wasn't carrying any packages. He noticed there was something very different about the way she was coming out to the car. She was walking at a mildly quick walk and was looking over her shoulder every few feet. As she got closer to the car he saw that she had a very upset look on her face and when she got closer, he could see the upset leaking down her face.

She was crying when she got into the car and Ronnie asked what the problem was. He was also wondering where the groceries were. Margret told him they wouldn't take her check because it was from out of town. When she had shown them her check cashing card from the same chain, she had been humiliated in front of a bunch of people that were checking out. Every one had been looking at her and she had been greatly embarrassed in front of all of the strangers.

Ronnie offered to go inside and try to straighten this matter out. After all, he had cash and if they wouldn't take a check, he knew they would damn well take cash. Along with the cash, he was going to give them a piece of his mind about being rude to a customer. Margret insisted he didn't have to do that and added she just wanted to go home. Margret knew the last thing she wanted Ronnie to do was to go inside and find out the other side of the story. Besides, she told him, after the way she had been treated, she wouldn't buy another thing at this chain even if it was the last store on the planet.

Ronnie started the car and was pulling out of the parking lot just as the manager came out of the store looking to see if Margret was still around. When the manager had called the main office and explained what had happened, he was instructed to see if she was still around and to detain her if possible. Then if he was successful in detaining her, he was to contact the police and have her arrested for theft.

Ronnie noticed on the ride home that Margret's mood had changed considerably since she had gone into the store. He thought back to the way she had been to him yesterday when she had been nice to him and last night she had been...well, she had been there for him. Even today she had been nice to him and now here she sat, sullen and moody. Ronnie was beginning to resent the fact that he had even stopped at that ill-fated store. Up until then, everything, last night, today, had been great.

Margret was sitting there greatly perplexed as to whether or not she should come clean with Ronnie and tell him about her little faux pas with the checks. She knew if she did, Ronnie might go off in some sort of rage that, although she had blamed her injuries on to Ted, had never seen Ronnie in before. So being afraid of the unknown, she kept her mouth shut. Still, it bothered her because she knew that sooner or later, the inevitable would happen and he would find out. It scared her wondering what his reaction would be when that day finally came.

Then she remembered that in two weeks, Ted was going to rid her of her problem and take care of Ronnie on a permanent basis. That is, if she continued to push the right buttons with Ted. If she could get through the next two weeks without screwing up again, she wouldn't have anything to worry about. She would be with Ted and her life would be set as an officer's wife. She would be able to just walk out of this miserable life and start anew in some place where nobody knew her. Next time, she wouldn't have anything to do with the checkbook and would let Ted handle all of the finances.

The whole time Margret was sitting there planning her future life, she gave not one thought to Nancy, who was sitting in her car seat asleep not more than three feet behind her. Margret should have been sitting there thinking about how to explain to Ted that she had a daughter and would not only be getting her, but becoming an instant father at the same time.

The rest of the ride was done in silence and by the time they got home, the mood was grim. Just before they got to the house, Ronnie stopped by a chicken place and got a bucket of chicken for dinner. Ronnie knew Margret liked this particular brand and was doing everything he could think of to try and recapture the mood Margret had been in earlier.

Margret just picked at her meal, the whole time she was eating, she was consumed with the thought of what Ronnie might do if he found out about the checks. She knew that she only had two weeks to wait, but to a person in her place, two weeks could seem like a mighty long time. She was amazed that so far, Ronnie hadn't figured out the telephones had been turned off in the house for over a week now.

The night got later and soon it was time to go to bed. There was no intimacy this night and Ronnie drifted off to sleep. This night there was a dream and Ronnie's life would never be the same.

51.

When Ronnie opened his dream eyes, he was sitting at the high place. He looked down and saw he was sitting with his legs crossed under him in the classic lotus position. He looked up and craning his neck, saw that the stars were out in abundance. Ronnie gazed up in amazement at the view, there were so many stars in sight it was hard to tell the individual stars and constellations. Even though Ronnie felt at peace here and the view was something to marvel at, he felt lonely. He marveled at the feeling he was having and wondered how the human race could be so vain to think humans are the only intelligent life around. Surely, there had to be someone else out there.

Almost as if in answer to his thoughts, a falling star blazed across the sky. It was low and the fiery streak stretched across the sky from one horizon to the other.

'Wow!' Ronnie said aloud.

Wow is right. A voice said beside him. At the same time, Ronnie felt a bony hand grip his leg. Startled, Ronnie jerked his head back down from the view and saw the Professor sitting beside him. With a shudder of disgust, he shoved the hand off of his leg.

'Cut that shit out.' Ronnie said flatly as he was shoving the hand off of his leg.

Awww, you never let me have any fun. The Professor replied.

'Just remember that and you'll keep all of your appendages.' Ronnie replied sarcastically.

Listen asshole. You had better watch your mouth. I don't feel like having to teach you a lesson tonight. All I want to do is talk.

'Then why didn't you drag me down in front of the computer like you always do?' Ronnie asked with a more respectful tone to his voice.

Because for now, I'm through writing. I finished my first book and I'm taking a small break before I write the next one. Besides, I don't need your help with the computer anymore.

'Well...I'm real happy for you. I figured you were working on your own when I found the pile of paper this morning. Have you got any ideas on what your next subject will be about?'

It really doesn't really matter what my next topic will be if I can't get you to mail the fucking things. The Professor replied, his voice rising as he said it until the last two words came out as a bone rattling shout.

'Sorry about that. But I had some questions. I did hand the columns in.' Ronnie stammered in reply.

Look boy, the only question you should have is 'How fast do you want me to drive to the post office?'.

'Wait a minute! We have never really talked about this. What exactly am I supposed to do?'

The Professor paused for a moment and after a brief thought said, *I guess you're right. It's real simple. I write them, give you a cover letter, and you send them off to the address I give you. Is that simple enough for you?*

'I understand, I'm not stupid.' Ronnie replied sharply and then added, 'Why did you write the cover letter the way you did?'

What do you mean?

'You wrote the book but you wrote the cover letter as if it was coming from me. Why did you do that?'

And you say you're not stupid. Look, the guy the letter is addressed to was one of my students also. Do you think you were the only student I ever had? The Professor paused for a second and then continued. *He's a big shot now at the publishing firm I gave you the address to. He knows me, or I should say he used to know me. He also knows that I'm long since passed from your world. What do you think he would do if he was to suddenly start getting correspondence from me?*

'Think it was a joke and trash what was sent?'

Bingo. I guess you're not so dumb after all. So tag, you're it. I write the letters as if they are coming from you. Hopefully he'll bite on the part that I sent you and actually read what you sent. If you had taken the time to actually read what I was writing, you would have seen that I pinned you as the author also.

'Okay. I promise that I'll send it out first thing Monday morning. Is there anything else I should know about or you want me to do?'

Since you mentioned it and promise to quit dicking around when I give you something to mail, I have some information you might be interested in. The Professor said. As he said the last part he acted excited.

'Well...I can see that you are dying to tell me something. What is it?' Ronnie asked mildly curious. He had never really seen the Professor acting like he was right now.

Okay. But I want you to promise me that you won't act on the information that I give you.

257

R. H. Gosse

'What?'

Promise that you'll pretend you didn't know anything about this when it happens.

'Whatever.'

Promise.

'Okay, I promise.'

Margret has been writing bad checks. You are also about to get a visit from the long arm of the law. The Professor replied matter of factually.

'What?!! Margret has been doing what?'

Writing bad checks. Hanging bad paper. Floating worthless tree pulp...

'I know what you're talking about.' Ronnie replied, cutting the Professor off and sounding clearly upset. 'How do you know this? What proof do you have?'

Do you think the little fiasco at the grocery store this afternoon was because they didn't like the out of town flavor of your checks? It was because that chain is tired of being ripped off by her and people like her. Had she stayed in the store a bit longer, they would have had her arrested today.

'Why are you telling me this?' Ronnie asked feeling defeated and like he had nothing to live for.

For two reasons really. First, to let you know before hand you are about to go through some rough weather in your smooth sailing. But you will come through it and things will be much better on the other side.

'And what is the other thing?' Ronnie asked after the Professor had fallen silent for a couple of seconds.

To give you a heads up. If you get on the horn Monday and call the bank and talk to them, you might be able to soften the blow headed your way. I think you'll find that alot of people will work with you if you're honest with them. Tell them you didn't know what your lunatic bitch wife was up to. It might even keep you out of jail.

'Why would I go to jail?' Ronnie snapped back. He was in a high state of pissed.

Because...In this state, you, being the man, are responsible for what your wife does.

'That's stupid. I didn't have anything to do with it.'

Sorry, but that's the law. Are you okay?

'Yeah, I'm okay. I just can't believe this. Why would she do this to me?' Ronnie asked glumly.

Because she's a first class selfish bitch. But don't worry, you'll come out of this all right and a much better person for the experience.

'Great, just what I need, more experience. Thanks for telling me.' Ronnie said in a small weak voice.

Nothing to it. I consider you the lover I never had.

Ronnie said nothing but just gave the Professor a dirty look along with the frown that was stuck on his face.

Oh yeah...One more thing Ronnie.

'There's something else?'

Yeah. That guy that Margret is still fucking is going to try to kill you. The Professor said nonchalantly. With no more emotion to his voice than as if he was saying the sky was blue.

'What?!! When?!!' Ronnie cried in disbelief.

Soon. So watch your ass. Okay?

'Great...Is there anything else you might want to lay on me?'

Nope. That just about does it. Remember, you can't act on this. You know, like beat her ass or something like that. Just call the bank and talk to them. Tell them you found a returned check notice and you want to find out what's going on. They will work with you.

'Thanks I guess.' Ronnie replied.

One more thing Ronnie. The Professor said as he stood up.

'Shit, now what?'

Mail the fucking book! The Professor said as he faded away from sight, leaving Ronnie to sit by himself under the stars.

Ronnie sat there wondering what it was that had caused Margret to go and do something like this to him. His first impulse was to rip her throat out and be done with her. If she was gone, out of his life forever he would be so much happier. Now he understood why she didn't want him to go back into the store and had wanted to leave so quickly.

Then his mind settled on the fact that the bitch was going to try and have him killed. So she hadn't stopped her affair after the talk he had with her like she had promised she would do. This made him madder than the business about the checks. Ronnie wondered what it was about this Ted guy that attracted Margret to him. Then Ronnie decided that it really didn't matter what it was, if the guy was stupid enough to try to kill him, then Ronnie would kick his ass. And when he was finished, Ronnie thought with a smile on his face, when he was finished with her lover he would go and kick Margret's ass also just to teach her a lesson.

When Ronnie came back from his deep thought he saw the sky was beginning to get lighter to what seemed to be the direction of east. It was getting time for the dawn to come and for the first time, Ronnie noticed a chill to the air and a slight breeze was starting to pick up. Ronnie stood and stretched with his arms raised above his head. Anyone looking at him would have thought he was raising his arms to greet the dawn and the coming of a new day.

Ronnie felt a calm, an inner peace he hadn't felt in a long time. But deep down, he was depressed at the thought of what was going to happen. There was nothing he could do now but try to stop the flow of bad checks and try to keep Margret as well as himself out of jail. He decided he would take the Professors advice and get ahold of the bank to work out some kind of a deal to pay the worthless checks off. Then if he survived Ted's plan to do him in, he would seriously re-evaluate his situation with Margret. The thought of a divorce was on the edge of his mind, but he pushed it off and told himself he would take one thing at a time.

He watched as the dawn revealed itself to him and it was a glorious morning. He looked down over the edge and saw the town far below him, still asleep. It looked so peaceful and serene, this sleeping town below him, and he began to wonder what town this was. What it must be like to live in a small sleepy little burg like this one below him.

Ronnie's mind returned to his earlier thoughts, then he really started to question what it was about Ted that was drawing his wife to him. Ronnie did everything Margret wanted when she wanted it. Hell, even the greasy chicken he bought on the way home was because she liked that particular brand. Although he now understood her lack of appetite tonight. But there had to be something that was a draw, some quality to Ted that Ronnie lacked. Unfortunately for Ronnie, he never thought of the attraction of forbidden fruit. And money.

The sun rose quickly and as if in high speed, he saw the town below wake up. The streets alternated between heavy and light with the flow of traffic. It was like some sort of concrete artery that was passing heavy metal blood. Ronnie looked and saw the sun was high and he could feel its radiant warmth. But it wasn't unpleasant. In fact, Ronnie felt quite comfortable.

Now that he felt calmer, he decided it was time to wake up. As he felt himself coming to consciousness, watching his dream world fade away, the last thing he thought he heard was the Professor say, *Keep your mouth shut and don't let on that you know. You promised!*

Ronnie became aware he was still lying in bed and he opened his eyes to the world of everyday reality. He felt slightly disappointed he wasn't still in his high place. As he lay there, he looked over and saw Margret was already gone.

His first thought was she was downstairs with her lover. No, he thought, she's probably on the phone with him right now. Ronnie craned his neck to get a look at the clock and saw it was almost ten in the morning. He hadn't slept this late in a long, long time.

Ronnie got up and headed for the shower to start the new day.

52.

Margret woke up at the crack of dawn, her close brush with destiny yesterday had given her a restless night. When she did sleep, she had the same dream about being chased across a giant checkbook. She would wake up in a sweat and it would take her a spell to get back to sleep. When she did sleep, she would return right back to the dream like she had never left. The dream combined with Ronnie's constant snoring, made sleep an elusive commodity that night. Around sunrise, Margret gave up on sleep and went downstairs to watch tv.

She sat there for a long time flipping channels, but as usual, there wasn't anything on. When the church hour hit, all of the channels were filled with preachers telling her she was going to hell unless she sent them lots of money so they could absolve her of her sins.

Margret sat there thinking and realized she had never really given a thought to good and evil, or her soul. She had just lived her life thinking about herself and not really giving a damn where the chips fell when they were thrown. That is as long as the chips fell in a direction that benefitted her. She sat there listening about salvation and how God was going to let her into the Pearly Gates and forgive her of her sins. All she had to do was put her hand over the hand the tv Preacher held up, confess her sins and then pray for a few minutes asking for Jesus and God to come into her life. By the way, please don't forget to send the preacher a thousand bucks as a love offering. Hallelujah.

Margret found it easy to cover the hand and repeat the words the good Reverend said. But she found it impossible to even consider parting with the money.

Now that Margret was feeling at peace with God, she sat there thinking about the next two weeks, and how cool she was going to play things. If she got lucky, she would be able to get a couple more grand before Ted took care of Ronnie.

Then she would just step right out of this life and into her new one with Ted. No one would know where she had gone and she would be able to start all over again. The checks were part of her old life and with her just disappearing, there would be no way anyone would be able to find her. That would stop the people from hassling her about the money they were owed.

261

R. H. Gosse

Margret sat there thinking about the next two weeks in a way that a mountain climber thinks about a mountain he is about to climb. Not this weekend, but the weekend after would be the peak. Then she would be swept away from all of this. She would have plenty of money and wouldn't have to write a check ever again. Even if she did write a check, it would be almost a year from now when she had a new name. Even if she still had her old name, she would at least be in a new location, far away from this shitty little town.

The thought of this made her happy and she smiled for the first time since the supermarket yesterday. A small voice she didn't recognize in the back of her mind asked a single question.

What if Ted decides to just walk and not do this for you?

That question stopped her dead in her mental tracks. What if Ted decided not to come back to her? Just dump her and not call her when he got back to town? She had no way of finding him at the base and she wouldn't be able to hang around his dorm room waiting for him to show up. For that matter, she had no way onto the base. Even the last time she had followed Ted and he had to sign her in at the main gate.

This thought took an edge off of her happy mood.

Well...I'll just have to make sure that if he does call, Margret thought to herself, I'll just have to make sure he wants to go along with my plans.

Now her smile was back and she started to fantasize about the things she would do with her body to Ted to ensure his obedience to her.

53.

As Ronnie finished getting ready for the day, his thought's kept going back to his dream. How much of what the Professor had told him was even true? How could he be sure he wasn't getting his chain pulled in some sick prank by the Professor? Still, a large part of him wanted to believe in what he had been told. The Professor had told him things before and they had proven themselves out. But how could he be sure this time? He could see Margret getting herself a lover, but to have that lover kill him? He knew she was mean but he couldn't fathom Margret going to that extreme. And the mess about the checks, he couldn't see her doing that. After giving it much thought, Ronnie decided to take one thing at a time and see how the days ahead would play out.

Still, there was a big temptation to go downstairs and confront her on the subject. But his promise to the Professor kept him from doing that. Ronnie didn't want to make the Professor mad by breaking his promise. Ronnie imagined there were things the Professor could do to him while he was asleep that might be really bad. Ronnie's hand crept up and touched his throat where the bruises had been when he had woken up that time and a cold shudder ran up his spine.

Ronnie put on his T-shirt and headed for the stairwell. As he passed by Nancy's room he saw that Nancy was awake and standing in her crib. Ronnie walked through the door and Nancy was all smiles and threw her arms open in her pick-me-up gesture. When he picked her up he could smell the surprise waiting for him in her diaper. He could also feel she was soaking wet.

Ronnie sat her back down, got some clothes out of her dresser and took them into the bathroom. Then he came back and got Nancy and took her into the bathroom. After giving her a bath and getting her dressed, they both went down the stairs.

Margret looked up and smiled at them when they reached the bottom of the stairs.

"Good morning." She said as she jumped up and took Nancy from Ronnie. "Did you have a good sleep?" She asked him.

"Fairly good." Ronnie casually replied, "How about you?"

"Okay I guess. I had some really strange dreams last night and woke up early this morning." Margret replied as she headed for the kitchen with Nancy in the crook of her arm.

"Tell me about it." Ronnie replied as a statement on his dream state. But Margret took it the wrong way and answered him.

"Well. It was nothing really, just a whole bunch of different things."

I bet. Ronnie thought to himself and then fought the urge to ask 'Did it have anything to do with your lover killing me or was it just about the bad checks?'

Margret came out of the kitchen a couple of minutes later with Nancy and her breakfast. She sat Nancy in her high chair next to the table and sat down. Nothing was really said for the next ten minutes as she fed Nancy her breakfast. After the feeding was done and Nancy was hosed off, Margret came into the living room and put Nancy down on the floor. Then Margret asked Ronnie what he wanted to do today.

Ronnie replied he hadn't really put much thought to it, but he was open for anything. Margret told him that if he didn't mind, she just wanted to lay around today and rest up. Ronnie agreed saying it sounded like a good idea. They spent the rest of the day laying around the house and resting. At one point, Ronnie decided to toy with Margret for a bit and told her he was really mad about the way she had been treated yesterday. In fact, he was so outraged he was going to call the chain tomorrow while he was at work and lodge a big protest about the way one of their loyal customers had been treated.

Margret was horrified. She had never considered Ronnie would do something like that. She had figured he would just forget about it and that would be the end of the subject. She quickly told him not to worry about it and that it was better to chalk this one up to experience and move on with their lives.

Her reaction was enough to confirm from Ronnie there might be some credence to what the Professor had told him. If this was the old Margret, she would have been the first one to scream for her pound of flesh in retribution. But now, here she was sitting next to him giving him a speech about how the meek will inherit the earth and it was better to turn the other cheek.

Ronnie almost slipped up on that point and said something else, something closer to home that would really make her wonder how much of her evil plans he knew. But as his mouth opened he heard the Professor say *You Promised*. Ronnie shut his mouth with a snap and just sat there looking at the tv.

Margret was in a quiet state of panic. What if Ronnie did call them tomorrow? What would they tell him? Or would he get lost in the bureaucracy that run the company and get his complaint quietly taken? The questions whirling through her mind was starting to give her a headache. She realized the best thing she could do was to divert his attention away from his idea.

Margret turned to Ronnie and said, "I do know one thing that I would like to do."

"What's that?"

"Something we haven't done during the day in a long time."

"What's that?"

"Come upstairs and I'll show you." Margret said as she got up, looking over she saw Nancy asleep in her playpen. When she saw that, she looked back at Ronnie and took off her clothes. Soon, she was standing there naked in front of him.

"Oh yeah?" Ronnie said as he sat there looking at her.

"Yeah. But there's a lot more to see and do upstairs." After saying that she turned and walked to the staircase. Looking back, she saw Ronnie stand up. When he did that, she went on up the stairs to the bedroom.

The rest of the afternoon was spent in the haze of sex. Ronnie was worn out when they finished the third time. Margret was insatiable. Ronnie thought it was because of him. Margret was thinking about how mad Ronnie would be if he knew the whole time they were together, she had been fantasizing about Ted.

The sex with Ronnie was okay, Margret thought to herself, but it was nothing compared to the sex she had with Ted. Then with a smile on her face she had the thought that having sex with Ronnie was like having an appetizer before a really good meal. It let you chew, but it didn't really fill you up.

Ronnie asked Margret what she was smiling about and she replied, "Just you baby." as she reached down and took his flaccid cock in her hand, trying to stir life back into it.

As Ronnie was beginning to respond to her advances, in his mind he heard the Professor ask him one question. *Does a Black Widow Spider smile during sex just before it eats its mate?* Ronnie started to become annoyed that the Professor was intruding on his private moment but by then it was too late. Margret's hand was working miracles and he submitted to her.

54.

Ted had been waiting in a staging area for a day now. The exercise he was on had gone totally SNAFU. He snickered to himself about the acronym SNAFU. It meant Situation Normal All Fouled Up. The exercise could have been described in stronger terms, but this seemed to fit the description the best.

By now, he should have already dangled on the end of a parachute while he was being dropped into the desert. Once on the ground, he was supposed to survive and avoid capture for three days. This was the highlight of his training, other than flying. Some of the guys who survived flight school, washed out or was rotated back when they failed this test. It was very rare that somebody actually died during this training, but it did happen every now and then. Ted had paid attention in the survival school and thought he knew how to use his survival vest to its fullest capability.

Ted thought back to water school. It had been a breeze compared to this. Floating in the open waters knowing you were going to be picked up was no challenge. All he had to do there was stay afloat and not succumb to hypothermia. Still, knowing there was a boat that would be picking you up at the end of the day had taken the edge off of the thrill.

But this was different. He had to actually survive on his own wits and make it to the pick up point thirty miles away from where he was dropped. The fun part would come with having to avoid the enemy. He knew the people who would be looking for him were on his side, but he could well imagine the humiliating situations they would put him through if they caught him. Of course there were the stories about what they could and would do to a person that was caught (partially spread by the Drill Instructor and partially grown from legends that had come from the men themselves), but Ted suspected those stories were spread as a part of the head game that was being played on his squad.

Ted thought back to a game he used to play when he was in the Boy Scouts. Late at night on a camp out, they would play a game of Capture the Flag. There was a flag set up in each 'Base' camp. The object was to protect your own flag while trying your best to get the other teams flag. Ted always considered himself the best at this game. When he was older and a more seasoned Scout, he was hardly ever captured. The few times he had been captured, he was able to evade like no one had ever been seen doing this feat.

Ted remembered one time he had been captured. He was standing in front of a tree and while the two Scouts were arguing about which one was going to take him to the 'Jail', he had slowly climbed the tree behind him. The best part was when the two Scouts had finally turned their attention back to him and found he was nowhere to be seen. It never occurred to either of the boys to simply look up. If they had, they would have seen Ted ten feet over their heads with a huge smile on his face. After the boys left, Ted came out of the tree and continued on his way.

Ted thought of this exercise as nothing more than a big government sponsored Capture the Flag game.

What was keeping Ted and the rest of his squad stuck in the holding area was a freakish low pressure front that had stalled in the area. The clouds were too low for a safe drop and the constant storms were causing flash flood problems in the surrounding valleys and desert. There was a rumor that if the frontal system didn't move out by tomorrow afternoon, the exercise would be scrubbed for two weeks until their squad could be put back into the system and rescheduled for the survival range.

The time on the ramp gave a lot of time to think about his situation with Margret. From his view point, the only thing that would take care of her problem would be for someone to give her old man a one ounce dose of lead poisoning. Since Ted didn't know anyone that would do something like that for him, it made him the most likely candidate for the job.

Part of Ted, the still sane human part, told him just to leave it alone and walk away. Everyone had a story, some happy, some sad. It was unfortunate Margret's story turned out to be a sad one and there would be other women in his young life. All he had to do was wait and see what time brought along. But Ted didn't want to wait, he wanted Margret, or at least his hormones wanted Margret. He was just too young, inexperienced, and stupid to know the difference.

Also playing against Ted's emotional state was the four hour bad-ass psych out speech from the Drill Instructor. The speech where he was a living, breathing, killing machine. There was none better than him (other than God himself), or none meaner. The speech went on to mention this was going to be nothing more than a mere stroll through the desert because he was rough and tough and there was none meaner or craftier walking on two feet. He was nothing more than a government issued weapon in combat boots.

Like a good football coach, the Drill Instructor got his team of men pumped up to win the battle. Since the playing field was over a thirty mile area, he had to get his men as pumped as possible. He was very good with the Rah-Rah speeches and had them pumped up to a fever pitch, even the delay on the ramp wasn't diminishing their drive for action. If anything, it was intensifying the aura of physical and mental strength. The DI knew if he got his men all psyched out before they left, they would do better on their own once they were out in the field. He wanted them the best he could get them to give them a better chance for survival.

Besides, the DI had money in the pool the other instructors had going on whose group was going to come out first with the least amount of captures and causalities. This time he had a good group of guys and it looked like he had a good chance of collecting the bet this time.

After almost twenty hours of waiting in the staging area pondering his problem, Ted thought he had what he was going to do to Ronnie planned out very well. He knew of a back street biker bar where he would most likely be able to get a gun for very little money. Then he would rent a car and do a simple drive by shooting. He would wait until Ronnie came home from work and when Ronnie got out of his car, Ted would pull up and ask for directions. Then, when Ronnie was right in front of the car window, Ted would simply put a lead slug between his eyes and just calmly drive away. He wanted Ronnie close so he could watch the look on the bastards face when he saw the gun go off in his direction.

He would then go wash the car and return it to where he had rented it. Ted decided it would be best if he rented the car in another town. After everything was done with, all he would have to do is lay low until he graduated. Then Margret and he would be in a different state and she would be able to start her life all over again.

Yes, Ted thought to himself, that's exactly what I'll do and the world will be rid of just one more piece of slime.

He noticed the guys around him were heeding the old Marine adage, 'Don't stand when you can sit. Don't sit when you can lay. Don't just lay there when you can sleep.' Most of the guys were catching as much sleep as they could in preparation for the big event. In war, one never knows when they will be able to get the next 'safe' sleep.

Everyone was outfitted the same. Parachute, survival vest, and nothing else but their helmets and the clothes on their backs. The survival vest was complete and had a small flare gun along with a couple of smoke flares and star flares. If you got out there and got into trouble or just couldn't take it anymore, you could just pop a flare and when the chopper came near, light up the smoke for a pick up.

Nobody had any intentions of using these five items, especially after the DI explained in no uncertain terms that "You had better be dead when you lit them up, rather than embarrassing him by wimping out and bringing shame on himself, his comrades, and the whole human race.' Then the DI had speculated about how none of the military greats ever admitted defeat. In fact, the last time he had looked, there was no such word as defeat in the military dictionary.

Several of the guys had tried to give their flare gun and flares back to the DI saying they weren't pussies, they were men, and being men they wouldn't need this instrument of defeat. They were men and real men get the job done. Hoo-Rah! But the DI refused them by saying it was necessary for them to carry these items in case they got seriously hurt. He then reminded them that there were rattlesnakes and scorpions out there. Also, if someone was stupid enough to do it, a person could fall into a washout or a gully and break a leg or worse.

Nobody bothered to ask what was in the 'or worse' category. They were too pumped up to care because they were invincible. They were the perfect fighting machine.

Ted was a dangerous man. He was dangerous because he was full of himself and had no regards for human life. In the big picture, it wasn't his fault. The head games that are played in the military can sometimes convince a man to put himself in harms way with no regard or thought of personal harm. That is what makes a good soldier, because when the chips are really down the job must get done regardless of the personal consequences.

55.

Ronnie had been at work for ten minutes when the phone rang, it was Floyd sounding all nasal and coughing. He explained to Ronnie that he had come down with the flu or something like it during the weekend and wouldn't be coming in at all today.

"Well Floyd, I'm real sorry you feel bad." Ronnie told him.

"That's okay," Floyd replied after a brief coughing fit, "Thought I had dodged the bug this year but the damn thing got me anyway."

"I don't want to add to your troubles Floyd, but I'm not sure I know what to do to keep this place running. I haven't had that much experience and I don't know all of the in's and out's yet."

Floyd started laughing loudly which led to another coughing fit. Once he calmed down and got his breathing under control he said, "Look kid, there's really nothing to it. If you see anyone screwing around, chase them off to do some work. Stay in the office and answer the phone if it rings, which most likely it won't. If anyone bitches about something, get the first person you see screwing around to go and fix it. Then in the afternoon, take my cart and make sure nobody's out sleeping in the woods instead of working."

"Basically, you want me to lay low and keep everyone from just standing around. Keep everyone busy."

"You got it kid. Welcome to the secret world of management. You'll do fine. I'll call you later to make sure everything is going well."

"No problem. Call if you want but do what you gotta do to get better."

"Talk to you later, bye." Floyd said and then hung up.

Ronnie hung up and then went outside to make sure everyone had a chore and was on their way to do it instead of standing around swapping lies about deeds of the weekend. Once everyone was gone and Ronnie was there by himself, he went back into the shack and waited for nine o'clock to roll around. When it did he got out the telephone book and looked up the phone number to the bank.

The phone was answered on the second ring by a woman he could hear the smile she was wearing in her voice. Ronnie was as polite as he could be and explained he was going through some things this weekend and found a check notice. He went on to explain, he had never seen the notice before and his wife wouldn't explain about it and just passed it off as a mistake the bank had made but it was taken care of. He was just calling to find out what was going on with his checking account. The pleasant young woman said that she would check on it for him and asked him what his checking account number was. Ronnie imagined the smile on her face when she said that and he told her the account number. He was then put on hold and listened to a Muzak version of a Deep Purple tune.

Ronnie didn't get to listen to the mind numbing groovy music for very long. A gentleman picked up and began talking to Ronnie.

"Mr. Fisher?"

"Yes."

"Hello. My name is Mr. Gates and I'm the Vice-President of collections. I understand that we have a little problem with you account." The man said in a voice that was authoritative and as cold as ice.

"Well Mr. Gates, that's what I was trying to explain to the young lady. You see, I was looking through some things this weekend and I found a returned check notice from the bank. Since I didn't know anything about it, I asked my wife about it and she got all defensive and wouldn't answer my question saying it was a mistake at the bank and it was already handled. Since I seem to be out of the loop here about what's going on with my money, I thought I'd call you guys and find out what was going on." Ronnie lied to Gates. After all, he couldn't tell the man that a dream ghost had told him to call because his wife was writing bad checks.

"Mr. Fisher. Are you telling me you have no idea what is going on with your account?" Gates voice had softened a little telling Ronnie his story was on it's way to being bought.

"Call me Ronnie, Mr. Gates, everyone calls me Ronnie. And yes, I'm ashamed to admit that I don't have the slightest idea what's going on with my account. You see, my wife handles the checkbook and all I do is put my paychecks in."

"Well Ronnie, we have a big problem with your account. It seems that somebody has been writing alot of checks out of it, several thousand dollars worth of bad checks I believe."

There was silence on Ronnie's end. He was sitting there with his mouth open in the state of shock.

"Hello...Ronnie, are you there?"

"Wha...What?" Ronnie managed weakly.

"Ronnie...Mr. Fisher, are you alright?" Gates asked sounding concerned.

"Did you say several thousand?" Ronnie asked timidly.

"Let me check the totals." After a brief pause he said, "The total after what came in last night is seven thousand, nine hundred and thirty nine dollars and some pennies."

"OhmiGod." Ronnie said, his state of mind had gone from shock to disbelief.

"The checks are all signed by a Margret Fisher, she's your wife isn't she?"

"Yes Mr. Gates. How could this have happened? What do I do? Doesn't anyone call to see if the checks might have been stolen or something?"

"We did call. There's a note here in your file that we talked to Mrs. Fisher the beginning of last week. She said she would come right in and take care of the problem. We haven't seen her and we have tried to call back, but the notation here in the computer say's that there was no answer."

"Mr. Gates, I want to get this problem taken care of as quickly as possible. Can I make payments? I really don't make that much but I will pay you what I can each payday until this matter is resolved."

"Of course we would want restitution on what we have here, we can hold the checks we currently have and you can pay them here. I just need to know we can resolve this as quickly as possible."

"Excuse me Mr. Gates, but what do you mean by the checks that you have there? Don't you have all of the checks that were written?"

"Goodness no. When a check comes through it goes back to the store it was written to for their collections department."

Another slug in the gut for Ronnie. He had never considered the checks would go back to the stores. "Mr. Gates, is there a way I can get a list of the places the outstanding checks were written to? I would like to contact the stores and make arrangements with them to pay these bad debts off."

"We usually don't do that." Gates said and then lowered his voice and continued, "But I guess we can make an exception in this case. Tell you what, I don't do this for everyone, but if you take care of this matter quickly, I'll wave the check charges. But I can only do that if you make a good effort. Do you understand?"

"Thank you Mr. Gates. I really appreciate your help in this matter. Could you please put some kind of freeze on my account and close it or something?"

"I'll freeze your account, but I can't close it until everything is paid up on this end."

"I understand. Again, thank you for your help. Listen, I can get off from work in an hour for lunch. Is there anyway I can come by and get the list then?"

"Sure. Just come by the bank and ask for me, tell them I'm expecting you."

"I sure will and I'll see you shortly. Good bye."

Ronnie hung up the phone and sat there in shock. He couldn't believe the Professor had been right and Margret had done so much financial damage. But at the same time he was shocked by the situation, he was also simmering in his own juices. Margret would die for this, Ronnie thought to himself. Had Margret been around that instant, he would have killed her.

How could she do this to them? He kept asking himself over and over again.

56.

After nearly thirty hours in the staging area watching the lightning and the tremendous amounts of rain falling, it was announced that the exercise was canceled for this week. Frustrated and ready to eat raw meat, some of Ted's comrades argued that this was just a little rain storm and they weren't afraid to get wet. There was a lot of "Yeah's", "Damn Right's", and "Amens" murmured through the group. The DI calmly listened to this and told them that this was the way it was going to be. If anyone had any problems with this, they could do laps around the huge hanger they were sitting in until the DI himself got tired.

In consolation, they were given leave to go into the local town and get a beer if they wanted to. They would have to be back in five hours because that's when they would be shipping back to their home base.

Once the group was dismissed, everyone quickly stripped out of their gear until they just had their utility uniforms. They piled the gear neatly where the DI told them to put it and then it was a foot race to find a phone they could call for taxi's. Twenty minutes later the group was on its way to town to check out the local talent.

Ted opted to tag along with Bud. Bud was a real bad ass from the ground up. Bud almost didn't get into flying school because of a small problem about an assault charge stemming from a bar fight. At the last minute the charges were mysteriously dropped and the other party (who had taken the worst part of the fight) just wanted to drop the matter and get on with his life.

At first, the DI had really given Bud a hard time, but when it was seen that the man had a natural talent for flying, the DI got off of his case and loosened up a little. Bud whizzed through the simulators with ease. Scenarios that were presented to him, engine fire, flame outs, wind shears during landing were a breeze for him. He was also a natural at dog fights and hit targets on the ground with ease. While the rest of his buddies were sweating bullets during the simulations, Bud actually seemed bored. But he was still a bad ass and if he told you he was going to kick your ass about something, he would find a way to do it.

Ted stayed with him more to keep him out of trouble than as a social thing.

When Ted and Bud got into their cab, the driver asked them where they wanted to go and Bud promptly informed the driver that he wanted to go to the sleaziest bar there was and still be able to get a cab. The driver told Bud there was only one place that fit that description, it was a biker bar and a pretty rough one at that. The driver added that unfortunately, they didn't cotton much to military types. Bud replied it was just the type of place he was looking for and added he didn't give a shit what they did or did not like, he wanted beer and lots of it.

The driver muttered something about it being their lives and they were off.

Five minutes later, the cab pulled up at a place that couldn't even qualify as a hole in the wall. Bud threw open the door of the cab and proclaimed he was home. Ted got out of the other door and saw, much to his distaste, just how scummy this place was. There were no windows, just a door leading into a faceless, cinder block building. Ted looked around and saw there were no high class cars parked in the dirt parking lot. Just a couple of cars that had various dents and scrapes, cars that most definitely had seen much better days a long time ago. But there were a dozen motorcycles parked in a row like a line of steel horses tied up at the water trough outside a saloon.

Bud gave the cab driver a twenty dollar bill and then looked at Ted. "Let's go maggot!" Bud yelled at him and then turned around, heading for the door.

Ted followed him and when he got to the door saw, much to his disdain, that someone had puked just outside the door. It didn't look like a normal puke. It looked as though Godzilla had tossed his cookies while leaning out through the door. Whoever had done the dastardly deed had missed a good part of the ground and had hit the wall. Bud pointed to it and remarked "The bastard that done that musta been so drunk he missed the ground." Then turned and went through the door.

Going inside, Ted decided the outside of the bar looked better than the inside. The inside was clean enough, but the clientele left a lot to be desired.

All heads turned in Bud and Ted's direction when they walked through the door. Whatever intellectual endeavors that had been going on before they walked in quickly ceased. No one said anything as Bud and Ted walked into the bar.

"I want beer!" Bud said very loudly, much to Ted's dismay. "And any man, or woman, that has balls enough to walk up here and stand in front of me, why...I'll buy them a beer too!"

A nervous laugh went through the group of people that were in there. The next five minutes was spent buying beer for everyone who took Bud up on his offer. This seemed the perfect ice breaker and after the first round, it was like they were all old drinking buddies.

"Man, when you opened your mouth when we first walked in, I thought we were going to be killed." Ted said in a low voice to Bud when the crowd finally subsided and they were drinking alone.

"You forget," Bud said in a loud voice as he threw open his arms, "These are my people."

Several of the people in the bar, who most likely hadn't heard exactly what Bud had said and just saw him throw his arms open, raised their beer bottles and gave him a thumbs up salute. It was almost as if they were paying tribute to what he had said.

"So what's the deal? How did you end up with this lifestyle?" Ted asked.

"I don't follow you, what are you trying to ask?"

"Well...Did you grow up on the streets or something like that? How did you end up with the biker lifestyle?"

Bud laughed out loud and then replied, "Hell no. My parents are stinking rich. I started hanging out in bars out of...rebellion. Yeah, that's it. I was pissed at my old man about something at the time and I just started hanging out in bars. I graduated to biker bars because the women are wilder."

"So you weren't some trailer trash that just ended up in the service?"

"Damn straight. I was meant to fly, to soar with the eagles. But I almost fucked it up when I got into a small disagreement in a bar one night."

"If you don't mind me asking, what was the disagreement about?"

"Not a'tall. Basically it was about life. The asshole I was arguing with wanted mine and I wanted to keep it." Bud said and then took a long hard pull from his beer.

"What did you do?"

"Kicked his ass from one side of the place to the other. You can't hang out in biker bars projecting a bad ass image and not expect to have to reinforce the persona from time to time. Any ways, I landed in jail three days before I was supposed to report."

"How did you get out of it?" Ted asked.

Bud looked surprised and asked, "How did you know that I got out of it?"

Ted looked at the floor sheepishly and replied, "Well, you know how scuttle butt travels."

"Of course, the jungle drums are quicker than the telephone. I'll answer your question if you answer mine. Deal?"

"Hoo-rah!" Ted snapped back.

"The old man got me out of jail and then paid the recipient of the whoop ass just to forget the matter. Wa-La, here I am."

"But I thought you were having troubles with your dad."

"I was." Bud replied reflectively, "But the day I told him I had joined the service, he slapped me on the back and said he was glad I had decided to become a man. Ever since then, we've been on good terms."

"So, why do you..." Ted started to say but was cut off by Bud.

"I answered your question. Now as per our agreement, you have to answer mine."

"You bet, what do you want to know?"

"What are the guys saying about me? What's the scuttle butt?"

"You're the mysterious bad ass of the group. You were in some kind of trouble, either a fight or a killing, and you got off for some reason."

Bud sat back laughing and when the guffaws subsided he said, "Of course, everything I told you is classified. I wouldn't want to ruin my image."

"Why do you keep up this image anyway?" Ted asked the question he had started to ask before he was cut off.

"Because it's easier than having to put up with other peoples BS. I have found that if people think you're bad, they have a tendency to leave you alone."

Ted sat there for awhile drinking beer and thinking about what Bud had told him. He could see how a negative image could be an asset. Ted realized he was sitting here with the one person who could help him get a weapon. After all, Ted was beginning to think of Bud as his own personal tour guide to the biker bars and that type of life style. What Ted mulled over in his mind the longest was how he was going to approach the subject with Bud. After a while of thinking about it and a couple of six packs later, Ted just flat out asked Bud.

"If I wanted to get a gun, something I could get right now and didn't have to register, do you know where I could look?"

"Go to a store and buy a rifle."

"No. I want a gun if I lost it, I wouldn't really care."

Bud looked at Ted for a second and then asked, "So you want a throw away gun, huh? Who are you going to off?"

"It's nothing like that. I just want something around for protection." Ted replied quickly.

"How much do you want to pay?" Bud asked.

"I don't know. How much would something like that cost?"

"How much do you have on you now?"

After a quick tally of his pockets Ted replied, "About seventy-five dollars."

"Hmm. I bet you could get a Saturday night special here for that. Wouldn't have much range to it, but up close it would make a good sized hole coming out."

"Are you serious? We could get one here? Now?"

Bud looked around surveying the room and said, "Yeah. I bet we could."

"Would you help me get one?"

"Only if you buy the next round."

The round was bought and after drinking most of his, Bud slid off the bar stool and walked to the end of the bar. He stood there for a second before flagging the bartender over to where he was standing. Ted watched as they talked for a minute and then the bartender pointed to a man sitting on the other side of the room in the corner.

Ted was surprised to see the man. The room wasn't that dark and he hadn't noticed the man when he had looked around before. Bud walked back and told

Ted to wait there until he was motioned over to where the dealing was going on. Bud then walked over to where the man was sitting and took a seat.

A little more than a minute passed before Bud motioned to Ted to come over. Ted walked over and took a seat at the table also. The man sitting in front of both Ted and Bud was much older and very scruffy looking. He had unwashed (by a few days) hair and was wearing a trench coat that Goodwill would have thrown away. Ted suspected the trench coat was more for keeping the man dry in the torrential rains outside than for a fashion statement. Unless filth was the intended statement.

"So...I understand you're looking for something in personal protection." The man said.

"Yeah, you could say that. Wha'cha got?" Ted replied.

"Fifty bucks will get you a.38. It's not in the best of shape, but it's dead accurate and fires every time."

"That sounds good. Where is it?"

"You give me the fifty and I'll go and get it." The man replied.

"Bull shit," Bud interjected, "We give you the money and that's the last time we see you. You get the gun and we'll give you the money when we see the goods."

"Been around awhile, huh? Lucky for you I have a sense of humor. As it just so happens, I have it with me right now."

"Is it clean?" Bud asked.

"Clean enough. Hasn't been used for a long time, couple of years if I recall. It might have got shown a few times, but not used. It was in a private collection if you know what I mean."

Ted didn't know what the man meant but wasn't about to let on that he was ignorant about such matters. Bud saved the day when he spoke up again.

"Hand me the gun and I'll look it over. If it's a good deal, he'll pay you." Bud said indicating Ted would be the payer.

"That sounds mighty fine boys, but, I would like to see some cash before I pull out my merchandise."

"Of course." Ted replied and pulled a wad of bills out of his pocket. Holding them so the rest of the bar couldn't see what he had in his hand, he showed the man the money.

Once the man saw the money, he reached into one of his coat pockets and after a moment of fumbling around, pulled the gun out of the pocket. For a brief moment Ted was afraid the man was going to pull out a police badge and arrest them for trying to illegally purchase a firearm. He was greatly relieved when he saw the gun come out of the pocket and was passed to Bud under the table.

Bud took a couple of minutes inspecting the gun and then gave Ted the nod to pay the man. Once the transaction was complete, they got up and went back over to where they had been sitting at the bar. When they were seated and saw that nobody was paying attention to their actions. Bud passed the gun to Ted and told him to put it away. Ted did just that, not even taking the time to look at his newly purchased lethal toy.

A couple more six packs later, it was time to return to the base for their ride home. The bartender called a cab for them and everyone in the bar waved and told them goodbye as they crawled out the door. Bud told the cabbie they wanted to go to the military base.

"You wanna go to Nellis?" The cabbie asked over the backseat.

"What?" Was Bud's semi-intelligent reply.

"Nellis...Nellis Air Force base. Is that where you want to go?" The cabbie asked, he was patient and was used to dealing with drunk Airmen.

"Is that where the Military is?" Bud asked as his head was doing the drunk bob, it seemed as if his neck muscles would no longer support his head.

"Yes it is." Was the cold reply from the front seat.

"Then that's where we want to go." Ted threw in before Bud could say anything. If he could say anything. At that moment, Bud looked as if he was either going to throw up or pass out.

"Tell your buddy that if he's going to blow, he better roll down the window first, or the ride is going to cost you a hundred extra." The cabbie said as he pulled out of the parking lot.

The rest of the ride back to the base was uneventful. Bud didn't toss his cookies and by the time they got back to the base itself, both of them were in much better shape. The fresh air on the ride went a long way in clearing their heads. Nothing was ever mentioned about the conversation nor the business transaction.

57.

Ronnie took lunch a few minutes early and arrived at the bank promptly in one hour. He walked up to the receptionist's desk, introduced himself and asked where he could find Mr. Gates. He added that Mr. Gates was expecting him. The young woman behind the desk picked up the telephone, dialed a number and spoke into the handset announcing Ronnie. After a brief pause, she hung up the phone and directed Ronnie over to a set of doors along one side of the bank. Once Ronnie arrived at the correct door, he knocked and was beckoned inside by Gates voice from the other side of the door.

Going inside, Ronnie walked up to Gates's desk. "Mr. Gates, I spoke to you an hour ago. My name is Ronnie Fisher." Ronnie said as he stuck out his hand in a gesture of goodwill.

"Mr. Fisher, Ronnie, so nice of you to come by so quickly." Gates replied as he stood up and taking Ronnie's outstretched hand. He gave it a couple of pumps and released it "Well, this is a very serious matter and I would like to get it taken care of as quickly as possible."

"Yes, I agree. Please have a seat." Gates said pointing to the chairs in front of his desk as he sat down himself.

"Thank you." Ronnie said as he sat down. So far the meeting didn't have a hostile air to it and Ronnie was glad for it. This might go better than I hoped, he thought to himself. "Mr. Gates, to be quite frank with you, I haven't got the slightest idea what has happened with the checking account. Like I told you earlier, Margret, my wife, takes care of the checkbook and the bills. If I hadn't found the check statement and called you, I would still be in the dark right now. Do you have any theories about this? Because if you do, I sure would like to hear them."

Gates had seen a lot of different reactions from people in this job. Over the eight years in this position he had seen people come in and give lame excuses for writing a bunch of bad checks. He had also seen the people who came in claiming that it was the banks fault. Yes, he had seen it all over the years and he thought of himself as a fair judge of people because of this.

He did get some enjoyment from dealing with the rant and ravers (as he liked to call them) when he pulled out their banking records and showed them the error of their ways. Usually, the people were mighty humble after that and he would give them a big lecture about how much trouble they would get into if they continued along the path they had chosen.

But Ronnie struck Gates as different, sincere. He really had no clue as to what was going on. Ronnie's promptness at coming to see him also said alot about Ronnie and helped to convince him of the sincerity. Gates decided to give Ronnie a break from the usual speeches and offered Ronnie the best scenario that he could think of.

"Well Ronnie, I really can't begin to tell you what went wrong with your account other than the obvious. We started getting a bunch of checks written to various grocery and department stores in this area. All of the checks were signed by a Margret Fisher. M-A-R-G-R-E-T, I've never seen that spelling of Margaret before. Is that really the way she spells it?"

"Yes," Ronnie replied, "That's the way she spells it. She told me that it was because her parents were young trailer trash with no education when she was born and her dad didn't know how to spell Margaret when he filled out the assistance forms. My wife also said that her mother couldn't read and never knew that it wasn't the correct way to spell Margaret."

"You never met her parents?" Gates asked.

"No, when I met Margret she told me that she was an orphan. I lost my parents when I was a teenager so I never questioned her on the matter."

"Hmm," Gates said after listening to Ronnie's story, then he continued as he leaned back into his chair, "I don't know and can't tell you why, but I have seen cases in the past where a spouse will go nuts, get ahold of the checkbook and start writing checks. I must admit though, I have never seen anyone rack up as high of a total as quickly as your wife."

"Lucky me." Ronnie replied in a small, weak voice.

"Take heart Ronnie, this is what I can do for you." Gates told Ronnie sympathetically. Then he went on to explain how the bank would honor the rest of the checks that came in, but Ronnie would have to start making payments as soon as possible. It was also imperative that the bank be paid off as quickly as possible. Gates went on to say that as long as Ronnie kept making the payments on the debt, the bank wouldn't prosecute Margret. That could lead to serious ramifications for Ronnie.

Ronnie replied he was aware of what could happen and wanted the matter handled as quickly as possible just like the bank. He then went on to explain that he could pay a hundred dollars every two weeks when he got paid.

Gates agreed it sounded like a good plan but added that Ronnie couldn't miss a payment or Gates's bosses would take matters into their own hands.

Ronnie replied he understood the banks position and would do what was necessary. He then asked for the list of stores Gates had told him he could have earlier.

Gates picked up his phone and a couple of seconds later it was brought in by a young woman that Ronnie assumed was Gates's secretary. Ronnie was handed the list and the woman left the room, closing the door behind her.

Ronnie sat there looking over the list and he couldn't believe what he was seeing. There were so many stores and so many checks that had been written. The list not only listed the stores the checks were written to, but also the check number and the amount along with the date the check had arrived at the bank. It was a couple of pages long and single spaced. Each line containing information about one check.

"The checks without an asterisk next to the check number are the ones the stores are holding themselves. You'll have to contact them individually and make the necessary arrangements to pay them off. The asterisks indicate which checks we are holding ourselves."

"Thank you." Ronnie said as he stood up and once again stuck out his hand, "This is more than I could have asked for and it will be a lot of help. Now if you'll excuse me, I have to get back to work so I can get those payments coming in."

"No problem." Gates said as he stood also and took Ronnie's offered hand. "If there's anything else I can do for you, please let me know."

"Do you want a wife? I can let the bank have her for collateral, but you'll have to keep her here." Ronnie offered jokingly.

"No thanks." Gates replied laughing, "I already have one and the bank can't take actual living people as a security."

"It's a shame. If you change your mind let me know." Ronnie said as he turned to leave, he mentally added, 'But don't wait too long. I don't know what kind of shape she'll be in after I see her.'

When Ronnie got back to the greens-keeper shack, he gave everyone their assignments for the afternoon and then advised everyone that they should leave as soon as they finished their lunches. He lied and told them that he had heard that Mr. Bernstien was planning to drop by sometime right after lunch. This little nugget of information went along way to speeding up everyone's lunches. Nobody liked to be around when Mr. Bernstien came. He had a powerful personality and tended to make you feel as though if you weren't working hard when he saw you, he would fire you on the spot.

Ronnie went on into the office and sat down at the desk. He checked the lunch area ten minutes later and found it to be deserted. He was happy with himself that his little trick had worked and marveled that everyone was now busy at their tasks. He turned around and went back into the small office and setting back down at the desk, unfolded the list he had been given at the bank. Ronnie got out the phone book and just as he was about to pick up the phone, it rang and startled him. He almost dropped the receiver as he picked it up. After a moment of fumbling around with it, he got it up to his ear and said hello.

It was Floyd calling to see how things were going. Ronnie told him not to worry, everything was being handled. Floyd then asked how many people were still around eating lunch and Ronnie told him that everyone had been working for the last twenty minutes. This impressed Floyd because he had figured the guys would be taking advantage of Ronnie and still sitting around after lunch.

Floyd told Ronnie that he was feeling better and would most likely be in tomorrow. But the way Floyd sounded told Ronnie more than what Floyd was saying. He was sounding worse than he had when he had called that morning and Ronnie doubted that Floyd would be in tomorrow. Once Floyd was assured everything was going well at the shop he told Ronnie he would see him tomorrow and hung up.

Ronnie sat there for another minute before he resumed what he was doing before the phone rang. He looked back at the list again and finding the first telephone number, dialed it.

"Hello," Ronnie said when it was answered, "I'd like to speak to someone about some bounced checks that my wife may have written at your store."

58.

Aaron McGuire had been wrestling with what to do about Ronnie's columns ever since Ronnie had left his office on Friday. By Sunday he couldn't stand it and had called to arrange a lunch meeting with John Whitfield on Monday. It wasn't a matter of the columns being bad or non-factual, they were good. Really good.

Too good.

Most of the stuff Aaron had read in the columns, he had taken with a grain of salt, assuming they must be true. But he had come across a story about how Fryer had taken an old woman for most of her dead husband's stocks and estate from the probate as fees and handling charges. By the time the woman found out about what had happened, it was too late and she had no legal recourse. Or at least by the time Bernie got through with her she thought she didn't. Bernie had gotten most of the stock by convincing the old man to change the name on the stock to Bernie's. This was to escape all of the high taxes and the transfer problems later. The stocks were cashed out with less than twenty-five percent going to the woman. The sale of the estate went towards paying the legal and medical bills.

Aaron normally would have passed the story by without a second thought, but he had heard this story before. One of the secretaries was the daughter of the woman that had been swindled and he remembered sympathizing with the daughter when he had first heard the story. At the time he didn't know who the lawyer had been, but he did now and wasn't surprised when he found out the name by reading the Gabby Column. This one story alone had galvanized his opinion what he was reading was true and all of the stories had an element of truth to them.

Aaron learned one thing for certain and that was Bernie Fryer had been one first class rat bastard. No matter how many charities Bernie gave to; how nice of a father he had been to his children; what a fine upstanding citizen in the community he gave the appearance to be, would ever change that fact. An old friend of Aaron's in Chicago had told him once, 'Once a rat bastard, always a rat bastard.' This certainly seemed to be a true statement now more than ever.

What was troubling Aaron was the question of how much of this he could print before igniting the good citizens of the community into a lynch mob. That's why he wanted to have this meeting with John. John had a better grasp of the deep roots pulse of the community. He had been living here a lot longer than Aaron and knew everyone's moans and groans.

Aaron planned on taking copies of the columns and let John read them over lunch. Then he would listen to what john had to say about them. Aaron still planned on running them, but he would feel better about doing it if John gave him some sort of thumbs up.

There was a possibility that John would read them and tell him there was no way the columns could be run. The thought of that happening left Aaron empty inside, it would be too much like censoring the news. Being in the newspaper business for so long, he believed that a paper should put the information out there and let the chips fall where they may.

Monday came and at the appropriate time, Aaron left his office and headed for his meeting at the Bistro with John. It was an hour after lunch time and he knew this time of the afternoon would guarantee it would almost be deserted. As he walked into the Bistro he thought about the irony of the situation. Here was the place Bernie Fryer loved to go the most. It seemed like every time there was a meeting, this is where he wanted to meet. But today Aaron would meet at Bernie's favorite place for the express purpose of discussing material that would destroy Bernie's good name.

Inside, Aaron saw John sitting at a table so he walked over and sat down.

"Afternoon Aaron. How are you doing today?" John said as Aaron sat down.

"Fine John, just fine."

"Well then, let's get down to the heart of the matter so we can enjoy lunch. What's up?"

"That's what I like about you John, always business first. Anyway, this is the problem, read these." Aaron said as he sat down the stack of columns in front of John.

John got his glasses out of his sports coat pocket and put them on as he picked up the stack of paper. Then he leaned back in his chair and started reading. A fair amount of time passed as he slowly read one column after another. A waitress wandered by and took their drink orders and wandered off. Still, John read on and offered no outward sign of the magnitude of the damaging information he was reading. They were both on their third round of drinks when John finally sat the papers down, took off his glasses and began rubbing his eyes.

"It's been a long time since I've had to read so much, feels like I'm out of practice. This is quite a little bundle of information you have here Aaron."

"Yes. It is disturbing, isn't it?"

"Not only that, but it clears up some of the things I've seen happen around here...Seems like Bernie was up to some schnanagans around here."

"So you believe there's some element of truth here?" Aaron asked.

"Aaron...What I said is that these papers give explanation to a lot of the things that have happened around here. As to whether or not these statements are true, you'll have to speak to the author of these fine papers. But knowing you, you already know about their authenticity. Don't you?"

"I have been assured every word is gospel."

"So what's the problem Aaron?"

"You can see by the sheer bulk of the material I can run the Gabby column for awhile."

"Let me guess." John said, cutting Aaron off. "You want me to tell you how much of this you can run."

"Bingo." Aaron said with a smile on his face.

"As far as I'm concerned, run every damn bit of it. Although he was a business partner, we should show him no special favoritism. We've slammed presidents in our pages, there's no reason why we should let a slime bucket like this pass by without a second thought. The fact he's no longer with us shouldn't be a deterrent either."

"I was hoping you'd say that."

"What else could I say? This is hot and will stay hot for a long time. I"m surprised you wanted my opinion."

"Well...You have a better grip on the pulse of the older community than I do. I'm just a new comer and I value your opinion."

"That may be true Aaron, but I have the feeling that even if I had said no, you would have run the columns anyway."

Aaron only smiled back sheepishly.

"That's what I thought. Now, are you going to buy me lunch or are we on a strict liquid diet today?" John said as he picked up one of the menus that had been lying on the table.

After lunch was finished and Aaron was safely back at his office, he felt much better. He was about to blow the lid off of this town with what had to be the biggest scandal most of these people had ever seen before. He had been given the go ahead by the one person he valued the opinion of when it came to how hot he could make things around here.

It is going to get hot around here. Aaron thought to himself. Very hot.

He felt giddy like a school kid again and the feeling was invigorating.

59.

Margret had been sitting around the house getting on her own nerves all morning long. She got up to discover she had forgotten to ask Ronnie for the car. After a while she began to get a trapped feeling. She knew she was losing money being at home when there were so many stores she hadn't gotten to yet.

She had turned the ringer on the phone back on right after she had gotten up. Almost immediately, the phone started ringing. Without thinking, Margret answered the phone and was confronted by a woman from the discount store where she had written a good portion of the checks to.

When the woman identified herself and asked to speak to Margret, a cold shiver ran up her spine and she pretended the woman had dialed the wrong number. The woman asked for verification of the telephone number and Margret gave her a number that was one digit off. The nice woman apologized and hung up. The second Margret hung the phone up it rang again. This time it was the grocery store calling. Margret pulled the same routine again but this time turned the ringer off before sitting the handset down.

That had been over four hours ago and now Margret could feel the walls closing in on her. Several times, she got up and paced the living room like a predator paces inside a cage. Two weeks, was the single thought on her mind, just survive two more weeks.

Two more weeks and I'll be free, Margret rationalized to herself. But doubt was beginning to poke its head into her thoughts. Could she make two more weeks? She didn't know if she could. If she slipped up now, everything would come crashing down. The big question in her mind, the one she refused to address, was whether or not Ted would take Ronnie out of her life forever so she could be free to start all over again.

Around two in the afternoon Margret picked up the phone and dialed Ted's phone number. She didn't know why she did it, she knew he wasn't there because he was still out on maneuvers. She just wanted to hear his phone ring and was secretly hoping Ted had an answering machine so she could hear his voice. After the fifth ring she was about to hang up the phone when it was answered.

"Jell-O?" A very sleepy sounding Ted said.

"Ted?!" Margret almost screamed at him.

"Margret?" A now sleepy and confused sounding Ted asked.

"Ted." A now sobbing Margret replied. "OhmiGod, I'm so happy you're here."

"Baby, what's the matter?" Ted was fully alert now, although he was still sporting a huge hangover from his culture trip with Bud and cheap beer. "Are you alright?"

"It's bad Ted. Please help me." More sobs and tears.

"Where are you? I'll come and get you."

Margret didn't know what to say and almost told him to come over, but at the last second she thought about the neighbors. It would look bad if a strange man shows up just before your husband disappears from the face of the planet. She realized that time was ticking by so she did what she does best, she threw her mouth in gear and started weaving a bigger and better tale of woe.

"You can't come here Ted. Ted...My sweet Ted. It's not safe here."

"Margret, is he hurting you again?"

"I'm okay." Was her cold reply.

"He's hurting you, isn't he?" Ted almost yelled over the phone.

"Ted, I can take care of myself. Don't worry about it. I was just so relieved to hear your voice. Why are you back early?" Margret asked making a very obvious change of subject.

"Look Margret...Don't change the subject on me. I know that bastard is doing something to you. I've been thinking about that little problem we discussed."

Margret's breath caught in her throat and her blood froze. She was sure he was going to tell her no.

"I'm going to take care of your problem and I'm going to fix it on a permanent basis." Ted told her.

"What are you going to do?" She asked feeling greatly relieved. Ted had taken her bait after all. She was careful not to let her excitement show in her voice.

"The less you know, the better off you'll be. Just tell me what time he gets home from work."

"Most times at four-fifteen. Unless he stops off at a bar first. Why?"

"Why do you think Margret? Is he working tomorrow?"

"Yes."

"Then don't be outside or come outside when he gets home no matter what you hear. Don't look outside either. Wait five minutes after you're sure he's home before you do and then call the police."

"What do I tell them?" Margret asked.

"Tell them your beloved husband is out in the front yard and you don't know what happened."

"Ted my love, thank you. I love you so much."

"One more thing Margret."

"Yes Ted?"

"You have to give me your address."

Margret managed a slight laugh and then gave him the address.

"Good. Now that we understand each other let me tell you one more thing. I'm leaving Wednesday so you won't be able to call me. The class I was supposed to be in got canceled and Wednesday we are leaving at five in the morning to go back and catch the next class. Also, whatever you do, don't call me tomorrow night. You are going to be busy with the police. It's going to get rough, but just keep reminding yourself that we are going to be together for the rest of our lives. Can you do that Margret?"

Better than you think, Margret thought to herself and then said, "Yes Ted. I can do it. I'll just keep telling myself this is the only way we can really be free together."

"Good. You keep your end up and we'll sail through this with no problems. But if you blow it, we'll both go down and never be together. Are you still sure you want me to do this?"

"Yes darling. I realize that it's like you said. This is the only way I can be free and we can be together. Everything will be fine. I love you, do you know that?"

"Yes baby, I do know that. I love you too."

That was the last of the planning stage of the conversation, the next hour and a half was devoted to syrupy love small talk. When they finally got off of the phone, Margret gave herself a mental high five and was in a very good mood. Being able to talk to Ted had lifted her spirits dramatically. She would only have to put up with Ronnie for another day. Not even that because he would be at work all day tomorrow and get his surprise as soon as he got home. The thought of this made her even happier and she found that just the thought of this was beginning to turn her on.

She went upstairs and spent the rest of the afternoon taking care other needs. Just before Ronnie was to arrive home, she went downstairs and cleaned Nancy up. Changing her diaper for only the second time that day.

60.

Ronnie spent the better part of three hours on the phone talking to different people about Margret's checks. He had found once the people he was talking to found out Ronnie wanted to take care of the problem quickly, they were more willing to work with him. He didn't give them a big tale of grief, he simply told them his wife had gone nuts and wrote a bunch of checks all over town.

The crowning feather in his cap was when he requested each of the retailers to put Margret on their permanent bad check list. That way, he explained to everyone, there would be no way she could continue to write checks at their stores. Since he had requested that one simple thing be done, the people he talked to believed him and told him they would do whatever was necessary to help him pay off his debts to them. One store went so far as to waive the bad check fees to help him out. He acknowledged it would be a big help since Margret had written twenty checks at their stores, it saved him a little over three hundred dollars.

When Ronnie got off of the phone, he had a massive headache and felt brain dead. When he saw what time it was, he realized it was late and he still hadn't rode the greens yet. Ronnie ran out of the office, jumped into the golf cart that was reserved for the Superintendent and roared from hole to hole out on the greens like he was an indy car driver. He did take time to stop and checked the pumps and timers to make sure that the irrigation would come on like it was supposed to tonight.

Once he was satisfied everything was in order with the irrigation, he went back to the office to set up who was working where tomorrow from the things he had seen while he was out. He had just finished when the guys started coming in for the day.

When everyone was back, Ronnie thanked everyone for doing a good job today and made comments to the fact that they were the best group of guys anyone could have working for them. A couple of guys asked if Floyd was going to be back tomorrow and Ronnie answered them saying Floyd had called and told him he would be back tomorrow. Ronnie also added that when Floyd had called and told him that, he was sounding worse than when he had called the first time this morning.

Then Ronnie went over what work was supposed to be done tomorrow and who was working where. When he was sure everyone knew what they were supposed to do in the morning he let them go home. It was five minutes early and the men weren't used to leaving early, they usually spent the last five minutes watching the second hand on the clock make it's painfully slow rotations.

Ronnie noticed even though they had been released early, they took longer to leave than they normally would have. Normally, five minutes after they had been released, the shack would be a ghost town. Today, the guys were still hanging around fifteen minutes after they had been told to leave. A couple of the guys even came up and told Ronnie he had been a pretty good boss today and they would be happy to follow him anywhere. At that moment, Ronnie just chalked it up to them being world class suck ups. But as he was driving home he began to feel good that the guys liked him.

It was on that ride home that he began to marvel about how far he had come in his job. Before, not too long ago, he had been a drunk riding around on a lawn mower believing, knowing, that everyone was laughing at him behind his back. Now he was a boss and everyone respected him. He had put the matter of the checks out of his mind for the time being because he knew the second he began to dwell on them again, it would drastically bring his mood down.

Ronnie wanted to be happy when he got home because he was afraid if he arrived in a bad mood, he wouldn't be able to contain himself and do something stupid to Margret. Not that she didn't deserve it.

Ronnie was jolted out of his thoughts when he passed by the post office and he realized that he hadn't mailed the Professor's book off like he had been instructed to do. He almost said the heck with it, thinking that he would just mail it tomorrow when the fear of the unknown made him turn around and go back to the post office. The unknown being that he was afraid of what the Professor would do if he found out that Ronnie had spaced his chore for a day.

After the book was mailed Ronnie returned to his car and drove straight home. He was in a good mood and decided to table the discussion of checks for now. He decided instead to toy with Margret and let her dig her own hole. But he also remembered that the Professor had told him not to act like he knew, so he decided to follow that advice instead.

When he got home he found Margret was in a very good mood. He also discovered there was nothing being prepared for dinner and Margret suggested they go out and eat. Ronnie quickly agreed it sounded like a good idea. Having missed lunch, he found he was now starving.

61.

As Margret and Ronnie were heading for a restaurant to get dinner, Ted was on his way to the next town over to buy ammunition for his gun. He had thought his whole plan through and decided it wouldn't be smart to buy the bullets in the same town he was going to use them in. Since he had to go 'next door' to get a rental car, he decided to get the ammunition there also.

Ted had gotten what he went for, paying cash at a discount store for the ammunition. He bought the smallest box he could find, telling the clerk a friend of his was having a birthday and this was the best thing he could think of to buy for him. Jokingly, he inquired if the store did gift wrapping and was surprised when the clerk replied it could be arranged for a small additional fee.

Next, Ted found the airport and put his car into long term parking. He took his package and made sure his car was secure before going into the terminal to rent a car that he could drive back to the base in.

On his way back to the base in the rental car, he went over his plans for tomorrow afternoon. He didn't have duty because of the survival school and there weren't any classes scheduled. He did have to go to muster first thing in the morning, but after that, his day would be his do whatever he pleased. When the afternoon rolled around, he would go to Margret's neighborhood and wait until he saw her car come by. Then he would follow it and stop in the street when Ronnie pulled into the yard. He would then roll the window down and call Ronnie over to the car acting like he was asking for directions. When Ronnie leaned down to talk to him, he would pull the gun out and give Ronnie a single dose of lead poisoning right between his beady eyes. He didn't know why he thought Ronnie had beady eyes, it just seemed to fit his mental picture of what an asshole like Ronnie would look like.

Once the gruesome task was done, he would simply drive away. If he was lucky and no one saw him do it, by the time anyone discovered what had really happened, he would be well out of town and on his way back to return the rental car. He would then pick up his own car and return to the base. After that he would be gone the next morning and wouldn't return for the next two weeks. Ted

292

also decided once he was out on the survival course and well out in the desert, he would dig a hole and bury the gun and what was left of the bullets.

Ted looked down at the bag containing the bullets. He took the box out of the bag and set it on the seat beside him, then he pulled the receipt out of the bag. He put the receipt in his mouth and chewed it like a big spitwad. As he chewed, he crumpled up the bag and tossed it out the window. When he was sufficiently satisfied the receipt was a well chewed, slobbery mess, he tossed it out the window as well.

Any fourth grade paper-chewing, spitwad-making boy would have been proud of the spitwad Ted so carelessly tossed from the window of the rental car he was driving. It had been just the right consistency and resembled nothing more than paper fiber and spit. There was no way that it could ever be proven that this particular wad of yuck had ever contained writing of any type. Had Ted thrown it at a wall or ceiling instead of tossing it out the window, it would have stuck and stayed there for a long time.

It was mid evening when he arrived back at the base and he flashed his ID to get through the gate. He had a moment of anxiety when he thought he was going to have to stop and get a visitors pass to register his rental car. But the moment passed as the gate guard gave Ted's ID a casual glance and waved him on through before snapping to attention and saluting. Ted returned the salute and drove on to the dorm. Normally he would have stopped and read the guard the riot act for not saluting first, but tonight, the last thing he wanted to do was to draw attention to himself.

Ted parked in the back of the parking lot behind the dorm well away from where he normally parked. After scanning the parking lot to make sure nobody was around, he got out of the car and walked quickly to the building and went inside.

62.

Ronnie did a good job at keeping his mouth shut and his temper under control. There were several times he was tempted to say something, anything, to let Margret know that as far as he was concerned, her goose was cooked. But he kept quiet even though his mind was a blur with thoughts.

Most of those thoughts were not nice and pretty.

In fact, most of Ronnie's thoughts were quite cruel and brutal. They also had a common thread to them and it was that he wanted to let Margret know she was busted. He saw himself reaching across the table and just with one hand, grab Margret's throat and crush it. Then he would tell her he knew about her bad checks and all of her evil plans as she sat there unable to draw a breath. He wondered how blue her lips would turn before she lost consciousness. Then he wondered if she would just sit there with her eyes bulged open or if she would slump forward into her dinner plate.

But he kept his mouth shut because the Professor had told him to keep his mouth shut. He just contented himself on his fantasy and began musing about how much of a tip for the waitress leaving Margret here dead would require.

Margret had been droning on and on about some meaningless crap and she mistook the smile on Ronnie's face as interest in what she was talking about. If she could have only read his mind, she would have left the restaurant in fear for her life.

On the drive home Ronnie began to think about the Professor. Since the Professor had been right about the checks, it might be in his best interest to heed the rest of the Professor's advice and just lay low in his knowledge of what was going on.

Margret was continuing with her monolog and mentioned she wanted to go to one of the discount stores to do some shopping. She didn't say 'Let's go!', it was more of a casual 'Wouldn't it be fun?' and Ronnie misunderstood the meaning of what she was trying to say. He just agreed with her and continued driving in the direction of home. A few minutes passed and she mentioned it again, but this time it was a 'Do you wanna?' and Ronnie remarked he was tired and wanted to get home. That's when she started whining.

Normally Ronnie would have given in to her and turned the car in the direction of the store she wanted to go to. But tonight, he was tired and all he wanted to do was to sit down and relax for the evening. The day had been draining on him.

Margret's whining continued and it got to the point where Ronnie was ready to reach over and just snap her neck. He looked at her and there was something in the look on his face that stopped her mouth amid flap. It was at that same time he was seeing himself just reaching over with one hand and snapping her neck like a dried twig. A firm grip on the back of the neck with his fingers digging deeply into the meat. Once he could feel her spinal column, then it would just take a firm, quick, twist towards the ground. He could hear the meaty crack as her vertebrae gave way and created a space where one didn't belong.

This time, she interpreted the smile on his face as something bad, sinister.

The silence became thick, very quickly inside the car.

Ronnie went back to his thoughts and began to think about the various conversations with different people he had this afternoon. It had been one of the most embarrassing days of his life. Humbling was a better description of what he had been through. To have to tell strangers he had no idea of what had been going on with his own personal finances. That he had no control over his wife and had no idea this could have even happened.

As he pondered his lesson in humility, a thought crossed his mind about the money. He realized he hadn't been seeing an influx of goods into the household from Margret's spoils. There was no outward sign Margret had gone off and spent the shitload of money she had. He added two and two and realized it meant that she either had the stuff stashed somewhere or had given it to someone else. He quickly discounted the last idea because he knew how selfish she was. The third option was she had returned the stuff and was sitting on a pot full of cash.

He also knew he had to get the checkbook away from her. He decided that in the morning before he went to work, while Margret was still asleep, he would simply open her purse, get the check book out and see if she had any money. What a surprise that would be for her tomorrow when she found the checkbook gone and her purse void of any cash he would confiscate if he found.

The rest of the night was tough, but he managed to get through it. After some mediocre sex, he fell asleep. The sex had been Margret's idea. Although she didn't say anything to Ronnie, she looked at it more as doing her duty for the condemned man. Her supercilious ego made her want to send her man off with a smile and it was her belief that all good soldiers deserved one last pokin' before being sent off to die in battle.

And as with anything that had to do with making Ronnie happy, she put about as much effort into it as she put into cleaning the toilet or refrigerator. It was something that had to be done, but it was still pretty disgusting.

Most of the night had passed before Ronnie began to dream.

When he opened his dream eyes, he found himself standing in a very small glen. The ground was thickly carpeted by a small leaf ivy. Directly in front of him was a pile of good sized rocks. From the top of the pile was a stream of water that flowed with enough pressure to arch the water a couple of inches before spilling down the front of the pile of rocks into a small pool. Although the fountain was right in front of him, it wasn't the first thing he noticed. It was the aroma, the air was sweet. Inhaling deeply, he recognized the sweet smells of Honeysuckle and Jasmine. The sweetness was as intoxicating as a lazy summer day.

Stepping forward as he was looking into the pool, Ronnie saw there was a spring coming up from the edge of the pool underneath the rocks. At first he had mistakenly thought the hole was from the water entering the pool there after cascading down the rock face from the top. But as he watched, he saw there was movement and he saw a good amount of water was coming out of the ground. He realized that somehow the pressure of the spring was forcing the water up through the pile of rocks. The small pool was about the size of two bathtubs and drained off creating a small stream that flowed away. A thick carpet of rich, green grass came up from the waters edge and ran out a few feet before ending abruptly where the ivy took over.

He marveled at the force of the spring because it put a fair amount of water into the pool and still have enough force to propel the water upward through the stone. He put his finger tips to the water coming out of the rock and found it surprisingly cool, almost cold. He collected a small amount of water on his finger tips and raised them to his lips. He tasted the water and found it sweet and refreshing.

Instantly, Ronnie was reminded of a time when he was little and still had a family. A real family with loving parents and a feeling of well-being and safety. His parents had taken him off into the woods to see an artesian well. His mind and taste buds remembered the water had been cool and sweet that day also. He remembered that day in the woods as if he were there right that second. He had been very young and the day was bright and hot. To Ronnie, at that age, it was just another something among the endless cascade of things he saw. He remembered the sweet cool taste of the water after an afternoon of bouncing around in the back of an old hot car that was driving down dusty dirt roads. It was a random memory he still had of his parents. Some of his memories were buried deeply and came floating up to the surface every now and then. The feeling he normally attached to these types of memories was of sadness, he missed his parents deeply. But when he thought of this memory there was no regret or remorse, it was as if he viewed a moment of time itself detached.

Ronnie stepped back from the rocks and looked around. He saw most of the glen was covered by the tops of conifer trees, which in the heat of the day provided a cool shady spot for a weary traveler to rest. The bottom branches of the trees were just a couple of feet over his head and thickly interlaced. Only directly over the spring itself was an area the thick overhead foliage didn't block out the sunlight. Looking up through that hole in the branches he could see the deep blue of the sky. He also noticed Honeysuckle and a vine with small white flowers that he recognized as Jasmine was running through the branches. The area he was standing in reminded him of something out of Tolkien. This area would be a place where you would find gypsies, fairies, and elves. The glen had a mysterious air about it. But Ronnie liked it, it wasn't as good as the high place, where the air was crisp and clean smelling and the view was spectacular. But it was an excellent second.

Ronnie walked over to where the ivy stopped and the trees started. He looked into the forest and saw nothing but trees. Trees as far as he could see, which wasn't more than forty feet, fifty in some places, into the woods. He started walking around the edge of the oval shaped glen and saw there were no trails or foot paths leading here. Everywhere were the trees. Even where the small stream disappeared into the woods it was impossible to follow. The branches of the trees were intertwined and hung to the very top of the water. He didn't look too closely because he didn't notice even though the branches hung to the top of the water, they didn't touch the it. Neither did the grass, there were scant millimeters of bare earth between the water and the blades of grass.

Ronnie realized there was no way into the glen, thus there was no way out. He figured he could plunge into the woods, but he thought from the looks of them, he would be hopelessly lost within a matter of seconds.

Ronnie walked over to the pool and sat down. It was peaceful and serene here. As he sat there, he could hear a sound off in the distance. It sounded like water flowing briskly over rocks and the sound was growing closer and louder. Ronnie noticed a breeze beginning to fill the glen and the tops of the trees began to sway. As the sound grew in intensity, the trees moved even more until even the bottom branches were moving back and forth. Then the breeze stopped and the air became still again. He listened as the sound of the wind moved away from him like a breaker passes a swimmer at the beach.

Ronnie laughed to himself as he laid back in the grass. There had been a moment when the sound was approaching and was about to overtake the spot where he was that he had an anxious feeling, almost afraid. There had been a small adrenalin rush as the sound passed directly overhead. There was also a sense of relief it had only been the wind. Listening as he laid there, Ronnie noticed that he could hear the wind all around him. He realized what he was hearing was not the wind itself, but its interaction with the trees. The force of the wind causing the leaves to rustle and rub against themselves.

Ronnie was beginning to like this place, the serenity here was very calming. He closed his eyes so he could use his other senses to observe the place he was in.

Without warning, Ronnie realized the sounds had changed, they were no longer the gentle sound of the wind in the trees and the bubbling sound of the water coming out of the stone and slipping into the pool. Now there were car sounds and he realized that he was standing. Ronnie slowly opened his eyes and found himself standing next to the Professor on top of the same overpass he had been to before.

He had opened his eyes just in time to watch the all too familiar scene of the car shooting off of the ramp and flipping over. Looking over at the Professor, Ronnie could see the intense concentration on the Professors face as he watched the events unfold below him. When the car battery fell out of the crushed hood and sparked the fire, the Professor yelled at the fireball.

Gawddamn I love this shit!!! The Professor yelled with as much enthusiasm as a picnicker watching a Forth of July fireworks show. *Isn't it great?* He yelled in Ronnie's ear as he slapped him on the back.

'Somehow I knew it was too good to be true.' Ronnie replied casually.

What's too good to be true? The Professor asked. *This magnificent scene below?* As the Professor said that he swept his arms open wide indicating the spectacle in front of them.

'No. That I can have a moment of peace without you showing up. What do I have to do to get you to leave me alone, die?'

Now Ronnie. Death wouldn't help you at all. Besides, that's a real shitty attitude to have towards seeing your old friend.

'Friend, ha. What a laugh.'

Ronnie...I'm shocked. I consider you one of my closest friends. Why...I rate you right up there with Hitler and Manson. I enjoy my conversations with you as much as I do with them.

'Bullshit!' Ronnie snapped right back at him, 'A lot you know, Manson isn't dead yet.'

Who do you think belongs to one of those voices he's always claiming to hear? The Professor snapped back, starting to sound angry.

'Okay, so you know Manson. Why did you bring me here?'

So you could thank me for telling you about the checks. Was the nonchalant reply.

'I don't know if "thank-you" is correct. There is a lot to be said about ignorance of a situation.'

Sometimes maybe. But in this case, getting a leg up on the situation was the only thing you could have done. I don't think you fully understand how far out of hand this could have gotten.

'How about giving me an example if you don't mind.'

Okay. How about constant phone calls at work hounding you about checks you know nothing about. Word would spread to your superiors and you would be fired.

'I doubt that would have happened. Too bad you can't show me what would have happened, oh Mister Time and Space.' Ronnie replied flatly.

Look boy...This ain't no Dickens story. The Professor said sharply. *We go when and where I want to go.*

'Never a truer word had been spoken. Everything is always on your terms isn't it?' Ronnie said and then added, 'What brings you here, or should I say, brings me here tonight?'

I don't know if I should tell you. You have such a bad attitude. The Professor said feigning indifference.

'Okay, be like that, I'm not going to beg. But I will tell you thanks for letting me know about Margret's doings.' Ronnie said, not really trying to console the Professor.

Well...Since you asked. The Professor replied sounding like a little kid with something to tell. *Tomorrow is going to be the big day.*

'What do you mean?'

It's time for you to go to work. The Professor said as he began to fade away. Ronnie noticed as the Professor faded, everything else faded away also. The last thing Ronnie heard before he noticed the alarm going off over his head was the words, *Watch your ass.*

Ronnie laid there in bed for a couple of minutes as he adjusted to the shift in reality. To him, scant seconds before he was on top of the overpass beam and now here he was in bed. But the words *"Watch your ass"* still echoed in his ears and mind. After a few moments Ronnie went ahead and got up to get ready for work. After showering and a quick breakfast, he was on his way out of the door when he remembered he wanted to go through Margret's purse before he left to get the checkbook and to see if she had any money.

He turned around at the door and went back into the house. After a minute of looking he found Margret's purse and opened it. As with most women's purses, it was littered with tissue and various other items that took up the valuable space inside. Ronnie quickly located the checkbook and removed it. Then he started looking through everything for Margret's stash of cash. Although he thought he was being thorough, he wasn't thorough enough. Had he looked a little closer at the bottom of her purse he would have found a spot where the lining had been ripped open along one seam. He had no way of knowing Margret's fortune was hidden inside that rip, nestled safely between the lining and the outer shell of the purse.

After checking her wallet and generally inspecting the contents of her purse, Ronnie decided his idea about Margret having a fortune hidden away was just that, an idea. Contented she wasn't sitting on a huge stash of cash, Ronnie put the things he had removed back into her purse (except the checkbook) and put the purse back where he had found it. He stuck the checkbook in his back pocket and resumed his journey to work.

63.

At the same time Ronnie began to dream about the glen, Ted began to dream also. In his dream, Ted was sitting in front of a house. He heard laugher and saw a black dot coming towards him at a rapid pace. Before he had time to register what the black dot was, it seemed to head straight for his forehead. His eyes crossed as they tried to track the path of the dot. At the same instant the dot hit his forehead, there was nothing and Ted found himself standing in a wide expanse of nothing. Looking around he saw there was black as far as he could see and he found he couldn't discern where the floor ended and the walls began or even where the ceiling started. Looking down, he could see himself. It was as if he was the only illuminated object in the center of a vast darkness.

When Ted woke up, he didn't remember the strange dream he had the night before. He jumped up and quickly put on his uniform so he could get to muster on time. After muster was over and roll call had been taken, he would be released with orders to report at this same spot at four-thirty in the morning. Then he would have the rest of the day to get prepared for what had to be done this afternoon.

Ted's plans were almost waylaid at muster. The Commanding Officer of the formation asked for volunteers to do a goodwill project for the community. With dread, Ted watched as his squad leader stepped forward to volunteer the squad for the duty. Fortunately, the squad leader was too slow and another squad leader spoke before he had a chance to speak. The other squad leader announced in a loud and proud voice that the 34th would be proud to donate their free time to the community. Ted's squad leader stepped back without getting a chance to open his mouth.

After some announcements, they were dismissed from formation and everyone went their separate ways. A couple of guys from Ted's squad asked him what he had planned today and he replied he was going to lay around and rest today and he might go out later. This brought snickers from his inquisitors and they made remarks to the fact that he was going to meet his mystery girlfriend. Although Ted had been fortunate and nobody in his squad had seen him with Margret, they had seen the change in his attitude and had speculated

Ted was now getting laid. The shit eating grin on his face and the fact he didn't deny it when they were rasing him nailed him to the fact the squad believed. As they parted, there were some comments made that he should save some of his strength for the survival course. Ted laughed and waved as he walked away.

The last thing Ted wanted to do today was see Margret, but it was also the one thing he wanted to do the most. He wanted to be with her so he could bolster his now sagging confidence in what he was going to do. But he told himself he had gone too far and had too much riding on this to stop now. How would he look in Margret's eyes if he told her he couldn't go through with his plans? What would his comrades think of him if they ever knew he had come so close to a plan to chicken out at the last minute? And more important, what would he think of himself?

He knew he had told Margret he was going to take care of her problem and he imagined how she must have felt with him giving her a ray of hope to a better life to hang on to. He felt if he told her that he couldn't go through with what he had promised it would crush her. It would almost be like him giving her a prison sentence to a really bad life. Besides, he loved her and couldn't imagine the rest of his life if she wasn't in it.

Ted spent the rest of the day in his dorm room with the door locked. His room mate had opted to go with the guys to see just how long it would take to get thrown out of as many bars as possible. Ted had gone out with them before when they were playing this game and he knew they wouldn't be back to the base until well after midnight.

Ted sat there with the door locked. He had his gun out and he would load it, then unload it and break it down. After inspecting the pieces individually, he would then reassemble the gun and load it again. The process repeated itself over and over again. It was a good thing he couldn't wear the parts out by the repeated disassembly, because the gun would have been completely worn out by the time it was time to use it. It was also a shame Ted didn't know enough about guns. If he had, he would have seen just how used and worn his gun was.

An hour before it was time, Ted took the gun and bullets and put them in a light windbreaker jacket and headed for the door. Ted had suddenly gotten the urge to try the gun before zero hour. He knew of a patch of woods about ten minutes away and he decided to drive to those woods and pop off a few rounds. Then, when he was done, he would go and wait for the return of Ronnie.

64.

Ronnie had an excellent day at work. Fran Fritz, Floyd's wife, called first thing and informed him Floyd had gotten worse during the night and there was no way she was going to let him out of the house. Ronnie politely thanked her for calling and told her to tell Floyd everything was under control and everyone at the shack hoped he would be feeling better soon. After Ronnie hung up the phone, he immediately went into the lunch area and chased everyone out to their jobs.

Now Ronnie had the office to himself and he mostly sat around thinking about what the Professor had told him and reading some of Floyd's magazines. The day had been an easy one and he kept finding his thoughts wandering back to the glen he had dreamed of last night. He kept thinking about how perfect it would be if he could be sitting in the glen right now. Then he heard the last utterance of the Professor, *Watch your ass.*

He wondered what was going to happen and knew he had to be ready for anything. Just what he had to be ready for was the thing that was eating away at him. Was she going to poison him? Should he not eat anything at home for awhile? Or should he be wary of any strangers? Just before the paranoia ate him up, Ronnie would push himself away from his thoughts like a full eater pushes himself away from the table.

"Ronnie," He would tell himself, "You gotta get a grip on yourself and just go with the flow. You don't wanna end up a paranoid basket-case by the end of the day."

Then he would take a second to relax and pick up another trade journal and start reading it. He found he was learning a lot about the business of maintaining the greens. Things he had just taken for granted and never thought about before. He found there was a lot more to this new job of his than he had ever considered, ph balances and parasites. Best times to water and the worst, what fungicides to use if the grass looked like this. The journal was full of color pictures. Ronnie was soaking up some knowledge.

After awhile of reading however, Ronnie would find his mind wandering back to the glen and the vicious little cycle of paranoia the thoughts would bring with it.

65.

Margret was going stir crazy in the house. She didn't dare turn the phones on because she didn't want to start dealing with the harassing calls for her to come and give the stores their money back.

Ironically, there were no phone calls coming to her house today because no one was trying to call her. Ronnie being on the phone yesterday had gone a long way to stem the flow of calls. The people that were owed money were satisfied there would be payments starting on Friday after Ronnie got his paycheck. From the business point of view, once the husband had been talked to and an answer given, there was no reason to keep calling.

Nancy had been crying all day long, she had woken up in a very fussy mood. Now Margret's nerves were stretched as far as they would go. If it hadn't been for the fact that Margret had put Nancy in her room and tied the door shut, she would have snapped and gone over the edge by early afternoon.

By all accords, this should have been the happiest day of her life because she was getting exactly what she wanted. But instead, she was nervous about what it was going to be like when she 'discovered' Ronnie's dead body out in the front yard. Margret was making mental notes about how she was going to act, she must assume the role of the grieving widow. She would have dinner cooking and the house would look like a happy little home a terrible thing had happened in front of.

Margret's immediate source of irritation was Ronnie's computer. After all of this time siting there, she had been drawn to it once again in the afternoon. She had no computer skills and barely found the on/off switch. After waiting for what seemed like forever for the thing to come on, it came on asking for a password. She spent the better part of a half hour typing things in, only to be rejected time and time again. Out of frustration, she typed in 'Piece of shit computer' and pressed enter. The computer promptly replied on screen with a message of 'FUCK YOU'. This ignited Margret and she pounded 'FUCK YOU TOO' into the keyboard and slammed her fist down on the enter key.

Immediately, something inside the computer began to whirr and a couple of seconds later she was presented with a menu. Scrolling down the list of things on the menu, she saw there was a ton of stuff in the menu. Not knowing it, Margret had stumbled into a menu Ronnie had not seen yet. She found there were all sorts of games and different files listed there. Every time she tried to load something, it would appear to load and then nothing else could be done. The computer would seem to lock up. Margret would have to turn the computer off and then back on again. Then she would re-enter her new found password back into the machine and go through the process again. After several times of doing this, her frustration level began to rise with each time she had to go through the process. Finally she slammed her fists down on the keyboard and yelled, "This piece of shit thing is fucking with me!!". Then she turned the computer off and just sat in front of it looking at the blank monitor.

To Margret, it seemed the computer was sitting there mocking her. In her mind, she imagined that it was laughing at her. Margret wanted to do something, but she didn't know exactly what to do. She felt a great need to hurt or damage the computer to show it who was the boss.

Looking around, Margret saw a wire coat hanger laying on the floor. Smiling, she picked it up. She twisted the hook end until it broke off, then she took the hanger apart. Twisting and turning the wire until it broke off in small pieces. When she had three pieces, including the hook, she looked at the computer and began dropping the pieces of thick wire into the computer through the ventilation strips on the top.

With each piece of the metal coathanger she dropped, she imagined that the computer was shrieking in pain. Luckily, she didn't hit anything important or she would have been electrocuted on the spot. The last piece of coathanger landed on the pile of wire and fell over, coming to rest against a coil on the modem part of the circuit board.

Now, Margret was in a much better mood, laughing the next time somebody turned the computer on, they were going to be in for a pretty good fireworks display. It never occurred to her the most likely person to turn it on, Ronnie, was supposed to be dead before the sun set.

The coil the piece of coathanger landed on happened to be part of the impedance matching network for the modem. All of the pieces touching each other became a good, short range antenna. A magnetic field created by the coil would be induced in the end of the coat hanger and the electrons would travel through the rest of the pieces of wire. The magnetic field would amplify itself through the mass of the coathanger pieces and the electrons would then be radiated into the air as a magnetic field similar to a small radio station. A transmit only device.

A circuit came on inside the computer, it rose in power and then lowered, then it repeated the process a couple more times. Each time it rose in power, the magnetic field increased in magnitude and got a little bigger. It was as if the computer was testing the range of its newly installed capability.

Margret had given up on the computer and had drifted back into the living room to the television. The magnetic field increased inside the computer and Margret saw static on the television screen just before the television turned itself off. Margret picked up the remote and turned the television back on. A couple of minutes later, just when the show she was watching was starting to get good, she saw static again and the channels changed. Again she picked up the remote and changed back to what she had been watching. A commercial came on and the television played just fine during the ads, but as soon as the program came back on, Margret saw static and the volume raised to a deafening pitch and the channels changed. Just as she was reaching for the remote, the television turned itself off.

"What the hell is wrong with this Goddamn thing?!" Margret yelled as she turned the television back on and adjusted the volume. When she was back to her show, she sat there with the remote in her hand waiting for something to happen again. After ten minutes she figured it had been just a fluke and set the remote down. When she did the television turned itself back off again. Margret shot out of her seat and almost ran to the set, when she was near it she drew her foot back and kicked the side of the console. Her attention was fixed on the television as she backed away from it with her full attention fixed on it waiting for something else to happen.

Now she was sure her kicking it had somehow magically fixed it, she sat down and started watching the show once again. This time nothing happened for thirty minutes. This time the volume wouldn't stay where she had set it. The volume would raise to a speaker splitting loudness and Margret would snatch the remote up and lower it again. A minute would pass and the process would repeat itself. Then the channel changing started again frustrating Margret to outrage. In the end, she gave up trying to watch the television. She couldn't understand why or how it was happening. Now, in a much truer sense, the computer was fucking with her.

66.

Max got to the station just before three in the afternoon, an hour before he was supposed to be there. He was working undercover tonight at the Junior League Baseball game. There had been some cars broken into, then left to be found vandalized with most of the sound equipment gone. Captain Waters had put uniforms out to patrol the parking lot and nothing happened. After awhile, the Chief had decided it had just been a couple of hit and runs and he canceled the parking lot security saying the resources were needed elsewhere. (That had been a polite way of saying he was tired of paying the overtime.) That very night, ten cars were broken into. Broken windows and slashed dashes. The Mayors brand new Cadillac was included in the ravaging. The Chief of Police was the second person to find out about the Mayor's car.

Max heard the ass chewing that the Chief had gotten was almost an hour long.

So here Max was. He was going to a baseball game and was going to see everything but the game. Actually, Max had volunteered for the duty. It meant he could wear civvies and would be able to drive his own car to the game. The best part was he would be off duty as soon as he was done. Those benefits aside, Waters begging Max to volunteer and crack this case had a little to do with him accepting the special duty.

Max wouldn't be at the game alone tonight, two other guys Max had handpicked would be there undercover also. They planned on meeting before the watch started, go over their game plan and then go their own separate ways for dinner. They would then go to the game separately and meet there. They had been ordered to continue doing this until the culprits were caught. To paraphrase the Mayor, 'Until they were of retirement age, if necessary.'

As Max passed by the Captains office, Waters looked up from his desk and saw him. Max was motioned into the office, Waters was on the phone and gestured for Max to sit down. Max sat and waited for Waters to finish his call.

"Looking spiffy Max." Waters said as he hung up the phone.

"Thought I'd go to the show in style tonight." Max answered with a smile on his face.

"Well, whatever you do, catch them bastards tonight. The Chief has been all over my ass about this."

"From what I hear, the Chief has been getting some pretty good motivation himself."

"Yeah, ain't rank a bitch." Waters replied snickering and then continued, "Just remember that shit rolls downhill. You got a game plan for tonight?"

"I figured we'd just roll up in a van, open the doors and yell, 'All you criminals get in, especially the assholes who broke into the Mayor's car.' Then we'll bring them all back and sort them out here."

If it had been anyone other than Max, Waters would have been all over their ass the second they opened their mouth with that reply. But Max and Waters went back along ways, joining the force at almost the same time. But Waters had been better at testing than Max and had advanced quicker. To Waters, it didn't mean Max was any less of the cop than he was. He knew some guys were better at the paperwork than others and some guys were better at sorting out the details and cutting through the bullshit in the field than the rest. Waters knew Max fell into the latter category. He also felt out of all of the guys that worked here, he would take Max above anyone else to watch his back.

"What's plan 'B'?" Waters asked.

"We're going to case the parking lots and check out all unusual activity without drawing attention to ourselves."

"What's your gut feeling Max?"

"If they're there and they hit, they'll be spending the rest of the night here doing paperwork."

"You got the guys you want and the equipment you'll need?"

"Yeah, Bubba and Junior are my back ups. We got radios with ear pieces and our own freq. Yeah, we're set."

"I know you'll do your best Max." Waters said and Max started to get up to leave but Waters stopped him. "Wait a minute. That's not the reason I called you in here."

"Okay, what's the problem boss?" Max said as he sat back down.

Waters sat there for a couple of seconds before replying. To Max, it seemed that the man was trying to choose his words carefully before he spoke. "Do you remember that Fisher guy? You know, the one where that Lawyer Fryer died in his house? The one that has the real nut case for a wife?"

"Yes, I remember him." Max replied coldly. When he heard Ronnie's name his heart skipped a beat, he was sure the next thing he was going to hear was that Ronnie had either been badly hurt or killed. "Why?" He managed to ask.

"How well do you know him?"

"Just through paperwork. Nice kid, real polite. But his wife is a piece of work. What's wrong?"

"Yeah, I remember her." Waters said, then spent the next five minutes telling Max about a couple of stores that had come in yesterday and started warrants to have Margret Fisher arrested for bad checks. But today, the stores had called and stopped the process. Also today, Margret's fingerprints had come through the print check from a pawn shop where she had pawned a large amount of high dollar jewelry. Waters wondered aloud if Margret had found a new line of work.

Waters explained he wanted Max to use his acquaintance with Ronnie and go over and find out what was going on from Ronnie's point of view. Since there was no one attempting to have Margret arrested, the police had no authority to talk to Ronnie. That's where Max's familiarity with Ronnie might prove useful to get the message across that if whatever was going on didn't stop, somebody would be spending a few nights locked up.

Max told Waters he would go by Ronnie's house on his way to the game and talk to him. Waters reminded Max that his main responsibility was to cover the parking lot. Max sat there looking confused and Waters said, "What I mean is just go by and have a small talk with the man, but make sure your ass is at the game."

"Never fear boss." Max said with a grin, "The next time you see me, I will have the perpetrators of this dastardly crime wave in my custody." Having said that, he got up and started to leave.

"If you catch them tonight, there might be something extra in it for you."

Max stopped his about face and asked, "Oh yeah? What's the bounty?"

"You know all those personal days you got saved up? I might let you take one of them off. But you'll have to do it on your weekend."

"Of course." Max replied with a huge grin, "Later." He said as he restarted for the door.

"Max...Be safe." Waters said as Max walked out the door.

"Always." Came drifting back through the door.

Waters sat there looking at the door thinking about Max. Max was one hell of a cop and if the guys could be caught in one operation, Max was the guy that could pull it off. Waters knew full well that if Max hadn't quit the force for that year back when they were younger, Max would be the one sitting in the Captain's chair instead of him. That and the test scores had held Max back in his career. Waters thought about how life wasn't fair and then put his attention back on his job.

67.

Ted shot through most of the box of ammunition and was satisfied that the gun was in working order. He reloaded the gun and snapped the chamber shut. Looking at the gun he told himself that it was time. Time to take care of business. Ted walked back to the car, took off his jacket and got into the car. He laid the gun on the front seat, covered it with the jacket and drove off to find Margret's house.

He drove to Margret's neighborhood and found her house. He drove on past the house and circled the block. The next time around he parked at the end of a hedge one house down the road. Ted looked at his watch and saw he had about fifteen minutes to wait.

Keeping it low, Ted checked the gun one more time.

68.

It was late in the workday for Ronnie and he had just returned from his inspection ride of the greens. Although he had found a couple of trouble spots, everything was looking great. On his way back to the shack, Ronnie decided the greens wouldn't fall apart if Floyd wasn't around for a couple of days.

When Ronnie got back to the shack, the phone was ringing and he answered it. It turned out to be Floyd's wife calling to say Floyd's cold had turned out to be pneumonia and Floyd would be spending a few days in the hospital.

Ronnie gave his sympathy and asked how Floyd was doing. He was told that Floyd was too tough to be anything more than kinda sick. It had been the doctor's idea that Floyd spent his sick time in the hospital in case the pneumonia took a turn for the worst. She then told Ronnie what hospital Floyd was in and gave him the room number.

Later, when the guys were back and getting the briefing for the next day, Ronnie told them about Floyd's condition and asked for donations for flowers to send to Floyd. The donations were heavy, everyone gave something. Ronnie thanked everyone and dismissed them, telling them they could go home.

On the way home, Ronnie stopped at a florist and ordered an arrangement of flowers to be delivered. He signed the card and handed it over to be put in the flowers. The florist told Ronnie he was in luck because there was one last delivery going out in a few minutes. The flowers Ronnie had just ordered could ride along and would be delivered in the next half hour.

Ronnie thanked the woman and left, feeling good about what he had just done.

R. H. Gosse

69.

Max met with Bubba and Junior and discussed the game plan for the night with them. Once everyone understood what they were supposed to do, Max got up and told them he had to go because he had to meet with someone before the game started. No one questioned him about the subject of his meeting, they just told him they would see him at the game.

Just before he left, Max told them no matter what they did tonight, when they got to the game not to act like cops and huddle around the snack bar. They were to find a seat in the stands with a good view of the parking lot and keep their eyes open. They had radios and Max would meet up with each of them later.

Max then left and headed for his car. As he was getting in, he looked at his watch and saw he would get to Ronnie's house at a quarter after four. He knew he was going to be early, but this way he could talk to Ronnie when he got home and not have to confront the shrew he was married to.

When he got to Ronnie's house, he drove slowly past and stopped on the other side of the driveway. He saw Ronnie's car wasn't there and wondered to himself if Ronnie's wife hadn't taken the car as soon as he got home from work. He let his car roll another couple of feet before stopping and parking. He sat there for a couple of minutes before getting out of the car and walking up to the front door. He stopped short of the front porch and looked around. The day was beginning to grow long and the evening shadows were beginning to form. The air was still and warm and breathing deeply, he could smell Honeysuckle in the air along with the aromas of dinner cooking.

Max turned and looked at the front door to Ronnie's house. He hoped Margret had indeed left for the evening and he would find Ronnie home alone. With a resigned sigh, Max started for the front door and began climbing the steps with as much enthusiasm as a man climbing the gallows.

70.

Margret was going crazy inside the house. Nancy had been hosed off and Margret had cleaned up the house. She even had dinner cooking in the kitchen. Although Ted had told her to stay away from the front windows, she couldn't resist the urge to sneak peeks through the front window blinds.

The fact Ronnie was now five minutes late coming home was eating at her. She wondered if the deed had already been done, but she doubted that because Ted had told her it would happen in front of the house. She was pacing the floor and looking out through the blinds every couple of minutes. She didn't see Max until he was standing in front of the porch. She didn't recognize him in his civvies with a days growth of beard on his face and was startled to see a strange man standing in front of her house.

Margret almost tripped on the plant stand as she jumped back from the window. Standing there in near panic, she suddenly thought Ted had hired a hit man. She expanded the theory and thought the hit man standing in front of the house was either waiting for Ronnie or was going to come up and ring the doorbell.

Margret decided she definitely wasn't going to answer the door if the bell rang. Quietly, Margret ran to the back of the house to the kitchen.

She would be safe here, Margret thought to herself.

71.

Ronnie looked at his watch as he rounded the corner down the street from his house and saw he was late getting home. He knew Margret was going to throw a fit because he was late and was wondering how he was going to handle it. After what he had been through in the last couple of days with her checks, he didn't know if he could keep a civil tongue if Margret started really ragging him. He just kept telling himself to keep his hands off her no matter how pissed he got and this was surely going to be an exercise in patience.

He slowed down and pulled into his driveway, noticing a rusted out, blue piece of crap parked at his property line on the other side of the driveway. He didn't see Max until he had turned off the ignition of the car. His blood froze when he saw the strange man approaching from his front porch. Ronnie instantly thought he was a hit man and Margret had been waiting for him. Ronnie imagined Margret bitching at the hit man when he hadn't arrived promptly on time. A sly smile crossed his lips as the thought maybe the hit man had gotten tired of listening to Margret and snuffed her on the side for free.

Still, as he fumbled to put the key back into the ignition, Ronnie suddenly realized he knew this guy. It was the policeman that had been here when Fryer fried and found he couldn't remember his name. It had been Max something. Ronnie opened the door and stood up, not noticing the new car as it pulled across the end of the driveway.

"Max?" Ronnie asked as he stood up from the car.

"Ronnie, you remember me, great! I really need to talk to you." Max said in a friendly tone as he quickly walked to Ronnie's car. He was relieved he hadn't made it all the way up to the door and rung the door bell before seeing Ronnie come home, the last thing he wanted to do was wake the sleeping beast within.

"Excuse me. I'm lost. Could you please help me?" Came a shout from behind Ronnie.

72.

Ted saw Max when Max pulled up and parked. It hadn't been Margret's car so Ted hadn't been concerned about it. From Ted's vantage point two full houses away, it looked as if Max had parked on the other side of Margret's house and had gone into the yard next door. He didn't know Max from anyone else that he hadn't met and just thought it was a next door neighbor.

Besides, the little piece of shit Ronnie was late coming home and that made Ted nervous, more nervous than he had been. He was afraid the extended amount of time he was spending sitting there waiting was giving him a bigger chance of being discovered or remembered by an observer. He kept turning the gun around in his hand while keeping it low so if anyone happened to look, they wouldn't see a man sitting in a car with a gun in his hand.

Ted finally resolved that he would sit there until Ronnie came home, no matter how long it took. This was too important and he had too much invested to give up now. Margret was depending on the word he had given that he was going to take care of her problem. Ted's conscience was telling him that it was no good, the whole plan had been blown and he should just cut and run and try again later when it was safe. His exposure here was too long and he was on the verge of being discovered, remembered. That's the part of himself he steeled against with the determination to carry through with the task.

He saw a car come around the corner behind him and when it passed him he recognized it as Margret's car. Ted started his car and put it into drive, easing down the street behind Ronnie. Ted wanted to get there just as Ronnie stepped out of the car.

Ted watched as Ronnie pulled into his driveway and parked the car. Ted continued his slow roll forward trying to gauge his reaching the driveway as Ronnie got out. He saw the car door open as he stopped at the end of the driveway.

With his attention on Margret's car, Ted never saw Max as he stepped off the front porch until long after he had rolled down the passenger's window and shouted at Ronnie for assistance. Ted's jacket was still lying on the front seat and with a firm grip on the gun, Ted slid his hand under the jacket to hide the gun

315

from sight. He wanted Ronnie right up next to the car to make sure it would only take one bullet. When he looked up from making sure the gun was out of sight he saw Max standing on the other side of Ronnie.

Ted's first impulse was to floor the accelerator and take off. He fought back the urge and thinking quickly, found he had a plan B. He would get both guys next to the car and nail them. There was no way he could leave a witness and he quickly decided it was worth two lives to be able to spend the rest of his life with Margret.

He also saw that his first shout had gone unheeded. Ronnie and the stranger were talking and Ted decided they hadn't heard him the first time, so he shouted again. This time both Ronnie and the stranger turned and looked at him and then started for Ted's car.

"Excuse me," Ted repeated, "I'm lost." He said as the men came closer.

"Where are you trying to get to?" Ronnie asked as they walked to the car sitting across the front of his driveway.

"Well...I'm trying to get to the shopping center and got turned around somehow." Ted replied. Both men had reached his car and were now squatting down to get a better look through the car window.

"I'll say you did." Ronnie said as he stood back up. He found that half squatting, half leaning down was making his lower back hurt. As he stood up, Ronnie took one step back to maintain his balance. Max continued to squat and lean into the car window as he was trying to give instructions to the supposedly lost Ted.

Ted looked up pretending he was paying attention to Max and saw he had a perfect shot. He would be able to nail Ronnie with the first shot and then nail Ronnie's friend with the second. Ted calculated the whole thing should take less than two seconds.

For everyone involved, this was going to be the longest two seconds in recorded history.

Ted pulled the gun up and aimed on the draw. The jacket pulled away from the gun as it came up off of the seat. When he had his shot, he pulled the trigger.

Max started pulling back from the window the instant he saw the gun come up from the seat. The gun went off with a very loud bang and even in his now deafened state, Max heard the bullet go past his right ear.

Ronnie didn't know what was happening, all he saw was Max suddenly pull away from the car window as a small explosion went off inside. The bullet dug a white hot furrow across the top of his left shoulder. Another couple of inches to the right and the slug would have hit Ronnie dead center of his throat. Ronnie fell backwards well after the slug had passed him by taking a two inch by a quarter inch wide and deep piece of meat with it.

As Max was pulling away from the window, he was reaching under his arm pit inside his sports coat to pull his own gun from its holster. Max looked at Ted and saw that Ted now had the gun pointed straight at his forehead. Max watched Ted as he pulled the trigger for his second shot. As Max was pulling his own gun out of its holster in one fluid motion, Max saw the hammer fall as he continued to pull his own gun up to the level of the window.

Nothing happened.

The hammer fell but the gun didn't go off. Nobody knew it then, but the firing pin had sheared off on the round Ted had fired at Ronnie. Ted could have pulled the trigger all day long and nothing would have ever happened. The next round would never fire.

Max yelled for Ted to drop the gun as he finally got his own gun. He took a quick bead on the gun in Ted's hand. Max knew that even if he missed the gun, he was going to hit this stranger in mid to lower torso. This guy had picked the wrong cop to shoot at, as Max was an expert shot. He had grown up with a BB gun when he was very little and graduated to other guns as he grew older.

Max watched as Ted squeezed the trigger again and saw the hammer go back to its cocking position. Max pulled his own trigger and his forty-five went off with a roar. Max was pointing his gun straight at the very end of the barrel of Ted's gun where the hole is. From this close proximity, there was no way Max could have missed.

But he did.

At the very instant the hammer fell on his gun, Max felt something grab the end of his gun. He was looking down the barrel and saw what looked like a shadow on either side of the barrel. In that split second the hammer fell, Max realized that he didn't have control of his gun. The gun itself seemed to jerk upward in his hand just before the natural recoil was going off.

The bullet, now loose of its confines, struck Ted right between the eyes, neatly breaking the sunglasses he was wearing into two separate and equal pieces. The bullet continued to travel through his brain and shattered the back of his skull as it exited his head. The bullet continued on, shattering the drivers side window and then fell to the street, its energy spent. Less than a quarter of a second later, the gore that had been Ted's brain and the back of his head, landed on the street all around the spent bullet.

Ted saw Max's gun go off and in the fraction of the last second he had left to live, he saw what appeared to be a black dot coming straight for his eyes. The dot was coming too fast for his eyes to track, but they did cross slightly in response to his brains effort to keep the encroaching bullet in focus. Ted died instantly, there were no afterthoughts, no reflexes, no flinching. There was no time for any of that. The force of the bullet caused Ted to sit back against the corner the seat and the door post created. He just sat there and Max watched as the broken sunglasses slowly slid down Ted's face on their way to his lap. Ted's gun hand dropped and the gun fell onto the car seat.

The car was still in drive, but Ted's foot was still holding the brake down. Even though he was dead, he still had control of the car.

Max looked at Ted for a couple of seconds, staring in disbelief of the shot he had just made. Then he looked at his own gun, not believing what had just happened. His mind cleared a little and he realized that Ronnie had been standing behind him. Max spun around and saw Ronnie trying to crawl away, belly down on the grass.

"Ronnie!" Max shouted, pumped up and full of adrenaline from what had just taken place. "It's safe! Are you okay?"

Ronnie stopped crawling and rolled over onto his back and sat up. He was now becoming even more aware of his wound. "No. Bastard got me in the shoulder. What the hell was that all about?" He yelled back at Max, his shoulder was a white-hot, dull throb now... He looked down and saw blood spilling down the front of his shirt.

"Shit!" Max yelled. "You don't know this guy?"

"Hell no, I just thought he was some stranger asking for directions." But I'll bet my wife knows him, Ronnie thought to himself. "Did you kill him?" He asked as he put his other hand to his injured shoulder.

"Permanently I'm afraid." Max replied as he looked into the car.

Ted's mouth had dropped open and his head was beginning to sag downward by the chin. With his eyes open, Max noted for himself that Ted was beginning to look like a ghastly version of the Joker out of an old time Batman comic book.

Still looking into the car, Max realized the engine was still running and saw that the car was still in drive. Max leaned in through the passenger window and slipped the gear shift lever quickly into park. Now that the car wasn't going to be subject to driving off by itself, he switched the ignition to the off position. Now that he was sure the car wasn't going to go away and Ted wasn't playing possum (Which would have been one of the world's best tricks), Max turned his attention back to Ronnie.

Turning around. Max saw Ronnie was still sitting there but now there was a fairly good sized amount of blood soaking the front of the shirt he was wearing. "Are you going to live?" Max asked as he quickly stepped to where Ronnie was sitting.

"I think it's just a scratch." Ronnie casually replied, now looking considerably paler.

"Stay with me Ronnie, don't pass out." Max said as he started the emergency first aid he had been trained to do. "I'm going to cut your shirt off," He said as he reached into his pocket and pulled out his pocket knife, "Then I can see how bad it is and I can use your shirt as a bandage."

Max didn't wait for a reply and started cutting the shirt, his knife easily slitting the cotton fabric.

"Whatever." Was Ronnie's reply as he began to swoon, the pain was too intense.

"Come on Ronnie, stay with me. Keep breathing, you're just trying to go into shock. Concentrate on your breathing, in-out, in-out."

Max peeled Ronnie's shirt off and he could see that Ronnie had a pretty good groove across the top of his shoulder. Relieved that the damage wasn't as bad as it could have been, he rolled up Ronnie's shirt and gently place it across the wound. He also saw that Ronnie was breathing deeply and was beginning to look better now.

"It's just a scratch. There's a lot of blood, but you are definitely going to live." Max told Ronnie trying to console him.

"Man, if this is just a scratch, I'd really hate to get hurt. This hurts like a bitch."

"I know, and it's going to hurt for awhile. I need to use your phone."

"Okay, it's in the house. Could you help me to the porch? I feel kinda stupid sitting here in the middle of the yard."

"No problem." Max replied as he bent over and helped Ronnie get to his feet.

Once Ronnie was situated on the porch, Max walked over to the front door.

"Just go on in." Ronnie said.

Max pulled out his badge and opened the door.

73.

Margret heard Ronnie when he pulled into the driveway. What seemed like a few seconds later, she heard something that sounded like firecrackers going off. Two of them. She smiled to herself thinking she was now free. Margret planned on waiting for a few minutes and then going to look out of the window, where she would find her beloved husband laying in the yard somewhere dead.

Oh the horror, she would cry to the police.

She was starting to walk towards the living room when the front door burst open. Margret froze in her tracks thinking the hit man had seen her looking out of the window earlier and was now coming to finish the job, the goal being to leave no witnesses. She knew that her best bet was to run. Turn and run out through the back door. But like a deer caught in a set of headlights, she found her feet refused to move.

The door finished opening and the strange man she had seen in front of the house earlier stepped in. Margret saw that he was holding something in one hand and she just continued to stand there with a look of surprise on her face. She found she could not formulate any other thought than to run, which her feet refused to respond to. It wasn't until the man spoke that her paralysis broke.

74.

As Max stepped into the living room, he saw Margret standing in the dining room looking at him. He saw the strange look on her face and mistook it as an expression of shock that a total stranger had just barged into her safe haven.

"Excuse me ma'am, I'm Sergeant Maxwell and I need to use your phone." He said as he held up his badge in plain sight and looked towards the telephone.

"What?" Margret asked confused.

"There's been a shooting outside and I need to use your telephone."

"What happened? Where's Ronnie?" She demanded pointing towards the phone as an indication that Max could use it. This was better than she could have hoped for, a witness to Ronnie's murder who could prove she didn't have anything to do with it.

"He's okay. Get a towel and take it to him." Max ordered as he strode over to the phone, "He was hit in the shoulder, but he's going to be just fine."

Margret's let down was tremendous. She knew she had to keep up a front, but she strained to keep the disappointment from her face. She quickly turned around and went to the kitchen and retrieved a dish towel. As she was heading for the front door she asked, "Where is he?"

Max diverted his attention from dialing the phone and replied, "On the front porch. Don't worry, I'll have an ambulance here in a couple of minutes."

Margret continued out through the front door. When she got outside onto the porch she stopped dead in her tracks and stood looking at the car sitting at the end of the driveway. It dawned on her that she had heard *two* firecracker pops. She forced herself to turn and face where Ronnie was sitting, slowly, she walked over to him and offered him the dish towel.

"Is Max using the phone?" Ronnie asked as he took the towel from Margret.

"Yes." She replied. She wanted so very badly to run down to that car and see who was in it.

"Good...Then I'll tell you something."

Silence from Margret, although she looked as if she was paying attention to Ronnie, her real attention was focused on that car.

Ronnie took her silence as a cue to continue speaking. "Your boyfriend Ted is dead. I told Max I didn't know him, I suggest you stick to the same story." Ronnie said, with no emotion to his voice, it was as if he was just reciting some boring fact.

"Ted who?" She asked innocently.

"Cut the bullshit Margret. You know damn well who. Looks like your little plan didn't succeed, your boyfriend's dead and I'm still alive. If I were you, I would forget that you ever knew him. I hope he was a better lover than a shot." Ronnie fell silent after saying that.

Margret starting crying. This time, unlike the rest of the times she cried on cue, the tears were real.

75.

Max called the police department, identified himself and explained the situation he was in. He then requested another unit and an ambulance. Max stayed on the line and when the uproar on the other end of the phone settled down, he asked to speak to Waters.

"Captain Waters speaking. May I help you?"

"Cap, this is Max. You ain't gonna believe what just happened."

"Max, all you alright? You sound funny."

"Hell no. I came over to Fisher's house to talk to him and just before we got a chance to speak, some asshole rolled up out front and started shooting."

"What? What did you say?" Waters asked in shocked disbelief.

"Some guy tried to shoot me and Fisher."

"Are you okay? Is everyone okay? Where is he?"

"The guy missed me, but Fisher caught it across the top of his shoulder. It looks bad, but I think it's just a flesh wound."

"Gawddamn!! What about the shooter?"

"Nailed him between the eyes with one shot. I tried to just wound him, but everything happened so fast..."

"Don't worry about it Max. As long as you're okay we can sort the rest out later."

"I'll start my report as soon as I get back to the station. I'll be coming back just as soon as the investigation's over."

"No...No you won't." Waters told him, "You already have your assignment. Investigate the crime scene until it's time for the game to start, then turn the investigation over to somebody else and get to the game. When everything is over with, come in and do your paperwork."

"If that's the way you want me to do it, then that's the way it will be done." Max replied.

"That's the word. Max, when you get finished with your paperwork, come see me."

"You got it boss." Max could hear the wail of the approaching sirens. "Sounds like everyone is fixing to arrive. I gotta go."

"Just make sure you get to that game on time, then come and see me later."
Waters said just before he hung up the phone.

Max hung up his end and went out to the front porch to direct the traffic that
was fixing to arrive. When he got outside he saw Margret standing next to
Ronnie crying. Max mis-interpreted what he saw, as he thought Margret was
crying about what had happened to Ronnie.

The first squad car arrived and was followed a half a minute later by the
ambulance. After checking on how Ronnie was doing, he walked down the lawn
to greet his comrades when the ambulance showed up.

Max told the paramedic as he pointed in the direction of what he was
describing, "The guy in the car is dead I believe, try not to disturb anything while
you check him out. The guy on the porch has a shoulder wound."

The paramedic just nodded and after a brief conference with his partner,
headed for the car while his partner headed for the porch. Max resumed his trip to
where his work mates were now standing.

"What the hell happened here Max?" One of the Officers asked.

Max explained to his friend that he had just stopped by to speak to Ronnie
and this guy had rolled up on the both of them asking directions. He further
explained that when he had stooped down to give directions, the man in the car
had opened fire.

The cop listening to the story was taking notes and commented that Max had
been very lucky to escape injury. Very lucky indeed. Max nodded his head yes
and then resumed speaking, explaining how when the first shot was fired, he had
grabbed his own gun and managed to fire off one round as the man in the car
tried to fire his gun a second time. For whatever reason, the guys gun had failed
to fire. Max knew the only reason he was standing there talking to them was
because of that failure to fire. Max told his friend that when the guy had pulled
the trigger, Max had been looking straight down the barrel of the other gun.

As Max was speaking, his thoughts were going over and over what had just
happened. He knew full well when he had pulled his own trigger, his shot should
have hit the gun in the other guys hand. He had been shooting long enough and
knew his gun very well. He also knew he had better keep his mouth shut about
the jerk he had felt on his gun and the shadows he had seen on either side of the
barrel.

As Max thought about those two shadows, he realized they had looked just
like fingers. Even though he had only seen them for a fraction of a second, that
image was burned into his memory forever. He could see every detail as plain as
if he was looking at the end of his gun that very second close up. He continued to
run the image slowly over and over in his mind.

While his mind was occupied with those thoughts, deep down he was also
remembering about seeing the trigger pulled and the first bullet passing his ear.
Then seeing the trigger pulled that second time and nothing happening.

324

Nothing with the gun that was pointed at him, that is.

Inside Max, at that very instant, he knew he was going to die, he had resolved himself to that fact. Now that it didn't happen, he felt changed. He had been in a few tight spots before, but nothing like this. Sure, he had seen a gun pulled and used before, but he had never had one pointed right in his face and the trigger pulled. He felt like he had been given a second chance, spared for some reason.

Max's mind had been wandering for a few moments and when he came back to reality, he realized the officer standing next to him had been talking and was now looking at him as if he was expecting a response.

"I'm sorry," Max said, "Did you say something?"

"I was asking if you were all right."

"Yeah, just shook up a little."

"No shit! How close was it?" One of the junior officers interrupted.

"I felt the first slug go by my ear and was looking straight down his gun barrel when he pulled the trigger the second time."

"And it didn't go off." The younger man said almost in awe.

"Yep, it didn't go off. But I was in the process of pulling the trigger on my gun at the same time. So for him, the results would have been the same." Max said as he looked towards the soon to be discovered rental car. "Anybody got an ID yet?" He asked.

"It's been called in." Somebody offered.

"Max, you are one lucky sum'bitch." Max's long time work mate said, "I can't imagine how you can be standing here so calm. I would have gone home and changed my pants, because if this had happened to me, I would have shit them full for sure."

"It's all in the training boy. What about the ID?"

"Homicide said not to touch anything until they showed. What about this Fisher guy, does he know him?"

"No. Ronnie said he didn't know him and I'm inclined to believe him." Max answered.

"Why's that?" The Officer taking notes asked.

"Because when this guy rolled up, he was acting like he was lost and just wanted directions. Ronnie didn't act like he knew him, there was no recognition that I saw."

"So you say that this guy just rolled up asking for directions and started blasting away?"

"Yep."

"Pissed anyone off lately?"

"Other than my wife? Nobody I can think of." Max replied as he turned his attention to the senior officer there and said, "Listen, the Captain has me on that ball park stakeout tonight and I need to leave in a little while. Can you finish the investigation and I'll file my report with you later tonight?"

"No problem." Was the reply without hesitation.

"Great. One more thing, go easy on Fisher, he's okay. His wife is a different story though."

"I think I remember her from a while back. Isn't she the one who called in and said that her old man was trying to kill her? If I remember right, didn't she proceed to tell Lewis how small his dick is?"

"You got part of it right. She was commenting about my dick. In fact, she was marveling about how big it is." Max embellished.

"Then you woke up." the officer said and everyone started laughing.

After the exchange was finished, Max went to see how things were going with Ronnie. Max found the paramedics were taking care of him and treating him for shock as well as for the wound on his shoulder. Max didn't think anything bad about Ronnie's lack of fortitude towards the bullet wound. Max knew different people had different reactions to this type of pain in addition to the trauma of the chain of events.

Max took a good look at Margret. She was standing there next to Ronnie acting all concerned for his welfare. For some reason, Max found her actions strange. He couldn't put a finger on it, but for some reason she didn't seem to be acting the way he thought she should be.

Max had no idea how she should be acting, but he just knew it should be different. Then he realized what it was. It was her tears, her crying, that was troubling him. She seemed to be crying and acting like she had just lost somebody close to her instead of being happy her husband was still alive. As Max watched her out of the corner of his eye, he noticed she kept stealing glances toward the car at the end of the driveway and then the tears would get a little heavier. He also noticed that not once had she asked why.

Why?

Why, is the most logical and the most asked question after something senseless like this happened. Hell, it was asked after just about anything that took a life or lives. Mankind has a need to believe that there is a higher authority in charge of all events that happens to every living thing. Why did the earthquake hit? Why did the factory burn down? Why did one kid shoot another over lunch money? Why does life suck? Mankind always demands an explanation for the events that sometimes overwhelm the mind.

But today, it seemed to Max, Margret had no questions to ask.

Max now stood there looking fully at Margret and he couldn't help but wonder how much of the concern she seemed to be showing for Ronnie was false. So he decided to ask Ronnie once again about the strange man in the car that was now assuming air temperature.

"How you doing Ronnie?" He asked.

"I've damn sure had better days, but I think I'll live." Ronnie replied as the paramedic applied another field dressing to his shoulder.

"I have to ask you again, are you sure you don't know the guy in the car?"

"No, I just thought he was some lost guy asking for directions."

"Okay." Max said, "What about you ma'am, do you recognize that car?" He asked Margret. The whole time Max had been speaking to Ronnie he had been looking at Margret, he was surprised by the total lack of emotion in her eyes.

"Pardon me? What did you say?" Margret replied, suddenly becoming animated. She hadn't heard a word Max had said because she was off in her own little world thinking about how cheap life really is.

"That's okay, there's alot going on right now." Max said as he slapped a smile on his face. "I'm sorry, but I have to ask. Do you recognize the car sitting in the street?"

"No." Margret replied flatly and honestly. She had no idea Ted was going to be in a different car than the one she had always seen him in.

"Didn't think so." Max commented. He hadn't expected her to admit to knowing the car so it was just a question he asked to gauge her reaction. He had to admit he was surprised, her reaction had been totally honest. He began to have second thoughts about his previous train of thoughts. "Well...Like I said, I had to ask for the paperwork." he said and then turned his attention back to the both of them, "As soon as homicide gets here, we'll get an ID on the guy and know who he was. You're probably going to get asked a few hundred more times tonight if you knew him. I imagine you'll get used to it."

"Of course." Ronnie replied and then added, "By the way Max, why did you come by tonight? Not that I mind that you did, you sure saved my ass."

Max thought for a moment because he didn't want to bring up the subject of the bad checks in front of Margret, he wanted to have a chance to talk to Ronnie alone. "Well...I haven't had a chance to talk to you after the last time I saw you. I just wanted to let you know the investigation into Fryer's death is closed. But don't worry about that right now, we can talk later."

"I hate to say this," Ronnie said, "But I hate to think what your opinion of me is. Everytime you see me something bad has happened. I bet you think I have the worst luck in the world."

"Don't sweat it Ronnie, shit happens."

"That is the truth and there's a really big pile of it right there to prove the statement." Ronnie answered as he nodded his head in the direction of the car in the street.

Ronnie's comment brought a smile from everyone standing there and a snicker from the paramedic. Everyone except Margret, Max noticed. Now he seriously began to wonder what her involvement in all of this was.

The paramedic announced that he was ready to transport Ronnie to the hospital to get some real treatment. Ronnie started to protest saying he wasn't that badly hurt, but Max just looked at him and told him he should go anyway to make sure he wasn't hurt worse than he thought he was. He also added that sometimes, looks can be deceiving. When Max said the word 'deceiving' he had full eye contact with Margret who quickly diverted her eyes.

Ronnie made no more protest and they helped him to walk off of the porch and out to the ambulance.

Looking around, Max saw a small crowd had gathered on the other side of the yellow police tape that had magically sprung up around the front of the house. Max walked over to a couple of policemen who were milling around and told them to start dispersing the crowd before evidence started disappearing. The two men went and started telling people to go home. Most of the neighbors who lived within looking distance were sitting on their front porches watching the show.

Once Ronnie was loaded into the ambulance, Margret went to Max and asked if she could go along. Max went over to the driver and after a couple of words with the man, told her to go ahead and get in and ride to the hospital with Ronnie. Margret was just getting into the ambulance when a policeman came out of the house carrying Nancy in his arms. In all of the hubbub, Margret had almost gone off and left Nancy sitting in her playpen. Not that she wouldn't have been safe with all of the policemen standing around.

As Margret walked towards the policeman coming down the walk towards her, she saw Heather's mother coming toward her out of the corner of her eye. She was on her way over to volunteer to get Nancy and keep her until Margret and Ronnie got back. With tear swollen eyes, Margret thanked the older woman and handed Nancy over to her. Margret then turned around to get into the ambulance.

After the ambulance was gone, Max took the last few minutes he had to go over and talk to the nice people that were so gracious to take the Ronnie's kid at a moments notice. Ten minutes later, he came back with a much different opinion of Margret. Not only was she a two-faced bitch, she was the queen of the herd. Ronnie on the other hand, was the nicest person they had ever met. They left the impression that they thought very highly of Ronnie.

Max looked at his watch and saw he had to go, so he went and found the officer he had been talking to earlier and turned the investigation over to him. As Max left, the cop told him he hoped Max cracked the case he was going to.

76.

Ever since Max had busted in on Margret to use the phone, she felt as if her mind had turned off. When Ronnie had told her Ted was dead, she found she felt nothing, nothing at all except pity. Pity for herself and pity that all of her plans had just been flushed and now she was stuck. There was no way she could now start her life over and she now felt the impending doom of the wall of checks that were going to collapse down on her.

On the ride to the hospital, she began to resent Ronnie. This was all his fault, if he had been killed like he was supposed to, then she could be planning her new life right now. But no...she was stuck with him. As she sat there deep in thought, she rationalized the bad checks were his fault as well. If he had paid more attention to her, she wouldn't have had to resort to such a drastic cry for help. She almost told Ronnie right then about the checks, but decided it would be better to wait until they were alone to do it. The last thing she wanted was for him to get really mad inside the ambulance. He might start telling people it was Ted, Margret's lover, that had just been killed in front of their house.

Thinking about that, she remembered Ronnie had told her Ted was dead. Not some guy had been killed, but TED had been killed. They had never met each other, so how did he know it was Ted? Margret began to have some hope it wasn't Ted at all, but someone Ted had hired to come and do the job right. Deep down she doubted it, but a girl has to have hope she told herself. And she hoped it was just some guy who had seriously screwed up a job. Maybe she would be able to start her new life after all.

Margret knew enough to keep her mouth shut while that pesky cop was around and she wondered why Ronnie had lied for her. What was he up to? There was no way he would do something like that just to let her off the hook. How had he known it was Ted that had tried to kill him? Now that she thought about it, she wondered how he had known someone trying to kill him was even tied one way or another back to her? But he had given her an out with the police and she was smart enough to take it. As long as he kept his mouth shut, she would keep hers shut also. At least until she figured out a way to shut his mouth permanently. If this wasn't Ted that was dead and this being a miss, there would be no way Ted would risk a second attempt at getting the job done. It had been hard enough for her to get him to do it the first time. Margret decided if Ted was somehow still alive, she intended to put in whatever time on her back with her legs spread it would require to change his mind for a second try.

Once they were at the hospital, Margret sat in the waiting room patiently waiting for someone to come out and tell her she could go in to Ronnie. The emergency room had taken Ronnie straight to the back where she assumed they were working on him. She had been banished to the waiting room when they had first taken him into the hospital, someone dressed in scrubs had told her to please wait in the waiting room. And that's where she had stayed.

Thinking.

As she sat there, she thought. As she thought, she planned. As she planned, she became bitter. She decided she had taken enough of Ronnie's shit and when they were back home and the light's were out, she would make his life hell. And that would be because he was making her life hell. It was hard for her to imagine she would be able to restart her life because she didn't know if her way out of this life was still walking and breathing.

Then it dawned on her that she wasn't supposed to call Ted from her house. But she wasn't home and she saw the pay phone over in the corner. She sat there looking at the phone trying to decide whether she should call or not and put an end to her wondering about his welfare. Finally she couldn't resist the temptation and picked up her purse. Digging around in it she found enough change to use the phone. She remembered something about Ted telling her he had to leave in the morning, so she decided he must be in his room waiting for the time to leave.

She casually walked over to the phone and dialed Ted's number. It rang. Then it rang again. After it had rung a dozen times she hung up and went back over to sit down. Part of her told her this was proof that Ted was dead, but the irrational part of her mind told her it was nonsense, he was more likely to be out eating or getting ready for his trip. Maybe he was even out with his buddies drinking beer, without the knowledge his plans to end Ronnie's life had failed.

Margret had been sitting there for forty minutes when a cop walked into the emergency room, walked up to the receptionist and spoke to her. The nurse at the window looked around and pointed at Margret. The policeman thanked her and walked over to where Margret was sitting.

"Margret Fisher?" The officer asked.

"Yes." Margret replied, her blood frozen in her veins, she just knew this man was here to arrest her.

"I'm Officer Bell, I have to ask you a couple of questions about what happened at your house this afternoon."

"I'm afraid I won't be of much help. I was inside cooking dinner when Officer Maxwell came inside my house and told me what happened."

"So you didn't see anything happen for yourself?"

"No sir. I didn't see a thing."

"Okay," Bell said as he wrote in a small note book. "Is there anyone you can think of that would want to cause you or your husband harm?"

"Nobody that I can think of. But I don't know what Ronnie's up to when he's at work. You really need to talk to him."

"Actually, I have to talk to the both of you, I just found you first. I have one last question." Bell stated, he couldn't believe the stories he had heard about this woman. The talk around was that she was mean and belligerent, but here she was talking to him in a civil manner and being respectful. Too bad he didn't know she had been scared shitless that he was going to arrest her for the attempted murder of her husband not less than thirty minutes ago.

"Ask away." She replied emotionless, she suddenly knew what his next question would be.

"Did you or your husband know a Theodore Tillman?"

Margret appeared to be thinking for a moment, but what she was doing was her best to not give Bell some kind of reaction he could read as her true emotions. When she had heard Ted's name she felt all of the life go out of her. "Sorry, I can't say the name rings a bell with me. Maybe Ronnie knows him."

Bell stood up and closing the small notebook he had been writing in, thanked her for her cooperation. As he turned to leave to go to where Ronnie was, Margret asked if he could find out when she could go and see Ronnie. She explained they had made her sit out here and wait.

Bell smiled and told her he would see what he could do. Then he walked off in the direction of where Ronnie was.

As soon as Bell got out of sight, the full gravity of what had happened settled on her. She felt like her life was slipping away from her, everything she had been working towards had failed in one miserable attempt.

For this, Ronnie would pay dearly. She decided that she would play it cool and when Ronnie was the least expecting it, wham! She would have her revenge.

77.

Ronnie was feeling sick to his stomach and his shoulder hurt very badly. It felt as though all of the nerve endings had been asleep were now waking up and letting him know full well their protest of the afternoons activities. Right after he got to the hospital, a doctor had looked at him and had given him a shot. Now he felt good. Deliciously good. He knew the pain was still there, but he didn't care, it was turned off.

He felt so good that if someone had come in and started sawing his legs off, he would have probably held the light for them to see what they were doing.

Even in his induced stupor, Ronnie was thinking about how lucky Max and he had been. For that matter, how lucky he had been that Max had even been there. If Max hadn't been there Ronnie knew full well the outcome of this would have been alot different. He couldn't believe Margret was behind all of this, but there wasn't a time he doubted it either. He knew what a calculating bitch she could be. He also knew if it hadn't been for the Professor, he would probably be dead right now. Somehow, the foreknowledge of what was going to happen had made him a little more cautious. Deep down he knew it had been that edge that had kept him from sticking his head into that car window to give directions. He had held back and let Max give the directions. Now here he was still alive and miraculously, Max had not been hurt either.

Ronnie decided he really didn't love Margret anymore. After all, it's hard to find love for someone who wanted to see you with a brand new asshole blown in the center of your forehead. He did feel sad though, he had tried to be the best husband he could be. He had gone to work and always handed over his paycheck. He didn't go out partying after work like alot of the other guys he knew did. He had always gone straight home.

Laying here in the sterile emergency room under the influence of some really good drugs, everything was crystal clear. He would talk to Margret and explain to her that she would have to get a job to help pay off her bad checks. He would also tell her after the checks were paid for, she would be able to go her own separate way. Then maybe she would be able to find the happiness he was unable to give her for whatever reason she found him lacking. He would also tell her as far as he was concerned, there would be no more conjugal interaction between them. He just wanted her to stick around and help clean up her mess before leaving.

Her alternative was to get the hell out now and take all of her checks with her. At least with his method, they would be able to pool their paychecks and get the debt paid off faster.

Still thinking about it, he realized Nancy would have to go somewhere, so he decided he would try to get custody and she could live with him. He would do his best to raise her right. Looking into the future, Ronnie just couldn't see life without Nancy. Unfortunately, this was the one thing Margret and he still had in common and he couldn't see Margret just giving up custody without a fight.

Not that custody would be a problem with Margret, he would just tell her she either hit the road alone or he would let Max know he had 'Just found out who was fucking the guy that had tried to shot him' was. Ronnie anticipated no resistance from Margret.

Ronnie did feel sad that his marriage had come to this point, but he realized Margret was not the same woman he had pursued while they were dating. Then, she had been feminine and demure, now she was just mean and vicious.

A couple of minutes after the doctor came in and started putting stitches in his shoulder, a policeman walked into the room and started asking questions about what had happened. Ronnie was very careful in his replies, making the excuse that the shot he had been given was making it difficult to concentrate. The doctor backed Ronnie on that point and the policeman walked away satisfied Ronnie didn't know the man who shot him or what the mans motives might have been.

Finally, the hospital was done with him and started the process of checking him out since Ronnie had refused the overnight stay. His mind was on the fact that he had to go to work in the morning. He also wanted to get Margret home so he could talk to her and let her know the party was now officially over.

As they wheeled him into the waiting room in the wheelchair, he saw a clock and saw he had been there for over five hours. His head was beginning to clear and the pain in his shoulder was now just a dull throb. Ronnie thought to himself about time flying when you're having fun and asked himself if he could call what he had just been through, fun. Other than the drugs, his answer was to himself was no.

Much to Ronnie's relief, Officer Bell was still there and offered Ronnie and Margret a ride back to their house. When they got home, the wrecker was just starting to tow Ted's rental car away and everyone was starting to disperse. The investigation was over and Ted's body had long been taken away.

It took all Ronnie's strength to get to the couch in the living room before he collapsed. Margret stood there for a moment before saying she was going next door to get Nancy. Without waiting for a reply she turned to leave. Being here and knowing it really had been Ted at the end of the driveway had brought a wave of remorse on again, she wanted to get outside because she felt as if she was going to cry. She didn't want that butt wipe, piece of trash Ronnie to see her crying.

As she turned away, Ronnie saw that Margret had a whipped puppy look to her, it was as if he was looking at somebody who had all of the life sucked out of them and for the first time, realized they didn't have anything left to live for.

Margret didn't get very far, as soon as she reached the door, there was a knock. It was Heather's mother bringing Nancy back, she had obviously been watching and saw them return home. Margret reluctantly invited the woman into the house and took Nancy from her. Margret went straight upstairs to put Nancy to bed.

Ronnie got to recant the events of the afternoon to Heather's mother and apologized for imposing on her. He was told not to worry about it and the older woman told him she hoped he would be feeling better quickly. Ronnie thanked her and told her he was sorry because he couldn't pay her for watching Nancy because he was broke. She replied she had taken Nancy because she was a good neighbor and hadn't expected any pay for what she had done. Ronnie thanked her again and after making the appropriate excuses, she left.

Ronnie laid there on the couch thinking about what he was going to say to Margret. That's when he began to notice she had been gone for a long time and almost as if in response to him thinking about her, Margret came back downstairs. Ronnie saw her eyes looked all puffy and red. He commanded her to sit down because they had a lot to talk about.

He waited until Margret sat down in her recliner before speaking. She just sat there looking at him with a blank look on her face. That blank look didn't help Ronnie formulate how he was going to slip into the subject he wanted to discuss. He didn't want to just blurt out that ultimately, she was going to hit the road. Ronnie wanted to open a line of conversation with her first and then ease into the subject.

But it didn't happen that way, Margret spoke first, catching him off guard.

"Ronnie, I know that right now, you probably won't believe me, but...I had no idea Ted was going to try something as stupid as this. I'm just glad you weren't hurt worse than you were." She said in a solemn voice.

"Well, I'm glad also. But you are right, I don't believe you."

"Do you think I tried to have you killed? Is that what you think?" She asked with a very emotional voice, but the tears that always came so easy for her, weren't flowing.

"What am I supposed to think, Margret? Your boyfriend shows up here when I arrive home from work and tries to give me a first class case of lead poisoning."

"I know how it looks. But there's a part of the story I haven't told you and you don't know yet."

"Here's your chance. I'm listening to everything you have to say." He replied. He was curious as to what kind of a lie she was going to tell him.

"I broke off the affair a couple of weeks ago. Ted went ballistic and kept calling me, but I always refused telling him it was over and to get over it. Then the other day he called and when I told him to get lost, he said maybe if you weren't around I would still be with him. At the time, I just thought he was talking trash. You know how people are sometimes, they talk big but never follow up with any action."

"So you're saying he was acting on his own?" Ronnie asked. He was beginning to feel stupid, he could see how this could have happened because her story had some plausibility to it.

"That's exactly what I'm saying. Ronnie, you have to believe me. If I had thought what he said had any merit to it, I would have told you and called the police myself."

"Okay." Ronnie replied flatly, now he didn't know what to think. He wanted to believe this had just been a random act by a man crazy with lust. But after everything he had been through with her...

"Ronnie," Margret replied as she got up and came over to where he was sitting, when she was very close to him she quietly said, "thank you for covering for me with the police. I have the feeling they would have tried to charge me as an accessory even though I had nothing to do with it. I love you and I don't want anything to happen to you." at least until I can figure out what to do to you, Margret thought to herself.

"I don't know why, I guess I'm a fool, but I believe you Margret. But there's still one little matter that we still have to discuss."

"What's that darling?" She asked smugly. She couldn't believe he had bought the bag of bullshit she had just handed over. This was good, she had disarmed him of his anger for her and any thoughts that he might have had that she was involved with Ted's actions. Now she would be free to get her revenge, and it would be sweet. It was also a testament of just how stupid she thought Ronnie was.

"Seems like you've had a small problem with writing checks lately."

"How...How did you find out about that?" Margret asked as her mouth fell open in disbelief. The wind had definitely been taken out of her sails.

"It doesn't matter how I found out, the point is...What do you have to say for yourself?"

"It's...It's true Ronnie." Margret said as she stood back up and stepped back from Ronnie. He had caught her off guard with his knowledge of her checks and she couldn't formulate a lie quick enough. "I did get stupid with the checkbook. But I was trying to take care of the problem myself." She added, her mind finally getting into gear and coming up with a better tale of woe.

"Well, I've taken care of it for you. I talked to everyone you wrote checks to and they agreed to take payments. Understand this, that is the only reason you are not in jail right now."

"Jail?" Margret asked, her train of thought derailed again.

"Yes Margret, jail. You don't know how many of those stores were swearing out warrants on you before I talked to them and set up a payment plan. You really don't know how close you came..."

"You did that for me? Why?" Margret asked. She was shocked he had done something like to protect her on his own. She never considered he had a spine to stand up to someone.

"Because you're my wife and for some stupid reason, I love you."

"I don't see how. I've been so bad to you. Can you ever find it in your heart to forgive me?" She said, clearly defeated.

"I guess. But you are going to have to get a job. The payment plans that are set up will eat up most of my paycheck."

"Then pay them less, they'll just have to understand. After all, we have to have some money for food and rent."

"Can't do it Margret. I'm paying as little as I can get away with now. You," Ronnie punctuated the word 'you' with his voice, "Are going to have to go to work to help with the expenses around here."

"I don't know Ronnie. Nancy is so young and the daycare bills will eat up most of my paycheck." Margret said trying to find a way to weasel out of having to spend her free time working.

"I'm afraid you have no choice in this matter. This is just how it's going to be. Tomorrow after work, I'll go next door and have a talk with Heather's mother, maybe I can work something out with her that won't eat up everything you make."

"Is this the only alternative that I have?"

"It's either this or go to jail for a good long time."

"Oh Ronnie, you do love me. This is the second time today you've saved me."

"Just tell me one thing."

"Only if you promise not to tell the neighbors why I'm going back to work."

"You don't have to worry about that. Just tell me why you did it."

"I didn't mean to do it, at first it was just a couple of checks. Then I wrote another check to cover the first couple. Then the whole thing just sort of snowballed on me. Next thing I knew, I was up to my ass in bad checks. I didn't know what to do."

"Why didn't you just tell me instead of trying to hide it?"

"I...I was afraid of what you might do."

"You're saying you were afraid of me?" Ronnie asked loudly. He had only raised his fist to her once and she had kicked his ass. He felt his ire raise somewhat at her inference.

"I'm not afraid, I was just scared you'd get really mad and leave. I couldn't imagine going through life without you. I guess that's what I was really afraid of."

"Margret, you should know by now that you don't have to be afraid to tell me anything. You're my wife, if something is happening to you, it's happening to me too." Ronnie said as he struggled to keep control of his temper.

While Margret was talking, telling him how afraid of him she was, Ronnie had imagined reaching out with one hand and just tearing her throat out. In his minds eye he saw himself looking down at her vocal cords in his hand. This mini vision helped to relieve his tension greatly and he felt that he could go on talking with her without the conversation degrading into a shouting match.

Ronnie suddenly realized the Professor was noticeably silent in his mind. The last time there had been such a rift between Margret and him, the Professor had almost been shouting in his mind. Not that Ronnie didn't mind the silence, in fact, he was grateful for it. Ronnie knew it would take very little coaxing for the Professor to bring the vision he had just had into reality.

"You're right Ronnie. Looking back on it now, it was very foolish for me not to come to you at the very beginning." Margret said as came back closer to him once again.

"Don't make a mistake Margret, I'm still very mad that you hid this from me. While I was sitting in the emergency room tonight I was thinking some very disturbing things. Not to say the least, was you had better not do this again, or your fears may not be unfounded next time." Ronnie said, hoping to let Margret know next time, he would be gone from her life.

But Margret didn't understand what he meant by the last thing he had said and she didn't care, because now she was off of the hook. Ronnie would take care of the checks and he had lied to the police by saying he didn't know who it was that had shot at him. She knew she would have to slip back into the role of devoted housewife for a little while, but she didn't mind. She knew she could slip back into that role as easily as slipping on an old pair of sneakers.

But let no one make any mistake, she did not intend to spend the rest of her life with Ronnie. She would be free.

78.

Max returned to the station as a hero that night. Bubba, Junior, and he hadn't been at the ballpark more than two hours when they had caught three teenagers smashing car windows and taking stereos.

The teenagers would wait at the edge of the parking lot and when the crowd was cheering a play, each one would break a window on three different cars. Then it was just a matter of rifling through the cars and taking what they wanted. Then the crowd would go berserk again and they would repeat the process.

The teens were being careful not to come any closer to the bleachers than the last two rows of parked cars. Max wouldn't have caught on to their game if he hadn't stopped by a tree about thirty feet from the edge of the parking lot to take a leak. He was standing there in the dark with matters in hand when he heard the roar of the crowd, at the same instant, he heard what he thought sounded like glass breaking. Unwittingly, one of the teenagers was between the bleachers and Max standing in the edge of the wood. If Max had been standing on the other side near the bleachers, he would have never heard the noise.

Max zipped up and started walking in the direction of where the sound had come from, when he spotted one of the teenagers at work. He quickly stepped back into the shadows and started watching what was going on. That's when he saw the kid had two other companions working on two other cars. Max quietly and quickly stepped back and keeping a low profile, made his way back towards where his coworkers were stationed. Once he was sure he was out of the teenagers earshot, he began calling Bubba and Junior on the radio to come and meet him.

They came out of the bleachers and met him. He quickly explained what was happening and the three of them went back out to the parking lot. They found the kids standing next to their next victims cars. Max and his men waited. The noise of the crowd rose again and the windows were smashed. Still they waited. Once the teenagers were busy with their task, Max, Bubba, and Junior each took one kid.

The bust was very smooth. Once the teenagers realized they were staring at the business end of whatever caliber gun was the flavor of the evening, they simply gave up. One of the teenagers led Max over to a rusted out Chevy van that had seen better days and looked as if it had been painted with a can of spray paint. Inside the van, Max found at least fifty car stereos and assorted items that had been stolen out of various cars. From the looks of things, Max decided the boys had a very busy shopping night.

As soon as they got back to the station, Waters made it plain he wanted to see Max ASAP. Max started the process of booking his guy and then turned it over to a flunky to get the names, addresses, and finger prints. Max would meet back up with them later after the background checks went through to finish the process. When he was assured the paperwork was going okay, he made his retreat to Waters office.

When Max got there he didn't have to wait. Waters was on the phone with someone and motioned Max in. As Max was sitting down, Waters cut his call short and hung up.

"Well...Marshal Dillon, seems like you've had one very busy and highly productive night." Waters said with a huge grin on his face.

"You bet boss. What do you want to hear about first?"

"Tell me about the three assholes you caught."

Max explained how he had been strolling through the parking lot, omitting the part about standing there taking a leak, when he heard glass breaking. He then outlined every step they had taken after that. Waters was pleased, very pleased. He had just felt a two-hundred and fifty pound weight crawl off of his ass.

The next topic of discussion was the shootout at Ronnie's house, where he once again outlined in detail how he had gone to Ronnie's house to talk to him and the guy had rolled up on them asking for directions. Max told how he had leaned down and started giving directions when the guy had whipped out a gun and started firing. Max explained how he had drawn his gun in self defense and fired one round. He added that unfortunately, in the heat of the moment, he had missed his target and nailed the guy in the forehead.

"Well, I.A. will want to talk to you. But I wouldn't worry too much, this is clearly a case of self defense."

Max knew Internal Affairs always checked out any crime where a gun was used by an Officer. So this would just be a routine grilling by them. "I kinda figured that would happen." He replied.

"Homicide ID'd the guy as Theodore Tillman. He was a student pilot at the base. I talked to his Commander and he told me as far as he knew, the guy was as stable as a rock."

"Couldn't prove it by me." Max replied.

"Wait, there's more and it gets better. Ballistics went over his gun and found that the firing pin had sheared off when it struck the first round. So there was no way the gun could have fired a second time. The coroner reported the shot you made was perfect. He was impressed because he had never seen anyone hit so dead square between the eyes."

Now, Max knew why the gun hadn't fired the second time and he felt sad that he hadn't been able to know that fact before he had pulled his own trigger. He knew if he had been able to know, a man wouldn't be dead right now. "I guess all those years of wasting ammunition shooting coke bottles had finally paid off." He offered as a response to Waters.

"I would say so." Waters said as he looked at Max. He had heard something in Max's voice that he had never heard before.

"How's Fisher?" Max said both trying to change the subject and find out about Ronnie.

"If what I've been told is true, he should be home right now sleeping off a load of pain killers. Other than that, he's in good shape. Did Fisher say whether or not he knew the Tillman guy?"

"He said he didn't and I believe him. I was standing right there and I didn't see any recognition on his face when he saw Tillman."

"Okay...What about his wife?"

"She said she didn't know him."

"Max, why is it that I hear a 'But' in your voice?"

"I don't know Cap. She said she didn't know who Tillman was, but I just have a feeling there's another side to this story."

"You think this might have been a contract hit?" Waters asked.

"Naw...I don't think she's that smart. I just think there's more to the story on her part than she's telling."

"What are you going to do?"

After a moments thought Max replied, "I'm still going to talk to her husband, maybe if I'm lucky he'll tell me what she's been up to."

Water thought for a couple of moments and then said, "Do what you gotta do. Now...Don't you have a shit load of paperwork to do? Get the hell out of my office."

Max just smiled as he got up and was interrupted on his way to the door by Waters.

"The Mayor is probably going to want to see you. You know how royalty always wants to meet the Dragon slayers."

"Whatever, whenever. Your wish is my command." Max replied with a bow and then resumed his path for the door.

"Max, one more thing."

"Yes?" Max said stopping again.

"I'm glad you're okay."

Max didn't answer as he left Waters office.

By the time the paperwork was finished, Max got home around three in the morning. Not as early as he wanted to get home, but it was about five hours before he would have normally gotten home. Max thought to himself that working undercover sometimes had it's perks.

When he got into bed, Max fell almost right to sleep. But he woke up at eight-thirty bathed in sweat from the dream he just had. In his dream, he was standing there looking down the barrel of Ted's gun again. In his dream, when the hammer fell on the gun the second time, it fired. Max saw his own sunglasses as they fell to the ground in two neat pieces, cut in half at the nose piece by the bullet Ted had just fired.

Max had to get up and towel himself off. While he was standing there he heard his wife fussing around with something in the kitchen. So he went to see what she was up to and they spent the next few hours pleasuring each other. Although she didn't say anything, Max's wife knew him well enough to know there was something troubling him. She didn't press him on what the problem was because she knew he would tell her in his own good time.

79.

Ronnie didn't have any problems falling asleep courtesy of some really good drug samples the emergency room doctor had given him. He went upstairs with Margret following him and she actually tucked him into bed. She told him she was too keyed up to sleep and was going back downstairs to read the want ads in the paper.

Ronnie had been asleep for awhile before he opened his dream eyes. He found himself lying on the stainless steel autopsy table in the warehouse once again. Looking over, he saw the Professor standing with his back to Ronnie. As Ronnie looked, he saw the Professor was looking at a blacken piece of meat on the end of a pair of hemostats.

'What's that?' Ronnie asked as he tried to sit up.

You're awake! The Professor said as he spun around to face Ronnie.

'That's kind of a strange thing to say considering that this is a dream.' Ronnie threw back at the Professor. 'Now, are you going to tell me what you have in your hand?'

What? This? The Professor said as he held up the hemostats. Ronnie saw its jaws didn't hold just a nondescript piece of meat. It was another black, fetal looking growth. *This is just another one of those growths I told you about last time.*

This time Ronnie didn't try to see who or what it looked like, he just simply said, 'Let me guess. You took it out for free, right?'

You bet little buddy. The Professor replied as he tossed it, hemostats and all, into the bucket with the other one. *However, there is one small problem.* He added.

'What's that?'

Well...If you remember, the last time I told you there were two growths left. When I was removing this one I found one more real small one.

'So what's that mean to me?' Ronnie asked.

Nothing right now. Hey...Let's get out of here and go have some fun. The Professor replied as he snapped his fingers.

Instantly, everything changed around Ronnie and he now found himself in a strange place he had never been before. All around him were things that reminded him of the things you would find inside a transistor radio. Except these things were huge. Standing up and looking around, Ronnie saw the Professor standing next to an enormous wall looking out through a huge slit in the wall. The Professor seemed to be manipulating something in his hands.

Ronnie walked over to the Professor to see what he was doing and saw he had what looked like an enormous computer chip in one hand and a bar of metal in the other. Ronnie saw the chip had Rockwell written on the top of it and he watched as the Professor ran the bar of metal up and down the legs of the chip. Then he would stop and look through the slit in the wall. The Professor would then laugh and after a few minutes, start the process all over again.

Either the Professor didn't notice Ronnie was there, or he didn't care. He made no motions to acknowledge Ronnie until Ronnie was standing right next to him.

Well...How's it going little Buck-A-Roo? The Professor asked as he was still looking out through the slit. *At least you're looking better.* He added.

'I've damn sure had better days, that's for sure.'

At least you're still alive to bitch about it. The Professor replied as he stepped back and started working the metal back and forth again.

'If you don't mind me asking, what the hell are you doing?'

Having some fun.

'I don't understand.' Ronnie said and then looked around. 'Where are we?' He asked.

Believe it or not, we are inside your computer.

'No way!' Ronnie replied surprised.

Yes we are. The Professor replied. *In fact, I've taken the liberty to use this for my residence since I'm doing your writing.*

'Great, live in the computer if you want to, but you still haven't answered me. What are you doing?'

Fucking with your old lady.

'What? How?'

Come here, look out and tell me what you see.

Ronnie stepped up to the slit and looked out. He could see his living room (though everything was enormous) and saw Margret sitting in her chair watching tv. He also noticed Margret was acting very irritated. 'Okay. I see my living room. There's Margret sitting in her chair looking pissed off. So, what are you doing?'

Do you see the tv?

'Yeah, why?'

Just keep your eyes on the tv. The Professor said as he began running the metal bar up and down the legs of the enormous computer chip.

343

Ronnie saw the channels suddenly change and then the set just turned itself off. Margret blew a load in response.

"God damn piece of shit!!" She screamed and then raised the remote over her head. For a brief moment, Ronnie thought she was going to throw the remote at the television.

'Hey...That's a pretty neat trick.' Ronnie remarked to the Professor, laughing, then he added, 'I want you to know if you ever pull this crap on me, I'll come over here and piss in your little home here.'

Not to worry. I have no reason to do it to you. It's your old lady I have the beef with.

'Yeah, right. The thought of you having any kind of beef with a woman is laughable. Why are you mad at her?'

Thinking with your dick as usual. But this time I'll forgive you. Small minds for small heads is your excuse. In this case, my trouble with your wife is easily explained. Look around.

Ronnie looked down and saw pieces of metal similar to the one the Professor was holding lying all around, but they were much larger. 'What is this stuff?' He asked.

You're beloved started playing around with the computer this afternoon. The voice security was on and she couldn't get it to do anything. So she got mad, tore up a coat hanger and then dropped the pieces in here.

'I didn't turn voice security on. Besides, why would she want to do something like that? I use this computer to earn extra money.'

I guess she wanted to short something out and burn the computer up. And yes, you didn't have voice security on. I turned it on when she turned the computer on. Next time, don't be so careless.

Ronnie just stood there looking at the Professor without saying anything. The Professor continued speaking.

You have to remember Ronnie. When she did this, you were still on your way to your date with fate. She had intended that by this time tonight, you'd be on your way to doing the worm wave at stiff stadium.

'Huh?' Ronnie mumbled, not understanding what the Professor meant.

Damn you're thick tonight. You know, taking the long dirt nap. Assuming room temperature. Dead.

'That bitch!' Ronnie almost shouted.

Good description and it fits too! Besides, this isn't about me. You're here so we can talk about you.

'Don't you mean I'm here so you can gloat about being right?' Ronnie asked.

That too maybe, I guess. Just a little.

'I knew it. But let me just go ahead and thank you. If you hadn't given me a heads up, this might have turned out worse than it did.' Ronnie said as he pointed to the bandage on his shoulder.

You're right, it would have been worse. I also wanted you to know the little conversation you had with her, well...she was putting on an act for you. I think she's still plotting your demise.

'Oh yeah?'

Yes. She definitely missed her calling. She should have been an actress.

'And what do you base your observations on?'

She told you she was coming down here to read the paper, correct?

'Yes she did.'

Well, she hasn't touched it since she came back down the stairs. She also told you she didn't have any idea what dear sweet Ted was going to try to do to you. Well, the last conversation she had with him was yesterday afternoon on the phone. It sure seemed like they were in a strategy session. Of course, I only got her side of the conversation.

'But she was so convincing. I thought she was telling the truth.' Ronnie said as he cast his gaze downward. He wanted to believe she had been telling him the truth.

Like I said, The Professor said in a consolatory voice, *She's good and you swallowed the whole story. Hook, line, and sinker.*

'What should I do?'

Ronnie old pal. If I were you, I would continue to watch my back.

'Great. Just what I need, a permanent case of paranoia.' Ronnie replied and then asked, 'What about the checks?'

What do you mean?

'What about her explanation about the checks? Was she lying then also?'

Don't know. I can't really see into her mind like I can with you. Besides, who really knows a woman's mind?

'Oh man, that's original. Did you think that one up on your own? Oh Mighty Sage of Wisdom? Besides, what do you mean you can see into my mind?'

Hey, The Professor replied defensibly, *You have to work with what you got. Don't worry about the mind thing, it's just a little trick I've been able to pick up since my untimely demise.*

'Is there anything else I should know about?'

Nope. Go back to sleep, you are going to have a tough day tomorrow.

As the Professor said that, the insides of the computer faded away along with the Professor. Ronnie opened his eyes and found himself laying in bed. From downstairs he heard the volume raise on the TV and then there was silence. Less than a second later there was a streak of profanity Ronnie recognized as coming from Margret. The TV came back on and the volume went back down quickly.

Ronnie smiled as he rolled over trying to find a comfortable position, momentarily forgetting about his shoulder. A sharp, stinging pain shot through him as the stitches holding his stretched skin together protested against the added strain. Ronnie quickly rolled back over onto his back. As he laid there waiting for the pain to subside, he thought about what the professor had told him. Ronnie decided there was no way he wanted to go through life having to watch his back.

As he laid there, he decided after the checks were paid for, he would indeed ask her for a divorce and they could go their separate ways.

As sleep finally started to overtake him, he heard the TV make a repeat of its earlier performance, followed by a repeat performance of Margret's mouth. As Ronnie drifted back off to sleep, he had a smile on his face.

80.

Ronnie was five minutes late when he got to work the next morning. He was stiff from sleeping in one position all night and his shoulder was very sore in general and tender to the touch. Although he still had some painkillers the doctor had given him the night before, he didn't want to take any in fear he would get too spaced out to work.

He had been in the office for about ten minutes when the phone rang and it was one of the ladies from the front office calling. She told Ronnie that Floyd's wife had called a few minutes ago and reported that Floyd's condition was worsening. Now there was no firm date when Floyd would be returning back to work and it seemed Ronnie was going to be the boss for awhile.

Ronnie thanked her and after hanging up, went out to address the troops. He gathered everyone together and told them about Floyd's condition. As an afterthought, he asked every one for a moment of silence so everyone could ask whatever deity they prayed to for help with Floyd's condition. This one act seemed to change the group somehow. Ronnie noticed the mood of the group change. It seemed they were no longer a group of individuals gathered together to do a job, but a close knit group of brothers working together on a cause.

After the moment of silence, Ronnie chased everyone out to go to their tasks. A majority of the guys came up to him individually and told him how touched they were for what he had done for Floyd. Then they would tell Ronnie about how they were given their first real break by Floyd. How they could never hold a job more than a week or a month, or had problems with booze or dope before Floyd had given them a chance to prove themselves as men. Ronnie remembered back to his days of crawling through the hole in the fence to walk to the liquor store. He also thought about the nightmare he had at home and found that he too, like everyone else that came up to him, had a story to tell.

The guys didn't have to be told a second time to get to work this morning. Ronnie noticed as he watched them leave, that for the first time since he could remember, they seemed to be helping each other out. There was one mower the guys called Satan. It was the hardest to start and the most difficult to operate. Everyone dreaded the days it was their turn to operate it. Today, a new kid barely nineteen years old, was outside cussing and yanking on the starter rope with no success. Ronnie was just about to go out and see what he could do to help when he saw a couple of the older guys walking over to give a hand.

Usually, everyone hauled ass as the victim of Satan would start to lose his religion trying to get it to start. It would always seem that just when all hope was to be abandoned, it would fire up and run a few licks before dying again. Just enough to afford a little hope. Then a thousand pulls later it would fire up with gusto and run all day long without troubles. At other times it seemed to have a mind of its own. You'd steer one way and it would go the other or not even turn at all. There was a pond on the front side of the fifteenth green that at least twice a month last summer, Floyd and whoever was handy at the time would have to go and fish the mower out.

The standing story was whoever was mowing would turn towards the pond and the mower would seem to just take off out of control and make a pretty good sized splash down. Ronnie remembered his turn to go help fish the mower out of the pond. A young man by the name of Mitch had come walking back to the shack dripping wet. He stuck his head in the door and explained, in no uncertain terms, that he quit. That's all he said, he quit and then he walked off towards the parking lot. Floyd didn't say a word, but just motioned for Ronnie to come with him. Sitting in Floyd's golf cart, they drove out to fifteen. There in the center of the pond, was Satan's steering wheel, seat, and gas tank standing proudly above the top of the water.

Ronnie watched as the guys finally got Satan started and the kid roared off in a cloud of blue smoke towards his job of mowing the rough. The guys had helped him get it started were laughing and applauding the kid on towards his task. It made Ronnie feel good when he realized he was the one who had put the motivation into them.

The rest of the day was uneventful, everyone doing their tasks and nobody was giving Ronnie any grief about anything. Around two-thirty in the afternoon, there was a knock on the door and Max stuck his head in. Ronnie, needless to say, was glad to see him.

"Max, come in." Ronnie said as he got up and walked over to Max and shook his hand.

"Looks like you're doing pretty good for yourself." Max said as he looked around the small office.

"It's okay. I got promoted to Assistant Superintendent and the boss is out sick in the hospital. So temporarily, I'm running the show. Have a seat."

"I'm sorry to bother you at work. To tell the truth, I'm surprised to see you here after last night."

"With the head boss out, I would have to be dead not to come to work today. So what brings you here?"

"I wanted to see how you were doing and I also wanted to talk to you without your wife around. So, how are you doing?"

"Hurting. But what else is new? What's on your mind Max?" Ronnie asked, curious about what would bring Max here to talk to him.

"It's hard for me to approach the subject, but I was doing some police work and I saw where several stores were swearing out warrants on your wife for bad checks. Then the next day the stores stopped the process. I...I just wanted to come by and tell you in case you didn't know what was going on." Max told Ronnie flat out.

Ronnie leaned back in his chair, touched because a casual acquaintance had taken the time to come and warn him about something his wife was up to. "It's okay Max. I found out about it Monday. Most likely the reason the process was stopped was because I talked to everyone and worked out payment plans."

Max looked relieved, "So you got a handle on it?"

"Yeah, and none too soon it seems."

"Do you know why she did it?"

"She said she bounced one check, then wrote another to cover the first. From there she said the whole thing seemed to snowball."

"Why do I get the feeling you don't believe her?" Max asked.

"Max," Ronnie said looking Max straight in the eye, "At this point, I don't know what to believe. But, she is my wife and I'm going to have to take what she says at face value. Other than that, all I know is I have a shit load of checks to pay off."

Max shook his head in sympathy and said, "I hope you don't mind if I ask you one more thing."

"What's that?"

"How did you ever get mixed up with a wild card like her?"

Ronnie was silent for a moment and then said, "Hormones and too much thinking with the wrong head."

"I can understand that." Max replied nodding his head in agreement. "That's how I got my first ex-wife."

They sat there looking at each other for a couple of seconds before Ronnie spoke, "Max, can I ask you something?"

"I guess that would be fair. What's on your mind?"

"What were you thinking last night? I mean, don't get me wrong, but how do you do it? You blew that guy away and sitting here now, it seems like it never happened."

"What was I thinking..." Max replied, his voice trailing off.

Sitting there, Ronnie suddenly thought Max looked alot older than he had just a few seconds ago. "Look man, I'm sorry. Just forget I asked that stupid question. Okay?"

"No, it's okay Ronnie. Actually, that's a very good question. To tell you the truth, I really don't remember thinking anything other than 'This guy is fixing to kill me'. I think I acted out of reflex more than anything else. I know if I'm in a situation like that and stop to think about what I'm doing, I could be killed. It's all of the training that the force puts you through. You learn to react to a situation without having to really think about what you're doing. There's always time for reflection if you're still around later."

"Well Max. My hat is off to you. If it hadn't been for you and your training, I feel this would have been much worse. I want to thank you again for saving my life."

Max sat there without speaking for almost a full minute, just long enough for Ronnie to grow uncomfortable about offering the thank you. Ronnie became fearful Max knew more than he was letting on, that Max knew Ted had been Margret's back door man.

"I think you can thank circumstances more than you can thank me." Max finally said.

"What do you mean by that Max?" Ronnie asked acting innocent.

"It seems when Tillman shot his first round, the firing pin sheared off the hammer. There was no way he could have fired the gun again. Not without doing some major work on it first."

"You sound like you're sorry for what you did." Ronnie said. He was relieved, what he thought was going to be his downfall was nothing more than a mans regrets. "Max," Ronnie continued, "You did the right thing. You had no way of knowing the gun was broken."

"I know. When that hammer fell that second time, I just thought it was a dud round in the chamber. I made my shot before he could pull the trigger the third time." Max said, but his voice held a strand of remorse in it.

"Like I said Max, you did the right thing. Do you have any ideas why someone would do a sick thing like he did? Just roll up on some folks and try to take their lives?"

"We may never know that Ronnie. I can't think of anyone that would be out after me, and you said you didn't know him."

"That's right. I asked Margret later and she didn't know him either. We never saw him before."

"Right. Who really knows what's in the heads of these sicko's. When I left work last night, the only things we knew for sure was that he was dead and the car he was driving was a rental. Not to mention the gun he was using was a piece of shit." Max said. For some reason he left out that they also knew he was a student pilot at the base.

Ronnie could now hear the remorse as plain as day in Max's voice. Even though he didn't know Max very well, he did think of the man as a friend. "Look," He said, "Even though I've never been through it, I know it must be hard for you to do what you did. And that's what I'm thanking you for, because I feel you did it to protect me."

Max looked up with a sly smile on his face that Ronnie could tell was faked and said, "I don't seem to remember your ass hanging through the window with me."

Ronnie chuckled, even though the man was hurting, he was still trying to be humorous. Ronnie thought to himself. "Well, I may not have been in the window with you," Ronnie said, "But I was there in spirit. As a taxpayer and therefore your boss, I thank you anyway whether you want me to or not."

"Anytime boss." Max replied, this time the smile was genuine. Max almost told Ronnie about how he hadn't been aiming quite where the bullet had struck, but he kept himself from doing it. He didn't know why he was compelled to tell Ronnie. For some reason, he just had the feeling Ronnie would understand. The urge to confess was compelling and Max was puzzled why he had the urge to confess to the man sitting in front of him. He also had the feeling if he told about the poor aim, then he would have to tell about the jerk he had felt and the two finger shadows he had seen on the end of the barrel at the same time.

"So Max, do you play golf?" Ronnie asked, breaking the small uncomfortable silence that had fallen between them.

"Only played it once, never really cared for it. Nothing personal. How about you?"

"Actually...I've never played. I just keep the playground for the rich and elite nice and clean. Or at least I try to."

"How's the writing coming along? I read your columns in the paper, you really hit some of those people below the belt. Not that they didn't deserve it. Remember that column about the Sheriff's kid and the City Councilman? That's when I became an instant fan. We had problems with the both of them in the past. But somehow whenever they got in trouble with the law, it would get swept under the carpet and everyone would go on like nothing ever happened. When I read that column, I told myself here's someone who has the balls to tell the truth the way it should be told. Up front and honest." Max said with enthusiasm.

"Do me a favor Max, don't speak of the column here. There's too many people that would like to find out who Gabby really is." Ronnie said quietly.

"Sorry...I didn't even think about it." Max offered.

"Don't worry about it. I'm glad to get some feedback, it's nice to know there are fans out there."

"I'm not the only one. There's always a lot of talk around the station on Mondays. Most of it positive, too."

"Great! The writing is going very well. In fact," Ronnie boasted, "I've just submitted a book hoping it's good enough to get published."

"Really?"

"You bet. But it's my first submission and I don't know how well it will be received. Writing for a small town newspaper is a lot different than writing to get a book published."

"Personally, I think that you'll do very well."

"Thanks. If it sells, I'll give you an autographed copy."

"That would be great." Max said and then looked at his watch. "I really got to get going." he said as he got up.

"Don't be a stranger, come by anytime." Ronnie said as he stuck out his hand.

Max took it and gave it a couple of pumps. "You bet."

"I'll walk you out. It's time I made my rounds to see who's sleeping where. You gotta stay on top of things around here or the work will never get done."

Max and Ronnie left the office and went out to Max's car that was parked on the service lane just outside the shack. They said their goodbyes and Max promised to come by and visit again. Just before Max left, Ronnie thanked him again. This time instead of thanking him for blowing away Margret's lover, he thanked Max for having enough concern to come by and tell him what Margret was up to.

Ronnie watched Max drive off and when the car had disappeared around the corner, Ronnie got into his golf cart and drove off to see how everyone was doing at their jobs. On his tour of the greens, he found everyone working hard and in good spirits. Ronnie checked the irrigation ponds and made sure the timers for all of the water pumps and sprinkler systems were set correctly. Happy that everything was looking good, Ronnie drove back to the shack and parked the cart.

Back inside his office, Ronnie sat back down and within a few minutes, started to get a headache. As much as he didn't want to admit it, today had been too much. His shoulder was very tender and it now felt as though he could feel his shirt rubbing against the bandage covering his wound. He opened the desk drawer and took out the bottle of aspirin he knew that Floyd kept there. He then went outside and got a soda out of the machine. Going back inside, he fumbled the top off of the aspirin bottle and downed a handful.

Resuming his position in the desk chair, Ronnie decided it wasn't just today that had been too much, it was the way his life had turned out for the duration of his married life. The last couple of months was just the cherry on top. He felt a pang of guilt about Max. Ronnie could see the man was nursing a spiritual hurt and all Ronnie had done was just cover his own tracks. And for what? If the roles had been reversed, Margret would have not only sold him up the river, but would have volunteered to pull the switch on old Sparky.

The question was starting to formulate in his mind was whether or not he wanted to even wait until the checks were paid to toss her out. Ronnie leaned back in his chair and closed his eyes as he thought about his new financial situation, courtesy of Margret.

81.

When Max got to the station, he checked his messages and went straight to see Waters. When Max got to Waters office, he knocked on the door and without bothering to wait for an invite, walked straight in and closed the door behind him.

"Come in, I guess." Waters said looking up from a pile of paperwork on his desk.

"Have you seen the ballistic report on the Tillman gun?" Max asked as he laid his copy of the report down on the desk.

"It's in this pile of crap somewhere." Waters replied opening his arms wide to indicate the massive pile of paperwork covering his desk. "Why?"

"Seems like the gun is more well traveled than I am."

"Explain." Waters said as he leaned back in his chair and gave Max his full attention.

"Ballistics sent a copy to the FBI and got a report back almost immediately."

Waters perked up at that news. "That's very unusual, the best we've ever done in the past was seventy-two hours."

"The first report of the same ballistics goes back to ten years ago. Since the first entry there has been an average of three murders a year in sixteen different states. From one coast to the other." Max summarized.

"Same M.O.?" Waters asked.

"No. A couple are the same, but most of them are different."

"So what do you think?" Waters asked, "Do you think Tillman was going around blasting away at will?"

"Not unless he started when he was twelve. I think this gun was a transient."

Waters thought about this theory for a moment and then said, "Sounds good to me. I suppose the FBI wants it."

"To say the least. It was flagged as an immediate surrender if we have the weapon. There's even a phone number here to call whether we have the gun or not." Max said.

"Okay, call the number. But don't let them have the gun unless they give us something."

"What are you thinking Cap?"

"Tell them they'll get their gun if they give us a full background check on Tillman. I bet they can give us a lot more details about him than we can get on our own." Waters said.

"Okay, let me get this straight. You want me to go fishing for information using the gun as bait? Sounds like fun."

"If you run into a wall, just explain what a backwoods society we are and the immense amount of paperwork you'll have to do just to turn the gun over. Lay it on thick so they'll think if they don't help you, it might take years before you can get through all of the forms." Waters told Max with a smile on his face.

"I follow you. But what are you looking for?" Max asked.

"Anything other than just some asshole who rolled up on one of my finest and started blasting. If there's anything to this, I want us to find it before the Feds."

"I'm on it." Max said as he turned to leave.

"One more thing Max."

"Why is it that I can never finish a conversation and just leave this office?" Max asked with a smile.

"The Mayor, Grand Pooh-Bah himself called and wishes to take you to dinner tonight. Seems like he's extremely happy about your bust last night. I hear he was even happier when half of his dash board was found in the van those guys were driving."

"What time?"

"His Royal Assholiness wishes to dine around seven. You, of course, will show up and six forty-five, shit, shined, and shaved."

"Of course."

"You are also relieved from duty tonight for this grand occasion. So don't bust your ass trying to get back here. And Max, take your wife, the poor woman could use a night out, especially since she has to deal with your sorry ass."

"Great. My first day off in a while and I have to spend it rubbing noses with the elite on behalf of the department." Max replied.

"Ain't fame a bitch." Was the reply Max heard from behind him as he walked out through Waters office door.

Max went to his desk and after a moments hesitation, called the number to the FBI that was listed in the report. Max identified himself and gave the reason why he was calling. The young lady who had answered the phone apologized that there were no agents available at the time, but she took his name and number and promised he would be contacted as soon as someone was available. Max thanked her and explained he would only be there for another hour.

After Max hung up, he called his wife to let her know about the new dinner plans. She freaked out when she heard who it was that they would be dining with. Knowing the Mayor like he did, he assured her that it would be semi-formal and as long as she showed some cleavage, the Mayor wouldn't care if she had showed up in a sweat-suit. After receiving the proper berating for the comment, he laughed and told her the truth, that she would look like a million no matter what she wore.

After exchanging 'luv you's', Max turned his attention to the pile of paperwork on his own desk. Less than five minutes had passed when his phone rang. A young man on the other end, sounding excited, identified himself as an FBI agent. Max turned on his charm and not only got the information he had been instructed to, but also an immediate fax of the files and a promise of hand delivery of the hard files from the agent himself tomorrow afternoon. Max was very happy by the time he hung up.

82.

At quitting time, Ronnie noticed that nobody had arrived back at the shack to clock out. Ten minutes passed, nobody. Fifteen minutes and the first of the group started arriving. By twenty minutes past quitting time, the group was now growing larger. Everyone was in a cheerful mood putting their tools and equipment away. Ronnie was asking everyone, individually, why they were late and the answer was almost universal, they didn't want to stop working until they were sure their jobs were complete.

This made Ronnie happy because never in the history of working there that he could remember, had everyone willingly gave of their free time to complete their tasks. Most of the time, the guys would start coming in a half hour before quitting time. Here they were, working hard and over on his tour of duty. Ronnie knew it wasn't thoughts of overtime that kept the guys there, everyone knew about the Club's strict policy on overtime; There was none.

When everyone had finally left, Ronnie locked up and headed home.

When he got there he found Margret sitting on the couch. She looked as if she hadn't bothered getting dressed that day. The house was a mess and when Ronnie got near Nancy, he could tell from the smell that she had been neglected also. Ronnie walked back over to Margret and asked her what her problem was. She just looked up at him with a blank look on her face and didn't answer.

Ronnie asked again what her problem was and was again rewarded with a blank stare and no answer. He explained he was concerned and if she had a problem, she had better fess up now.

"I'm sorry Ronnie." Margret finally said, "I just don't feel very well today."

"Sorry to hear that." Ronnie replied. He was looking at the stack of dishes next to her chair and thought to himself that whatever it was that was making her not feel well, certainly hadn't affected her appetite.

"I'm sorry I didn't look for a job today, I just feel really sick." Margret offered as an excuse.

"That's okay Margret. Tell you what, don't even worry about finding a job right now. You can start looking next week."

"Are you sure that's okay with you?" She asked timidly.

"Yeah sure. Enjoy the rest of the week and on Monday morning, you can start off fresh, looking."

"But what if I don't find a job?"

Ronnie looked at her for a couple of seconds and said, "I'm sure that you'll find something." His voice was cold and unfeeling.

Something about the tone of his voice changed Margret. Ronnie saw the change. She flashed him a hateful look that was very reminiscent of the old Margret. Out of reflex, Ronnie almost pulled a duck and cover. He was sure the blows were soon to follow. But in an instant. The old Margret was gone and replaced by the new and improved Margret.

"Sit down and rest Ronnie. I know you must be really tired from work today." Margret said as she got up.

"Well, I was going to start dinner." He replied.

"Nonsense. You were working hard all day and I haven't been doing anything. I'll do it."

"Then I'll take care of Nancy." He offered.

"Don't be silly. I'll get her first and then cook some dinner for you." Margret said as she picked up Nancy and started for the stairs.

"In that case, I think I'll go next door and try to arrange for babysitting. If it's okay with you?"

"That would be great." Margret called back down the stairs. But he could tell from the tone of her voice that maybe she didn't think it was so great.

Ronnie stood there for a minute trying to decide what she was up to. He had noticed the remarkable improvement in her when he had told her not to worry about the job this week. He decided that's what her game was. She was going to play lame until he had either given up on the job for her or...Well, he didn't know what the "or" was. He knew he was damn well not going to find out because she was going to get a job whether she wanted one or not. With that thought, he left the house and went next door.

The conference with Heather's parents went much better than he had anticipated. They were sorry to hear that Ronnie was having financial troubles, but they were more than happy to help out with Nancy while Margret was working. They even told Ronnie not to worry about paying them right now, they would work out something later, when Ronnie could better afford it.

Then the conversation turned to the events of yesterday and Ronnie told what had happened from his point of view. The story he gave them pretty much matched up to the one Max was working on. They listened to what he had to say and agreed this was a sick world they were living in these days. They also mentioned they were very happy that he hadn't been hurt worse than he was. To that, Ronnie agreed.

Glancing at his watch, Ronnie saw he had been there for a little over forty minutes. He excused himself, telling them Margret was waiting dinner on him. Getting up, he thanked them for their help and left.

When Ronnie walked back into his house, he could smell the savory aroma of food cooking. The smell instantly made his mouth water and his stomach gave a loud rumble. Walking into the kitchen, Ronnie was expecting to find Margret there. But she wasn't. There was macaroni and cheese sitting in a pot simmering. There were hotdogs sitting in another pot beside the macaroni. Ronnie picked up a spoon and went to stir the macaroni. He found the bottom half inch burned to the bottom of the pot. He checked the hotdogs and found they were still frozen. Upon further inspection, he found the dogs were still frozen because nobody had turned on the heat under them.

Ronnie became mad looking at the dinner on the stove. He turned on the heat under the hotdogs and turned off the macaroni. He then went to look for Margret. It was obvious that she wasn't downstairs, so he climbed the stairs to see where she was.

At the top of the stairs, he saw the bedroom door was closed. Going to the door, he found it locked.

"Margret, are you in there?" Ronnie called through the locked door.

"Go away." Was her cold reply.

"Are you okay? Open the door." He said as he rattled the door knob.

"I said go away!!" Margret screamed from the other side of the door.

Ronnie stood there for a second debating what he should do and made his decision. "Margret! I said open the door right now!" He yelled back.

"Go to hell, you asshole!"

Ronnie felt rage rising in him like a giant bubble. He raised his foot thinking one well placed kick next to the door knob would open the door. But just as he started to kick, he stopped. Breathing deeply, he began to feel calmer. He turned and went to the hall closet. Unknown to Margret, after the last time he had kicked the door in, Ronnie had stashed a screwdriver that was small enough to fit through the hole in the door knob. With this tool, he would be able to unlock the door in a matter of seconds. He took the screwdriver and walked back to the door.

"Margret, this is your last chance. Open the door." Ronnie said calmly.

"And just what the hell are you going to do about it? I'll tell you what. Not a God damn thing, you spineless prick." She yelled back taunting him.

Without reply, Ronnie stuck the screwdriver through the hole as quietly as he could and tripped the lock. Stepping through the open door into the dark room he asked, "You were saying?"

There was no reply. Ronnie caught a movement out of the corner of his eye and managed to side step the telephone as it came sailing through the air. The telephone hit the wall approximately where his head had been just a half second before. Ronnie said "Missed." as he tried to see where Margret was. This was a mistake and he knew it when he did it. He realized what he should have done was keep his mouth shut and retreated from the room, or at least turned the light on. But he wanted to stand his ground and not let Margret see him in what she would think of as cowardice. Ronnie was facing the direction of the bed assuming that was where Margret was when he heard running footsteps coming towards him from his side. He turned just in time to receive the full force of Margret slamming into him. The momentum carried Ronnie backwards with the full weight of Margret on top of him.

Stumbling backwards, he hit the side of the bed. Now, over-balanced with no sure footing, he went down with Margret still on top of him. There wasn't enough time to say anything even if he could, the weight of Margret had knocked the wind out of him when he hit the floor. Then she was off of him and moving away in the dark.

"What the fuck is your problem?" He managed to gasp out. Not only could he not catch his breath, but his shoulder was stinging like he had been stung by a killer wasp. He raised his hand to his shoulder and it felt wet. Great, he thought to himself, I blew a stitch. He looked at his hand and although it was dark, he could see the blood on his hand.

"I'll show you what my fucking problem is, dickless!" Was the reply that came out of the darkness. Once again, Ronnie could hear footsteps coming towards him. At the last moment he rolled over twice and heard the alarm clock hit the floor with force where he had just been. Ronnie didn't know it, but Margret had swung the alarm clock while holding onto the cord. The momentum of the arch put a lot of force behind the small clock and when it hit the floor, it exploded into pieces. "You son of a bitch!!" Margret howled in rage when she realized she had missed him.

Ronnie tried to regain his footing to get up as quietly and as quickly as he could. He now knew his only recourse was to get back out of the room and into the hallway. But his time her aim was much better and she hit him with full force in the small of his back. He had no doubt in his mind that it was the alarm clock she had hit him with. She hit him with enough force to finish off the alarm clock and Ronnie could hear clock parts falling to the floor all around him. This ended his struggle to get up. All he could do in the blinding pain he was in was try to crawl out of the room. An endless string of profanity was coming from Margret and in Ronnie's sensory overloaded state, it sounded almost like a chant.

The only other conscious thought he had was the door. He had to make it to the door because she was going to kill him. He felt certain she would if she was given a chance. Not that her actions of the last few seconds were doing anything to disprove his latest theory. Looking up, he could see the door ahead of him, gathering the last of his will and summoning the last of his strength, he managed to half-way get to his feet and bolted. Three feet from the door, he stumbled and actually slid out through the open door on his knees.

When he realized he was outside in the hallway, all he could think of was 'Victory!' and he tried to stand up. Now the profanity had reached a fevered pitch inside of the room he had just escaped from. Ronnie decided for his own health, maybe it would be better if he was downstairs. So he grabbed the banister and pulled himself up, standing finally at the top step just in time to receive the full brunt force of the table lamp hitting him in the back.

There was no way that anyone could have kept their balance on the top of those stairs after getting hit by the heavy lamp. Ronnie watched himself in slow motion horror as his footing was lost and he fell. He was aware of every bone jarring thump and bounce as he cartwheeled down the stairs. With detached amazement, he watched the foot of the stairs coming closer and closer until he was there. The impact with the floor was tremendous and everything went black. The last thought Ronnie had before he blacked out was he was now dead.

Ronnie didn't know how long he was unconscious, but when he opened his eyes, Margret was standing over him crying. When he first saw her, he thought she was there to finish the job. But when he saw her tears, he was confused. He lay there knowing every bone in his body must be broken. There was no way anyone could have survived the fall down those stairs without breaking something. He began to take stock of what hurt and what didn't. Everything hurt and nothing didn't hurt. To Ronnie, it was a good sign. If his back was broken, it stood to reason he wouldn't be feeling any pain from the break down. His pain made him happy and gave him hope that he was going to survive.

"Margret." He managed to croak out.

"Oh Ronnie, you're okay." She said through a fresh gush of tears. "I was so afraid you were badly hurt."

"Margret." He said again.

"Yes Ronnie, what is it?"

"You fucked up. I'm still alive."

"How could you say such a horrible thing?" Margret said as she pulled away a little.

"Let me get this straight," Ronnie said as he tried to sit up, "This is all my fault. Right?"

"Let me help you." Margret said as she tried to give him a hand, ignoring what he had just said.

Ronnie shrugged her off and used the wall to pull himself up. As he stood on unsteady feet, he looked down and saw that his shirt was covered with blood. There was a few seconds of disorientation before he realized he must have pulled out all of his stitches instead of just one or two. His shoulder and back were pure agony as he stood there trying to make sense of what had just happened.

"What the hell is your problem?" Ronnie yelled angrily at Margret.

"I don't know. I'm so sorry. For some reason, I just couldn't help myself." She said through yet another fresh onslaught of tears.

"Save it for somebody who will believe you." He told her. There was no way he was going to let this pass.

"Ronnie, I'm so sorry."

"Look...Go in the kitchen and turn off the stove."

"Why?" She asked.

"Just fucking do it!" He yelled at her.

Without a word, Margret turned around and retreated to the kitchen. A couple of seconds later she was back.

"Now, go get Nancy and get your ass back down here." Ronnie commanded.

Margret complied without saying a word. When she was gone, Ronnie struggled to get into the bathroom and get a towel to try to stem the flow of blood from his shoulder. When he came out of the bathroom, Margret was standing in the middle of the living room looking pale and scared. Nancy was in her arms looking sleepy.

"Get your car keys." He told her.

"Why?" Margret asked timidly. Ronnie didn't think that it was possible, but Margret was now looking even more scared than she had been just a few seconds ago.

"You are going to take me to the hospital." Ronnie told her matter of factually.

"Why would I want to do that?" Margret asked. Her fear seemed to deepen as she remembered the time Max had told her if she ever did anything to Ronnie again, she would be in jail. To her, the last place she wanted to go was to the hospital. "You seem to be alright." She said.

"My stitches are torn out! You are going to take me to the hospital so they can sew me up again." He told her. His voice was a mix of anger, pain, and venom. He had come to the point he now matched Margret's hatred she had shown towards him so many times in the past.

"Oh." Margret replied. It was the only thing she said. Even on the trip to the hospital, she didn't say a word. She just drove, looking over at him every now and then like she wanted to say something. But instead of speaking, she would just turn her attention back to the road.

When they finally arrived, Ronnie got out at the emergency room and went in while Margret found a parking place.

Standing in front of the check-in desk, Ronnie explained that he had tripped as he was going down the stairs in his house and had pulled some of the stitches that had been put in last night. The emergency room was almost empty and they took him right in. Once he was inside and after an orderly had helped Ronnie remove his shirt, the doctor stepped in, looked at his wound and told the orderly to clean Ronnie up.

Ten minutes later, the doctor came back in, stitched Ronnie up and then ordered a bunch of X-Rays. Once the wound was dressed, an x-ray technician came in with a portable unit and took a bunch of films of Ronnie's body. A half hour after the technician left, the films were back and the doctor came back in to tell Ronnie he was a very lucky man. Other than some bruises on his back and pulling his stitches out, Ronnie was alright.

That was when Ronnie asked if he could have a couple of seconds alone with the doctor. The doctor looked over at the orderly and the orderly left.

"So, what's on your mind?" The doctor asked.

"This is kind of embarrassing, but it's my wife."

"What about her?"

"Don't you have some kind of confidentiality thing you are bound to?" Ronnie asked.

"If you are asking me whether or not I can repeat what you tell me, the answer is no. It's the same as a lawyer. So, what's on your mind?"

"My wife goes through these incredible mood swings."

"Did she do this to you?" The doctor asked.

"Kind of, but no. I fell down the stairs on my very own."

"Okay, I'll accept that. Now...You were telling me about her mood swings."

"Yeah. I really don't know how to describe it."

"Then let me try to describe it for you. She's an angel one minute and a raving bitch the next. Right?"

"Exactly." Ronnie told him. He couldn't believe this man who had never met her, had hit the description of her dead center.

"These mood swings are every month?"

"Yes." Ronnie replied.

After a moment's thought the doctor said, "Sounds like she's suffering from PMS."

"What?"

"Pre Menstrual Syndrome. PMS. Some women have violent mood swings just before their periods."

"Is there anything that can be done about it?" Ronnie asked, he knew what PMS was, now he thought it would give Margret an excuse to be the total bitch she was.

"Tell you what, let me talk to her. We've found we can treat this very effectively with drugs. If this is what her problem is, there's no reason you have to suffer anymore."

"Don't you mean that she doesn't have to suffer?" Ronnie asked.

"I don't know about that. I do know that this is the second time I've had to stitch you up in as many days."

"What do we have to do?" Ronnie asked. If this PMS thing was really her problem, then it would go a long way in explaining her behavior.

"Let me talk to your wife and see if she fits the profile." The doctor said as he pulled off his surgical gloves and threw them into the hazardous waste container.

"What do you mean by profile?" Ronnie asked.

"There are several common threads that manifest themselves in all cases of severe PMS. If you want, I can ask your wife a few questions to find out if she's a candidate for treatment."

Ronnie thought for a moment and told the doctor he wanted to talk to his wife before the doctor did. The physician thought about it and decided maybe it would be for the best and offered a small lounge around the corner that could be used for privacy.

Walking out into the waiting area, Ronnie walked up to Margret and told her he needed her to come with him. She got up, gathered Nancy into her arms and followed Ronnie down the hall. Ronnie found the lounge and went inside with Margret following him. Closing the door behind Margret, he turned and told her to sit down. After a brief moment while he gathered his thoughts, he spoke.

"Margret...I was talking to the doctor while he was sewing me back up and he seems to think maybe you're suffering from a condition known as PMS." Ronnie said flat out.

"You did what?" Margret asked in a raised voice. Ronnie could tell that she wasn't happy about his discussion with the doctor about her.

"Shut up and listen." Ronnie told her, the volume for his voice matched hers. "There is some kind of syndrome that affects some women and the doctor wants to talk to you for a couple of minutes to see if you fit the guidelines for it."

"I can't believe you would do something like that." Margret said, clearly mad now. But the volume of her voice was lower.

"Let me put it another way Margret. You either talk to the doctor or when we get home, you pack your bags and get the hell out." Ronnie told her. He felt greatly relieved. He had been avoiding the subject of divorce with her, telling himself that there wasn't a good time to bring it up. But he found he felt much better now that his cards were out on the table.

Margret started to open her mouth to say something, but closed it. After almost a minute she said, "Alright. I'll talk to him if that's what you want me to do." Her voice was greatly subdued and her tone was one of defeat.

"Yes Margret, that is what I want. And as far as I can see, this is the only way YOU can save our marriage." Not that there's anything left to save, Ronnie thought to himself. Then he added, "I told the doctor I tripped going down the stairs. Don't ask me why I'm covering your ass again, but I am covering it this one last time. Now, are you going to talk to the doctor and try to find out what your problem is?"

"Whatever you wish." Margret told him, she didn't look at him but stared at the floor instead.

"Good. Wait here and I'll be back with the doctor in a minute." He told her as he went out the door to search for the doctor. Ronnie found the doctor towards the rear of the emergency room sitting at a desk reading a book. Ronnie assumed the book was a medical journal of some sort, but in reality, it was a book on repairing televisions. The doctor saw Ronnie approach and closed the book. He sat there looking at Ronnie approach.

"She's decided she'll talk to you." Ronnie said when he got within earshot.

"Okay." Was the doctors reply as he got up from behind the desk.

"Just one thing," Ronnie said, "I don't think she's going to be in a very receptive mood to you. She seems to be having one of her moods."

The doctor just smiled at Ronnie and assured him he would take that into account. He then turned and went off in the direction of the lounge. Ronnie stood there for a couple of seconds and then went back to the front desk to see what he had to do to settle up for this visit.

When he was finished, Ronnie went and sat down in the waiting room and waited for Margret to come out. Fifteen minutes went by. Then thirty minutes. Thirty-five minutes later, Margret, escorted by the doctor appeared in the waiting room. The first thing Ronnie noticed was the smile on her face. Ronnie looked at the doctor and saw that he was smiling also.

"I think everything will be just fine now." The doctor said to Ronnie when he was near and then turned and disappeared back into the emergency room.

"He's telling the truth." Margret told Ronnie as she watched the doctor leave.

When they were in the car on their way back to the house, Margret told Ronnie she now understood what had been happening to her and the doctor had given her a prescription to take when she felt like she was losing control again. She told Ronnie she was sorry for making his life a living hell and she would do everything she could to make up for her past ways of treating him. Ronnie just smiled back at her and was beginning to feel happy the problem was just a medical one. Ronnie thought that now, everything would be much better from then on out.

It's too bad Ronnie couldn't read Margret's thoughts. Because the whole time Margret was telling him how rosy their lives would be from that moment on, she was thinking about how she was going to fuck him over. She had talked to the doctor and gave him all of the answers he was looking for. And when they had come out of the lounge into the waiting room, just like now, she was putting on the greatest act of her life. She wanted Ronnie to think everything was going to be great. That way, when she blind sided him, she would be able to get the satisfaction from the look of surprise on his face.

After they had been home for awhile and Nancy had been tended to and put to bed, Ronnie took one of his pain pills and went to bed himself. Ronnie decided even if he had missed dinner, he was going to get a good nights sleep. He lay there in bed for twenty minutes before the pill took affect and Ronnie closed his eyes in a drug induced sleep.

To Ronnie, it seemed as if he closed his eyes and opened his dream eyes almost immediately. He found himself sitting next to the small stream in the glen. The air was cool and a small breeze stirred the trees in a manner that made them creak and rustle, creating a noise that was both soothing and familiar. Ronnie found that even here in his dream, he was having trouble keeping his eyes open.

Ronnie laid back in the soft grass and closed his eyes. Soon, he was asleep in the glen of his dream.

Ronnie, time to wake up. A voice said after awhile. Ronnie stirred slightly in response to the voice.

Ronnie awaken! This time he heard the voice and sat up, fully awake. Sitting next to him was the Professor. Ronnie noticed the Professor was dressed in a costume that looked like something out of an Errol Flynn Robin Hood movie.

Ronnie sat there looking at the way the Professor was dressed, from the pointed cap on his head, complete with feather. Down to the shoes on his feet that had long toes that ended with an upward curve. Ronnie realized this was the first time he was aware of what the Professor wore as clothing. He thought back to the other dreams and realized there wasn't a single time he could remember what the Professor had been wearing. Although he couldn't help it, a smile crept on his face that broadened into a laugh with time.

What's so funny? The Professor asked.

'Nothing,' Ronnie said between giggles, 'Unless you're going out for the role of Robin Hood.'

Making fun of the way I'm dressed?

'Why would I do that? You look very...woodsy. Where's your bow?'

Didn't think to bring it. Enough about me, how are you feeling? The Professor asked.

Ronnie thought about it for a second and realized for the first time, he felt really good. Although his shoulder was still sore, it wasn't hurting like it had been when he first had gotten home. He also found his back felt much better. Ronnie also found he felt very rested, more rested than he had felt in weeks. 'I feel really good, if I say so myself.' He replied.

How's the shoulder?

'It's a little sore, but other than that, great.' Ronnie replied as he slowly raised his arm almost to shoulder level. A sharp, stabbing pain emanating from his shoulder shot through him and he suddenly felt sick.

Well, you don't look so great. From the way you just paled before my eyes, I'd say it's still bothering you quite a bit.

'Just a bit.' Ronnie replied as he felt his strength start to slowly return.

Why haven't you fixed it yet? The Professor asked.

'What do you mean? I can only heal so fast.'

So much energy, so little intelligence. The Professor remarked. *You really don't know, do you? Take your shirt off and I'll show you.* He said as he got up and stepped closer to where Ronnie was sitting.

When Ronnie had stripped off his shirt, the Professor reached down and gently removed the bandage that was covering Ronnie's wound. When it was exposed to the open air, the Professor walked over to where the water was forcing itself from the top of the pile of rocks. Ronnie watched as the Professor took off his hat and filled it from the small arch of water, being careful not to let the hat touch the rocks and only collecting the water while it was still in the air.

When the hat was full, the Professor turned and walked back to where Ronnie was. Once he was behind Ronnie, he began to slowly pour the water over Ronnie's wound. At first, the shock of the cold water on his shoulder and back made him flinch, but it was quickly replaced by a burning feeling that was replaced by a more pleasant tingling sensation.

That almost did it. The Professor remarked and then went back and refilled his hat. Then he came back and repeated the process. This time he only poured half of the hats contents on Ronnie's shoulder and then poured the rest down Ronnie's back. This caused Ronnie to pull forward because he wasn't expecting it.

'What are you doing?' Ronnie demanded.

Hold still, I'm trying to take care of these bruises on your back. The Professor replied, *Looks like she got in a good shot on you this time.*

'I guess I got lucky.' Ronnie replied, 'I think it could have been alot worse.'

Think again. I don't see how this could be worse.

'Well...She could have crippled or killed me.' Ronnie replied.

I guess I can see your point. But Ronnie, you have to remember that this was this time. What about next time? The Professor said as he stood up.

'There isn't going to be a next time. Tonight, while I was at the hospital, I talked to the doctor and he said there was a medical reason for the way she's been acting. He talked to her and gave her a prescription.'

Are you finished? The Professor asked.

'What?' Ronnie asked confused.

Are you finished? Because I want to wait until you're finished talking to laugh in your face. The Professor said just before he burst into laugher.

For the next few minutes, Ronnie had to endure the Professor laughing at him. Ronnie waited until it seemed the laugher was winding down and Ronnie asked, 'What the hell are you laughing at?' There was a great deal of irritation in his voice.

I can't believe you fell for it. You are so stupid, what would you do if I wasn't around? Do you think they can just write a prescription to relieve someone of being a bitch? That would be the most popular prescription around. Popular demand would force it to be an over-the-counter drug. The Professor said, mocking Ronnie.

Ronnie looked the Professor straight in the eyes and held his gaze there for a couple of eternity long seconds. For the first time, he saw something in those eyes. He didn't know exactly what it was, but he did know that it was something evil and malignant. The Professor's eyes reminded Ronnie of a picture he had seen a few years ago. It was a picture of another crazy, evil person. Ronnie remembered the eyes most of all, they had the same look to them that the eyes he was presently looking into had. Those eyes had belonged to a party animal by the name of Adolph Hitler.

A cold shiver ran up Ronnie's spine.

'I admit you've been helpful in the past,' Ronnie managed to say, 'But I think that you're way off base this time. I think she was actually relieved to find out there is a solution to her problem.' Ronnie told the Professor. His mind was still comparing the Professors eyes to Hitler's and Ronnie began to get a feeling of anxiety about it.

The Professor stood there looking back at Ronnie for a couple of minutes before sitting back down. *You can put your shirt back on.* Was the only thing he said.

Ronnie picked his shirt up and started to put it on, but he stopped and asked, 'What about the bandage?'

You're right. Even though you no longer need it, I would suggest you keep it on to avoid questions.

The Professor reapplied the bandage and Ronnie finished putting his shirt on. This time Ronnie noticed he had a much better range of motion from his shoulder. There was just a little sting, but other than that, he felt really good.

'So why are we here tonight?' Ronnie asked after he was finished flexing his shoulder.

A couple of reasons. The Professor replied nonchalantly and then fell silent.

'Do I have to guess them, or are you going to tell me?'

Okay, I'll make it easy on you. First, there's another book coming, so make sure there's plenty of paper around. I'm going to need it.

'Another book? We still haven't heard back from the first one. What's the new book about?'

It's about a real dip-shit who has a wife beating him and writing bad checks. But the clincher is she has her boyfriend try to kill him.

'Very funny.'

Not really. Kind of pathetic if you ask me. But I have no opinion, I just write them like I see them.

'You're serious? You're really writing about that? You're writing about me?'

Sometimes Ronnie, the Professor said as he leaned close to Ronnie, *Life, real life, makes better reading than all of the fiction you can create.*

Ronnie thought about this for a couple of seconds before replying, 'I really hope you plan on changing the names.'

To protect the innocent? You haven't been innocent since you were sixteen. But as a personal favor, I will change the names of the characters.

'Okay, you want paper. Anything else?'

Not at the present moment.

'No, I mean, what's the second thing?'

Just for you to keep watching your ass. If you think all of the answers she gave to the doctor were real, then I've been giving you too much credit as a thinking member of the human race.

Ronnie just sat there in silence, unable to formulate a thought.

Don't be shocked. The Professor continued, *Sometimes it's hard to see what's in the heart of the cold, dark beast. But I do know she's still planning to do something to you. I don't know what. All I could get from her was she wanted to savor the look of surprise on your hurting face. That thought came from a darkness that is darker than any other I've encountered. So you must be careful.*

'You don't know what she was, or is, going to do. Just that she wanted to see the look of surprise on my face? Shit, that could be anything. Maybe she wanted to do something nice for getting her some help with her condition.' Ronnie argued.

Man...You are impossible. She tore you up, tried to kill you, and you still persist on trying to find a ray of sunshine in the storm that is her mind. Let me tell you something, nice happy thoughts don't come from the darkness that her thoughts are coming from. Happy things that come from happy places in peoples minds are bright and as clear as day. Unhappy or evil thoughts come from dark places in the mind. I don't know how or why, they just do.

'How do you know this?'

Well boy, when you're on my side of the fence, you'll find you know a lot of things. Not the least of them is the realization of the evil man can conceive all by himself.

Ronnie sat thinking about this and then said, 'Okay, I'll watch my backdoor.'

And don't forget about the paper. I have to start printing tomorrow night.

'And the paper.' Ronnie repeated.

They sat there in the glen for a long time, enjoying the cool breeze and the whisper of the trees. Neither said anything, all of the conversation had been spoken and was out of the way. Finally, the Professor stood and told Ronnie it was time to go back. Ronnie didn't want to go, he just wanted to continue to sit there and enjoy himself. Here, there were no cares, no troubles, no worries. It was the perfect place to relax. But the Professor was adamant about getting back, so Ronnie got to his feet and started to walk.

369

He had only gone about ten feet when he stopped, realizing there was no place to go. You couldn't just walk out of here. He turned and saw the Professor standing there with a huge grin on his face.

Forget something? The Professor asked.

'Yes, I...I seem to have forgotten how to leave here.' Ronnie admitted.

It's understandable, especially here. Just close your eyes and tell yourself that it's time to return to the real world.

Ronnie did as he was instructed, but when he opened his eyes, he was still standing in the glen.

I forgot to tell you. The Professor said, *You have to want to go back. Even if you have to make yourself want, you must return to your world now. Close your eyes and make yourself believe you want to return to the real world.*

Ronnie closed his eyes once again and with all of the determination he could muster, willed himself back to his world. His reality, his life.

83.

Ronnie became aware he was laying down as he opened his eyes again. He found himself in his own bed with the alarm clock going off. Margret shifted and asked angrily, "Are you going to turn that damn thing off?"

Now Ronnie knew he was back where he was supposed to be, although it wasn't where he wanted to be.

He got out of bed and walked to the bathroom, tenderly trying to touch his shoulder. He quickly found his shoulder didn't hurt at all. So when he was in the bathroom with the door closed, he stripped off his shirt and looked at the bandage on his shoulder. The pad of the bandage looked as if it was almost soaked through with blood, so he decided he would change the dressing and put on a new one when he got out of the shower.

He reached up and carefully pulled the old dressing off and tossed it into the garbage can before looking at his shoulder in the mirror. He froze. The wound looked completely healed. The stitches were still there, but now they looped over a fresh looking scar. Ronnie could see no evidence of the seam where the skin had been pulled together. There was no redness, just a fresh pink colored scar.

Ronnie turned so he could see his back in the mirror and found the bruises that should have been covering the lower part of his back were also gone. In disbelief, his eyes kept going from the scar on his shoulder to the place where the bruises should have been. Ronnie stood there in amazement for almost ten minutes before he realized time was getting away from him. So he quickly got into the shower and started his morning ritual knowing he had better hurry or he would be late.

When Ronnie arrived at work, everyone was there waiting for him. Ronnie couldn't believe it because he was twenty minutes early himself. Usually, everyone would start arriving in the next ten minutes, the older, more dedicated workers getting there first. Then everyone would filter in from there with the last guy just barely getting there on time. But today, here they all were, this time waiting for him to arrive. He also noticed everyone was in a really good mood.

After ushering everyone out to do their tasks, Ronnie settled down in the office and began his daily routine of looking busy. He started going through the books and saw a thick book on the shelf behind his desk. He pulled it out and saw it was put out by a company named Ortho, this book showed examples of grass and told about every malady and pest problem that could befall a lawn. In addition, it also gave solutions to the problems it showed. Ronnie smiled to himself when he realized this one book would help him more than any other in the whole building.

Ronnie spent the next hour going through this new found treasure and when he was finished, decided he would go around and look for trouble spots. Just as he was leaving the office, the phone rang and halted his progress. He answered it, and it was one of the administrative assistants from the club house calling to see if he could come for a meeting. Now that he had been interrupted, Ronnie told the woman he could be there in five minutes. After hanging up the phone, Ronnie drove up to the club house in his golf cart.

84.

Ever since Aaron had started printing the last set of Gabby columns Ronnie had dropped off to him, his phone rang constantly in a firestorm of controversy. People would either call and tell him what a bastard he was for printing such vile things about a deceased upstanding member of the community, or they would praise him for having the courage to print the truth. The praise phone calls were far outnumbering the others and the general consensus was that Fryer was a low life, money grubbing, snake in the grass.

Aaron paid no heed to the phone calls, in the last week, he had seen his circulation increase by another ten thousand. But he was getting nervous because he didn't want the popularity of the newspaper to be solely dependant on the life and times of one man. He quickly realized he would have to get Ronnie to write some other columns to space the Fryer columns out. Thinking about it, he decided he would run two Fryer columns and then a column about how the mayor was a dickhead or something like that. He hoped Ronnie would be able to get into the groove he had been in before he handed in all of those columns in mass.

Aaron decided that instead of waiting for Ronnie to come in on Friday, he would call Ronnie to see what he was up to and discuss his new plans. Aaron sat there looking at the phone with the sudden realization that he couldn't just pick up the phone and call Ronnie at work. Aaron didn't know about Floyd's condition and Ronnie's new assignment of being chained to a desk. So after pondering his dilemma for a while, he decided today looked like a good day to go golfing. That way, he could hang around the golf course and hopefully catch Ronnie working.

But what if Ronnie wasn't working today? Aaron thought about it for a few moments and came up with a solution. He called the clubhouse and explained he was doing a credit check on a Ronald Fisher. He asked all of the usual questions, did Ronnie work there, how long had he been working there. Anything to make himself sound legitimate. The young lady that answered the phone was more than happy to help Aaron out and answered each question as he asked.

After a couple of minutes of what could only be called chit chat, Aaron zeroed in on what he really wanted to know, was Ronnie there today. The young lady continued her brief history of telling everything she knew, answered quickly, saying that yes indeedy, Mr. Fisher was at work today.

Aaron smiled to himself, making a mental note that all of these years of being out of the field and behind a desk hadn't dulled his ability to get people to tell him what he wanted to know. The last time he had used tactics like this, he had been a cub reporter and many years had passed under the bridge since then. He quickly thanked the young lady and hung up.

Now secure in the knowledge that Ronnie was at work, Aaron went out to the receptionist and told her he would be out of the office for the rest of the afternoon. He told her to take his messages and just to keep track of whether or not people supported the Gabby column. When she asked him where he could be reached in case there was an emergency, Aaron just looked at her and told her there had better not be any emergencies because he wouldn't be able to be reached where he was going.

With a big smile on his face, he turned around and went to find the head printer. When Aaron found him, he pretty much repeated what he had told the receptionist, except the part about the messages and about where he could be reached. He said this in a loud voice, loud enough to be clearly understood by anyone who might overhear the conversation and take time enough to try and listen to it. In a much lower voice, he told the printer he would be at the Country Club chasing down a lead.

The printer just nodded and told Aaron to have fun. Aaron turned around and headed for the door. When he reached the back door to the loading dock, he found Avery chasing and picking up trash that was blowing out of the dumpster.

"Hey kid!" Aaron yelled at him.

"Yessir?" Avery answered, clearly startled because he hadn't seen Aaron come out of the building.

"Don't let this go to your head, but you are doing one hell of a good job." Aaron answered as he kept walking.

Avery didn't reply as he kept to his task, but he was definitely puffed up with pride from getting a compliment from Mr. McGuire. It was something that didn't happen very often, so when you got some praise, it tended to make you feel larger than life.

What Avery didn't hear was the comment Aaron made under his breath. After the word 'job', Aaron added "For a total dip-shit".

Avery continued picking up trash as he watched Aaron get into his car and drive off. As soon as he was sure the boss was gone, he decided it was break time. In his ramblings around the office, he had found a corner in the paper storage room was secluded. It was that corner that he headed for and spent the next two hours.

85.

Ronnie arrived at the clubhouse and went straight to the assistant administrators office. He was motioned into the office on the first knock and gestured to sit down. Ronnie made himself comfortable and sat there looking around the richly decorated office. He saw photos hanging on the walls of what he assumed to be celebrity golf players. He also recognized the holes the photos had been taken at and surmised the majority of these photos had been taken a long time ago.

The assistant administrator was an older woman who looked as if she had helped man the oars on Noah's Ark. She was on the phone, but kept going out of her way to smile at Ronnie.

Ronnie was slowly becoming uncomfortable being in this office. He had no idea why he was there, but he had the feeling that most children get when they are sent to the principle's office, a spiral down into a sense of dread.

All too quickly, she was off of the phone and sat there for a moment looking at Ronnie before speaking. That long moment did alot to boost the feeling of dread that Ronnie felt. He wanted to confess, to what he could confess to he didn't know, but he just wanted to jump up and take credit for all of the sins of the world. He would gladly do this just to break this spell of silence. Then the Gabby column crossed his mind and he felt all of the wind go right out of his sails. He now thought he knew why he was there, he was going to be fired for writing those columns. Somebody had told on him, ratted him out and he was going to lose his job.

"Mr. Fisher," this living mother of Moses finally spoke, "I am so glad you could take time to stop by for this little meeting."

"You called, I came." Ronnie replied, trying to sound respectful.

"Yes, you certainly did. And so promptly too. So...How do you like your job now that you've moved up?"

"Just fine ma'am. A lot of responsibility since Floyd's been sick." He told her. Now, he really had a sinking feeling he was about to be given the boot. He thought that this was just her way of softening the blow. Ronnie's paranoia was increasing by the second.

"I can only imagine. The reason I called you here today," Oh-oh, Ronnie thought, here it comes. "Was because I wanted to apologize to you."

"Pardon me?" Ronnie half said, half asked. Confused because he had never been fired with an apology before.

"When somebody gets promoted around here, I make a point to visit them and congratulate them. Unfortunately in your case, I've been too busy to get down to your office."

"That's quite alright." Ronnie told her, "I've been kind of busy myself."

"That's what I understand and that's also another reason I've called you in here today. Floyd's condition has worsened. Now we don't know when or even if he will return to work. I just wanted to tell you myself so you didn't hear any wild rumors first."

"Thanks for letting me know, I really appreciate it." Ronnie told her, now greatly relieved that his worse fears had been nothing more than his overworked imagination.

"I would like to ask you a question, if you don't mind."

"Of course. What's on your mind?"

"What did you do to your work crew?"

"Excuse me? I don't follow you." Ronnie said puzzled.

"Yesterday, some of your guys came in here after work and reported you are the best boss they had ever worked for. Now, I've been around a long time and I've seen some of the grounds keepers put their guys up to coming up to the front office singing their praises for the boss. And I'm afraid that's what I thought at first..."

"Let me assure you that I never even considered doing anything like that." Ronnie interrupted.

Grandma Moses held up her finger in a quiet gesture and Ronnie instantly shut his mouth. When he was quiet she continued, "I just said that's what I thought at first. But then something else happened to make me think differently. A couple of patrons, old time members will take any chance they can to criticize anything and everything, came by here and said they had seen a vast improvement in the course over the last few days. They also commented on how courteous and helpful your staff was yesterday. They also made the comment that the superintendent was doing a fine job of motivating his staff."

Ronnie just sat there not knowing what to say, he was beginning to see this as a very big compliment.

"I just wanted you to know that is what made me take notice of the job you're doing. Well done!"

"Thank you." Ronnie replied back proudly.

"No Mr. Fisher, thank you. That was the first time I ever heard any compliments out of those two patrons about anything having to do with this club.

Please keep up the good work and please pass the compliments along to your crew."

"You can rest assured that I will bring it up in our meeting this afternoon. But I also want to assure you that I never put anyone up to coming to see you. To tell you the truth, I never even considered it."

"I know that now, but you still haven't answered my original question. How did you do it?"

Ronnie thought about it for a couple of moments and then replied, "To tell you the truth, I'm not sure. I just treat them like men and let them do their jobs. I give them their task for the day and let them figure out how they will accomplish them."

"So...Are you telling me you motivate them by letting them motivate themselves?"

"I guess you could call that a fair assessment." Ronnie replied.

The vision of extreme old age just sat there thinking for a minute and then said, "Then you have my congratulations also. You have done something I haven't seen done for a very long time around here. Keep it up."

"Once again ma'am, thank you." Ronnie said. Sensing that the conversation was coming to an end, Ronnie added, "If there's nothing else ma'am, I need to get back to my duties. You can never tell when I will be needed."

"Of course." She replied and stood up, offering him her hand, "Remember to let your crew know what a good job they're doing and keep up the fine job also."

Ronnie took her hand and assured her he would and then almost as an afterthought, told her that anytime she wanted a tour of the greens, to call him and he would personally chauffeur her around. She smiled and told him she just might take her up on his offer.

When Ronnie was safely out of her office and on his way back to the shack, he allowed himself a smile and a "Hell Yeah" to accommodate his ego. As he was driving back, he decided not to go back to the shack, but to ride around the course to announce there would be a meeting this afternoon for his guys.

This time on his rounds, instead of starting at the first hole, he took aim and set sail for the eighteenth hole.

86.

As Ronnie was heading down the path that would take him to where the first of his work crews would be, Aaron was pulling into the club parking lot. He unloaded his clubs out of the trunk of his car and headed for the Pro shop.

Fortunately for Aaron, it was still early in the day and he was able to get right out on the course. Not that it really mattered, he intended on riding around in the golf cart until he found Ronnie. But he would play a round of golf to make his being there look legitimate, as if that was his only intention for being there.

Aaron teed off from the first hole playing what could only be described as the quickest round of golf that would ever be played. He barely sighted where his ball had landed when he jumped into his golf cart and took off. He drove straight to where his ball was, jumped out of the cart and blasted the ball once again. The rest of the game followed the same pattern, Aaron roaring up to the ball in his golf cart, taking about a half of a second to get his bearings and then putting. It was a shame Aaron wasn't keeping score, because ironically, he was playing the best game he had ever played. Would ever play, as a matter of fact.

He found Ronnie at the tenth hole. Aaron was so intent on looking through the woods for Ronnie that he almost drove his golf cart head on into Ronnie's cart on a curve that went around a small stand of trees. There was a brief moment of confusion before recognition hit.

"I see you've graduated from a lawn mower to a golf cart now." Aaron said as he stopped next to Ronnie.

"And I see that you're taking the day off. Are you sure the paper can run without you?" Ronnie asked with a big smile on his face.

"Just barely," Aaron replied, "The reason I'm here is you. We need to talk." He told Ronnie quietly.

Ronnie was silent for a moment and then said, "Follow me". Ronnie drove around to the other side of the stand of trees and to a secluded spot. Ronnie stopped his cart and sat there watching as Aaron parked his cart next to Ronnie's. "So what's so important that you had to come find me?" Ronnie asked after Aaron got himself arranged.

"Ronnie. I'm really sorry for bothering you at work, but I need to talk to you about the column."

"Is there a problem?" Ronnie asked, suddenly worried that Aaron was going to tell him he had decided to drop the column. Ronnie knew if that happened, he would never be able to keep the payment schedules he had arranged with all of the stores Margret had written checks to.

"Yes and no," Aaron said, "Could you write some more columns?"

"What? You want more?" Ronnie asked relieved that his gravy train would still be rolling down the tracks.

"Well...The problem is the stuff you gave me is too good. It's creating controversy like you've never seen before. I would like you to write some different stuff so I can space the columns about Fryer out. I'm afraid that if I keep with the Fryer story week after week, people will grow tired of us hammering on the same old SOB all of the time."

"So you want something as a spacer."

"Exactly. It doesn't have to be this week, but if you could give me a column or two next week, I would be really happy."

Ronnie thought for a second and said, "I see no problems with those arrangements. Do you want anything in particular for the subject matter?"

"Not as long as it's up to the same fine set of standards the rest of the Gabby columns adhere to."

Ronnie started laughing, "So it doesn't matter as long as it's total trash."

"That's my boy. You know, if you ever want to quit cutting grass for a living, you'd make one hell of a reporter."

"Didn't I tell you? I don't have to cut grass anymore, I got promoted."

"As a matter of fact, you did tell me that. How's the new job going?"

"Really good. But the best news is the boss is sick and now this is my grass...Don't take me wrong, Floyd's a great guy and I hate to see him sick, but now I'm responsible for all of the greens."

Aaron could see Ronnie was really proud of his new position and replied, "So now you're king of your own empire. I'm really happy for you."

"Yep, it's all mine. Just remember that next time you're pissing on one of the fairways."

Now it was Aaron's turn to laugh, "I promise I'll only pee in the woods from now on."

Ronnie was laughing also, "Yeah, you say that now. Knowing you, you'll probably try to pee in the cups from now on."

The image of Aaron standing at a flag peeing in the hole only made them laugh harder. When the laughter had subsided, Ronnie explained he had to get back to work and whipped out his hand in friendship. Aaron took it and told Ronnie he was looking forward to reading whatever he had to offer. Once the goodbyes were said, Ronnie restarted his cart and drove off.

379

Ronnie finished making his rounds and telling everyone about the meeting. It was well past lunch time when he got back to the shack.

Ronnie went inside his office and sat down at his desk. As he sat there, he let his mind wander and reflected on everything that had been happening to him. This time, instead of lamenting about how Margret was a bitch, he mostly thought about last night. The dream where the Professor had repaired his shoulder, and this morning the proof of what had happened in his dream, was real. After everything that had happened in those dreams, he realized that he just accepted them as fact, never questioning the events that transpired. He wondered what it was that kept him from running away and losing his mind, the Professor and the dreams certainly qualified as beyond normal.

Ronnie also felt as if he could no longer hold the secret in. He felt an overwhelming need to tell someone, to reveal the dark secret he was living with. But who could he tell? Who could he trust to tell that wouldn't be on the telephone within a second trying to get the number of the local looney bin to come and make a pick up?

As he thought about it, Ronnie realized there was absolutely no reason why he should tell anyone. The Professor had helped him more lately than not. After all, it had been the Professor that had warned him about Margret's indiscretions, first with Ted and then with the checks. Of course there was that little matter of Ted trying to kill him. The Professor had written the columns about Fryer that Aaron was creaming in his pants about. And it was also the Professor that was now writing books in Ronnie's name, using contacts Ronnie could have never hoped to have to hopefully get them published. So the main question on his mind now was, "Why did he feel so guilty?"

The rest of the day passed as Ronnie busied himself studying the Ortho manual. He decided he wanted to be a walking, talking, expert on grass ailments. He surmised that this knowledge would do nothing but help to promote his own cause and make him a valuable asset. Finally looking up from his desk, he saw it was almost time for the meeting. So he closed the book after marking the page and went outside to the lunch area to await the return of his guys.

Everyone showed up promptly except for one guy, Bill. It was Bill's turn to drive Satan today, so they waited for him to arrive. Everyone was laughing and there were several remarks that Bill was probably swimming out of one of the ponds at that moment. After a couple of minutes, they could hear the sound of an engine backfiring and everyone went to the door to see what was making so much noise. In the distance, they saw Bill coming, driving at almost a walking speed. Just when it seemed like he was picking up some speed, Satan would back fire a couple of times, belching out thick clouds of blue/black smoke. Then Bill would be slowed down to a crawl again and as he picked up speed again, the whole noisy, smoky process would repeat.

The group watched as Bill drew nearer and finally was at the shack. Bill stopped Satan with the other mowers and switched it off. But the mower refused to quit running. It would backfire, belch out its cloud of smoke and just when it seemed that the engine would finally quit, it would rev up again and repeat the process. Bill crawled off of the mower and stood there watching the festivities the mower was putting on. Then Bill stepped back, pulled his left foot behind him and kicked the engine as hard as he could. Satan emitted one last backfire (Which Ronnie swore later that he saw a six foot flame shoot out of the exhaust) and the machine died. Bill walked inside and the only thing he said was if he had to drive that damn thing again, he would quit.

When everyone had calmed down from laughing, Ronnie took his position in front of the group. He told them he had been called to the main office because of the way they had been acting. A murmur ran through the group, they were thinking Ronnie had gotten into trouble and were speculating on what had happened to cause his grief. Ronnie let the speculation go on for a minute and then raised his hands to quiet the group. Almost instantly they grew silent. Then Ronnie told them he knew exactly what the trouble was and if they would be quiet for a minute, he would tell them. The suspense in the small room was thick as everyone strained to hear what Ronnie had to say. When he felt he could no longer stretch their patience, Ronnie told them he had been told they were doing a spectacular job and to keep it up. Then he told them they had actually gotten compliments from the patrons on the good job they were doing.

A nervous laugh ran through the group and one of the older guys spoke up and said to quit messing around with them and tell them what the problem really was. Ronnie was astonished, he told them the truth and they didn't believe him. The crew was so unused to hearing compliments when they heard one, they didn't believe it. So Ronnie assured them he was telling the truth, that everyone in the front office was very happy with their performances, but he also added he had been told some of them had gone up to the front office to give Ronnie raving reviews about his job performance as a boss. This he explained, was neither expected nor wanted, but it was appreciated.

Everyone sat there like they didn't know what to do and Ronnie finally said, "Shit guys. For the first time that I can remember, they gave us a compliment. Be happy."

That was the ice breaker and everyone started cheering and slapping each other on the back. Ronnie's hand was shook until it felt as if it was going to fall off. Ronnie found he was also swept up in the reverie. When the guys started calming down, Ronnie held up his hands once again and everyone was instantly silent. Then Ronnie told them about Floyd, that his condition was getting worse and no one knew for sure when he would return. The group was silent and Ronnie asked for another moment of silence for their stricken leader. After the moment of silence, Ronnie mentioned that it might be nice if they went and visited Floyd, or at least make the effort to do so. Then he dismissed everyone to go home.

Ronnie waited for the actual quitting time to leave himself. On his way home he stopped at an office supply store and bought a couple of reams of paper, when he arrived at home, he found Margret in the same position he found her in yesterday. But when she saw him walk into the house, she jumped up and went into the kitchen to start dinner. The whole time she was cooking, she was keeping a monolog going about the way her day had gone and asking Ronnie questions about his.

Ronnie told her his day had been real busy and listened to everything she was telling him. He was happy about the way she was acting today, and she was so much different than the way she had been yesterday and Ronnie thanked God for small miracles. Within the half hour, Margret laid dinner out on the table. Ronnie stepped up to the table and saw she had cooked one of his favorite meals, Tater Tots and Corn dogs. Ronnie had commented one time that it may not sound like much, but he did like them and enjoyed them the few times he got them.

As Ronnie munched on a corn dog, Margret kept up the running commentary of what she had been doing since he had walked through the door. Finally, when there was a break in the one sided conversation, Ronnie asked her if she had looked through the newspaper to see what the employment opportunities were looking like. Margret replied she had looked, but didn't see much she was qualified for. Ronnie told her it was alright, there would be alot more listings in the Sunday paper. When that was said, it seemed to kill all of the conversation. Margret was silent for most of the rest of the night.

When bedtime came around, Ronnie made sure to lay the two reams of paper on the desk next to the computer. That night there were no dreams and Ronnie slept the night through. The next morning after going downstairs, Ronnie found that almost one whole ream of paper had been printed on. Ronnie took the stack of paper without reading any of it and put it where he always did, in the lower desk drawer. Then he went to work to finish out the work week.

87.

When Ronnie got home that evening Margret was in a strange mood, almost jumping up and down with excitement. When Margret calmed down, she told Ronnie that a man from a publishing company had called and left his phone number, asking Ronnie call him back as soon as possible. Collect if need be. At first it didn't register with Ronnie what she was talking about. But then he heard an all too familiar voice in his mind say, *The book asshole!*

Ronnie took the piece of paper from Margret and after telling her to please calm down and give him a few minutes, he went into the dining room and dialed the number.

"Phantom Press, may I help you?" A feminine voice on the other end answered the phone.

Ronnie explained who he was and told her he had received a phone call from one of the gentlemen that worked there, gave her the name, and then told her he was returning the call. He was then told to wait and put on hold. Margret was standing right next to him straining to hear both ends of the conversation. A couple of seconds later, the phone was answered once again and Ronnie explained who he was. The man on the other end sounded glad to hear from him and acted as if Ronnie was his long lost buddy.

For the next ten minutes, they talked about their old alma mater. Yes, it had been a blast to go there. Yes, the party potential had been incredible. And yes, it had been very unfortunate what had happened to their old Professor, but no, Ronnie didn't know exactly how the man had died. But yes, it was a great blow to the literary community that the Professor had never been able to write the books he had planned on writing.

When the magical mystery tour through the past was complete, Ronnie was told they were planning on publishing his book. It was also explained that normally the publishing company wouldn't have moved so fast on a book, but when the man had seen they shared a common past, he had put Ronnie's book ahead of the rest they were reviewing. Then Ronnie was asked if there was another book on the horizon and Ronnie explained he was just about halfway through the next one. There was a startled silence on the other end of the phone before Ronnie was asked if he was serious, to which he replied 'yes'.

What Ronnie was told next brought a startled silence from him, the publisher would buy the book for ten grand and also lay out another five grand on top as a retainer for the next one. After a couple of seconds, Ronnie sputtered out that it sounded great to him. Then he was asked if the address was correct for his mailing address and Ronnie, not thinking because he was still in a state of shock, asked why. To which he was answered, "So we can send you a check and a contract."

Ronnie thought about it for a moment and replied that yes, the address was correct, but to please send any correspondence to his work address for now. He was told that it wouldn't be a problem and Ronnie gave the address to the Country Club. They continued chatting for another ten minutes and it was explained to Ronnie about the contract and how book buying business worked.

As they talked, Ronnie began to think about the Gabby column and realized if there was suddenly a book with his name on it, someone might put two and two together and realize Ronnie was really Gabby. He quickly asked if he could be published under a pen name. Ronnie was asked why he wanted to do that and he replied this was his first attempt and he would rather have it listed under a pen name than his real name. It was agreed it could be worked out that way. Then Ronnie was asked if there was a particular name he wanted to be published under, to which he replied, "How about 'The Professor'?"

It was agreed upon and the deal was set. Ronnie was told to make his submissions directly to him and if he had any questions, not to hesitate to call. Ronnie was also told if anyone tried to give him the runaround when he called, to let the man know.

When Ronnie got off of the phone, Margret (who had only caught bits and pieces of the conversation) wanted to know what was going on. Ronnie thought about it for a moment and decided to lie to her. He told her he had submitted a book to be published and the publisher had called to iron out some details before deciding whether or not they were going to publish it. Margret was about to dance around in anticipation and asked him what they had said, whether the book was going to be published or not. Ronnie told her it was looking good, but they were going to send him some paperwork that needed to be signed before they could move any further.

This seemed to satisfy Margret's curiosity and she didn't ask about the money or bring up why he was having them send the paperwork to his job. Ronnie did, however, feel a pang of guilt about not telling her the truth. But he quickly squashed it by telling himself that no matter how much money he was going to make on the book, he still wanted her to take some responsibility for her actions and get a job to help pay the bills. To Ronnie, that would mean more to him than her on her knees begging forgiveness for her actions.

Now, with his money troubles over and nothing but good things on the horizon, he was beginning to have second doubts about divorcing her. That night as he lay in bed, he lay there awake for a long time thinking long and hard about his decision. Before he finally drifted off to sleep, he decided to hold off on any decision about divorce. Because if the change he had seen in her for the last couple of nights held out, his problems with her abusing him would be over. Ronnie decided from that moment on, he would take life one day at a time.

The rest of the weekend was great. Margret was attentive to his every need and actually seemed to go out of her way to make him happy. Sunday morning came and when Ronnie came downstairs, he found Margret already down there going through the newspaper want ads. He looked over her shoulder as he kissed her good morning and saw she had circled a dozen entries. Ronnie asked her what she was doing and she replied she had decided to get an early start and see what was going on in the world of employment. Secretly, this made Ronnie happy to see her doing this because he was afraid he was going to have to have another showdown to motivate her to get a job.

Ronnie smiled at Margret and told her how proud he was of her. She didn't say anything back to him. In fact, Margret was holding her breath hoping Ronnie didn't look too closely at what she had circled, because she hadn't.

When Margret had heard Ronnie walking around upstairs, she had quickly turned off the television and grabbed the newspaper. She then ran over to the table and opened the paper, quickly finding the want ads. Then she took a pen and just started circling things. When she had a few circled, then she started actually looking at what she was doing and started circling things that were kind of in the realm of possibility for her. But in most cases, she really didn't pay too much attention to what she was circling and the things she had circled and there wasn't a snowballs chance she could get those jobs. She hardly qualified as a head administrator for an experimental compound lab.

As with most Sunday mornings of late, Margret had gotten up very early today. After watching the tv preachers preaching their words instead of God's and channel hopping to find the sermons that made her feel good, she decided she would go through the motions of trying to find a job. After all, she told herself, Ronnie would be at work and wouldn't be with her on her interviews. She figured after a couple of weeks of riding around 'Looking' for a job, Ronnie would give up on his crazy idea that she had to work and drop the subject. So she decided she had time on her side and if Ronnie was close to having a book published, then they would be millionaires and their money troubles would be over.

While she had been getting her dose of spiritual inspiration this morning, she had also decided if Ronnie was going to be rich, there was no reason why she couldn't stay with him awhile longer. She would wait until he had amassed a huge fortune, then she would leave him and take him for everything she could in the divorce settlement. She sat there thinking about that and then she realized if she went for the divorce, there was a good chance she could come out of it with nothing. That thought alarmed her and after careful thought, she decided if she had almost gotten him killed once, she could easily do it again.

Except next time, she would find someone that would do the job right.

After Ronnie saw that Margret was hard at work looking through the want ads, he found the section of the paper that the Gabby column ran in and then went to pour himself a cup of coffee. He went and sat down and began reading the column. This particular column was about how Fryer had bilked an old lady out of most of the money she had won in an insurance settlement.

After he had read the column and drank his coffee, Ronnie went back upstairs to the bathroom. The bandage that was covering his well healed shoulder wound was beginning to bother him. So, with the bathroom door securely closed behind him, he peeled off his shirt and removed the bandage. A close inspection of his shoulder revealed the wound itself looked pretty good, the problem was where the stitches came out of the skin and crisscrossed the pink scar. The spots where the stitches exited the skin was starting to become puffy and red looking. Ronnie decided it was time to remove the stitches. So he opened the drawer under the sink, found a pair of tweezers and a pair of scissors.

During his marriage with Margret, he had a lot of stitches both put in and taken out of various places of his body, so he knew what to expect. He reached up with the tweezers, grabbed a hold of one of the stitches right next to the knot, then he brought up his other hand with the scissors and cut the stitch on the other side of the knot. That having been done, he gently pulled the stitch out of his shoulder with a gentle, constant, pulling motion. The stitch slipped out with just a slight pulling sensation. Once it was out, he looked at it and then dropped it into the garbage can next to the sink. Then he repeated the process again and again on the remaining sutures, dropping each one into the garbage can with the others. When he was done, he looked back at the overall wound and saw he was bleeding from a couple of the holes the sutures had come out of. So he picked up a wash cloth, wetted it, put soap on it and gently cleaned the entire wound. When he was done, Ronnie stood there looking at his handy work and was pleased it had stopped bleeding altogether. He put on a clean shirt and went back downstairs.

When he got back downstairs, Margret asked him what he had been doing and Ronnie replied he had been taking care of his shoulder. She then asked him how his shoulder was doing and Ronnie told her it was doing surprisingly well. Which of course, was the understatement of the century.

Then, just as he had done Saturday morning, Ronnie looked at the pile of paper that had accumulated overnight next to the computer. He took this new stack and put it on top of the growing pile of paper in the desk. He hadn't bothered reading any of it because he had decided to wait until the Professor told him it was done, or when he saw the cover letter.

The rest of the weekend was uneventful and early Monday morning, Margret took Ronnie to work and dropped him off because she needed the car to go job hunting. Ronnie stood there watching as she drove away, hoping she was going to be looking for a job today instead of repeating her earlier pattern.

Ronnie winched at the thought of Margret out writing more bad checks. But then he realized he was being silly, there wasn't anyplace left in town that would accept a check from her and besides, he had the checkbook. He didn't like doing something sneaky like taking the checkbook without telling her, but he also didn't want her to be out there running amuck on the chance she was able to find someone she could write a check to.

Ronnie also decided when he got home, he would put the checkbook on the desk or someplace semi-obvious. Someplace that would be safe from her. But he ultimately hoped she would get into a situation where she would wonder where the checkbook had gone.

With a smile on his face, Ronnie finished his walk into his office and started his day.

88.

Margret, after dropping off Ronnie, went home for a while and tried to decide what she was going to do for the day. She still had a good chunk of money left she had 'collected' from the second go around with the checkbook. So she got Nancy ready and took her next door. Margret tried to be nice, but got a very cold reception from Heather's mother. She took Nancy from Margret and almost shut the door in Margret's face. Margret barely noticed because she was in too much of a hurry to get started on her day of freedom.

Margret spent part of her day window shopping at the mall, but for the most part, she spent her day just riding around. At one point, she found herself out by the base and pulled into Acehole's parking lot to get some lunch. But as she sat there in the car, her thoughts returned to Ted and she found that suddenly, she wasn't very hungry.

Aceholes had been his place and she found that her thoughts wouldn't let go of him. As she sat there looking at the little restaurant, she vowed one way or another, she would get revenge for Ted's unfortunate and untimely death. She felt rage starting to build inside of her, the rage of how unfair her life was. Rage from being saddled with a loser like Ronnie and the brat kid. Rage that the only real man that had come into her life who had some authority to change her miserable life had been killed by Ronnie. Oh, Ronnie will pay, she thought to herself.

Or at least she thought she had thought that to herself. A patron walking into the restaurant overheard her thoughts as they escaped from her lips and looked at her for a second wondering what she was talking about. But Margret was too absorbed in her own thoughts to notice the man.

Margret knew she wouldn't be able to do anything this quickly to Ronnie, but she would wait. Then she remembered she would have to wait anyway, if Ronnie got his book published and made enough money, she would hire someone to do the job right next time. And since she was going to be picking up the bill on this, she would make sure his death was a slow and painful one. A slight smile crossed her lips as she went deeper into her fantasy and decided that she would offer a bonus for every hour Ronnie suffered.

To her, it hadn't been Max that had pulled the trigger on the gun that killed her beloved Ted, it had been Ronnie. Max never entered her thoughts, he had just been an unfortunate bystander that had been there when Ronnie had killed her love. And even though there was a smile on her lips, there were silent tears streaming from her eyes. Margret knew she couldn't go into Aceholes. That part of her was a memory that was as dead as the man she really loved was. That is, what Margret regarded as love.

Margret started the car, slipped it into reverse and pulled back out of the parking space and drove away. She resigned herself to put up with the shovels full of crap that Ronnie would heap on her until the time was right. Then she would strike back at him with a revenge that was deadlier and colder than any known in the history of mankind.

Margret visited a few more stores and then rode around until it was time to get Ronnie from work. Her first instinct was to let the bastard walk home, but she decided against it because she wanted him to be happy and content. Now, more than ever, she needed to see that look of surprise on his face.

When Ronnie came out to the parking lot, he found Margret waiting for him. It had been a long day and was glad he didn't have to wait for her. One of the well pumps had gone out during the weekend and the back up pump had sucked all of the water out of one of the irrigation ponds that also served as a critical landscaping feature of the course.

Needless to say, management was highly pissed the pond was empty. But after Ronnie pointed out the reason the ponds were there was for this type of emergency situation, management calmed down somewhat. Then Ronnie asked why he hadn't been notified about this when it had first been noticed and only got "We didn't think of it" as a reply. Ronnie then went further to point out that not only had he been home all weekend, but the club also had and paid a great deal of money for an emergency maintenance contract that would have gotten the irrigation company to send a guy out to the course the day the problem had occurred. This was met with silence and then a feeble apology that Ronnie had not been allowed to do his job. Ronnie then went back to his office and called the irrigation company and the irrigation guy got there early and fixed the pump. It was still in the process, but the pond was refilling nicely and barring any unforseen circumstances, would be full long before morning.

All Ronnie wanted to do was go home and put his feet up. Instead of showing his frustration to Margret, he asked her how her first day of job hunting had gone. She replied she had put in about a dozen applications but didn't have a feel who was going to call her back for interviews. Had Ronnie not been as tired as he was, he would have pressed her harder on where she had put the applications in to. But he decided to let the matter drop, consoling himself that at least she had been out trying to find a job.

389

Although Margret was prepared to further her lie, she was relieved Ronnie didn't delve too deeply into her days activities. Ronnie on the other hand, was relieved that Margret wasn't screaming she had misplaced the checkbook.

That night as Ronnie lay in bed trying to go to sleep, his mind wandered back to the checkbook matter. He decided if he stayed on a strict cash basis when paying his bills, he would have no record of where his money was going. So he decided he would go and open another bank account with just his name on it. That way, Margret wouldn't be able to write any checks and the responsibility would fall solely on his shoulders to pay the bills. To him, this plan sounded like a good one, so he decided he would open his new account with the three hundred dollars he would collect on Friday from Aaron. Then Ronnie realized he hadn't collected his money last Friday, so Aaron owed him six hundred. Ronnie made a mental note to call Aaron tomorrow about the money he was owed.

Now that he was content about his financial future, he drifted off to sleep.

89.

It seemed as if he opened his dream eyes as soon as he had went to sleep. Ronnie stood in the glen next to the stream. He looked up and saw there were small, puffy clouds going by overhead. He inhaled deeply and smelled the sweet smells of the flowers overhead. It was almost as if the smell itself was intoxicating and Ronnie soon found he had to sit down before he fell down.

As he laid on the cool grass watching the clouds drift lazily across the sky, he almost jumped out of his skin when a voice next to him suddenly asked him if he was ever going to visit the high place again. He looked up and over, and without surprise, saw the Professor sitting in the grass next to him.

'I should have known you'd show up.' Ronnie remarked as he turned his attention back to the sky.

Least I could do. So, how's things going for you? The Professor asked.

'Why are you asking me? I thought you were the almighty seer of all things.'

Thought that I'd give you a chance to lie about it. The Professor replied after a moment of reflection, then he continued, *So, how's the shoulder?*

This question brought Ronnie to a sitting position, 'Much better.' He replied, 'What's the deal with this stream? I couldn't believe it healed my shoulder so quickly. So it heals wounds and refreshes the thirst, can't get much better than that. The all purpose water. Too bad I can't bottle and sell it.'

The Professor jumped up and said, *This is so much better than just common old all purpose water.*

'What do you mean?'

Why Ronnie, I'm surprised you asked me that. Don't you know about this stream?

Ronnie didn't want to, but he admitted that he didn't.

I'm so disappointed in you. I guess you never studied mythology while you were in school.

'The only mythology I studied was how fast money goes away while getting a view of the world from people that were hardly qualified to show it. I also learned when you paid enough money, they tell you there is no more education they can give you for that price and you are now an expert in your field. Of course they'll tell you that if you give them some more money they'll give you a bigger world view and make you a bigger expert.' Ronnie quickly replied, the sarcasm dripping from his voice.

It's a shame you take that point of view. A closed mind is a true sign of the lack of intelligence.

'You think I have a closed mind?' Ronnie asked laughing, 'Here I am sitting in a glen in my dreams talking to a man that has been dead for quite a few years. And I haven't lost my mind yet. Yeah, sounds to me like I've got a closed mind.'

Well, you have a good point there. But please, I'd rather think of myself as metabolically challenged. And since you seem to be ignorant of your surroundings, I guess I'll have to assume the position of teacher again and tell you about where you are exactly.

'Teach on.' Ronnie replied, his curiosity now aroused by the way the Professor was acting about the glen.

If I must. The Professor replied and after a moments thought, started speaking, *How much do you know about the River Styx?*

'Are you talking about the mythological boundary between life and death? The river you must cross to get to the underworld after death?'

Very good. You get an A+. Well guess what, you are standing at the headwater of that river.

'What?' Ronnie asked in disbelief, 'I never heard about a headwater for the River Styx. I thought it existed in a never ending form, no beginning and no end.'

Well here it is chief. Everything has a beginning and an end, that is one of the laws of reality that is unchangeable. On this side of the river is life, the other side is the region of death. Haven't you noticed that every time you come here, you're always on this side of the stream?

'Damn, I guess I've never really thought about it. But what about you? You're dead and here you are on this side.'

That, Ronnie, is because I choose to be here. If I were to cross the stream here, I would never be able to return. Don't tell anyone, but if you have a strong will, you can resist the pull of the other side.

'Okay, I can understand that if you cross the stream you can't come back, but what would happen if you simply walked around the pile of stone there that the stream comes out of?' Ronnie asked pointing to the stone fountain.

Good question. To tell you the truth, I don't know. Would you care to take a walk and find out? The Professor asked taunting him.

'Sure, I'll go if you go first.' Ronnie told him, now thinking he had a way to rid himself of the Professor once and for all.

Good try. But I don't think so. The Professor replied, apparently seeing through Ronnie's rouse.

"So, the water heals and it's the ultimate boundary between life and death. That's so cool."

It only heals if you collect it after it comes out of the rock and before it touches either the rock on the way down or the ground itself.

'So...This well of life comes with a few rules huh?'

A few. You can drink a little, but if you drink or even get too much on you, it has a tendency to make you forget.

'Forget what?'

Everything. Who you are, what you were doing. Things like that. Remember the last time you were here? You were just about stuck here. That was just from the water being poured on your back. When you drink it, the effects are more potent and quicker, more permanent also I'm afraid.

'Explain.' Ronnie said.

I will. When we were here last, I poured a couple of hat fulls down your back and you almost forgot how to get back to the real world. If you were to drink more than a couple of hands full of water, you wouldn't even know who you are. Of course you wouldn't care, but as far as you would know, you wouldn't have an identity anymore. There is also the possibility that it could wipe your memory so clean that you would forget how to breath.

'Shit!' Ronnie exclaimed.

Yeah, that just about sums it up.

'But that is when you collect the water before it hits the stone and the ground. What if you drank from the stream itself?'

Another good question. Here, let me show you. The Professor said as he stood up and walked over to where some flowers were growing. He reached down, picked one and walked back over to where Ronnie was sitting. *Watch this.* He said as he bent down and dipped the flower into the water as he held onto the stem. The Professor didn't leave the flower in the water but just a half of a second before pulling the flower back out and extending it in Ronnie's direction. Ronnie saw that the flower that had been beautiful and alive less than a second ago, was now black, withered, and dead.

'Let me guess,' Ronnie said as he brought his gaze up from the flower to the Professor's face, 'Poisonous.'

More than that. The Professor replied as he threw the flower back into the stream. *Poisonous would be an easy but far too inaccurate way to describe it. The ground surrounding the stone is vile. It's vileness from the heart of man that creates this ground. And as the years go on, the ground gets a little higher around the stones.* Then the Professor leaned close to Ronnie as if he was about to tell a secret that was not to be overheard. *I hear that there is a time when the ground will cover the stones and the river will stop flowing. Can you guess what will happen then?*

Ronnie could only shake his head no.

That will signal the end of the world Ronnie my boy. Yep, when that happens, when the stones are finally covered with the vileness of mankind, poof. No more world, no more people, no more reality.

'So that will be the end of everything?'

Nope. The Professor replied.

'Huh? I thought you said that will be the end of everything.'

I did and it will. But you have to understand that it will also be the beginning too.

'Shit. I give up!' Ronnie said as he threw his hands up, 'You have totally lost me.'

Well, without having to explain a whole bunch of stuff that I think you wouldn't understand anyway, I'll explain it like this. The reality that mankind lives in is closer in resemblance to a circle than a straight line. Let me show you. The Professor said as he pointed a finger in the air to represent a point. *Here we are at the beginning, where everything is new.* Now he started moving his finger slowly in a circle, *And here we are at the half way point.* He said when he got to the bottom of the circle. *And finally, here we are at the top, which I might add, is also the beginning. So, everything starts again.*

'I think I understand.' Ronnie said and then asked, 'Where are we now?'

Who knows and really, who cares? The Professor replied nonchalantly.

Ronnie sat there silently mad, he hated it when the Professor did this. 'Then what was the point of this exercise?' He finally asked.

Hopefully, to make you realize that you can't live every moment of your life worrying about what's going to happen. You have to just live it as if this is your last day and try to get the most out of each day. Besides, you're the one that picked the location, I just showed up to see what you were up to. And to also tell you to leave some more paper out, I need to print out a bunch of stuff tomorrow night.

Ronnie thought about what the Professor had told him for a few minutes before he replied. The Professor had laid alot of information at his doorstep about things Ronnie hadn't thought about in a long-long time. Ronnie had entertained the question of what happened to you when you die during his party days in college, but the question had sorta died within him after his days of settling into a routine of going to work everyday and making a living. He could remember a few times, later in his working years, of wondering if this was all there is to life. Especially when Margret was at her worst. Ronnie thought of a few more questions he wanted to ask.

'You say that reality is a circle.' Ronnie said trying to clarify what he had been told.

For most people, Yes, it is.

'What do you mean by that?'

If you learn enough in life, you are supposed to be able to 'graduate' to the next level.

'What's the next level?' Ronnie asked.

The Professor looked at Ronnie for a second debating whether or not he really wanted to get into this discussion with Ronnie, then he replied, *You really must think on a multi-dimensional level. I said that your reality is like a circle. Yours is not the only circle out there. There are circles within your circle and outside your circle. There are circles for infinitum. That's how I'm able to be here, you can call it an overlap of our separate circles. I'm bound by some of the physical laws of your realm and since I haven't really crossed all the way over yet, some of the physical laws of my realm. The old theory about we are the universe that makes up the atom that makes up an atom isn't too far off.*

'So the stream is more of a boundary between the physical worlds, or circles, of your reality and mine?'

It's about time you got that last brain cell fired up. Congratulations, you have figured out one of the greatest mysteries of mankind. But let me give you some advice. I wouldn't go spreading it around if I were you. People might think you're crazy or something and Margret won't have to go through all of the hassle of trying to kill you. She can just divorce your sorry ass after they tote you off to the looney bin. Then she can piss away your fortune in style.

Ronnie frowned at the prospect of Margret deriving pleasure from his misfortune. Then he asked, 'You said if you learn enough you can pass through to the next level. What happens if you don't learn enough?'

The Professor took a long time before he answered Ronnie's question. Just when Ronnie was beginning to give up hope of getting an answer, the Professor spoke, *Think of crossing the stream as a test. If you pass, you continue on. But if you fail, you get to go to summer school and ride the rock around the sun for another life.*

Suddenly Ronnie understood what the Professor was telling him. "You're talking about reincarnation." He said excitedly.

It's been called that also.

'Then if all of the people that are around are reincarnated, then why don't they remember their previous lives so they can learn from their past mistakes?'

Some do, vague recollections of something that you've seen or done before. Where do you think the term 'De ja vue' comes from? Everyone has experienced times when a trace memory breaks through. But for the most part, if you fail the test, you get your memories wiped clean on the transition back.

'What if you pass?'

Then you get to remember from all of your past lives. That's how you learn. The old story about there being no memory in heaven is bull. That is, if you call the next level heaven.

'How do you know all of this?' Ronnie asked.

Full of questions tonight huh? To answer your question, I don't know how I know, I just know.

'What's the next level like?'

That's one question I can't answer because I don't know. There are limits to my knowledge. If you're so curious, step over the line and find out for yourself. The Professor replied as he pointed to the stream.

'Naw...I don't think so. I think I'll hold onto my life until it's my turn to cross.'

No balls huh? Well, that's okay. Don't feel too bad, you see I'm still here don't you?

'Where did you say the vile that grows the ground comes from?'

This is the last question or I'll have to charge you for a personal consultation. The vile is basically a culmination of all of the evil, perverted, sick, and twisted things that all of humanity does. It's also from the small evils, drug abuse, self abuse, self pity, ignoring the plight of others. Hell, the ovens at Auschwitz added almost an inch on their own. Anything that goes against the positive Karma of the universe creates this as a byproduct.

'I understand.' Ronnie said and he did, suddenly everything was crystal clear to him.

Good. It's almost time for you to return. Don't forget the paper, okay?

'How's the book going?' Ronnie casually asked.

Haven't you been reading it?

'Well, I've been kinda busy.' Ronnie quickly said as he diverted his eyes from the Professor's gaze.

Some gratitude, don't even take the time to read what's going to make him rich and famous. And judging from the phone call the other night, that's not too far off in the future. The Professor replied bitterly.

'I swear I intended to read all of it before I mailed it off. I was just waiting for your cover letter before I read it.' Ronnie replied defensively.

Okay-okay, at least I'll give you credit for having them send the check directly to your work. That way you can get it before little miss bitch gets her hands on it. You realize if that happened, you wouldn't have anything left to pay off her bad checks. You be sure to get that paid off and behind you so you won't be distracted and we can get some serious work done.

'You know it.' Ronnie replied.

One more thing bean-head. Don't forget the paper.

'Hey, I almost forgot. Aaron McGuire told me he wanted some more columns so he can stretch out the Fryer columns.'

Sorry, can't help you with that. I'll spell check and do your rewrites, but you're going to have to put some time in on the keyboard yourself. I can't do everything for you.

'I never intended for you to write them for me.' Ronnie replied defensively, 'I just wanted you to know why I would be doing some work on the computer before the week end.'

You lie so well. the Professor said, and then looked at his watch and said, *Hey, I really gotta go. Elvis promised to show me how to make something called Fried Nanner Sandwiches, whatever that is. He really seemed to be so happy about those things, kept saying something about a sandwich isn't a sandwich without the zip of miracle whip, whatever that means.*

The Professor faded away and as he did, the glen faded away from Ronnie. He suddenly found himself standing on the deck of the small fishing boat once again. He recognized the boat from the first time he had been there. Standing there on the deck, he looked at the small fishing boat following him off to port. He stood there straining his eyes to see who was piloting the boat behind him. Just as he thought he recognized the pilot of the boat, his boat lurched and Ronnie found himself falling overboard once again. This time when he hit the water, he woke up in his bed to find the alarm clock going off.

90.

Ronnie hit the off button on the alarm clock and lay there thinking about the image of the pilot while it was still fresh on his mind. He could have sworn it looked like that Fryer guy was the pilot of the other small fishing boat. Ronnie would have thought about it longer, but he had other things on his mind. The Professor had given him alot to think about.

Ronnie rolled over and woke Margret up, telling her it was time to get up so she could take him to work. Then he got up and started his daily ritual.

This day was almost a carbon copy of yesterday for Margret. From going to the mall to sitting in Aceholes parking lot, Margret retraced her steps and did everything but look for a job.

For Ronnie, this was a much better day and it went along as smooth as glass. He did, however, find his mind wandering during what Ronnie would have called his slump time. This was just after lunch and Ronnie found himself alone with nothing to do. He had put much of last nights conversation with the Professor aside during the morning, when he was busy. But now, with nothing better to do, he went over the conversation again and again in his head. On top of learning the true fate of man and the universe, he had also found a possible way to get rid of the Professor if he had to.

Ronnie realized he had to conceal, especially in his mind, any thoughts of attempts to send the Professor on to his final destination. He also realized any plan he came up with would have to be so simple it wouldn't require any forethought, just simple action. He continued along that train of thought and came up with the idea that all he had to do was simply stand by the stream and when the time was right, give a simple hard push towards the stream. If he was successful in the element of surprise, the Professor would travel backwards from being caught off balance and land in the stream across the center. Then, if Ronnie understood correctly what he had been told, the Professor would be sucked into his next life with no hope of return because he was on the other side.

Ronnie felt safe making plans at work, the Professors range of thought interception only seemed to be around the house and its immediate vicinity. The Professor had known about the phone call from the Publisher, but had made no mention of Max's visit to Ronnie here at the shack. He didn't know if it was because the Professor was too preoccupied with his writing or if it was because the Professor had limitations to his power of knowledge. He quickly put his plan out of his mind just in case. Then he remembered he was owed money and called Aaron to see if he could come by after work and collect his earnings for the last column. Aaron told him there wasn't any problem with that and he would look forward to seeing him.

91.

The week went by without any major blow-ups. Floyd was still in the hospital and Margret wasn't any closer to finding a job (which was the cause of a few minor blow-ups). The check and the contract hadn't arrived at his office yet and Ronnie got a couple of juicy stories for his column. He dropped them off a couple of days after picking up his money at the paper. Aaron was extremely happy after reading the columns, complete with the Professor's rewrites and polishing.

Saturday morning, Ronnie got up early and started his rounds, paying the money to the people Margret had written the checks to. He stopped by a new bank and tried to open a new account with just his name on it. At first, the bank wouldn't open the account because of the account at the other bank. But after explaining to the manager of the bank what had happened and showing the man the checks he had collected that morning, along with the explanation that he just wanted his name on the account and it would be primarily used to pay bills and rent, the manager relented and agreed to let him open an account. On a trial basis of course. Ronnie, who would have agreed to anything to get the account opened, readily agreed to it and forked over his last hundred dollars and received his starter checks. Instead of putting his home address, he gave his work address and made a mental note to get a post office box first thing Monday morning.

Monday came and Ronnie took some time in the morning from work to walk a couple of blocks to a small post office to get a post office box. Ironically, he had parked his golf cart in the same place he used to park his mower to go to the liquor store, but instead of heading down the street like he had used to after crawling through the same hole in the fence he headed in the opposite direction to the post office. When he got back to his office he called the bank and gave them the new address with his work address as a back up.

It was a few minutes after one in the afternoon when one of the go-fers from the Main Club House came down with the mail. Ronnie tore through the advertisements for grass seed, fertilizers, and pesticides to find what he was looking for. Near the bottom of the stack he found it, the envelope from the publisher. Ronnie went back into his office and closed the door, sitting down in his chair before opening it. He carefully opened the envelope and took out the folded paper from inside. It was a hand written letter that had been carefully folded around a certified check. Ronnie sat there for a long time just looking at the check itself. Fifteen thousand dollars, Ronnie had never conceived of being able to look at a check for that much money, let alone have one that was made out to him.

Ronnie carefully folded the check in half and put it in his shirt pocket, he would take care of it later when he got a chance. Looking over the contents of the envelope, he saw there was a form included along with the letter and check. He read the form and saw it was a release for the company to print his book, which he signed quickly. Then he read the letter from his newfound old college bud. It was personal and sounded like the guy was starving for some news of better days gone by. But mainly, it just went back over the majority of the conversation they had on the telephone. It also sang praises for the memory of the Professor. Ronnie sat back, smiling to himself and wondered if this guy would be singing as many praises as he was if he had been saddled with the Professor's ghost as Ronnie was. Ronnie went further to wonder if this guy would even have any of his sanity left after toting the note on the Professor's ghost.

That thought amused Ronnie, instead of being saddled with the Professor's ghost, he was totin the note. His amusement quickly faded when he realized there always came a time when notes came due and had to be paid. Ronnie silently wondered what the payment would be on this note and a cold shiver ran up his spine because he knew that for a ghost, the Professor had alot of freedom to do as he pleased. To Ronnie, that just meant the final cost would be enormous. That thought pretty much killed Ronnie's happy mood until he looked down at the check folded in his shirt pocket. At that moment he decided the Professor mattered only in his dreams and now with some money in his pocket, he was going to indulge in some dreams of his own.

When Margret picked him up that afternoon, after her day of riding around and wasting time, Ronnie told her he needed the car tomorrow. At first she protested, but he quickly reminded her he still needed to pay off some of her checks and she quickly shut her mouth. For the rest of the night, Margret was cold to him, only responding to his questions after he had asked them a couple of times, and then her voice would sound angry and hateful.

Ronnie was becoming annoyed with her attitude and decided she was digging her own grave. After the checks were paid off tomorrow, there wouldn't really be anything keeping him there. He would be free just to go and start his life all over again. But then he thought about Nancy and realized that she was the one thing that was keeping him there. He didn't want her to grow up without a mother, because he knew that if he ever did leave Margret, there was no way he could leave his daughter behind. He was scared what Margret would do to her if he wasn't around to be the brunt of her abuse and the focus would be shifted away from him and onto her because she would be a captive audience.

The next morning, when Ronnie went downstairs to go to work, he saw there was another stack of paper next to the computer. On top of the stack was the cover letter he had been waiting for, signifying that the book was complete. Ronnie opened the desk drawer, got out the stack of paper and added the new addition to it. Then he took the whole thing with him to work, where he spent most of the morning reading it. This book was as good as the last one and it was also good that Ronnie had been a disciple of Evelyn Woodhead during his college days (although 'daze' was a better description) and had learned her speed reading course. If he hadn't, it would have taken him at least three days to get through the new book. He knew that wouldn't do, when the Professor printed out the cover letter, it was time for the book to be put in the mail and shipped off.

At lunch time, Ronnie called up to the front office and told them he had some business to take care of and would be gone for a couple of hours. There were no objections and Ronnie headed for the bank. Instead of going to his new bank to cash the check, he went to the old one that was still holding some of Margret's checks. He was sitting in the office that he had been in before and found his old bank was more than happy to cash this monster paycheck for him, providing they got their cut off the top first.

When he was back in his car, he started going down the list of stores and was fortunate enough to get to the last one just before his two hours were up. He quickly paid for the checks and hurried back to work. On the way back he decided to stop by his new bank on his way home and deposit the rest of his money into his new account. That way, he wouldn't be walking around with a big wad of cash in his pocket.

So, after work, he stopped at his bank and put five thousand into his checking account. His next stop was at the post office and he mailed the new book off to the publisher. Ronnie found that after the book had been mailed, he felt as if a weight had been lifted from his shoulders. He didn't feel that way when he had single handedly wiped out Margret's debts that afternoon. He found it curious that he would feel relief from mailing the book, but no relief in paying off the checks.

When Ronnie got home, Margret was still in a bitchy mood. She told him one of the stores she had applied to had called for an interview that afternoon, but since he had the car, she didn't go and lost her chance for that job. Of course, she hadn't really gotten a call, that would have required actually putting in an application somewhere and she just wanted Ronnie to feel bad that he had caused her to miss her big break in life.

Ronnie just stood there looking at her without saying anything. When she finished her ranting, he looked her straight in the eye and replied, "Well, there's always tomorrow."

Margret opened her mouth to say something else smart and realized she was looking at the back of Ronnie's head because he had turned around and was walking away from her. That simple act was like throwing a lit match into a gasoline tank to see how full it is. She exploded and started telling him, at a very loud volume, about his ancestry. Then she moved on to speculation about how he could technically be a man without any testicles.

Ronnie was doing his best to keep his mouth closed and not provoke Margret more than she was. But on the third time she called him dickless, he stopped, turned around and looked at her for a second before he spoke.

"That may be so," He said in a quiet voice, "But I've seen what you call a man, remember? Let me see, if memory serves me right, he was the dip shit who left his brains laying around in the street out front."

Margret stood there silent with a look of shock on her face. She didn't know it, but Ronnie was standing there looking back at her with the same feeling of shock on his insides. He couldn't believe what he had just said to her. He remembered opening his mouth to make a retort and couldn't believe what had come out. But since he had said it and it shut her up, he decided to do the only decent thing he could think of. He remained silent and resumed his trip to the kitchen. All the while expecting her to attack him from the rear.

When he was safely in the kitchen without being pummeled from the rear, he snuck a peak around the corner and saw that Margret was no longer standing where she had been, she was now moving back towards the couch to sit back down. Ronnie genuinely felt bad about what he had said, it had come out so mean sounding and what was worse, he had never intended to say anything like that to her. He pondered whether it had been a Freudian slip as he turned his attention towards the stove and saw there was absolutely nothing being prepared for dinner. So he rummaged around in the freezer and found some food to cook. Using what he could find, he prepared a meal that even Margret commented on how good it was.

When Ronnie had said what he did about Ted to Margret, it had stopped her in her tracks. She supposed as she sat down, that she should be mad. But she wasn't, she felt herself withdraw and decided to sit down before she did something stupid. After all, Ronnie's time was coming and he would pay. She would make sure he would pay dearly with the only thing that, in her eyes, he held dear. His life. And he would pay that debt very slowly.

Margret sat very quietly looking in the direction of the television while Ronnie was in the kitchen banging pots and pans around. The whole time she sat there, she was fantasizing about different ways Ronnie could be killed. After awhile, the noise in the kitchen became less, until finally, Ronnie set the table and laid out the meal. He had found some old pot roast and had made a stir fry out of it. As she ate, Margret found it was very good. But it didn't change the fact that Ronnie wasn't very long for this world.

Later that night, Ronnie was going through the trash looking for a spoon he had accidentally dropped and found an overdue notice from the power company. The notice was written on paper with a red border around it. The notice explained that the account was three months behind and the power would be turned off if the bill wasn't settled in full by noon on Friday. At first, Ronnie wanted to storm into the living room and demand an explanation for what the hell was going on. But he managed to push his rage back down inside himself and dug deeper into the trash. He found another bill, this one from the gas company with a similar threat.

Ronnie found himself becoming madder, but managed to push his rage away, to contain it. He decided that tomorrow, he would call all of the people they owed money to and see how far this trend of not paying the bills went. He also decided that while he was at it, he would give all of them his new PO Box and have them send the bills there from now on. That way, he could make sure they were being paid.

Ronnie went back into the living room after fishing the missing spoon out of the garbage and without drawing attention to himself, started finding the telephone numbers to the couple of credit cards they had. When that was done, he sat down in his chair and decided he would let the utilities go until he was at work tomorrow. At work, in the solitude of his office, he would be able to make notes and phone calls without having to explain himself to Margret.

Not that there would be much of an explanation, Ronnie imagined as soon as she asked what he was doing and he told her he was checking on the bills that she was supposed to be paying, the fight would be on. Doing his calling from work tomorrow would go a long way to prevent the fight tonight.

That night, there were no real dreams to speak of. There was only a brief moment that Ronnie found himself standing in front of the Professor. He looked around and found that he was standing in the middle of nowhere. It was dark as far as he could see and the only light that there was, was the one illuminating him and the Professor. The Professor only said one thing to him, *I have more stories. I need more paper.*

Then Ronnie found himself in the middle of another forgettable dream that wouldn't be remembered the next morning. The only thing he did remember was the Professor's request for more paper.

92.

It was early in the day when Ronnie decided to start calling around to find out just how bad his finances really were. Had he any idea what he was about to find out, he would have just hung up the phone and stayed blissfully ignorant.

Ronnie called the power company first, talked to a customer service representative and found out that the shut-off notice was real. When he asked why they had let it go on for so long, he was informed it had been two months late when it was paid and the check had bounced. Ronnie felt that weight coming back on him and he explained that his wife had gone nuts and written a lot of bad checks around town. He also explained he now had his own checking account and was now trying to pick up the pieces. He further explained he would be into their office within the next two days to pay the bill in full.

Next, he called the gas company and got basically the same story. The water company was no different, but it was the telephone company that astonished him. The bill was only two months late, but it was over three hundred dollars. He never made long distance calls and couldn't understand who Margret had been calling. As far as he knew, she didn't know anyone who lived out of state.

The two credit cards were a different matter entirely. He was told in both cases the accounts had been closed after the cards had been maxed out and now the companies were considering legal action for non-payment. After a fair amount of pleading on his part, they reached an agreement and he would pay the accounts off in full within the next seventy-two hours. Ronnie wanted that time buffer in there because he knew there was no way he could afford to pay everything off without the three hundred from Aaron. He had done a quick calculation in his head and knew it would be close.

After he got off of the phone, Ronnie sat there adding up what all was owed and found that yes, it would take a large part of the money he was owed from his column to finish off his debts. Even the money he had from the book wouldn't be enough. He was sitting there in shock from the information he had just learned. This time though, the shock wasn't as bad as when he had learned about the checks the first time. Ronnie just felt like somebody was heaping some more load onto his back. As he sat there, he suddenly felt old and there was also the feeling he couldn't go on, that he had enough. Everywhere he turned, there was somebody hanging their hand out for money and it was all because of Margret. He sat there debating how long he was going to remain married to her when he noticed the guys coming in for lunch.

He walked out into the lunch area for a change of scenery and overheard a couple of guys remarking that they were going out for lunch because they had to go to the water company to pay their bills. Ronnie asked if he could tag along because he had to pay his bill also. There were no problems and he ran back into his office to get the sheet of paper he written the totals down on and to also get his checkbook. He walked out of his office folding the piece of paper and put it into his shirt pocket. Then they were off to the gas company.

When Ronnie got back to his office, there was a note on his telephone asking him to call the main office. He was scared when he did because he thought he was going to get in trouble for taking so long for lunch. Instead, he was shuffled around for a few moments before Grandma Moses got on the phone. In a soft voice, she told him she needed him to come to the front office because she needed to talk to him in private. After hanging up the phone, Ronnie shot over to the Club House as fast as his golf cart would take him.

When he got there, he was ushered right into her office. He stood there for a moment trying to decide what the problem was when she asked him to sit down. He sat for an uncomfortable few moments before she finally spoke. Ronnie noticed she looked as uncomfortable as he felt. She finally told him that Floyd had passed away that morning from complications from his pneumonia. Then her expression changed, and as if what she had just told him had been nothing, she congratulated him because he was now the new Superintendent. Ronnie barely heard that because he was shocked about the news about Floyd. All he could think of was how he was going to break the news to his crew.

Even after all of the things he had been through himself that morning, Ronnie's only thoughts were of Floyd and Floyd's wife. He looked up and saw Grandma Moses looking at him in a strange way. Ronnie realized she must have asked him a question and was now waiting for an answer. Judging from the look on her face, Ronnie realized she must have asked the question awhile back. He apologized saying the news about Floyd was a shock and he hadn't caught what she had said.

She smiled and commented it was perfectly natural, but she wanted to know how the grounds department was going to treat Floyd's death. Ronnie was confused and once again she smiled and asked him if he wanted to shut the whole department down for the day of the funeral, or just part of the day.

Ronnie thought about it and quickly decided they would take the whole day off for Floyd. After all, Floyd had been there long before anyone else had been, even the long timers said that Floyd had come with the course. Grandma smiled and told him it was a wise decision, the entire office staff had planned on doing the same. Ronnie was relieved when he heard that, he hated to think his first official decision about a day off would make management angry. But he decided when he told her of his decision that he would take it as far as he had to, to make sure there was a proper and fitting remembrance of Floyd's contribution to the club.

Grandma made it clear she was through with Ronnie and he left. He took his time going back to his office and when he was almost there, he decided to pass the word around the course of another meeting this afternoon. So he set sail in his golf cart for the greens and passed the word around about the meeting. He didn't tell his guys what the meeting was about, even though they asked. He fended them off by telling them he wanted to start a weekly meeting and left.

Ronnie spent the rest of the afternoon thinking about how short life really was and wondering if Floyd had passed his final test, or if he was going to have to spend another life in this reality. Ronnie decided from what he knew about Floyd's nature, there was no way he wouldn't have moved on to the next plain.

When he wasn't thinking about Floyd, he was wondering what drove a cold, dark hearted bitch like Margret to do the things she had done. Thinking about Margret made him feel depressed. How could she write all of those checks and not pay the bills either? What had she done with the money? Ronnie didn't know, but he did know that tonight, he was going to find out.

The men came in from the greens when they were supposed to. When they were all inside and the room grew quiet, Ronnie simply told them what he had to say.

"I called all of you in early this afternoon because I have an important announcement to make." There were several comments made in speculation of what the announcement was and Ronnie waited for the room to grow quiet again before he spoke. "This morning, Floyd Fritz passed away from complications of his pneumonia. We will be taking the day of his funeral off and everyone is encouraged to attend whatever service there is to honor him. I don't know when it will be, in fact, I don't have very many details other than Floyd is no longer with us."

No one said a word and Ronnie could feel his eyes beginning to moisten. Looking around the small room, he saw he wasn't the only one.

"Although attendance at the funeral is not mandatory," Ronnie continued when he felt he could go on without crying like a baby, "It would be a nice thing to do to show respect for the man that had the greatest positive influence in all of our lives."

When he finished saying that, he looked around and saw several of his guys were silently weeping. The depression in the room was catching and spreading like wildfire. Ronnie saw guys that never showed any type of emotion sitting there with watery eyes.

"That's all I have to say. If anyone has anything else to add, go ahead. If there's nothing else, then clock out and go home. There will be at least a days notice before the funeral. See you tomorrow."

The instant Ronnie was finished speaking, he turned around and walked straight back into his office, shutting the door behind him. Leaning against the back of the door, Ronnie put both of his hands to his eyes and found that not only were his eyes damp, but his cheeks were wet as well. He looked down and realized he must have cried more than he thought, because the front of his shirt was tear soaked.

It was at that moment Ronnie had the insight that he didn't know if he was crying because of Floyd or because of his own circumstances. It was with that awareness he stopped feeling depressed and got mad. Life was far too short to put up with what he had been putting up with. Hell, Ronnie thought to himself, it's too short for what I will have to put up with. That thought forced him to take a stand. That afternoon when he got home, it was all going to end. He didn't know what was going to happen, but he felt the whole situation with Margret was going to come to some sort of climax.

The death of Floyd served as a catalyst for his emotions. Even though he now had a better understanding of what really happens to a person after they die, he also now had a better understanding that walking around in the physical form was a hell of alot more fun. The old saying about life being too damn short was a very true and accurate one.

Ronnie found he no longer felt sad, or mad, or happy. He felt nothing. It was as if someone had found the switch on his emotions and flipped it off. He was beginning to see things around him in a sort of detached way. It wasn't like one of those mind out of body experiences or anything like that. He saw things through his own eyes and heard things through his own ears, but it was as if his brain was now processing information in a different format. Nothing really registered.

When Ronnie walked out of the building, there were several of his crew standing around outside the shack. He saw them standing there and saw they were talking amongst themselves.

The guys were standing around reminiscing about Floyd when Ronnie came out. They saw him lock the door just like he always did and turn around. Immediately, they saw Ronnie had a strange look to him. It wasn't that the mischievous smile he always wore on his face was gone, that was to be expected after the chain of events about Floyd. It was the fact that he had no emotions on his face. It was so blank that it was almost unsettling to look at him. Then he walked right by them without acknowledging they were even there. If the kid hadn't stepped out of Ronnie's way, Ronnie would have walked right over him as he walked by on his way to the parking lot.

All Ronnie would remember later was going outside, locking the door and seeing his guys standing there. He didn't remember the walk to the parking lot nor the guys moving out of his way. The next thing he remembered was standing out in the parking lot waiting for Margret to come and pick him up.

The guys just stood there looking at Ronnie as he passed by and then disappeared in the direction of the parking lot. They returned to their conversation with a remark that Ronnie was really taking Floyd's death in a rough way. Someone else commented it was understandable because Ronnie and Floyd had known each other for a long time and had been through a lot together. Then they each lapsed into their own stories about Floyd's heroic deeds and their own adventures with the man.

Margret was twenty minutes late picking Ronnie up. She wasn't sweating the fact that she was late. As far as she was concerned, the bastard could wait all night for her and she would get there when she damn well felt like it.

"There he is." Margret said to herself when she saw Ronnie standing on the other side of the parking lot, "The king of the dip-shits."

She noticed, with some ire, that he was standing on the other side of the parking lot and had not walked out to the street where she could pick him up and not have to drive all of the way into the parking lot.

When she pulled up to where he was, she actually said "Howdy king!" followed with an excuse she was late because of a job interview as he was getting into the car. But her voice trailed off amid the lie when she saw him seated next to her. She saw he looked different and had an air about him that was almost as thick as a concrete wall.

Margret took advantage of the silence and had driven almost halfway home before she couldn't stand it anymore and asked him what the problem was. Then she added that she hoped that he hadn't gotten fired because they needed the money. Ronnie just looked at her with blank eyes and said nothing. The way he appeared when he had looked at her was unnerving and Margret immediately stopped her end of the conversation. The only thought that crossed her mind was that somehow, he had been away from work and had seen her wasting time not looking for a job.

The only time Ronnie did speak was when they passed by a discount store. Ronnie asked her to stop because he wanted to get something. Normally, Margret would have ignored him and drove on by. But there was something in his voice, something almost not human and she obeyed immediately, pulling into the parking lot and parking the car.

As he got out of the car, Margret asked him if he wanted her to go in with him. But he didn't answer and just walked away and into the store. Margret was way past the point of being concerned and was now becoming scared, she had never seen him like this before. And she just knew that somehow, he had followed her around today and saw she hadn't been looking for a job. Why he had wanted to stop by the store, she didn't know, but she did know she felt safer by herself in the car. So she just sat there waiting for him to come out.

A few minutes later, Ronnie came out and Margret saw he was carrying a bag that looked like it was heavy. For an instant, she wondered if the state they lived in had a waiting period when you bought handguns. But when he got into the car, she saw he had bought three reams of paper and felt a wave of relief sweep over her.

She decided to take her chances and asked him once again if there was a problem. This time, he looked at her and told her in a voice that was devoid of all emotion, that Floyd had died this morning and he was now the Superintendent. For an instant, Margret was both relieved that it wasn't her that was on the hot seat, and extremely happy and told him so. She wasn't happy that Floyd had died, but she was happy that Ronnie had been promoted. The look he gave her silenced her once again. After a moment, Ronnie added there were other things and they would talk later. The rest of the trip home was made in silence.

When they got home, Ronnie went next door to get Nancy while Margret hurried into the kitchen and threw together a quick meal. They ate and most of the evening passed by without conversation.

After Nancy had gone to bed, Margret was coming back down the stairs and saw Ronnie sitting in his chair with a piece of paper in his hands. She didn't know it then, but the paper Ronnie was holding was his tally sheet of the bills he had gotten today. Margret came on down the stairs and sat on the couch facing him. A few minutes passed before Ronnie spoke.

"So...How was the job hunting today?" he asked her.

"It went well." She told him and decided she had better cover her inactivity during the day. "I only had a couple of applications to put in today. I called around earlier this morning and got specific times to be somewhere to put the application in and also get the interview. I'm tired of putting in applications and waiting for the call that never comes. Sorry I was late, the last interview went longer than I thought it would and time caught up with me."

"That's nice." Ronnie replied in an indifferent tone as if he hadn't been listening to her. "Guess what I found out today." He said as he fixed his gaze on her.

Margret was taken aback by Ronnie's attitude and falling into his trap, asked, "I dunno, what did you find out today?" She was beginning to feel uncomfortable under his stare.

"You haven't been paying the bills like a good little girl. Have you?"

Margret was flabbergasted. She could only sit there looking back at him feeling her cheeks flush to a dark crimson. All the while, her mind was going sixty miles an hour to come up with a good excuse for this new charge.

"In fact," Ronnie continued, "We were just a few days short of getting the power, water, telephone, and everything else around here turned off. Seems like there was a bunch of past due notices you ignored. Threw them away maybe, I don't know. I do know we were just a few days away from losing all of the comforts of home." The whole time he told her, his voice was flat and still void of emotion.

Margret still couldn't think of anything to say in her defense, so she slipped back into her old standby defense, she started crying. Now that the tears were flowing, she could think. The tears served as a shield for her to hide behind while she thought of a counter defense. She had used this one on Ronnie before and knew it was somewhat effective on him. It had always slowed him down enough for her to figure out a way to get the upper hand with him. She finally decided on her strategy.

While Margret was deep in thought, Ronnie was making a few observations of his own. The one he was currently dwelling on was how Margret could turn on the tears so quickly and easily.

"I'm so sorry Ronnie." She explained between sobs, "I know I'm a terrible person. I can explain...Please let me explain." She seemed to get herself under better control and continued, "When the checks got all messed up, some of the checks for the bills bounced. I thought I could get this under control before you found out."

"How in the hell did you think you could get it under control?" He yelled at her as he came partially out of his seat in her direction.

As Ronnie was coming out of the chair, Margret got a good look in his eyes and was instantly petrified with fear. She had never seen eyes that looked so cold and lifeless. In those eyes, she saw a man that could easily reach up and snap her neck, or, at the very least, crush her throat. In those eyes, she saw that then, he would just sit back down in his chair and watch her turn blue and flop around on the floor as she fought for breath. She felt relief when she saw Ronnie stop and settle back down in his chair. Along with the relief, she had no doubts about how close she had just come to dying.

"I thought," Margret said quickly to keep the conversation going. She knew more conversation equals less action, "that I would have a job by now and would be able to pay the bills and get them caught up. Honestly, I know how much stress you're under with your new job and the checks I wrote. I just didn't want to add to it with this."

Ronnie could see her point and she seemed to be telling the truth. It was a shame that he didn't know that he had just been played. Margret's ploy had taken some of the wind out of his sails, but he still told her this, "Margret, is there anything else I should know about? Because if there is, you had better tell me now. I don't know how much more of this I can take and I'm tired of being pushed."

"No Ronnie." Margret said as she stood up and walked over to where he was sitting. She got down on her knees in front of him as she continued speaking, "I promise there's nothing else."

"Good." Ronnie replied as she began to play with the zipper of his pants. "There had better not be anything else and you better get a job damn fast." He told her as she unzipped his pants, reached in and began to massage his cock to life.

"Trust me." Margret said as she slipped Ronnie's cock out of his pants and into her mouth. In a sudden burst of inspiration, Ronnie decided not to tell her he had taken care of the delinquent bills. He decided if he wasn't going to tell her about the checks, then he wasn't going to tell her about the bills. This was the last thought he had before a wave of sexual feelings swept over him. The rest of the night was a carnal playground.

93.

The funeral for Floyd was on Friday. It was held in a small church about ten miles from town. Everyone from work was there. Looking around, Ronnie decided the only people running the Country Club today were the new cooks and food servers. But as he looked around the church, he saw a lot of patrons from the club there also. All of the old time players were there and Ronnie noticed quite a few of the new faces he always saw playing on the course. So he decided business at the club was pretty slow today. Besides, the people from the country club weren't the only ones there. Ronnie was amazed at the amount of people attending he didn't recognize.

The church was small, but still good sized for its location. He figured it could easily hold a hundred people. But today, it was standing room only. Women dressed in black and elderly sat in the pews, while younger men lined the walls and part of the aisle in the rear of the church. There wasn't a dry eye in the house and halfway through the service, Ronnie found it hard to keep himself from crying also.

Ronnie learned from the Preachers eulogy that there was alot more to the man they were burying. On top of giving hopeless people a new chance on life, he had been deeply involved in the community and helping with troubled youth. Many times paying for a young person to go to a special camp or activity out of his own pocket, never giving a second thought as to repayment.

After the memorial service was over, the casket was wheeled out and the whole funeral was moved out to the cemetery behind the church. At the grave site, words were said and an Honor Guard of Boy Scouts played Taps as the casket was lowered into the ground.

Afterwards, Ronnie walked back to his car after giving Floyd's wife his condolences on her loss. On the trip to his car, Ronnie wondered what he would have to do to get to the level of greatness Floyd had achieved. During the service, Ronnie had noticed he was the only one there without a partner. Even the new kid from the shack had brought his girlfriend to the service. Margret had stayed home today saying she didn't want to go and face the people that she had worked with. After a heated discussion on the subject, it was agreed she could stay home while Ronnie went to the service.

Margret had been behaving herself since the showdown Ronnie had with her. She wasn't any closer to getting a job because she still wasn't looking for one. But Ronnie didn't know that, he only saw her leaving with the car after dropping him off in the mornings. At night, he would listen to stories from her about how she had went here and there putting in applications.

On the way home from the funeral, Ronnie took the opportunity to stop by the paper and get his weekly installment of money. After another quick stop at the bank, he went around and paid the utility bills off. Then he stopped by the department stores and paid the credit cards off. He should have been mad at Margret when he got home for not coming with him and supporting him, but he wasn't. Ronnie was in a good mood. He had found Margret a job.

While Ronnie had been talking to Aaron, he had mentioned that Margret was looking for a job, but was having no success. Aaron asked him what she was looking for and Ronnie told him anything that had a steady paycheck behind it. Aaron told him if she wanted to work fast food, he could pick up the phone and get her a job with one call. Ronnie was intrigued as to how Aaron could get her a job sight unseen.

Aaron smiled and explained he had a friend, a poker buddy, who was opening a fast food joint on Monday and was still hopelessly short on help. Besides, Aaron added, the man owed him money and a favor for not telling the guy's wife why he was owed money. Ronnie didn't ask, but assumed the debt was owed because of the before mentioned poker game.

Ronnie told Aaron if he could get her a job, then he would let Aaron print next weeks column for free. Aaron, being a man that couldn't pass up a chance to get something for free for the paper, was on the phone in less than a heartbeat. After five minutes of talking, Aaron hung up the phone and handed Ronnie a piece he had been writing on during the conversation. On the paper was an address and a time to be there tomorrow.

Ronnie thanked Aaron and told him next week was on him. He further explained he would have given the money back today, but he needed it for bills. Aaron just smiled and told Ronnie not to worry about it, just to make sure she was at the right place at the right time.

Although the day had been overshadowed by Floyd's funeral, Ronnie felt today was turning out to be a great day.

It was a shame Margret wouldn't share his view of life when he got home. In fact, it could easily be said that she was very unhappy with the joyful news of her new job.

When Ronnie arrived home, he was all smiles. Margret noticed he was in a very good mood for someone who had just come from a funeral. Margret was glad for the change, Ronnie had been acting like an asshole all week and she was tired of bending over and trying to kiss his backside to keep him happy. Little did she know of the bombshell he was fixing to drop on her.

"How was the funeral? Sure did last a long time." Margret said as she walked around the house trying to look busy.

"It was a very nice service, very touching. Too bad you couldn't be there with me."

"Now Ronnie. I thought we had that all settled before you left. Somebody had to stay home with Nancy." Margret replied in a caring, but condescending tone.

"Well...You sure did miss a nice thing." Ronnie replied non-combatantly and then added excitedly, "You'll never guess what I was able to do for you."

"You're right. Since you did it and I wasn't around to know what you did, it would be hard for me to guess what it was you did. So let's not waste any time and you just tell me what you did."

"Margret," Ronnie said as he took a step closer to her, "I know how difficult it's been for you, putting in applications all over town and nothing ever coming of them." Ronnie paused trying to build up some suspense.

Margret could see the excitement in his eyes. Maybe he's going to tell me to quit looking, she thought to herself. "Yes...So?" She asked trying to keep the hope out of her voice.

"Well...You can stop looking."

Oh joy of joys, she cried to herself, I knew if I waited long enough, I would be able to wait out his crazy idea that I needed a job. "Really?" She asked.

"Yep. Today, when I was picking up my money at the paper, Aaron told me about a friend of his that was trying to get help for a restaurant he's opening. I told Aaron you were looking for a job, he made a phone call and wa'la." Ronnie said as he pulled the piece of paper out of his pocket and handed it to Margret. "He got you a job. You need to be there tomorrow to meet your new boss and get trained." Ronnie saw her face freeze.

"Really? That's great." Margret said as she took the paper from him.

Ronnie could tell from her voice she thought otherwise. Her voice sounded strained and the expression never changed on her face. Then realization hit and he knew she had been expecting him to tell her to quit looking for a job. "Look Margret, if it was up to me, I'd say you could stay home as long as you like." Like Hell! Ronnie's inner voice said. "But with all of the bills we have, we can't make it without you helping also."

"Even with your new promotion?" She asked him, her eyes beginning to tear.

"My new promotion just means I can pay everything off quicker. We talked about this before, remember?" he felt a small pang of guilt about saying that. He felt he should have just told her about him paying everything off already. But with all of the things she had done to him, his inner child had decided it was time for her to dance.

"No. You talked about it. You never listened to what I had to say on the subject." Margret replied defensively, almost to the point of trying to start an argument.

But Ronnie wasn't going to bite on that hook. "Margret...Your little charade isn't going to work, but you are. I'm not going to get into an argument with you. This is an excellent opportunity for you to get in on the ground floor of a new business. With your experience at the club, I wouldn't be surprised if you make management real quick." Then Ronnie threw one extra bone on the pile. Later, he wouldn't remember why he did it, maybe it was to give her a slim thread of hope to hang on to. The instant he said it, the small pang of guilt he was feeling rolled over and became a large lump in the pit of his stomach. "Besides, if this book deal comes through, neither one of us will have to work very much longer."

Margret perked up when she heard that. "Do you really think it will come through? I mean the book, do you think it will come through?" She asked.

He didn't want her to know it was an already done deal, so he simply said, "It's really looking good."

That seemed to stop the feedback from Margret, who now believed there was now a silver lining to the cloud Ronnie had hung over her head. Watching her reaction about her new job, Ronnie decided when she had earned enough to cover the value of the checks, he would tell her she could quit her job. He also decided that he would sock the money she earned away and they would buy something elaborate with it. Hell, maybe he would just give her the money and tell her to go and have a good time with it. More likely though, he would give her the money and tell her to get the hell out of Nancy and his lives.

The next day, Margret went to her job interview and did everything she could not to get hired. She was rude and abrasive, in short, she was her normal self. But Mr. Richard MacGrewder (Everyone called him 'Big Dick,' he announced when he met Margret), was originally from New York and found something in her attitude that was familiar and he liked it. There was no way she was going to walk out of that fast food place without a job. Big Dick MacGrewder even offered her a buck fifty more than he was willing to go on her wages to get her to work for him. Begrudgingly, Margret agreed to work for him and spent the rest of the day learning how he wanted the job done.

Margret decided she would work for this guy, especially since the money was alot better than she would have found elsewhere. But if she found that the job cut into her personal life too much, she would simply quit and tell Ronnie she had gotten fired. Besides, Ronnie's book deal would come through soon and this whole discussion of her working would be academic. Ronnie had promised she would be able to quit.

But she didn't quit. Margret found her new job gave her alot more freedom than she could have had staying at home. Sure, the job sucked, like all jobs do, but after a couple of months Margret found she could tell Ronnie she had to go to work, then go out all evening and do as she pleased.

Big Dick gave Margret the freedom to set her schedule as she wanted it. So after the initial start up period, she just worked the lunch and dinner crowds. When she was really late coming home, she would just tell Ronnie she had worked over because they had been short handed.

When the second book hit the publisher, it was an instant success and Ronnie got another fifteen grand. Six months went by and Ronnie decided to call off the debt and tell Margret that all of the bills were paid. He did that partially because of the way she had been working without complaint and turning her checks over to him for the good of the family. Had she given him any grief, he probably wouldn't have done it. But she had been good and it was time for her reward. But she turned down his offer to quit saying her job made her feel more satisfied than she had felt in a long time. As a reward for her turn around in attitude, Ronnie took her car shopping so they wouldn't have to keep doing the car shuffle every day. And Ronnie could easily afford it now. Along with the fifteen grand he got from the up front money of his second book, the royalties were now starting to come in from his first book. Since the books were being published under a pen name, Margret had no idea just how popular they were becoming. Even though his checking account was by no means fat, it was getting well stuffed with the money that was now coming in on a weekly and monthly basis. It was a good thing Margret didn't know about the money, because if she had, she would have went through it like water through a colander.

The car shopping trip was almost a look back at the old days with Margret. Ronnie had taken her shopping with the intentions of buying her a nice used car. But she found a new car she just couldn't live without. Ronnie suggested she take another look back through the used lot and Margret almost pitched a fit in front of the salesman. But she caught herself in time and with a great deal of restraint, told Ronnie this was the only car for her. The car was nice and had very few options on it, plus the price wasn't that unreasonable. So he bought it for her, not knowing as he did so, he was giving her unlimited mobility.

Ronnie never really kept up with her work schedule, he was too absorbed with keeping the Country Clubs grass as green as he could get it, but the money she brought home seemed to be the right amount for the amount of time she said she was working. It might have helped if Ronnie had known how much Margret was making an hour, but she had lied about that to him right off from the start. He thought she was making minimum wage and had never considered her tips. Margret however, was keeping up with it and when her regular paycheck wouldn't cover the hours she had supposedly worked, she supplemented her checks with her tips.

For Ronnie, there were hardly any dreams anymore. The only time he saw the Professor was when he had forgotten to leave the nightly supply of paper.

417

R. H. Gosse

And those times were few and far between. The visits in dreamland were getting more and more violent. It was almost as if the nicer Margret got, the worse tempered the Professor got. After the last confrontation Ronnie had with the Professor, he made sure there were two reams of paper on the desk at all times.

During that last dream, the Professor had unloaded on Ronnie when Ronnie told him he had forgotten to get paper on the way home from work. The Professor went berserk, grabbed Ronnie by the throat and started lifting him off of the ground. The Professor's face turned beet red and spittle flew from his lips as he explained to Ronnie, in no uncertain terms, the reason he was being kept around was so the Professor could finish the work Ronnie and his meddling had interrupted.

As he dangled there in the Professor's grasp, Ronnie couldn't help but notice that as the saliva flying from the Professor's mouth touched his skin, he could feel more than hear the hiss from where the saliva burned into his skin like an acid. That pain was secondary to his inability to breath.

The Professor didn't seem to take any regard to Ronnie's predicament and continued to explain that if Ronnie didn't fly right, he would be 'taken care of' and the Professor would find somebody else to help him finish his work. Ronnie felt himself passing out from the lack of oxygen and the last image he saw was a close up view of the Professor's mouth.

To his horror, Ronnie saw the machete teeth were back.

Ronnie felt the same sinking feeling he had felt in the dream when he had fallen off of the boat and was drowning. This time when he opened his eyes, instead of being in another dream, he was in his own bed. It was morning and time to get up. His throat hurt like hell and he saw in the bathroom mirror he had a nice set of bruises around his neck. Fortunately for Ronnie, everyone at work mistook the bruises for a world class set of hickeys and the guys kidded him unmercifully about having a wild night of sex last night. Ronnie just let the rumor go because there was no way he could have countered it with the truth and sounded sane.

94.

Ronnie now knew the Professor was getting dangerous again and might have to be dealt with. Ronnie had a few dreams at the glen, but the Professor never showed. Ronnie never got the opportunity to try and shove him across the small stream.

Margret had come home the night after the dream where Ronnie's neck had gotten bruised, very late and half drunk from a party she had just come from. She saw the bruises on his neck and freaked out thinking she had done something to him during her sleep. So she was extra nice to him that night.

Another month passed by and now Margret was in danger of losing her job. She spent too few hours at work and the business was expanding. Big Dickhead (That's what Margret called MacGrewder behind his back) was demanding she spend more hours working instead of partying. Margret complied for a few days before slipping back into her old ways. Margret had better things on her agenda than work, she had met another guy and was busy being his party favor. To Margret, work was just an excuse to get out of the house.

A couple more weeks went by before MacGrewder reached his limit. He was getting big enough to expand his business and needed someone to supervise the waitresses. Other than himself and the cook, he knew Margret had been there the longest and was the most logical choice for the new position, but she was too unreliable. So he gave the position to another waitress that had started a couple of weeks after Margret.

When Margret found out the joyful news, she went ballistic and told MacGrewder that it was her job. He tried to explain as tactfully as he could that he needed somebody he could rely on and she literally blew up in his face. For a brief second, he thought she was going to attack him, but she didn't. She did however, follow him out of the kitchen area and call him 'Big Dickhead' to his face in front of a couple of customers. That's when it was his turn to go ballistic. He did everything but pick her up and throw her out of the front door. When he saw she wasn't going to leave and her mouth was getting more abusive, he grabbed her by the arm, pulled her to the front door and pushed her out. He told her to never return and told her, her final paycheck would be mailed to her at home. He then sent a waitress to gather Margret's things and carefully watched as her stuff was handed to her through the front door.

After getting her stuff, Margret stood in front of the restaurant for a couple of minutes shouting obscenities and flipping MacGrewder the bird through the front windows before she left.

Instead of going home, Margret went to her new boyfriend's house and partied until she was almost too drunk to stand up. She got home very late, much later than she had come home in the past from her job. Ronnie saw just how hammered Margret was the instant she walked through the front door. He started to tell her she should have called him and he would have come and got her instead of running the risk of getting busted driving drunk. She cut him short, got right in his face, telling him she was a big girl and she would do whatever she wanted to do. Then she promptly turned around and went upstairs to bed.

Ronnie stood there in a mild state of shock from her outburst, then he followed her up the stairs. When he got to the bedroom, he found the door locked. So he went downstairs and fell asleep on the couch. The next morning, Margret acted as if nothing had happened the night before. Ronnie only brought the subject up long enough to tell her he would rather have to get out of bed to come and get her than to have and go bail her out of jail for DWI. Margret glared at him and told him she would remember that next time.

Everyday for the next two weeks, Margret left as if she was going to work. Every night, she would come home later and later in various states of intoxication.

She did however, start to grow worried about her future. She knew soon, Ronnie was going to be expecting to see a paycheck. One that would never come because there wasn't a job to provide it. MacGrewder was true to his word and mailed her last paycheck the day after he had fired her and now that money was beginning to run out. Over the months, Margret had gone through all of the money she had gotten from writing the second batch of bad checks by always being the life of the party. Nothing was too good or too expensive for her 'friends' and now she was close to being broke.

Then one day while she was getting ready to go to 'work', she was going through Ronnie's desk drawers to see if he had any money squirreled away and found the original book of starter checks that Ronnie had gotten when he opened the new bank account. So that day when she left, Margret was going to a different sort of job, one she knew she was good at.

First, she went to the grocery store, bought some things and wrote her name in on the top of the check. The clerk took the check and never said a word. Then Margret stopped by the service desk on her way out of the store and cashed a check for a hundred dollars. It was too easy and since this was a different account number, no one tried to stop her. By the end of the day, she had written almost a thousand dollars worth of checks.

Once again, Margret was back in business.

Ronnie found out about Margret getting fired by accident. Fortunately for him, it was the same day she had embarked on her new/old career. He was sitting in Aaron's office getting his weekly installment when Aaron brought the subject up.

"Sorry to hear about your wife." Aaron said after giving Ronnie his money.

"What do you mean?" Ronnie asked. He had no idea what Aaron was talking about.

"About her getting fired awhile back. I know that must be a strain on the old budget."

Ronnie had never discussed his book deals with Aaron, so he didn't know Ronnie was sitting on top of a growing pile of money. "Yeah, it's been rough." Ronnie replied, stunned at the news. "How did you find out?" He asked, trying to be careful not to let the look on his face give away the fact he hadn't had the slightest idea Margret had been fired.

"I was playing poker with MacGrewder the other night and he told me."

"Well, I think we'll survive." Ronnie told him. "You know how these things work out sometimes. Some people just don't work out." He said, still as cool as a cucumber. Then he looked at his watch and said, "Hey, I gotta go. See you next week?"

"You bet. I'll be here." Aaron said as he watched Ronnie get up and head for the door.

Ronnie just barely made it outside of the building before his rage took over. He sat in his car for a good, long time because he was too mad to drive. When he finally got himself under control, he started the car and went straight home. There were no outward signs of how he felt, he was still raging inside with emotions, but anyone who would have seen him would have said Ronnie looked as if he was at peace with himself and the universe.

When he got home, Margret wasn't there. Ronnie went next door and Heather's mother told him Margret had left early in the day. Ronnie thanked her and gave her a hundred dollar bill. At first, she refused it saying Nancy wasn't a bother and she really enjoyed watching her. Ronnie insisted and told her they were at the end of their money troubles for the time being and it was time that she got paid for her troubles.

Again, she protested being paid and Ronnie looked her straight in the eye and told her she was going to keep the money one way or another. This time she took the bill without saying a word. There was something in his eyes she saw. She didn't know what it was, but the look definitely wasn't the normal run of the mill Ronnie. She could see that he looked deeply troubled. Then she realized he had the look of a man that had finally run out of rope and didn't know where else he could go. She had recognized the look of hopelessness.

She got Nancy for him and he thanked her as he took Nancy from her. She watched him start to leave and saw him stop at the top of the steps leading off of the porch.

"If something happened to me and Margret, would you be interested in keeping Nancy?" He asked as he turned back to face her.

"Whatever do you mean by that?" She asked, suddenly afraid Ronnie was going to do something drastic.

"I was thinking...You see, Margret and I have no family Nancy could go to if something were to happen to us. I couldn't stand to think she would end up in an orphanage. She seems really happy with you guys and you seem to be happy with her..." Ronnie's voice trailed off into nothingness.

"Why, of course we would be happy to take care of her!" Heather's mother cried out, "I couldn't bear to think of her going anywhere else." She was greatly relieved her fears were unfounded.

"Thank you." Ronnie said and Heather's mother could see his eyes were tearing up. "I'll see to it there is a will made out that names you guys as benefactors." With that said, Ronnie left.

Heather's mother watched Ronnie as he walked across the yard with Nancy. Even though his explanation about Nancy's fate seemed normal on the outside, she was still worried something bad was going to happen next door. Later, her husband asked her why she felt that way and she told him she didn't know why, it was just female intuition. He told her she was watching too much television.

95.

Margret got home around midnight, so drunk she couldn't open the front door. How she ever navigated the car home without decorating a few trees or lamp posts will remain one of man's greatest mysteries. Here she stood in all of her glory at the front door, instead of knocking, she stood out on the front porch shrieking for Ronnie to 'Quit fucking around and open the Goddamn door!' Which, after a few minutes of listening to her bellow and now hearing the neighborhood dogs beginning to bark, he did.

She just made it to the couch before collapsing, the whole time telling Ronnie what a piece of shit he was. Ronnie just stood there at the front door listening to what she had to say. Waiting for her to get it all out of her system before he confronted her about the job. Her tirade didn't last very long, when she landed on the couch she started passing out.

Ronnie didn't know she was passing out as he closed the door and walked back into the living room. All he knew was she was quiet and he saw that her eyes were closed. He asked her if she was finished and in her semi-conscious state she mumbled she was. So Ronnie asked how her job was and not giving her a chance to answer (which she couldn't because she was now officially out), told her he knew she had been fired. Then he asked where the hell she had been going to everyday. His question was answered by a sloppy sounding snore.

That snore was like throwing a match into a can of gasoline. The rage within him built so fast it over came him and he couldn't control it. The next thing he realized, he was standing there with both shoulders of Margret's shirt were bunched up in his hands and had lifted her up off of the couch by the shirt. He was standing there shaking her, her feet dangling a couple of inches off of the floor. The looseness of her muscles under the influence of the alcohol let her head bob around on her neck like one of those toy dogs you sometimes see in the back of car windows. The fact that she wasn't awake to enjoy this new side of Ronnie only made him madder. A few long seconds passed before the fact he was getting nowhere with her sunk into his brain. Enraged, Ronnie threw her back onto the couch.

Then, as he stood there looking down at her, he felt ashamed for what he had just been reduced to and had done. He had acted like her, using force to express his anger. So Ronnie lifted Margret's feet onto the couch as he took off her shoes and then he arranged her into a more comfortable laying position. The whole time, Margret continued to snore away. The whole thing was too much for Ronnie to bear, so he went upstairs and went to bed, knowing he had to go to work in the morning and they would settle this whole matter tomorrow when he got home.

96.

When Ronnie opened his dream eyes, he found himself laying on the stainless steel examination table he had been on before. This time, instead of the room being brightly lit, everything was dark. He strained his neck around to look up through the massive skylights and saw that the sky was dark and overcast. He started to get up off of the table and found himself strapped to it and unable to move. So he decided not to fight it and just laid there waiting to see what was going to happen next. He didn't have to wait long.

Off in the distance, somewhere deep inside the massive building, Ronnie could hear someone whistling a tune. Listening to the tune as he lay strapped to the table, Ronnie quickly recognized the person who was whistling was either the worlds worst whistler, or was just whistling aimlessly. Either way, Ronnie could tell it was getting closer. Just as he was beginning to feel frustrated he couldn't move, over the top of his feet he saw the Professor come walking around the corner.

Well...Here you are again. The Professor said without giving Ronnie a chance to say anything first.

'Howdy to you.' Ronnie replied, 'I didn't call you, I was asleep, you called me. Let me up off this table and tell me what you want.'

Yes...You're right, I did call you here. The Professor answered, *And I'll let you up when I want to.*

Ronnie took a good look at the Professor and saw in the eyes and sadistic grin looking back at him that the older, more evil Professor was back. 'Look, quit playing games and let me up.' Ronnie tried to say forcefully, but what came out sounded more like he was pleading.

Do you realize how much work I've got to get finished? And here you are interrupting me. The Professor said as he turned away from Ronnie and walked over to a table about four feet away.

'Okay, you're a busy man and you're not going to let me up. What do you need from me?'

Cooperation. Was the Professor's only reply as he picked up a rusty looking meat cleaver off of the table and held it close to his face, carefully inspecting the edge of the blade.

'Hey, I make sure there's paper there for you every day. Is there something else you need?' Ronnie asked, looking at the cleaver in the Professor's hand as intently as the Professor seemed to be.

Yes, you do. You're a very good boy. The Professor said as he walked back over to the table Ronnie was on. *But you left that bitch wife of yours down stairs and I can't get any work done.*

'Fuck her!' Ronnie snapped back, 'She's passed out drunk, she won't bother you. Besides, I'm not getting up to carry her ass upstairs.'

The Professor's face turned crimson and he leaned very close to Ronnie's face. Ronnie could see the little machete teeth in the Professor's mouth and smell the toxic breath coming from behind those teeth. *Look asshole,* The Professor said really sounding mad, *It's hard enough to work when your dead ass is with me. I cannot work when someone else is there.*

'Sor-ry.' Ronnie replied.

The instant Ronnie said that, the Professor stood up straight and grabbed Ronnie's right hand. He pulled Ronnie's arm out as far as the restraints would allow and with a quick motion, raised the cleaver above his head and brought it down in a sweep. Ronnie felt a thump just above his wrist and didn't comprehend that anything had happened until the Professor, with a post orgasmic grin on his face, raised Ronnie's severed right hand into the air.

It was at that millisecond Ronnie felt the blinding, white hot pain and what had happened registered in his mind. Ronnie's howl of pain was deafening.

Quit crying, you big baby. You haven't lost anything. Your hand is right here. The Professor said tauntingly as he tossed Ronnie's still warm, still bleeding hand onto Ronnie's chest.

Ronnie looked down at his hand and then tried to look down where his hand should have been. He couldn't see the stump, but he could see the spurts of blood that was beginning to soak the sheet that was covering his legs. In his pain confused state, Ronnie never thought to simply pull his arm free of the restraint, which now without the obstacle of his hand to obstruct his arms progress, would have slid easily out of the restraint. Each spurt of blood was shooting from the force of Ronnie's own heart beat. Ronnie could feel shock starting to set in and his vision began to tunnel, the world he was in was beginning to fade away.

The instant the room Ronnie was lying in faded away, he found himself standing up in darkness. He looked down, and he thought he was still having tunnel vision. Then he realized the ground was far below him. He began to lose his balance and fall forward, unable to stop himself. Instantly, he felt a slap on his back and his forward and downward motion halted.

Ronnie looked over his shoulder behind him and saw the Professor standing there holding the back of his shirt. Ronnie righted himself and stood up straight, regaining his balance. He also realized his hand had stopped hurting and raised his right arm, afraid to look at the damage that had been inflicted there. To his relief, he saw his arm and hand were intact. Although, his hand felt numb from the wrist down.

Sorry about that. The Professor said nonchalantly. *It was getting pretty intense back there and I decided it might be nice to get a little fresh air. Hope you don't mind.*

Ronnie recognized he was back on top of the interstate overpass support. He felt his rage rise within him and he said, 'Not at all.' in a calm voice. As he said that, without thinking he took a half step backwards, placed his hand in the middle of the Professor's back and gave him the hardest shove that he could.

The Professor, not expecting this, was immediately propelled forward and fell over the edge of the concrete beam they were standing on.

Ronnie took a step forward and watched with fascination as the Professor fell, arms cartwheeling all the way down to the ground below. The Professor hit the ground and actually splattered like an over ripe tomato hitting a wall after being thrown really hard. Ronnie felt more satisfaction at looking at the splat the Professor had just made than anything else he could ever remember.

Ronnie was startled from his warm fuzzy thoughts by a voice from behind him, *I give it a four on form, but I give it a ten on splat-ability.*

Ronnie turned and saw the Professor standing there, now looking down to where his body was supposed to be lying. Ronnie could feel himself go white as the blood drained out of his body in fear.

Calm down little buddy. The Professor said. *I suppose I deserved that, I was being somewhat of a shit earlier. But Ronnie, really, how do you think you're going to kill me a second time?*

'Too bad we're not at the creek right now, I'd show you how.'

Now it was the Professor's turn to feel fear and he covered it by saying, *Yes, I would suppose you would consider that death. But you wouldn't be killing me, you'd just be sending me on to my destiny.*

'Whatever it would be, I wouldn't have to put up with your bullshit anymore. You'd be gone and I'd be free.' Ronnie said with a great deal of sarcasm in his voice.

Ronnie, The Professor said with a slight chuckle to his voice, *You'll never be free as long as you're married to that harpy you call your bitch...Excuse me, I mean wife. She plays you for a fool, and you know it. You think I'm the one tying you down and making your life hell. Look in your own backyard first.*

Ronnie had no reply because he knew the truth when he heard it.

The ball's in your court big guy. What call are you going to make? The Professor inquired.

After thinking for a second, Ronnie replied, 'There is no call. I'll deal with Margret in my own way. In the meantime, why are we here?'

You like the Glen and the High Place, as you call them, so much. Well, I like it here and I demand equal time.

'I thought your favorite place was the liquor store.'

Well, yeah, it is. But you have to have variety to be a well rounded person. Besides, you have a couple of different places. Three, if you count your little fishing trip. So quit bitching and enjoy the scenery.

'Okay. But are we going to have to watch the car crash again?'

Hey boy...You don't go to the theater and not stay for the show. Of course we're going to watch the car crash. The Professor said. Then he stopped and put his hand up to his ear in a mockery of trying to listen for something in the distance. *In fact, here it comes now.*

Ronnie looked up the road and saw the all too familiar pair of headlights making their way in his direction. He stood there silently and watched them grow closer until the car could finally be seen. He continued to watch as the car went up and off the ramp, flip over in the island and come to rest on it's roof after doing it's back bumper handstand. A few seconds later, as he knew it would, the battery did its slow fall out of the crushed engine compartment and touched off the fatal spark. The warm concussion from the explosion pushed against him as a soft breeze and he felt the pressure change in his ears. He could hear the glass cracking in the intense heat and then there was a small muffled explosion inside the car.

'Satisfied?' Ronnie asked after the first car stopped a couple of seconds after the crash and explosion.

Hell yes! The Professor cried exuberantly. *Gives me a boner every time I see it!*

'Great, glad to know that. Now that you're in such a happy mood, tell me why I'm here.'

Why is anybody here? That's the one question no one really knows the answer to. The Professor replied in a more than obviously playful mood.

'You know what I mean, smart ass. What was so important you had to drag me here, assault me, insult me, and make me watch that damn car blow up again?' Ronnie replied in a less than playful mood. The ire dripping from the words he said.

The Professor looked at Ronnie for a long moment before exclaiming, *You really are a stick in the mud, aren't you? I have never seen a man go to such extremes not to have fun.*

'Extremes?' Ronnie shouted, 'You're the one who chopped MY hand off. Remember?'

Yes, that's true. But I put it back. Besides, we're even, you pushed me off. The Professor said as he pointed down towards the ground. *See?* He said.

Ronnie looked down and saw the splat the Professor had made earlier. 'Okay, we're even. What do you want?'

If that's the attitude you're going to take, then I won't tell you Margret's writing bad checks again. Oops, there I go spilling the beans again.

Ronnie was stunned, 'What did you say?' Was all that he managed to croak out.

I really hate to tell you this little buddy, seems like I'm always the one that brings the bad news. The Professor said and then drew in a deep breath, exhaling he said, *God that's so much fun.*

After a couple of moments of silence Ronnie said, 'You were saying something about Margret and checks.'

Oh yes. The Professor answered, *I seem to get sidetracked so easily. Anyway, Margret found your starter checks and took them. I can only imagine what she's been up to.*

That bit of startling news set Ronnie off into a fit of profanity. He was cussing and pacing back and forth on top of the narrow space they were on. During his ranting and raving, discussing Margret's lineage, without seeing he almost stepped off of the beam several times.

When Ronnie was finally running out of steam, the Professor said, *Hey there big boy, you better watch where you step. It's a long way down.*

Ronnie stopped his pacing, looked at the Professor and asked, 'What?'

You almost stepped off a couple of times. You wouldn't want to do that.

'Didn't seem to hurt you none.'

I'll let that bit of stupidity pass. Let's just say it's a lot harder to kill me than it is for you to fuck up and kill yourself.

'Has she written any checks yet?' Ronnie asked.

What am I? The all knowing oracle?

'Cut through the bullshit.' Ronnie demanded, 'Has she written any checks yet?'

I'll only tell you because I like you. Yes, about a grands worth.

'Oh shit!' Ronnie said and then was off on another rant. This time, he did so without pacing.

Once again, the Professor waited until Ronnie was done before saying, *That's not really the reason I called you here tonight.*

'What? What other jolly news do you have?' Ronnie asked, his voice loud with the rage he was feeling about Margret.

Nothing serious, really. You know that little trick I can do to the TV?

'What about it?'

I've improved it. Now, I can change the channel on the television next door. I've also found I can change the channels on a digital radio also.

'Well, ain't that a hoot!' Ronnie said, clearly mocking the Professor. 'You call me here, put me through hell, tell me Margret's writing checks again, just because you wanted to tell me you can fuck with other people's TV's. That just makes my day. I really want you to know that.'

The Professor, his more than usual jolly nature now strained from Ronnie yelling at him, glared at Ronnie and simply said flatly, *Sometimes you get what you deserve, asshole.*

Without another word, the Professor turned, stepped over to the edge of the beam and stepped off. Ronnie watched him disappear and stepped over to the edge himself. He watched as the Professor dropped and then landed on the ground. He saw the Professor's landing looked as if he had done nothing more than step off of a curb.

Ronnie almost followed the Professor. Just before he took the long step, he remembered the Professor's warning about falling off. So he just stood there, contented to watch the Professor stroll towards the burning car. Ronnie looked at the burning car and realized this was the first time he had been there so long after the wreck. He looked around and saw there were now at least a dozen cars stopped on both sides of the interstate. There were a couple of people now at the burning car and looking carefully, he could see that a couple of guys were holding fire extinguishers. They were squirting the undercarriage of the car in a feeble attempt to control the intensity the gasoline was burning.

Ronnie could see the small extinguishers were no match for the inferno and looking around, saw there were a couple of other men standing there with extinguishers in their hands. He supposed since they were not helping, they must have exhausted their extinguishers earlier. As he watched, he began to feel irritated the Professor had left him standing by himself up there. He looked around for the Professor and saw he had joined the crowd of people that were beginning to accumulate around the flaming wreck.

When the Professor had stepped off of the concrete beam, he did so because he was afraid he would do something stupid and actually kill Ronnie. He decided it would be better to just get away from Ronnie. Besides, he was missing the best part of the festivities. There was a bitch roast going on and he wanted to be there. He just hoped he wasn't too late to savor the snap and popping sounds of fat and muscle burning off of the bone. There would be a smell also, almost indistinguishable from the burning smell of gasoline, rubber, and plastic. He knew that the men standing around would not notice it, but he would. He knew what to look for and would look for it. It would be a fleeting smell just a tad tangier than hair burning with a slight hint of pork. It was the savory smell of a person burning to almost carbon.

As glad as that would have usually made him, the last part of this meeting with Ronnie was bothering him. How could he have missed that Ronnie was fixing to push him off? Normally, he would have read Ronnie's thoughts and would have reacted to the threat. Oh, he might have hurt Ronnie a little in the process, but Ronnie would have been put in his place and be alot more submissive than he had been. Then he smiled, content in the knowledge that Ronnie wouldn't be going anywhere until he, the Professor, decided Ronnie could go.

As the Professor walked around the wreck to get downwind of the smoke, he suddenly realized he had forgotten to tell Ronnie one of the reasons, the main reason, the Professor had brought him there. So after he got his little whiff of heaven, he decided to have some more fun with Ronnie.

Ronnie had watched (because he had no other choice) the Professor walk around to the other side of the burning car and disappear into the smoke. He was beginning to feel a little more than just irritation. He disliked the spectacle going on before him and wished he was either in the glen or the high place. Any place but here. Ronnie turned around and was startled by the Professor standing right behind him.

Ronnie lost his footing and began to fall backwards, cartwheeling his arms in a vain attempt to regain his balance. There was a critical moment when Ronnie thought he was going to over come gravity, but he found he didn't have enough of a footing or the strength in his legs to magically right himself. He watched in horror as the Professor just stood there and didn't make any move to grab him. The milliseconds ticked away like days be fore Ronnie surmised he had lost the war against gravity and began to fall further and further back.

At the very last possible moment, the Professor's hand shot out and grabbed the front of Ronnie's shirt. Ronnie's rearward movement stopped and he just stayed there, his feet straight out against the edge of the beam and nothing between him and the ground but the Professor's hand holding his now stretched shirt.

I forgot to tell you something. The Professor said nonchalantly with no sound of strain in his voice from holding onto Ronnie.

'Pull me up God dammit!' Ronnie yelled.

I forgot to tell you I need some diskettes. The Professor continued.

'What? PULL ME UP!' Ronnie shouted, now sounding near panic.

You know, computer storage disks. Five and a quarter inch and a bunch of them. The Professor said, not paying attention to Ronnie's demands.

Ronnie tried to grab ahold of the Professor's arms but the Professor just extended his reach out another quarter of an inch, throwing Ronnie that much further off balance. 'Bastard!' Ronnie shouted.

Seems like I've been working faster than my ability to print. I've got two more books done and I want to save them on disk until I can print them.

'Okay-Okay, I'll get you the disks. Please pull me back up.' Ronnie begged.

You make sure I get them tomorrow night.

'I will, I will. I promise. Please pull me up, please.'

The Professor looked at Ronnie for a long second and said, *Not this time Bucky.* Then he let go of Ronnie's shirt.

431

Ronnie had a sick feeling in the pit of his stomach as he resumed his backwards journey down. He felt his heart speed up and it felt as though it was going to burst out of his chest. Ronnie braced himself for the sudden stop that was to come. The instant that he felt himself hit the ground, he woke up with a start.

He found himself sitting bolt upright in his bed with his heart pounding in his chest. Then he noticed the sheets and him were soaking wet. Ronnie thought for a moment he had wet the bed, but the fullness of his bladder convinced him the moisture was only sweat.

Ronnie sat in bed for a few minutes trying to regain his composure before going to the bathroom to take care of his needs. As he sat there, he thought about what a bastard the Professor was for dropping him like that. Now, in his awakened state, Ronnie found his right hand was still numb, as numb as it had been in his dream. Now he felt a slight tingling sensation in a line around and slightly above his wrist. He looked over at the clock and saw that even though it was still early, it was almost time to go to work.

Then Ronnie remembered he had a bigger bastard downstairs and he hoped she was still asleep so he wouldn't have to deal with her before he left. As he brushed his teeth, which wasn't so easy with his right hand still totally numb, he decided sneaking out of the house without confronting her was ridiculous. His dream had woken him almost an hour earlier than he normally would have been up, so he decided he would go downstairs and start Margret's day off right. He took a quick shower, got dressed, and went downstairs.

Margret was still on the couch, pretty much in the same position Ronnie had left her in. She was still snoring loudly. Big old wet, sloppy snores. Ronnie tried to wake her for a couple of minutes, but was only successful in making her roll over.

Frustrated in his inability to wake Margret up, Ronnie went and made himself breakfast. Then he sat down at his computer desk while he ate it. He went through the desk drawer his starter checks had been hidden in. After rummaging around for a couple of minutes, he couldn't find them where he had hid them.

When Ronnie had finished with his meal, he went and got Margret's purse. He took it to the center of the living room floor and dumped the entire contents onto the floor. There, lying on top of the pile of stuff, was his book of starter checks. Ronnie picked the book up and saw most of the checks were missing. He could see the impression of the last check she had written in the top check of the book. Although it was hard to read, he could tell that the amount she had written out had been a long one.

Ronnie got mad and stood up, leaving the contents of Margret's purse lying on the floor. This time when he tried to wake her, he wasn't as gentle as the first time. Still, he couldn't wake her.

Frustrated in his inability to rouse his wife, Ronnie left the house heading for work, slamming the door as he left. He stood on the porch for a minute as he looked at Margret's car. That car meant mobility for Margret and at that moment, mobility was the last thing he wanted her to have. After careful thought, Ronnie went to her car and opened the door. He decided he would pull the wire on the distributer cap to disable the car. He knew by doing that, the car would be reduced to nothing more than a paperweight with wheels and he just hoped Margret would call him at work for a ride to her supposed job. Then he would come home early and the fight would be on. Ronnie found the hood release and pulled it.

He walked back around and opened the hood, looking at the engine to locate the correct wire. But the engine was a new type with a full electronic ignition. He couldn't find the distributer cap although he did see the spark plug wires. Remembering his dream, he realized that Margret's car had the same type of engine compartment the car that crashed had. So he went to his car, got a pair of pliers and disconnected one of the battery cables.

There, Ronnie thought to himself, that ought to keep the bitch at home. Satisfied she wouldn't be going anywhere today, Ronnie went to work.

97.

It was a little after ten-thirty when Margret finally woke up. The first thing she heard was Nancy crying upstairs, the second thing she heard was the pounding in her head. Her mouth was dry and her headache was apocalyptic. She couldn't remember how much she had to drink last night, in fact, she could just barely remember driving home. But she knew from the size of her hangover she had either drunk some really cheap booze, or drunk just way too much of the moderately priced stuff.

Nancy was crying louder now, doing like all little kids do, cry for a few seconds and then stop and listen to see if anyone was responding to her cries. When she didn't hear anything, she would cry again, this time louder. Now her cries were so loud they almost sounded like screams. The sound was going into Margret's ears and straight to her toenails, making them feel as if they wanted to peel off of her toes just to get away from all of the pain and misery Margret was going through.

"I hear you God dammit! I'll be there in a fucking second." Margret screamed and was instantly sorry she had even opened her mouth. The wave of nausea was overwhelming and it was all Margret could do to keep from vomiting.

Nancy, hearing Margret yell at her, was silent for a couple of minutes while she waited for Margret to come to her room. But when she saw Margret wasn't showing up, she resumed her crying at a decibel louder than she had been before she had stopped to listen.

Margret tried to stand up, but quickly found that her head was too far away from the floor. She quickly dropped to her knees and waited for the room to stop spinning. When it finally did, she crawled over to the stairs and started up. The whole time she had been awake in the living room, she didn't see the contents of her purse spread out on the floor.

98.

Ronnie's morning was slow. He got his paperwork done quickly and found himself waiting until nine for the banks to open. His intention was to call the bank, tell them what had happened and ask them to please hold the checks until he could get there to pick them up. He didn't know what he was going to do with them, maybe take them home and throw them in Margret's face, but he wanted them just the same.

When nine finally rolled around, he waited for a few more minutes before making his call. He explained what had happened and the lady on the other end, once she saw Ronnie's huge balance, was more than helpful. She told him she would mark his account and as soon as the checks started arriving, they would be pulled and he would be called. Then they would wait until he came down to either okay the checks or press charges for theft. Ronnie felt much better when he got off of the phone. The offer of pressing charges sounded like a nice idea, but he doubted he would let it go that far. More than likely, he would get the names of the places the checks had been written to, the amounts, and then okay them to be paid from the account. Then he would deal with Margret later.

Just before lunch time, Ronnie took a ride around the golf course to see how everything was going. As he neared the middle of the first nine holes, he saw an old man carrying his golf bag. Ronnie recognized the man as the judge he had written about in one of his earlier Gabby columns. He also saw the judge looked very hot and tired. Ronnie pulled along side the judge and asked him if he was headed for the Clubhouse. The judge replied saying he was going that way because he was having a rotten day and decided to call it quits. He further explained that it was just too damn hot to play golf.

Ronnie agreed it was a hot one indeed and then asked the judge if he wanted a ride. The judge, a wise man, told Ronnie it sounded like the thing to do as he put his clubs in the caddy on the back of the cart.

Since the Clubhouse was a good ways away, Ronnie was able to strike up a pretty good conversation. Soon, both of them were laughing over a very crude joke the judge told. Now Ronnie was feeling comfortable in the presence of the judge, he asked the judge how he could go about writing up something to ensure his daughter would be taken care of in the event something happened to his wife and him. The judge thought for a minute and replied for the price of lunch, the judge would write something up for him then and there that would be just as binding and as good as any will that a high priced lawyer could do. Ronnie agreed and asked the judge if he minded stopping by his office first and writing the necessary document. There were no objections and the deal was struck. So Ronnie changed course and headed for the shack.

When they got there, Ronnie let the judge have his desk while Ronnie sat in the other chair answering the questions the judge asked every now and then. Ten minutes later the document was done and the judge asked Ronnie if he could get three witnesses. Ronnie replied it wasn't a problem and then went out to the break room where some of the crew was beginning to gather to eat their lunches. Within a minute, he had the correct amount of bodies and went back into the office. Everyone signed where the judge had hand drawn the spaces for them to sign. Now that everything was in order, Ronnie took the judge to the Clubhouse to fulfill his part of the agreement.

99.

Margret managed to make it to the top of the stairs before her need to vomit became overwhelming. She managed to stand for the last ten feet as she bolted for the bathroom. Just making it in time to toss her cookies into the sink. Since she had been on a liquid diet last night, there was no food in her stomach to throw up, so the bulk of her vomit was liquid. When she finished throwing up, she felt a lot better, but still not up to human standards.

Margret got Nancy out of her room and almost vomited again when the smell of the over ripe diaper assaulted her nose. She took Nancy into the bathroom and after stripping her bare, gave her a bath. After the bath was over, Margret got Nancy dressed and took her back downstairs to feed her before getting her ready to go next door.

When Margret reached the bottom step and turned to go into the living room, she froze. She saw the contents of her purse for the first time. Margret felt a hot flush creep over her as she went to where her stuff was lying and started putting it back into purse. Immediately she saw the only thing that was missing was Ronnie's book of starter checks. The flush deepened and she felt a sweat break out on her arms and forehead. A slight wave of nausea swept over her again and she began to quickly stuff all of her junk back into her purse. The nausea quickly passed leaving fear in its wake.

She knew that up until now, Ronnie was too much of a wimp to really do anything to her. But now he had found his checkbook in her purse, there was no telling what he would do to her in retaliation. She knew he wasn't stupid enough (just barely) not to notice that some of the checks were missing.

Now, with her hangover forgotten, the knowledge she had gained about the missing checkbook lit a fire under her. Margret quickly fed Nancy, gathered up the things Nancy would need for the day and took her next door.

Margret got the usual cold shoulder when she dropped Nancy off next door. Usually Margret didn't notice, or pretended not to notice the way Heather's parents treated her. Today was no exception, she walked away pretending she hadn't noticed the way Nancy had been quickly taken away from her, she didn't notice the way the door had a little extra force behind it as it had closed in her face. The pretense was for public view only. As she walked away today, it was different. Today, she hadn't been so self absorbed in what she was going to do that she could ignore the things she had just noticed. She began to wonder if Ronnie hadn't stopped by earlier that morning and told them about finding his checkbook in her purse. She told herself to stop being silly, Ronnie hadn't stopped by their house. Ronnie always left for work right after the sun came up and that was too early to go visiting. That rationalization seemed to appease her, but the doubt was still there.

As Margret walked to her car, she realized she didn't know where she was going to go. All she knew was that she had to get away. Anywhere. By leaving, she would leave all of her troubles behind her and that was a good thing, even if it was just for a few hours.

When she got into her car, Margret didn't notice the dome light didn't come on. She quickly jammed the keys into the ignition and tried to start the car. Nothing happened. She tried to start the car again and was still met with the silence only an ignition system with absolutely no power could provide. She pulled the keys out of the ignition and stuck them back in again, almost as if she was thinking she had put it in wrong the first time. Still nothing. Frustrated, she ripped the keys out of the ignition in a cloud of profanity.

Her profanity continued as she stuck the keys into the ignition for the third time. It was as if she was chanting to provoke the God of Mechanical Things with her verbal offering. If her intensity was an indicator and the profanity was a chant that would have worked, everybody on the block would have had their cars start when Margret turned those keys again. But it wasn't to be. Nobody's car started, especially Margret's.

She pulled the keys out and just sat there looking at them in her hand. Ronnie did this, she thought, he did something to the car to trap me here. He found out about the checkbook and he wanted to make sure she stayed there until he came home.

Margret got out of the car and went into the house. The fear of what Ronnie was going to do to her ran unchecked through her mind. Her thoughts were an absolute blur. Then it dawned on her she couldn't be at home and still leave Nancy next door without raising a number of questions. She had to make things appear as normal as possible. She also realized Nancy was her protection. Surely, Ronnie wouldn't do anything to her while his precious child was there. Most likely, he would wait until they were alone to *Kill* her.

That thought froze her in her tracks. Where had it come from? She had never really considered Ronnie as someone capable of murder. But who really knows the human soul? When she pondered the question as to whether or not Ronnie could kill someone, she found that the only answer she could come up with was yes. Yes, he was capable of inflicting death. All men are, it's part of their nature, some are just better at it than others.

Margret went back next door and got Nancy, explaining she had gotten her days confused and she was really off today. Heather's mother didn't say anything as she collected Nancy and handed her over to Margret. Margret continued to apologize as she left.

Heather's mother, watching Margret walk off of her porch and head back to her house, turned to her husband and remarked that she hoped one day, Margret would get what she deserved.

Once Margret was back inside the safety of her house, began to pace the floor. She just knew Ronnie was plotting to do something to her. After awhile had passed, she decided to call Ronnie at work and test the water, to see how he would react to her.

The first couple of times she called Ronnie's office, she had just missed him by a couple of minutes. Then, on the third time, it was during the time Ronnie was at lunch with the judge. Although the young man who answered the phone didn't know when Ronnie would be back, he was a bundle of information anyway. When he told Margret that Ronnie was at lunch with a judge, Margret's surprise was reflected in her voice. To which, the young man told her not to worry because Ronnie and the judge had been signing some papers before they went to eat lunch. When Margret asked how he had known what they had been doing, the young man quickly (and proudly) replied Ronnie had needed some witnesses for some kind of legal document the judge had written for Ronnie.

Margret's heart was beating very fast and the only thing she could think of was Ronnie was drawing up divorce papers. Then Margret had a heart stopping thought, since she had been so mean to him for so long and he had found his checkbook, he was going to divorce her and leave her penniless. The thought that he would go behind her back and do something like that made her mad. With a very controlled voice, she thanked the young man for being so helpful and hung up.

The small voice inside her that was what was left of her reason, told her not to worry, Ronnie was probably working on something pertaining to his job. She quickly quenched that thought and determined Ronnie was indeed going to leave her on the streets without a dime to her name.

How could he do that? She asked herself and after a bit of self reflection, determined that if it wasn't for her, he wouldn't be making the kind of money he was with his writing. After all, she was the one that had allowed him to buy that piece of shit computer she rarely saw him working on. The whole time these thoughts were going through her mind, she found herself becoming madder and madder.

With the computer as her new focal point in her wrath, she decided she was going to do something to it like Ronnie had done to her car. Turnabout was fair play in her book. So she sat down at the desk and sat there looking at the computer for awhile trying to decide what to do to it to ensure the next time

Ronnie sat down to work on it, it would be as dead as her car was now. At first she wanted to stick something in through the ventilation strips that would short something out. She remembered the last time she had done that, it had been a wasted use of energy. Nothing had shorted out. There was no shower of sparks and/or the burning smell of fried electrical components.

She decided the best way to monitor whatever she was going to do was having any effect, was to turn on the computer and watch it as she messed with it. So she flipped the power switch on and sat there waiting for the thing to warm up and come on before proceeding. Margret had developed a dislike for the computer stemming back to the first time she had tried to use it and couldn't get anything to work. Now, the simple fact it was in the same house, sharing the same space as her was unthinkable. Never mind it was a tool that had showered down a large sum of cash through the things Ronnie had created on it. As time ticked by, it was becoming a larger and larger source of irritation for her. To her, there was no logical reason Ronnie should be successful while her life stagnated in Ronnie's shadow.

With a hum and the crackle of static electricity, the screen came on. Margret just stared at the screen trying to decide what to do until she saw the icon for the menu. Then it hit her, instead of doing something physical to the computer, she would get into the files and do some house cleaning. That way, Ronnie would just think something had happened to the memory of the computer.

Margret poked around on the keyboard for a couple of minutes before she was able to get into one of the files that was listed in the menu. A couple of minutes later, she was able to delete the file. It was just a game file she had wiped out, but she felt a great sense of accomplishment in doing so just the same. Then she got into another file and wiped it clean as well. The second file gave her even more satisfaction.

The Professor became aware something was wrong when he noticed the file buffer was beginning to have more space in it. His second indication was when he noticed it was as if there was something wrong with his own memory, he didn't know what it was he had forgotten, he only knew part of his memory was gone. He didn't know what was going on until Margret deleted the second file. That was when he saw a huge jump in available RAM and almost at the same time, he felt as if someone had reached inside his mind and had torn a huge chunk of his memory away. He quickly checked the internal clock and saw that at this time of day, Ronnie would still be at work. Which only meant one thing, that bitch Margret was messing around with the computer again. For a brief second, he was worried his writing files were in danger of being wiped clean, but he remembered his writing files were encrypted with a password and she wouldn't be able to get into them far enough to do any damage. So, as if he had all day long to do it, he went over to the ventilation grid and looked out to see what she was up to.

He saw Margret sitting there looking like she was having the best time of her life. He could see the smile she wore was almost as evil as the one he put on from time to time. He got lost in her smile until he felt the third file deleted. This time it felt as if someone had shoved a bamboo stick into the side of his head. The pain was sharp and overwhelming. The Professor dropped to his knees with his head cradled in his hands. The pain was so immense he couldn't form a thought in his head other than to make the pain stop.

Now the situation wasn't so fun anymore now that she was actually doing something to his computer, his home. His mind. The third file was an operational file, although Ronnie would never know it because he never used it, Margret had just wiped out the drivers for the fax function. The Professor knew he had to act fast because he had misjudged Margret's ability to get into things, so he sent a simple message to the screen just before shutting the system down.

The message was 'FUCK OFF MARGRET!' and then the screen went black and the computer turned itself off.

Margret was having a good time, she was doing more with the computer this time than she had been able to do the other times she tried to use it. Then, right after she deleted the third file, the computer printed the message that was especially for her and turned itself off. Margret tried to turn it back on, but like her car, no matter what she did, nothing worked. In a fit of rage, Margret pounded on the keyboard with her fists hoping she would be able to break some of the internal workings of the keyboard and render the computer useless.

But with the computer turned off, she was unable to gauge how effective her blows were being. When she finished with the keyboard, she slapped the side of the monitor unknowingly breaking a speaker mount. Then, she reached around and grabbed what cables she could get her hands on and yanked as hard as she could. The cables wouldn't come out of their connectors because they were the type that had screws on the sides and not the type that simply plugged in. But Margret didn't know that and kept pulling as hard as he could. She felt a cable come loose and was satisfied she had done some damage there also. What she had felt was a cable that was trapped behind the edge of the desk come free of it's captor and release the six inches of slack that had been hanging down.

The Professor endured the punishment Margret was inflicting on the computer. He felt every slap on the monitor. He couldn't understand why everything she was doing to the computer was transferring over to him. He could actually feel the blows. When she hit the side of the monitor with enough force to break the speaker mount, it knocked him to the ground. As he stood up, he found his nose was bleeding and it almost sent him into a howling rage. Before he got a chance to start screaming, Margret reached around behind the computer and started pulling on the cables.

As her hand gripped the cables, the Professor felt it as someone getting a tight grip on his throat, while at the same time, it also felt as though someone had their hands in his bowels and was trying to twist and pull them from his body. The world was beginning to grey out as he slowly sank to his knees, unable to do anything for himself. The only thoughts on his mind were this was impossible, that this couldn't be happening to him. There was one more thought, much further back in his mind and much more basic than the first one. It was that one way or another, he was personally going to kill that bitch.

Just as the Professor thought his existence was going to finally end, the cable trapped behind the desk gave way and Margret released her grip on the cables. This gave the Professor a much needed gasp of air. He still remained on his knees trying to catch his breath, while he was formulating his plan of how he was going to deal with Margret. Right then, he decided since she liked to yank on cables so much, then he would use those cables to finish her.

The Professor started concentrating on planting a thought into Margret's mind. The thought was to grab the power cable and pull on it. Then, while she had the power cable in her hand, he would send her a little surprise via the power company. Something she would get a real 'charge' out of.

With the satisfaction that she was starting to do some real damage, Margret decided to give the cables another pull. Almost as if someone whispered it in her ear, she thought it would be much better to pull on the power cable and do some damage to it. Once again, she reached behind the computer and started grabbing cables. Then her fingertips came upon a cable that felt warmer than the rest. She decided this must be the power cable and started to wrap her fingers around it. As she did so, the cable began to feel increasingly warmer. The instant the cable began to change temperature, Margret released it and tried to yank her hand back out, only to find that her hand was now tangled in the nest of cables. She could now feel the hot power cable as it brushed across the back of her hand. To Margret, it became a race to pull her hand free. But she found the harder she pulled it, the tighter the cables became around her wrist. The power cable was now hot enough to burn her hand where it touched it.

The Professor, no doubt, thought he had her trapped and her seconds were numbered.

Margret, in a sudden burst of inspiration, quickly jammed her arm forward as far as it would go. The cables lost their grip on her arm and just as quickly as she had thrust her hand forward, she snatched it back. She was free!

The momentum of pulling her hand out of the nest of cables overloaded her balance on the desk chair and she toppled over backwards. As she did so, she could have sworn she heard something that sounded like a growl come out of the computer. There was also a crackling sound and the definite smell of ozone in the air. When she hit the floor, Margret rolled over her right shoulder and away from the chair.

Margret never saw the blue spark that leapt from the computer and traveled in a straight line to the same outlet it had connected itself to when Bernie Fryer had completed the circuit. The spark missed the back of Margret's head by a good six inches on the way to the other outlet. Although it had missed her, the small blue fireball had been close enough to her hair to singe the ends. It was a good thing it had happened on the back of her head, that way, she wouldn't be able to see the damage that had been done, immediately.

Like a cat, Margret was instantly on her feet and backing away from the desk as fast as her feet could carry her. She was filled with the fear that somehow, the computer was trying to kill her for the things she had done to it. The air was filled with the smell of ozone and burnt hair. Margret quickly inspected herself (what she could see of herself) and found that she was okay. She stood looking at the computer from across the room and after her initial fear subsided, which took about a minute, started laughing. There was no smoke in the air, just a smell that was already beginning to fade.

She stood there laughing at herself, thinking she was being silly for thinking the computer was trying to kill her. How could it? She asked herself. It was just a big calculator with some higher level capabilities. At least, that's what she told herself to calm her nerves.

When Margret was much calmer, she contented herself with the thought she had caused enough mischief with the computer. So she decided to sit down and watch TV. Margret started to reach for the phone and stopped, deciding not to call Ronnie to find out how his day was going. She decided when he got home, she would just tell him that she had the day off, hopefully, that would frustrate whatever plans he had by trapping her there. The idea he was going to come home and do something to her, along with the reason why he would have a reason to do something to her in the first place, was gone from her mind like a wisp of smoke blown by a gentle breeze.

The Professor on the other hand, was livid that he had missed on his attempt to deal with Margret on a permanent basis. He stormed around inside the computer in a vain attempt to do further damage to her. After awhile, he gave up because he knew there was nothing he could really do to her without being in direct contact with her. He sat down on a resistor and thought about the discussion he was going to have with Ronnie tonight. He was trying to decide how much he was going to make Ronnie hurt when he saw the metal bar and the computer chip lying next to the ventilation strip where he had left them.

A sly smile crept across the Professor's face when he realized that maybe there was something he could do to irritate Margret. He casually strolled over, picked up his toys and began to play with them. A couple of minutes later, a small burst of profanity came from Margret as the channels on the television began to change.

100.

After Ronnie's lunch with the judge, the rest of his afternoon was uneventful. After making his rounds, he came back to his office and called the bank to see if any of Margret's checks had started coming in yet. After being put on hold for a couple of minutes, the young lady came back on the phone and apologized to him saying that nothing had come in today. She offered the notion that the checks would probably start coming in tomorrow. Ronnie started to thank her and hang up when he had another thought.

"When do you think they would start coming in tomorrow?" He asked.

The young woman explained she had no way of knowing, but assured Ronnie as soon as any checks did come in on his account, she would call him immediately at his office number.

Ronnie thanked her for being so helpful and hung up. So, he thought to himself, it's going to be tomorrow before I find out how naughty Margret had been. Then, as he was thinking about Margret, he realized she hadn't called today to complain about her car not working. Ronnie immediately began to wonder what Margret had been up to all day.

Finally, quitting time rolled around and Ronnie was out of there like a shot. He was almost home when he remembered the Professor's request for computer disks and had to turn around and go back to the nearest discount store.

Inside the store, he found what he was looking for and had to endure standing in line as the check out lady gave two teenage boys a ration of crap about buying a shopping cart full of international orange spray paint. They kept explaining to her that they were on an errand for their mother, but the older woman behind the counter kept going on and on about how it was a shame taxpayers had to foot the bills for kids spray painting graffiti on public property. As he stood there listening to her drone on, Ronnie noticed the teenagers were exhibiting alot more patience than he would have if the roles had been reversed.

Even when it was finally his turn to check out, the clerk continued the banter about the paint.

"I just know them boys are gonna paint the trestle tonight." She lamented.

"Well, there's one possibility you haven't considered yet." Ronnie replied as she rang up the disks.

"What's that?"

"Maybe they are on an errand for their mother." That seemed to make her think for a moment. "Besides," He continued, "you have to be mindful of what you say to boys like that."

"Why's that?"

"Let's say they do get caught tonight painting something. They can always tell the police they were buying some paint for their mother's project when the nice check out lady suggested they go paint something public."

"Why...I never suggested anything like that." She countered as Ronnie handed over the money for his purchase.

"Maybe not directly, but you are an adult and whatever plans they had before, you planted a mighty powerful suggestion in their minds." Ronnie explained as he took his change from her.

"Oh." The clerk said in a weak voice, "I never thought about it that way."

Ronnie took his package from her and leaned across the counter to get closer to her and said, "Have a nice day." Then he turned and walked out of the store without looking back.

When Ronnie left the store, he saw the boys walking towards the grocery store empty handed, so he assumed they had stashed their loot in one of the cars in the parking lot. He fondly thought back to his high school days and about all of the paint he and a couple of friends had spread around town announcing that their class year was the best. As he got to his car, he surmised that some traditions took on a life of their own and always repeated without prompting from anyone.

With that joyful thought, he started the car and headed home.

445

101.

Max was suspended with pay for a couple of weeks after the shooting in Ronnie's front yard. He wasn't in any trouble, it was just a standard procedure in the police department when there was a shooting involving any of the officers. Especially when the shooting had proved to be a fatal one. It gave time for the department's internal affairs to investigate the shooting and determine if excessive force had been warranted in the case. Mostly, this was a paperwork review and if something proved to be suspicious, then it would result in interviews with the witnesses. The ultimate end result could be charges would be filed on the offending officer.

In Max's case, it never got past the paperwork stage. The Mayor had been so pleased with Max's performance in catching the parking lot bandits and the case for the deadly force was so airtight that internal affairs gave up and rubber stamped the whole thing as closed. The gun itself had been linked to many crimes almost from the time it first hit the streets. The investigators couldn't decide if the crimes were the work of one man, Ted, or if he had just been the unfortunate current owner of the gun when he had his fatal meeting with Max. Since Ted was dead and the FBI now had the gun in their possession, they decided to just close the whole matter.

With everything seemingly in Max's favor, he still couldn't find peace with himself about what had happened. Up until the night he shot Ted, he had always prided himself in being able to hit any target he was aiming at. Whether he was looking directly at the target or not, he could always count on putting the lead where he wanted it to go.

But in Max's dreams at night, it wasn't two shadowy fingers guiding the barrel of his gun. It was a gruesome skeletal fist wrapped around the barrel of his gun guiding it out of Max's control. Pieces of dead flesh and maggots dripped off of the bones as Max wrestled for control of the gun. Just as he thought he had won, the gun would go off in his dream and he would look up to see Ted's head blown completely off of his shoulders. Max would look down at the head lying in the seat. To his horror, the eyes would suddenly open and Ted would ask in a gaspy voice, "Is this your idea of gun control?"

Max would wake at that point every time and find himself sitting upright in bed bathed in sweat. Now, after the months of the same dream taking its toll on him, he was beginning to think he needed the help of the counselor the police department kept on hand to deal with these types of problems and stress. The only thing he wondered about was if he should tell the counselor about the shadowy fingers he had seen. That was the one point he had left out of his report concerning the incident.

Just when Max began to question his future on the police force, Captain Waters personally took him to see the counselor and ordered him to stay there until he got his shit together. Max would find the counseling would help him with problems he didn't realize he had and it would ultimately make him a better policeman. By going to the counseling. He also helped to break down the stigma that was attached to going to the shrink within the department. For many years after that, the department had no problems with its patrol force that many police departments have due to stress.

The counselor, on the other hand, was busy for the first time since he had been hired there. Ironically, after a couple of years, the counselor started having problems at work due to stress. His work load was staggering.

102.

When Ronnie arrived home from work, he found Margret sitting in the living room reading a magazine. Margret watched over the top of the magazine as Ronnie walked in and sat a paper bag down on the computer desk.

"I'm surprised to find you here. I thought you had to work today." Ronnie said coolly, he didn't want to tip his hand too quickly.

"That's the funny thing." Margret answered him, not suspecting what he was up to. "I thought I had to work today, but it wasn't until after I had taken Nancy next door I remembered I was off today."

When Ronnie heard Nancy's name, he remembered he had paperwork for Heather's parents. He quickly made an excuse and went next door. After talking to Heather's parents for a few minutes, he handed over the document and then went back to his house for more fun with Margret.

"I have just one question to ask you." Ronnie said as he walked in through the front door.

Oh-oh, Margret thought to herself, here it comes about the checkbook. "What would you like to know?" She asked.

"When you realized you were off today, just what job were you off from? From what I understand, you got fired about two weeks ago." Ronnie said as he looked Margret straight in the eye.

Margret's mouth fell open and she sat there dumbfounded. There was no way he could have found out from anyone she knew. When she was at work, she had been careful to keep the information about her home life to herself. "How...How did you find out?" She finally managed to ask.

"Margret," Ronnie said as he got real close to her face (which knowing her track record, probably wasn't the smartest thing to do.), "You'd be real surprised who I know and what I can find out." He said in a quiet voice.

Margret started the tears and said, "I was afraid to tell you. I didn't know how you'd react."

"THAT has got to be the biggest load of BULL SHIT I've ever heard!" Ronnie exploded. "Don't drag that tired excuse out again. Since when have you ever been afraid of what I would do or think?" He shouted at her.

"I've been out everyday trying to find a new job." Margret sobbed.

"You can cut those fake tears out, they don't impress me anymore." Ronnie said coldly and was amazed how quickly after he said that, Margret's tears stopped. "So I guess when you were out looking for this mythical new job, you just needed to carry my checkbook around with you."

"Yes, I had your fucking checkbook!" Margret snapped back at him. She had been working on a defense for this one all afternoon, so she knew exactly what she was going to say. "I was leaving the house one day and found it laying behind the desk. I picked it up and put it in my purse. I just forgot to give it back to you."

Ronnie thought about this for almost a microsecond before he spoke. "So Margret, you say you just found my checkbook. How many checks found their way out of my checkbook with your handwriting on them?"

"I swear I didn't do anything," Margret pleaded, "It was just in my purse. I learned my lesson from last time. I wouldn't make the same mistake twice."

"I know you're lying to me. Why can't you just tell me the truth for once in your life?" Ronnie asked pointedly.

"I am telling you the truth." She said as she got up and started walking towards the kitchen.

"I didn't say you could go anywhere." Ronnie yelled as he got between Margret and her destination.

"I didn't know I had to ask!" She yelled back, except this time, instead of just talking to him, she punched him in the chest.

Punching Ronnie in the chest was the exact one wrong thing to do. She watched as he grew beet red with rage. Ronnie had been having a hard time controlling himself as it was, but when she punched him, he could control himself no longer. Margret began to get scared, she had seen Ronnie in various states of emotion, but this time, it was so much different. For a second, she knew she was going to die. She would die and it would be her fault because she had pushed him over the edge. Her punch had been the final shove.

What was really pushing Ronnie over the edge was he now had the Professor's voice screaming in his mind.

KILL HER KILL THE BITCH BREAK HER NECK KILL HER KILL HER KILL HER MAKE HER PAY MAKE HER HURT MAKE HER BLEED RIP HER HEART OUT KILL HER

Margret stood and watched the emotion's crossing Ronnie's face even though she knew she had better run. Run long, run swift, but run for her life. She watched as he balled his hands into fists and she got ready for the blows about to rain down upon her. She saw Ronnie draw his right fist back and she closed her eyes, waiting for the blow.

Ronnie was barely aware of what he was doing, the mantra going through his mind was blocking out all rational thought. What the Professor was telling him made more sense than anything anyone had ever told him before.

THAT'S IT RONNIE BEAT HER TO DEATH KILL HER THE WAY SHE DESERVES IT MAKE HER SUFFER KILL HER KILL HER KILL HER KILL HER GIVE HER WHAT SHE DESERVES DO IT NOW

Ronnie watched as his fist drew back and saw it go forward, feeling the momentum behind it as he threw his weight behind it. At the last possible instant, he pulled the punch. He hit the closet door with enough force to split the solid wood panel and spring the latch. A glass like, sharp pain shot from his knuckles and straight up his arm. That served to bring Ronnie back to reality. He looked at Margret and saw her standing there with her eyes closed waiting for the blow that would never come.

YOU PUSSY YOU WIMP FAGBOY KILL HER NOW WHILE YOU STILL HAVE A CHANCE KILL HER KILL HER KILL HER

Ronnie raised his fists to either side of his head and screamed "NO!" He knew if he stayed there, he would do something stupid. So he did the one thing he could think of, he turned around and ran to the front door. When he got to it, he turned back and looked at Margret again, she was standing there looking back at him with a look of amazement on her face. Then Ronnie turned back and walked out of the front door.

Margret had been standing there braced for the punch to come and heard the crunch from Ronnie hitting the closet door. She opened her eyes and saw Ronnie standing there with his fists pressed to the sides of his head. When he screamed no, she took a step back away from him. The look on his face was almost inhuman and she knew if she stayed close to him, she would die. But Ronnie had simply turned around and ran to the front door. When he turned and looked at her just before going out the door, she saw something in his face that was totally different than what she had just seen while he was standing in front of her. There was a look of confusion and hurt. Then he left.

Margret went to the window and saw Ronnie walking down the street. She smiled to herself because in her book, she had just won this round. Had Margret known just how close she had come to having her life ended, she would have been upstairs packing her stuff.

As soon as Ronnie was outside the house, he found he could think clearer. The Professor's voice was no longer a deafening roar in his mind. As he walked, he found the further from the house he got, the quieter the voice became in his mind. Soon, Ronnie realized he was running down the street. Out of breath, he stopped and realized he had run at least ten blocks. The wind ripped in and out of him and made his throat feel raw from just the effort of trying to breath.

He saw a bus bench on the next corner so he walked to it and sat down to rest. He sat there and watched the sun go down, the street lamps come on without really seeing. His mind was busy the whole time trying to figure out where he had blown it and why the Professor had chosen this time to re-enter his mind to add his two cents worth. Ronnie knew just how close he had come to really doing some serious harm to Margret and it scared him. He had never intended for this fight to go as far as it did, but he also knew the Professor had done alot to provoke his rage. The hit Margret had gotten in on him was nothing compared to the things that she had done to him in the past, but with that and the Professor throwing logs on the fire, he had lost total control.

Ronnie surfaced from his thoughts like a deep sea diver coming to the surface and he realized it was late. He was surprised he had been sitting there for so long without realizing it. He got up and as he was walking home, promised himself no matter what happened when he got home, he would stay in control of himself.

Margret sat in the living room waiting for Ronnie to return. She had been through a full range of emotions since he had left. At first, she was relieved he was gone, then she became annoyed he had left and left her with Nancy. Then, she became mad at the simple thought that he was gone. Now, she was afraid he wasn't going to return. She promised God she would be good if he just let her meal ticket return to her safe and sound.

At ten o'clock, Ronnie walked through the front door looking tired and hot.

"It's about time you showed back up." Margret said sarcastically, forgetting the deal she had made with God earlier.

"I thought I'd go for a walk." Ronnie replied as he walked straight through the living room on his way to the kitchen.

"You mean you decided to run away like a little boy, don't you?"

Ronnie stopped and looked straight at Margret, "If I were you," He told her through clenched teeth, "I would shut my mouth now and not continue this line of conversation."

"You broke the closet door." Margret announced as if it was the worst thing had ever happened in the history of mankind.

"Just be glad it wasn't your neck." Was the cold reply.

"Like you're man enough to do it." She replied taunting him.

"Look bitch, I've had enough of your bullshit for one night. Now, I'm going to get myself something to eat and then I'm going to bed. If you have a problem with that, eat shit."

Margret, now happy with herself she had been able to provoke Ronnie again, simply said, "Do what you feel is necessary."

Ronnie went into the kitchen, looked in the refrigerator and couldn't find anything to eat that was to his taste. So he settled for his old standby, peanut butter. When he was finished eating, he walked back through the living room and started climbing the stairs on his way to the bedroom. Margret stopped him.

"Ronnie, I know you did something to my car. Could you please fix it?"

"Why?" He asked, "So you can run the streets and party?"

"No Ronnie. I really am looking for another job."

"Yeah right, I bet you are."

"Please Ronnie. I'll do anything if you'd fix my car. I mean it, anything."

"Okay Margret, I'll fix your car. But remember, you're the one that said anything." after saying that, he turned and went outside to Margret's car. Within a couple of minutes, he had it fixed and was on his way into the house.

"Did you fix it?" she asked.

"Yes I did."

"Then what would you like for your reward?" She asked as she stepped up to him and put her arms around his neck.

"Just one little silly, simple thing."

"Oh yeah?" Margret said with a big smile on her face, "And what's that?"

"That you start telling me the truth." Ronnie said as he pulled her arms off of him and resumed his trip up the stairs.

Margret looked as if she had been slapped in the face. "Ronnie...I do tell you the truth. It hurts me when you say things like that." She said up the stairwell to Ronnie as he climbed the stairs.

Ronnie stopped dead in his tracks and thought about what Margret had said, he couldn't remember one single time he had said anything remotely resembling what he had just said to her. He slowly turned and looked at her.

"I see you're off to a good start on your part of the bargain." He said quietly.

"Just what does that mean?"

"I'll tell you what that means." Ronnie said as he came back down a couple of steps. "I asked you for honesty in payment of fixing your car and you repay me by the first thing that comes out of your mouth is a lie."

"And just what the hell do you mean by that?" Margret said, this time she didn't bother to hide her disgust mixed with a hint of rage in her voice.

"I mean," He said as he took one more step down, "I have never made a simple request out of you for the truth. Even when you wrote all of those checks I told you that you shouldn't be afraid to tell me the truth."

"I knew you'd throw those checks up in my face when you got a chance!" Margret yelled at him angrily.

"If you are finished," Ronnie said doing his best to stay in control and not get mad, "I have never put truth as a condition on anything." He finished.

"You are the biggest bastard on the planet." Margret said, the tone of her voice would have made a polar bear run off in fright.

"That may be so, but I'd rather be a bastard than not to have anything I said be trusted." He said calmly. He could see in a way, he had Margret on the run.

"Oh...And since when have you been elected the champion of the truth? Seems like I can remember a few times you've told some good ones." Margret replied in her defense.

"Yes Margret, that maybe true. But I have never lied when it came to important things that affected our happy little family."

Margret didn't have a reply for this and only stood there looking at him. Ronnie saw she was deep in thought to come up with something that would pin his ears back like he had pinned hers. The only thing she could come up with was a hearty "Fuck-you!" before turning around and going back to the living room.

Ronnie stood there on the steps debating whether he should go back down stairs and finish this argument or just let the matter drop. Part of him wanted to confront her again about the checks and the other part of him was just glad he had been able to keep his cool during this argument. After a moments thought, he decided to wait until he had gotten the information back from the bank about the amounts of the checks that had been written. With that decided, Ronnie turned, resumed his journey back up the stairs and went to bed.

That night as he slept, Margret laid awake downstairs for a long time thinking about what Ronnie had said. A small (very small) part of her felt bad about the things that she had done. She knew she couldn't call Ronnie a loser anymore. His promotion to Superintendent at the country club gave them a sense of financial stability the first time. While she had done just about everything in her power to destroy that stability.

The rest of her decided to hell with Ronnie, all she cared about was herself. If she wrote checks, then Ronnie would just have to pony up some of his precious loot and take care of the problem. That was the way with everything she did, if she found herself in trouble, she always knew someone else would bail her out.

It took a long time, but Margret finally fell asleep on the couch in the early hours of the morning.

103.

Shortly after Margret fell asleep, Ronnie opened his dream eyes and found himself sitting in front of the computer. The computer was on, but instead of the usual display, the Professor's face filled the monitor screen.

Good evening Ronnie. The Professor said in a heavy electronic voice.

'At least I'm not strapped to a table this time.' Ronnie replied. There was a strange noise was coming and going in the background he couldn't identify.

Hey! I was just having some fun.

'Just like you were having fun tonight?' Ronnie asked in a loud voice.

Shhh...You'll wake the beast.

Ronnie turned and looked in the direction of the couch. He saw Margret lying there asleep and he now knew where the strange sound was coming from, it was Margret snoring. 'Okay, why am I here?' He asked in a hushed voice.

Why is anyone here?

'Don't start that shit again. What do you want? I'm supposed to be sleeping right now.'

You are sleeping. But okay, I'll tell you why I brought you here. I need some help storing my books on the disks.

'Since when? You've been able to put paper in the printer, why do you need my help with the disks?'

The Professor's gaze shifted down and in a small voice said, *Could you please open the package for me?*

'Is that all you want?' Ronnie asked, his tone mocking the Professor's helplessness.

Don't get smart you little prick. The Professor said angrily. *I've had a real shitty day because of your wife, I would just appreciate a small amount of help from you.*

'I don't understand how you could have had a bad day because of Margret. I'm the one who has to deal with her.' Ronnie said as he opened the box of computer disks for the Professor.

Let's just say as soon as she found out you messed with her car, she decided to retaliate by messing with my home away from home here. The Professor said as he reached out of the monitor and put a disk into the drive.

'What did she do?'

Apart from beating and banging on the computer and deleting some files, not much. The Professor answered, being careful to leave out the part where he had been choked when Margret had grabbed the cables.

'She did what? Did she wipe out anything important?'

As far as the books go, no. I have those buried in a processing program and encrypted so no one but you and me can get into them. She wiped a couple of game files and broke a speaker mount in the monitor.

'I can't believe it, she did what?' Ronnie asked bewildered.

Don't sweat it. Would you mind flipping that disk over please. This side is full.

Ronnie pulled the disk and flipped it. 'What games did she delete?'

Nothing important, just a couple of crappy games and a fax driver.

'Didn't you try to do something about it? Something to stop her?'

I tried. I swear she has more luck than a four leaf clover. I lost my head and tried to zap her. Missed her as you can very well tell, but the hair on the back of her head is going to take awhile to look right again.

'Really? I didn't notice.'

Damn, I guess I wasn't as close as I thought I had gotten. Oh well, I have other things in mind for her. Better things.

'Like what?'

Let's just say it's my little gift to you. I think you'll like it when it happens.

'What have you done? What's going to happen?'

Don't worry Ronnie. Hey, you need to pull that disk out now, it's full. Put in another one please. Mark that disk you're taking out as books one and two. Anyway, I think you're really going to like what happens.

Ronnie was concerned about what the Professor's surprise for Margret was, but it was also clear to him that the Professor wasn't going to say. Ronnie and the Professor made small talk as Ronnie kept changing the disk and flipping them over. Each time a disk was full, he was instructed to mark that disk similar to the first one. The Professor never made an attempt to come out of the computer and remained on the screen with his visual representation, it was clear to Ronnie the Professor was running the whole show from inside the computer. An hour and a half later, all ten disks were filled up, the second side of the last disk was only half full.

During that time, Ronnie tried to find out what the Professor had done to ensure Margret's fate. But the Professor had been adamant about not telling him what his plans were.

455

When the task of storing all of the Professor's work on disks was complete, Ronnie put all ten of them back in the box they had come in and set the box back down on the desk. The task complete, the Professor commanded Ronnie to go back to bed.

Ronnie, when you get back to bed you need to wake up. I accidentally reprogrammed your alarm clock today when I was messing around with T.B.

'T.B.? What the hell's TB?'

The Bitch...Your Bitch. The Professor said as he faded away, taking the surroundings Ronnie was sitting in with him.

Ronnie woke almost immediately, he laid there for a moment waiting for his eyes to focus before sitting up and flipping on the light. Through light blinded eyes he inspected his digital alarm clock and found that although the alarm time looked right, it had been set to the afternoon instead of morning. When the alarm was set to the correct time, Ronnie went back to sleep for the last hour and a quarter he had left before the alarm would go off to start another day.

When Ronnie woke the next morning, he vaguely remembered the incident about the alarm clock. He rushed to get himself ready and left for work without stopping to eat breakfast. Part of it was because he didn't want to be around when Margret woke up. He didn't want to start the day by getting in a fight with her about beating on the computer. That one little fact the Professor had told him was eating away at him more than any of the other things she had done. How dare she mess with his computer? It was the only thing in the house that was bringing in good money and it had saved her bacon with her last bout with checks. Just as it was going to save her bacon with the checks whose amounts Ronnie still had yet to find out about. To his way of thinking, that meant the computer was a sacred thing and should be treated with kid gloves. Not beating on it hard enough to break things inside, its internal workings.

The other reason he wanted to get out of there quickly was so he could get to work early. He wanted to get his work out of the way as soon as possible so he could take off whatever time he needed to go to the bank and take care of checks that would be coming in.

Ronnie's morning was uneventful and his work went quickly. By lunch time he was caught up with all of his work for the day. He called the bank and asked for the young lady that was helping him yesterday. When she got on the phone she told him she was just getting ready to call him to let him know the first of the checks had started arriving.

They talked for a couple of minutes and she confirmed it was Margret's signature on the checks, Ronnie thanked her and said he would come in later that afternoon to take care of what they had and see what the total was up to by then.

After getting off of the phone, Ronnie sat back and marveled to himself that having a big wad of money in his account really made a difference in the treatment he was getting. Not to say he had been treated shabbily the first go around of checks, this time nobody approached the subject of service charges. Instead, he was getting the "anybody can make a mistake" treatment.

At the same time Ronnie was on the phone to the bank, Margret woke up. The first thing she did after opening her eyes was to grab the remote and turn the television on. Almost immediately, it started changing channels and when the volume started going higher and lower as well, she turned it off and threw the remote at it in frustration.

The commotion with the television started Nancy crying. With a few select cuss words, Margret got up and went upstairs to get Nancy out of her room. The mess that greeted Margret in Nancy's room far surpassed the mess Ronnie had been greeted with that time in the past. There was crap everywhere and the room smelled of urine. Clothes had been scattered everywhere along with books and toys, giving the room that cozy feel of Carpeted by Garbage. Looking around, Margret saw 'Finger Painting with Crap' had been this mornings handicraft for Nancy. The drawings were primordial, there was the classic 'Dung Handprint' along with something that looked like a huge blob (also made of the same material) repeated several times around the room on the walls.

Margret went ballistic and started whipping Nancy with the handle of a push toy that had been lying on the floor. The attack on Nancy did little to clean the room and only accomplished in making Nancy cry harder and louder.

Margret, in a fit of anger, snatched Nancy off of the floor and took her into the bathroom and threw her into the bathtub. She then turned on the water at full blast without first checking its temperature, or allowing it to warm up first. The cold water sent Nancy into a fit and made her protest even more. Being just over a year old, she didn't understand the reason for the rough treatment she was receiving was simply because her mother was a bitch. Margret on the other hand, didn't care about the water, she just wanted Nancy to stop screaming and regretted the fact she was having to tend to the child.

When Nancy was bathed and dressed, Margret took her downstairs for lunch and to finish getting her ready to take next door. The only thing Margret was concentrating on was getting out of the house and going somewhere, anywhere.

After lunch, Margret was stuffing Nancy's diaper bag with the necessary items for the day when she noticed the box of computer disks Ronnie had foolishly left out on the desk. This was something new and she picked up the box to examine it. Opening the box, she saw the disks were labeled in such a manner that suggested they contained information.

Margret's first impulse was to throw the box of disks away. She smiled at that because she wanted to see Ronnie tearing up the house looking for the missing box of disks. But she had a second thought, she decided it would be better to hide the disks than throw them away in case Ronnie got out of hand like he had done last night. She thought for a couple of moments on where to hide them when Nancy started getting fussy again. She tried to come up with a hiding place, but found there was nowhere she could put something Ronnie wouldn't find in a couple of minutes. Meanwhile, Nancy was getting louder in her protests.

With a smile on her face, Margret picked up the diaper bag and stuffed the box of disks to the very bottom. Now that she was pleased with herself for finding a good hiding place, she picked Nancy up, took her next door and dropped her off. When she went back to the house, she dressed quickly and went out to her car to leave.

But this morning was a repeat of yesterday morning and the car wouldn't start. Frustrated and mad, Margret went into the house and called a cab to come and get her. The cab arrived ten minutes later and Margret went to the mall.

104.

A little over an hour before quitting time, Ronnie got a call from the bank. It was the young lady again and she explained that all of the checks that were missing from his checkbook were finally in. Ronnie told her to hold that thought and he would be at her location in twenty minutes. He also told her he would settle up the account when he got there. After hanging up, he called the clubhouse and told them he had to go and take care of some pressing business. No one protested.

Fifteen minutes later, Ronnie was walking into the bank. He found the young lady that had been assisting him and they went into her office. The damage to his checking account was worse than he had imagined. He had expected to be down in the account by a couple of hundred dollars, but when he found out he was actually down almost a grand, he felt the floor shift beneath his feet and had to sit down.

The concerned young woman ran out of her office and returned a second later with a paper cup full of cold water. Ronnie thanked her as he took it and sipped the water slowly. When he was feeling better, they began to discuss what he wanted to be done about the checks. His first thought was to have Margret arrested and thrown in jail for theft, but decided to just let the checks be paid from his account and he would deal with Margret himself. But he did ask the young lady if it was possible for her to make copies of those checks for him and she was more than happy to oblige.

On his way home, Ronnie decided this was the end. He would confront Margret about the checks and then tell her she had to find another place to live. If she protested too much, then he would simply go, pack his bags and leave. There was no way he could go on living with Margret the way she was acting. He dwelled on that thought for a moment and decided the hell with her, he wouldn't leave his own house, shortly after arriving home, Margret WOULD be leaving. Nancy crossed his thoughts and he made his decision then and there in the car, she would stay with him. He knew it would be a major strain, but he also knew Heather's mother would help him out with the child care. He knew he could count on Heather's mother because he knew there was no love loss between her and his soon to be ex-wife.

Ronnie also decided just to make it easier to get Margret gone, he would take all of the bills and pay for the divorce itself. He just wanted her out of his life no matter what the cost. As he drove along, he tried to steel himself that Margret would try anything to change his mind. Including when she saw whatever tactics she was using was failing, violence. He decided if he had to, he would call Max and try to have her arrested, or at the very least, taken away.

Ronnie kept telling himself he was doing the right thing. He turned on the radio and almost as if the radio itself was trying to lend a hand of support for his cause, 'Harden My Heart' came back at him through the car speakers. He listened carefully to the words and for the first time, understood their meaning. Or at least his interpretation of them. He found what his weak point with Margret was. He had a soft spot in his heart for her and no matter what she did to him, he still loved her. He now knew if he was going to pull this off and not cower to Margret, then he was going to have to harden his heart.

When Ronnie finally pulled into the driveway, he parked beside Margret's car. When he saw it still parked there, he thought to himself this was better because he could get it over quickly. The sooner the better.

Ronnie picked up the copies of the checks from beside him on the front seat, went to the front door and found it locked. He unlocked the door, went into the house and started looking for Margret. After searching the house, he couldn't find Margret or Nancy and he couldn't understand why Margret would leave and not take her car. He had put the battery cable back on last night, so there wasn't a reason why she shouldn't have been able to drive it. Then, almost as an after thought, he realized maybe Margret hadn't gone anywhere and was just next door with Nancy.

He decided maybe it was better that way, he could just go and get her while they left Nancy there while they came back home and discussed the problem at hand. So leaving the house, he went next door to start the process of cleaning up his life.

Heather's mother answered the door on the second knock and looked relieved to see Ronnie standing there. Ronnie asked her if Margret was there and was told no, the she had left much earlier to go to work. But she quickly added they needed to talk and invited Ronnie in.

"Ronnie, there seems to be a small problem." She said as soon as Ronnie sat down.

"I hope you're not going to tell me you can't watch Nancy anymore." Ronnie replied.

"Heavens no, nothing like that. The problem is with Nancy."

"What do you mean? Is she alright? Where is she?" Ronnie asked quickly with a great deal of concern in his voice.

"She's okay now...Ronnie, I don't know how to bring this up. I don't want to seem like a nosey neighbor, but I think Margret is abusing Nancy."

"What?!!" Ronnie almost shouted.

"It's hard to believe myself, I don't know how a parent can do something like that. Especially a mother."

"What makes you think she's doing something like that?" Ronnie said in disbelief.

"Today when your wife brought Nancy here, she seemed to be in more of a snit than usual. When I was changing Nancy later, I found a bunch of fresh bruises on her, especially her back."

"I just can't believe that bitch would do that to her." Ronnie exploded.

"Neither can I. At first I thought they were just from Nancy being too rough while she was playing. Kids will do that sometimes, play too hard or fall off something and get bruises that make them look as if they were the most abused child on the planet. But later, I looked at Nancy again and saw the bruises were still coming up on her. So they must be fresh. You know, new bruises."

"Is Nancy okay?" Ronnie sputtered. His mind seemed to be vapor locked on the revelation that Margret would do something like that.

"Oh yes, she's napping right now. I am ashamed to admit it, but at first I thought you were the one who had done it to her. But when I saw the bruises were still coming up on her, I knew they were too fresh for you to have done it. Also, there were the finger prints."

"Finger prints? What finger prints?" Ronnie asked, relieved to hear that Nancy was more or less okay, but he was also highly pissed off that this had been done to her.

"Both of her arms look as if they had been grabbed hard and squeezed. Maybe she had been jerked around by her little arms. I don't know. All I know is that later, when I was checking her for more bruises, I found more on both of her arms that resembled hand prints. You could see the four fingertips in a row and on the other side of her arm was the thumb print. The hand print is too small to be yours, so it has to be Margret's."

"I just do not believe this!" Ronnie exclaimed. But he did believe it, he thought back to the bruises the Professor had left on him and wondered if it had been the Professor or Margret that had given him those nice bruises on his throat.

"Neither do I. I hope you understand why I had to tell you. If someone else had seen them, the police might have been called and I couldn't bear to think you might get into trouble for something she had done."

Ronnie sat there and thought for a moment, then decided to let Heather's mother in on his plan. Right now, he felt as though he could use an Ally. So he explained that Margret had been getting into some evil things. He told her about Margret's boyfriend and explained about the checks she had written. He continued to explain about the book deals and how he had taken care of the first batch of checks. Then he told her about how Margret had gotten fired but still continued to act as if she was still working. And then there was the new matter with his new checking account.

The older woman sat there and listened to everything Ronnie had to say. She couldn't believe what she was hearing and told him so. He agreed saying if he hadn't been living with Margret, he would be inclined not to believe his story either. Then he told her he was going to put an end to it today when he came home and throw Margret out, but she hadn't been home for him to do that. He was still intending to do it when she returned, but wanted to know if she would still watch Nancy after he became a single parent.

She quickly agreed and put his fears to rest, then she went one step further, she suggested he let Nancy spent the night. That way, he could do his business with Margret and not subject Nancy to the turmoil that would be going on in his house. Ronnie thanked her, for the first time realized just how much Heather's mother cared for him (in a motherly sort of way) and just how much she disliked Margret.

Ronnie thanked her again and told her he was going back to his house to wait for the return of Margret.

"Ronnie, just one more thing." She said as she stood also.

"What's that?"

"Don't do anything stupid. Don't lay a hand on her, just tell her to get lost so you can restart your life."

"If she tries to come over here..." Ronnie started to say.

"Don't worry about that. I'll kick her ass off of my doorstep myself. Then again, I just might let David handle my light work for me."

"Well...Just be careful," Ronnie told her, "she's alot meaner in a fight than she looks like she can be."

"Don't worry about me, this old girl can still can still kick butt when she wants to. Just worry about yourself. Now, promise me you'll do like I said."

"I will."

"Promise."

"I promise I won't kill my bitch of a wife or do anything stupid. No matter how much fun it would be. Scout's honor." He said as he put his hand up in an attempt to make a Scout Sign with his fingers.

"Good. Now go get 'em."

Ronnie was feeling good as he walked out of the house and headed back to his. He was surprised to discover that talking to Heather's mother had taken such a load off of his mind. He was still outraged about Margret's abuse of Nancy, but now he felt like he could face her without trying to rip her head from her shoulders upon first sight.

When Ronnie was back inside of his own house, he quickly went into the kitchen to get something to eat. He didn't want to face Margret on an empty stomach and his dinner consisted of the usual peanut butter and jelly. He ate quickly, afraid Margret was going to walk into the house while he had his mouth crammed full of sandwich. Had he known, he would have taken his time eating. Margret wouldn't be home for quite awhile.

Quite awhile indeed! It was almost midnight before Ronnie heard a car pull up out front and a door slam. He quickly hurried to the front window, looked out and saw a taxi dropping Margret off. Within a few seconds, Margret walked in through the front door.

"It's about time you got home." Ronnie said as he stood in the middle of the living room. "Where have you been?"

"You aren't my keeper. I'll do as I please." Margret said in a defiant tone.

Ronnie could tell by the way she was swaying on her feet she had been drinking. "Where have you been?" He demanded this time.

"Eat shit Ronnie. I don't have to stand here and listen to your crap. But I will tell you where I was. I went out looking for a job this afternoon and ran into a couple of friends of mine. We went to dinner and I lost track of time. If that isn't good enough for you, then kiss my ass."

"What friends?"

"What?" Margret asked.

"What friends were you out with? Where did you go?" Ronnie asked. He was having an excellent time of keeping his temper. Much better than he had hoped to.

"Friends. I don't have to tell you. Besides, what's the idea of messing with my car again?" Margret asked trying to change the subject of the conversation and turn it around to some sin Ronnie had committed. The times she had given Ronnie a B.S. story to cover her whereabouts and Ronnie not pressing the issue had made her lax. Margret hadn't put any thought to her alibi.

"I didn't mess with your car. I fixed it last night and that was the last time I touched it." Ronnie quickly said, defending himself against the charges.

"Bull-shit!" Margret yelled at him. "I tried to use it today and it wouldn't start."

"I'll check it." He told her and then walked outside to Margret's car. She followed him to the front porch and watched as he pulled his keys from his pocket, got into her car. The car started as soon as he turned the key. Having satisfied himself Margret had been lying about the car for whatever reason, he went back inside.

"Seems okay to me." He said as he walked back in through the front door.

"That doesn't prove anything, you could have fixed it as soon as you got home. I had to use a cab because I heard about a job and I went to apply for it." Margret told him, now she had a pouty tone to her voice. When Ronnie had been outside, she decided she was going to disarm him with sex. Since she had been drinking, she now found herself becoming aroused.

"Where?" Ronnie asked, the tone of his voice was flat and controlled.

"What?" Margret asked, she hadn't been expecting Ronnie to call her on that one, so she wasn't prepared with an answer. Her lack of a workable alibi was getting her in deeper.

"Where did you go for a job? What was the name of the place where you put your application into? Can't tell me, can you?"

"Yes I can!" Margret all but shouted defensively. Ronnie's constant questioning was beginning to more than irritate her. How dare he question anything she told him? Her arousal was now turning into anger.

"Then where was it?" Ronnie quickly asked. He knew she was lying and he had her on the run. "In fact, name two or three places you've put applications in to."

Margret didn't answer and only stood there with a blank look on her face. She couldn't think fast enough to keep up with Ronnie's questioning and the large amount of Tequila she had drunk wasn't helping her mental facilities any.

"What's the matter Margret?" Ronnie asked, not really giving her time to think of an answer. "Can't think of anywhere? That's because you are a liar. You haven't been putting in applications all over town, you've been out writing bad checks."

"I have not!" Margret quickly replied. It was becoming clear to her this fight was not going her way. Just when she thought she was going to get the upper hand in the argument, Ronnie would change the direction of the fight, throwing her off balance.

"Are you sure?" He asked her and in doing so, set the trap for her to fall into.

"Yes, I'm sure. I learned my lesson last time." She replied, her eyes becoming watery.

"Apparently Margret," He said as he reached into his pants pocket and pulled out the copies of the checks he had gotten from the bank, "It was a lesson you didn't learn very well." Unfolding the paper, he held it up and asked, "Do you know what this is?"

"How could I? What is it?" She asked, holding her tears in check.

"These are the copies of all of the checks you wrote out of my checking account when you were supposedly holding onto my checkbook for safe keeping."

Margret could see the check outlines and the handwriting the copier had reproduced without fail. She said nothing because she was suddenly afraid. Afraid she had been caught in one of her bigger lies. Without saying anything in her defense, she suddenly turned and ran for the stairs. As she got to them, she looked behind her and saw that Ronnie was following her. She raced up the stairs two at a time and when she got to the top, stopped and saw that Ronnie hadn't followed her. He was standing at the foot of the stairs.

"I just have one question for you." He called up the staircase, "Why did you do it?"

Whether she was trying to be funny or smart, or just trying to piss him off, Ronnie would never find out. "Because I felt like it." was the reply that came back down the stairs to him.

Ronnie was standing there with his left hand on the banister and when she said that, he instantly saw red with rage. His only thought was that he wanted to hit her with something. Since his hand was on the banister, it was the weapon at hand (no pun intended). Without realizing what he was doing, he gave the banister a yank. The bottom and middle mounting brackets ripped free of their moorings but the top one refused to let go. Ronnie was standing at the bottom of the stairs with the long pole in his hand.

Margret's eyes widened in fear because she realized once again, she had pushed Ronnie over the edge. She watched in amazement as Ronnie ripped the banister off of the wall without any effort at all. She realized the top mounting bracket had stopped her from getting hurt. She didn't know what he was trying to do with the banister, but quickly decided she didn't want to find out and she was in the wrong place for that. She turned and ran into the bedroom, locking the door behind her. Now that she was safe behind a locked door, she relaxed.

When Margret disappeared around the corner and he heard the bedroom door slam, Ronnie decided this was the end and he was going to finish it. Ronnie calmly climbed the stairs and went to the bedroom door. He gently tried the doorknob and found the door was locked. Ronnie took a step back, turned around and raised his right foot. Then he kicked backwards placing his foot just below the doorknob, trying to back kick the door open. The door only protested on the first kick, so Ronnie did it again. This time, he felt a huge surge of adrenaline and applied alot more force to the door via the sole of his foot.

The lock on the bedroom door was a cheap interior door lock and not designed to withstand alot of force. The door exploded inward on the second kick. Not that it really mattered how much force the lock could withstand, the door frame around the bolt shattered inward from the force. Ronnie turned around slowly and was just in time to duck a lamp that Margret threw at him.

"Stay away from me you asshole!" She screamed at him.

"That's no problem." Ronnie calmly replied. All of his anger had been vented on the door and he felt strangely calm and in control.

"I mean it! Get out of here!" She continued screaming.

"No Margret." He told her, "This time it's your turn to leave. I'm throwing you out. Get your stuff and then get the hell out of my house. As far as I'm concerned, this marriage is over. I'm through with your lies and your bull shit. I'll take the bills and Nancy. You get to keep whatever you can haul out of here in the next ten minutes and your car. But make no mistake, you are leaving here one way or the other."

"Where...Where will I go?" Margret stonewalled. She didn't, couldn't, believe he was actually doing this to her.

"Since it never concerned you where I went all those times I left to get away from your abuse, I can only tell you that I don't give a damn where you go, just get out! You now have nine minutes and forty-five seconds."

Margret stood there looking at him wide eyed and gap mouthed, she couldn't believe the change she was seeing in Ronnie. Normally by now, she would have been able to provoke him into a shouting match, but here he stood in front of her so calm. His demeanor wasn't the only thing that was different about him, his face was somehow different, especially his eyes. They were dark and cold, unfeeling. She sensed that at that moment, it wouldn't take very much and he would squash her with as much regard as mashing a bug. "Fine, I'll go, you dickless piece of shit!" She finally screamed at him, "I just want you to know I'll get a lawyer and we'll see who gets what. By the time I'm finished with you, you won't have a damn dime left to your name."

"If that's what it takes to get rid of you, then fine. But let me give you some advice. Pay your lawyer in cash...Because when your check bounces, you'll be without counsel." Ronnie said calmly.

Margret went ballistic, she was weaving together a tapestry of profanity that any sailor would have been proud to lay claim to. She picked up the first thing she saw, a good sized bottle of cheap perfume and threw it at him. Ronnie was once again successful in ducking the missile. It flew across the stairwell and shattered against the wall. The hall and stairwell quickly began to fill with the overpowering smell of very cheap perfume.

Ronnie remarked if she was finished, she now only had nine minutes to get the hell out before he called the police and told them about the checks. Then he told her how he would also tell them he had just found out the guy Max had killed out front was Ted, her lover. He told her he would tell them he had confronted her about this new batch of checks and she had made a remark about Ted not doing the job right. Of course, he would say, he had found out Margret had a boyfriend and guess who he was. Why Ted, of course! As a cherry on top he added he would tell them she was trying to kill him.

He then turned around (a dangerous thing to do, turning his back on Margret) and went back downstairs. Ronnie sat in a chair facing the stairwell and the front door and listening to things crashing and banging around upstairs as Margret did her best to trash the bedroom. Then there was silence and Ronnie heard Margret coming down the stairs. He quickly picked up the receiver of the phone and held it up to his ear in a bluff that he was on the phone to the police.

Margret appeared with an armload of clothes and upon seeing him on the phone, told him he could hang up because she was leaving. Ronnie slowly lowered the receiver and watched as she walked out of the door. Ronnie then got up and walked over to the open front door. Watching as Margret threw her clothes in the back seat of her car. As she got into her car, she said one more thing.

"I'll see you rotting in hell!" She yelled at him.

"It would be a pleasure meeting you there, just to know you finally got to where you belong." He yelled back at her with a small amount of cheer to his voice.

With her car door still open, Margret looked down and saw a rock that was part of the border between the driveway and the grass. It was a smooth one just smaller than the palm of her hand. She leaned down out of the car and picked it up. From where Ronnie was standing, he couldn't see what she was picking up and thought she was picking her keys up from the ground. Margret got back out of the car and stood up as if she had something else to say.

"Ronnie, there's just one more thing." She said in a normal tone of voice.

"What's that?"

"DIE YOU PIECE OF SHIT!!" she screamed as she threw the stone. Whipping it like a baseball at Ronnie in a modern day imitation of David and Goliath.

Being dark outside and the stone smooth, dark blue almost black in color, Ronnie never saw the rock coming until it glanced off of the side of his head. Ronnie was surprised that she had hit him from her distance and a little less surprised he actually saw stars as he fell backwards onto the porch, dazed.

Heather's parents had been watching the show next door from the relative safety of their front porch. They saw Margret pick up something and throw it at Ronnie. They watched in sickened horror as Ronnie's head snapped over to one side and he fell backwards. David was instantly on his feet and starting down the steps of the porch as Connie pleaded with him to stay out of it.

"What the hell is going on here?" He yelled as he quickly walked across the yard.

Margret watched in delighted surprise as the rock she had thrown hit Ronnie in the head and he fell down, not moving. The next thing she knew, the next door neighbor was coming off of his porch yelling something at her. Margret took one more look at Ronnie and saw he still wasn't moving, then she looked over at David and saw he was coming towards her.

Margret's only thought was she had gotten lucky and had killed the rat bastard. She didn't want to hang around, so she jumped in her car and started it after locking all of the doors. She saw David wasn't coming after her after all, but was going to Ronnie's aid. She shifted the car into reverse and floored the accelerator.

She laid two separate patches of rubber on the ground as she left. One patch was from the tires burning out in reverse into the street. The second should have been from where she tried to lock up the breaks, but the ABS system refused to let the wheels lock. So her second patch was from where she had slammed the shifter into drive and floored the accelerator once again.

Margret had two separate emotions going on inside of her. First, she was ecstatic she had gotten in the last major damage to Ronnie before she left. Second, she was afraid she had killed him and didn't want to be anywhere around to be arrested. She knew that even if he wasn't dead, with the intrusion of David, the police would be called. So she decided to put as much distance between her and the town as quickly as possible.

As she drove, Margret took stock of what she had. She knew she still had about six hundred dollars from the checks she had written. She cursed herself for being so stupid and blowing the rest of her money on the bar flies she had been hanging around with. She had a full tank of gas, so she knew she could go a long way before she had to stop and refill the tank with gas.

Up ahead of her, she saw the sign for the interstate and without hesitation, she turned onto the first on ramp she came to and headed west. Once she was on the interstate, she set the cruise control for five miles an hour above the speed limit and cruised on.

105.

At the same time Margret was taking stock of her purse, Ronnie was being helped to his feet by David. Ronnie was still somewhat dazed and the side of his head hurt like hell. He saw Connie standing at the bottom of his porch steps, she had come out of her hiding place on her porch as Margret tore out of her driveway. As Ronnie became more aware of his surroundings, he realized she was asking him if he wanted her to call an ambulance. In a weak voice, Ronnie told her he didn't think it would be necessary and he would be okay.

David helped Ronnie into the house as Connie went back to her house to get an ice pack. Ronnie sat down heavily onto the couch as his headache deepened and seemed to take over his whole being. His vision kept blurring and then going back to normal. Ronnie noticed every time his vision blurred, his headache would do the impossible and worsen. When his vision returned to normal, the pain would ease off to a somewhat bearable level.

A few short minutes later, Connie was back with the ice pack. She gently applied it to the side of Ronnie's head and stepped back, remarking to her husband that she was worried about the swelling on the side of Ronnie's head. Ronnie told her he would be alright once he got some rest.

She went back home after telling David to stay there, all night if he had to, and make sure that Ronnie didn't lapse into a coma or something. David told her he would and also promised to call her if Ronnie's condition worsened.

106.

Margret had been running steady for almost an hour and found the further away she got from Ronnie, the better she felt. As she thought about it, she now realized she would be able to start her life over again like she had planned to do with Ted.

Tears, real tears this time because there was no one around to put on a show for, began to seep from her eyes as she thought about Ted. It was unfair he had been taken away from her just as they were getting their first real chance to start a new life together. Never mind that he had lost his life trying to take Ronnie's. She began to hope Ronnie was dead, it would be a small payback for taking the life of the one man she truly loved. Not to mention the earning potential Ted would have been able to achieve. Up ahead, she could see the lights of an overpass where two interstates crossed each other. With tears blurring her vision, she approached the first series of off ramps to the overpass and went into the oasis of light in the darkness.

As she neared the first overpass, the radio suddenly switched itself on and began to rapidly change stations. Margret reached over and switched the radio back off, but it didn't go off and just continued to change channels. Finally, it settled on one station just as the song 'Another one Bites the Dust' by Queen came on. Margret, who had been looking at the radio and not the road, looked up and saw that she was drifting to the right towards one of the off ramps.

She tried to steer the car back to the left, but found the steering wouldn't respond and seemed to be locked into a slight right hand drift. Frantically, she pulled on the steering wheel, first left and then right, but it wouldn't budge. It was as if the car was riding on a set of rails and she was powerless to control it. She knew her speed was too great for the ramp and couldn't understand why after she had taken her foot off of the accelerator, the car refused to slow down. She was now beginning to drift into the actual ramp lane when she remembered the reason the car wasn't slowing down was because she had the cruise control on. She tapped her foot on the brake expecting it to disengage the cruise control, but nothing happened and she continued on her journey under full power.

Margret quickly reached down and found the controls to the cruise control. She switched the on-off switch to off, but still nothing happened. Margret had no way of knowing it, but the computer control module under the hood had been reprogrammed by the Professor and there was nothing she could do to stop the car.

As she saw the actual ramp itself ahead, Margret jammed on the brakes as hard as she could. The computer module over rode the ABS module and locked the bleeder valves in the open position. So, as hard as she pressed, the brake fluid bypassed the brake cylinders because of those bleeder valves, which normally opened and closed several times a second to keep the brakes from locking under emergency stops and didn't actuate the plungers that would press the brake pads against the rotors. The car did slow down a couple of miles an hour though. The computer sensed the slow down and compensated, increasing the speed of the car back to what the cruise control had been locked on.

As the curve of the ramp came rushing towards her, Margret had the sickening feeling she wasn't going to make the curve. Even if she could steer the car, her speed was too fast and she knew she would flip over on the curve. Just as she started up the ramp, she grabbed the shift lever in a vain attempt to shift the car out of drive and into neutral, but she found the shift lever seemed to be locked into position. She now accepted the fact there was nothing she could do to stop the inevitable. So she grasped the steering wheel tighter and tried to brace herself for the wreck that was about to happen.

Margret saw the concrete post with the steel guard rail attached to it just before the front of the car struck it. She felt the car lift up as she crashed through the guard rail. There was a brief, seemingly eternal feeling of weightlessness as the car, now off of the ramp, sailed through the air to the ground that was a good ten feet below it. In that ten feet of downward air, she was propelled a hundred feet forward before the nose of the car came in contact with the soft ground.

The jolt of the crash was tremendous and everything inside of the car flew forward. If Margret hadn't been wearing her seatbelt, she would have been propelled forward also, although her head bobbed down scant millimeters in front of the steering wheel. But the seatbelt functioned as the manufactures had intended it to and Margret was held firmly in her seat. The glove box however, was never intended to take such forces and sprang open, spilling it's contents.

As the front of the car buckled at the bottom of the windshield from the overwhelming stresses it was never designed to withstand, Margret felt the bottom edge of the dashboard scrape along the tops of her legs just above her knees as the dash was forced downward towards her legs. She thought it felt like someone was trying to rip her skin off of the tops of her legs using a salt grindstone. For a brief moment, Margret felt her weight triple as the car stood on its nose and she was still being forced downward. She could feel the center of the steering wheel as it pressed against the top of her head and it felt as if all of her weight was being supported by the seatbelt and her neck.

Then the feeling of the G Forces let up and once again she was weightless. Her head fell back and hit the headrest. Looking out of the windshield, she marveled that the glass was still intact and she saw that the world looked strange, the ground was where the sky should have been and there was no way she could look down to see if the black sky was also out of place, but she assumed it was as the car was now flipping over to make another handstand on its rear bumper.

The next jolt was worse than the first when the car settled into the ground on its rear end. Margret felt the car stand straight up. It was like being inside a tornado as the stuff flew around the interior of the car. A can of Root Beer, more than rock solid from the pressure that had built up inside of it from bouncing around in the floor board in the heat and now the tremendous shaking it had just received from being airborne with the car, hit her in the chin and Margret felt the needle sharp pain as her chin was crushed and her lower front teeth shattered. For a brief instant, she thought the car was going to remain standing on its rear bumper as it settled deeper into the soft ground. The seat under her protested from the shift and increase in body weight, but didn't give way and held firm. A passing thought of an astronaut being strapped into his chair before blast off passed through Margret's mind. She couldn't see anything through the windshield because the hood was lying back over the top of the car. The impact of the hood falling against the top of the car put spider cracks all through the windshield itself.

Margret could feel her weight beginning to press against the shoulder strap of her seatbelt as the car, having lost its momentum and unable to complete its next part of a loop, fell back onto its top. Margret saw the door post crunch outward, making a gap between the edge of the door and the door frame, her senses were overloaded from the white-hot pain of the dash board coming down on both of her legs and crushing them. Just before she grayed out, she could feel both sides of her hips snap as the dash pushed her legs flat against the floor and pinned them there.

Margret came to quickly, only being out for a second or two at the most. She tried to move and found the pain from her legs short circuited any idea of movement. She was being held upside down by her seatbelt and her legs. Her legs, being crushed, had the rigidity of cooked spaghetti. What was really holding her legs was the dashboard across the tops of her thighs.

Margret marveled she was still alive and found she could move her head slightly. She could see out of the side window and a small part of the windshield. Her breath caught in her throat.

Outside of the car, kneeling towards the hood of the car, was the figure of a person. Margret thought someone had seen the wreck and was here to save her. Then she realized with horror that the side view of the person she was looking at was Ronnie. He seemed not to be intent on getting her out, but instead, was watching something in the engine compartment. Even though her jaw was crushed and flopping against the roof of her mouth because she was upside down, she began to laugh hysterically at the thought of Ronnie being there.

Her laughter became louder and more uncontrollable when she saw the flames start racing around on the ground around her. It was then she became aware of the thick smell of the gasoline fumes that were now filling the car and a cold, burning wetness of fluid pouring down her body into the car.

Margret's hysterical shrieks of laughter were drowned out by a FAW-WHUMP sound as the gasoline fumes inside the car ignited through the buckles in the door frame. The pressure on her ear drums was unbearable as the fireball expanded inside the car, swapping fire for oxygen.

Her breath was white-hot with heat and Margret could feel her lungs shrivel inside her chest as she tried to draw in one more lung full of air. All over her body, her skin felt as if someone was holding a giant magnifying glass to the sun with her as the focal point as her skin heated up to the boiling point of the blood it contained. She could feel herself being consumed by the fire, burning alive, as she passed out from the lack of oxygen and shock.

Margret may have passed out from the lack of oxygen and shock, away from the outside world, but she was far from dead. She still had a few precious moments to think as she hung upside down in the inferno that just a short while ago had been the interior of her car. Those few moments she had to think before her brain began to cook inside her skull, boiled in its own pot as it were.

Her mind was now disconnected from the physical world as her body was being consumed by the fire and she thought about Ronnie. The rat bastard was somehow alive and had escaped her. Hate filled her mind and a darkness came over her thoughts, Margret accepted she was dying for sure, no reprieves this time. She wondered where the light was, she had always heard that a person sees a light they go towards as they died. But she saw none. The only thing she saw was the after image of the flames burning her that were held in her memory. Even more hatred filled her mind bringing on even more darkness as she thought she had been lied to, there was nothing special that happened when you died. At the very end, her maternal instinct finally pushed its way to the surface and her last thought was how she had been a failure as a parent to Nancy.

In a space of time less than the length of one song, Margret's life ended. The radio played on for a minute or two before the power cables and speakers began to melt and burn. Just enough time for Queen to finish their immortal song.

The fire raged to such a point that after the glass in the windows began to break, it started to melt. It would be forty-five minutes before a fire truck would arrive and finally douse the flames. Which by then, had almost burned themselves out except for the tires. They continued to burn sootedly until the firemen quenched their flames.

R. H. Gosse

After the fire truck arrived, the loose crowd of people who had gathered at first to try and lend some assistance, but stayed to watch the fire, quickly dissipated when the policeman who had accompanied the fire truck started asking questions. Within a couple of minutes a couple more local cops arrived along with a couple of State Troopers. Since the ground was soft and it was only a couple of more hours till dawn, the senior State Trooper and the local Fire Marshal (who had just arrived himself after hearing his men whoop and holler about how bad this fire was on the radio) decided any investigations could wait until sunrise. They used the excuse that they would have to wait until the car itself had cooled. Another Trooper called back to base and requested a decision on whether to have forensics come out and take a look.

The State Trooper Watch Commander asked the junior Trooper if it looked like there had been anyone in the car. He was able to be completely honest when he reported that it was impossible to tell. The Commander told him to wait until the local Fire Marshal determined if there had been a fatality, then, if there had been one, a team would be dispatched immediately.

107.

At the same time a State Trooper was calling back to report they had found some teeth and bone fragments in the car, Ronnie was beginning to surface from the almost catatonic state he had been in. His head hurt like hell and he was mildly surprised to see David there with him.

Ronnie tried to sit up, but quickly found the change in position made him so dizzy he began to feel sick and quickly laid back down. The only thing he could remember was throwing Margret out and then Margret picking something up off the ground outside. The rest of his memories from the night were strange and fuzzy.

"That's a mighty nasty looking bruise on the side of the old noggin you got there." David remarked in what seemed to Ronnie to be an unusually loud voice.

"Shhh." Ronnie said as he attempted to raise a finger to his lips. "This is a beauty of a hangover and everything is really loud." he said quietly.

"Sorry," David said in a much quieter tone of voice, "But that ain't no hangover you're sportin son. Your wife damn near kilt you with a rock she chucked at you. If she'd been a quarter inch over, she'd had put your temple out. Course, if she'd done that, we'd not be havin this conversation right now."

"Is she gone?" Ronnie asked not paying attention to the news about his near miss with death at the hands of Margret.

"Ain't seen her since she tore outta here last night. How are you feeling? One point last night I thought I'd have to tote you to the hospital. The side of your head swoll up and got big. I see some of the swellin is gone now, but you're gonna have a beaut of a bruise for awhile." David rambled on, looking relieved that Ronnie had survived the night and seemed to be making sense now.

"Nancy?"

"She's safe next door with Connie. Probably still asleep."

"What time is it?" Ronnie asked, suddenly realizing it was light outside and he had a job to go to.

"Almost seven-thirty." David replied after a quick glance at his watch.

"Oh shit." Ronnie said as he tried to sit up again, "I'm late for work." Ronnie found if he sat up more slowly this time, it wasn't as bad as the first time. He was moving almost slow enough to say he was sneaking up on being vertical.

"Hold on there big boy." David said as he put his hand on Ronnie's chest stopping him, "I don't think your in any shape to go anywhere. You got any sick time saved up?"

"Sure, loads of it." Ronnie replied as he sat there leaning back against the couch cushions.

David picked up the phone and asked, "Who do I call?"

Ronnie told him the phone number and asked for the receiver when the phone started ringing. After a few rings, the phone was answered on the other end and Ronnie asked to speak with Grandma Moses. A couple more seconds sneaked by and she answered the phone. Ronnie explained he had an accident at his house and had hurt his head. The old lady on the other end asked if he was okay just as Ronnie felt another wave of nausea building again and he knew he had to lay down or toss his cookies.

David saw what was happening and took the receiver away from Ronnie and held it up to his own ear. He listened for a second and then interrupted the woman on the phone, explaining who he was. He told her he was Ronnie's next door neighbor and had been helping watch Ronnie all night to make sure he wasn't going to die. He went on to further explain that Ronnie had gotten hit in the side of the head and couldn't sit upright for more than a couple of minutes at a time, much less stand or drive himself to work. David was asked how it happened and he told her he really couldn't discuss it. But he could attest to the fact that Ronnie was not playing and was indeed, seriously hurt. David was told to tell Ronnie if he had to take a couple of days off, it would be alright. He was also told if there was any question to Ronnie's health, to tote him to the hospital whether he wanted to go or not. He thanked her and then hung up, relaying the concern that he had been told to relay to Ronnie.

David asked Ronnie if he was okay and Ronnie told him yes, he just didn' feel very well. David replied he needed to go back to his house for a few minutes to change clothes and Ronnie merely waved him on.

David quickly went to his house and found Connie sleeping on the couch. The second David walked in, she sat bolt upright and asked how Ronnie was doing. He told her Ronnie was now awake and making alot more sense than he had last night, but he was still weak and suffering from the effects of the blow to the head. Connie got up and without saying a word, went next door to check on Ronnie for herself.

As soon as she had walked out the front door, David picked up the phone and called the Country Club himself. When it was answered, he asked for the administrator. When she got on the phone he explained as best he could, what had happened the night before. He told her how as Margret was leaving, she had gotten a lucky shot off with a good sized rock and nailed Ronnie in the side of the head, almost killing him. He went on to explain about how delirious he had been last night and had just come back to the land of the living less than a half hour ago.

She was horrified to hear it and told him not to let Ronnie come back to work until he was better. David then asked if this could be kept confidential and she told him as far as anyone would be concerned there, Ronnie was just out sick with the flu. David thanked her and after hanging up, quickly went and changed clothes. Fifteen minutes later, he was on his way back next door.

When he arrived, he found that Ronnie was looking better and was now sitting up with his feet on the floor.

108.

At sunup, the fire marshal started going through what was left of the burned out car. He had remarked to the Troopers standing around that he hoped nobody had been in the car. All of them agreed.

The crash scene, under the light of day, bordered on unbelievable and surreal. Yellow police tape seemed to grow around the scene and now that it was light, the Troopers began taking pictures in an effort to document what had happened.

The car, still lying on its top, had sagged and almost melted from the intense heat of the fire that had consumed it. It had sagged down on its roof and was now just over three feet tall. Low enough that the fire marshal had to get down on his knees to start trying to go through the car. His mission was simple. He was to go through the car as carefully as possible and at the first sight of human remains, he was to stop and report it. Then his duties would be over and the crime lab would be called in to go through the rest of the car.

Lying on his belly he crawled in through where the windshield had been, the heavy protective fireman's jacket and pants protecting him from the still hot car frame, and within a couple of minutes of poking around found the first few teeth and pieces of bone. He didn't say anything and kept looking. Being careful not to disturb anything, he poked his Maglite under what had been the dash. Now that all of its coverings and panels had been burned away, it was easy to look under what remained of the support structure. He found what appeared to be a pair of burned up sneakers. Nothing in the car really bothered him, not the teeth nor the bone. But when he saw those sneakers, he felt the vomit raise in his throat like a freight elevator. The shoes were more or less intact and a couple of inches of charred bone were sticking out. To his horror, he realized the rest of the feet were contained inside those shoes.

The fire marshal rolled out of the car and crawled a couple of feet before vomiting. The State Troopers were gathered around and he was asked what he had found. Between gags, he said there were teeth and bone inside the car. Then after vomiting again, he told about the shoes.

It was then the senior Trooper went and made the call for the forensic team. The rest of the Troopers started to document the crash site in earnest. There was a small debate about how they were going to identify the remains, let alone what type of car it had been. The fire had been very thorough in its destruction. One Trooper speculated it might never be known who had met their fate, he recalled a time when a car had been found almost in this same state and to this day they still didn't know who had been killed.

Ten minutes later, another important discovery was made. In the hole in the ground the rear end of the car had made, was the license plate of the car partially covered by dirt. It had been torn off of the car when the car had made its rear end handstand. Dirt, scooped out by the rear bumper, had fallen onto the plate partially covering it as the car fell back onto its roof.

Since the car had rolled back towards the hood with the engine of the car weighing the front end down, all of the gasoline that had poured out of the ruptured gas tank had spilled down the undercarriage of the car towards the engine and passenger compartments. What gas had spilled and burned in the hole the rear end made, had left the license plate unharmed because of the dirt covering it. Pictures were immediately taken and the plate was retrieved for examination.

The plate was out of state since Margret had crossed over the state line twenty minutes before the accident. Another message was sent back to headquarters for a license check.

At the State Troopers Headquarters, the plate was run for outstanding warrants. None was found so a phone call was made to the county the plate was from for a stolen car check. The local county ran the plate and found it wasn't hot, but they did have an address the car had come from. The young civil servant gave the information about the address back to the Troopers who then called the city police to further the information along.

109.

Max had been doing some paperwork when Officer Bell came into the small cubical in which he had been sitting. Max used the paperwork story to stay long after his shift and wait for the company shrink to get to work.

"Sergeant Maxwell?" Bell asked.

"Yeah, what's up?" Max asked without looking up from the paperwork he was supposedly so hard at work.

"The Captain is having a shit fit looking for you." Was the reply.

"Thanks, you can leave now." Max said.

Max had no idea what Waters wanted, but he wasted no time in finding Waters himself. Waters wasn't the type of person who was looking for anybody unless it was really important.

"In my office, we have to talk." Was the only thing Waters said when he saw Max.

Once inside, Max closed the door and said, "Honestly boss, I didn't have a thing to do with it."

"I know, you never do." Waters said with a smile on his face. Then he turned serious. "You know that kid I sent you over to and you decided to have people shoot at you for fun?"

"Fisher? Of course I remember. Why?"

"There's been an accident." Waters said and Max felt his blood freeze in his veins, he was sure the next thing he was about to be told was that Ronnie had been killed. It was the only logical thing he could think of and the most likely chain of events.

"Is he dead?" Max asked not really wanting to know.

"That's what we need to find out."

"What's going on?" Max asked puzzled.

Water explained the information as he knew it about the accident and burned human remains. Basically, he wanted Max to go over to Ronnie's house, find out who was there and if the car had been stolen. But whatever he did, he was to find out who, if anyone, was missing by personally looking at the both of them husband and wife. Even if it took the rest of the day. The motivation behind this was the State Troopers from the neighboring state were in a hurry to close this case as quickly as possible. The more they were helped, the more they would appreciate it.

Max told Waters he was on the job as he got up and walked out of the office. Waters watched Max leave thinking this was the first time he had told Max to do something and Max had straight out left without shooting the breeze for a couple of seconds at least. He also thought Max's question was a strange one, 'Is he dead?' wasn't a question he had expected. He wondered why Max would ask a question like that. Of course, he didn't have Max's knowledge of Margret's continuing physical abuse of Ronnie. Although he had first hand knowledge of the legend of Margret's mouth.

Max walked straight out of the building without stopping to straighten the cubical he had been using. The whole time he was walking out to the patrol car he was about to use, he was wondering what Margret was up to. He was very afraid he was about to find out she had killed Ronnie and then ditched his body in the burning car. Although Waters had filled him in with as much information and as many facts as he knew, the jungle drums had omitted alot of information in the translation.

When he got to Ronnie's house, Max was partially relieved to see Ronnie's old junker car sitting in the driveway. He hadn't seen Ronnie since the day after the shooting and didn't know there had been another car bought. He walked up to the front door half thinking there had been a mistake and somebody had screwed up calling the plate in from the scene of the crash.

Max knocked on the door and it was answered by David. Max instantly recognized David as Ronnie's next door neighbor. Deep down inside, he heard that little voice he sometimes listened to go 'Oh-oh'.

"I am Sergeant Maxwell, is Ronald Fisher here?" He asked in an official voice.

"Yes. But I don't think he is able to come to the door right now." David answered.

"Well...I really need to see him." Max replied as he pushed his way past David into the living room.

"Come on in." David said as he closed the door behind Max.

Max saw Ronnie laying on the couch with his eyes closed as he stepped into the living room. Instinctively, he dropped the palm of his hand to the butt of his gun just in case something funny was going on. Ronnie opened his eyes when David closed the door.

"Max!" Ronnie said, truly glad to see him. "What brings you here?"

Max relaxed when he saw Ronnie's eyes open. He took a couple of steps toward where Ronnie was with his hand outstretched in greeting. "Unfortunately, business." He replied.

"It's really good to see you." Ronnie said as he took Max's hand and gave it a couple of pumps.

Max started to say something when he realized just how bad Ronnie looked. He looked weak and his head was different, lopsided. "What happened to you?" He asked.

"Had a small accident." Ronnie replied.

Instantly, Max thought he had it wrong, Ronnie had gotten rid of Margret Which was unusual, the abused gave out a dose of medicine to the abuser. But before he got a chance to ask anything, he was interrupted by David.

"Accident hell!" David said loudly, "His wife almost killed him last night."

Max turned his attention to David.

"Max, meet David, my next door neighbor. Max-David, David-Max." Ronnie added from his place on the couch.

"We've met." Max replied to Ronnie and then asked David, "How do you know that?"

"Cause I saw it." David replied and started to elaborate when he was interrupted by a knock on the front door. David stopped and answered the door. It turned out to be Connie, who came over when she looked out of her front window and saw the police car parked in front of Ronnie's house.

"You were saying something about seeing Margret try to kill Ronnie?" Max asked not wanting to let this line of questioning drop.

"Me and the Misses were sitting out on the front porch last night. Ronnie and Margret were having a fight, they were outside you see and I saw her pick up that rock and hit Ronnie in the head with it." He told Max and pointed towards the fist sized smooth stone laying on the coffee table.

Max glanced at the rock and asked, "Where is she now?"

"Margret?" David asked back and then said, "Couldn't tell you. After she beaned old Ronnie there, she saw me coming to help him and took off in her car."

"You have a second car now?" Max asked Ronnie.

"Yep. Things are doing alot better these days."

"Ronnie, do you know where Margret is?" Max asked him.

"Wish I could help you on that one. I threw her out last night and told her to hit the streets. So I guess in retaliation, she hit me with the rock. The rest of what happened, I couldn't tell you. I was knocked goofy and spent the night on the couch with David and Connie watching over me to make sure I didn't stop breathing. I don't really remember Margret leaving. In fact, I don't remember much except waking up here on the couch this morning."

"Is that pretty much how it happened?" Max asked Connie.

"Pretty much, except for the part about me being here. I was staying at my house because of the kids and didn't come over here until this morning." She told him.

Max had a sick feeling, "Ronnie," He asked, "Where's your daughter?"

"She's at my house next door. Why?" Connie said.

Max, greatly relieved, stood there for a moment not knowing what to say. Finally, he said, "Ronnie, the...Your car was found in another state. It was involved in some sort of accident and burned. They also found what they think are human remains inside the car."

"Oh no!" Connie cried out and Ronnie just at there not comprehending what he had just heard.

"What did you say?" Ronnie finally managed to ask.

Max sat down in a chair next to the couch and began to explain what he knew. He told Ronnie to expect a visit or a call from the State Troopers after he (Max) reported in. Ronnie was in a mild state of shock, he had wanted to get rid of Margret, but he had never considered anything like this.

Max asked Ronnie a few more questions; what time did she leave, had she been drinking? Connie told Max the time and Ronnie said Margret had been drinking before she had come home. Max speculated she had probably fallen asleep at the wheel before the wreck.

Then Max told Ronnie he was sorry to have to be the first one to give him the happy news. Ronnie told Max he couldn't think of anyone else he would rather have told him and then thanked him for doing what he had done. Max felt bad for Ronnie, but at the same time, he was kind of glad. He knew what Ronnie had been living with and he knew it was better that Margret checked out on her own instead of at the hands of Ronnie, or even worse, before she did something bad like killing Ronnie in a fit of rage.

Max had half expected Ronnie to jump up and yell "Alright!", but he didn't miss the small smile that crept across Ronnie's face for a brief instant when the news Max had given him sank in. Fixating on that point for a second, Max realized it wasn't a smile he saw on Ronnie's face, but more the look of relief. Knowing the things Ronnie had been through in the past, Max selectively let Ronnie's look pass without further question. He was just glad Ronnie seemed to have an airtight alibi and Margret had been alone when her mishap happened.

Ronnie was in a mild state of shock from the news Max had brought, not to mention the killer headache that was now making his teeth hurt with every pulse of his beating heart. Ronnie sat there for a few minutes before he politely asked if Connie and David would leave and let him have a few minutes alone with Max.

There was no fuss as Connie made the excuse she had to check on Nancy and left with David in tow. For an awkward second, Max was afraid Ronnie was going to do something stupid and confess to killing Margret after the next door neighbors left. Max almost said so as they sat in silence for a moment, but he thought better of it and also sat there in silence.

"Max, I don't know what to say." Ronnie finally said after a couple o
minutes. "I know that I should feel bad about what happened, but I don't. I'ı
glad the bitch is dead and out of my hair forever."

"I know Ronnie. I don't blame you for the way you feel. I'm not surprised ā
it either. It happens like this sometimes. I'm just surprised you didn't jump u
and yell Ya-Hoo when I told you." Max told him, relieved Ronnie only wanted t
reflect and not confess.

"But...Does this mean that I'm a bad person?" Ronnie asked as he looke
Max straight in the eye.

"No." Max answered after a moment, "But I suppose yelling Ya-Hoo woul
have gone a long way for qualifying you for the bad person title."

"But I feel bad about the way I feel. Does that make sense?"

"Not really, but yeah, it does. It's only natural you would feel this way afte
you were told the biggest instigator of abuse and oppression in your life had bee
removed permanently. Happy, but at the same time, ashamed you're happy.
Max told Ronnie trying to console him.

"That's exactly how I feel." Ronnie remarked and Max noticed that Ronni
seemed to brighten up somewhat.

"I know Ronnie, believe me, I know."

"Max, there's one more thing I think I should come right out and say to you.

"What's that?"

"I had nothing to do with her accident. We just fought, I threw her out an
she left. I had no knowledge of what had happened until you showed up and tol
me."

Max was surprised Ronnie had said that, but at the same time, he wasn'
surprised. He knew Ronnie was an up-front type of guy with a terrible secret a
home. "I know that Ronnie." He replied and saw Ronnie looked confused, so h
continued, "I saw it in your face when I told you. I could see you had no ide
why I was here. Being in this job awhile, you develop a sort of sixth sense abou
people. You have to so you can stay alive for as long as I have. Anyway, yo
start to be able to tell when someone's telling you the truth and when they'r
trying to shovel a load of bullshit on you."

"Thanks man." Ronnie said and then fell silent.

"No problem." Max replied and then fell silent also. He was only silent for
minute before he began to tell Ronnie what to expect to happen in the nex
couple of days. First, the State Troopers would send an investigator to ask him
bunch of questions about what happened the night Margret left. Max suggeste
Ronnie tell the truth and let the investigator know about the next door neighbor
who would collaborate his story and Max himself. Then, if there were enoug
remains to do so, they would ask him to identify them. Lastly, they would as
Ronnie what he wanted done with the remains, so he had better think about tha

last one. If there was a funeral home his family normally used, he might want to contact them soon, just in case.

When Max finished telling Ronnie this, he said one more thing, "Ronnie, you really look like shit. Are you sure you don't need to go to the hospital? I'll take you if you want to go."

"Nah., I'll be alright. She's done worse to me and I've survived before." Ronnie stopped speaking for a moment and then said, "I guess I'll never have to worry about that again, will I?"

"No, you won't. It's really over and you're free. You can start all over again. Did she have any insurance?"

"Not that I know of. I couldn't afford to put her on my work policy. Now that I've got a fairly decent income rolling in, I really haven't thought about getting some kind of policy."

"Good." Max replied, "That rules out any motive of financial gain. You're going to be okay Ronnie, but are you sure you don't want me to take you to the hospital?"

"No Max, I don't want to go to the hospital. But you could do me a favor."

"Name it."

"I've been on this couch ever since they plopped me here last night, my back teeth are floating. Could you help me get to the bathroom?"

Max agreed at once and Ronnie's knees almost buckled after he got standing up. Ronnie did notice as he stood up, his headache toned down somewhat and he took it as a good sign he was getting progressively better. By the time Max got Ronnie to the bathroom door, Ronnie found he was more able to stand on his own. Walking was another story, he required Max to act as a counter balance.

Inside the bathroom, Ronnie went straight to the toilet and did his business. As he was zipping up, he turned around slowly and caught the first glimpse of himself since Margret had nailed him with the rock, in the mirror behind Max. Immediately, he could see why Max kept asking him if he wanted to go to the hospital.

The rock Margret hit Ronnie with was smooth, so there was no gaping gash along the side of his head, but the area she had hit him was swollen, making the side of his head seem lopsided. In the mirror, he could see almost a quarter of his head was covered by a bright, blood red bruise that was starting to turn an alarming shade of black along the edges. Looking at the swollen area itself, the angry red looked as if he was bleeding just under the skin. He figured the rock must have ruptured some capillaries and they were still bleeding under the skin causing the red. Ronnie figured it was better to rupture a few capillaries in his skin than to rupture his skull.

After the inspection of his war wounds, Ronnie carefully washed his face and found the cold water soothing. He started to get some aspirin for his headache, but just before he took them, he remembered something about a warning about aspirin not letting blood clot. So he put the pills back into the bottle and just drank the water he had drawn to wash the pills down instead. Ronnie found he was very thirsty and drank two more glass fulls. Drinking the cold water reminded him of the fountain in the glen.

The glen, he thought, of course! Why hadn't he thought of it sooner? All he needed to do was to get rid of everyone and get some sleep. He felt if he could do that, he could will himself to go to the glen. Once there, he could wash his head with the water from the fountain and heal himself. He remembered the risks that were involved in doing that, but he decided he would risk anything to get rid of the headache he was sporting.

A few minutes later, he re-emerged from the bathroom feeling a little better than when he had gone in. More important, his almost terminal feeling of having to urinate was taken care of. On shaky feet, he walked back into the living room. Max had stepped out of the small bathroom and was waiting for him just outside the bathroom, but Ronnie resisted Max's attempts to help and managed to walk into the living room under his own power.

The trip from the bathroom was exhausting and Ronnie sat down heavily onto the couch. Max was at his side the whole time in case he was needed.

When Ronnie was settled, Max asked if he could use the phone to make a couple of calls. Ronnie told Max he didn't have to ask and to help himself.

110.

Max's first call was to the police station. He identified himself and asked for the Captain. He was on hold only three seconds before Waters picked up. Max gave the fullest report he could in front of Ronnie. He explained there had been a fight, Margret picked up a rock, knocked Ronnie for a loop and Ronnie had been passed out all night on the couch. He listened for a couple of seconds and then quickly added that there were witnesses to what had happened. There were a few more minutes of talking before Max broke the connection. The next call he made was to his house. He told his wife the readers digest version of what was going on and told her he would be home in a bit.

After Max hung up, he went back over and sat down in the chair next to the couch. Ronnie was still sitting upright and looked much better than before the trip to the bathroom. Max told Ronnie he should go to the bathroom more often if it improved his looks this much.

Ronnie chuckled at that and they shot the breeze for a long time. Ronnie asked Max if he was working days now and Max told him no, he had just gotten off of the night shift when the Captain asked him to come over here and check on Ronnie's sorry butt. Ronnie remarked that Max must be tired and needed to go home to get some rest, but Max wouldn't hear of it, saying he was going to stay there as long as he wanted to.

Since Max already knew about Ronnie's Gabby connection, Ronnie decided to tell him about the books that had been written. Max was amazed to hear that and even more amazed to find out how much money Ronnie had made from those books. Ronnie than told Max about the box of disks that contained more books he was waiting to print off. Max congratulated Ronnie on his success and said he admired Ronnie for having the imagination to write. Then Max asked him how he did it. Ronnie thought about this for a moment and said, "Easy. I just write one word at a time."

After an hour of small talk, Ronnie told Max he was tired and wanted to catch a nap. Max replied that he understood and gave Ronnie another one of his business cards after writing his home phone number on it. He told Ronnie that if he needed anything, no matter what time of day or night, he was to call him. Ronnie thanked him and assured Max he would.

Max left and Ronnie settled back onto the couch, waiting to doze off. Sleep caught up with him within a couple of minutes.

When Max left Ronnie's house, he went straight next door. He told Connie Ronnie was starting to look better, but was over there getting ready to take a nap. He suggested somebody needed to go next door periodically and check on Ronnie's condition. Then he gave her one of his business cards with his phone number on it and told her that if there was any change in Ronnie for the worse, or if he needed anything, she was to call him immediately.

Connie thanked him and remarked that it was nice Ronnie had friends like him. It was Max's turn to thank her and then he left to go home.

When Max got home, he ate his breakfast his wife had made for him as soon as she heard him drive up. He then instructed her to get him up if either Ronnie or Ronnie's neighbor called. That having been said, they both went to bed. It was Max's wife's routine to return to bed with him after he got home from work and this morning was no different, even though Max was really late getting home. Thirty minutes later, Max was snoring like a chainsaw.

111.

Ronnie had been asleep for almost a half hour before he opened his dream eyes and found himself standing in the glen. Ronnie had no idea that as he slept, Connie had come back over to his house and was sitting in the chair next to him reading.

Ronnie saw what he was after and walked up to the fountain. He didn't have a hat to catch the water like the Professor had when he was there with the stitches, so Ronnie cupped his hands and thrust them into the stream of water, being careful to collect the water just like he had been instructed to. The water was cold to the touch and he splashed it onto his forehead. There was an instant tingling, burning sensation. But Ronnie also found he felt alot better. So he scooped up another couple of hands full and repeated the process.

Connie just happened to look up from her reading at the exact same moment Ronnie splashed himself in his dream the first time. With widening eyes, she watched as part of the bruise faded away and the swelling went down noticeably. Then, just as she was telling herself she wasn't seeing what she thought she was seeing, the bruise faded again. This time, a much larger area simply disappeared. She jumped up and ran next door to get David so he could see what was happening. By the time they got back, Ronnie's bruise was completely gone and the swelling had disappeared as well.

Ronnie had splashed himself three times from the fountain and he felt better than he had felt in a long time. As Ronnie looked around the glen that surrounded him, he found that he was having a hard time concentrating. He couldn't really remember his name, although he felt as if it was on the tip of his tongue. He knew he was in a glen, but he couldn't remember how he had gotten there. All he did know was he felt really good.

David was alarmed Ronnie had returned to a normal looking state so quickly, so he reached over and shook Ronnie's shoulder to wake him up to see if he was okay. Ronnie wouldn't rouse from his sleep. David shook him harder and ended up screaming in Ronnie's face as he was shaking him hard. David was becoming afraid Ronnie had slipped into some kind of coma due to his head wound.

Ronnie was standing in the glen admiring the beauty of his surroundings when he got the sudden urge that he was needed elsewhere. He could almost hear someone calling his name, or at least he thought it was his name. He really couldn't remember. After a moment, the urge to leave got more intense and his surroundings began to fade away.

Ronnie opened his eyes and found he was still lying on the couch and he was looking straight into David's face. David had a surprised look on his face and his eyes were opened wide.

"Ronnie...Ronnie, how do you feel?" David asked excitedly.

"Fine, why?" Ronnie replied. He immediately noticed he did feel fine, better than he had felt in quite awhile. But he also noticed there were gaps in his memory. Although he knew he was lying on his couch, he couldn't remember how he had gotten there. He also couldn't remember who David was when he first saw him, but Ronnie found his memory was returning quickly.

"Ronnie, you ain't gonna believe it, but something's happened to your face. You were sleeping so soundly, I thought you had slipped away from us." David stammered.

Looking past David, Ronnie saw Connie standing there with the most amazing look on her face. "What's wrong with my face?" Ronnie asked, his mind still dull from the after affects of the fountain and being woken up.

"The bruises, they're gone. Connie saw it first, she was over here watching you while you slept. Any ways, she came bustin over to the house saying your face was mutatin. I came back over here and sure enough, your bruises were gone."

"Gone?" Ronnie asked as he stood up to find a mirror. He had expected to be unsteady on his feet, but found his stance to be rock solid. There was no more dizziness and his thinking was very clear. More important than that, Ronnie realized his headache was gone.

David had been expecting Ronnie to need assistance with his standing and walking. He stood there looking at Ronnie with utter astonishment on his face. He watched as Ronnie walked, by himself, unassisted, to the bathroom.

Ronnie walked into the bathroom, shut the door behind him and then took a good look at himself in the mirror. The angry redness that had covered a good portion of the side of his head was gone. There was still a slight twinge of yellow from where the bruise had been, but Ronnie saw that the water from the fountain had done its job. Healing that should have taken weeks had come to pass in a few minutes when he had washed his head with the all purpose water. Carefully Ronnie tested the side of his head with his fingertips and found it was no longer even sore. In fact, a small hard lump at the point where the rock had hit him was the only outward sign (other than the slight twinge of yellow) that remained.

"It's a miracle!" Connie exclaimed as Ronnie walked out of the bathroom and into the living room.

"Not really." Ronnie replied. "I've always been an extremely fast healer."

"Oh." Connie said, sounding as though she was going to have to cancel her plans to build some sort of shrine to Ronnie.

"It's true. Remember when I got shot? Well, I had healed up in a couple of days and took the stitches out myself." Ronnie told her feeling his story needed a little more backing to it.

"Well, I'll be. I never saw anything like it." she remarked, "Have you David?"

"Can't say as I ever did." he replied. "How does it feel? Do you feel okay?"

"To tell you the truth, it feels really good and I feel really great." Ronnie answered David.

"Ronnie...I'm really sorry about Margret." Connie said, finally broaching the subject.

Looking at Connie, Ronnie replied, "Yeah, I know. It's really hard when something like this happens." Connie saw just how sad he looked when he said that.

"Well, I just want you to know not to worry about anything. I said it before and I'll say it again, we'll do whatever it takes to help you through this. You can count on us to help you with Nancy." Connie announced to him.

"I'm really glad to have friends like you guys."

"What are you going to do now?" David asked.

After a moments thought, Ronnie said, "I guess I'll take it one day at a time."

"That's the best attitude to have." David replied.

They made small talk for a few minutes before Ronnie told them he was still really tired and wanted to get some more sleep. They told him they understood and left. Ronnie laid back on the couch after they were gone and tried to get back to sleep.

Instead of rest, Ronnie could only think this was some kind of a big joke. Sometime soon, Max was going to come back through the door and tell him he was only April foolin'. But Ronnie knew this was just wishful thinking making him feel that way. If Max said Margret was dead, then she was stone cold dead.

Almost as an act of mercy, Ronnie did fall back to sleep.

Ronnie opened his dream eyes and found he was in the Professor's world. He was in the warehouse again, but this time he wasn't strapped to the table, he was sitting on it as if he was waiting for the Professor to show up. Within a minute, the Professor came.

So, how are we doing today? The Professor asked in a cheery voice.

'Shitty.'

Seems to me you would be in a really good mood right now.

'Why's that?'

Because I took care of the biggest problem you had. The Professor said as he held up another pair of hemostat's with another growth locked in its grip. Ronnie saw that this growth looked like the other two he had seen, except this one was larger, almost solid black and more malignant looking. Instinct told Ronnie what he was looking at was more sinister and evil than the others the Professor had shown him in the past.

'What?!' Ronnie snapped, 'You killed Margret? How?'

Ronnie, what do you take me for? The Professor said as if he had not a care in the world. He tossed the pair of hemostat's nonchalantly into the bucket at the end of the table with the two other pairs of hemostat's that were already there.

'I don't take you for anything. How did you do it? How did you kill her?'

Okay, if you want to know so badly, then I'll show you.

Instantly, the surroundings changed and they were standing atop the concrete pillar that supported the overpass bridge. It was day now and Ronnie could see a group of police and firemen gathered around the burned out frame of a car. Some of the people that he saw were busy going through what was left of the car. Ronnie instantly recognized where he was.

Recognize it?

'Are...are you telling me the car crash you kept dragging me to was Margret's accident?'

Funny how that is, don't you think? The Professor replied with a tone of disinterest in his voice.

'But, how did you do it?'

Since you want to know so bad, then I'll tell you. Remember how I was playing around with changing the channels on the television? Well, I found something better to play with. I found by increasing my power output, I could actually access the computer in Margret's car.

'That's impossible!' Ronnie yelled at him.

Impossible you say! Here you are standing here looking at the outcome of all my hard work and all you can do is doubt me? Take another good long, hard look. Keep this in mind as you do so, I did it all myself.

'It's just so hard to believe. Why should I believe you?'

Okay, I can see that you're going to be a hard sell. Do you remember having to reset your alarm clock the other night? Well, I did by accident while I was playing around with Margret's car computer.

Ronnie felt as if he had been punched in the stomach and all of his wind was gone. He only stood there with his mouth open and had nothing to say.

You look as if you need a change of scenery. The Professor said and then they were no longer on top of the pillar. They both now stood on the bridge of the small fishing boat.

'Where are we?'

Beats me. This is something from your dreams.

'Well, wherever we are, I kind of like it here.' Ronnie said as he looked out through the windows and saw the wall where he would have to make the left

492

hand turn was a long ways off. So he settled back against a shelf that was behind him. Now more relaxed, he began to ask questions. 'Why did you do it?'

Because she deserved it. She was hurting you.

'I don't buy that answer. She deserved it long before this. Her pattern of hurting me hasn't changed much since you've been around. So...Why did you do it?'

You want to know why? I'll tell you. The Professor screamed at Ronnie, seeming to finally lose his temper. *Because she hurt me. You're right, I don't really give a shit what happens to you. But when she brought the war to my neighborhood, I kicked her ass!*

Ronnie asked the only question he could think of, the remark about Margret hurting the Professor raised more questions than it answered. 'How could she hurt you?' Ronnie asked as he turned face to face with the Professor.

Since the Professor was still full of steam, he answered Ronnie without thinking about what he was doing first. *When she was beating on my home, the computer...* His voice trailed off as he realized what he was saying.

Ronnie heard enough to realized what the real answer was and pretended like the Professor's comment about the computer had passed over him without notice. 'Did she hurt you bad?' Ronnie asked, faking concern.

No, not really. The Professor said, downplaying his last comment hoping that Ronnie had missed it. *It was more like she pissed me off and I decided it was time to put an end to it. For me and for you. But if you really need to know, it was mostly for me.*

'I guess if that's the case, then the only thing I can say is thanks.' he told the Professor. Now, Ronnie's only motive was to get out of this dream and back to the real world.

There is one more thing.

'What's that?'

What did you do with the box of disks?

'What?'

The box of disks we stored all of the books to come on is missing. What did you do with them after we were finished the other night?

Ronnie thought back and remembered he had left the box sitting on the desk. 'I didn't do anything with them. Last time I saw them, they were sitting on the desk.'

The Professor didn't want to hear that as an answer. *Look boy. You better go back and find them. I can't believe you lost them!*

'I didn't lose shit! Usually, you're the one that puts things away after you're finished with them. I thought you were going to put them away.' Ronnie said defensively.

Well...I'll tell you what I'm going to do. You either go back and find them or else.

'Or else what?'

The Professor got right in Ronnie's face and said, *I already got rid of one bitch in your family, I can easily get rid of another. Remember when I got rid of that twit Ted? Right after I removed him from you, I told you there were two more growths...*

Ronnie knew immediately the Professor was talking about Nancy. 'You can't do that, she's just a baby.'

Then you do as you're told! The Professor said and then faded away. Ronnie stood there for another minute and then his surroundings faded away also.

112.

Ronnie laid on the couch thinking about what he had just been told. At first, he couldn't believe the Professor would threaten Nancy's life. Then he realized it was just the type of thing the Professor WOULD do. He sat up and looked over to where the computer sat on the desk. Looking past the computer to where he had sat the box of disks down, he saw they were no longer there.

Ronnie got up, went to the desk and started looking around, thinking the box of disks had just been moved. With a feeling of apprehension, he saw they were gone and he had a thought that froze the blood running through his veins.

What if Margret had picked up the box of disks to get back at him? Then they must have burned up in the car along with her. Ronnie knew the Professor would not take that as an answer and he stood there for a moment trying to decide what to do next.

At once, Ronnie knew. If Margret had hurt the Professor by beating on the computer, then he was going to finish it now. At the same time Ronnie began to formulate his plan, he heard the computer turn itself on and begin to warm up.

Ronnie knew he had to work quickly before the computer came on. So he grabbed the monitor off of the top of the computer casing and tried to throw it on the floor. The cables attached to the back of the monitor kept it from hitting the floor with enough force to break it. Even though the screen was still black, the computers voice, the voice of the Professor, came out of the speakers.

WHAT ARE YOU DOING RONNIE?

"If you don't know the answer to that one, then you're a dumber dead fag than I thought you were." Ronnie said as he was busy putting his arms around the whole computer so he could lift it up and throw it.

I WOULDN'T DO THAT IF I WERE YOU. The Professor's electronic voice said to him.

"Tell you the truth," Ronnie answered as he picked the computer up, "I really don't give a damn what you think I should or shouldn't do. But I'll tell you this, this is the end of you!"

Ronnie now had the computer up and was holding it over his head between his hands. The monitor lay at his feet and was beginning to glow. Ronnie looked

like a weight lifter at some nerdy computer camp as he stood there with th
computer over his head. The only reason he didn't throw the computer on th
floor behind him was because of the power cable that was firmly welded into th
power socket. He decided if he couldn't throw it against the wall on the othe
side of the room, then he would just throw it against the wall in front of him.

STOP OR ELSE! Came one more warning from the computer.

"Or else shit!" was Ronnie reply. As he said that, Ronnie felt the hummin
inside the computer change and deepen. It wasn't so much that he heard th
change inside the computer, but felt it through his hands and arms. Ronni
glanced at the cables coming out of the rear of the computer and saw that th
power cable was beginning to glow a faint red. The insulation of the cable bega
to smoke and drip off of the wires, leaving the two conductors of bare wire tha
were glowing a hot, angry red.

Just as he was about to give the computer the toss of its life, Ronnie heard
static, crackling sound coming from the keyboard. Ronnie looked down to the to
of the desk where the keyboard was still lying and watched in what seemed to b
slow motion as a blue spark leapt from the keyboard, traveled through the air an
hit him square between the eyes. Just before he died, Ronnie felt a pullin
sensation and he felt himself being drawn into the computer. There was
sensation that his whole mind and soul, everything that made Ronnie who an
what he was (except for his physical self), being loaded into the memory of th
computer. He was aware the Professor was there and in some small parts of th
memory, what hadn't been printed of Fryer, was there also. Ronnie felt th
Professor's presence here was so immense he was overwhelmed.

Ronnie's mind was wiped clean and his life ended. His body continued t
stand there for another second with the computer still over his head. The spar
continued through the back of his head to the wall socket behind him.

When the spark left his body, his muscles relaxed and he fell ove
backwards. As he fell, the computer was at the end of the arc that his arms made
There was an electronic scream as the computer came down with Ronnie's dea
hands still gripping it. The very overheated conductors of the power cable bega
to come apart as easily as someone pulling licorice whips apart.

The computer hit the floor with enough force to split the floorboard. Th
casing of the computer split wide open and a couple of the circuit boards cam
spilling out in a shower of sparks. Some of the boards survived the fall, but mos
of them were broken, cracked. Others were just broken at the connectors that ha
attached the boards to the motherboard itself.

As the power cable came apart, it fell across the cable that fed the monito
The two conductors of the power cable, as it came in contact with the monito
cable, began to heat up again as the current flow from the outlet resumed. Th
red hot conductors began to melt through the plastic protective coating of th
monitor cable. When the bare conductors melted through the last of th

insulation, a power surge was crated when they came in contact with the wires the monitor cable contained. The surge ran through those wires, which had been designed for carrying video signals only and started blowing components off of the circuit boards inside the monitor itself.

When everything stopped flying around, the computer lay on the floor over Ronnie's head as dead as he was.

113.

David found Ronnie laying on the floor thirty minutes after the main event. He had been sent over by Connie to see if Ronnie wanted to come over for some lunch. After calling the police, David called Max at home and explained what he had found.

Almost a week later, Connie found the box of disks that had been hidden in the diaper bag. A second call was made to Max asking what should be done. Max had some friends that were computer hackers and he took the box of disks to them to see what they could do. All of the books were retrieved along with the cover letters to the publishing firm.

Two months later, a court ruled Ronnie's power of attorney the judge had made up would serve as his will. It also ruled that David and Connie would be able to keep and care for Nancy as their own. It was also ruled that any proceeds from the books that had been found and the ones that were already in print, would go into a trust fund for Nancy. All except for a generous stipend that would serve to offset the costs of raising her. The publisher Ronnie had been dealing with suggested that arrangement and was more than happy to find out the court had gone along with it.

They also changed the name of the author on all of the books to Ronald Fisher, even the ones that were going through their second and third printings.

114.

Ronnie stood atop the high place and watched the small town below him. He now had the knowledge of everything and there were no mysteries to life left to wonder. He knew Nancy was well taken care of and by the time she was of legal age, rich. She would never have to learn lifes hard lessons and get a real job. He knew she shared her wealth with the parents she had grown up with and saw to it they were well taken care of in their old age.

The knowledge she had grown up to be a caring person and nothing like Margret made Ronnie feel proud.

He thought back to the day he had lost his life. He had been loaded into the computers memory in a conscious state and when the computer died when it hit the floor, he was set free. Ronnie never saw nor heard of the Professor again and assumed the Professor had been sent on to his final destination when the computer was destroyed. But none of that mattered now, he was at peace with himself and the world he surveyed so far below him.

He stood on the high place for a thousand generations and watched the small town below him flourish and prosper, the checker board pattern of civilization spreading to cover the valley. He watched as the air below him grew yellow with the stink of man.

As Ronnie watched, the civilization withered and he saw the green vegetation as it slowly crept back into the valley from the north and south. From time to time, he felt great rumblings to the west. They came from the east also, but not as frequent. He felt mankind as it died away, not with a catastrophe or event of epic proportions, but the reign of man come to its end with time itself. Just another species of animal that had become extinct. He saw the streets empty and grow still with no further movement of man. He continued to watch as vegetation grew up and took the town over, reclaiming what had once been its own, and saw that after awhile, the floor of the valley grew to look like a jungle.

He could feel life there again, in the valley below. This time not human, but animal instead. Another thousand generations passed before Ronnie decided he was bored and thirsty, so he went to the glen. When he got there, he saw the glen hadn't changed much in all of the years he had been absent. The grass was longer

and the tree line seemed to be closer to the stream now, but the water still flow
from the fountain as cold and clear as the day he had used it to heal his he
wounds.

Ronnie saw the Professor had been wrong. The evil and vile that made up t
ground hadn't grown high enough to cover the stone pile and spring. In fact,
hadn't gotten more than a couple of inches higher since the last time he had se
it.

Inhaling deeply of the Honeysuckle and Jasmine smell that always seemed
be there, Ronnie bent down and drank long and deep from where the water car
from   the   roc